THE

LYLE

OFFICIAL

ANTIQUES

REVIEW 1996

D0862000

THE

LYLE

OFFICIAL
ANTIQUES
REVIEW 1996

A PERIGEE BOOK

Perigee Books
are published by
The Berkley Publishing Group
200 Madison Avenue
New York, NY 10016

ISBN 0-399-52164-X
First edition: December 1995

Cover design by Jack Ribik

Printed in the United States of America
1   2   3   4   5   6   7   8   9   10

This book is printed on acid-free paper

INTRODUCTION

T his year over 100,000 Antique Dealers and Collectors will make full and profitable use of their Lyle Antiques Price Guide. They know that only in this one volume will they find the widest possible variety of goods – illustrated, described and given a current market value to assist them to BUY RIGHT AND SELL RIGHT throughout the year of issue.

They know, too, that by building a collection of these immensely valuable volumes year by year, they will equip themselves with an unparalleled reference library of facts, figures and illustrations which, properly used, cannot fail to help them keep one step ahead of the market.

In its twenty six years of publication, Lyle has gone from strength to strength and has become without doubt the pre-eminent book of reference for the antique trade throughout the world. Each of its fact filled pages is packed with precisely the kind of profitable information the professional Dealer needs – including descriptions, illustrations and values of thousands and thousands of individual items carefully selected to give a representative picture of the current market in antiques and collectables – and remember all values are prices actually paid, based on accurate sales records in the twelve months prior to publication from the best established and most highly respected auction houses and retail outlets in Europe and America.

This is THE book for the Professional Antiques Dealer. 'The Lyle Book' – we've even heard it called 'The Dealer's Bible'.

Compiled and published afresh each year, the Lyle Antiques Price Guide is the most comprehensive up-to-date antiques price guide available. THIS COULD BE YOUR WISEST INVESTMENT OF THE YEAR!

Anthony Curtis

While every care has been taken in the compiling of information contained in this volume, the publisher cannot accept liability for loss, financial or otherwise, incurred by reliance placed on the information herein.

All prices quoted in this book are obtained from a variety of auctions in various countries during the twelve months prior to publication and are converted to dollars at the rate of exchange prevalent at the time of sale.

The publishers wish to express their sincere thanks to the following for their involvement and assistance in the production of this volume:

EELIN McIVOR (Sub Editor)

ANNETTE CURTIS (Editorial)

CATRIONA DAY (Art Production)

ANGIE DE MARCO (Art Production)

JAMES BROWN (Graphics)

DONNA RUTHERFORD (Advertising)

MATTHEW OLYKAN

SONIA KARAITIANA

CONTENTS

ANTIQUES REVIEW

ACKNOWLEDGEMENTS

AB Stockholms Auktionsverk, Box 16256, 103 25 Stockholm, Sweden
Abbotts Auction Rooms, The Auction Rooms, Campsea Ash, Woodbridge, Suffolk
Academy Auctioneers, Northcote House, Northcote Avenue, Ealing, London W5 3UR
James Adam, 26 St Stephens Green, Dublin 2
Jean Claude Anaf, Lyon Brotteaux, 13 bis place Jules Ferry, 69456 Lyon, France
Anderson & Garland, Marlborough House, Marlborough Crescent, Newcastle upon Tyne NE1 4EE
Antique Collectors Club & Co. Ltd, 5 Church Street, Woodbridge, Suffolk IP 12 1DS
The Auction Galleries, Mount Rd., Tweedmouth, Berwick on Tweed
Auction Team Köln, Postfach 50 11 68, D-5000 Köln 50 Germany
Auktionshaus Arnold, Bleichstr. 42, 6000 Frankfurt a/M, Germany
Barber's Auctions, Woking, Surrey
Bearnes, Rainbow, Avenue Road, Torquay TQ2 5TG
John Bellman, New Pound, Wisborough Green, Billingshurst, West Sussex RH14 0AY
Biddle & Webb, Ladywood Middleway, Birmingham B16 0PP
Bigwood, The Old School, Tiddington, Stratford upon Avon
Black Horse Agencies, Locke & England, 18 Guy Street, Leamington Spa
Boardman Fine Art Auctioneers, Station Road Corner, Haverhill, Suffolk CB9 0EY
Bonhams, Montpelier Street, Knightsbridge, London SW7 1HH
Bonhams Chelsea, 65–69 Lots Road, London SW10 0RN
Bonhams West Country, Dowell Street, Honiton, Devon
Bosleys, 42 West Street, Marlow, Bucks SL7 1NB
Michael J. Bowman, 6 Haccombe House, Near Netherton, Newton Abbot, Devon
Bristol Auction Rooms, St Johns Place, Apsley Road, Clifton, Bristol BS8 2ST
British Antique Exporters, School Close, Queen Elizabeth Avenue, Burgess Hill, Sussex
William H Brown, The Warner Auction Rooms, 16–18, Halford Street, Leicester LE1 1JB
Butterfield & Butterfield, 220 San Bruno Avenue, San Francisco CA 94103, USA
Butterfield & Butterfield, 7601 Sunset Boulevard, Los Angeles CA 90046, USA
Canterbury Auction Galleries, 40 Station Road West, Canterbury CT2 8AN
Central Motor Auctions, Barfield House, Britannia Road, Morley, Leeds, LS27 0HN
H.C. Chapman & Son, The Auction Mart, North Street, Scarborough.
Chapman Moore & Mugford, 8 High Street, Shaftesbury SP7 8JB
Cheffins Grain & Comins, 2 Clifton Road, Cambridge
Christie's (International) SA, 8 place de la Taconnerie, 1204 Genève, Switzerland
Christie's Monaco, S.A.M, Park Palace 98000 Monte Carlo, Monaco
Christie's Scotland, 164–166 Bath Street Glasgow G2 4TG
Christie's South Kensington Ltd., 85 Old Brompton Road, London SW7 3LD
Christie's, 8 King Street, London SW1Y 6QT
Christie's East, 219 East 67th Street, New York, NY 10021, USA
Christie's, 502 Park Avenue, New York, NY 10022, USA
Christie's, Cornelis Schuytstraat 57, 1071 JG Amsterdam, Netherlands
Christie's SA Roma, 114 Piazza Navona, 00186 Rome, Italy
Christie's Swire, 2804–6 Alexandra House, 16–20 Chater Road, Hong Kong
Christie's Australia Pty Ltd., 1 Darling Street, South Yarra, Victoria 3141, Australia
A J Cobern, The Grosvenor Sales Rooms, 93b Eastbank Street, Southport PR8 1DG
Cooper Hirst Auctions, The Granary Saleroom, Victoria Road, Chelmsford, Essex CM2 6LH
The Crested China Co., Station House, Driffield, E. Yorks YO25 7PY
Cundalls, The Cattle Market, 17 Market Square, Malton, N. Yorks
Clifford Dann, 20/21 High Street, Lewes, Sussex
Julian Dawson, Lewes Auction Rooms, 56 High Street, Lewes BN7 1XE
Dee & Atkinson, & Harrison, The Exchange Saleroom, Driffield, Nth Humberside YO25 7LJ
Garth Denham & Assocs. Horsham Auction Galleries, Warnsham, Nr. Horsham, Sussex
Diamond Mills & Co., 117 Hamilton Road, Felixstowe, Suffolk
David Dockree Fine Art, 224 Moss Lane, Bramhall, Stockport SK7 1BD
William Doyle Galleries, 175 East 87th Street, New York, NY 10128, USA
Downer Ross, Charter House, 42 Avebury Boulevard, Central Milton Keynes MK9 2HS
Hy. Duke & Son, 40 South Street, Dorchester, Dorset
Du Mouchelles Art Galleries Co., 409 E. Jefferson Avenue, Detroit, Michigan 48226, USA
Duncan Vincent, 92 London Street, Reading RG1 4SJ

ANTIQUES REVIEW

Sala de Artes y Subastas Durán, Serrano 12, 28001 Madrid, Spain
Eldred's, Box 796, E. Dennis, MA 02641, USA
R H Ellis & Sons, 44/46 High St., Worthing, BN11 1LL
Ewbanks, Burnt Common Auction Rooms, London Road, Send, Woking GU23 7LN
Fellows & Son, Augusta House, 19 Augusta Street, Hockley, Birmingham
Finarte, 20121 Milano, Piazzetta Bossi 4, Italy
John D Fleming & Co., The North Devon Auction Rooms, The Savory, South Molton, Devon
Peter Francis, 19 King Street, Carmarthen, Dyfed
Fraser Pinney's, 8290 Devonshire, Montreal, Quebec, Canada H4P 2PZ
G A Property Services, Canterbury Auction Galleries, Canterbury, Kent
Galerie Koller, Rämistr. 8, CH 8024 Zürich, Switzerland
Galerie Moderne, 3 rue du Parnasse, 1040 Bruxelles, Belgium
Geering & Colyer (Black Horse Agencies) Highgate, Hawkhurst, Kent
Glerum Auctioneers, Westeinde 12, 2512 HD's Gravenhage, Netherlands
The Goss and Crested China Co., 62 Murray Road, Horndean, Hants PO8 9JL
Graves Son & Pilcher, 71 Church Road, Hove, East Sussex, BN3 2GL
Greenslade Hunt, Magdalene House, Church Square, Taunton, Somerset, TA1 1SB
Halifax Property Services, 53 High Street, Tenterden, Kent
Halifax Property Services, 15 Cattle Market, Sandwich, Kent CT13 9AW
Hampton's Fine Art, 93 High Street, Godalming, Surrey
Hanseatisches Auktionshaus für Historica, Neuer Wall 57, 2000 Hamburg 36, Germany
William Hardie Ltd., 141 West Regent Street, Glasgow G2 2SG
Andrew Hartley Fine Arts, Victoria Hall, Little Lane, Ilkley
Hauswedell & Nolte, D-2000 Hamburg 13, Pöseldorfer Weg 1, Germany
Giles Haywood, The Auction House, St John's Road, Stourbridge, West Midlands, DY8 1EW
Muir Hewitt, Halifax Antiques Centre, Queens Road/Gibbet Street, Halifax HX1 4LR
Hobbs & Chambers, 'At the Sign of the Bell', Market Place, Cirencester, Glos
Hobbs Parker, Romney House, Ashford Market, Ashford, Kent
Holloways, 49 Parsons Street, Banbury OX16 8PF
Hotel de Ventes Horta, 390 Chaussée de Waterloo (Ma Campagne), 1060 Bruxelles, Belgium
Jacobs & Hunt, Lavant Street, Petersfield, Hants. GU33 3EF
P Herholdt Jensens Auktioner, Rundforbivej 188, 2850 Nerum, Denmark
Kennedy & Wolfenden, 218 Lisburn Rd, Belfast BT9 6GD
G A Key, Aylsham Saleroom, 8 Market Place, Aylsham, Norfolk, NR11 6EH
George Kidner, The Old School, The Square, Pennington, Lymington, Hants SO41 8GN
Kunsthaus am Museum, Drususgasse 1–5, 5000 Köln 1, Germany
Kunsthaus Lempertz, Neumarkt 3, 5000 Köln 1, Germany
Lambert & Foster (County Group), The Auction Sales Room, 102 High Street, Tenterden, Kent
W.H. Lane & Son, 64 Morrab Road, Penzance, Cornwall, TR18 2QT
Langlois Ltd., Westaway Rooms, Don Street, St Helier, Channel Islands
Lawrence Butler Fine Art Salerooms, Marine Walk, Hythe, Kent, CT21 5AJ
Lawrence Fine Art, South Street, Crewkerne, Somerset TA18 8AB
Lawrence's Fine Art Auctioneers, Norfolk House, 80 High Street, Bletchingley, Surrey
David Lay, The Penzance Auction House, Alverton, Penzance, Cornwall TA18 4KE
Lloyd International Auctions, 118 Putney Bridge Road, London SW15 2NQ
Brian Loomes, Calf Haugh Farm, Pateley Bridge, North Yorks
Lots Road Chelsea Auction Galleries, 71 Lots Road, Chelsea, London SW10 0RN
R K Lucas & Son, Tithe Exchange, 9 Victoria Place, Haverfordwest, SA61 2JX
Duncan McAlpine, Stateside Comics plc, 125 East Barnet Road, London EN4 8RF
McCartneys, Portcullis Salerooms, Ludlow, Shropshire
Christopher Matthews, 23 Mount Street, Harrogate HG2 8DG
John Maxwell, 75 Hawthorn Street, Wilmslow, Cheshire
May & Son, 18 Bridge Street, Andover, Hants
Morphets, 4–6 Albert Street, Harrogate, North Yorks HG1 1JL
D M Nesbit & Co, 7 Clarendon Road, Southsea, Hants PO5 2ED
John Nicholson, 1 Crossways Court, Fernhurst, Haslemere, Surrey GU27 3EP
Onslow's, Metrostore, Townmead Road, London SW6 2RZ
Outhwaite & Litherland, Kingsley Galleries, Fontenoy Street, Liverpool, Merseyside L3 2BE

ANTIQUES REVIEW

J R Parkinson Son & Hamer Auctions, The Auction Rooms, Rochdale, Bury, Lancs
Phillips Manchester, Trinity House, 114 Northenden Road, Sale, Manchester M33 3HD
Phillips Son & Neale SA, 10 rue des Chaudronniers, 1204 Genève, Switzerland
Phillips West Two, 10 Salem Road, London W2 4BL
Phillips, 11 Bayle Parade, Folkestone, Kent CT20 1SQ
Phillips, 49 London Road, Sevenoaks, Kent TN13 1UU
Phillips, 65 George Street, Edinburgh EH2 2JL
Phillips, Blenstock House, 7 Blenheim Street, New Bond Street, London W1Y 0AS
Phillips Marylebone, Hayes Place, Lisson Grove, London NW1 6UA
Phillips, New House, 150 Christleton Road, Chester CH3 5TD
Andrew Pickford, 42 St Andrew Street, Hertford SG14 1JA
Pieces of Time, 1–7 Davies Mews, Unit 17–19, London W17 1AR
Pooley & Rogers, Regent Auction Rooms, Abbey Street, Penzance
Pretty & Ellis, Amersham Auction Rooms, Station Road, Amersham, Bucks
Peter M Raw, Thornfield, Hurdle Way, Compton Down, Winchester, Hants SC21 2AN
Rennie's, 1 Agincourt Street, Monmouth
Riddetts, Richmond Hill, Bournemouth
Ritchie's, 429 Richmond Street East, Toronto, Canada M5A 1R1
Derek Roberts Antiques, 24–25 Shipbourne Road, Tonbridge, Kent TN10 3DN
Rogers de Rin, 79 Royal Hospital Road, London SW3 4HN
Russell, Baldwin & Bright, The Fine Art Saleroom, Ryelands Road, Leominster HR6 8JG
Rye Auction Galleries, Rock Channel, Rye, East Sussex
Schrager Auction Galleries, 2915 N Sherman Boulevard, PO Box 10390, Milwaukee WI 53210, USA
Selkirk's, 4166 Olive Street, St Louis, Missouri 63108, USA
Skinner Inc., Bolton Gallery, Route 117, Bolton MA, USA
Soccer Nostalgia, Albion Chambers, Birchington, Kent CT7 9DN
Sotheby's, 34–35 New Bond Street, London W1A 2AA
Sotheby's, 1334 York Avenue, New York NY 10021
Sotheby's, 112 George Street, Edinburgh EH2 2LH
Sotheby's, Summers Place, Billingshurst, West Sussex RH14 9AD
Sotheby's Monaco, BP 45, 98001 Monte Carlo
Southgate Auction Rooms, 55 High St, Southgate, London N14 6LD
Henry Spencer, 20 The Square, Retford, Notts. DN22 6BX
Spink & Son Ltd, 5-7 King St., St James's, London SW1Y 6QS
Michael Stainer Ltd., St Andrews Auction Rooms, Wolverton Rd, Boscombe, Bournemouth BH7 6HT
Mike Stanton, 7 Rowood Drive, Solihull, West Midlands B92 9LT
Street Jewellery, 5 Runnymede Road, Ponteland, Northumbria NE20 9HE
Stride & Son, Southdown House, St John's St., Chichester, Sussex
G E Sworder & Son, Northgate End Salerooms, 15 Northgate End, Bishop Stortford, Herts
Taviner's of Bristol, Prewett Street, Redcliffe, Bristol BS1 6PB
Tennants, Harmby Road, Leyburn, Yorkshire
Thomson Roddick & Laurie, 24 Lowther Street, Carlisle
Thomson Roddick & Laurie, 60 Whitesands, Dumfries
Timbleby & Shorland, 31 Gt Knollys St, Reading RG1 7HU
Venator & Hanstein, Cäcilienstr. 48, 5000 Köln 1, Germany
T Vennett Smith, 11 Nottingham Road, Gotham, Nottingham NG11 0HE
Duncan Vincent, 92 London Street, Reading RG1 4SJ
Wallis & Wallis, West Street Auction Galleries, West Street, Lewes, E. Sussex BN7 2NJ
Walter's, 1 Mint Lane, Lincoln LN1 1UD
Ward & Morris, Stuart House, 18 Gloucester Road, Ross on Wye HR9 5BN
Warren & Wignall Ltd, The Mill, Earnshaw Bridge, Leyland Lane, Leyland PR5 3PH
Dominique Watine-Arnault, 11 rue François 1er, 75008 Paris, France
Wells Cundall Nationwide Anglia, Staffordshire House, 27 Flowergate, Whitby YO21 3AX
Peter Wilson, Victoria Gallery, Market Street, Nantwich, Cheshire CW5 5DG
Wintertons Ltd., Lichfield Auction Centre, Fradley Park, Lichfield, Staffs WS13 8NF
Woltons, 6 Whiting Street, Bury St Edmunds, Suffolk IP33 1PB
Woolley & Wallis, The Castle Auction Mart, Salisbury, Wilts SP1 3SU
Worthing Auction Galleries, 31 Chatsworth Road, Worthing, W. Sussex BN11 1LY

ANTIQUES

REVIEW 1996

T HE Lyle Antiques Price Guide is compiled and published with completely fresh information annually, enabling you to begin each new year with an up-to-date knowledge of the current trends, together with the verified values of antiques of all descriptions.

We have endeavored to obtain a balance between the more expensive collector's items and those which, although not in their true sense antiques, are handled daily by the antiques trade.

The illustrations and prices in the following sections have been arranged to make it easy for the reader to assess the period and value of all items with speed.

You will find illustrations for almost every category of antique and curio, together with a corresponding price collated during the last twelve months, from the auction rooms and retail outlets of the major trading countries.

When dealing with the more popular trade pieces, in some instances, a calculation of an average price has been estimated from the varying accounts researched.

As regards prices, when 'one of a pair' is given in the description the price quoted is for a pair and so that we can make maximum use of the available space it is generally considered that one illustration is sufficient.

It will be noted that in some descriptions taken directly from sales catalogues originating from many different countries, terms such as bureau, secretary and davenport are used in a broader sense than is customary, but in all cases the term used is self explanatory.

ACTORS & ACTRESSES

Bette Davis, signed and
inscribed 8 x 10in., half length
seated.
(Vennett-Smith) $170

Audrey Hepburn, signed 5 x
7in., half-length with Gregory
Peck.
(Vennett-Smith) $112

Harrison Ford, signed 8 x 10in.,
as Han Solo, from The Return of
the Jedi.
(Vennett-Smith) $82

Marisa Tomei, signed color 8 x
10in., half-length from 'My
Cousin Vinny'.
(Vennett-Smith) $104

Laurel and Hardy, excellent
signed and inscribed 10 x 8in.,
by both, half-length at music
stand.
(Vennett-Smith) $960

Harold Lloyd, signed German
film brochure for 'The
Catspaw', signed to cover.
(Vennett-Smith) $122

Audrey Hepburn, signed 7 x
11in., head and shoulders in
strapless dress.
(Vennett-Smith) $192

Lon Chaney Jnr., signed album
page, alongside 2³/₄ x 6³/₄in.
photo of Chaney as
Frankenstein's Monster.
(Vennett-Smith) $164

Marlene Dietrich, signed
postcard, full vintage signature
in green.
(Vennett-Smith) $83

14

Gertrude Lawrence, signed sepia 5½ x 8½in., photo by Georges.
(Vennett-Smith) $62

Groucho Marx, signed and inscribed, 10 x 8in., first name only.
(Vennett-Smith) $246

John Wayne, signed 8 x 10in. magazine photo, as Davy Crockett (?).
(Vennett-Smith) $426

Vivien Leigh, signed postcard, as Scarlett O'Hara, half-length seated.
(Vennett-Smith) $992

Buster Keaton, signed card, overmounted in red beneath, 7½ x 8in. photo.
(Vennett-Smith) $148

Nastassja Kinski, signed and inscribed color 8 x 10in.
(Vennett-Smith) $148

Charles Chaplin, early signed sepia 7 x 5in., wearing bowtie.
(Vennett-Smith) $541

Arnold Schwarzenegger, signed color 8 x 10in., as Hamlet.
(Vennett-Smith) $40

Bing Crosby, signed and inscribed sepia 8 x 10in.
(Vennett-Smith) $66

Spencer Tracy, signed sepia 5 x 7in., head and shoulders. (Vennett-Smith) $120

Danny DeVito, signed color 8 x 10in., as the Penguin. (Vennett-Smith) $41

Burt Lancaster, signed and inscribed 8 x 10in., half length. (Vennett-Smith) $421

Marilyn Monroe, signed album page, mounted beneath 5¹/₂ x 7in. photo. (Vennett-Smith) $1,782

Jean Gabin, a good signed and inscribed 8 x 10in., wearing cap and smoking cigarette from 'Moontide'. (Vennett-Smith) $361

Clark Gable, signed bank check, drawn on Security-First National Bank of Los Angeles, 10th May 1950, for $11.75. (Vennett-Smith) $416

Burt Lancaster, signed 8 x 9¹/₂in. pencil sketch, head and shoulders, 1951. (Vennett-Smith) $131

Errol Flynn, signed and inscribed 5 x 7in., three quarter length. (Vennett-Smith) $418

Will Rogers, signed sepia 8 x 10in., head and shoulders, wearing hat. (Vennett-Smith) $279

ACTORS & ACTRESSES

Edward G. Robinson, signed and inscribed 8 x 10in., 1938?.
(Vennett-Smith) $259

Oliver Hardy, signed and inscribed sepia 10 x 8in., showing Hardy seated while fishing, 1934.
(Vennett-Smith) $544

Charles Chaplin, signed postcard, in white ink.
(Vennett-Smith) $288

Oliver Hardy, a fine sepia signed and inscribed 8 x 10in., by Oliver Hardy, early, half-length wearing cap and sports jacket.
(Vennett-Smith) $583

Bogart and Bacall, a good signed and inscribed color 8 x 8½in. magazine photo by both individually.
(Vennett-Smith) $1,640

Rudolph Valentino, a good signed sepia 8 x 10in., head and shoulders, wearing suit.
(Vennett-Smith) $1,279

Vivien Leigh, a fine signed postcard as Scarlett O'Hara, three quarter length seated.
(Vennett-Smith) $1,183

Richard Burton, signed 8 x 10in., from a scene from Exorcist II.
(Vennett-Smith) $128

Robert De Niro, signed color 8 x 10in., half-length with barbell from 'Cape Fear'.
(Vennett-Smith) $104

Don, Deauville, on linen, 160 x 120cm.
(Onslow's) $580

Lamport & Holt Line Sunshine Cruises, double royal.
(Onslow's) $400

Jean Gabriel Domergue, Monte-Carlo, 100 x 63cm.
(Onslow's) $510

Paris à Londres via Calais Boulogne Traversee Maritime en 60 minutes, with timetable information, 1895, on linen, 95 x 66cm.
(Onslow's) $450

Brynhild Parker, Shell poster, The Quay, Appledore, No. 341, 1932, 76 x 114cm.
(Onslow's) $160

Paint decorated tavern sign, American late 18th century, 'Phillip's Inn' with an American shielded eagle, reverse with American eagle above a rising sun, 62 x 27in.
(Skinner) $5,175

Castrol Kaye Don Miss England III, color poster, pub by Gottschalk Paris, on linen, 78 x 59cm.
(Onslow's) $400

E. McKnight-Kauffer, Summer Time In The Country, pub by London Transport No. 497 1000 4/23/25, quad royal.
(Onslow's) $1,220

Great Northern Railway advertisement, 'If You Need A Holiday', advert reverse, published 1915.
(Vennett-Smith) $104

Frys advertisement, 'Highway Robbery', by Tom Browne. (Vennett-Smith) $64

Greig, P&O Cruises The Strathnaver, double royal. (Onslow's) $770

Peter Behrends, Blumen Hüber, lithograph in colours, framed and glazed, 68 x 45cm. (Christie's) $496

Le Fervre, Chemins de Fer de L'Ouest et de Brighton Paris à Londres 1895, on linen, 123 x 85cm. (Onslow's) $320

C. Felkel, Shell poster, Bristol Bombays, No. 530, 1938, 76 x 114cm. (Onslow's) $670

Carreras, poster, 18 x 27in., for Craven 'A' cigarettes, showing lady smoker in green dress and bonnet. (Vennett-Smith) $131

Laurence Bradshaw, Epsom Spring Meeting, 1937, double royal. (Onslow's) $180

E. McKnight-Kauffer, Read Cricketer in the Manchester Guardian, double crown on linen. (Onslow's) $460

Theo Doro, Chemins de Fer de L'Est, 1929, double royal, on linen. (Onslow's) $830

ADVERTISING

A color concert poster from the London Palladium, featuring Mama Cass With Her Musicians, along with The Debbie Reynolds Show. (Christie's) $230

A painted and gilded iron and sheet metal clock trade sign: J. F. Krieft, American, circa 1875, painted on both sides with a clock face, 41in. high. (Sotheby's) $3,450

Alphonse Mucha, 'Monaco, Monte Carlo', 1897, lithograph backed on linen, signed and dated, 109.5 x 71.5cm. (Sotheby's) $5,962

An early and unusual Kynoch Military and Sporting cartridge display-board, cartridges and components arranged radially around a Kynoch railway alarm and fog signal, oak framed, 37^1/$_2$ x 26^1/$_4$in. overall. (Christie's) $3,452

Alphonse Mucha, Job Cigarette Papers, (B. A. 6, R.W. 15), 1896, lithograph, printed in colors on wove paper, printed by Champenois, Paris, with margins, 20^3/$_8$ x 15^5/$_{16}$in. (Butterfield & Butterfield) $9,200

Leslie Carr, Royal Automobile Club Club Prix de Europe incorporating British Grand Prix Silverstone May 13th 1950, color lithographic poster, 76 x 51cm. (Onslow's) $350

A metallic gold, green, yellow and blue psychedelic 'Save Earth Now' poster, 1960's, by Hapshash. (Bonhams) $620

St. Julian Tobacco All Records Broken for Quality, shaped color lithographic standing three dimensional, 27 x 15cm. 1920s. (Onslow's) $40

Paul Nash, Mansard Gallery The Friday Club Exhibition of Prints and drawings, Paintings, Sculpture etc., double crown. (Onslow's) $270

ADVERTISING

Ralph Terry, The Man with the Mysterious Fingers, colored lithographic poster, 26¼ x 35½in.
(Christie's) $270

A circa 1950s color concert poster for The Fabulous Platters, at the London Palladium, 29³/₄ x 19³/₄in., framed.
(Christie's) $920

Gaston Stephane (French, 20th century), 'Cognac Briand', color lithographic poster on paper, sheet size 63 x 47in., framed.
(Skinner) $2,645

Albert Bergevin, Avranches, lithograph printed in colors on wove paper, printed by Imprimerie du Syndicat d'Initiative d'Avranches, 39⁹/₁₆ x 29⁵/₈in.
(Butterfield & Butterfield) $920

A Carlton ware Guinness three piece condiment set, decorated panels of glasses of Guinness and 'Guinness for You'.
(Anderson & Garland) $34

Jules Cheret, Quinquina Dubonnet (B. 873), 1895, lithograph printed in colors on wove paper, printed by Chaix, Paris, chalk additions in the center left area of the image, 21¹/₁₆ x 14³/₄in.
(Butterfield & Butterfield) $920

Life's a joy with a Kodak, an 18¹/₂ x 28¹/₂in. colored lithographic poster, mounted on board.
(Christie's) $305

Blackpool Winter Gardens, color lithographic vignette, text mentioning programme of events for July 19th 1886, double royal, on linen.
(Onslow's) $610

Through the World and Back Again 15,000 Miles in Nine Days at 68mph, color lithographic poster, 76 x 51cm.; and Daily Sketch vendors stand poster.
(Onslow's) $190

21

ADVERTISING

Frys advertisement, The Diver, slight corner rounding.
(Vennett-Smith) $38

Singer, unusual shaped circular chromo booklet, for the Pan-American Exposition at Niagara Falls, 1901.
(Vennett-Smith) $36

S. W. le Feaux, Raleigh The Gold Medal Motor-Cycle, double crown.
(Onslow's) $190

After Beligond, 24 Heures du Mans Juin 1958, on linen, 39 x 29cm.
(Onslow's) $190

Gallaher Limited 'A Tip to Remember, Smoke Park Drive Cigarettes', colored ithographic, hanging card, 37 x 24cm. 1920s.
(Onslow's) $80

After Geo Ham, 2e Grand Prix de Paris 24 Avril 1949 Montlhery, 60 x 40cm.
(Onslow's) $530

Ein Volk, ein Reich, ein Fuhrer!, published by Carl Werner Reichenbach, 1939, on linen, 119 x 86cm.
(Onslow's) $900

Lucien Bernhard, Internationale Automobile Ausstellung Berlin 1911, pub by Hollerbaum & Schmidt Berlin, on linen, 70 x 96cm.
(Onslow's) $1,360

Frank Newbould, Shopping by London Transport, LT, 1934, double royal.
(Onslow's) $180

Even, Near East (Air France), double royal. (Onslow's) $420

Air France Amerique du Sud, double royal, on linen. (Onslow's) $460

Renluc, Air-Fer, 1949, on linen, double royal. (Onslow's) $320

A German World War II sheepskin lined leather flying helmet made by Siemens, complete with throat microphone, ear phones and electrical connector with plug. (Andrew Bottomley) $367

Whitlock, Empire Air Day Saturday May 20th 1939, Come to the Annual At Home of the RAF Warmwell near Dorchester, 76 x 51cm. (Onslow's) $400

German World War II airman's watch, signed *Laco*, the gilt finished bar movement numbered *2556* with 22 jewels and bimetallic balance, 55mm. diameter. (Christie's) $1,140

Lucien Boucher, Air France Great Britain, 1952, on linen, double royal. (Onslow's) $260

Prout, Air France Paris-Mexico, 1952, on linen, double royal. (Onslow's) $320

S. Horfespringer, Venez En Suisse Par Avion, 1937, double royal, on linen. (Onslow's) $510

Aeroplane Supply Company First Aviation Catalogue The Aeroplane and Everything For It, compiled by Bernard Isaac, 1st ed., November 1st 1909. (Onslow's) $100

Imperial Airways The Empire Flying Boat The Most Luxurious Flying Boat In The World, 1936, double royal. (Onslow's) $960

Ottomer Anton, Across The Atlantic In Two Days Deutsche Zeppelin-Reederei Hamburg-Amerika Linie, 84 x 59cm. (Onslow's) $1,440

Zepps Reported Over London Many Fires (Official Tuesday June 1st), newspaper vendors stand letterpress poster, on pink paper, 63 x 45cm. (Onslow's) $350

A Smith's Air Ministry Swiss made chronometer, the black dial marked Mk II 4688/39 Ref No. 6A839, 9cm. diameter. (Onslow's) $560

Handbook on Rigid 23 Class Airships, pub by HMSO for Admiralty Airship Department, May 1918, plates, rubber stamped Airship Station Pulham Norfolk. (Onslow's) $300

Armee de L'Air, indistinctly signed, pub by Lang Paris, on linen, 81 x 58cm. (Onslow's) $160

E. McKnight Kauffer, Miles-Whitney Straight Lubrication by Shell No. 477, 76.5 x 114cm., 1932. (Onslow's) $800

The Daily Mirror Zepp Raid, pictorial newspaper vendors stand poster, 63 x 45cm. (Onslow's) $480

AERONAUTICAL ITEMS

D'Orcy (Ladislas) D'Orcy's
Airship Manual An
International Register of
Official Souvenir Program of   Airships with Compendium of
the London Aerodrome Hendon,   the Airships Elementary   TWA Across The Atlantic and
pub by The Grahame-White Co.   Mechanics, pub by Century New Across USA You Can Depend
1913.   York, 1917.   on TWA, double royal, on linen.
(Onslow's) $90   (Onslow's) $320   (Onslow's) $340

Plaquet, Great Civil Air Display   A Second World War khaki
at Brooklands Saturday May   cloth D-Type Summer issue
28th 1932, blue letterpress, 51 x flying helmet, complete with ear   Herbert J. Williams, Jersey
38cm.   phones and lead; and a pair of   Airways Ltd. Regular Services
                                   Mk VIII goggles.   Paris Jersey $2^1/_2$ Hrs, 76 x 51cm.
(Onslow's) $70   (Onslow's) $100   (Onslow's) $720

Pan American World Airways   Aeroplanes Bleriot G. Borel &
The System of the Flying   Cie 25 Rue Brunel Paris, pub by   Aero Vias Guest Miami Mexico,
Clippers, double royal, on linen. Louis Galice Paris, 76.5 x   on linen, double royal.
(Onslow's) $320   100cm.   (Onslow's) $320
                             (Onslow's) $480

Sioux beaded moccasins, fully-beaded with buffalo tracks on the vamp, the remainder with concentric stepped pyramids on a pale blue ground, 10³/₄in. long. (Butterfield & Butterfield) $978

'Tecumseh' Presentation Pipe tomahawk, on an expansive wood haft of oval section, with a carved horn mouthpiece, the iron blade with an inset gold cartouche inscribed *Techumseh* (sic) in flowery script, length of haft 20³/₈in. (Butterfield & Butterfield) $18,400

Mono Lake Paiute polychrome basket, of flattened globular form, depicting a pair of opposing frog figures with trident tongues, 6¹/₄in. diameter. (Butterfield & Butterfield) $3,738

Navajo classic wearing blanket, woven in a banded pattern, alternating narrow stripes of contrasting colors with solid color panels, size approximately 5ft. 9in. x 4ft. 9in. (Butterfield & Butterfield) $11,500

Apache pictorial olla, the barrel-shaped vessel with pinched neck and flaring rim, worked with solid color and negative half diamonds, deer and smaller creatures in the reserves, 15¹/₂in. high. (Butterfield & Butterfield) $3,738

Navajo chief's style rug, woven in a Third Phase variant pattern, in gray, gray-brown, dark brown, red and white, size approximately 4ft. 10in. x 6ft. 3in. (Butterfield & Butterfield) $2,875

Eskimo woman's beaded cap, the domed hat consisting of rows of beads in alternate colors, separated by thin hide spacers, 7in. high. (Butterfield & Butterfield) $1,380

Pair of Arapaho beaded leggings, the soft hide with fully beaded panels, drawn with diamonds, boxes and bands, 23in. long. (Butterfield & Butterfield) $1,610

Flathead beaded vest, showing identical panels of floral arrangements in varied styles and colors on a sky blue ground, 24¹/₂in. long. (Butterfield & Butterfield) $1,955

Tlingit moccasins, soft-soled and tapering to the toe, the instep and applied cloth cuffs decorated with stylized floriforms, 9in. long.
(Butterfield & Butterfield)
$920

Southern Plains bow case and quiver, made from wolf hide, decorated with fringe, a tapering red trade cloth-lined tab covering the mouth of the quiver, the case carrying Osage double-curved bow, 54in. long overall.
(Butterfield & Butterfield)
$4,600

Northwest Coast basketry hat, of domed construction with slight concave top, painted allover to depict a stylized sea monster, $6^{1}/_{2}$in. high.
(Butterfield & Butterfield)
$863

Large Navajo rug, the central cruciform medallion lined with latchhooks and enclosed by borders of floating diamonds and reciprocal serrated devices, size approximately 14ft. 5in. x 10ft. 5in.
(Butterfield & Butterfield)
$13,800

Apache pictorial olla, decorated with a diamond lattice pattern of multiple stepped outlines, showing two rows of standing human figures at top and bottom, $14^{1}/_{2}$in. high.
(Butterfield & Butterfield)
$2,300

Navajo crystal rug, with central box medallion, displaying an angular geometric figure, flanked by four-corner box and whirling log motifs, size approximately 8ft. 2in. x 6ft. 10in.
(Butterfield & Butterfield)
$3,450

Sioux beaded vest, fully-beaded on canvas, with cloth lining and trim, profusely decorated with pennants, triangle and geometric motifs on a white ground, 21in. long.
(Butterfield & Butterfield)
$2,300

Tlingit copper rattle, comprising a pair of sun faces in bold relief, joined by copper rivets about the scalloped perimeter, one side of the wood handle remaining, $9^{1}/_{2}$in. long.
(Butterfield & Butterfield)
$8,050

Ojibwa beaded shirt, the fringed buckskin shirt with applied black felt panels at the shoulders, about the collar, on the two front pockets and as a bib, 28in. long.
(Butterfield & Butterfield)
$2,588

Human scalp lock, circa 1876, with decorative covering of red wool with contrasting blue wool cross, 18in. long.
(Butterfield & Butterfield)
$7,150

Paiute beaded cradle, consisting of a basketry frame and hood, covered with hide partially-beaded in floral depictions, 36in. long.
(Butterfield & Butterfield)
$1,150

Historic pipe tomahawk from Battle of Slim Buttes, circa 1876, attached faded label reads: *A Black Hills Indian Tomahawk and Pipe*.
(Butterfield & Butterfield)
$16,500

Cabinet photo of Ute Chief Piah, circa 1885, wearing wool shirt with medal around neck, caption reads: *Piah, Chief of Middle Park Band of Utes*, 4¹/₄ x 6¹/₄in.
(Butterfield & Butterfield)
$660

Pair of Sioux moccasins recovered from Wounded Knee, circa 1890, partially beaded with cruciform and stepped panels of blue, red, green and yellow beadwork.
(Butterfield & Butterfield)
$4,950

Cabinet card photo of Rain-In-The-Face by D. F. Barry, circa 1881, Rain In The Face most likely did not kill General Custer but rather may have killed Tom Custer.
(Butterfield & Butterfield)
$1,870

Copper arm band belonging to Sioux warrior Short-Bull, circa 1876, with locking device, engraved inscription reads: *Short Bull/Ischta Maza*, adorned with two scalp locks.
(Butterfield & Butterfield)
$7,700

Mounted photo of Sioux chiefs by D. S. Cole, circa 1901, studio view, subjects are seated and standing dressed in full regalia with weapons, 7 x 9in.
(Butterfield & Butterfield)
$2,750

Cabinet card photo of Uncpapa Sioux Chief Gaul by O. S. Goff, circa 1881, one of the most important of Sitting Bull's Chiefs, size: 6¹/₂ x 4¹/₄in.
(Butterfield & Butterfield)
$2,475

Stereo photo card of Sioux Chief Spotted Tail with wife and daughter by S. J. Morrow, circa 1881, 4 x 7in., being the Chief that signed the treaty giving away the Black Hills.
(Butterfield & Butterfield)
$550

Historic wood pipestem and catlinite pipe belonging to Sioux Chief Big Foot, killed by members of the 7th Cavalry in what is now known as the Massacre at Wounded Knee, December 29, 1890, 24³/₄in. long.
(Butterfield & Butterfield)
$26,400

Hide tobacco pouch belonging to Sioux warrior He-Dog, circa 1876, the rectangular pouch of composite construction, edges laced with orange and yellow quillwork.
(Butterfield & Butterfield)
$6,600

Cabinet card photo of Sioux Chief White-Ghost by J. N. Templeton, circa 1880[?], caption reads: *White Ghost, Head Chief./Sioux located at Fort Thompson, D.T.*, 4¹/₄ x 6¹/₄in.
(Butterfield & Butterfield)
$770

Cabinet photo of Sioux Chief Gaul by D. F. Barry, circa 1884, 4¹/₄ x 6¹/₂in.
(Butterfield & Butterfield)
$2,200

Extremely rare dual-signed photo of Sitting Bull and Buffalo Bill Cody, circa 1885, this rare and important photograph depicts Sitting Bull and Bill Cody in full costume for Cody's Wild West Show, 7 x 11in.
(Butterfield & Butterfield)
$11,000

Large photo including Sioux warriors Crow-King and Low-Dog, circa 1881[?], penned, 6 x 8in.
(Butterfield & Butterfield)
$2,750

Pair of Sioux moccasins recovered from Wounded Knee, circa 1890, partially beaded with diamond lozenge motifs.
(Butterfield & Butterfield)
$3,850

Cabinet photo of Sioux Medicine Man Sitting Bull by D. F. Barry, circa 1880, 4¹/₄ x 6¹/₂in.
(Butterfield & Butterfield)
$2,475

Cheyenne beaded moccasins, on thick hide, fully-beaded with depictions of a spread-winged eagle between buffalo tracks on the toes, 10³/₄in. long.
(Butterfield & Butterfield)
$1,955

Yurok elk horn spoon, consisting of a shallow ladle, the handle deeply grooved on both sides and narrowing down to end in a zig-zag and flat oval finial, 7¹/₄in. long.
(Butterfield & Butterfield)
$1,150

Tlingit pictorial basket, false embroidered to depict a pair of large stylized killer whales following a pair of box-like totemic faces, 10in. diameter.
(Butterfield & Butterfield)
$2,185

Chemehuevi basket, in olla form, having large globular body, pinched neck and raised rim, worked with an open design of three perpendicular sets of double ckeckered lines, 9¹/₂in. diameter.
(Butterfield & Butterfield)
$2,875

Southern Plains beaded leggings, with beaded panels about the ankle and extending up the seam, showing a series of pendant diamonds along a solid color band on white, 19in. long.
(Butterfield & Butterfield)
$1,610

Panamint polychrome pictorial bottleneck basket, with flaring sides, tapering shoulder and raised neck, depicting various birds perched in the branches of trees, 5in. diameter.
(Butterfield & Butterfield)
$4,600

Nootka wood mask, Tyee Maquinna, (Jimmy John), a sun mask, with central humanoid face flanked by a pair of coiling serpentine creatures, with abalone shell inlays, 35in. long.
(Butterfield & Butterfield)
$1,093

Hopi kachina doll, representing Hemis kachina, the black-painted figure wearing traditional casemask surmounted by basketry cap and tableta, 19¹/₄in. high.
(Butterfield & Butterfield)
$2,875

Maidu tray, the shallow vessel woven with a three-directional device lined with plumed hooks, similarly plumed bands converging from all three sides, 15¹/₄in. diameter.
(Butterfield & Butterfield)
$1,725

Northwest Coast Chilkat blanket, of characteristic pentagonal form, having a schematised depiction of a killer whale, in yellow, slightly faded turquoise blue, black and white, 30 x 40in.
(Butterfield & Butterfield)
$10,925

Bella Bella raven rattle, comprising a principal raven figure, a recumbent human upon its back, surmounted by a frog, in black, red, oxidised blue and blue-green pigments, 15½in. long.
(Butterfield & Butterfield)
$9,200

Cheyenne beaded possible bag, the rectangular container with fully-beaded central panel, showing polychrome crosses on a green or white banded background, 21in. wide.
(Butterfield & Butterfield)
$2,300

Sioux beaded girl's dress, the deerskin garment with fully-beaded bodice, showing box crosses and eight-pointed stars on a light blue ground within a white frame, 39in. long.
(Butterfield & Butterfield)
$3,163

Pair of Blackfoot beaded leggings, with wide fully-beaded panels on canvas, worked with an elaborate arrangement of concentric and connected diamonds, triangles and squares, 11½in. long.
(Butterfield & Butterfield)
$1,035

Plateau Parfleche container, the rawhide packet folded to meet in the center, each flap painted in mirror-image linear patterns of polychrome diamonds and triangles, 25in. long.
(Butterfield & Butterfield)
$1,725

Ute beaded shirt, the soft hide garment open at back with brass buttons for closure, a triangular edge-beaded fringed bib below the neck, rubbed allover in ocher stain, 35in. long.
(Butterfield & Butterfield)
$8,625

Apache basket, of deep tray form, woven with stepped diagonals of graduated size scrolling out from the small dark center, 13in. diameter.
(Butterfield & Butterfield)
$978

Sioux beaded pictorial boy's vest, displaying a pair of confronting roosters and fence devices on the front, a pair of soldiers and American flags on the reverse, 10½in. long.
(Butterfield & Butterfield)
$2,070

A Canosan teracotta figure of the goddess Artemis, clasping a spear in her right arm, Greek South Italy, circa 3rd century B.C., 9in.
(Bonhams) $966

A gold ram head attachment in sheet gold, the curved ribbed horns separately made, Parthian-early Sasanian, circa 2nd–3rd century A.D.
(Bonhams) $6,118

A light brown granite upper torso of a noble wearing a bag wig, two vertical columns of hieroglyph on the back pillar, 7th–6th century B.C., 5in.
(Bonhams) $2,415

The upper half of a painted wooden sarcophagus lid of a woman wearing a feathered Mut vulture headdress, Late New Kingdom, 19th–20th dynasties, circa 1300–1200 B.C., 19^1/$_2$in. high.
(Bonhams) $1,771

A substantial Roman bronze rein guide from a chariot, consisting of a hollow central column, a square platform above, supporting a polyhedron with rosette motifs, circa 2nd–3rd century A.D., 6^1/$_4$in. high.
(Bonhams) $2,415

An Egyptian polychrome painted limestone stele, with the standing figure of a noble holding a tall staff, 1st Intermediate Period, 1st dynasty, circa 20th century B.C., 20^1/$_2$in.
(Bonhams) $1,771

A Red-Figure volute krater, Apulia, Greek South Italy, late 4th century B.C., from the workshop of the White Saccos Painter, 26^3/$_4$in. high.
(Bonhams) $3,542

An Apulian Red-Figure knop-handled patera on a stepped ring base, Greek South Italy, later 4th century B.C., 15^1/$_2$in. diameter.
(Bonhams) $3,220

An Etrusco-Corinthian storage amphora, the piriform body painted and incised with a single frieze of animals, later 7th century B.C., 24in., repaired.
(Bonhams) $7,728

A large and complete example of a British Acheulian flint hand axe of pointed form, circa 250,000–200,000 B.C., 9³/₄in. long.
(Bonhams) $1,932

A Luristan bronze adze-axe, the central shaft-hole decorated with zig-zags and grooves, 1st millennium B.C., 7in. long, mounted.
(Bonhams) $451

An over life-size Roman marble head of Socrates, with high domed cranium and thickly curled beard and hair, 14¹/₂in. high, mounted.
(Bonhams) $12,075

The upper two thirds of an Ur III clay tablet, three columns on each side of an administrative text in Sumerian cuneiform, 2112–2004 B.C., 15 x 13 x 2.2cm.
(Bonhams) $4,186

An Egyptian wooden pylon-shaped black painted shabti-box, complete with lid, an inscription on one side, Thebes, early 22nd dynasty, circa 900 B.C., 37 x 41.7 x 19.2cm.
(Bonhams) $3,220

An Egyptian wooden upper portion of a sarcophagus lid, with tri-partite wig and ritual beard, Ptolemaic Period, 300–30 B.C., 17¹/₂in.
(Bonhams) $1,932

An Apulian Red-Figure bell krater, both sides with a meander pattern on the base line, Greek South Italy, mid 4th century B.C., 15¹/₂in.
(Bonhams) $2,737

An Apulian black-glazed Red-Figure fish plate with undecorated depressed tondo surrounded by bream, Greek South Italy, later 4th century B.C., 7¹/₄in. diameter.
(Bonhams) $1,288

A Boeotian buff-colored terracotta seated female figure, the hollow body of flattened form with fully modeled head and arms, circa 600–550 B.C., 6in. high.
(Bonhams) $1,288

An Iranian terracotta pot stand with a central columnar support dividing into three struts, 1st millennium B.C., 1³/₄in. high.
(Bonhams) $365

A Luristan bronze axe-head, the cylindrical shaft-hole decorated with two standing rams, North West Iran, 1st millennium B.C., 6³/₄in. long.
(Bonhams) $465

A Canosan pottery askos, surmounted by the upper half of a male, circa 3rd century B.C., 13¹/₄in. high.
(Bonhams) $564

A Cypriot bichrome ware amphora, the neck decorated on either side with two panels, Iron Age, 10th-8th centuries B.C., 14in.
(Bonhams) $764

A Saite bronze seated cat, with pierced ears and finely detailed incised whiskers and broad collar with a rear loop, 26th Dynasty, 664–525 B.C., 6¹/₄in. high.
(Bonhams) $10,200

A sizeable Cypriot bichrome ware amphora, the neck decorated on either side with two panels, a four-leaf flower in each, Iron Age, 10th-8th centuries B.C., 21in.
(Bonhams) $2,400

A large Gnathian Ware black-glazed hydria, with ribbed body, Greek, South Italy, circa 3rd century B.C., 18in.
(Bonhams) $1,461

A finely modeled Alexandrian style bronze of a naked acrobatic negro with Afro-hairstyle, 3³/₄in.
(Bonhams) $3,000

An Etruscan hollow terracotta head of a female wearing a diadem and earrings, circa 4th-3rd century B.C., 9in.
(Bonhams) $830

A large Etrusco-Corinthian pottery olpe, the body decorated with five registers of animals, with wine-colored and umber slip, circa 600 B.C., 17½in. high.
(Bonhams) $4,200

A rare group of four squatting wooden servant figures, with white painted details, all wearing layered wigs, Middle Kingdom, 12th Dynasty, 20th century B.C., 6in.
(Bonhams) $7,200

A terracotta double horse and rider group, the horses attached centrally, their heads facing away from one another, 6in. high, Parthian, circa 1st-2nd century A.D.
(Bonhams) $581

A Daunian double askos, the handle joining the necks, both with strainers to restrict pouring, Greek, South Italy, circa 3rd century B.C., 7½in. high.
(Bonhams) $570

A sizeable Apulian knob-handled patera on a stemmed foot, with two long handles and enlivened with white and yellow showing the Greeks fighting the Amazons, Greek, South Italy, 4th century B.C., attributed to the Baltimore Painter, 10in. high.
(Bonhams) $8,250

An Orientalizing black-figure Greek amphora, the upper body decorated on side A with a centrally seated female Sphinx, a lion standing before her, 6th century B.C., 12¾in. high.
(Bonhams) $3,750

A buff-colored Messapian ornamental nestoris or torzella, umber decoration on the body, late 5th century B.C., 11¼in. high.
(Bonhams) $332

A large buff-colored askos with wide spout, the upper body decorated in umber, Greek, South Italy, second half of the 4th century B.C., 11¼in. high.
(Bonhams) $332

A substantial upper portion of a wooden sarcophagus lid, the tripartite wig painted blue, the face flesh colored, Ptolemaic Period, 18½in. mounted.
(Bonhams) $3,320

ARMOR

An early 17th century English pikeman's armor, comprising two piece pot, breastplate, backplate, tassets embossed. (Wallis & Wallis) **$2,318**

The breast plate and tassets from a mid 17th century English pikeman's harness, of munition quality with turned edges. (Andrew Bottomley) **$1,071**

A good set of French cuirassier's breastplate, backplate and helmet, 1845 pattern steel helmet with brass Medusa fronted crest. (Bosley's) **$4,590**

A composite German fluted 'Maximilian' full armor, partly early 16th century, together with a shaffron and saddle. (Christie's) **$20,746**

A white laced o-yoroi, the helmet bowl of twenty-plate hoshi bachi (knobbed bowl) of low rounded form. (Christie's) **$75,843**

A copy of the Innsbruck foot-combat armor of Giuliano de Medici, of bright steel, the cuff of the right gauntlet dated *1515*. (Christie's) **$22,218**

A Victorian officers' helmet, cuirass, shoulder belt and pouch of the Royal Horse Guards (The Blues), the silver plated helmet with gilt mounts.
(Wallis & Wallis) $4,017

An English mid 17th century pikeman's breastplate with tassets, raised medial ridge, turned over borders to neck and arm cusps, incised line decoration.
(Wallis & Wallis) $927

A Georgian officers' 1817 pattern helmet, and cuirass, of the Life Guards, silver plated helmet, skull and high comb.
(Wallis & Wallis) $6,335

An iron mogami do, the thirty-two plate russet iron helmet, covered with printed leather, late Edo period, 19th century.
(Christie's) $6,948

A German half-armour, comprising a cuirassier helmet, single deep gorget-plates, almain collar, cuirass and one-piece tassets, early 17th century.
(Christie's) $4,906

A well made miniature copy of a Gothic full suit of armor, 36in. overall, fluted salet with hinged visor, fluted two part breastplate, one piece tassets.
(Wallis & Wallis) $1,705

ARMOR

A Japanese half mask menpo, of black lacquered iron, red inside, copper teeth, bristle 'moustache' to detachable nose.
(Wallis & Wallis) $975

A fine 17th century Indian chainmail and lamellar shirt, composed of alternate rows of thick solid and riveted rings of various sizes, rectangular front plates with six embossed fish shaped buckles.
(Wallis & Wallis) $1,170

A 19th century Persian Qjar helmet khula khud, bowl chiseled with cartouches of Islamic script around base.
(Wallis & Wallis) $899

An English mid 17th century pikeman's breastplate of conventional form struck with crowned *IR* (Jacobus Rex) storekeeper's mark, raised medial ridge, turned over borders to neck and arm cusps.
(Wallis & Wallis) $1,003

A pair of articulated gauntlets from a black and white armor of the mid 16th century, the cuffs with pointed roped edges.
(Andrew Bottomley) $918

An English mid 17th century pikeman's breastplate, of conventional form, struck with crowned *IR* (Jacobus Rex) storekeeper's mark, medial ridge, turned over neck and arm cusps.
(Wallis & Wallis) $775

A breast-plate, of flattened globular form with bold angular turns at the neck and arms, circa 1490, 20^1/$_2$in. high.
(Christie's) $3,018

A fine and heavy Indian 17th century mail and lamellar shirt, the mail of alternate rows of thick solid forged ring and thick riveted rings.
(Wallis & Wallis) $991

A Victorian breast plate, made in imitation of a late 16th century North Italian example, with roped edges and finely etched bands of decoration.
(Andrew Bottomley) $719

ARMOR

A complete lower leg defence from a German full suit of armor, in the style of the early 16th century.
(Andrew Bottomley) $612

An Italian fingered gauntlet for the right hand, with one-piece cuff turned and roped at the border, circa 1540, attributed to the workshop of Filipo Negroli of Milan, 11¼in.
(Christie's) $22,632

A pair of Cromwellian style riding gauntlets, mid-19th century, with some finger elements lacking to right.
(Bonhams) $247

A 17th century cavalry troopers' breastplate, distinct medial ridge, turned over neck and arm cusps, painted in gilt and red with *From the Plains of Waterloo*.
(Wallis & Wallis) $358

A small chain mail vest, composed of small steel links, with simple butt joints, 26 x 16in.
(Andrew Bottomley) $428

An English Commonwealth period trooper's breastplate, of conventional form, struck with Commonwealth Armorers Company stamp, raised medial ridge, turned over neck and arm cusps.
(Wallis & Wallis) $562

A good heavy early 17th century cavalry trooper's breastplate, deeply struck with oval armorer's mark, distinct medial ridge, deeply incised *HC*, turned up borders pierced for lining.
(Wallis & Wallis) $612

A fine and heavy Indian 17th century mail and lamellar shirt, the mail of alternate rows of solid forged rings and riveted rings of various graduated sizes.
(Wallis & Wallis) $977

A rare Ottoman shaffron, formed of a single piece of steel with a horizontal flange at the top and shaped flanges round the eyes, circa 1512–20, 21⅛in.
(Christie's) $12,825

BAYONETS

An 1857 Whitworth rifle experimental bayonet, blade 23in., hexagonal muzzle ring, diced black leather grip.
(Wallis & Wallis)

$536

An 1879 Martini Henry artillery carbine sword bayonet, saw backed blade 25½in., marked with crown, *VR* and inspection stamps, steel mounts, in its leather scabbard.
(Wallis & Wallis)

$290

A rare marine artillery 1858 pattern sword bayonet, slightly curved blade 26in., by *CK*, steel mounts, diced black leather grips.
(Wallis & Wallis)

$337

A rare Bowie bladed bayonet, clipped back blade 8¼in., back fuller, maker *F.H*, steel mounts, diced black leather grips.
(Wallis & Wallis)

$291

A scarce brass hilted 1836 pattern constabulary carbine bayonet, blade 11¼in., short fuller, ribbed grip, the blade with inspection stamp, also stamped *2 BGG*.
(Wallis & Wallis)

$367

A scarce German World War I trench knife bayonet, clipped back blade 6in., King's head and knight's head trade mark of *WKC*, blackened finish to mounts, diced black grips.
(Wallis & Wallis)

$31

An 1837 pattern brass hilted Brunswick rifle bayonet, blade 22in., marked at forte crown, *VR*, *Enfield 1846*.
(Wallis & Wallis)

$222

A rare 1857 brass hilted constabulary bayonet, straight blade 21in. with central fuller, down turned crosspiece, ribbed grip.
(Wallis & Wallis)

$811

BOWIE KNIVES

A large Bowie style knife, probably American late 19th century, the hilt with brass pommel and guard, grooved leather grip and large clip pointed blade, blade 12in.
(Andrew Bottomley) $612

A Victorian Bowie knife, straight double edged blade 6in. by H. G. Long & Co., Sheffield, short German silver crosspiece, staghorn grips, mounted with German silver blank shield.
(Wallis & Wallis) $138

Fine English Bowie knife, 9in. clip point blade with *J. Rodgers & Sons No 5 Norfolk St Sheffield* stamped on one side on blade at ricasso, brass cross guard with ball quillons, steel handle.
(Butterfield & Butterfield) $1,320

A fine classic Bowie knife by George Wostenholm, polished clipped back blade 9¹/₄in., stamped *G. Wostenholm & Son Washington Works*, scalloped back edge, white metal crosspiece, two piece ebony grips.
(Wallis & Wallis) $612

Large Bowie knife marked *Arnachellum, Salem,* 10in. clip point blade with sharpened false edge, steel cross guard with rounded quillons, stag antler grip with steel ferrule.
(Butterfield & Butterfield) $1,210

Sheffield Bowie knife, Civil War era, the 7¹/₂in. clip point blade with etched panel *Death to Traitors* and marked at the ricasso *Manhattan/Cutlery/Sheffield*, small German silver quillons, length overall 12in.
(Butterfield & Butterfield) $550

CASED SETS

Cased pair of Colt Third Model 'Thuer' derringers, London proofed, serial numbers 10812 and 19316, .41 caliber, blued barrels with nickel plated frames, varnished walnut grips. (Butterfield & Butterfield) $3,575

Colt Model of 1911 pistol, Capt. C. G. Howe, Ordnance Dept. U.S.A., serial No. 190250, .45 ACP, 5in. barrel, 1913 patent dated slide, Rampant Colt without circle. (Butterfield & Butterfield) $1,980

Cased Lindsay Young America two shot superposed percussion pistol, serial No. 70, .41 caliber, 4in. barrel with floral engraving at breech, engraved brass frame, varnished walnut grips. (Butterfield & Butterfield) $3,300

Cased factory engraved Colt London single action army revolver, serial No. 53371, .450 Boxer caliber, 5¹/₂in. barrel marked *Colt's Pt. F. A. Mfg. Co. Hartford, Ct. U.S.A. Depot 14 Pall Mall London*, profusely scroll engraved. (Butterfield & Butterfield) $13,200

Cased pair of factory engraved Remington Model 1871 single shot pistols, serial numbers 3052 and 3054, additionally serial numbered 9 and 10, .50 caliber, 8in. silver plated barrel with scroll engraved panels. (Butterfield & Butterfield) $27,500

Cased English double barrel derringer by Woodward, serial No. 802, .30 Cf caliber, 2¹/₄in. gold plated swivel barrels, scroll engraved silver plated frame, ivory grips with engraved silver screw plates. (Butterfield & Butterfield) $4,400

Rare cased factory engraved Colt Model 1862 pocket navy percussion revolver, serial No. 5570 IE, .36 caliber, 4¹/₂in. barrel with New York address, ivory grips finely relief carved. (Butterfield & Butterfield) $13,200

Fine cased and Gustave Young engraved Smith & Wesson Model No. 1¹/₂ Second Issue revolver, serial No. 63752, .32 caliber, 3¹/₂in. barrel, blue finish, profusely engraved·with floriate scrolls. (Butterfield & Butterfield) $15,400

Rare cased pair of factory engraved Starr Model 1858 double army revolvers, serial numbers 6806 and 6613, .44 caliber, nickel plated finish, 6in. barrels with engraved panels at the breeches and on the barrel lugs, checkered walnut grips. (Butterfield & Butterfield) $12,100

An unusual pair of small flintlock pistols with rebrowned twist octagonal barrels signed in gold and with silver fore-sights, patent recessed breeches each with back-sight, by Joseph Egg, London, each barrel numbered 2151, London hallmarks for 1815. (Christie's) $9,430

Fine cased pair of French percussion salon pistols by Devisme, each 9¹/₂in. octagonal barrel with polygroove rifling in .52 caliber and profusely overlaid with gold, ebony half stock with relief scrollwork panels. (Butterfield & Butterfield) $26,400

A pair of Belgian percussion target pistols with sighted rebrowned twist octagonal multigroove rifled barrels, case-hardened breeches, engraved case-hardened tangs, signed case-hardened locks, by J. B. Rongé, Liège proof, circa 1850, 15³/₄in. (Christie's) $5,658

CASED SETS

A fine cased 7.65mm. Luger Swiss model 1900 commercial self-loading pistol by D.W.M., No. 474, old model receiver and toggle assembly with flat breech block and 'dished' toggle knobs, 4³/₄in. barrel.
(Christie's) **$5,451**

A fine pair of French percussion target pistols with sighted fluted octagonal barrels each signed in gold and decorated with encrusted silver and gold at the muzzle and breech, by Houllier Blanchard à Paris, circa 1860, 16¹/₄in.
(Christie's) **$14,145**

Cased Colt London single action army revolver, serial No. 37286, .450 Boxer caliber, 5¹/₂in. barrel with Pall Mall Depot markings, nickel plated finish, varnished walnut grips.
(Butterfield & Butterfield) **$7,700**

Boxed factory engraved Smith & Wesson Safety First Fourth Model double action revolver, serial No. 145433, .38 caliber, 3¹/₄in. barrel, nickel plated finish, mother-of-pearl grips.
(Butterfield & Butterfield) **$1,870**

An unusual pair of German percussion rifled saloon pistols with blued sighted octagonal barrels inlaid with silver and gold and with gold-inlaid signature on the top flat, by Carl Stiegele in München, circa 1870, 10³/₄in.
(Christie's) **$4,149**

A good quality pair of boxlock flintlock pocket pistols, signed *Baucheron Pirmet à Paris*, 1¹/₂in. turn off barrel with name inlaid in gold, folding triggers and lockwork engraved with floral leafwork.
(Bonhams) **$3,399**

CASED SETS

A Westley Richards patent 54-bore five-shot self-cocking percussion revolver, No. 266, with blued octagonal sighted rifled barrel fitted with Westley Richards patent rack and pinion rammer on the left side, 11¼in.
(Christie's) $2,263

A Colt 1851 model navy percussion revolver, No. 1611/. for 1853, the blued barrel with London address, the blued cylinder with naval engagement scene, silvered brass trigger-guard and grip-strap, 13in.
(Christie's) $8,487

Smith & Wesson Model No. 1 First Issue revolver with rare gutta percha case, serial No. 8909, .22 calibre, 3¼in. barrel, blued and silver plated finish, varnished rosewood grips.
(Butterfield & Butterfield) $6,050

Cased Kolibri automatic pistol, serial No. 27, 2.7mm., 1⅜in. barrel, marked with Austrian proof marks and numbered 27 on barrel, slide and trigger.
(Butterfield & Butterfield) $4,400

An unusual set of four Swiss percussion pistols, converted from flintlock, comprising a pair of dueling pistols and a pair of overcoat pistols, by F. Ulrich in Bern, early 19th century, 13½in. and 7¼in.
(Christie's) $4,904

Boxed Smith & Wesson K-22 masterpiece double action revolver, serial No. K15075, .22 caliber, 6in. barrel, blue finish with casehardened hammer and trigger, checkered walnut grips with silver S&W medallions.
(Butterfield & Butterfield) $715

American inlaid dagger, 6in. blade stamped *US* at ricasso, steel handle inlaid with ebony and mother of pearl in floral motif.
(Butterfield & Butterfield) $303

A scarce gunner's stiletto, circa 1650, triangular section blade 8in., with traces of engraved scale on one face, baluster forte, spirally carved solid horn grip inlaid with ivory pellets and brass piqué work.
(Wallis & Wallis) $228

A scarce Indian double katar, being a large katar 16in. overall, made hollow to receive a 14¹/₄in. solid steel katar which slides into it.
(Wallis & Wallis) $295

A Javanese kris, with waved pattern-welded blade chiseled (and originally gilt) with flowers and scrollwork, gilt wooden hilt carved as a figure of raksha, 22³/₄in. blade.
(Christie's) $1,414

Fine ivory hilted South American dagger, 19th century, straight 7¹/₂in. single edged blade with 3in. false edge, silver ferrule marked *Sterling* and engraved with the monogram *EF*, bulbous ivory grip relief carved, length overall 13¹/₂in.
(Butterfield & Butterfield) $770

A Nazi Luftwaffe officers' 1st pattern dagger, by SMF, plated mounts, navy blue leather wire bound grip, in its blue leather covered sheath with plated mounts and original suspension chains and belt clip.
(Wallis & Wallis) $326

DIRKS

Rare horsehead pommel American naval dirk, narrow single edge 8in. blade with 5in. double fullers and gilt floral decoration, spirally fluted ivory grip wound with three strands of twisted silver wire, length overall 12in.
(Butterfield & Butterfield) $1,980

An Imperial German naval officers' dirk, watered steel blade 8in., etched with sailing ships, fouled anchor and crown, and floral pattern, some gilding, lacquered brass mounts, crown pommel, ivory grip with brass wire binding.
(Wallis & Wallis) $815

A post 1902 Cameron Highlanders officer's dress dirk, single edged blade 11³/4in. with scalloped back edge, carved ebony grip with strapwork, bonnet and crossed swords in low relief, gilt fittings with thistles and acorns in relief.
(Wallis & Wallis) $310

Fine silver mounted English naval dirk by Dudley, the 9⁷/8in. blade of diamond section etched overall with scrolling florals, oval silver crossguard with lobed sections, silver ferrule, ivory grip, length overall 13¹/4in.
(Butterfield & Butterfield) $1,870

Fine gold and tortoiseshell mounted English naval dirk, narrow 15¹/2in. blade of diamond section with partially flattened median ridge, narrow recurved 18ct. gold quillons, faceted one piece tortoiseshell grip, length overall 19¹/2in.
(Butterfield & Butterfield) $3,575

English naval dirk, the 8¹/2in. blade with ³/4 blued and gilt decoration, gilt bronze hilt with oval dish, flattened spatulate quillons, ebony grips of tapering square section, length overall 12¹/4in.
(Butterfield & Butterfield) $1,540

Unusual Springfield marked flintlock carbine, round 26in. barrel in .69 caliber smoothbore and marked with *VP* and eagle head proof marks, lockplate marked *Spring/Field/1840*, full walnut stock.
(Butterfield & Butterfield) $2,475

A Dutch double barreled flintlock fowling-piece in the French taste, the twist sighted barrels with grooved rib and engraved tang, platinum vents, by Jan Frank, Amsterdam, Liège proof, early 19th century, 40³/₈in. barrels.
(Christie's) $3,206

A good late 18th century Indian matchlock gun torador, 72¹/₂in., deeply etched damascus twist barrel 52¹/₂in., chiseled cartouche at breech, raised rib, swollen polygonal muzzle gold damascened.
(Wallis & Wallis) $1,221

A Caucasian miquelet-lock blunderbuss-pistol with belled barrel damascened with silver and gold scrollwork at the muzzle and breech, Circassian walnut full stock inlaid with brass and horn rosettes, button trigger, 19th century, 16in.
(Christie's) $1,886

A good early 19th century Algerian toe-lock flintlock gun jezail, 75in., octagonal barrel 58¹/₂in. with Spanish makers marks, threequarter stocked, lock with applied foliate chiseled brass decoration.
(Wallis & Wallis) $763

A Liège double barreled flintlock sporting gun with twist sighted barrels, plain tang also forming the back-sight, signed flat beveled locks, reinforced cocks, by Jean Baptiste Heuseux à Liège, early 19th century, 31¹/₂in. barrels.
(Christie's) $2,640

A flintlock blunderbuss by Clarke of Dublin, graduated brass barrel, stepped lock, brass mounts.
(Bonhams) $386

FLINTLOCK GUNS

An early English dog-lock musket with three-stage sighted barrel, signed flat beveled lock, the cock engraved with the arms of the city of Dartmouth, signed *James Barker Fecit*, London proof marks, circa 1660, 46¼in. barrel.
(Christie's) $7,544

A Spanish miquelet-lock blunderbuss with belled three-stage barrel inlaid at the breech, patilla lock with fluted bridle on the cock and pan, walnut full stock with Catalan butt, second half 18th century, 18½in.
(Christie's) $4,526

A flintlock carbine with an earlier two-stage barrel from the Munich court workshop, finely chiseled in relief on a gilt ground, signed *Gandon*, the barrel almost certainly by Daniel Sadeler, early 17th century, the remainder circa 1740–50, 29½in.
(Christie's) $15,088

A Spanish miquelet-lock blunderbuss with Dutch two-stage brass barrel, octagonal breech struck with Amsterdam town mark on the top flat, signed patilla lock, late 18th century, 28in.
(Christie's) $2,452

A brass barreled flintlock blunderbuss circa 1700–1710, 32in., flared barrel 16¼in. octagonal at breech with raised ring, London proved with maker's mark of sun above EN, fullstocked, flattened lock with traces of engraving.
(Wallis & Wallis) $1,224

American flintlock musketoon, round 24in. barrel in .69 caliber smoothbore, engraved lock marked *Wilkes* and fitted with roller mounted frizzen spring, walnut full stock, length overall 40in.
(Butterfield & Butterfield) $2,090

A scarce 10 bore Tower Short Land pattern flintlock musket, 58in. overall, barrel 42in. with Tower proofs at breech, rounded lock with swan-neck cock, walnut stock.
(Wallis & Wallis) $1,224

Fine French wheellock holster pistol, early 17th century, the 11⁵/₈in. part round/part octagonal barrel in .62 caliber smoothbore, front sight set in engraved panel with stippled gold ground, walnut stock with horn fore-end cap.
(Butterfield & Butterfield) $5,500

An extremely rare French long wheel-lock holster pistol, with slender two-stage barrel with gilt ribbed muzzle-ring and stepped gilt molded breech engraved with conventional foliage and two rosettes, early 17th century, 32³/₄in.
(Christie's) $51,842

U.S. Model 1826 flintlock navy pistol, the 8¹/₂in. barrel in .54 caliber, lock marked *U.S./S. North* and dated *1826*, steel furniture.
(Butterfield & Butterfield) $990

A rare German wheel-lock hand mortar with heavy brass two-stage barrel recessed at the breech, iron trigger-guard, and baluster trigger, circa 1600, 18⁵/₈in.
(Christie's) $22,218

Fine French flintlock pistol by Peniet, circa 1805, octagonal 8in. sighted barrel with swamped muzzle and polygroove rifling in .54 caliber, walnut full stock profusely inlaid with roped silver ropes, checkered grip, length overall 13¹/₂in.
(Butterfield & Butterfield) $22,000

A Turkish over-and-under flintlock holster pistol with two-stage barrels each retaining traces of original blueing and gold-damascened at the octagonal breech with trophies of arms, counterfeit London proof marks, 19th century, 19¹/₈in.
(Christie's) $2,829

An 18th century brass mounted flintlock holster pistol by Henry Hadley, swamped barrel London proved, with maker's stamp, fullstocked, shell carved behind the barrel tang.
(Wallis & Wallis)   **$1,197**

American silver mounted 'Kentucky' flintlock pistol, octagonal 9¼in. steel barrel rifled in .38 caliber, top flat marked *Cochran* and fitted with rear sight and silver front sight, length overall 14in.
(Butterfield & Butterfield)   **$9,900**

A Caucasian miquelet-lock pistol, the etched twist barrel with sighting flat, chiseled details at the muzzle and breech, full length tang incorporating the back-sight, figured Circassian walnut full stock, 19th century, 18in.
(Christie's)   **$2,452**

An officers' 16 bore flintlock holster pistol by Rigby of Dublin, 13½in., browned octagonal twist barrels 8¼in., twin gold inlaid breech lines, silver vent plug.
(Wallis & Wallis)   **$1,120**

A 22 bore silver mounted cannon barreled flintlock holster pistol by R. Willoughby, 12in., turn off barrel 5½in., London proved, maker's stamp *RW*, foliate engraved breech.
(Wallis & Wallis)   **$1,043**

A fine German silver-mounted flintlock pistol with sighted barrel retaining traces of original blueing and chiseled in low relief at the breech with rococo ornament, unsigned, mid-18th century, 14¼in.
(Christie's)   **$2,829**

German type steel sallet with elongated tapering neckpiece, forger's mark at rim, 1450–60. (Auktionsverket) $1,830

A Cromwellian trooper's lobster tail helmet with triple bar face guard, two piece skull, one piece neck guard with embossed 'articulations'. (Wallis & Wallis) $1,262

Indian Army, an officer's white Wolsey pattern Foreign Service helmet complete with blue pagri, brass spike to top. (Bosley's) $291

East Yorkshire Militia, a Napoleonic officer's bicorn hat with fire gilded regimental button to front with 'Y' above EM to center of an eight-pointed star. (Bosley's) $1,912

An early 17th century Continental cuirassier close helmet, the skull of two pieces, joined together at the comb, incorporating small plume holder to rear. (Andrew Bottomley) $3,366

A Cromwellian officer's helmet, two piece skull with embossed vertical ribs, hanging ring to apex. (Wallis & Wallis) $367

A Georgian officer's 1817 pattern helmet of the Household Cavalry, silver plated skull and high comb, in its original shaped case. (Wallis & Wallis) $2,745

A Prussian M 1895 other ranks' Pickelhaube, white metal helmet plate, spike and mounts, both cockades. (Wallis & Wallis) $314

Coldstream Guards Boer War other rank's Foreign Service helmet, khaki body with brass rosettes to sides. (Bosley's) $415

HELMETS

An Imperial German 'Death's Head' Hussar officers' busby, German silver busby badge.
(Wallis & Wallis) $2,163

A good Imperial German officers' busby of the Leib Garde Hussar Regiment, silvered and enamel busby badge.
(Wallis & Wallis) $2,009

An Italian morion, in one piece, the rounded skull with roped comb, down-turned brim pointed fore and aft, circa 1550, 8¹/₂in. high.
(Christie's) $2,452

An Imperial German officers' Pickelhaube of the 3rd Battalion 92nd Brunswick Regiment, gilt helmet badge with silvered skull and crossbones.
(Wallis & Wallis) $1,545

A cuirassier helmet with ovoidal ribbed two-piece skull, bevor and pointed fall, single gorget-plate at front and rear, circa 1630, probably German, 11¹/₂in. high.
(Christie's) $1,886

A 19th century Prussian copper Pickelhaube, the conical spike issuing from a nickel plated elliptical spike base.
(Spencer's) $428

A burgonet, circa 1600, with old repair to the body and replacement cheek pieces.
(Bonhams) $742

An Artillery officer's blue cloth helmet with King's Crown Militia helmet plate, in original tin.
(Bonhams) $170

A cabasset circa 1600, formed in one piece, 'pear stalk' finial to crown.
(Wallis & Wallis) $245

HELMETS

A late 16th century Italian high comb close helmet adapted for the Pisan bridge festival, one piece skull with roped comb.
(Wallis & Wallis) $1,521

A scarce Nazi NSKK despatch rider's black leather helmet, metal eagle helmet plate, transfer Edelweiss badge to side of helmet.
(Wallis & Wallis) $244

Indian Army officer's lungi of blue and gold, together with gold embroidered kulla with red velvet base.
(Bosley's) $1,224

A North Italian barbute, made in one piece, the rounded skull arched over the face and rising to a central ridge, circa 1450, 10in. high.
(Christie's) $9,807

A close-helmet, comprising one-piece skull with roped comb, the pointed visor with single roped vision slit and fitting into the upper-bevor, circa 1560, 11$\frac{1}{2}$in. high.
(Christie's) $6,412

A Victorian officers' helmet, worn 1853–55, of the Durham Artillery Militia, black patent leather skull with silver plated copper peak binding.
(Wallis & Wallis) $2,936

A good 19th century Indo-Persian devil's head kulah khud, bowl finely silver damascened overall with intricate flowers and foliage within geometric cartouches.
(Wallis & Wallis) $1,140

An Imperial Prussian Jäger Battalion Reservist officer's M1897 shako, gilt helmet plate with Landwehr cross.
(Wallis & Wallis) $736

A scarce Victorian other ranks gray cloth spiked helmet of the Queen's Westminster Volunteers, darkened Maltese Cross helmet plate on scarlet backing.
(Wallis & Wallis) $913

HELMETS

An Imperial Prussian M1897 Tschapka of a Reservist officer of the Garde Ulanen Regiment (as worn by Nos 1 and 3). (Wallis & Wallis) $611

A German black and white comb morion, the two-piece skull with high roped comb, circa 1600, 10½in. high. (Christie's) $1,320

An Imperial Prussian Artillerymans Pickelhaube, brass helmet badge with *Colberg 1807*. (Wallis & Wallis) $556

An officer's gilt metal helmet of The 5th (Princess Charlotte of Wales's) Dragoon Guards, gilt mounts, ear to ear wreath, gilt and silver plated helmet plate. (Wallis & Wallis) $1,677

16th century close helmet with high comb, pointed visor with single vision slit, ringed and studded neckplate. (Auktionsverket) $1,923

A good Imperial Garde Du Corps officers' helmet, gilt skull, silvered helmet badge with enameled center. (Wallis & Wallis) $5,253

An Imperial Prussian Volunteer Private Purchase M 1897 tschapka, as worn by the 9, 10, 11, 12 Uhlan Regiments, single cockades. (Wallis & Wallis) $685

A pre World War II black cloth helmet of the West Sussex Constabulary, blackened helmet plate with German silver central device. (Wallis & Wallis) $126

A lobster-tailed pot, the adjustable bar nasal struck with an S mark, second quarter 17th century, probably German, 12in. high. (Christie's) $1,320

ARMS & ARMOR

A scarce German World War II trench fighting knife, blade 8in., wood grips containing corkscrew, pricker and screwdriver, in its black painted steel sheath.
(Wallis & Wallis)   **$202**

English dirk knife, straight 4¹/₂in. blade of diamond section, silver plate quillon block with short, recurved fluted quillons, octagonal ivory grip, 8¹/₂in.
(Butterfield & Butterfield)   **$660**

A good 19th century Spanish folding knife navaja, blade 8¹/₂in. stamped *Valero Jun Saragoza*, gilt sides of alternate brass plates and horn.
(Wallis & Wallis)   **$130**

World War II Special Forces knuckleduster fighting knife with brass grip, large steel cross-guard, double edged blade, probably NZ/Australian made.
(Bosley's)   **$1,170**

An English agate hilted silver mounted knife, 2 prong fork circa 1660, swollen blade 5¹/₄in. stamped with maker *Brown*, foliate engraved silver ferrules, swollen smokey agate octagonal handles with engraved silver buttons.
(Wallis & Wallis)   **$518**

An unusual diver's knife, shallow diamond section blade 6¹/₂in. stamped *Siebe & Gorman*, flattened mahogany grip, screw thread around bottom mount allows knife to screw into cylindrical brass sheath.
(Wallis & Wallis)   **$295**

A 19th century Ceylonese knife piah-kaetta, blade 7¹/₄in. with applied silver decoration, scroll brass mounts with silver decoration, scroll carved horn grips with engraved silver mounts. (Wallis & Wallis) $588

A gold mounted Nepalese kukri, blade 13³/₄in., horn hilt with gold ferrule, in its black leather covered sheath with large gold mounts, locket embossed and chased with the arms of Nepal. (Wallis & Wallis)
                                                                        $407

A large late 19th century Spanish clasp knife, navaja, folding blade 17¹/₂in. with pronounced clipped back tip, etched with foliate pattern and engraved around edge of panel. (Wallis & Wallis)
                                                                        $520

Silver mounted gaucho knife, straight 7in. single edged blade with etched panels of cattle drive and gauchos, hollowcast silver hilt of tapering hexagonal section. (Butterfield & Butterfield)
                                                                        $248

A German World War I hunting trench knife, clipped back blade 5¹/₂in., WKC trade mark, reversed steel crosspiece, all metal imitation staghorn hilt, in its steel sheath. (Wallis & Wallis)
                                                                        $93

Elaborate English dirk knife, acutely pointed 5¹/₄in. blade of diamond section, elaborate silver plated German silver scrollwork hilt, brown velvet covered silver mounted scabbard, length overall 9in.
(Butterfield & Butterfield)
                                                                        $770

A Nazi metal desk ornament made to commemorate the 'Pact of Steel', (the Axis Alliance), central globe surmounted by brass eagle bordered with swastika and fasces.
(Wallis & Wallis) $352

An extremely rare pair of English enameled rowel spurs, of brass cast and chased with scrolling vine leaves and grapes, third quarter 17th century, 6¼in.
(Christie's) $12,259

Rare Barney and Berrys Patent three barrel Rapidfire saluting cannon, early 20th century, brass 9in. barrel cast in one piece in 3 bore Cf calibre.
(Butterfield & Butterfield) $7,150

A fine Eley Sporting and Military cartridge display-board, with metallic and paper dummy-cartridges and components arranged radially around an Eley medallion, oak framed, 31 x 25¾in. overall.
(Christie's) $4,543

Paint and gilt decorated drum, America, mid 19th century, labeled *Porter Blanchard, Concord, New Hampshire*, with ebony drumsticks, 16¾in. diameter.
(Skinner) $8,050

A Nobel cartridge display-board, the selection of proprietary sporting cartridges arranged radially upon a cloth shield, oak framed, 28¾ x 19½in. overall.
(Christie's) $3,634

Unmarked four pound powder tin, oval shaped with brass screw off top, marked in gold paint *4lb. GUNPOWDER*.
(Butterfield & Butterfield) $440

A pair of late Victorian back-to-back buff silk pipe-banners of the 1st Battalion The Seaforth Highlanders.
(Wallis & Wallis) $811

A Victorian officers sabretache flap only of the 1st (Royal) Dragoons, circa 1850, broad gilt lace border embroidered *Peninsula* and *Waterloo*.
(Wallis & Wallis) $978

MILITARIA

A Georgian other ranks black leather shoulder belt and pouch, probably for cavalry, belt with tooled line to edges, pouch with rounded inner flap.
(Wallis & Wallis) $897

A scarce double cavity steel bullet mold for .56in. Colt revolving rifle, the sprue cutter stamped *Colts Patent* (faint).
(Wallis & Wallis) $232

An extremely rare German bolt-quiver, of wood flaring toward the base and of plano-convex section covered on the front with pigskin, late 15th century, 17$^{1/4}$in.
(Christie's) $10,939

A Victorian officers' full dress embroidered sabretache of the Lancashire Hussars, crimson cloth, gilt lace border, embroidered crown and rose on VR cypher.
(Wallis & Wallis) $839

A rare Indian shield boss with concealed percussion pistol circa 1825, truncated conical body with hinged lid reveals boxlock percussion pistol.
(Wallis & Wallis) $793

Walker Patent powder bucket, the cylindrical copper bucket with bail handles at the sides, having two copper and one wooden lid, 8$^{1/2}$in. high.
(Butterfield & Butterfield) $990

A very rare Bohemian pavise, of wood covered with gesso-covered canvas, late 15th century, 50in. high.
(Christie's) $54,694

A rare Winchester cartridge display-board, the large selection of metallic, brass and paper-case rifle and shot cartridges arranged in the form of an extended 'W', oak framed, 39$^{3/4}$ x 57$^{1/4}$in. overall.
(Christie's) $6,178

A Victorian officers' full dress embroidered sabretache of the 8th The King's Royal Irish Hussars, circa 1856.
(Wallis & Wallis) $2,009

ARMS & ARMOR

A large back action percussion punt gun with 1¼in. bore diameter, 81in., heavy barrel 72in. with brass foresight, stock 36in. long, back action lock.
(Wallis & Wallis) $439

Marlin-Ballard No. 6½ Rigby off-hand mid range rifle, serial No. 3583, .38–50 caliber, 28in. round barrel, Rigby breech with engraved band at muzzle, windgauge globe front sight.
(Butterfield & Butterfield) $4,125

Rare engraved Sharps-Borchardt long range rifle, serial No. 364, .45 caliber, 30in. octagonal barrel marked *Old Reliable, Sharps Rifle Co. Bridgeport Conn.* and *Cal. 45*, windgauge spirit level front sight.
(Butterfield & Butterfield) $25,300

Rare Gustav Young engraved Sharps Model 1851 box lock sporting rifle, serial No. 1510, .45 caliber, heavy 28in. octagonal barrel marked *Robbins &/Lawrence* and finely scroll engraved.
(Butterfield & Butterfield) $18,700

U.S. Model 1841 Lindner Alteration 'Mississippi' percussion rifle, the 28in. barrel rifled in .54 caliber, lock marked *Robbins/&/Lawrence/U.S.* and *Windsor Vt./1850*, walnut furniture with brass furniture and patch box.
(Butterfield & Butterfield) $6,050

Rare inscribed and engraved Sharps Model 1852 percussion carbine, serial No. 2953, .52 caliber, 21in. browned barrel engraved with floral scroll panels, tang mounted peep sight, varnished walnut stock and fore-end.
(Butterfield & Butterfield) $33,000

U.S. Navy Jenks-Merrill conversion carbine, .54 calibre, 25in. browned barrel equipped with single standing and double folding leaf rear sight, breech mechanism marked *Jas. A. Merrill/Balto Patented/July 1858*, walnut stock.
(Butterfield & Butterfield) $7,150

Winchester Model 1876 Deluxe rifle British proofed, serial No. 39635, .50–95 Express caliber, 22in. round barrel with ramp front sight, two folding and one standing leaf express rear sight.
(Butterfield & Butterfield) $6,050

Winchester Model 1876 lever action rifle, serial No. 9568, .40–60 caliber, 26in. octagonal barrel with full magazine, blue finish, single set trigger.
(Butterfield & Butterfield)

$4,125

Winchester model of 1917 rifle, serial No. 21622, .30–06, 26in. barrel marked *W 8–17*, together with Winchester 1917 bayonet.
(Butterfield & Butterfield)

$1,430

Deluxe Parker Bros. double barrel hammerless shotgun, serial No. 82343, 12 gauge, 30in. barrels with bead fore-sight on matte rin inscribed *PIDGEON GUN PARKER BROS. MAKERS. MERIDEN. CONN. WHITWORTH STEEL.*
(Butterfield & Butterfield)

$220

A percussion blunderbuss by Raper, 14in. graduated brass barrel with sprung bayonet, brass mounts, scroll engraved bar lock.
(Bonhams)

$927

Scarce Maynard Model 1873 Improved mid-range and hunting rifle, caliber .35–30 Maynard, 32in. part round/part octagonal barrel equipped with unmarked telescopic sight, checkered fore-end and pistol grip stock, Swiss buttplate.
(Butterfield & Butterfield)

$2,475

Parker Bros., double barrel hammer gun, serial No. 90825, 12 gauge, 30in. browned single twist damascus barrels with matte rib, simple bead fore-sight and engraved breech borders.
(Butterfield & Butterfield)

$3,025

Winchester Model 1895 lever action rifle, serial No. 92888, .303 caliber British, 28in. round barrel, blue finish overall, plain straight walnut stock.
(Butterfield & Butterfield)

$4,400

Winchester M1 carbine, serial No. 133389, .30M1, 18in. barrel, early type front band, operating rod, bolt and rear sight.
(Butterfield & Butterfield)

$770

An early 16 bore double barreled percussion pistol by Deakin of London circa 1825, 15in., twist browned barrels 9¹/₄in. with gold breech line, top rib engraved *London*, engraved breech, platinum safety plugs to breech drums.
(Wallis & Wallis) $980

A 6 shot 80 bore self cocking bar hammer transitional percussion revolver, 10¹/₂in. overall, octagonal barrel 4¹/₂in. with Birmingham proofs, the hammer with sighting slot, rounded scroll engraved frame.
(Wallis & Wallis) $839

A 9mm. Mauser model 1898 semi-automatic pistol, 11¹/₂in. overall, tubed barrel 5¹/₄in., number 815157, rearsight to 1000m., flat sided hammer with large hole, ribbed wood grips with traces of figure *9*.
(Wallis & Wallis) $704

U.S. Model 1842 percussion pistol by H. Aston, caliber .54, breech marked *U.S./S.M.P.*, lockplated dated *1848*.
(Butterfield & Butterfield) $605

A 16 bore rifled military style percussion holster pistol, 16in., barrel 10in., Birmingham black powder proof stamped 25, breech stamped *R Jones Manchester St Liverpool*, fullstocked.
(Wallis & Wallis) $649

American 'Kentucky' mule ear percussion pistol, octagonal 7in. barrel in .44 caliber smoothbore, unmarked lock, curly maple full stock, length overall 12in.
(Butterfield & Butterfield) $3,300

PERCUSSION REVOLVERS

Forehand & Wadsworth New Model army revolver, serial No. 489, .44 Russian caliber, 6³/₄in. barrel, blue finish, walnut grips. (Butterfield & Butterfield) $3,575

Rogers & Spencer percussion army revolver, serial No. 2238, .44 caliber, 7¹/₂in. barrel, blue finish, oil finished walnut grips with *RPB* inspector's cartouche. (Butterfield & Butterfield) $2,750

Rare Colt 1847 Walker Model percussion revolver, E Company no 120, .44 caliber, 9in. barrel, walnut grips. (Butterfield & Butterfield) $187,000

A Webley .455 Mk VI Service revolver, No. 262049, dated *1917*, Enfield grips, bearing release marks, backstrap engraved *J. D. Hignett.* (Bonhams) $151

A 6 shot .44in. Remington New Model Army single action percussion revolver, 14in. overall, barrel 8in., number 77621, large number 751 stamped on left side of breech, walnut grips with government inspector's initials. (Wallis & Wallis) $624

A 6 shot 54 bore self cocking percussion pepperbox revolver, 9in., barrels 4in., Birmingham proved, foliate engraved round frame, bar hammer, backstrap engraved *Philip Webley London.* (Wallis & Wallis) $1,144

PERCUSSION REVOLVERS

A 6 shot .44in. Starr Arms & Co. Army percussion revolver No. 35720, 13½in., round barrel 8in., underlever rammer, one piece wooden grip with government inspectors initials.
(Wallis & Wallis) $667

Colt Model 1851 navy conversion revolver, serial No. 54294, .38 Cf calibre, 7½in. barrel marked *Address Saml Colt New York City*, blued and casehardened finish with silver plated trigger guard/grip strap.
(Butterfield & Butterfield) $8,250

Starr Model 1858 double action navy revolver, serial No. 896, .36 caliber, 6in. barrel, blue finish, walnut grips.
(Butterfield & Butterfield) $1,320

A rare Belgian/French 5mm. Dolne Apache combination revolver knuckle-duster knife pistol, circa 1880, folding trigger and hinged dagger blade with flamboyant edge.
(Andrew Bottomley) $1,473

A 6 shot .455in. Webley Mark VI double action service revolver, 11½in. overall, barrel 6in., number 398470, the frame dated *1918*.
(Wallis & Wallis) $193

A 6 shot .36in. Savage Navy percussion revolver, 14in., octagonal barrel 7in., underlever rammer, heart shaped trigger guard, ring cocking trigger.
(Wallis & Wallis) $695

PERCUSSION REVOLVERS

Rare 1876 Centennial Winchester revolver, not serialized, .50 caliber, 7¹/₂in. barrel, fluted bottleneck six shot cylinder, full nickel plated finish.
(Butterfield & Butterfield) $82,500

U.S. Colt Artillery single action army, David F. Clark, serial No. 116375, .45 Colt, 5¹/₂in. barrel, dough-nut style ejector, trigger guard serial number 1892 A, backstrap 11294.
(Butterfield & Butterfield) $3,300

Factory engraved Remington New Model pocket conversion revolver, serial No. 24814, .32 caliber, 3¹/₂in. barrel, scroll engraved on barrel, cylinder and frame, mother-of-pearl grips.
(Butterfield & Butterfield) $2,750

A scarce 5 shot .31in. Colt Pocket 'Little Dragoon' percussion revolver No. 14266, 9¹/₂in., barrel 5in. stamped *Address Saml Colt New York City*, underlever rammer, cylinder roll engraved with stage coach hold up scene.
(Wallis & Wallis) $3,708

A good 5 shot .31in. Colt Pocket Model percussion revolver No. 253095, 9¹/₂in., octagonal blued barrel 5in., London proved cylinder roll engraved with stage coach hold up scene.
(Wallis & Wallis) $757

A 6 shot .36in. Colt Navy single action percussion revolver, No. 126903/2, 12¹/₂in., barrel 7¹/₂in. stamped *Address Col Saml Colt New York US America*, underlever rammer (numbered 9999), cylinder faintly roll engraved.
(Wallis & Wallis) $980

ARMS & ARMOR

Shell sporting powder flask, shell motif on both faces, complete with carrying cord. (Butterfield & Butterfield) $154

An engraved powderhorn, possibly Siege of Boston School, signed *Roxbury, Massachusetts*, and dated *1775*, inscribed, *Elisha Taylor*, 13³/₄in. high. (Christie's) $8,050

Fluted sporting powder flask, overall full fluted on both faces. (Butterfield & Butterfield) $220

A German circular copper priming-flask, the front domed with a central boss embossed in relief with a grotesque mask, probably mid-16th century, 4³/₄in. high. (Christie's) $1,886

Fine gold and silver inlaid bronze powder flask by Henri Le Page, with relief panel on one side depicting Diana reclining, length overall 9in. (Butterfield & Butterfield) $20,900

A German 'musketeer's' powder-flask, of triangular form, with wooden body covered with black velvet and with blackened iron mounts, early 17th century, 9⁷/₈in. high. (Christie's) $1,697

U.S.N. fouled anchor powder flask, top marked *N.P. Ames 1843 W.A.T.* (Butterfield & Butterfield) $413

Fluted sporting powder flask, screw-off top marked *G. & J. W. Hawksley*, 3¹/₂ x 7⁵/₈in. (Butterfield & Butterfield) $440

Colt's Patent cannon and flags KM Model 1851 navy powder flask, lacquered body, marked *KM 313*. (Butterfield & Butterfield) $935

ARMS & ARMOR

A rare Dixon's copper powder flask in the form of a gun stock, with registration mark.
(Bonhams) $139

U.S. Peace flask, screw off top marked Batey 1847.
(Butterfield & Butterfield) $3,850

Rare elaborate cast sporting powder flask, screw off top marked *G. & J. W. Hawksley.*
(Butterfield & Butterfield) $3,300

Dead game sporting powder flask, hanging game with fern and grain motif on one side, over the legend *James Dixon & Sons.*
(Butterfield & Butterfield) $440

Fine European powder flask probably French, dated *1581*, of triangular form, the black velvet covered wooden flask enclosed in a gilt copper frame, 10¼in. high.
(Butterfield & Butterfield) $8,800

Rare elongated three compartment pistol powder flask, screw off top, swinging covers for ball and cap receptacles at base.
(Butterfield & Butterfield) $330

Dolphin pistol powder flask, body in the form of entwined dolphins, measuring 1½ x 3in.
(Butterfield & Butterfield) $880

Colt Dragoon sloping charger powder flask, cannon, flags, panoply-of-arms over crossed rifles, pistols and *Colt's Patent* riband motif.
(Butterfield & Butterfield) $5,225

Large violin shape sporting powder flask, screw-off top marked *G. & J. W. Hawksley,* 9in. high.
(Butterfield & Butterfield) $330

ARMS & ARMOUR

U.S. James bolt, missing sabot, 3.8in. caliber, 7in. long. (Butterfield & Butterfield) $2,090

Confederate Archer bolt, missing lead sabot, 3in. caliber, 6in. long. (Butterfield & Butterfield) $385

U.S. James canister round, with canvas covering. (Butterfield & Butterfield) $4,125

French rifled projectile, circa late 19th century, two rows of lead studs, missing fuse, 6½in. long. (Butterfield & Butterfield) $302

German Krupp canister, portion of tin side cut away to expose the canister balls for display, wooden sabot intact, circa late 19th century, 8³⁄₈in. long. (Butterfield & Butterfield) $137

U.S. 12-pound howitzer canister, for the howitzer cannon, wooden cylinder is longer than standard canister, 4.62 caliber. (Butterfield & Butterfield) $3,300

U.S. Sawyer pattern projectile, iron body covered by a lead jacket, missing fuse, 9⁵⁄₈in. long. (Butterfield & Butterfield) $1,870

Solid shot with metal banded wood sabot, 4in. in diameter. (Butterfield & Butterfield) $1,760

Late 19th century French rifled projectile, approximate 4.5in. caliber, large lead studs in two rows, missing fuse, 9¹⁄₈in. long. (Butterfield & Butterfield) $275

SHELLS

British Blakely projectile, three vertical flanges, missing fuse, 10in. long.
(Butterfield & Butterfield)
$1,980

32-pound stand of grapeshot, complete with top and bottom plate 6.4in. caliber, 8¹/₂in., long.
(Butterfield & Butterfield)
$2,200

U.S. Hotchkiss bolt, missing lead sabot, 3.67in. caliber, 7¹/₄in. long.
(Butterfield & Butterfield)
$165

U.S. 2.6in. canister round, portion of tin side cut away to expose the canister balls for display, wooden sabot intact, 6¹/₄in. long.
(Butterfield & Butterfield)
$3,575

U.S. 1-pound Ketchum hand grenade, complete with paper fins marked: *Patented Aug. 20 1861*, 10⁵/₁₆in. long.
(Butterfield & Butterfield)
$3,300

U.S.N. 12-pound canister round, portion of tin side removed to expose canister shot, wooden sabot on base intact, 4.62in. calibre.
(Butterfield & Butterfield)
$2,090

Rare stand of pre Civil War quilted grape, 13 balls wrapped in canvas with wooden base, 3³/₄in. long.
(Butterfield & Butterfield)
$1,760

British Whitworth rifled spherical solid shot, first appeared in 1867 Whitworth's manual, 5⁷/₁₆in. diameter.
(Butterfield & Butterfield)
$1,650

British Britten projectile, 4.5in. caliber, missing fuse, lead sabot, 8in. long.
(Butterfield & Butterfield)
$715

A good Victorian 1821 pattern light cavalry officer's undress sword, slightly curved blade 34in., reputedly the sword of John Wilkie, 10th Hussars, commanded the regiment in the Crimea. (Wallis & Wallis) $644

A good 19th century Chinese Manchu sword, 28in., slightly curved bi-fullered single edged blade 18½in., brass tape bound sharkskin grip, brass pommel, ferrule, circular guard and scabbard mounts all cast with dragons and clouds in low relief. (Wallis & Wallis) $295

A French late 18th century officer's Napoleonic era saber, plain curved blade 33in., narrow back fuller, clipped back point, brass hilt, plain double side loop. (Wallis & Wallis) $736

A well made 19th century Moro sword barong, swollen single edged blade 17¼in., brass ferrule with finely woven bindings, foliate carved finely figured wooden pommel. (Wallis & Wallis) $237

A fine silver-gilt presentation small-sword, scabbard and case, with slender blade of hollow-ground triangular section etched, blued and gilt throughout its length, London silver hallmarks for 1798, maker's mark of Moses Brent, 35in. blade. (Christie's) $41,492

A Chinese river pirate's double sword, shallow diamond section blades 18in. inlaid with brass pellets, cast brass makarra crosspiece, pommels cast with dragons amidst scrolls, fluted horn grips. (Wallis & Wallis) $474

A George V 1865 pattern Scottish officers' military broadsword, straight blade 33in., with central fuller, by Henry Wilkinson, Pall Mall (No. 643638), etched with Royal cypher, thistles, Regimental badge and *Queen's Own Cameron Highlanders*. (Wallis & Wallis) $618

A Victorian 1865 pattern Scottish officers military broadsword, straight, double edged, double fullered blade 32in. by Utrecht, George St. Edinburgh, etched with crown, VR, strung bugle, *'90th Highland Borderers'*.
(Wallis & Wallis) $604

A rare Viking sword, in excavated condition, with broad slightly tapering pattern-welded blade of flat section, the iron hilt comprising short straight quillons and 'tea-cosy' pommel, 10th/11th century, probably Rhenish, 29¹/₄in. blade.
(Christie's) $11,693

An Imperial German train battalion officer's sword, curved plated blade 33in. by W. Dame Magdeburg, etched within panel upon blued background *Magdeb. Train Bataillon No 4*.
(Wallis & Wallis) $267

A German sword, in excavated condition, the long slightly curved single-edged blade cut along the back with a series of shallow steps, circa 1500, 35³/₄in. blade.
(Christie's) $1,886

A Nazi naval officers' sword, plain, curved pipeback, clipped backed blade 31in., by E. & F. Horster, in its brass mounted leather scabbard, locket with repeated number and eagle stamp above *M*.
(Wallis & Wallis) $342

An Italian sword of the Historismus period in early Renaissance style, the broad triangular blade with two wide shallow fullers on each face, the hilt of gilt iron, mid-19th century, 33¹/₂in. blade.
(Christie's) $5,555

A mid 17th century English basket hilted backsword, bi-fullered blade 35in., hilt foliate chiseled with broad thumb scroll, side bars screwed to foliate chiseled pommel.
(Wallis & Wallis) $689

TSUBAS

A Mito school tsuba, decorated and carved in relief with a teakettle, the reverse with a Chinese teapot, late Edo period, 19th century, 8.5cm.
(Christie's) $1,233

A rounded-square shibuichi tsuba decorated with a silver dragon in takazogan, late Edo period, 19th century, 8cm.
(Christie's) $1,280

A rounded-square iron ishimeji-tsuba depicting a scene of aritoshi with a man carrying a lantern and an umbrella, signed *Katsuhei* (1804–1886), 8.1cm.
(Christie's) $7,314

A shibuichi tsuba by Teikan, of rounded-square form decorated with an elephant and a karako holding a hoe in takabori and iroe takazogan, signed, late Edo period, 19th century, 7.1cm.
(Christie's) $4,934

A circular silver shibuichi tsuba by Masatoshi, pierced and carved with a dragon in nikubori and ji-sukashi with gold flames, signed *Suifu ju Masatoshi*, late Edo period, 19th century, 7.9cm.
(Christie's) $2,277

A rounded-square copper tsuba, depicting the Old Hag of Adachi-ga-hara, gold details, signed *Kitokuan Keiou heiin aki* and a gold seal, late Edo period, 19th century, 8.5cm.
(Christie's) $3,036

An iron bizen shoami tsuba, of irregular shape pierced with pine trees in marubori and gold nunome-zogan, mid Edo period, 18th century, 8.6cm.
(Christie's) $1,328

An irregularly-shaped sentoku tsuba, in the form of a coiled snake attacking a monkey in marubori, signed *Ichiryuken Shjin kore o tsukuru*, late Edo period, 8.2cm.
(Christie's) $3,416

An Akao school iron tsuba, pierced with gohei and reeds, the thick mimi in the form of a rope, late Edo period, 19th century, 7.8cm.
(Christie's) $759

TSUBAS

A rounded-square shibuichi tsuba decorated with Kwanyu mounted on a horse, Mito school, signed *Fujitoshi*, late Edo period, 19th century, 6.4cm. (Christie's) $1,097

An irregularly-shaped iron tsuba decorated with a bird perched on a grape vine, with signature *Kazutsura*, late Edo period, 19th century, 7.3cm. (Christie's) $639

A Fujita Toshinaga tsuba, in the form of a toad in nikubori, the eyes inlaid with gold and shakudo, signed *Koshi nen* (1864), late Edo period, 7.1cm. (Christie's) $2,467

An oval iron Soten tsuba, depicting the battle on the bridge of the Uji river in ji-sukashi and iroe zogan, with signature *Goshu Hikone ju, Soheishi nyudo Soten sei*, mid Edo period, 18th century, 7.3cm. (Christie's) $1,139

An aoi-gata copper tsuba by Yoshinori, decorated with mokume patterns of mixed soft metals comprising silver, shakudo and copper, signed *Bushu ju Yoshinori*, late Edo period, 8.6cm. (Christie's) $2,277

A large iron rounded-square tsuba by Yoshitoshi, depicting Hotei and his sack in silver, shibuichi and iroe takazogan, signed *Shizen, Yoshitoshi ro* and a gold seal, late Edo period, 8.6cm. (Christie's) $1,898

An irregularly-shaped iron tsuba decorated with tall grasses against the moon in takabori, signed *Kongosai Gassan* (1815–1875), 7cm. (Christie's) $914

An iron tsuba, of irregular form forming a well with a bucket in very high relief, signed *Sempu Genjuryo Nagakiyo*, mid Edo period, 18th century, 6.5cm. (Christie's) $1,139

An aori-gata iron tsuba, decorated with a female demon, signed *Shorakusai Katsusada* and a gold seal, late Edo period, 19th century, 8.8cm. (Christie's) $4,554

ARMS & ARMOR

A circular shibuichi Nanako tsuba, depicting a plover beside a stream, late Edo period (19th century), 7.5cm.
(Christie's) $3,312

A copper Hirata Hikozo tsuba, of multi-lobed flower shape (kiku), 17th century, 7.2cm.
(Christie's) $6,440

An Umetada shakudo tsuba, forming two small shoulder drum heads decorated with cherry blossoms, early Edo period (circa 1700), 6.4cm.
(Christie's) $1,747

A daisho pair of rounded-square shakudo nanako tsuba, each depicting Minamoto no Yoshitsune playing the flute on a horse, both signed *Kikuoka Mitsumasa* (1759–1824), 8.1cm. and 7.5cm.
(Christie's) $5,486

An irregularly-shaped iron tsuba by Arai Teruyuki, forming a group of monkeys at play in nikubori, copper and gold details, signed *Ryuchiken Teruyuki* (Arai), 8cm., late Edo period.
(Christie's) $2,087

A circular iron tsuba, decorated with Kappa and a cucumber floating on a stream in the rain in silver and iroe takazogan, signature *Otsuryuken Miboku*, mid Edo period, 18th century, 8.5cm.
(Christie's) $1,708

A stylish circular Kaga tsuba, the copper plate inlaid with shakudo and silver shippo patterns, with signature *Haruaki Hogen* and *Kao*, late Edo period, 8.3cm.
(Christie's) $2,392

A shakudo nanako Ko-Mino tsuba, of circular form, the nanako plate decorated with shakudo and gilt takazogan, Momoyama period (16th century), 7.4cm.
(Christie's) $1,379

An oval shibuichi tsuba by Masayuki, the plate decorated with a flying crane with silver wings, shakudo body, signed, late Edo period (19th century), 7.8cm.
(Christie's) $3,680

74

TSUBAS

A circular iron Kyo-Sukashi tsuba, the large plate pierced with wild geese in flight, early Edo period (17th century), 8.8cm.
(Christie's) $2,208

A gourd-shaped tsuba, the iron plate depicting a young lady enticing her baby to breast feed, with signature *Katsuryuken Masayoshi*, 19th century, 8.2cm. (Christie's) $1,472

An oron lacquered Kenjo Higo tsuba, of oval form decorated with fuji flowers and leaves in gold hiramakie, late Edo period, 7.8cm.
(Christie's) $1,011

A large red lacquered tsuba by Hokei, decorated with Buddhist priests and symbols in nikubori, signed *Toto ju Okutani Hokei saku*, late Edo/Meiji period, late 19th/early 20th century, 9.5cm.
(Christie's) $9,108

A square Sentoku tsuba by Ryuso, portraying three shakudo kappa with gilt grass skirts, signed, late Edo period (19th century), 8.2cm.
(Christie's) $1,472

A rounded-square iron tsuba by Teikan, depicting a temple guardian with three eyes and a sleeping bozu in takabori and gold zogan, signed *Teikan* and a gold seal, late Edo period, 8.9cm.
(Christie's) $10,626

A rounded-square copper tsuba by Nobukatsu, the hari-ishimeji plate carved and decorated with kappa trying to catch a floating cucumber, late Edo period (19th century), 7.3cm.
(Christie's) $1,472

A Mokkogata Ko-Mino tsuba, of shakudo nanako plate decorated with flowering shrubs and insects, early Edo period (17th century), 7.9cm.
(Christie's) $1,195

A circular shakudo tsuba by Goto Mitsutomo, a large plate carved with the design of dragon and wave in katakiribori, late Edo period (19th century), 7.9cm.
(Christie's) $1,195

A New Hampshire Civil War uniform, a black wool coat with eight brass buttons inscribed *New Hampshire*, 32½in. long. (Christie's) $1,093

Nurse's dress World War I period, blue cotton full length, pleated front, no buttons. (Bosley's) $125

South Wales Borderers, 1902 pattern officer's service dress tunic, with high-necked collar, complete with Sam Browne belt. (Bosley's) $529

A Drum Major's full dress scarlet tunic, circa 1908, of the 4th Bn. The Prince of Wales's Vols. (South Lancs. Regt.), white facings and piping, silver lace trim to collar and wings. (Wallis & Wallis) $298

An extremely rare early 19th century Georgian officer's coatee of an Inspector of Yeomanry and Volunteers, scarlet cloth with dark blue facings to both collar and cuffs. (Bosley's) $872

A World War I Major's khaki service dress tunic of the Denbighshire Yeomanry (TR), rank badges to cuffs, bronze collar badges with TR below, POW's feathers on buttons. (Wallis & Wallis) $314

A rare Imperial Prussian General's M1861 full dress navy blue tunic, full dress bullion sash and double tassels.
(Wallis & Wallis)　　　$1,293

A Lieutenant's (Reserve) full dress scarlet tunic of the Welsh Guards, blue facings, buttons in 5s to chest.
(Wallis & Wallis)　　　$458

3rd Dragoon Guards officer's 1864 pattern scarlet tunic with yellow facings to cuff, collar and piping to front.
(Bosley's)　　　$377

Army Service Corps Ammunition Column, 1902 pattern other rank's khaki serge tunic with formation signs of the 14th Siege Battery Royal Garrison Artillery.
(Bosley's)　　　$716

A good Lieutenants full dress blue uniform dated *1911*, of the Army Service Corps, comprising: helmet, tunic, gilt lace shoulder belt and black PL pouch.
(Wallis & Wallis)　　　$1,349

104th Bengal Fusiliers 1868– 1880 pattern officer's scarlet tunic, pair of gold bullion flaming grenades with single bullion QVC (denoting rank of Lieutenant-Colonel) to collar.
(Bosley's)　　　$592

An extremely rare William IV period officer's coatee of an Inspector of Yeomanry, scarlet melton cloth with dark blue facings to both collar and cuffs. (Bosley's) $965

A flying jacket of 'The Flying Tigers', painted leather 14th AF roundel to chest, with name tag 'C. D. Moizahn' above. (Wallis & Wallis) $487

A rare Boer War period lance corporal's Service Dress tunic, scarlet on white chevron to right sleeve. (Wallis & Wallis) $564

An Imperial German officer's full dress navy blue tunic of the Prussian Guard Grenadier Regiment No. 2 to the rank of Captain. (Wallis & Wallis) $1,254

A good World War II US leather flying jacket of the 14th Army Air Force, 'The Flying Tigers', large cloth 14th AF roundel to right chest. (Wallis & Wallis) $565

Earl of Chester's Yeomanry, officer's full dress short tailed coatee of Yeomanry pattern circa 1840, dark blue cloth with scarlet facings to cuff. (Bosley's) $514

Northumberland Yeomanry, late 19th century Hussar pattern officer's tunic worn by Lord Ravensworth, Honorary Colonel of the Regiment.
(Bosley's) $1,760

A sergeant's full dress rifle green tunic of the 1st Vol. Bn. The Essex Regt., eleven embroidered badges to left sleeve.
(Wallis & Wallis) $1,019

A good late Victorian uniform of The Gordon Highlanders made for a boy, including: scarlet doublet, Gordon tartan kilt and plaid.
(Wallis & Wallis) $1,373

A Hussar Captains' (Reserve) full dress blue tunic, gilt gimp and braid trim, including six loops with olivets and purl buttons to chest.
(Wallis & Wallis) $440

Royal Air Force First Pattern khaki officer's service dress tunic, lieutenant (Flying Officer) rank lace to cuff, gilt metal eagle and crown above.
(Bosley's) $604

A sergeant's full dress scarlet tunic of the Essex Regt., white facings, brass collar badges, five embroidered badges to left sleeve.
(Wallis & Wallis) $978

An all steel European cavalryman's mace, circa 1560, the head comprising several flanges, of tapered form and terminating in a square sectioned point, the shaft in two stages, overall 24in.
(Andrew Bottomley)

$2,295

A good Ceylonese polearm Patisthanaya, 77in. overall, head 12¼in., wavy blades, inlaid with brass and silver pamels, foliate chiseled and with brass and silver ⟍ lines.
(Wallis & Wallis)

$915

A Georgian halberd, 92½in. overall, pierced blades with fleur-de-lys device, square section top spike faceted at base, reinforced socket, riveted side straps.
(Wallis & Wallis)

$534

A scarce mid 16th century German claw backed halberd, head 24½in. overall, diamond section top spike, slender crescent blade struck with 'T' shaped maker's mark, with a pair of three piercings, three pointed claw to rear.
(Wallis & Wallis)

$741

A North American Plains Indian pole axe tomahawk, the head with curved axe blade and top and rear spikes, the wooden shaft decorated with brass headed nails, possibly 18th century, overall 24in.
(Andrew Bottomley)

$1,913

An Indo Persian horseman's battle axe, probably early 19th century, the head with sharply down curved blade, decorated overall with gold koftgari work flowers and foliage, the round shaft terminating in large pointed finial, overall 21in.
(Andrew Bottomley)

$337

ARMS & ARMOR

A small German stonebow (Schnepper), with slender steel bow, two fore-sight pillars, folding back-sight mounted on the built-in gaffle, early 17th century, 18^{1}/$_{2}$in.
(Christie's) $1,886

A fine and rare gothic sporting crossbow, with robust composite bow covered with birch bark overlaid with paper, retained by cords and fitted with oval blackened iron stirrup at the front, late 15th century, 30^{3}/$_{4}$in.
(Christie's) $22,632

A scarce German pistol sized crossbow circa 1700, 19in., reinforced span 14^{3}/$_{4}$in., fruitwood stock, iron nut released by setting trigger, iron trigger guard and suspension loop.
(Wallis & Wallis) $977

A German sporting crossbow, with associated steel bow struck with a mark, wooden tiller veneered with panels of staghorn, early 17th century, 24^{1}/$_{2}$in.
(Christie's) $1,886

A German sporting crossbow, retained by its original cords, wooden tiller swelling towards the middle and inlaid in white staghorn, small iron stirrup and nut, late 16th century, 24^{1}/$_{4}$in.
(Christie's) $4,814

Nat King Cole, signed sepia 5 x 7in., seated at piano with the trio.
(Vennett-Smith) $192

Chester W. Nimitz, Admiral, signed and inscribed 8 x 10in. reproduction of Japanese Surrender.
(Vennett-Smith) $525

Leo Tolstoy, signed sepia postcard in Russian script, head and shoulders, 1910.
(Vennett-Smith) $907

Josephine Baker, signed and inscribed postcard, half length in costume, first name only, 1936.
(Vennett-Smith) $154

Pablo Casals, signed and inscribed 9 x 9½in. page from a program (artists sketch), 1964.
(Vennett-Smith) $82

J. R. Tolkein, autograph signed letter, one page, 13th May 1925, to Miss Basleigh, apologising for mislaying her application.
(Vennett-Smith) $656

Leonard Bernstein, signed 7 x 9½in., head and shoulders smiling.
(Vennett-Smith) $82

Karl Donitz, typed signed letter, one page, 16th December 1972, on Grossadmiral headed notepaper, in German to Mr Gray.
(Vennett-Smith) $134

Franz Lehar, signed copy of the sheet music entitled 'Melodien fur Akkordeon'.
(Vennett-Smith) $89

Lillie Langtry, signed postcard, three quarter length in semi profile.
(Vennett-Smith) $295

Mother Teresa, two signed letters, each one page, 28th September 1993.
(Vennett-Smith) $83

Harry Houdini, signed postcard, with surname only, half length in profile.
(Vennett-Smith) $1,345

Boris Yeltsin, signed hardback edition of 'Against the Grain' First Edition, signed to title page.
(Vennett-Smith) $356

Signed 7 x 7in. by both Lyndon B. Johnson and Willy Brandt individually, half length talking to each other.
(Vennett-Smith) $344

Roald Amundsen, signed letter, one page, 29th January 1926, to Miss Sams, mentioning the date he reached the South Pole.
(Vennett-Smith) $205

Pablo Casals, autograph letter, one page, 7th June 1914, in French.
(Vennett-Smith) $128

Harry Houdini, hardback edition of The Unmasking of Robert-Houdin, by Harry Houdini, New York 1908, signed to flyleaf.
(Vennett-Smith) $761

David Hockney, signed color 6 x 4in. of the painting 'Peter Schlesinger'.
(Vennett-Smith) $103

Graham Hill, signed postcard, in motor racing car.
(Vennett-Smith) $88

Charles Dickens, signed, check, made payable to Messrs. Flower and Sons for £21, dated 13th February 1861.
(Vennett-Smith) $525

Oscar Wilde, signed piece, 4¹/₂ x 2in., small attached photo.
(Vennett-Smith) $448

Juan Peron, autographed signed letter, on one side of a correspondence card, Madrid, 19th September 1964.
(Vennett-Smith) $164

Signed 8 x 6in., by James Callaghan, Jimmy Carter and Helmut Schmidt, standing outside Downing Street, 1977.
(Vennett-Smith) $122

Adolf Hitler, signed Christmas greetings card, December 1943, with typed inscription SS Oberfuhrer Georg Bochmann.
(Vennett-Smith) $1,640

Enrico Caruso, signed concert program to the cast list, Aida, at the Royal Opera House, Covent Garden, 11th July.
(Vennett-Smith) $192

Napoleon Bonaparte, framed document dated December Milhunsensix, appointment Certificate to the Legion of Honor for Mareschal de Sauvagney, signed Napoleon, one page, folio, framed with original large wax seal.
(Eldred's) $2,310

Corinne Luchaire, French actress who was convicted as a Nazi Collaborator after World War II, signed and inscribed sepia 7 x 9¹/₂in.
(Vennett-Smith) $148

Leonid Brezhnev, signed picture postcard, also signed by Gustav Husak and Ludwig Svoboda.
(Vennett-Smith) $312

Hans Ulrich Rudel, signed original 7 x 5in., talking to another airman, in uniform.
(Vennett-Smith) $156

Benjamin Disraeli, autograph signed note, June 1861, admitting bearer to the Gallery.
(Vennett-Smith) $397

General Charles Gordon, signed piece cut from letter as Governor General of Sudan. (Vennett-Smith) $240

Andy Warhol, signature on white card, 8 x 3in. (Vennett-Smith) $107

Charles Darwin, signed piece, 4³/₄ x 2¹/₂in., dated in his hand 25th March 1870. (Vennett-Smith) $405

Alexander Fleming, an excellent signed 7¹/₂ x 5¹/₂in., showing Fleming seated working in his lab. (Vennett-Smith) $778

Harry Houdini, signed card, 'Harry Handcuff Houdini, 7th February 1909, Glasgow Scotland'. (Vennett-Smith) $672

Princess Diana, signed invitation card for Her Birthday Luncheon in aid of Rainbow House, at the Savoy Hotel, 1st July 1991. (Vennett-Smith) $615

Paul Robeson, signed sepia 8 x 10in., three quarter length standing alongside his wife at Waterloo. (Vennett-Smith) $90

Prince Charles and Princess Diana, signed Christmas greetings card by both individually, featuring color photo of them, with Princes William and Harry. (Vennett-Smith) $2,624

Marconi, a black and white head and shoulders photographic postcard of the 'Rotary' series, 5³/₈ x 3¹/₂in., signed in black ink. (Bonhams) $354

Alfred Hitchcock, signed Royal Academy Summer Exhibition 1948 Order Form for tickets. (Vennett-Smith) $152

Louis Armstrong, signed album page, early example, with attached newspaper photo. (Vennett-Smith) $90

Steve McQueen, signed 7¹/₂ x 9¹/₂in. to reverse, head and shoulders in profile. (Vennett-Smith) $288

Yuri Gagarin, first man in space, signed 9 x 6½in., head and shoulders in uniform. (Vennett-Smith) $262

Mahatma Gandhi, signed 7 x 5in., three quarter length in crowd arriving at St. James Palace for the India Round Table Conference. (Vennett-Smith) $640

P. T. Barnum, a good signed sepia 12½ x 16in., 24th October 1885. (Vennett-Smith) $512

Adolf Hitler, fine signed document, at base, one page, Berchtesgaden, 23rd July 1935, in German, relating to Dr. Fritz Freiherrn Von Maffenbach. (Vennett-Smith) $1,804

Laurel and Hardy, an expremely fine pair of individual signed and inscribed sepia 8 x 10ins. (Vennett-Smith) $2,296

J. R. R. Tolkein, signed menu for the Annual Dinner at the Mermaid Club in Oxford, 25th February 1933. (Vennett-Smith) $443

Winston S. Churchill, small signed piece, beneath calligraphic reproduction quotation *Never in the field of human conflict*. (Vennett-Smith) $256

Walt Disney, large hardback edition of 'Fantasia', U.S. edition 1940, signed by Disney to title page B. (uenos) A. (ries), 1941. (Vennett-Smith) $1,886

Adolf Hitler, signed piece, in pencil, overmounted in black beneath contemporary postcard photo and printed caption, Munich, 1936, 10 x 6½in. overall. (Vennett-Smith) $787

AUTOGRAPHS

Nelson Mandela, signed card, 12th July 1990, overmounted in burgundy beneath 4 x 4in. magazine photo.
(Vennett-Smith) $134

William H. Taft, signed typed letter, one page, War Dept., Washington, 4th March 1908, to M. D. Fritz.
(Vennett-Smith) $167

Sir Winston S. Churchill, signed 7 x 11in., to mount, full signature, half length wearing bowtie.
(Vennett-Smith) $1,574

Helen Keller, signed typed letter, one page, 8th February 1958, to Mr. Konigsmark.
(Vennett-Smith) $208

Two black and white 11 x 14in. portrait photographs of Winston and Clementine Churchill, both signed, mounted, framed and glazed.
(Bonhams) $1,705

S.S. Gruppenführer, Hermann Preiss, Commander of the First S.S. Panzer Corps, won swords to the Knights Cross, signed 8 x 10in., head and shoulders in uniform.
(Vennett-Smith) $148

Prince Charles, signed hardback edition of Highgrove: Portrait of an Estate, signed to title page 1994.
(Vennett-Smith) $1,017

Wallis, Duchess of Windsor, autographed signed letter, sixteen pages, Boulevard Suchet, Paris, 19th November, no year (1940's), 'The Duke is so near the breaking point'.
(Vennett-Smith) $1,246

Sarah Bernhardt, signed postcard, three quarter length standing, arms resting on ornamental table, 1910.
(Vennett-Smith) $120

Duke of Wellington, autograph letter, one page, 20th May 1838, to Lord Lowther.
(Vennett-Smith) $168

Josephine Baker, signed postcard, full length in top hat and tails.
(Vennett-Smith) $288

ABBA, signed 8 x 11in. promotional magazine photo by all four.
(Vennett-Smith) $88

George Bernard Shaw, autograph letter, on one side of a correspondence card, 21st April 1914, to Constable & Co. London.
(Vennett-Smith) $240

Adolf Hitler, a signed document, with signature struck through with instruction in another hand that he wished to remove it, two pages in German.
(Vennett-Smith) $1,440

Winston S. Churchill, large signed color 21 x 28½in. print of Churchill, being a reproduction of the painting by Frank Salisbury.
(Vennett-Smith) $992

Jascha Heifetz, signed concert program to inside page, 1936.
(Vennett-Smith) $120

W. C. Handy, signed and inscribed sheet music, 'Memphis Blues', 1946.
(Vennett-Smith) $112

Margot Fonteyn, three postcards and signed letter, one page, 1955, referring to 'Sylvia'.
(Vennett-Smith) $104

AUTOMATONS

No. 45 Clown Violinist by Lambert, with turning and nodding composition head, 66in. high.
(Christie's) $3,198

Gilt bronze singing bird automaton, the base set with 'Sèvres' plaques depicting figural scenes against a turquoise ground, 17in. high.
(William Doyle) $4,887

A Gustave Vichy musical automaton bust of a gypsy lyre player, French, circa 1900, 20in.
(Sotheby's) $10,833

A mid-19th century portable barrel piano, the keyboard later converted to ten automaton figures in national costume, stamped inside *Hicks, Maker, Bristol*, 37½in. high.
(Woolley & Wallis) $1,264

An electrically driven automaton, of two monkeys at the breakfast table, constructed by The Fife Engineering Co. Ltd., 23in. wide, circa 1935.
(Christie's) $673

Copurchic No. 213 by Roullet & Decamps, revolving on his right foot while turning his head, 22in. high.
(Christie's) $5,330

J. H. Animations, England, an electrically-powered automata of a holidaying photographer with a Sunpet 826 camera.
(Christie's) $460

Palibois' three juggling clowns, with painted composition faces, original spangled costumes, 26in. high, circa 1880.
(Christie's) $6,751

Vichy Rabbit Magician, holding a cabbage from which a monkey's head appears, 19in. high.
(Christie's) $7,106

A rosewood Transitional barometer, Davis, Worcester, circa 1850, 38in.
(Bonhams) $968

A Charles X eglomise barometer, signed *Ortoli à Rouen*. (Hôtel de Ventes Horta) $895

A brass Standard barometer working on Fortin's principle by F. Darton & Co. Ltd., 51in. high.
(Spencer's) $765

A Regency mahogany and inlaid wheel barometer, signed *J. M. Ronketti*, 1m. high.
(Phillips) $582

A 19th century rosewood wheel barometer/ thermometer by R. Mears, Boston, 108cm. high.
(Spencer's) $612

A Regency mahogany bow-front stick barometer, signed *J. Ramsden London*, 38¹/₂in. high.
(Christie's) $5,055

An Empire rosewood wheel barometer and thermometer, signed *Leydecker, Quay des Augustins, 55, Paris*, 41in. high.
(Christie's) $903

A George III mahogany and checkerstrung stick barometer, signed *Campione, Oxford*, 3ft. 3¹/₂in. high.
(Phillips) $1,349

A Victorian mother-of-pearl inlaid rosewood banjo clock barometer, signed *Calderara, London*, 51½in. high. (Christie's)
$5,417

A George III mahogany stick barometer, the brass dial signed *C. Lincoln, London*, 1.03m. high. (Phillips) $1,155

A 19th century French giltwood wheel barometer, with oval painted wood dial, 88cm. high. (Phillips) $524

An important Queen Anne walnut column barometer, signed *Daniel Quare, London, No. 24*, 39¼in. high. (Christie's)
$67,981

Mahogany barometer, signed *Solaro en Butti fec*, Dutch, 19th century. (Kunsthaus am Museum)
$1,516

A 19th century French ormolu mounted wheel barometer, the replaced card dial signed *Gleizes, Paris*, 1.13m. high. (Phillips) $2,926

Rosewood carved and brass mounted gimbal barometer, J.B. Leroy, Jersey, circa 1869, 37in. high. (Skinner) $3,737

A good late George III wheel barometer/thermometer/timepiece by C.A. Canti of Town Malling, Kent, 51in. high. (Spencer's) $4,000

A hanging decorated woven basket, American, 19th century, the double handled crest over a rounded rectangular woven body, 17¼in. long.
(Christie's) $345

A leather key basket, initialed *J.R. McK.*, probably Richmond, Virginia, circa 1830, 7⅛in. high.
(Sotheby's) $41,400

A blue-painted and decorated woven basket, American, 19th century, with wooden handles at either end, 12in. long.
(Christie's) $173

A wicker picnic basket, containing a fitted interior with flasks, sandwich boxes, stamped *A. Barrett & Sons.*
(Christie's) $1,100

Nantucket basket, early 20th century, some splint breaks, 10in. diameter.
(Skinner) $431

A red and blue-painted woven basket, American, 19th century, the rectangular basket with a shaped wooden handle, 14¾in. long.
(Christie's) $368

A red-painted woven and handled diminutive buttocks basket, American, probably Virginia, first half 19th century, 5in. high.
(Sotheby's) $1,380

Large Nantucket basket, late 19th century, branded *C.W. Chapin* on handle and twice on base, swing handle, 13in. diameter.
(Skinner) $1,495

A rare tooled leather key basket, probably Shenandoah Valley, Virginia, mid 19th century, the shaped sides heightened with decorative tooling, 8½in. high.
(Sotheby's) $1,955

BOXING MEMORABILIA

Mohammed Ali, signed color
8 x 10in., full-length in boxing
pose.
(Vennett-Smith) $118

The Gold Medal of the
International Sporting Club of
New York, 17th January 1921,
Middleweight (160lbs), contest
won by H. Mallin.
(Bonhams) $1,320

Robert Duran, signed color
8 x 10in., half length in jubilant
boxing pose.
(Vennett-Smith) $74

Mike Tyson, signed color 8 x
10in., half length in boxing pose.
(Vennett-Smith) $128

Muhammed Ali, gloves by
Goldsmith of Cincinnati (these
gloves were from the contest
against Joe Bugner on February
14th, 1972, at Las Vegas).
(Bonhams) $1,808

Mike Tyson, signed color 8 x
10in., full-length in boxing pose
in ring.
(Vennett-Smith) $104

Joe Bugner, gloves by Baily's
(from a fight in
Wolverhampton).
(Bonhams) $226

Frank Bruno, gloves by Bryan
(the fight versus Larry Frazier,
4th December, 1985 at the Royal
Albert Hall).
(Bonhams) $362

Rocky Marciano, gloves by
Goldsmith of Cincinnati (from
Mickey Duff via the National
Sporting Club).
(Bonhams) $1,658

A French bronze study of a lion, cast from a model by Thomas-François Cartier, late 19th/early 20th century, 20½in. wide. (Christie's) $731

Hagenauer, stylised female head, 1930s, in lightly beaten, electroplated metal, stamped with *WHW* monogram, 26.5cm. (Sotheby's) $3,353

A German bronze study of a bear, cast from a model by D. Moldenhauer, late 19th/early 20th century, 11¾in. wide. (Christie's) $1,004

A bronze figure, signed *P.T.M.RENDA* and with *CHIURAZZI NAPOLI* foundry mark, of a naked and drunken boy, Neapolitan, early 20th century, 18in. high. (Christie's) $1,102

A pair of ormolu candlesticks, each with central tapering fluted and reeded shaft flanked by three upturned entwined dolphins, 5½in. high. (Christie's) $6,279

Demetre H. Chiparus, Dancer, 1920s, in cold painted bronze and ivory, on stepped, faceted red marble base, marked, 23in. (Sotheby's) $22,356

Dakon, stylized woman's head, 1930s, modeled in cold painted bronze as a female face with hair composed of twists of metal, marked, 27.5cm. high. (Sotheby's) $2,422

Demetre H. Chiparus, 'Kneeling Dancer', 1920s, cold painted brown, silver and gold with ivory face and hands, marked, 58cm. high. (Sotheby's) £27,600 $44,712

A French bronze bust entitled 'La Pensée', cast from a model by Gustave Michel, showing a lady looking to her right, late 19th century, 12½in. high. (Christie's) $456

A bronze figure after Giambologna, of Kneeling Venus, probably French, late 19th century, 9¼in. high. (Christie's) $1,745

A life size French bronze portrait figure of Emma Bierne, cast from the model by Hippolyte Moreau, last quarter 19th century, 50½in. high. (Christie's) $45,712

A gilt-bronze figure of a naked fisherboy emptying a pot, Neapolitan, early 20th century, 20½in. high. (Christie's) $2,021

An American bronze figure of Sophocles, cast from the model by John Talbott Donaghue, the young naked Greek playing a lyre, late 19th century, 44½in. high. (Christie's) $31,084

A pair of English bronze thoroughbred horses, cast by Elkington and Co. probably from models by Sir Joseph Edgar Boehm, late 19th century, 12¼in. and 14½in. high. (Christie's) $6,948

A French bronze and parcel-gilt bust of Helen of Troy, cast from the model by Jean-Baptiste Clesinger, third quarter 19th century, 30½in. high. (Christie's) $14,628

A bronze figure, signed *A. Sorgi* and with *CHIURAZZI NAPOLI* foundry signature, of a naked fisherboy, Neapolitan, early 20th century, 13¾in. high. (Christie's) $2,021

Hagenauer, kneeling woman, 1930s, one arm outstretched, the other raised, in hammered, patinated brass, stamped with *WHW* monogram, 94.5cm. (Sotheby's) $5,589

Raoul Larche, Loie Fuller lamp, circa 1900, gilt bronze, the dancer with raised arms, wearing a flowing gown, 46cm. high. (Sotheby's) $17,699

Alexandre Kelety (French, fl. 1918–1940), Exotic Dancer, unsigned, bronze with various patinas, silvered and gilded, 18¹/₂in. high.
(Skinner) $13,800

Beatrice Fenton (American, 1887–after 1982), The Acrobat, signed and dated *1926*, bronze, 5¹/₂in. high.
(Skinner) $3,450

Patinated bust of Longfellow, after a model by Thomas Brock, signed and dated *London 1884*, further inscribed *Elkington & Co. Founders*, 32in. high.
(William Doyle) $1,955

Paul Howard Manship (American, 1885–1966), Seated Nude, signed, bronze with brown patina, 12⁵/₈in. high.
(Skinner) $5,750

Pair of Louis XVI gilt bronze figures, each modeled as a classically draped woman, 12in. high overall.
(William Doyle) $2,185

Donald Delue (American, b. 1897), Eve, signed, bronze with golden brown patina, 11 x 11 x 6in.
(Skinner) $4,025

A bronze warrior in classical Greek armor, on rectangular variegated black marble base, 8in. wide.
(Christie's) $282

Abastenia St. Leger Eberle (American, 1878–1942), Seated Scribe, signed, bronze with brown patina, 7 x 7in.
(Skinner) $1,725

Attributed to A. Kelety, bronze stag, 1930s, modeled as a stylized stag poised with his head bent back, 41.5cm. high.
(Sotheby's) $1,341

A bronze Marly horse after Coustou, French, late 19th century, 23¹/₄in. high. (Christie's) $2,119

Art Deco cold painted metal and ivorene woman with dogs, after George Gori, France, circa 1930, cold painted decoration in black and gold with ivorene on brown onyx veneer base, 20⁵/₈in. high. (Skinner) $2,185

J. A. Hatfield after Chantry, bronze bust of Queen Victoria in the classical style, 17in. high. (Cheffins Grain & Comins) $988

Chinese archaic bronze covered vessel, Fanghu Han dynasty (206 B.C.–220 A.D.), surmounted by a square cover with four animal form finials, 16¹/₄in. high overall. (William Doyle) $1,265

Pair of Louis XVI style gilt bronze mounted malachite covered urns, each shield shaped body with elongated handles, 24in. high. (William Doyle) $6,612

Gilt bronze and ivory figure of a dancer, her costume with polychrome and enamel decoration, signed *Omerth*, on marble base, 14in. high. (William Doyle) $4,600

Hagenauer, female mask, 1930s, cast in bronze with stylized features, stamped *Hagenauer*, 21cm. (Sotheby's) $745

Maude Sherwood Jewett (American, b. 1873), 'Dancers', an orchid holder, signed, dated and stamped, bronze with green/ brown patina, 10¹/₄in. high. (Skinner) $4,370

Bronze and ivory figure of a dancer, after a model by P. Philippe, circa 1900, set on an onyx base, 12in. high. (William Doyle) $4,600

Donald Delue (American, b. 1897), Leda and the Swan, signed, bronze with golden brown patina, 8 x 11in. (Skinner) $4,025

George Edwin Bissell (America, 1839–1920), Bronze bust of Abraham Lincoln, signed, cast by *The Henry-Bonnard Bronze Co. Founders. N.Y. 1899*, 25½in. high. (Skinner) $2,530

Tiffany bronze figural crab inkstand, dark original patina on full bodied crab with hinged body holding beaded pot inkwell with natural seashell cover, 8in. diameter widest. (Skinner) $4,313

A Victorian gilt-bronze inkwell, the detachable cover modeled as a stag and two deer, interior inscribed *PUBLISHED FEB.Y 5.TH 1850 BEN.N W. HAWKINS*, 9in. wide. (Christie's) $565

Pair of Louis XV style bronze chenets, each in the form of a lion resting on a shield, 21in. high. (William Doyle) $7,475

Bronze figural group 'Gloria Victus', after a model by Antoine Mercie, titled, signed and further inscribed *F. Barbedienne Fondeur Paris*, 36½in. high. (William Doyle) $8,050

Bronze allegorical group, late 19th century, depicting a woman astride an eagle, signed *Carrier*, 19½in. high. (William Doyle) $5,750

A bronze okimono of two Chinese sages tasting wine from a huge jar, signed *Harumitsu saku*, late 19th century, 43.2cm. high. (Christie's) $3,657

Bronze bust of Caesar, stamped *F. Barbedienne. Founder*, dark patina, on a walnut plinth, 19⅛in. high. (Skinner) $1,265

A 19th century German bronze cigar smoking male figure, with walking stick wearing clogs, signed *G. Jaeger*, 12³/₄in. high. (Dee, Atkinson & Harrison)

$291

A bronze statue of samurai wearing eboshi and posturing with a spear, 19th century. (Christie's)

$1,829

Gertrude Vanderbilt Whitney (American, 1875–1942), Satyr, bronze with black/brown patina, 13in. high. (Skinner)

$1,840

A bronze figure, indistinctly signed, of a half-naked young woman, seated on a rock, English, mid 19th century, 17¹/₂in. high. (Christie's)

$971

A pair of ormolu mounted bronze candelabra, the columns formed as the winged Victory holding two cornucopia, Thomire, Paris, early 19th century, 72cm. high. (Finarte)

$20,714

Bruno Zach, study of a dancing Pierrot carrying Pierrette in his arms, ivory faces, gilt bronze on veined marble socle, signed, 16in. high. (G. A. Key)

$3,875

Brown patinated bronze figure of a standing warrior with sword and helmet, 'Vincere avt. Morior', signed *E. Picault*, 67cm. high. (Herholdt Jensen)

$1,809

Austro-German school, 20th century, five-man bobsleigh taking a corner, burnished bronze, 10¹/₂in. high. (Bonhams)

$13,200

A bronze inkwell modeled as Rachel at the well, standing under a palm, an amphora at her side, 19th century, 14¹/₂in. high. (Christie's)

$441

Henri Alfred Marie Jacquemart, a bronze group of a horse and dog, the stallion looking at the dog lying below, late 19th century, 37cm.
(Bearne's) $2,907

A pair of gilt-bronze figures, signed *A. LE VEEL*, of soldiers in late 16th century costume, French, late 19th century, 24³/₄in. high.
(Christie's) $1,478

A French bronze and champlevé enamel onyx marble tazza, Paris, circa 1880, in the manner of Barbedienne, sculpted by Eugène Cornu, 44cm. high.
(Sotheby's) $10,057

A French olive green patinated bronze bust of a young girl entitled 'Cendrillon', cast from a model by Emmanuele Villanis, late 19th century, 20¹/₄in. high.
(Christie's) $1,646

A pair of French bronze Marly horses on ormolu-mounted boulle pedestals, the bronzes cast after the models by Guillaume Coustou, late 19th century, 23¹/₄in. wide.
(Christie's) $10,057

A French bronze bust of a lady, in the eighteenth century style, with elaborate coiffure and lace-fringed décolleté dress, third quarter 19th century, 26in. high.
(Christie's) $4,023

A Japanese bronze figure of a seated monkey, holding an inro in his left hand and gazing intently at the attached netsuke, Meiji period, signed, 27cm.
(Bearne's) $1,836

Pair of Empire gilt and patinated bronze urns, of campana form, the reeded handles with ram's head terminals, 13in. high.
(William Doyle) $2,990

A French bronze figure of a mastiff, cast from the model by Charles Valton, early 20th century, 7¹/₄in. wide.
(Christie's) $2,925

A French bronze figure entitled 'Coureur Japonais', cast from a model by Georges Coudray, late 19th century, 18½in. high.
(Christie's) $5,486

An English bronze relief plaque entitled 'Cathal and the Woodfolk', cast from the model by Charles Sergeant Jagger, first quarter 20th century, 30½in. wide.
(Christie's) $4,754

A French bronze group of two putti and a goat, in the manner of Clodion, late 19th century, 13in. high.
(Christie's) $2,194

A polished and patinated bronze head of an African woman, her neck elongated by ritual metal rings, circa 1930, 41cm. high.
(Christie's) $1,362

A pair of French gilt-bronze vases and covers, Napoléon III, Paris, circa 1865, the ovoid white carrara marble bodies cast by ribbon-tied summer flowers, 56cm. high.
(Sotheby's) $6,583

A gilt-bronze figure of a naked fisherboy in a hat, carrying lobster pots, *CHIURAZZI NAPOLI* foundry mark, Neapolitan, early 20th century, 18¾in. high.
(Christie's) $1,378

A French bronze model of a horse entitled 'Cheval Turc', cast from a model by Antoine-Louis Barye, third quarter 19th century, 11½in. high.
(Christie's) $24,685

A pair of French bronze figures of an Arab tribesman and a water-carrier, cast from the models by Jean Jules Salmson, second half 19th century, 21½in. high.
(Christie's) $10,971

A bronze figure of a seated classical lady, in the manner of Pradier, wearing flowing drapery, 19th century, 16in. high overall.
(Christie's) $3,108

French gilt-bronze and ivory group of four children playing blindman's buff, cast and carved after a model by Demetre Chiparus, circa 1920, 8in. high. (Butterfield & Butterfield) $9,775

French Art Deco patinated and gilt-bronze and onyx figural group, cast after a model by Armond Lémo, circa 1930, the maiden shown wearing a headdress of interlocking medallions, 18¼in. long. (Butterfield & Butterfield) $2,875

French gilt-bronze and ivory group of three girls under an umbrella, cast and carved after a model by Demetre Chiparus, circa 1925, 9in. high. (Butterfield & Butterfield) $7,475

French patinated bronze figure of a feather dancer, cast after a model by Fayral, circa 1930, charcoal brown patina, 19⅛in. high. (Butterfield & Butterfield) $920

Pair of bronze and ivory figural bookends, cast and carved after a model by Roland Paris, circa 1930, 6¾in. high. (Butterfield & Butterfield) $1,610

French patinated bronze and ivory figure, Starlight, cast after a model by Demetre Chiparus, circa 1925, depicting an exotic dancer wearing a beaded bodice with flaring skirt, 23in. high. (Butterfield & Butterfield) $5,750

Austrian patinated bronze group of two children kissing behind a screen, cast after a model by Tereszczuk, early 20th century, 7⅛in. high. (Butterfield & Butterfield) $2,185

French patinated bronze group, Bacchante and Faun, cast after a model by Paul-Jean Sebastian Guéry, circa 1925, green brown patina, 7in. high. (Butterfield & Butterfield) $1,092

Patinated bronze figure of a child playing blindman's buff, cast after a model by Cesare Mario Ferarri, circa 1920, 8¼in. high. (Butterfield & Butterfield) $690

A George III mahogany and brass bound plate bucket, with brass handle, 36cm. diameter.
(Phillips) $1,040

A pair of George III brass-mounted mahogany plate-buckets, each with open circular top with loop handle and ribbed sides, 14in. diameter.
(Christie's) $7,268

A Regency brass-bound mahogany bucket-on-stand, the rotating bucket with dished top and tapering pierced body, 14in. wide.
(Christie's) $4,450

Walker Patent powder bucket, wooden and two copper lids, tinned interior containing ten black painted tin powder containers, 9^{1}/$_{2}$in. high.
(Butterfield & Butterfield) $1,430

A pair of painted leather fire buckets, Boston, dated *1797*, each with leather swing handle, inscribed and dated *R. MORSE, 1797*.
(Christie's) $25,300

A George III brass-bound mahogany peat-bucket, the arched handle above a removable zinc liner and a ribbed tapering body, 14^{1}/$_{4}$in. diameter.
(Christie's) $2,347

A George III mahogany plate-bucket, the circular top with loop handle, later copper-lined and side opening, 14^{3}/$_{4}$in. diameter.
(Christie's) $3,430

A pair of Irish George III brass-bound mahogany peat-buckets, each with open circular top with loop-handles above tapering ribbed sides, 8^{1}/$_{4}$in. diameter.
(Christie's) $16,500

A George III brass-bound mahogany bucket, the open circular top above tapering slatted sides with ring-handles, 30^{3}/$_{4}$in. diameter.
(Christie's) $2,000

A George III green-stained fruitwood tea-caddy, in the shape of a squash, the hinged lid enclosing a zinc-lined interior, 5¹/₂in. high.
(Christie's) $6,139

A pair of ormolu-mounted Chinese blue and white porcelain tea-canisters in a rosewood box, the porcelain Kangxi, 8¹/₂in. high.
(Christie's) $14,352

After Franz von Stuck, Amazon box, circa 1900, the hinged lid enameled in shades of blue, 6.25cm. diameter.
(Sotheby's) $2,422

Emile Gallé, marquetry wood box, circa 1900, inlaid with various fruitwoods with a steaming cauldron and a dog wearing a hat with feathers, 62cm. wide.
(Sotheby's) $1,396

A pair of Federal burl walnut and tiger maple veneered knife urns, probably Philadelphia, 1800–1810, the squared domed top with veneered panels divided by patterned stringing with acorn finials, 28in. high.
(Christie's) $5,750

A mid Victorian silver castle top calling card case, chased and repoussé with a view of York Minster, Birmingham 1856, by David Pettifer.
(Spencer's) $693

A Chinese Export mother-of-pearl and reverse painting-on-glass tea-caddy, decorated overall with engraved blind tracery of birds and butterflies, early 19th century, 10in. wide.
(Christie's) $6,861

A Regency burr yew and satinwood strung tea caddy of rectangular form with domed lid, the interior fitted with two lidded canisters, 19cm. wide.
(Phillips) $537

A Momoyama domed coffer decorated in gold and aogai on roironuri ground with birds among flowers, late 16th/early 17th century, 70 x 46 x 37cm.
(Christie's) $7,314

A needlework casket, depicting scenes from the life of Venus worked in colored silks and chenille, the inside lid fitted with a mirror, with key, $9^{1}/_{2}$ x $11^{1}/_{2}$ x $7^{3}/_{4}$in., English, 17th century. (Christie's) $10,824

A paint-decorated pine document box, New England, early 19th century, the lid painted with a flower- and leaf-filled basket in shades of green and red on a yellow ground, $13^{1}/_{4}$in. long. (Sotheby's) $8,337

An early 19th century tortoiseshell veneered tea caddy, with a domed lid inset with a silver inscription plate, the interior fitted with two lidded canisters, 17.5cm. wide. (Phillips) $1,305

A paint-decorated pine and poplar small butter firkin, probably New Jersey, circa 1775, of circular form with fitted lid, the top decorated in polychrome with a flowerhead, 5in. diameter. (Sotheby's) $4,600

A George III mahogany and engraved marquetry knife-box, the domed stepped circular top surmounted by an ivory urn-shaped finial and with twelve floral medallions to its side, $22^{1}/_{2}$in. high. (Christie's) $3,250

An early 19th century penwork tea caddy, the lid and side panels extensively decorated with Arcadian scenes, the interior with two lidded canisters, 25cm. wide. (Phillips) $1,151

A paint-decorated pine document box, Rufus Porter, early 19th century, the rectangular hinged lid with stenciled name *P. Porter* within a shaped rectangular reserve, $13^{1}/_{4}$in. long. (Sotheby's) $68,500

Putto box and cover, circa 1910, the hinged lid with a circular ivory panel carved in high relief with a putto, 13.5cm. diameter. (Sotheby's) $2,422

A Chinese Export silvered metal-mounted mother-of-pearl tea-caddy, decorated overall with pierced foliate panels with scallop-shells, late 18th/early 19th century, $11^{1}/_{2}$in. wide. (Christie's) $3,972

An exceptional sarcophagus shaped rosewood tea caddy, fitted with two canisters and the original glass liner, on bun feet. (Dee, Atkinson & Harrison) $367

Mahogany and brass fitted Victorian coal scuttle. (G. A. Key) $151

Oak stationery cabinet, sloping front opening to reveal a fitted interior, circa 1910, 11½in. wide. (G. A. Key) $153

An early Victorian shellwork sailor's Valentine, of typical form, the octagonal oak box opening to two glazed panels, each 13¾in. wide. (Christie's) $3,365

A scattered kimpun ground suzuribako decorated with egrets in a stream among reeds, 19th century, 21.3 x 17cm. (Christie's) $2,560

A George III fruitwood tea caddy of urn shape with a brass acorn finial and an oval steel escutcheon plate, 8¼in. high. (Hy. Duke & Son) $6,068

A George III satinwood oval tea caddy, the hinged cover inlaid with floral basket within ebony stringing, 6in. (Hy. Duke & Son) $525

A whalebone and sealskin box, American, possibly Connecticut, second quarter 19th century, the domed hinged rectangular lid with sealskin covering, 9¾in. wide. (Christie's) $1,150

A late Regency mother of pearl tea caddy of rectangular form, the lid with a silver colored metal cartouche, 5in. wide. (Hy. Duke & Son) $759

A paint-decorated dome-top box, probably New England, 19th century, the top painted with a green, red and white oval reserve, 21in. long. (Sotheby's) **$2,875**

Rare painted wood ship's box, with decoration of the 'Ship Flying Fish', 18½in. long. (Eldred's) **$605**

Regency rosewood sewing box, sarcophagus formed lid with molded raised center with mother of pearl inlay, 12 x 10in., English, early 19th century. (G. A. Key) **$488**

A roironuri ground karabitsu (armour box) with six legs decorated with stylized foliate crests on the continuous shippo hanabishi mon ground, 18th century, 68cm. wide. (Christie's) **$5,303**

A Regency tortoiseshell-veneered tea caddy of hexagonal bombé form inlaid with pewter stringing and with a mother of pearl foliate finial, 5¼in. high. (Hy. Duke & Son) **$2,731**

Brass casket of sarcophagus form, the border chased with keyhole design and applied with a rope twist, by Charles Asprey of London, 19th century, 7in. wide. (G. A. Key) **$308**

A George III fruitwood tea caddy in the form of an apple, 5³/₄in. high. (Hy. Duke & Son) **$3,337**

Polished iron strongbox with gilt plate concealing lock, signed *Gudmun Cederberg, 1785*, 73cm. wide. (Stockholms Auktionsverk) **$10,133**

A George III oval satinwood tea caddy crossbanded in tulipwood edged with ebony and boxwood stringing, 6¼in. wide. (Hy. Duke & Son) **$303**

A Regency painted box in the form of a country cottage, inscribed on the base *from Mr Alice (?) to LHM, August 16th 1809 ... Tenby SW*, 5¹/₂in. wide. (Hy. Duke & Son)

$3,337

An ebony and palisander traveling chest, with six drawers, Portuguese, 18th century. (Galerie Moderne)

$3,023

Art Crafts Shop copper and enamel jewelry box, Buffalo, New York, circa 1905, original bronze patina with green, red and yellow enamel floral decoration, 8³/₄in. long. (Skinner)

$2,185

A Regency tortoiseshell-veneered tea caddy by Lund of Cornhill, London, with a bombé hexagonal body and conforming hinged lid with turned ivory finial, 5¹/₄in. high. (Hy. Duke & Son)

$3,034

A Reeves & Sons ceramics decorator's paint-box, the stained deal box with two internal trays containing approximately forty-six glass phials of 'Hancock & Sons Worcester China Colours', 12³/₄in. wide, circa 1860. (Christie's)

$397

Japanese lacquer portable smoking set, Tabakobon, Meiji period, 19th century, fitted with a chased silver koro and tobacco container above two narrow drawers and one wide, 9in. wide. (William Doyle)

$3,450

A George III painted bookstand, with an arrangement of three drawers, decorated with baskets of flowers, and rustic vignette, 17¹/₂in. wide. (Hy. Duke & Son)

$2,240

A late Regency amboyna work box of architectural form with ebonized moldings and a mother of pearl panel in the lid, 14¹/₄in. wide. (Hy. Duke & Son)

$1,214

A roironuri ground kodansu decorated in black and iroe takamakie simulating various tsuba, unsigned, late 18th/early 19th century, 31.3cm. wide. (Christie's)

$6,948

Rosewood cased vanity box containing ten glass and silver lid fittings, Birmingham 1855 and three later manicure items.
(G. A. Key) $630

Victorian walnut tea caddy of domed casket form, brass and ivory mounts, the interior with two divisions, 9in.
(G. A. Key) $225

A Napoleon III ebonized liqueur box, the hinged lid and front inlaid in brass with cartouches, 13in. wide.
(Hy. Duke & Son) $910

A 1920's lady's crocodile skin traveling case by Finnigans of Bond Street, containing a wide range of fittings, London 1928, 61 x 39cm.
(Cheffins Grain & Comins) $1,216

A good 19th century Celanese coromandel wood work casket, of undulating rectangular form, the hinged cover opening to reveal a vizigapatam panel to the inner cover, 16in. wide.
(Spencer's) $668

A Victorian papier mâché and mother-of-pearl sewing/writing and jewelry cabinet, the black ground with serpentine shaped doors, 13½in. wide.
(Hy. Duke & Son) $928

Sheraton small mahogany knife box, sloping top, ornate brass handles and key escutcheon, 7in. wide, English, mid to late 18th century.
(G. A. Key) $258

A late Victorian mahogany games compendium, the cover with folding leather chessboard, the divided interior with draughts, dominoes, miniature gavel and associated cribbage board, 12¾in. wide.
(Christie's) $496

Victorian figured rosewood decanter box, rectangular form, containing four cut glass decanters, each with globular stoppers, English, mid 19th century.
(G. A. Key) $501

Seischab, Germany, a metal-body Esco camera with a Steinheil Anastigmat Cassar f/3.5 3.5cm. lens no. 168571 in a dial-set Compur shutter.
(Christie's) $3,542

Leica M2 no. 990734, black, with a Leitz Summicron f/2 5cm. lens no. 1587571.
(Christie's) $4,250

Leica IIIf no. 684742 red-dial, the top-plate engraved *Canada Limited, Midland, Ontario* with a Leitz Elmar f/3.5 5cm. lens.
(Christie's) $5,313

Thornton-Pickard Mfg Co. Ltd., Altrincham, a half-plate brass and mahogany Triple Imperial Extension field camera with a brass bound Beck-Steinheil Unofocal Series I No. 5 7.2 inch lens.
(Christie's) $336

Zuiho Optical Instrument Co. Ltd., Japan, a 35mm. Honor SL camera no. 90614 with a Zuiho Optical Co. Honor f/1.9 50mm. lens no. 61591, in maker's box.
(Christie's) $2,349

A Twin-Lens Contaflex camera with a Carl Zeiss, Jena Sucher-Objektiv f/2.8 8cm. viewing lens and a Carl Zeiss, Jena Tessar f/2.8 5cm. taking lens.
(Christie's) $1,594

Eastman Kodak Co., Rochester, NY, a 7 x 5 inch No. 4 Kodak folding camera with rollfilm holder and a brass bound lens.
(Christie's) $708

A 6 x 9cm. wood-body tailboard camera with a brass bound lens.
(Christie's) $219

Leica I(c) no. 48766, with non-standardised mount, a Leitz Elmar f/3.5 50mm. lens, and a Leitz Elmar f/3.4 13.5cm. lens.
(Christie's) $7,438

A Challenge Dayspool tropical camera by J. Lizars of Glasgow, for 3¼ and 4¼ on roll film, with Beck lens, red leather bellows. (Spencer's) **$734**

A detective camera by W. Watson & Sons of London, the black leather covered box containing a quarter plate bellows and double plate holder, Rapid Rectilinear lens. (Spencer's) **$427**

A whole plate folding field camera by G. Hare of London, mahogany body, rack and pinion focusing, with Ross Rapid symmetrical lens. (Spencer's) **$291**

Nikon F2AS no. 7739424, with an AS Photomic head, Nikon MD-2 motordrive no. 436450 and Nikon MB-1 battery pack. (Christie's) **$1,328**

Leica I(a) no. 18778, with a Leitz Elmar f/3.5 50mm. lens, in maker's case, in maker's box. (Christie's) **$1,771**

Nikon F2 no. 7113985, chrome, with a DP-1 photomic head no. 403799, Nippon Kogaku Nikkor-S f/1.4 50mm. lens no. 731549. (Christie's) **$1,328**

C. P. Goerz, Berlin, an 110 x 45mm. Photo-Stereo-Binocle camera no. 376 with a pair of Goerz Doppel-Anastigmat Series III 75mm. lenses. (Christie's) **$3,896**

Houghtons Ltd., London, a metal-body Ticka watch camera and lens cap. (Christie's) **$402**

Le Coultre et Cie, Switzerland, a 35mm. Compass II camera no. 1446, and a CCL3B Anastigmat f/3.5 35mm. lens, in a maker's blue purse. (Christie's) **$1,505**

111

A chrome Nikon S3 camera no. 6300222 with a Nippon Kogaku Nikkor-S.C f/1.4 5cm. lens no. 318562.
(Christie's) $767

A Leica III camera no. 164413 with a Leitz Elmar 5cm. f/3.5 lens no. 232730 in maker's original box.
(Christie's) $767

A Leica I(a) camera with no. 308 with 'mushroom' release, and Leitz Elmar f/3.5 50mm. lens and cap.
(Christie's) $10,043

An 18th-century wood-body sliding-box reflex camera obscura with hinged top, 5 x 4in.
(Christie's) $4,017

A green-body Canon F1 camera no. 578203 with a Canon FD 50mm. f/1.4 lens no. 1089692.
(Christie's) $1,004

A Leitz Canada 16mm. gun camera type N-9 no. 4957 and a Leitz 35mm. f/2.8 lens.
(Christie's) $347

A red-dial Leica IIIf camera no. 795891 with delayed action and a Leitz Summaron f/2.8 35mm. lens no. 1678823, in ever ready case.
(Christie's) $1,278

Marion & Co., London, a 5½ x 3½in. tropical reflex camera no. M1111 with polished teak body, and a Carl Zeiss, Jena Tessar f/4.5 18cm. lens.
(Christie's) $1,604

Goltz & Breutmann, Dresden, a 127-rollfilm Mentor Dreivier camera with a Leitz Hektor 5cm. f/2.5 lens no. 150691 in a rimset Compur shutter.
(Christie's) $5,478

Folmer & Schwing Division, Rochester, NY, a 5 x 4in. Aero Camera model AII with an Eastman Kodak Co. Hawk-Eye Aerial f/4.5 254mm. lens no. 0112.
(Christie's) $428

Londo Stereoscopic Co., London, a 4½ x 6cm. Physiograph Binocular camera no. 1816 with a Krauss/Zeiss Tessar f/4.5 52mm. lens no. 88064.
(Christie's) $2,739

A. Boreux, Switzerland, a 13 x 6cm. Nanna 1 collapsible stereoscopic camera no. 356, with a pair of Carl Zeiss, Jena Tessar f/6.3 7.5cm. lenses nos. 144634 and 144633.
(Christie's) $876

Leica 250GG Reporter no. 352366 motorized, two 250 cassettes and a Leitz Elmar f/3.5 50mm. lens.
(Christie's) $12,397

A Leica I(a) camera no. 1699 with a Leitz Elmar f/3.5 50mm. lens, in leather purse.
(Christie's) $1,497

A Leica III camera no. 165935 with a Leitz Summar 5cm. f/2 lens no. 257276, in maker's leather ever ready case.
(Christie's) $548

A wood-body sliding box reflex camera obscura with single element lens and wood lens cap, 7 x 4 x 3in.
(Christie's) $3,208

A Leica M3 camera no. 973670 with Leica-Meter MR, a Summicron 5cm. f/2 lens no. 1578696, lens hood, and a Summaron f/2.8 35mm. lens no. 2049850.
(Christie's) $1,735

Vega S.A., Switzerland, a 6½ x 9cm. Vega camera no. 378 with internal twelve-plate holder.
(Christie's) $1,604

Le Coultre et Cie, Switzerland, a 35mm. Compass II camera no. 2957 with a CCL3B Anastigmat f/3.5 35mm. lens.
(Christie's) $2,317

C. P. Stirn, Germany, a 4cm. diameter nickel-plated Concealed Vest camera no. 11873 with lens.
(Christie's) $1,782

A Leicaflex fiftieth anniversary SL2 camera no. 1416117 and commemorative number 348-C with instructions, in maker's box.
(Christie's) $5,478

A chrome Leicaflex camera no. 1082041 with pie-shaped exposure counter and a Leitz Summicron-R f/2 50mm. lens no. 1940620, in maker's ever ready case.
(Christie's) $548

A 24 x 32mm. Nikon I camera no. 60997, the baseplate engraved *Made in Occupied Japan*, with a Nippon Kogaku Nikkor-H.C f/2.5 5cm. lens no. 6099.
(Christie's) $20,086

J. D. Möller, Germany, a 16mm. CamBinox combined camera/binocular no. 321266 with a Möller Idemar f/3.5 90mm. lens no. 322611.
(Christie's) $1,461

A. Darlot, Paris, a 13 x 18cm. mahogany-body collapsible camera with red-leather bellows, removable viewfinder, and brass bound Darlot lens.
(Christie's) $499

Contessa-Nettel, Germany, a 10 x 15cm. tropical Deck Rullo camera with a Carl Zeiss, Jena Tessar f/4.5 18cm. lens no. 492047 and three double darkslides.
(Christie's) $535

A 9 x 7cm. wood-body Dubroni camera with internal ceramic processing chamber, red window, and a brass bound Dubroni lens.
(Christie's) $2,317

Thornton-Pickard Mfg. Co. Ltd., Altrincham, a half-plate brass and mahogany Crown stereoscopic camera with a pair of brass bound Thornton-Pickard Crown Rapid Rectalinear lenses.
(Christie's) $624

A. Lehmann, Berlin, a metal-body Ben Akiba walking stick camera no. 772 with decoratively-engraved exterior, winding key and engraved exposure counter 1–20.
(Christie's) $21,912

A $8^{1}/_{2}$ x $8^{1}/_{2}$in. wet-plate wood-body tailboard camera with a brass bound rack and pinion focusing lens, the cap stamped *A. Coiffier, Paris* and Waterhouse stops.
(Christie's) $1,370

A Leica M2 camera no. 1138549 with a Leitz Elmarit f/2.8 90mm. lens no. 1692177, and E. Leitz, New York motor unit no. 2731.
(Christie's) $5,478

Cie Française, Paris, a 9 x 12cm. metal-body Photosphere camera no. 2286 with removable viewfinder, helically-focusing lens and retailer's label.
(Christie's) $1,693

Schmitz & Thienemann, Dresden, a $4^{1}/_{2}$ x 6cm. Uniflex SLR camera with a Rexar f/4.5 7.5cm. lens no. 80657 in an Ibsor shutter and single metal slides.
(Christie's) $876

American Camera Co., London, a 3¹/₄in. metal-body No. 2 Demon camera with flap shutter, lens and back cover.
(Christie's)   **$2,922**

An 18 x 10cm. walnut-body sliding-box stereoscopic camera with a pair of Richebourg rack and pinion focusing lenses.
(Christie's)   **$4,990**

Tourtin, France, a 9 x 12cm. Detective Lynx reflex camera model 1897 with a Darlot, Paris lens no. 16021.
(Christie's)   **$584**

Ross Ltd., London, a 6¹/₂ x 3¹/₄in. stereoscopic reflex camera no. R712 with a pair of Ross, London Homocentric f/6.3 5in. lenses nos. 66695 and 66694.
(Christie's)   **$1,278**

Franke and Heidecke, Braunschweig, a 127-rollfilm gray baby Rolleiflex TLR camera 2048680 with a Heidosmat f/2.8 60mm. viewing lens and a Schneider Xenar f/3.5 60mm. taking lens.
(Christie's)   **$499**

Gandolfi, London, a 5 x 4in. brass and mahogany field camera with red bellows, universal back and a Voigtländer Technika Heliar f/4.5 15cm. lens.
(Christie's)   **$1,604**

Varimex, Poland, a 35mm. aqua blue Alfa 2 camera with a WZFO Emitar f/4.5 45mm. lens no. 18490, in maker's case.
(Christie's)   **$219**

H. J. Redding & Gyles, London, a rollfilm mahogany-body Luzo camera no. 1301 with shutter and maker's plate.
(Christie's)   **$1,693**

A 35mm. twin-lens Contaflex camera no. Y.84448 with a Carl Zeiss, Jena Sucher-Objective f/2.8 8cm. viewing lens no. 1513337.
(Christie's)   **$2,191**

1951 Austin Atlantic 2-door coupe, green with gray leather interior, engine: four cylinder, in-line, overhead-valve, 2,660cc, 88bhp at 4,000rpm; gearbox: four speed manual; brakes: drum; suspension: independent front, semi-elliptic rear.
(Christie's) $3,130

1984 Daimler Sovereign 4.2 saloon, metallic gray with gray leather interior, engine: six cylinder, double overhead camshaft, 4,235cc, 198bhp at 5,500rpm; gearbox: automatic transmission; brakes: four wheel disk; suspension: independent all round.
(Christie's) $1,350

1950 Lea Francis 2$^{1/2}$ litre sports, black with red leather interior, engine: four cylinder, 2,496cc, 110bhp at 5,200rpm; gearbox: four speed manual; brakes: four wheel drum; suspension: front, independent rear, semi-elliptic leaf springs.
(Christie's) $23,450

1962 Jaguar E-Type Series 1 Roadster, black with red leather interior, engine: six cylinder, double overhead camshaft, 3,781cc, 265bhp at 5,500rpm; gearbox: four speed manual; brakes: disk all round; suspension: front, independent, torsion bar, anti-roll bar.
(Christie's) $33,750

1932 Studebaker President Four Seasons Roadster, two-tone brown with red striping and brown leather interior, engine: straight eight, 337ci, 122bhp at 3,200rpm; gearbox: three speed; brakes: four wheel drum; suspension: semi-elliptic leaf springs front and rear.
(Christie's) $79,500

1971 Ferrari 365 GTB/4 Daytona, black with beige leather interior, engine: V12, four overhead camshafts, 4,390ccm 355bhp at 7,500rpm; gearbox: five speed manual; brakes: four wheel disks; suspension: independent all round, left hand drive.
(Christie's) $78,000

1952 Alvis TA 21 drophead coupe, coachwork by Tickford, maroon with new brown leather interior, engine: six cylinder, 2993cc, overhead valve, 93bhp at 4,000rpm; gearbox: four speed manual; brakes: Lockhead hydraulic system, drum front and rear.
(Christie's) $16,250

1979 Maserati-Type 117 'Bora', coachwork by Ital Design, red with beige leather interior, engine: V8, 4,930cc, 280bhp at 5,500rpm; gearbox: five speed manual; brakes: four wheel disk; suspension: independent all round, left hand drive.
(Christie's) $40,000

1930 Willys-Knight Great Six Model 66B 'Plaid Side' Roadster, coachwork by Griswold, black with green, plaid striping and green interior, engine: six cylinder, in line, Knight sleeve valve, 255ci, 82bhp at 3,200rpm; gearbox: three speed manual.
(Christie's) $79,500

1959 Chevrolet Corvette, snowcrest white with black soft top and red interior, engine: V-8, 283ci, 290bhp at 6,200rpm; gearbox: four speed manual; brakes: four wheel drum; suspension: front, independent, rear, live axle with semi-elliptic leaf springs.
(Christie's) $27,600

1967 Lincoln short wheelbase Executive Limousine, coachwork by Lehmann Peterson, black with green striping and gray interior, engine: V8, 462ci, 340bhp at 4,600rpm; gearbox: three speed automatic; brakes: four wheel hydraulic disk/drum.
(Christie's) $14,950

1966 Mercedes-Benz 230SL Roadster, white with black interior, engine: six cylinder, 2,300cc, 150bhp at 5,500rpm; gearbox: four speed manual; brakes: front, disk, rear, drum; suspension: front, independent, rear, single joint swing axel, coil strings, left and drive.
(Christie's) $63,000

1951 MG TD Roadster, black with red leather interior, engine: four cylinder, overhead valve, 1,250cc, 45bhp at 5,500rpm; gearbox: four speed manual; brakes: four wheel drum; suspension: front, independent coil, rear, semi-elliptic leaf springs.
(Christie's) $28,750

1935 Morris Isis coupe, green with original green leather interior, engine: six cylinder, overhead camshaft, 2,468cc, 21hp; gearbox: 4 speed syncromesh; brakes: 4 wheel drum; suspension: semi-elliptic springs front and rear, right hand drive.
(Christie's) $14,450

1963 Mercedes-Benz 190SL Roadster, cream with gray hardtop and red leather interior, engine: four cylinder, single overhead camshaft, 1,897cc, 105bhp at 5,700rpm; gearbox: four speed manual; brakes: four wheel drum, left hand drive.
(Christie's) $48,300

1931 Cadillac Model 452B V-16 Sport Phaeton, coachwork by Fleetwood, two shades of gray with red wheels and gray interior, engine: V-16, 452.6ci, 165bhp at 3,400rpm; gearbox: three speed; suspension: semi-elliptic leaf springs with hydraulic dampers front and rear.
(Christie's) $310,500

Circa 1939 Morgan 4–4 drophead coupe, chassis No. MA4/4862783, engine No. A10306, white with black interior, engine: four cylinder, 1,122cc, 35bhp at 4,500rpm; gearbox: four speed manual; brakes: four wheel drum; suspension: front, independent coil, rear, semi-elliptic, right hand drive.
(Christie's) $19,987

1971 Triumph Herald 13/60 convertible, red with beige vinyl interior, engine: four cylinder, overhead valve, 1296cc, 61bhp at 5,000rpm; gearbox: four speed manual; brakes: front disk, rear drum; suspension: front, independent coil springs, rear independent transverse leaf springs, right hand drive.
(Christie's) $4,500

1935 Lagonda M45 tourer, coachwork by Lagonda Ltd., chassis No. Z11363, engine No. M45R 107 (Rapide), red with black wings and black leatherette interior, engine: six cylinder, overhead valve, 4,453cc, c.140bhp at 4,000rpm; gearbox: four speed manual; brakes: four wheel drum; suspension: semi-elliptic, right hand drive.
(Christie's) $52,693

1939 Bentley 4¼-litre MX series drophead coupe, coachwork by Barker, chassis No. B73MX, engine No. V2BJ, black with gray leather interior, engine: six cylinder, overhead valve, 4,257cc, 125bhp at 4,500rpm; gearbox: four speed manual with overdrive; brakes: four wheel drum; suspension: semi-elliptic, right hand drive.
(Christie's) $92,746

1960 Bentley S2 standard steel saloon, chassis No. B280AM, engine No. 302AB, black and white with gray leather interior, engine: V8, overhead valve, 6,230cc, 200bhp at 5,000rpm; gearbox: four speed automatic; brakes: four wheel drum; suspension: front, independent by coil springs and wishbones, rear, semi-elliptic, right hand drive.
(Christie's) $23,621

1973 Citroen SM Maserati 2.9 litre two-door sports saloon, engine: V-6 dual overhead-camshaft, 2965cc, 180bhp at 6,250rpm; gearbox: five speed manual; brakes; four wheel disk; suspension: front, hydropneumatic with parallel control arms and anti-roll bar, rear, hydropneumatic with trailing arms and anti-roll bar.
(Christie's) $17,150

1968 Jaguar 340 saloon, cream with black vinyl interior, engine: six-cylinder, in-line double overhead camshaft, 3,442cc, 210bhp at 5,500rpm; gearbox: four speed manual with overdrive; brakes: four wheel disk brakes; suspension: front, independent, rear, live axel, semi-elliptic leaf springs, right hand drive. (Christie's) $7,600

1950 Lagonda 2½ litre drophead coupe, gray with red leather interior, engine: six cylinder, twin overhead camshaft, 2,580cc, 105bhp at 5,000rpm; gearbox: four speed manual; brakes: hydraulically operated drums, rear brakes mounted inboard; suspension: independent front and rear, right hand drive. (Christie's) $25,250

1953 Lanchester LJ200 14hp saloon, dark green with green leather upholstery, engine: four cylinder in-line, overhead valve, 1,968cc, 60bhp at 4,200rpm; gearbox: four speed pre-selector manual; brakes: girling hydromechanical, front/rear drum; suspension: front, independent torsion bar, rear, rigid axel with semi-elliptic leaf springs. (Christie's) $1,000

1930 Alfa Romeo 6C–1750 supercharged grand sport tourer, coachwork by James Young, chassis No. 8513089, engine No. 8513089, engine: six cylinder, twin overhead camshafts, Memini supercharger, 1,750cc, 85bhp at 4,500rpm; gearbox: four speed manual; brakes: four wheel mechanical drum; suspension: semi-elliptic, right hand drive. (Christie's) $78,948

1978 MGB GT, chassis No. GHD5461056G, engine No. 18GB-11-H 80159, black with black and gray interior, engine: four cylinder, 1,798cc, 95bhp at 5,400rpm; gearbox: four speed manual with overdrive; brakes: front, disk, rear, drum; suspension: front, independent, rear, semi-elliptic, right hand drive. (Christie's) $4,361

1961 Aston Martin DB4 sports coupe, chassis No. DB4/573/R, engine No. 370/582, dark green with ivory leather interior, engine: six cylinder in-line, double overhead camshaft, 3,670cc, 240bhp at 5,500rpm; gearbox: four speed manual; brakes: four wheel disk; suspension: independent all round, right hand drive. (Christie's) $45,425

1955 Rolls-Royce Silver Dawn saloon, sand over metallic dark brown with beige leather interior, engine: six cylinder, 4,566ccm overhead inlet valves, 145bhp at 4,000rpm; gearbox: four speed automatic; brakes: four wheel drum.
(Christie's) $36,800

1976 Cadillac Eldorado Bicentenial convertible, white with red and blue 'Bicentenial Stripes' and white interior, engine: V-8, overhead valve, 500ci, 190bhp at 4,400rpm; gearbox: Turbo Hydra-matic; brakes: front, disk, rear, drum.
(Christie's) $30,475

1931 Packard Model 840 Dual Cowl Phaeton, tan with green and biscuit interior, engine: straight eight, 384.8ci, 120bhp at 3,200rpm; gearbox: four speed manual; brakes: four wheel drum; suspension: semi-elliptic leaf springs front and rear, left hand drive.
(Christie's) $134,500

1959 Mercedes-Benz 220S Convertible, silver over black with red leather interior, engine: six cylinder, 2,195cc, 106bhp at 5,200rpm; gearbox: four speed manual; brakes: power assisted drums; suspension: front, independent, rear, single joint swing axel and coil springs.
(Christie's) $48,300

1969 Jaguar 340 saloon, blue with red leather interior, engine: six cylinder, double overhead camshaft, 3,442cc, 210bhp at 5,500rpm; gearbox: four speed manual with overdrive, right hand drive.
(Christie's) $4,000

1931 Pierce-Arrow coupe model 41, coachwork by LeBaron, the 1931 New York Auto Show car, two tone blue with red wheels and blue mohair interior, engine: straight eight, 385ci, 132bhp at 3,000rpm; gearbox: four speed manual.
(Christie's) $68,500

1929 Bentley 4¹/₂-litre dual cowl Phaeton, coachwork by Vanden Plas, green with green leather interior, engine: four cylinder, 4,398cc, overhead camshaft, 100bhp at 3,500rpm; gearbox: four speed and reverse.
(Christie's) $365,500

1931 Cadillac Model 370A Sport Phaeton V-12, coachwork by Fleetwood, light blue over dark blue with red leather interior, engine: V-12, 368ci, 135bhp at 3,400rpm; gearbox: three speed manual, left hand drive.
(Christie's) $151,000

1931 Cadillac Model 355 Sport Phaeton V-8, coachwork by Fleetwood, midnight blue with red wheels and red interior, engine: V-8, 353ci, 95bhp at 3,000rpm; gearbox: three speed manual; brakes: drums all around.
(Christie's) $96,000

1949 Chrysler Town and Country Convertible, thunder gray and white ash with tan cloth and red leather interior, engine: straight eight, 2506ci, 114bhp at 3,600rpm; gearbox: four speed column shift.
(Christie's) $79,500

1937 Talbot Ten drophead coupe, chassis No. BE 2049, engine No. MRG 44971/2038, dark green with green interior, engine: four cylinder, 1,185cc, 41bhp; gearbox: four speed manual; brakes: four wheel drum; suspension: semi-elliptic, right hand drive.
(Christie's) $6,813

1931 Lincoln Model K convertible coupe, red with dark brown wings and red trim, engine: V-8, four cylinder, side valve, 6,294cc, 120bhp at 2,900rpm; gearbox: three speed manual; brakes: drums all round; suspension: semi-elliptic leaf springs.
(Christie's) $78,000

1934 SS II four seat tourer, light blue over dark with aquamarine leatherette interior, engine: four cylinder, side valve, 1,608cc, 38bhp at 4,000rpm; gearbox: four speed manual; brakes: four wheel drum; suspension: semi-elliptic.
(Christie's) $18,000

1931 Morris Minor tourer, red with blue vinyl upholstery, engine: four cylinder, side valve, 847cc, 8hp; gearbox: three speed manual; brakes: four wheel drum; suspension: semi-elliptic, right hand drive.
(Christie's) $3,250

1958 Rolls-Royce Silver Cloud I saloon, metallic dark brown over beige with tan leather interior, engine: six cylinder, overhead inlet valve, side exhaust, 4,887cc, approximately 175bhp at 4,500rpm; gearbox: four speed automatic.
(Christie's) $32,200

1947 Rover 12hp open 4 seat tourer, ivory with green leather interior, engine: 4 cylinder in line, overhead valves, 1,496cc; gearbox: 4 speed synchromesh; brakes: four wheel drum; suspension: semi-elliptic springs front and rear.
(Christie's) $11,750

A silvered brass chandelier, the five scrolling branches radiating from a bulbous part-fluted column, 20th century, 20¹/₂in. high.
(Christie's) $807

A Restauration tôle peinte chandelier, the corona with green ground gilt-heightened with leaves and pierced borders, 26¹/₂in. high.
(Christie's) $1,040

A gilt-brass ceiling light, with wrythen rod to rocky ceiling suspension, above foliate corona with tied rope-work struts, 20th century, 45in. high.
(Christie's) $1,345

An Empire ormolu and cut-glass forty-two-light chandelier, the foliate-cast scrolled corona hung with faceted drops, 68in. diameter.
(Christie's) $17,043

A pair of brass chandeliers, with eight scrolling branches supporting circular drip-pans, radiating from baluster bodies, modern, 30³/₄in. diameter.
(Christie's) $620

An Empire ormolu and glass twenty-four light chandelier, the laurel corona with crossed palm leaves and chain suspension, 71in. high.
(Christie's) $144,319

A Louis-Philippe ormolu hexagonal hall lantern, with a foliate-cast corona issuing six scrolling foliate branches, 42in. high.
(Christie's) $7,314

One of a pair of molded and cut glass eighteen-light chandeliers of George III style, 20th century, 45¹/₂in. diameter.
(Christie's)
(Two) $24,374

A French gilt-bronze chandelier, Paris, circa 1890, in Louis XIV Boulle manner, the square central baluster with ram's heads, 114cm. high.
(Sotheby's) $9,508

CHANDELIERS

A thirty-two light ormolu-mounted chandelier, France, 19th century, 150cm. high.
(Finarte) $13,105

A gilt-bronze chandelier, with scrolling supports to square frame with fluted scroll twin-light fittings to the angles, 20th century, 35¹/₂in. high.
(Christie's) $574

A French gilt-bronze chandelier, Paris, circa 1900, made for electricity, with sixteen lights, 122cm. high.
(Sotheby's) $16,822

A six light chandelier, the gilt bronze cage form stem hung with a variety of lusters, Swedish, 18th century, 93cm. high.
(Stockholms Auktionsverk)
                    $7,220

A Meissen rococo-scroll-molded chandelier, fitted with two tapering tiers of scrolling arms entwined with flowers, late 19th century, 37¹/₂in. high.
(Christie's) $15,542

One of two similar brass twelve light chandeliers, the branches issuing in two tiers from bulbous baluster knopped columns, probably English, 20th century, 30in. high.
(Christie's)
                    (Two) $2,217

A brass six light chandelier, the scrolling branches issuing from a bulbous baluster knopped column, probably English, 20th century, 23in. high.
(Christie's) $924

A Victorian cut-glass gas chandelier, the corona with five shepherd's crook branches hung with drops above the cascade of drops, 51in. high.
(Christie's) $3,089

Gilt metal and frosted glass umbrella chandelier, triple tiered gilt metal ceiling lamp fitted with frosted glass interlocking triangular panels, 36in. high.
(Skinner) $2,300

AMERICAN

Carl Walters pottey rooster, for Stonelain, high glaze with decoration in maroon and black on white ground, impressed marks, 11¹/₈in. high.
(Skinner) $288

North Dakota Art pottery vase, dated *1953*, in squat globular form with pink floral design, signed *Lebacken*, 7¹/₂in. high.
(Eldred's) $385

A painted chalkware cat, Pennsylvania, 19th century, the hollow molded figure painted white with red-painted stripes, 10¹/₂in. high.
(Christie's) $1,725

Grueby pottery vase, Boston, circa 1904, modeled by Marie Seaman, matt-ocher glaze on repeating high-relief foliate decoration, impressed mark, 10¹/₂in. high.
(Skinner) $1,725

Buffalo Pottery Deldare Ware jardinière and stand, Buffalo, New York, W. Foster and W. Forrester, 1908 and 1909, Ye Lion Inn, stamp marks, jardinière 9in. high.
(Skinner) $3,450

Newcomb pottery vase, New Orleans, circa 1915, Henrietta D. Bailey, matt glazed pale-pink, blue and green on low-relief pine cones and needles, 6⁷/₈in. high.
(Skinner) $1,495

A brown-glazed earthenware pitcher, American, probably 19th century, molded in two parts in the form of a human head, 10¹/₂in. high.
(Christie's) $3,450

Important Marblehead Pottery vase, matt blue ground glaze, incised decoration at shoulder consisting of five panels, each with a stalking panther, 7¹/₂in. high.
(Skinner) $11,500

Grueby Pottery vase, Boston, circa 1910, designed by George P. Kendrik, matt yellow glaze on high relief decorated form, 10³/₄in. high.
(Skinner) $23,000

AMERICAN

Fine Parian figure group, depicting a woman and Cupid with doves, this once stood in the living room of Jabez Gorham, founder of the Gorham Silver Co., 15in. high.
(Eldred's) $1,540

A Rookwood pottery jardinière, the oviform creamware body enameled in black and white with bats flying over fields, dated *1882*, 21cm. high.
(Christie's) $496

A rare 'elephant' crackle ware pottery paperweight, by Dedham Pottery, modeled as an elephant, painted with features in blue, 4in. high.
(Christie's) $6,670

Rare and important Greuby pottery vase, Boston, circa 1900, designed by George P. Kendrick, modeled by Wilhelmina Post, matt green glaze on high-relief decorated form, 12¹/₂in. high.
(Skinner) $34,500

An important pair of Tucker and Hulme porcelain 'vase' shape pitchers, Philadelphia, dated *1828*, initialed and dated *JWM.LM 1828*, 9¹/₂in. high.
(Sotheby's) $27,600

Grueby pottery vase, Boston, circa 1902, designed by George P. Kendrick, modeled by Wilhelmina Post, matt cucumber-green glaze on low-relief foliate decoration, 16¹/₂in. high.
(Skinner) $20,700

Rare and important Teco Pottery vase, Terra Cotta, Illinois, circa 1905, shape 119, designed by Fritz Albert, matt green glaze on ovoid form, 13in. high.
(Skinner) $14,950

A slip and sgraffito-decorated redware dish, Rock Hill Township, Bucks County, Pennsylvania, dated *1838*, 12in. diameter.
(Christie's) $18,400

Gouda pottery vase, matt glaze decorated rim and base in black with pale blue/gray, neck and shoulder brick-red with black over light green, 16³/₈in. high.
(Skinner) $1,035

ARITA

An Arita model of a hare, seated on rockwork decorated in iron-red, green, brown enamels and gilt, early 18th century, 22cm. high.
(Christie's) $13,800

An Arita blue and white jardinière depicting a three clawed dragon amidst scrolling clouds, late 17th century, 37cm. diameter.
(Christie's) $2,194

An Arita model of a leaping carp, decorated in iron-red and black enamels and gilt on underglaze blue, late 17th century, 30.2cm. high.
(Christie's) $3,680

An Arita blue and white pear-shaped tankard and silver cover decorated overall with peonies issuing from rockwork, late 17th century, silver mounts later, 20cm. high.
(Christie's) $3,657

A pair of Arita models of carp, decorated in iron-red and black enamel, gilt and underglaze blue, late 17th century, each approximately 19cm. high.
(Christie's) $2,390

An Arita blue and white oviform jar, decorated in underglaze blue with figures in a water landscape with plantain trees and shrubs issuing from rockwork, late 17th century, 29cm. high.
(Christie's) $2,200

An Arita blue and white oviform jar, decorated with two birds on rocks flanked by flowering plants, late 17th century, 27.5cm. high.
(Christie's) $3,680

A large Arita blue and white bowl, decorated with scrolling foliage and peonies surrounding the central roundel, late 17th century, 39.9cm. diameter.
(Christie's) $7,360

An Arita blue and white choshi (wine pitcher) in the Kakiemon style decorated with a continuous scene of flying ho-o birds, late 17th century, 22cm. high.
(Christie's) $2,743

BERLIN

A Berlin (later decorated) circular tureen, cover and stand, painted in the manner of Teniers with peasant revelers, the porcelain 18th century, the stand 17¼in. wide.
(Christie's) $1,553

A finely painted Berlin cabinet plate after a 17th century Dutch painting, with a lady seated and holding a small dog, 24.5cm., scepter and KPM in blue.
(Phillips) $2,254

An amusing Fromery Berlin snuff box modeled as a pair of lady's 'bloomers' with flat top and two 'legs' painted with buildings, 7cm. wide.
(Phillips) $1,048

A Berlin rectangular porcelain plaque painted after Murillo with Boys Playing Dice, impressed *KPM*, circa 1880, the plaque 11 x 8¾in.
(Christie's) $5,119

A pair of Berlin fayence red lacquer beaker-vases with flared rims, decorated in enamels, Funcke's factory, circa 1720, the lacquer circa 1800, 50.5cm. high.
(Christie's) $6,417

A large Berlin rectangular plaque painted after Rubens with The Rape of the Daughters of Leucippus, impressed *KPM*, circa 1880, the plaque 15¼ x 13in.
(Christie's) $17,919

Round footed Berlin beaker vase painted after Bendemann and C. F. Sohn, with two girls at a well, circa 1837, 17.2cm. high.
(Lempertz) $9,043

KPM porcelain plaque, depicting Christopher Columbus, impressed marks, 9 x 6in.
(William Doyle) $3,680

A German fayence blue and white helmet-shaped ewer with a bearded mask lip and shaped ribbed handle, circa 1730, probably Berlin, Funcke's factory, 21.5cm. high.
(Christie's) $1,961

BOW

An early Bow six-shell sweetmeat stand with three large and three smaller shells in two tiers on an open rockwork base, 20.5cm.
(Phillips) $1,148

A pair of Bow porcelain figures of a sheep and a ram with orange markings, 13cm. high.
(Bearne's) $1,109

A good Bow figure of Autumn, as a youth in lilac and blue drape, with goblet of wine and dead hare, 26cm. high.
(Tennants) $536

A pair of Bow figures of a fisherboy and girl, modeled by John Toulouse, after the Meissen originals, by Kaendler, 16cm.
(Phillips) $1,377

A Bow white large shell salt, circa 1755, the bowl formed as a deep scallop shell on a base of shell-encrusted coral, 7^5/8in. wide overall.
(Christie's) $920

A pair of Bow porcelain figures of nuns, each seated reading from books, the text headed 'Of Purgatory' and 'Of Absolution', 12.5cm. high.
(Bearne's) $1,209

An 18th century Bow tub of flowers, the ribbed pot painted with a loose bouquet and with scattered sprigs, circa 1765, 3in. high.
(Cheffins Grain & Comins) $471

A Bow square dish painted in blue with the popular 'Golfer and Caddy' pattern within a dark blue border, 18cm.
(Phillips) $367

A Bow white figure of Kitty Clive in the rôle of The Fine Lady from Garrick's farce Lethe, circa 1750, 27cm. high.
(Christie's) $3,209

A 19th century pottery sugar bowl, printed in black and decorated in colors with two scenes of a cricket match, 5¹/₂in. diameter.
(Bonhams) $330

A Ruskin high-fired vase on stand, shouldered body with tall tapered cylindrical neck and rolled rim, marked Ruskin, England, 1920s, 43.3cm. high.
(Christie's) $4,724

A 19th century pottery mug of large size, printed in black and decorated in colors with two scenes of a cricket match, 5in. high.
(Bonhams) $182

A rare David and John Philip Elers red stoneware mug, circa 1695, the slip-cast cylindrical body mold-applied on the front with a flowering branch in relief between two borders of lathe-turned horizontal reeding, 4in. high.
(Sotheby's) $8,625

After Privat Livemont, Johnson, Walker & Tolhurst Ltd, as retailers, large pot and cover with girl with yellow roses, 1901, the cover with the head and shoulders of a young girl, stamped with maker's mark, 7.5cm. diameter.
(Sotheby's) $2,422

An extremely rare English brown stoneware enameled mug, probably London, 1690–1710, the body thickly enameled on the front with a blue- and black-delineated white hare, 3in. high.
(Sotheby's) $20,700

A pearlware group of 'The Raising of Lazarus', of Sherratt-type, modeled with Christ standing between Lazarus, and Mary, 8in. wide, circa 1820.
(Christie's) $4,959

A pair of Davenport two-handled baluster vases, circa 1835, each with gilt handles molded as swan heads, 19³/₈in. high.
(Christie's) $5,750

A massive stoneware 'Thistle' vase, by Hans Coper, dimpled disk-shaped body with flared rim, on cylindrical foot, circa 1960, 45.6cm. high.
(Christie's) $9,994

BRITISH

A majolica-ware bowl modeled
by Delattre, as a gray bird's nest
with turquoise interior, 16cm.
(Phillips) $398

Beswick Ware Atlantic salmon,
pattern No. 1253, 9in., English,
20th century.
(G. A. Key) $130

Beswick model of a cougar,
pattern No. 1702, white
polychrome glazes, 12in.,
English, 20th century.
(G. A. Key) $154

A Bristol porcelain figure by
William Cookworthy's factory,
modeled as a man in rustic
dress of feathered bonnet, short
coat and breeches standing
playing the hurdy-gurdy, 7½in.
high, circa 1770.
(Christie's) $1,263

Pair of Miles Mason urn vases,
each painted with two landscape
panels on blue ground, 6½in.
high.
(Russell, Baldwin & Bright)
                    $2,149

Copeland parian ware bust,
'Hop Queen', sculptured by J.
Durham, published by Ceramic
& Crystal Palace Art Union,
1873, 13½in. high.
(G. A. Key) $237

A Nottingham pottery
Gravelware jar and cover in the
form of a bear holding cub,
inscribed *Thomas Bowen, 1753*,
12½in. high.
(Russell, Baldwin & Bright)
                        $1,873

A Copeland & Garrett two-
handled pottery footbath, 55cm.
diameter and a matching large
water jug with a grip under the
spout.
(Bearne's) $918

Coalport porcelain molded
milk jug, painted with floral
reserves, scrolled borders,
6½in., English, second quarter
19th century.
(G. A. Key) $135

BRITISH

Copeland pottery large soup tureen, cover and stand, decorated in sepia design of scales, flowers and lakeland landscape, circa 1857.
(G. A. Key) $124

A Beswick Green Woodpecker, No. 1218, 8½in. high.
(Dee, Atkinson & Harrison) $107

A Wade ship's decanter, British Navy Pusser's Rum, full and sealed complete with stopper.
(Dee, Atkinson & Harrison) $84

A very large Goodwins & Harris jug printed in blue with a View of Colnbrook from the 'Metropolitan Scenery' series, 30cm.
(Phillips) $428

Two Plymouth porcelain figure groups by William Cookworthy's factory, each of two scantily-draped putti before flowering bocages, enriched in colors, 7¾in. high, circa 1770.
(Christie's) $1,172

An English glazed Parian copy of the Portland vase, the figures in white relief on an apricot ground, circa 1880, 9½in. high.
(Christie's) $658

A bust of 'W: Shakespear' (sic), with gray beard and moustache and curly gray hair, 42.5cm.
(Phillips) $1,454

A Coalport porcelain 'jeweled' teapot and cover, milk jug and sugar basin, decorated with alternate jeweled turquoise panels on a gold ground.
(Bearne's) $918

An attractively colored Lord Howe toby jug, the man seated on a manganese barrel, his dog and his pipe at his feet, 25.5cm.
(Phillips) $3,060

BRITISH

A porcelain pastille-burner, modeled as a two-storey house with a single chimney, 4¹/₂in. high, circa 1840. (Christie's) $213

An English pearlware teapot and hinged cover, circa 1800, probably Yorkshire, of cylindrical form, the domed cover with swan finial, 7in. wide. (Christie's) $345

A porcelain pastille-burner, modeled as a twin turreted castle, applied with foliage, 3³/₄in. high, circa 1840. (Christie's) $142

A good North Devon slipware harvest jug, dated *1748*, the brown-red earthenware body dipped in cream slip and decorated in sgraffito technique, 12in. high. (Sotheby's) $18,400

Samuel Lear blue and white Jasper Ware Stilton dish and cover with figures in classical relief, impressed mark, circa 1877–86, 8¹/₂in. (G. A. Key) $375

A large earthenware jar and cover, printed and painted with panels of pheasants and highland cattle in the manner of John and Harry Stinton, 14in. high. (Spencer's) $1,020

A porcelain pastille-burner and cover, modeled as a cottage, the thatched roof with two chimneys, 4³/₄in. high, circa 1835. (Christie's) $496

An Andrew Stevenson pearlware plate printed and painted to commemorate the death of Princess Charlotte, printed with a portrait of the Princess, 6in., circa 1817. (Christie's) $397

An H. and R. Daniel presentation jug attributed to William Pollard, of baluster shape with gilt leaf-molded lip and handle terminals, 22.5cm. (Phillips) $435

BRITISH

An Edwardian blue Jasperware biscuit barrel, the cover with acorn knop finial.
(Dee, Atkinson & Harrison)
$85

Oval drainer dish, painted in colors with oriental pattern on a cream ground, 12in. long.
(G. A. Key) $177

Pottery ornament formed as a basket weave container, having two cats peering from the top, 8in., late 19th century period.
(G. A. Key) $167

A Moore Brothers comport modeled as a leaf-shaped dish, with three cupids at the base playing musical instruments above a trefoil base, 12³/₄in. high, circa 1890.
(Christie's) $902

An English brown stoneware mug, Nottingham or Derbyshire, mid 18th century, the cylindrical body decorated with horizontal ring turnings above a slightly flared foot, 3⁵/₈in. high.
(Sotheby's) $460

An English ironstone vase and cover twin-handled, the handles modeled as grotesque beasts, enriched allover with a dark-blue-ground painted in gilt, 19in. high, circa 1825.
(Christie's) $866

English blue and white pearlware jug, decorated with chinoiserie panels, mask spout, 7¹/₄in., English, 19th century.
(G. A. Key) $225

Paragon Coronation plate, the molded border decorated between gilt lines with King George VI and Queen Elizabeth, dated 1937, 10¹/₂in. diameter.
(G. A. Key) $138

Earthenware ale jug in the form of head and shoulders of 'Mischievous Fellow', his hat forming the spout, 19th century, 9in. high.
(G. A. Key) $274

CANTON

Antique rose medallion garden seat, 18¹/₂in. high.
(Eldred's) $1,980

An ormolu-mounted Canton famille rose bowl, the interior and exterior painted with panels of figures, flowers and birds, late 19th century, 20in. high.
(Christie's) $5,485

Canton porcelain mug, decorated in typical colors with family scenes on balconies and in gardens, 19th century, 5in. high.
(G. A. Key) $80

A Cantonese garden seat, of barrel shape painted all-over design of flowers, fish and birds in famille rose enamels, 19in. high, on ebonized wood plinth.
(Russell, Baldwin & Bright) $865

A pair of 'famille-rose' cache pots and stands, Qing Dynasty, Canton, 19th century, the upright sides painted with ladies in pavilions, 27.5cm. high.
(Sotheby's) $4,410

A Cantonese porcelain large vase and cover of inverted baluster form, with four mask lugs, decorated in famille rose et verte enamels, 42cm. high.
(Spencer's) $770

Canton porcelain baluster jug, with armorial panel and decorated throughout in typical colors with figures on a balcony, 5in. high.
(G. A. Key) $208

A pair of Cantonese vases with enameled polychrome decoration, circa 1830, 90cm. high.
(Hôtel de Ventes Horta) $7,138

Canton porcelain teapot, decorated in typical colors with panels of figures, birds and butterflies, 19th century, 7in. high.
(G. A. Key) $64

CAUGHLEY

Caughley oval two handled basket, the pierced latticed border encrusted with flower petals, late 18th century, 7in. wide.
(G. A. Key) $208

An early Caughley coffee pot and cover, of plain pear shape with unusual scroll finial, 17cm.
(Phillips) $452

A rare Caughley inkwell of waisted drum shape with a separate central well fitting within four holes for quills, 9.75cm. diameter.
(Phillips) $995

A fine Caughley blue and white cabbage-leaf jug, dated 1783, molded around the ovoid body with overlapping leaves and on the fluted neck with a border of leaves and caillouté, 8⁵/₈in. high.
(Sotheby's) $2,760

Caughley blue and white porcelain coffee can, painted with chinoiserie scene, crescent mark, 2¹/₂in., English, circa 1775–90.
(G. A. Key) $225

A fine Caughley blue and white eye-bath, 1785–95, with a scroll-molded lozenge-shaped bowl and baluster-form stem above a fluted oval foot, 2¹/₈in. high.
(Sotheby's) $1,725

An early Caughley mask jug of plain pear shape, the mask lip with cross-over beard, printed in blue, 14cm.
(Phillips) $387

An early Caughley teapot and a coffee pot, the coffee pot printed with the 'Three Flowers' pattern, thinly glazed base, 13cm.
(Phillips) $323

An early Caughley mask jug, of plain baluster shape with a cylindrical neck, printed in blue with flower and fruit sprays, 14.5cm.
(Phillips) $774

A rare Chelsea model of a hound, modeled seated on an oval grassy base, wearing black collar, 5cm., red anchor mark.
(Phillips) $2,580

A Chelsea-Derby desk set, circa 1770, gilt D and anchor marks, comprising an inkwell and cover, taperstick, and pounce pot, 8¹/₂in. wide, the stand.
(Christie's) $1,150

Harry Parr, an amusing Chelsea pottery figure of a cherub riding on the back of a large toad, signed and dated *1930*, 7in. high.
(Spencer's) $659

A Chelsea gold and enamel-mounted bonbonniere, modeled as a lady's head, her lace mob-cap enriched in blue and with a puce rose and three feathers at the front, circa 1758, 8cm. long.
(Christie's) $4,904

A pair of Chelsea groups of gallants and companions emblematic of the Seasons, gold anchor marks, circa 1765, 33cm. high.
(Christie's) $12,478

A Chelsea figure of a woman emblematic of Smell, from a set of the Senses, wearing puce headdress, flowered robe, iron-red, yellow and turquoise flowing drapery, circa 1758, 25.5cm. high.
(Christie's) $800

A very rare Chelsea group of Mercury and Argus, the former seated before a tree playing a pipe and lulling Argus to sleep, 18.5cm.
(Phillips) $689

A fine Chelsea Plate, circa 1755, of 'Warren Hastings' type, painted in soft shades in the center with a floral bouquet, a large leaf sprig and eight scattered floral sprigs, red anchor mark, 9⁷/₁₆in. diameter.
(Sotheby's) $2,070

A Chelsea figure of a flautist, the girl seated on a flower-encrusted tree-stump wearing iron-red-lined yellow bodice and pale-lilac skirt, circa 1756, 15.5cm. high.
(Christie's) $700

CHINESE

Oriental porcelain ornament of a nodding seated figure, brightly colored and designed, the hands also articulated, late 19th century period, 6in.
(G. A. Key) $246

A Chinese blue and white two-handled oviform fish bowl with flattened rim, painted allover with pagodas in fenced gardens, late 18th century, 24in. diameter.
(Christie's) $7,360

Chinese amber glazed biscuit roof tile, Ming Dynasty, 17th century, depicting a celestial deity mounted astride a phoenix, 13³/₄in. high.
(William Doyle) $690

A fine pair of Chinese export peony-form water droppers, dated *1882* and *1883*, each lightly molded with peony petals delineated in black, 7³/₈in. long.
(Sotheby's) $3,162

A Yixing-style stoneware wine pot and cover, probably Continental, late 18th or 19th century, each side of the hexagonal body with a slightly recessed panel molded with a dragon, incised *1788*, 6¹⁵/₁₆in. high.(Sotheby's) $1,725

Pair of Chinese famille verte porcelain ormolu mounted parrots, Kangxi period, 18th century, perched on a pierced aubergine rockwork base, 9in. high overall.
(William Doyle) $1,840

An early 18th century Chinese blue and white coffee pot and cover, of tapering form with loop handle and side spout, 23cm.
(Tennants) $689

A pair of Chinese porcelain, double gourd reticulated vases, the alternate pierced panels in turquoise and red enamel, 14.3cm. high, Qianlong.
(Bearne's) $428

A Chinese 'cherry pickers' tea caddy, of arched form, enameled and gilt with European figures, iron red borders, 11cm. high, Qianlong.
(Tennants) $918

CHINESE

A Han Dynasty funerary sculpture of a seated dog, 23cm. high.
(Stockholms Auktionsverk) $823

A pair of large Chinese famille rose jardinières, each enameled on one side with two cockerels amongst peony, 19th century, 24³/₄in. diameter.
(Christie's) $35,880

Enamelled porcelain figure of a seated dog with collar, Chinese, 18th century, 18cm. high.
(Stockholms Auktionsverk) $2,407

A Chinese famille rose porcelain monkey, Qianlong period, holding aloft in one hand a pink-tinged green peach, 8¹/₂in. high.
(Christie's) $3,680

A pair of Chinese porcelain spaniels, Qianlong period, with heads turned to one side in alert expression, 9¹/₈in. high.
(Christie's) $20,700

Sancai figure of a saddled horse, Tang Dynasty, 50cm. high.
(Galerie Koller) $24,181

A Chinese porcelain seated figure of Budai, the rotund monk with long lobed ears and smiling face, 23cm. high, Transitional.
(Bearne's) $5,712

A good pair of Chinese export fluted hexagonal wine coolers, circa 1765, painted with a duck in flight, 7³/₄in. high.
(Sotheby's) $9,775

A Chinese famille rose porcelain duck, Qianlong period, his long body with feather details picked out in brown enamel, 7in. high.
(Christie's) $6,900

A Chinese export 'Canton' blue and white platter, 19th century, painted with landscape scene showing an arched bridge and three sampans, 14¼in. wide. (Christie's) **$633**

A pair of ormolu-mounted Chinese blue and white porcelain vases, each with ribbon-tied laurel wreath collar, 14¼in. high. (Christie's) **$7,535**

A Qianlong famille rose and gilt edged barber's bowl, decorated with peonies, 30.4cm. long. (Stockholms Auktionsverk) **$886**

An ormolu-mounted and parcel-gilt Chinese porcelain jardinière, the pierced floral and C-scroll rim above the tapering vase-shaped body, the porcelain late 17th century, 16½in. diameter. (Christie's) **$5,741**

A pair of famille rose baluster jars and covers, the domed covers surmounted by seated gilt Buddhistic lion finials, the porcelain Yongzheng/early Qianlong, 61½in. high. (Christie's) **$53,820**

An ormolu-mounted Chinese armorial porcelain bowl, with lion-mask and ring-handles, with pierced and block-feet, the porcelain early 18th century, 11¼in. wide. (Christie's) **$4,664**

A pair of ormolu-mounted turquoise Chinese porcelain ewers, each with the water-cast everted spout above a paired set of two upright carp, the porcelain 18th century, 16¾in. high. (Christie's) **$73,369**

An ormolu-mounted Chinese blue and white porcelain tankard and cover, the domed-lid with spreading husk-trails and fluting, the porcelain Qianlong, 8¼in. high. (Christie's) **$1,794**

A pair of Chinese famille rose porcelain pheasants, Qianlong period, proudly standing on tree trunk form pierced bases, 14⅛in. high. (Christie's) **$20,700**

CHINESE EXPORT

A Chinese export punch bowl, circa 1780, the exterior with an iron-red and grisaille trellis diaper ground, 38.5cm. diameter.
(Sotheby's) $4,025

A Chinese export 'faux bois' shallow fish bowl, 19th century, painted on the interior with two cranes above two ducks, 40cm. diameter.
(Sotheby's) $1,265

A Chinese export 'Tobacco Leaf' pattern oval platter, 1770–80, painted with a green-centered rose and yellow tobacco blossom, 34.2cm. long.
(Sotheby's) $2,587

A Chinese export yellow-ground garden seat, the barrel-shaped body pierced on the top and sides with pink-ground cash medallions, 18in. high.
(Sotheby's) $632

A rare pair of Chinese export shell-shaped sauceboats and stands, circa 1775, painted in rose, purple, green, iron-red and blue, 9in. and 8³/₈in. long.
(Sotheby's) $6,325

A Chinese export reticulated oval lemon basket and a pedestal, 1765–75, the pedestal modeled as a tree runk with two putti, 15in. high overall.
(Sotheby's) $2,300

A Chinese export blue and white fish bowl, 18th century, painted around the circular body with lotus blossoms, 27.8cm. high.
(Sotheby's) $1,150

A pair of Chinese export blue and white quatrefoil tea caddies and covers, 19th century, painted with two butterflies amidst peony, 20.1cm. high.
(Sotheby's) $920

A Chinese export 'Judgment of Paris' plate, 1745–50, the rim painted with alternating views of Plymouth Sound and the Pearl River, 23cm. diameter.
(Sotheby's) $2,875

CHINESE EXPORT

A Chinese export blue and white large leaf-shaped dish, 1780–85, painted with bouquet, spray and five sprigs of peonies, 13in. long. (Sotheby's) $1,380

Chinese Export porcelain teapot, decorated with scale and floral pattern in the Worcester manner, the lid with bud finial, 6in., early 19th century. (G. A. Key) $153

A rare Chinese export blue and white chamfered rectangular small soup tureen and cover, circa 1785, 29cm. long. (Sotheby's) $4,600

A pair of Chinese export blue and white silver-shape oval platters, circa 1750, each painted in underglaze-blue with a box, a vase and a censer, 29cm. long. (Sotheby's) $1,035

A pair of Chinese export figures of cocks, early 19th century, standing astride lustrous dark brown rockwork, 31cm. and 30.3cm. high. (Sotheby's) $6,325

A pair of Chinese export famille-rose ginger jars, mid 18th century, each painted with a kingfisher, 8½in. and 8¾in. high. (Sotheby's) $862

A Chinese export 'Mandarin Palette' large cylindrical mug, circa 1785, loop handle with a gilt ruyi-head thumbpiece, 5⅝in. high. (Sotheby's) $805

A Chinese export blue and white chamfered rectangular soup tureen, a cover and a platter, circa 1770, 36.7cm. and 22.1cm. long. (Sotheby's) $2,300

A Chinese export blue and white ribbed ginger jar mounted as a lamp, early 18th century, 11½in. high. (Sotheby's) $2,300

CLARICE CLIFF

A 'Bizarre' washbasin and ewer painted with a band of red diamonds bordered with a yellow and brown triangles.
(Christie's) $1,050

A 'Bizarre' Clog in the 'Swirls' pattern, painted in colors, printed factory marks, 14cm. long.
(Christie's) $490

'Libra' a star sign, painted in colors, printed factory marks, 17cm. wide.
(Christie's) $670

A 'Bizarre' charger in the 'Oranges' pattern, painted in colors, printed factory marks, 45.5cm. diameter.
(Christie's) $4,575

A pedestal trumpet vase, molded in relief with twin handles, in the 'Crocus' pattern, painted in colors, printed factory marks, 29cm. high.
(Christie's) $563

An Appliqué 'Bizarre' charger in the 'Etna' pattern, painted in colors, remains of painted mark, 45.5cm. diameter.
(Christie's) $19,360

An Isis vase in the 'Anemone' patterns, painted in colors, printed factory marks, 29cm. high.
(Christie's) $845

'Flora' a wall mask molded in relief in the form of a womans head with flowers and foliage in her hair, 35cm. high.
(Christie's) $1,760

An Inspiration 'Bizarre' jug, of ovoid form, the orange ground covered with a running turquoise glaze, 20cm. high.
(Christie's) $335

CLARICE CLIFF

An Inspiration 'Bizarre' ribbed vase in the 'Caprice' pattern, painted in colors, printed factory marks, 25cm. wide.
(Christie's) $1,320

A 'Bizarre' Tankard coffee set for six in the 'Crocus' pattern, painted in colors, printed factory marks.
(Christie's) $740

A 'Bizarre' Bonjour teapot and cover designed by Eva Crofts, painted with a red breasted bird amongst flowers and trees.
(Christie's) $528

A 'Bizarre' twin-handled Lotus jug, painted in shades of orange, blue, green and yellow, 29cm. high.
(Christie's) $1,672

A pair of Fantasque 'Bizarre' book ends, shape No. 405, in the 'Sunrise' pattern, painted in colors, 16cm. high.
(Christie's) $2,100

A 'Fantasque Bizarre' single-handled Lotus jug in the 'Blue W' pattern, painted in colors, printed factory marks, 30cm. high.
(Christie's) $7,040

A 'Bizarre' ribbed vase, shape No. 356, in the 'Mushroom' pattern, painted in shades of red, green and black on a cream ground, printed factory marks, 24cm. diameter.
(Christie's) $2,640

A 'Bizarre' plate designed by Dame Laura Knight, the well printed and painted with three performing acrobats, 23cm. high.
(Christie's) $1,400

A 'Bizarre' single-handled jug, shape No. 634, in the 'Delecia Pansies' pattern, painted in colors, 16cm. high.
(Christie's) $915

DEDHAM

A large 'poppy' crackle ware pottey Chinese cut bowl, by Dedham Pottery, of flared form with cut edge, decorated in blue, 10in. diameter.
(Christie's) $1,495

A 'rabbit' pattern crackle ware pottery No. 1 creamer and No. 1 covered sugar, by Dedham Pottery, decorated in blue in the rabbit pattern, creamer 3¹/₂in. high.
(Christie's) $863

A 'Crab' crackle ware pottery serving platter, by Dedham Pottery, decorated in blue with a single large crab and a bit of seaweed, 17⁵/₈in. long.
(Christie's) $3,220

A rare crackle ware pottery dinner plate, by Dedham Pottery, the blue border design of turtles alternating with clover, 10in. diameter.
(Christie's) $4,140

A 'rabbit' pattern crackle ware pottery No. 3 covered sugar bowl, by Dedham Pottery, the octagonal body molded with two handles, 6¹/₄in. high including cover.
(Christie's) $748

A crackle ware pottery dinner plate, by Dedham Pottery, the center painted in blue with a white terrier posed in a landscape, 9³/₄in. diameter.
(Christie's) $1,035

A rare crackle ware pottery breakfast plate, by Dedham Pottery, the raised border decorated in blue with long-beaked ibis birds, 9in. diameter.
(Christie's) $1,265

A 'rabbit' pattern crackle ware pottery covered egg cup, by Dedham Pottery, egg-shaped on shallow dish base, 4¹/₄in. high.
(Christie's) $1,265

An 'elephant' pattern crackle ware pottery whipped cream bowl, by Dedham Pottery, the blue border design of a procession of elephants, 7¹/₂in. diameter.
(Christie's) $748

DEDHAM

A 'lobster' crackle ware pottery breakfast plate, by Dedham Pottery, decorated in blue with two lobsters, 8¹/₂in. diameter. (Christie's) $863

A rare crackle ware pottery dish, by Dedham Pottery, modeled with a naked lady reclining, 4¹/₂in. long. (Christie's) $1,610

An 'elephant' pattern crackle ware pottery child's mug, by Dedham Pottery, decorated in blue, 3in. high. (Christie's) $4,025

A 'lion' pattern crackle ware pottery dinner plate, by Dedham Pottery, the border decorated in blue in the tapestry lion pattern, 10¹/₈in. diameter. (Christie's) $1,265

A rare crackle ware pottery ashtray, by Dedham Pottery, signed by Charles Davenport, modeled as the figure of a little boy urinating, 4⁷/₈in. high. (Christie's) $920

A 'tiger lily' crackle ware pottery bread and butter plate, by Dedham Pottery, the center decorated with white lilies against blue, 6in. diameter. (Christie's) $1,610

A crackle ware pottery coaster, by Dedham Pottery, the small lobed dish painted to resemble a wild rose blossom, 3¹/₂in. diameter. (Christie's) $173

A 'rabbit' pattern crackle ware pottery teapot, by Dedham Pottery, decorated in blue in the rabbit pattern, 5¹/₂in. high. (Christie's) $1,380

A 'rabbit' pattern crackle ware pottery ashtray, by Dedham Pottery, decorated in blue in the rabbit pattern, 3⁷/₈in. diameter. (Christie's) $81

DELFT

A Lambeth delft 'Persian blue' posset pot, encircled with white painted landscapes and seated Chinamen, 11cm. high, late 17th century.
(Bearne's) $14,994

A well-painted Dutch delft quintal vase with shield-shaped body painted in blue within a black outline, 21.5cm.
(Phillips) $1,989

A Dutch delft blue and white barber's bowl, circa 1780, boldly painted in the center with flowers and a stylized rock by a garden fence, 9¹/₁₆in. diameter.
(Sotheby's) $690

A London delftware polychrome William III equestrian portrait charger, circa 1690, the King wearing an ocher crown flanked by the initials *K W*, astride a blue rearing steed, 12¹³/₁₆in. diameter.
(Sotheby's) $11,500

A London delftware white salt, probably Southwark, circa 1675, the circular top with a hemispherical well and flat rim supporting three 'ram's-horn' scrolls, 4⁷/₈in. high.
(Sotheby's) $19,550

A London delftware blue and white posset pot and cover, 1670–90, the cylindrical body painted in a slightly runny blue with three Chinamen seated amidst shrubbery in a rocky landscape, 6¹⁵/₁₆in. high.
(Sotheby's) $7,475

A Bristol delftware polychrome Queen Anne portrait charger, circa 1710, the monarch wearing a blue and yellow crown and dress, holding a yellow scepter and orb, 13³/₈in. diameter.
(Sotheby's) $12,650

A tin-glazed earthenware Documentary triangular salt, Southwark, dated *1674*, painted on a white ground in shades of blue, green , turquoise and yellow, 5³/₄in. high.
(Christie's) $16,100

An English delft blue dash polychrome 'Adam and Eve' charger, painted with the two nude figures flanking the green tree, 33.5cm.
(Phillips) $2,295

DELFT

A rare London delftware blue and white cup, 1655–75, painted around the ovoid body with the inscription *DRINCK* ᵛ•ᵖ *YOVR* • *DRINK* • *AND* • *SE* • *MY* • *CO[N]E*, 2³/₈in. high.
(Sotheby's) $14,950

A London (Southwark) delft dated blue and white mug, with strap handle and molded with five bands of raised dimple ornament, 1653, 19cm. high.
(Christie's) $51,693

A delft blue and white flower brick, probably Liverpool, the rectangular top pierced with eight holes, 12.5cm. wide, circa 1760.
(Bearne's) $773

A Dutch delft polychrome birdcage plaque, 19th century, the recessed central section painted with a blue-shaded yellow canary in a manganese, blue and yellow cage within blue-striped yellow drapery, 16⁵/₁₆in. wide.
(Sotheby's) $5,175

A pair of tin-glazed earthenware Documentary shoes, probably London, dated *1695*, each court shoe with a bow at the instep, 4⁷/₈in. long.
(Christie's) $8,625

A London delftware blue and white octagonal pill slab, mid 18th century, painted with the arms and rhinoceros crest of the Worshipful Society of Apothecaries above a blue-ground scroll-edged cartouche, 12¹/₄ x 10¹/₄in.
(Sotheby's) $3,737

A Southwark delftware white posset pot and cover, 1655–75, the compressed spherical body dimpled and molded with bosses, 6¹/₈in. high.
(Sotheby's) $28,750

An English delft blue and white mug, painted in a bright palette with flowering water-lily beside bamboo, circa 1750, perhaps London, 16.5cm. high.
(Christie's) $3,387

A Bristol delft shallow dish, boldly painted in underglaze blue, brown and green enamels, 34cm. diameter, mid-18th century.
(Bearne's) $2,688

DERBY

A jeweled and gilt Royal Crown Derby vase and cover by Desire Leroy, signed, of oval shape with double scroll handles, 11cm. high, date code for 1901.
(Phillips) $4,838

A Derby miniature teapot and cover of compressed form with a scrolling handle, applied with flowers on a green ground, iron-red mark, Robt. Bloor, 4¹/₈in. high, circa 1830.
(Christie's) $451

A Derby fluted lozenge-shaped dish, circa 1815, iron-red crown mark, painted with a loose bouquet within a wide border, 12in. wide.
(Christie's) $575

A pair of Derby blue-ground two-handled vases and covers (Lebes Gamikos), circa 1770, painted front and back en grisaille with a dancing nymph, 9³/₄in. high.
(Christie's) $5,520

A Royal Crown Derby jeweled vase and cover painted by Albert Gregory, with pearl bordered panels of flowers and swags, 34.5cm., date code for 1911.
(Phillips) $7,740

A pair of Derby male and female figures, she holding flowers in her apron, he holding a bowl of fruit, 9¹/₄in. high, circa 1765.
(Anderson & Garland) $1,836

A Royal Crown Derby campana shaped vase painted by William Mosley, signed, with vases and festoons of flowers in colors, 26.5cm., date code for 1903.
(Phillips) $3,064

A fine Derby dessert plate, painted with a border of roses and flower garlands, the center painted in puce with a Cupid, by Richard Askew, 21cm.
(Phillips) $1,129

Derby porcelain figure of a young lady seated by a bocage playing a lute, rococo base, English, early 19th century.
(G. A. Key) $244

148

DOULTON

'Ard of 'Earing' D6588, a Royal Doulton character jug, printed factory marks, 19cm. high.
(Christie's) $1,170

Four Doulton Lambeth stoneware decanters in original wicker basket, the shoulder molded in relief with fruiting vine, 21cm. high.
(Christie's) $809

A Doulton Lambeth stoneware mug of waisted form, applied with molded white figures of a bowler, 5¾in. high.
(Bonhams) $462

A Doulton Lambeth Holbein ware charger, by Charles Noke, the center paintd with a bust portrait of a medieval gentleman, 39cm. diameter.
(Christie's) $480

Three Doulton Lambeth graduated jugs, molded in relief with portrait medallions of Queen Victoria between bands of flowers and foliage, largest 23cm. high.
(Christie's) $800

'Good for Fifty' 'There's Style', a Royal Doulton vase, circa 1920, of money bag form, 7¼in. high.
(Bonhams) $5,280

'The Coming of Spring' H.N. 1722, a Royal Doulton figure, printed and painted marks, 33cm. high.
(Christie's) $576

A Royal Doulton figure of a bulldog, modeled smoking a cigar and wearing a brown derby hat and blue bowtie, and two graduated bulldogs.
(Christie's) $755

'Miranda' H.N. 1818, a Royal Doulton figure, printed and painted marks, 21cm. high.
(Christie's) $504

DOULTON

A Doulton stoneware vase by Hannah Barlow, incised with sheep in a hilly landscape, 14cm. high, dated *1887*.
(Bearne's) $244

Pair of Royal Doulton tapering cylinder vases with ocher rims, over a band of molded stylized flowers, 13in. high.
(G. A. Key) $289

A Royal Doulton character jug, Granny, 6½in. high, toothless version.
(Dee, Atkinson & Harrison) $459

A Doulton & Co. 'Simplicitas Wash Down' lavatory, the exterior molded in relief with swirling foliage, 58cm. wide.
(Christie's) $504

A Royal Doulton character jug 'Captain Hook', numbered D6597, 18.5cm. high.
(Spencer's) $290

A Doulton stoneware biscuit barrel by Hannah and Lucy Barlow, incised with an encircling scene with ponies in a moorland setting, 17cm. high.
(Bearne's) $453

A Royal Doulton figure, 'The Land of Nod' modeled by H. Tittensor, decorated in pale gray, yellow and blue, 26cm. high.
(Spencer's) $2,002

Pair of Doulton Lambeth Art pottery vases, circa 1900, in squat globular form with floral banded design, by Mark Marshall, 5¾in. high.
(Eldred's) $467

A Royal Doulton 'flambe veined' rounded cylindrical vase, the lower portion decorated with wispy blue luster glazes, 27cm. high.
(Bearne's) $302

DOULTON

A Doulton Burslem 'Blue Children' ware plaque, of oval form, printed and painted in blue with three childern in Edwardian dress, 24.5cm. high.
(Christie's) $540

A pair of large Royal Doulton ceramic baluster vases, early 20th century, painted in shades of brown, green and amber with pastoral landscapes, 22in. high.
(Christie's) $2,429

A Royal Doulton character jug 'Old King Cole' registered number 832354 with yellow crown, 5½in. high.
(Anderson & Garland) $1,279

Doulton Lambeth silicon ware brown ground simulated leather tankard, incised *Here's Luck*, hallmarked silver band, London 1910, 6in.
(G. A. Key) $52

A pair of Royal Doulton 'Chinese Jade' porcelain vases, by Charles Noke and Harry Nixon, covered in a streaked white and green glaze to simulate jade, impressed *3.12.30*, with ebonized stands, 25.2cm. high.
(Christie's) $1,635

Royal Doulton 'Aubrey' patterned slop pail and top with bound cane handle, English, early 20th century.
(G. A. Key) $294

A Royal Doulton figure, 'A Mandarin', wearing a yellow and green patterned tunic, HN611, 10in. high.
(Spencer's) $2,120

Royal Doulton sampler water jug and teapot, pattern No. D3749, English, early 20th century.
(G. A. Key) $195

A Royal Doulton figure entitled 'The Bather', style one, impressed date *3.2.29*.
(Bearne's) $672

DRESDEN

A Dresden clock-case, with a replacement pietra dura top inlaid with three bouquets, imitation blue crossed swords and dot mark, the porcelain circa 1880, 10in. high.
(Christie's) $1,863

Dresden porcelain ornament of a man displaying ribbons to a young girl, 6in., German, mid 19th century.
(G. A. Key) $619

Dresden cup and saucer of quatrefoil form, gilt edge, encrusted throughout with flowers, crossed swords mark in underglazed blue, late 19th century.
(G. A. Key) $431

A Dresden porcelain figure group modeled as a courting couple, the gentleman embracing the lady from behind as a young man looks on, circa 1900, 12½in. high.
(Christie's) $2,274

A pair of Dresden baluster Schneeballen vases and covers, applied overall with rows of yellow-centered white mayflowers, circa 1880, 22¼in. high.
(Christie's) $7,825

Dresden porcelain group, a regal man wearing a flowing puce cape, carrying a partially clad woman, (possibly The Rape of the Sabines), 19th century, 10½in. high.
(G. A. Key) $400

A Dresden figural clock-case, with a detachable top modeled after J. J. Pradier as Sappho wearing striped and flowered clothes and sandals, circa 1880, 22¾in. high.
(Christie's) $4,658

A Dresden porcelain clock-case, circa 1880, modeled as a broad scroll-molded column applied with garlands and a putto scantily clad in pink drapery, 23in. high.
(Christie's) $5,485

A Dresden pink-ground globular jar and domed cover, painted with lovers in 18th century-style dress in idyllic gardens, late 19th century, 11¼in. high.
(Christie's) $1,005

Demetre H. Chiparus porcelain box, Paris, circa 1930, for Etling, semi nude figure with leopard spot skirt, 8¹/₈in. long. (Skinner) **$460**

A pair of Continental figures of Malabars, bearing blue crossed sword marks, on circular rocky bases, 14in. high. (Christie's) **$7,475**

An Amphora pottery figural vase, surmounted on the shoulder by a large figure of a cockerel, painted in shades of brown, 43cm. high. (Christie's) **$1,328**

Two Continental mythological figures, late 19th century, bearing blue crossed swords marks at the back, possibly for Achille Bloch, 25¹/₄in. high. (Christie's) **$2,990**

A Marieberg oviform vase applied with meandering branches of flowering rose and painted with a yellow butterfly and a moth, circa 1765, 23cm. high. (Christie's) **$1,783**

A late 19th century Continental porcelain figure of a batsman standing before a tree stump, together with the companion figure of a young woman playing croquet. (Bonhams) **$858**

A rare Portuguese 'Hamburgtype' water jug in the form of a sphinx with the tail forming the hollow handle, 24cm. (Phillips) **$6,773**

A pair of Tournai white glazed vase groups, each baluster vase with pierced neck and applied with trailing plants, 18cm. high, late 18th century. (Bearne's) **$1,344**

Julius Dressler ceramic jardinière on pedestal, Austria, circa 1905, matt and glass green with tan flambé glaze on high relief stylized Art Nouveau floral decorated two-part form, 32¹/₈in. high. (Skinner) **$460**

Emile Gallé, crouched nodding cat, circa 1880, pale pink-colored tin glazed earthenware decorated with flowered jacket and a medallion, 15.5cm.
(Sotheby's) $10,750

A pair of ormolu-mounted famille rose Samson porcelain vases and lids, each with domed hexagonal lid, the porcelain late 19th century, 17in. high.
(Christie's) $3,229

A St. Clément faience desk tray, the design attributed to Emile Gallé, modeled with a heraldic lion, shield and armor, circa 1870, 35.5cm. wide.
(Christie's) $727

A Lallemant pottery vase, painted with a scene of Chopin playing at the piano before two devoted lady admirers, 28cm. high.
(Christie's) $620

A pair of Samson models of pugs, 19th century, faint blue marks at back, both with pink collars fixed with bells and attached at the back with blue bows, 4¼in. high.
(Christie's) $1,589

A Paris blue and green-ground parcel biscuit centerpiece, first quarter of the 19th century, modeled in the Empire style with two addorsed griffins, 18³/₈in. high.
(Christie's) $10,925

A pair of French two-handled vases, mid-19th century, the mouth extending into side handles in the form of a Sèvres vase oreilles, 12in. high.
(Christie's) $2,429

A René Buthaud earthenware vase, decorated with floral reserves and bands in turquoise, black and brown, 1920s, 19.8cm. high.
(Christie's) $1,180

A pair of fine Paris 19th century male and female figures, he holding two white doves, she holding a damaged urn, 27in. high.
(Anderson & Garland)
                               $1,469

FRENCH

A Theodore Deck jardinière, painted in colors on a cream ground with birds and flowers, 41cm. diameter.
(Christie's) $620

A pair of figurines of a Turk and his lady in polychrome enameled porcelain, attributed to Jacob Petit.
(Hôtel de Ventes Horta) $2,982

French porcelain ornament formed as cockerel and hen within an ovoid formed plaque with chicks to rear, oval base, 7in., late 19th century.
(G. A. Key) $106

A Boch Frères vase, by Charles Catteau, incised with stylized deer between borders of abstract roundels, 40.5cm. high.
(Christie's) $850

A pair of French green-ground cache pots, 19th century, each of rectangular form, with pierced gilt rim, raised on four lion paw feet, 6¹/₈in. high.
(Christie's) $1,776

J. Martel for Edition Lehmonn, stylized water carrier, 1920s, in cream crackle glazed earthenware heightened with metallic silver glaze, marked *J. Martel*, 28.5cm.
(Sotheby's) $2,049

A French blue and white faience cream-jug, probably Moustières, painted with a coat-of-arms within stylized pendant and scroll borders, 2³/₄in. high, circa 1740.
(Christie's) $505

A pair of Samson figural candelabra, late 19th century, bearing gold anchor marks, modeled in the Chelsea style with Neptune and Amphitrite, 14³/₄in. high.
(Christie's) $3,738

A French white group of a youth and companion, he holding a basket of grapes and she holding a bunch of grapes, perhaps Orléans, circa 1750, 21.5cm. high.
(Christie's) $980

GERMAN

A Fulda sporting group of a huntress, standing holding a rifle before a pair of billing doves, circa 1780, 16cm. high.
(Christie's) $16,934

Sitzendorf porcelain figure in white and gilt of a lady standing by a horse on oval base, 9in., German, 19th century.
(G. A. Key) $174

Continental porcelain comport, the bowl with pierced lattice border, the pedestal formed as a winged putto, 13½in. high.
(G. A. Key) $413

A brown salt glazed bellarmine, pear shaped with inscription band flanked by portrait medallions, Cologne, 16th century.
(Kunsthaus am Museum) $933

A pair of late 19th century Continental porcelain comports, the pillars surmounted frolicking cherubs and climbing roses on rococo base, 14½in. high.
(Dee, Atkinson & Harrison) $765

A Frankenthal figure of a trinket-seller modeled by Johann Friedrich Lück, in a green hat, orange bodice and puce-striped skirt, circa 1758, 18cm. high.
(Christie's) $4,278

A Bayreuth faïence blue and white plate, 1730–40, painted with two birds perched on a bowl of fruit and foliage within foliate lappets, 8¾in. diameter.
(Sotheby's) $805

An Erhardt & Söhne biscuit barrel, of cylindrical form, wood inlaid in brass with floral cartouches, 23.5cm. high.
(Christie's) $319

A Flörsheim fluted bough-pot with flared rim, painted in grand feu colors with flowering plants, manganese F monogram mark, circa 1775, 15.5cm. wide.
(Christie's) $801

GERMAN

Continental porcelain group of two lovers, he wearing a puce tunic and she holding a dove on her arm, late 19th century, 9in. high.
(G. A. Key) $447

Continental porcelain comport, supported on a single column with putti attendants and encrusted flowers, 12in., German, circa 1900.
(G. A. Key) $397

A Kloster Veilsdorf figure salt modeled by L.D. Heyd, with a figure of a seated lady, flanked by two white basket salts, 11.5cm.
(Phillips) $581

Art Nouveau ceramic ewer, attributed to Johan Marsch, Germany, circa 1900, high relief decoration, 17³/₄in. high.
(Skinner) $690

Pair of 19th century Continental porcelain cabinet plates, the central circular panels painted with bust length portraits of a young boy and girl in 16th century attire, 30cm. diameter.
(Spencer's) $1,078

A Continental scent bottle modeled as a man holding a pug dog in his right arm, the dog's head forming the stopper, 8.5cm.
(Phillips) $837

Continental porcelain group of 'Blind Mans Buff', a couple together with a child, probably German, 19th century, 8¹/₂in. high.
(G. A. Key) $162

Pair of Sitzendorf figures of 'Gainsborough Blue Boy' and 'Sarah Siddons', he mainly dressed in blue and cream, 11in. and 12in. high.
(G. A. Key) $426

Muller Art Deco mottled vase, bulbous body of transparent glass internally layered with gold flecks and green and red-orange cluthra-type inclusions, 9¹/₂in. high.
(Skinner) $547

GERMAN

A Künersberg oval barber's bowl painted in manganese, iron-red, yellow, pink and green with scattered fruit, circa 1740, 27cm. wide.
(Christie's) $8,021

A Frankfurt dated barrel-shaped spirit-flask painted with three scenes from the life of Christ, 1685, 20cm. high.
(Christie's) $6,417

A Continental creamware oval barber's bowl, circa 1830, the bowl inscribed in blue *Johañes Rubli* within a crescent of rose, blue, green and gray flowers and leaves, 10⁹/₁₆in. wide.
(Sotheby's) $632

A faience blue and white fluted dish, German, painted to the centre with a seated Oriental figure, the well with stylized flowers, the border painted with vignettes of figures in landscape, 13in. diameter, 18th century.
(Christie's) $395

A Künersberg rectangular plaque, the center painted en camaieu rose with the Penitent Magdalene before the Cross, circa 1750, 16.5 x 13.5cm.
(Christie's) $23,173

A Bayreuth glazed brown stoneware teapot and cover, circa 1730, the pear-shaped body decorated in gilding on either side with a cluster of three blossoms and foliage, 5¹¹/₁₆in. high.
(Sotheby's) $1,380

A Volkstedt fluted pear-shaped coffee-pot and cover, painted with trailing garden flowers from the shaped purple-scale borders, circa 1770, 26cm. high.
(Christie's) $1,336

A Strasbourg hexafoil plate finely painted in petit feu colors, the center with a tied bouquet, circa 1748, 24.2cm. diameter.
(Christie's) $11,052

A Frankenthal group of a Chinese family, modeled by Joh. Peter Melchoir, the man standing in a gilt and white conical hat and loose shirt, circa 1775, 26cm. high.
(Christie's) $3,500

GERMAN

A German porcelain basket, with pierced sides, painted to the center and to the exterior with named landscape view, 10¹/₂in. wide, 19th century.
(Christie's) $517

A Kelsterbach pewter-mounted pear-shaped jug painted with a hunting scene, faint HD mark, circa 1770, 31.5cm. high.
(Christie's) $6,774

A German porcelain model of a putto riding a dolphin, with red tail and fins, scantily draped in a flowered gilt-edge cloth, circa 1770, perhaps Höchst, 10.5cm. wide.
(Christie's) $880

A good Frankfurt faïence polychrome silver-mounted jug, 1670–90, the baluster-form body affixed with a scroll-tipped loop handle issuing from beneath a molded ridge below the rim, 10¹¹/₁₆in. high.
(Sotheby's) $10,350

Four Limbach figures emblematic of the Seasons, each modeled as a gallant, two with puce and one with sepia crossed L marks, circa 1775, 15.5–17cm. high.
(Christie's) $6,774

A German porcelain figure of Augustus III after the Meissen original modeled by J.J. Kändler, standing with his right arm akimbo, late 19th century, 30in. high.
(Christie's) $5,119

Mettlach pottery covered punch bowl with undertray, late 19th century, with grapevine and gnome decoration, 17¹/₂in. high.
(Eldred's) $632

Continental porcelain candelabrum in gilt, lemon and white, the column attended by two dancing figures, 15in. high, German, circa 1900.
(G. A. Key) $127

A Durlach blue and white fluted oval two-handled tureen, cover and stand molded with flutes and on four scroll feet, circa 1750, the stand 40.5cm. wide.
(Christie's) $12,834

GOLDSCHEIDER

A large Goldscheider terracotta vase, as a young girl holding a pet rabbit, standing upon an ivy encrusted bank, 60cm. high. (Henry Spencer) $1,200

Goldscheider ceramic figural, Austria, designed by Dakon, decorated in rose and black on white ground, 8⅞in. high. (Skinner) $488

A Goldscheider polychrome terracotta bust of a young turbanned Arab, signed, late 19th century, 78cm. high. (Finarte) $3,755

A Goldscheider terracotta head, of a young woman with pale green combed and curled hair, tin glazed in shades of white, orange and green, 29cm. high. (Christie's) $2,340

A large Goldscheider terracotta group of three boys, each seated, two wearing caps and all with jackets and trousers, circa 1890, 22½in. high. (Neales) $3,225

A Goldscheider terracotta wallmask, modeled as a young woman with green coiled hair and orange features, 25cm. high. (Christie's) $500

A Goldscheider terracotta wallmask, in the form of a young woman holding an apple to her throat, impressed 6774, 19cm. long. (Christie's) $508

A Goldscheider pottery Art Deco figure 'Butterfly Girl', striding with arms outstretched, 12½in. high. (Spencer's) $1,280

A Goldscheider terracotta wallmask, modeled as a young woman with orange flowing hair, holding a bluebird to the throat, 31cm. long. (Christie's) $625

GOSS

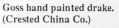

Goss swan.
(Crested China Co.) $192

W. H. Goss pin box, the lid
molded with a reclining figure
of a young lady in 1920's
costume, 4¹/₂in. wide.
(G. A. Key) $650

Goss hand painted drake.
(Crested China Co.) $312

Goss third size Aberdeen bronze
pot with arms of Owen
Glyndwr.
(Crested China Co.) $60

Goss trinket tray with arms of
Camberwell.
(Crested China Co.) $57

Goss toby jug.
(Crested China Co.) $280

Goss hand painted cup and
saucer.
(Crested China Co.) $136

W. H. Goss model of
Shakespeare's house, printed
marks, 3¹/₂in. high.
(G. A. Key) $92

Goss fruit dish.
(Crested China Co.) $104

IMARI

An Imari model of a cockerel, decorated in iron-red, green, aubergine and black enamels and gilt, late 17th century, 24cm. (Christie's) $5,152

A pair of large ormolu-mounted Japanese Imari dishes, each decorated in four colors, the center with flowers within a landscape border, the mounts 19th century, 20½in. diameter. (Christie's) $11,178

An Imari octagonal vase, decorated with two ho-o birds among peony and rockwork, early 18th century, 48cm. high. (Christie's) $14,720

An Imari blue and white pear-shaped bottle vase, decorated with flowering plants beneath a band of geometric patterns and plantain leaves, late 17th century, 35.5cm. high. (Christie's) $11,040

A pair of Imari decorated Japanese plates of lobed circular form, 19th century, 64.5cm. diameter. (Stockholms Auktionsverk) $4,307

An Imari coffee pot and cover, decorated in iron-red and gilt on underglaze blue with ho-o birds among flowering boughs, late 17th century, 25cm. high. (Christie's) $2,760

An Imari tureen and cover, decorated with four shaped panels of chrysanthemum, peony and cherry tree issuing from rockwork, late 17th century. (Christie's) $15,640

Two Imari square bottles and covers decorated in various colored enamels and gilt on underglaze blue, late 17th century, 26.7 and 25.6cm. high. (Christie's) $6,217

An Imari jar and cover, the upper part decorated in underglaze blue with pine and plum tree beneath a band of shippo pattern, late 17th century, 21.5cm. high. (Christie's) $8,832

IMARI

An Imari bowl decorated in various colored enamels and gilt over underglaze blue, early 18th century, 22cm. diameter. (Christie's) $1,454

A large pair of 19th century Japanese Imari bottle vases, each decorated with leaf shaped panels of pine branches and prunus blossom, 66cm. high. (Spencer's) $5,236

A fine, large Imari charger, the cavetto painted with a scroll like panel depicting a woman and her servant, 60cm. diameter. (Bearne's) $4,590

An Imari model Oniwa Komaru on a carp, decorated with underglaze blue, iron-red, green and aubergine enamels, late 17th century, 24cm. high. (Christie's) $4,600

A pair of Imari plates, each molded in relief with a sumo wrestler standing on a dohyo, 19th century, 34cm. diameter. (Christie's) $5,152

An Imari model of a standing bijin decorated in iron-red, green, aubergine, and black enamels, late 17th century, 30cm. high. (Christie's) $4,754

An Imari foliate rimmed bowl decorated in iron-red and green enamel and gilt on underglaze blue, late 19th century, 32.1cm. diameter. (Christie's) $2,011

A pair of Imari baluster jars and covers, Imari, early 18th century, each decorated with shaped panels of blossoming prunus, peony and bamboo sprigs, 56cm. high. (Sotheby's) $7,725

An Imari charger, the central roundel with peony and plum blossoms in a vase on a terrace, late 17th century, 53.4cm. diameter. (Christie's) $7,360

ITALIAN

An Italian porcelain figure group, modeled as a lady and gentleman, standing arm in arm, in fashionable dress, 5¼in. high, circa 1800.
(Christie's) $307

An Hispano-Moresque large circular dish painted in blue and pale-copper luster, Valencia, third quarter of the 15th century, 46cm. diameter.
(Christie's) $12,121

A Doccia coffee pot and cover with animal headed spout, the masso bastardo body painted all over with sprays of fruit and flowers, 25.5cm.
(Phillips) $677

A Ferdinand IV Naples porcelain plate painted with a philosopher in a landscape, circa 1785, 24cm. diameter.
(Finarte) $2,207

A Montelupo two-handled oviform wet-drug jar and a cover, with dolphin handles, painted with a shield with the initials *D.F.* below a Maltese cross, mid 16th century, 46cm. high overall.
(Christie's) $4,635

A Cantagalli globular jar twin-handled, painted with peacocks on a ground of peacock feathers beneath a flared neck, 11in. high, circa 1900.
(Christie's) $1,173

A blue painted Sarona albarello, the inscription between bands of putti in landscapes, 18th century.
(Kunsthaus am Museum) $320

Two Castelli wall plaques painted in colours with coastal landscapes, 18th century, 20 x 28cm.
(Kunsthaus am Museum) $2,158

A Venetian albarello, painted with a three quarter length figure of a Saint holding a book and a leaf, 32.5cm.
(Phillips) $4,838

ITALIAN

A dated Savona drug jar of baluster shape, with the drug label in dark manganese Gothic letters between bands of flowers and birds, date *1683*, 20cm.
(Phillips) $419

A Naples 'Fabbrica Reale Ferdinandea' cup and saucer, painted with classical scenes.
(Bearne's) $4,437

A Castelli portrait wet-drug jar of 'Orsini-Colonna' type and baluster form, with a strap handle and dragon's head spout, early 16th century, 25.5cm. high.
(Christie's) $17,825

A pair of Viterbo circular dishes painted in green, ocher, yellow and brown with a portrait of a girl and a warrior, 17th century, 28.5cm. diameter.
(Christie's) $4,635

A pair of Venetian decorated and parcel-gilt caryatid figures, each with one hand supporting a cushion and the other on the hip, on a rockwork base, 18th century, 80in. high.
(Christie's) $70,980

A Venice armorial berretino-ground shallow circular dish, the center with the Arms painted in ocher, yellow, black and green, mid-16th century, 26.5cm. diameter.
(Christie's) $10,339

A Fornasetti pottery biscuit barrel, of cylindrical form decorated with transfer-printed arches and doorways, printed factory marks, 30.5cm. high.
(Christie's) $496

A Savona faïence polychrome teapot and cover, Albisola Factory, circa 1765, the bullet-shaped body with a powdered manganese ground reserved on either side with a yellow-edged quatrefoil panel, 5¼in. high.
(Sotheby's) $1,265

A good Sicilian (Sciacca) drug jar, painted with a circular panel of a Roman soldier in profile, 24cm.
(Phillips) $3,825

JAPANESE

A globular teapot and cover, with upright bamboo handle, painted and gilt with flowers attached to canes, 5in. high. (Christie's) $105

A squat globular tripod koro, with molded mask handles, painted and gilt with shaped panels, dark blue ground decorated with scattered kiku heads, 2¹/₄in. high; and a pair of spherical hat pins. (Christie's) $230

A small flattened kettle and cover, with cane handle, painted and gilt with panels of seated ladies and children within foliate borders, 3¹/₂in. long. (Christie's) $315

A globular tripod koro and domed cover, with flowerhead finial and pierced handles, painted and gilt with shaped panels, on a dark blue ground reserved with stylized butterflies and scattered flowerheads, 6¹/₂in. high. (Christie's) $1,230

A fluted dish, painted and heavily gilt with a coiled dragon entwined among Kannon and Buddhist priests, the underside with mon and foliage, 10¹/₂in. diameter. (Christie's) $563

A tripod globular koro and pierced domed cover, with shishi lion and brocade ball finial, painted and gilt with shaped panels of Immortals and Buddhist priests on a ground of broken cell pattern and floral designs, 7in. high. (Christie's) $563

A Makuzu Kozan baluster vase and cover on tripod feet decorated in iron-red and blue-and-white, signed, Meiji period (1868–1912), 26.5cm. high. (Christie's) $5,486

A fine Kyoto pottery canted square dish, painted and richly gilded with a group of musicians, 16.2cm., six character seal mark, circa 1900. (Tennants) $1,071

A broad pear-shaped tripod koro and pierced cover, painted and gilt with a coiled dragon among Buddhist priests in a rocky landscape, 4in. high. (Christie's) $230

KAKIEMON

A Kakiemon style blue and white conch shaped tureen, with scattered flowerheads among stylized clouds and a stream, late 17th century, 21.5cm. long.
(Christie's) $9,200

A Kakiemon dish, decorated in iron-red, blue, green and black enamels and gilt on underglaze blue with quail, late 17th/early 18th century, 21.6cm. diameter.
(Christie's) $18,400

A Kakiemon teapot, the lobed body decorated in iron red, green, blue and black enamels and gilt, late 17th century, the mounts 18th century, 14.5cm. long.
(Christie's) $4,000

A Kakiemon oviform vase and cover, decorated in various colored enamels on underglaze blue with peonies and other flowers, late 17th century, 31cm. high.
(Christie's) $11,000

A pair of Kakiemon cockerels standing on rock work bases displaying their plumage, late 17th century, 23cm. and 24.5cm. high.
(Christie's) $89,835

An early enameled Kakiemon vase decorated in iron-red, blue, green and yellow enamels with a pair of stylized pheasants, late 17th century, 26cm. high.
(Christie's) $98,580

A Kakiemon incense-burner, decorated with flowers below a flared lip with half-circles, late 17th century, 13.5cm. high.
(Christie's) $5,152

A Milan faïence polychrome soup plate, Felice Clerici factory, circa 1770, painted in a Kakiemon palette with a bird perched on a branch of a flowering prunus tree, O mark in manganese, 9¹/₁₆in. diameter.
(Sotheby's) $2,300

A rare Kakiemon model of a boy sitting on a shogi table holding a puppy, late 17th century, 18cm. high.
(Christie's) $65,349

KINKOZAN

A Kinkozan vase and cover, decorated in various colored enamels and gilt on a dark blue ground, signed, late 19th century, 25.5cm. high.
(Christie's) $4,232

A set of five dishes, painted with shaped panels of exotic birds among prunus, irises, daisies and other flowers, 7in. diameter, signed and sealed *Kinkozan*.
(Christie's) $2,640

A Satsuma circular box and cover, signed *Kinkozan*, Meiji period, decorated in enamels and gilding with a design of samurai and ladies at leisure, 5.75cm. diameter.
(Phillips) $951

A fine and impressive Kinkozan hexagonal vase decorated with three kakemono of river landscapes alternated with three panels of cherry blossoms, signed *Kyoto Kinkozan zo*, late 19th century, 30.3cm. high.
(Christie's) $27,428

A Satsuma-style part tea set, signed *Kinkozan*, Meiji period, consisting of four tea cups and four saucers, each cup with a different samurai.
(Phillips) $805

A blue ground Kinkozan oviform vase decorated in various colored enamels and gilt with two panels, signed *Kinkozan zo*, late 19th century, 38cm. high.
(Christie's) $11,885

A Satsuma square section tea caddy and cover, signed *Kinkozan*, Meiji period, resting on four low feet, 9.5cm. high.
(Phillips) $1,554

Four Kinkozan plates, decorated in various colored enamels and gilt each depicting a season, signed *Kinkozan zo*, late 19th century, 22.3cm. diameter.
(Christie's) $4,023

A Kinkozan koro and cover, decorated in various colored enamels and gilt with two panels, signed, late 19th century, 20cm. high.
(Christie's) $2,760

LEACH

A St. Ives stoneware bottle vase, by Bernard Leach, covered in a mottled brown and olive green glaze, with incised decoration of a weeping willow, circa 1955, 19.6cm. high.
(Christie's) $1,453

A large and two smaller St. Ives stoneware bowls, attributed to Bernard Leach, each covered in a pale mushroom colored glaze with painted 'Z'-shaped iron-brown brushwork, circa 1945, 24cm. wide and 13.7cm. wide.
(Christie's) $365

A St. Ives stoneware vase, by Bernard Leach, incised decoration of two pairs of leaping salmon and birds in flight, circa 1960, 22cm. high.
(Christie's) $1,635

LENCI

A Lenci pottery box and cover, painted in shades of green with a gingham pattern, 12.5cm. long.
(Christie's) $390

A Lenci pottery vase, by Beppe Ferinando, painted in shades of orange, yellow, brown and black with geometric pastoral village scene, dated *1933*, 25.5cm. high.
(Christie's) $1,000

'Amore Paterno', a Lenci pottery group, modeled by Sandro Vachetti, of a man clasping a young baby to his lips, painted in colors, dated *1931*, 17cm. high.
(Christie's) $1,240

LIVERPOOL

A Liverpool creamware transfer-printed jug, circa 1799, printed darkly in black on one side with a scene of cows, 9in. high.
(Sotheby's) $1,150

Liverpool blue and white pottery plate, Oriental figure and pagoda pattern to centre, 9¹/₂in., English, 19th century.
(G. A. Key) $119

Liverpool creamware transfer-printed and enameled large jug, 1795–1800, the barrel-shaped body printed in black on one side with a full-rigged ship, 11¹/₄in. high.
(Sotheby's) $18,400

LOWESTOFT

A Lowestoft blue and white eye-bath of boat shape painted with flower-sprays within molded floral cartouches, circa 1765, 5.5cm. high.
(Christie's) $4,991

A good pair of Lowestoft models of pugs, with curled tails, decorated with sponged underglaze manganese, 8.5cm.
(Phillips) $5,805

A rare Lowestoft cylindrical mug, painted in the style of Thomas Curtis with a border of garlands above flower sprays, 7cm.
(Phillips) $1,129

LUDWIGSBURG

Porcelain group of two canaries, flanking a birds nest, possibly Frankenthal or Ludwigsburg, late 19th century, 4in. high.
(G. A. Key) $293

A Ludwigsburg group emblematic of the Seasons perhaps modeled by Pierre François Lejeune, the four figures about an arbor, circa 1770, 19cm. high.
(Christie's) $12,478

A Ludwigsburg group of a bacchanalian scene, 19th century, 20cm. high.
(Arnold Frankfurt) $485

MARTINWARE

A good large Martin Brothers jug, the tall cylindrical body incised with a continuous scene of horses and hounds, circa 1880, 14in. high.
(Neales) $1,280

A Martin Ware two handled vase of baluster form, decorated with fish and seaweed, signed and dated *1888*, 9in. high.
(Russell, Baldwin & Bright) $1,320

A Martin Brothers stoneware jug, the ovoid body incised and painted with birds and flowering branches, 16.5cm. high.
(Bearne's) $520

MEISSEN

A Meissen Kakiemon pipe-head, the bowl of baluster form and with short cylindrical stem painted with indianische Blumen, circa 1735.
(Christie's) $1,693

Two Meissen figures of cockatoos, after the original models by J. J. Kändler, with white plumage, painted faces and iron-red feathers around their necks, circa 1890, 14¼in. high. (Christie's) $5,888

A Meissen model of a large swan, 19th century, blue crossed swords mark, after a model by J. J. Kändler, 14in. high.
(Christie's) $13,081

A Meissen group of a maiden and a youth, on a shaped square base painted with grass and water, Pressnummer 107, incised G129, circa 1880, 7½in. high.
(Christie's) $2,422

A pair of Meissen articulated figures of pagodas, the grinning male and female figures with 'nodding' heads, tongues and hands, circa 1880, 12¼in. and 12¾in. high.
(Christie's) $14,904

A Meissen model of an elephant and warriors, circa 1880, blue crossed swords mark, the African animal draped n a 'jeweled' and tasseled saddle-cloth, 14½in. high.
(Christie's) $6,541

A Meissen model of 'pigs hunt', dated 1910, blue crossed swords and commemorative date mark, after a model by J. J. Kändler, 9in. high.
(Christie's) $1,495

Two Meissen figural four-light candelabra, 19th century, underscored blue crossed swords marks, 17¾in. high.
(Christie's) $3,924

A large Meissen figure group 'Lessons in love', 19th century, blue crossed swords marks, after a model by C. G. Jêchtzer, 21in. wide.
(Christie's) $14,950

MEISSEN

A Meissen figure of Harlequin teasing a dog modeled by J.J. Kändler, in yellow-edged green hat with a red rosette, circa 1740, the figure 16.5cm. high. (Christie's) $10,695

A Meissen group of shepherd lovers modeled by J.J. Kändler, she with a sheep on her lap and he with a dog at his side, circa 1740, 15cm. high. (Christie's) $6,239

A Meissen cream-pot and stand, and a cover of squat baluster form with foliage-molded gilt spout, circa 1728, the stand 17.8cm. diameter. (Christie's) $9,269

A Meissen gold-mounted blue-mosaic ground snuff-box, circa 1745, by Johann Jacob Wagner, the top and sides painted with Classical figures within gilt foliate cartouches, 3 x 2^{1}/$_8$ x 1^{1}/$_2$in. (Christie's) $13,800

A Meissen chinoiserie large dish, the centre painted in the manner of C. F. Herold with Orientals at various pursuits, blue crossed swords mark, circa 1735, 30.5cm. diameter. (Christie's) $35,650

A Meissen (K.P.M.) chinoiserie teapot and cover of pear shape, painted in the manner of J. G. Höroldt, one side with a couple at a table, circa 1723, 13.5cm. high. (Christie's) $9,804

A Louis XV ormolu-mounted Meissen porcelain pot-pourri center-piece, the vase and cover decorated with roses, peonies and others on a white ground, the vase circa 1755, 13in. high. (Christie's) $13,352

A Böttger porcelain pagoda, circa 1715, luster script B inside, modeled seated with his right hand resting on his knee, 3^9/$_{16}$in. high. (Christie's) $7,475

A Böttger silver mounted porcelain tankard, decorated in relief with prunus and chrysanthemums, circa 1730, 17.5cm. high. (Stockholms Auktionsverk) $76,852

MEISSEN

A Meissen bourdaloue, circa 1730, blue enamel crossed swords mark, of typical shape, enameled in the Kakiemon style, 8½in. wide overall.
(Christie's) $6,900

A Meissen figure of Hofnarr Fröhlich, dated 1737, blue crossed swords mark, from the model by J. J. Kändler, 10in. high.
(Christie's) $10,925

A Meissen crinoline group of The Rest during the Chase modeled by J.J. Kändler, the couple seated embracing before a tree with a squirrel in the branches, circa 1745, 20cm. high.
(Christie's) $15,686

An ormolu-mounted Meissen tobacco box, circa 1755, traces of blue mark, painted on each of the four sides with a gallant and his lady in a garden, 5¾in. high.
(Christie's) $2,530

A Meissen armorial circular dish from the Swan Service, modeled by J.J. Kändler and J. F. Eberlein for Count Brühl, molded with two swans swimming, 1737–41, 30cm. diameter.
(Christie's) $26,738

A Böttger silver-gilt mounted Goldchinesen ribbed cylindrical tankard with Augsburg silver-gilt cover, decorated at Augsburg in the Seuter workshop, the porcelain circa 1720, 17.5cm. high.
(Christie's) $9,804

A Böttger red-stoneware bust of Vitellius perhaps modeled by Paul Heermann, half turned to the right, circa 1712, 10.5cm. high.
(Christie's) $4,991

A pair of Meissen chinoiserie two-handled beakers and saucers painted by Johann Gregor Höroldt with half-length figures, blue enamel crossed swords mark, circa 1725.
(Christie's) $96,100

A Meissen covered baluster vase, the violet ground with a reserve painted with the Flight into Egypt, circa 1730, 38.5cm. high.
(Finarte) $22,073

MEISSEN

An elaborate ormolu mounted brûle parfum with two Meissen figures of sedan-chair carriers probably by Reinicke, 20cm. long.
(Phillips) $12,240

A pair of Meissen Commedia dell' Arte figures of Harlequin and Columbine, both seated, the latter playing a hurdy-gurdy, 13.7cm.
(Phillips) $2,295

A late Meissen group of two musicians seated on an elaborate settee with a pug-dog between them, 23cm.
(Phillips) $1,224

A Meissen pot-pourri vase, modeled as an urn supported on a branch-molded support applied with a figure of a seated lady with a pug dog, blue crossed swords mark, 7¼in. high, circa 1745.
(Christie's) $992

A Böttger porcelain beaker and saucer painted in the manner of J. G. Heroldt, with Chinese figures.
(Phillips) $1,071

A gilt-metal mounted Meissen circular snuff-box and cover, circa 1760, attributed to the 'Master of the Gray Landscape', 3¾in. diameter.
(Christie's) $8,050

19th century Meissen group, decorated in blue and gilt depicting five children with animals around a central column, 7in. high.
(Lawrences) $1,323

A fine and large pair of French figures of a lady and gentleman in Meissen style, wearing elaborate 18th century costume, 20in. high.
(Spencer's) $1,288

An extremely large late Meissen model of a turkey, after a model by Kaendler, standing with its tail feathers raised, 59cm.
(Phillips) $5,049

MEISSEN

A Meissen figure of a cockatoo after the original model by J. J. Kändler perched on a tree-stump, circa 1890, 14¹/₄in. high. (Christie's) $2,743

A pair of Meissen figures of Malabar musicians, sword mark, 31cm. and 32cm. high. (Arnold Frankfurt) $1,383

A Meissen jug in the form of a man seated beside a baluster jug wearing a flowered yellow coat, circa 1890, 7¹/₂in. high. (Christie's) $1,097

A late Meissen scent bottle and metal bird stopper, modeled as a lady being embraced by a man, 7.5cm., crossed swords mark. (Phillips) $1,095

A pair of late Meissen busts, after the models by Kaendler, of Prince Louis Charles de Bourbon and the Princess Marie Zephirine de Bourbon, 23cm. (Phillips) $1,836

A Meissen tea-caddy of lobed square section, painted in the Kakiemon palette with flowers and foliage within shaped panels, 4¹/₄in. high, circa 1740. (Christie's) $1,148

A Meissen group of Leda and the Swan, the young maiden drawing a garland around the swan's neck, circa 1880, 6³/₄in. high. (Christie's) $2,742

Pair of 18th century Meissen porcelain figures, of cockatoos standing on floral decorated tree trunks as a mouse observes, 14¹/₂in. high. (Eldred's) $1,155

A Meissen group of two children emblematic of Autumn after the original model by J. C. Schönheit, wearing 18th century rustic dress, circa 1880, 6in. high. (Christie's) $1,463

A Minton game pie dish and cover, modeled as a wicker basket, with twin oak branch handles and branch feet, date code for 1861, 13¹/₂in. wide. (Christie's) **$811**

A Minton's parian figure of Cupid, modeled ice-skating, his arms folded across his chest, 12in. high (with glass stand), circa 1860. (Christie's) **$685**

A rare Minton 'majolica; cockerel teapot and cover with bright green tail feathers forming the handle, the head with red coxcomb, 19.5cm., date code for 1876. (Phillips) **$3,709**

Mintons blue and white jardinière on stand of circular form, the flared neck with keyhole border, impressed date cipher for 1879, 11¹/₂in. diameter. (G. A. Key) **$408**

A pair of Minton twin-handled 'cloisonné' vases, designed by Dr. Christopher Dresser, gilt and polychrome enamel decoration of floral reserves on a turquoise ground, numbered *1592*, circa 1871, 28cm. high. (Christie's) **$6,359**

A large Minton Art Pottery jardinière, probably designed by Leon V. Solon, slip-trailed and painted with three colorful peacocks, 37cm. high, date code for 1915. (Bearne's) **$826**

Minton porcelain plate

A Minton stoneware encaustic bread plate, designed by A. W. N. Pugin, the rim with the text *Waste Not, Want Not*, circa 1849, 33cm. diameter. (Christie's) **$1,544**

An unusual Minton pottery figure of a cat, seated upon a maroon and orange decorated base, striped fur in light and dark gray, 13in. high. (Spencer's) **$2,464**

Minton porcelain plate, the center painted with a view of boats, jeweled and gilt pink border, English 1876, 9¹/₂in. (G. A. Key) **$202**

MINTON

A Minton walnut-encrusted center dish, 1830–35, the dish pierced around the circular rim with gilt-edged circlets and triangles, mounded in the center with brown walnuts, 7¹/₂in. diameter.
(Sotheby's) $2,530

A rare Minton 'majolica' Chinaman teapot and cover, he holds a grotesque aubergine mask from which the green spout emerges, 13.5cm., impressed *Mintons*.
(Phillips) $1,613

A Minton majolica 'crab tureen' and cover, naturalistically modeled and colored as a crab with a central seaweed frond handle lying on a bed of seaweed, 16³/₄in. wide, circa 1865.
(Christie's) $3,968

A. W. N. Pugin, pair of garden seats, 1868, manufactured by Minton & Co., in polychrome glazed earthenware of hexafoil section, 48cm. high.
(Sotheby's) $1,863

Majolica glazed Stilton cheese dish and stand, probably by George Jones or Minton, molded leaf floral detail, 11in. high, English, late 19th century.
(G. A. Key) $222

A pair of Mintons bleu celeste two-handled slender oviform vases and covers with gilt conical finials, each painted by J. E. Dean, circa 1895, 6in. high.
(Christie's) $731

A Minton Majolica cheese stand and cover molded with lilies, and having flower finial.
(Russell, Baldwin & Bright) $476

A Minton majolica ware centerpiece, with large turquoise interior bowl, supported by two playful Bacchic boys, 36cm. diameter, date code for 1867.
(Phillips) $2,295

A Minton majolica group of a young man pushing a wheelbarrow, modeled by J.B. Klagmann, date code for 1873, 12¹/₂in. high.
(Christie's) $2,194

PEARLWARE

A pearlware group of a tiger and hind, the tiger dragging the hind by the neck in its jaws, 14¹/₂in. wide, early 19th century. (Christie's) $14,168

A pearlware figure of Antony, wearing a cuirass and cape above a rocky molded mound base, 11³/₄in. long, circa 1790. (Christie's) $443

A pearlware 'Bull Baiting' group, the tethered bull bearing down over a crouching terrier, 12¹/₂in. wide, early 19th century. (Christie's) $2,834

An early 19th century Documentary pearlware blue and white 'Grazing Rabbit' pattern large jug, overpainted in brown *William and Jane Baldwin, 1815*, 24cm. high. (Spencer's) $832

A pair of Staffordshire pearlware bocage groups, circa 1815, modeled as a man and a woman in contemporary dress standing before bocage, 7¹/₂in. high. (Christie's) $1,725

A commemorative blue and white pearlware tankard, applied with a medallion, flanked by full length portrait of Lord Rodney and Lord Hood, 4⁵/₈in. high, late 18th/19th century. (Christie's) $283

A rare Pearlware figure of a lady with a girl riding a dog, on molded scrolled base, painted in bright colors, 19cm. (Phillips) $1,048

A pair of Sherratt-type pearlware portrait busts of William IV and Queen Charlotte, modeled wearing formal dress, 8in. high, circa 1817. (Christie's) $4,428

A pearlware group of a girl and hound modeled seated, wearing simple dress before a flowering bocage, 5⁷/₈in. high, circa 1815. (Christie's) $266

PEARLWARE

A Staffordshire pearlware model of two lions, circa 1820, with brown mane, iron-red body, modeled walking, 12⁷/8in. wide.
(Christie's) $1,380

A pearlware model of a lion, his paw resting on a ball, his tail curled, 6¹/2in. high, circa 1800–20.
(Christie's) $1,771

A pearlware bull baiting group, the standing bull tethered by a rope to a post and worried by a small dog, circa 1790, Staffordshire or Yorkshire, 30.5cm. wide.
(Christie's) $1,961

A Walton pearlware group of the 'Return From Egypt', typically modeled with Joseph leading a donkey ridden by the Virgin, 6³/4in. high, circa 1820.
(Christie's) $1,594

A pair of Staffordshire pearlware figures, circa 1790, one a gardener in black hat, his companion as a fish monger, in yellow smock, 6⁵/8in. high.
(Christie's) $460

A pearlware figure of Jeremiah, of Sherratt-type, modeled standing, an arm raised, wearing long robes, 11in. high, circa 1820.
(Christie's) $744

A pearlware group of the 'Sacrifice of Isaac', of Sherratt-type, with Abraham raising a dagger above his son, 10³/4in. high, circa 1820.
(Christie's) $886

A rare transfer printed early 19th century pearlware jug made to commemorate the Battle of Trafalgar, of baluster form with scroll handle, 18cm. high.
(Spencer's) $400

A pearlware group of the 'Flight into Egypt', typically modeled with Joseph leading a donkey, before a flowering bocage, 7in. high, circa 1820.
(Christie's) $797

PRATTWARE

A Pratt-type oval plaque, molded with two sleeping lions within molded bands, 11¹/₈in. wide, circa 1800.
(Christie's) $1,151

Two rare Prattware elephant money boxes, decorated with blue sponging and yellow and green pheasant's eyes, 20.5cm. high.
(Phillips) $20,156

A Pratt-type portrait mug of Lord Rodney, typically modeled facing forward, his eyes looking upward, 6¹/₂in. high, late 18th century.
(Christie's) $354

ROCKINGHAM

A Rockingham porcelain figure of John Liston as 'Lubin Log', wearing a lilac jacket and holding a hat box, umbrella, striped bag and coat, 18cm. high.
(Tennants) $4,284

An attractive pair of Rockingham models of pugs, both seated on oval maroon scrolled bases, 6.5cm., impressed marks.
(Phillips) $1,532

A Rockingham bulbous pot pourri two handled jar, painted in colored enamels with a view in Cumberland, 25cm. high.
(Tennants) $4,590

ROSENTHAL

A Rosenthal figure of a postillon by T. Kärner, 1920–21.
(Arnold Frankfurt) $211

A Rosenthal figure 'Merry March' of a woman in carnival costume, circa 1920, 36cm. high.
(Kunsthaus am Museum) $746

Rosenthal polychrome figure 'Girl Drinking', signed Ernst Wenck, 1865–1929.
(Arnold) $294

ROYAL DUX

A Royal Dux bisque porcelain figure of a young ploughman, holding a plough beside a harnessed cow, impressed *836*, 34cm. long.
(Spencer's) $616

A Royal Dux figure, as a girl wearing a pale maroon dress, holding a large shell, impressed triangle mark, 17in. high.
(Spencer's) $770

A large Royal Dux group of a plow boy and two bullocks, decorated in pale ocher, green and gilt, 17in. long.
(Spencer's) $1,232

A Royal Dux group in the form of a camel, with its rider leaning over in conversation, 50cm. high.
(Bearne's) $1,932

Royal Dux porcelain figural vase, early 20th century, with two Art Nouveau maidens clinging to the sides, 21½in. high.
(Butterfield & Butterfield) $1,955

A Royal Dux equestrian group, as an elegantly dressed horseman talking to a young peasant girl, impressed pink triangle mark, 16in. high.
(Spencer's) $1,287

A Royal Dux figure of an Arab horseman, holding a rifle, with dead game hung from his saddle, 19in. high.
(Spencer's) $1,225

A pair of Royal Dux figures, in the form of a gardener, his lady companion holding a posy, 40.5cm. high.
(Bearne's) $1,101

Royal Dux, Art Nouveau porcelain simulated marble bust of a girl wearing a floral bonnet and dress, with applied pink seal mark, 20in. high.
(Lawrences) $2,720

SATSUMA

A pair of slender double gourd Satsuma vases, with molded dragons to the necks, painted and heavily gilt with Kannon and Buddhist priests, 11in. high. (Christie's) $740

A Satsuma figure of a monkey trainer seated on a tree trunk with a monkey, unsigned, late 19th century, 33cm. high. (Christie's) $4,388

A pair of Satsuma vases with widely flaring rims and molded dragon handles, painted and heavily gilt with Buddhist priests entwined with dragons, 11in. high. (Christie's) $670

A large Satsuma vase, decorated with two panels surrounded by foliage, brocade lappets to the rim, late 19th century, 60.5cm. high. (Christie's) $13,800

A set of six cups and saucers, painted and gilt with fan-shaped panels of ladies and children at leisure on grounds of pavilions on the banks of a river, the saucers 4¼in. diameter. (Christie's) $1,232

A Satsuma oviform vase decorated with girls playing in a field of flowers, signed *Shuzan*, late 19th century, 28.7cm. high. (Christie's) $3,657

A pair of Satsuma vases, decorated depicting an array of vases, boxes, koro, jardinières and bowls, signed, Meiji period (1868–1912), 24.5cm. high. (Christie's) $3,496

A large Satsuma tripod koro and a cover, decorated depicting a dragon amidst stormy seas, late 19th century, 28.4cm. high. (Christie's) $3,496

A pair of cylindrical Satsuma vases, decorated in various colored enamels and gilt, depicting chrysanthemums and peony trees, signed, late 19th century, 18.5cm. high. (Christie's) $3,128

SEVRES

A Sèvres styled jeweled coffee can and saucer, the cup painted with a portrait of the Dauphin, Tournai or St. Amand les Eaux. (Phillips) $2,093

A massive Sèvres green-ground two-handled volute krater, circa 1810, painted in colors with Cephalus and Procris or Adonis and Venus and signed *Georget*, 27¹/₂in. high. (Christie's) $19,550

Sèvres porcelain three-piece demitasse set, 1872–99, red circle mark, polychrome decoration, reticulated outer shell, 7⁵/₈in. high. (Skinner) $2,415

A pair of French 'Sèvres' vases, Louis-Philippe, Paris, circa 1840, each with a painted scene of scènes galantes, 86cm. high. (Sotheby's) $24,685

Pair of 'Sèvres' cachepots, each of cylinder form, painted with reserves of rustic lovers and floral sprays against a bleu celeste ground, 6³/₄in. high. (William Doyle) $1,265

A pair of large giltmetal-mounted 'jewelled' Sèvres-pattern vases and covers, painted by Sepin in the manner of Boucher with lovers attended by playful cherubs, late 19th century, 47¹/₂in. high. (Christie's) $75,843

A Sèvres white biscuit group of La Pêche after the original model by Falconet, formed as two maidens and putti with fish, printed marks for 1886 and 1892, 13in. high. (Christie's) $2,011

Pair of 'Sèvres' porcelain figures, each depicting a seated putto writing or reading, set on a flambé glazed square base, 17in. overall height. (William Doyle) $37,950

A Sèvres bleu celeste ewer and basin, the ewer of pear-shape on a quatrefoil foot and with foliage-molded handle, date letters CC for 1780, the ewer 23.5cm. high. (Christie's) $17,825

SPODE

A Spode 8¼in. oval basket with pierced sides and two rustic handles, painted with Kakiemon pattern.
(Anderson & Garland) $459

A pair of Spode porcelain ice pails with gold scroll handles, liners and covers, 30cm. high.
(Bearne's) $6,730

Spode blue and white well and tree platter, 19th century, impressed mark, floral border, Rebecca at the Well center design, 20⁵/₈in. long.
(Skinner) $431

A pair of Spode ornithological pale-green-ground two-handled ice-pails, covers and liners, the ice-pails painted with specimen birds in landscape vignettes, circa 1820, 28cm. high.
(Christie's) $6,080

A Spode blue-ground potpourri-vase of squat form, the pierced rim with four richly gilt grotesque masks, painted with garden flowers on a dark-blue ground, 11cm. high, circa 1820.
(Christie's) $1,320

Rare pair of blue and white Spode covered cache pots, first quarter 19th century, in Tower pattern, two handles, 10in. high.
(Eldred's) $1,650

A Spode 'barrel scent jar' and covers, with inner cover and outer pierced cover, brightly decorated in Imari colors, 24cm.
(Phillips) $968

A pair of Spode sauce-tureens, with covers, stands and ladles, painted in colors, 10in. wide, circa 1810.
(Christie's) $499

A Spode vase modeled as an iris, the opened flower, surrounded by a blue bud and two slender leaves, circa 1820, 19.5cm. high.
(Christie's) $2,139

184

STAFFORDSHIRE

A brightly decorated
Staffordshire creamware cow
creamer and cover, with
milkmaid on a stool, 14cm. high.
(Bearne's) $680

A pair of models of spaniels,
seated, enriched with black
patches with gilt collars, 6¹/₈in.
high, 19th century.
(Christie's) $620

A Staffordshire pearlware blue
and white spittoon, circa 1780,
of globular form, painted with a
Chinese pavilion beside a fence,
5¹/₈in. diameter.
(Christie's) $552

A Staffordshire group, modeled
with two spaniels seated flanking
a clock-face, one with black and
white fur, the other with iron-
red and white fur, 1860–80,
9¹/₂in. high.
(Christie's) $736

A pair of Staffordshire white-
glazed figures of spaniels, with
painted features and baskets of
flowers clasped in their mouths,
1860–80, 9³/₄in. high.
(Christie's) $2,576

A Staffordshire pearl-ware jug,
in the form of a seated night
watchman holding a lantern on
his knee, 20.7cm. high.
(Bearne's) $168

A 19th century Staffordshire
pottery group, of a batsman and
wicket keeper, 6³/₄in. high.
(Bonhams) $594

A pair of creamware copper
luster curly dogs, Staffordshire,
19th century, with green
decorations and copper luster
highlights, 12³/₄in. high.
(Christie's) $2,185

A pair of figures of a sailor and
a girl, modeled standing beside
bollards, 9¹/₂in. high, 19th
century.
(Christie's) $620

STAFFORDSHIRE

A Staffordshire creamware figure of Saint George and the Dragon, circa 1790, mounted on a green and brown spotted horse above the writhing dragon, 11¼in. high.
(Christie's) $1,150

Antique English Staffordshire teapot, in the 'Canova' pattern by Mayer, pink and green decoration on a white ground, 6in. high.
(Eldred's) $330

A clock-face group of Daniel in the lion's den, modeled kneeling, flanked by two rearing lions, 10in. high, circa 1860.
(Christie's) $886

A Staffordshire pearlware tea-canister and cover, circa 1800, of Pratt-type, molded and glazed in blue, green, brown and ocher, 6¼in. high.
(Christie's) $276

Two rare Staffordshire models of elephants, standing foursquare and with her calf at her side, 14.5cm. and 13.5cm. high.
(Phillips) $918

An early Staffordshire tea canister, applied with quasi-heraldic roses on trailed stems, 11.5cm.
(Phillips) $1,148

Staffordshire child's mug for the American market, circa 1820, the cylindrical body transfer-printed with the Great Seal of the United States, 1⅞in. high.
(Sotheby's) $805

A Staffordshire yellow-ground teapot and cover, circa 1810, after prints by Adam Buck, the conical cover printed in black with vignettes, 5½in. high.
(Christie's) $276

A Staffordshire creamware cauliflower tea-canister, circa 1765, naturalistically molded with overlapping green leaves beneath white cauliflower, 4⅛in. high.
(Christie's) $460

STAFFORDSHIRE

A colorful Staffordshire pottery group of Samson killing the lion with his bare hands, 31.5cm. high.
(Bearne's) $134

A Staffordshire red stoneware punch pot and cover, mid 18th century, the spherical body sprigged with fruiting grapevines issuing from the gnarled and knotty stem handle, 6⁵/₁₆in. high.
(Sotheby's) $4,600

A theatrical group of the 'Death of the Lion Queen', modeled with Ellen Bright, being attacked by a tiger, 13¹/₄in. high, circa 1850.
(Christie's) $708

Antique blue and white historical Staffordshire coffee pot, 'Commodore MacDonnough's Victory', 10in. high.
(Eldred's) $880

Pair of antique Staffordshire spaniels, in brown and white, 12in. high.
(Eldred's) $688

A Staffordshire creamware cauliflower hot-milk jug and cover, circa 1765, with green foliate scroll handle, 6¹/₄in. high.
(Christie's) $1,380

An Obadiah Sherratt pottery model of 'The Red Barn' in which Maria Marten was murdered by William Corder on May 8th 1827, 19.5cm. high.
(Bearne's) $1,042

A rare Staffordshire saltglaze yellow-ground teapot and a cover, circa 1750, the hexagonal body molded on each side within a recessed oval panel with a chinoiserie scene, 5¹/₈in. high.
(Sotheby's) $1,265

A Staffordshire coffee-pot and cover, circa 1765, with white flower finial, the domed cover molded with overlapping leaves, 8¹/₈in. high.
(Christie's) $4,025

STAFFORDSHIRE

A rare Staffordshire figure of William Macready as 'James V of Scotland', wearing an ermine-edged cloak, tunic and short trunks, 21cm.
(Phillips) $484

A pair of models of seated spaniels, typically modeled facing left and right, wearing gilt collars and chains, 12¹/₂in. high, 19th century.
(Christie's) $797

A figure of Daniel O'Connell, Samson Smith, modeled standing, his hand resting on a draped plinth, 17³/₈in. high, circa 1875.
(Christie's) $443

A Staffordshire glazed red stoneware coffee pot and cover, 1765–70, the tapering cylindrical body engine-turned all over with a diamond and chevron pattern, 9¹/₁₆in. high.
(Sotheby's) $2,645

A pair of Staffordshire saltglaze white cornucopia wall vases, circa 1750, each with a spirally-fluted body beneath a valanced rim molded with a naked boy amongst fruiting vines, 9in. high.
(Sotheby's) $2,185

A Staffordshire red stoneware coffee pot and cover, circa 1765, the pear-shaped body decorated on either side with mold-applied reliefs of a moustachioed 'Drama' mask, 7⁵/₁₆in. high.
(Sotheby's) $862

Staffordshire flat back figure of a cavalier wearing a puce hat, ocher robe and black boots, circa 1850, 13¹/₂in. high.
(G. A. Key) $99

A pair of Staffordshire models of chickens, circa 1790, modeled as a rooster and a hen, with blue sponged plumage, standing on grassy mound bases, 8³/₄in. high, the rooster.
(Christie's) $1,380

An early Staffordshire equestrian figure of William III astride a trotting gray horse, on a rectangular base, 19.2cm.
(Phillips) $2,741

STAFFORDSHIRE

A theatrical group from the 'Bride of Abidos' modeled as Mr. Barton and Miss Rosa Henry as 'Giaffier & Zuleika', 12¹/₂in. high, circa 1847.
(Christie's) $708

Pair of Staffordshire porcelaneous figures of Harlequin and Columbine, 7¹/₂in., English, 19th century.
(G. A. Key) $300

Longton Staffordshire group of 'Tam O'Shanter' and 'Souter Johnny', base incised *Samson & Smith, Longton, Staffordshire, England*, 1892, 13in. high.
(G. A. Key) $230

A Staffordshire porcelain D-shaped bulb pot and cover, circa 1805, finely painted on the front with a fashionable couple strolling with their dog near a stream in a deer park, 8¹/₄in. wide.
(Sotheby's) $2,415

A Staffordshire red stoneware milk jug and a cover, 1765–70, the pear-shaped body and spout engine-turned in 'rose', diamond and chevron patterns above a flared and fluted foot, impressed pseudo-Chinese seal mark, 6¹/₄in. high.
(Sotheby's) $345

A Staffordshire copper luster canary-yellow-ground commemorative jug, 1825–35, portrait of La Fayette, 7¹/₈in. high.
(Sotheby's) $575

Staffordshire pottery figure of a man with raised drinking vessel, standing by a spill tree, 9in., English, late 19th century.
(G. A. Key) $175

A pair of spill-vases modeled as circus elephants, each wearing an orange and green caparison, 6¹/₈in. high, 19th century.
(Christie's) $2,657

A Staffordshire figure of Sir Isaac Newton, circa 1800, of Ralph Wood type, wearing a rose colored coat with spotted lining, 12in. high.
(Christie's) $863

VIENNA

'Vienna' porcelain vase, circa 1900, of pilgrim flask form, painted with a maiden, ruby luster borders, 10¹/₂in. high.
(William Doyle) $1,725

A finely painted and exceedingly large Vienna dish, painted by and signed *D. Wagner*, Wien, after Titian, entitled *Une Allegorie*, 55cm., shield mark in blue.
(Phillips) $5,202

A Vienna-style claret-ground two-handled oviform vase and square stand, painted on the front with Grazien, blue shield marks, circa 1890, 28in. high.
(Christie's) $6,440

A pair of Vienna-style dark-blue-ground tapering oviform vases, covers and waisted stands, painted in a bright palette by W. Pfohl, circa 1900, 38¹/₂in. high.
(Christie's) $40,986

A Vienna-style rectangular box and cover, the interior of the cover painted with Leda and the Swan in a secluded watery landscape, circa 1890, 5³/₄in. wide.
(Christie's) $2,049

Two Vienna style claret-ground vases, late 19th century, decorated with the Choice of Paris and the Graces, the claret ground gilt with floral swags, 10in. high.
(Christie's) $1,495

A Vienna style cabinet plate painted with 'Die Luft' (Air), with lady in décolleté white dress, 24.2cm.
(Phillips) $1,047

A 19th century porcelain plaque of the Abduction of Galatea, signed *Sacha...* and dated *1867*, possibly Vienna, in carved giltwood frame.
(Finarte) $3,479

A Vienna style plate painted in the center with Ruth after Landelle, signed *Deliuror*, within a lime green border, 24.5cm.
(Phillips) $419

WEDGWOOD

Wedgwood black basalt oval wall plaque, depicting The Three Graces, 9 x 7in.
(G. A. Key) $182

A rare Wedgwood teapot and cover, with unusual ovoid body decorated in white relief with 'Bacchanalian Boys', 13cm.
(Phillips) $1,377

Wedgwood Fairy luster vase, in baluster form with gilt butterfly design, 9in. high.
(Eldred's) $1,430

A Wedgwood creamware crested large oval settling pan and skimming spoon, circa 1790, the shallow dish with a spout at one end, and printed in brown on one side of the well with the crest of the Palk family of Haldon House.
(Sotheby's) $1,380

A green-dip Jasper two-handled biscuit barrel and cover, the handles scrolling, decorated with the 'Dancing Hours' below swags of flowers, the interior glazed, impressed marks, inscribed *McVITIE AND PRICE 1906*, 8in. high.
(Christie's) $685

A Wedgwood Fairyland luster charger, designed by Daisy Makeig Jones, in the Ghostly Wood pattern, printed and painted in colors and gilt printed factory marks, 38cm. diameter.
(Christie's) $23,400

Rare Wedgwood Etruscan majolica milk pitcher, with raised decoration of two baseball and two soccer players, 7½in. high.
(Eldred's) $1,320

A black basalt encaustic-decorated teapot and cover, Wedgwood & Bentley, the oval body painted with drapery swags with two pendant medallions, circa 1775.
(Christie's) $7,200

A Wedgwood black basalt copy of the Portland vase, the oviform body applied in white with classical figures at various pursuits, circa 1880, 25.5cm. high.
(Christie's) $3,565

WEMYSS

A large Wemyss tyg, the white ground painted with three sprays of peaches and foliage, the handles and rim outlined in green, 20cm. high, (cracked).
(Spencer's) $457

WESTERWALD

A Wemyss bedroom-service, painted with oranges and foliage within green-line rims, script and impressed marks, circa 1900. (Christie's) $1,600

Wemyss two bottle ink stand in the form of a heart, the border painted with turquoise dentil design, on a cream ground, impressed *Wemyss Ware RH & S*, 6^{1}/2in. wide.
(G. A. Key) $575

A gray and blue painted bellied jug, applied with marguerites, pewter cover, Westerwald, circa 1700.
(Kunsthaus am Museum)
$1,632

WOOD

A German saltglazed stoneware font-shaped salt cellar, probably Westerwald, 18th century, the compressed spherical bowl applied with spiraling borders of boss-molded gadrooning, 3^{1}/2in. high.
(Sotheby's) $1,725

A rare German saltglazed stoneware figural salt cellar, probably Westerwald, early 18th century, modeled as a man wearing a curly wig, a jabot and a frock coat, holding a circular dish, 7^{5}/8in. high.
(Sotheby's) $1,955

A Ralph Wood group of St. George and the Dragon, the helmeted warrior wearing pale-yellow tunic, seated astride a manganese stallion, circa 1785, 29cm. high.
(Christie's) $2,317

A pair of Ralph Wood figures of a shepherd and shepherdess, he standing beside a brown tree-stump, his companion standing placing a flower in her corsage, circa 1785, about 23cm. high.
(Christie's) $3,387

A Ralph Wood equestrian figure of King William III in the guise of a Roman Emperor seated on a rearing dun stallion, circa 1785, 40cm. high.
(Christie's) $11,586

WORCESTER

A Worcester blue and white oval sauce-tureen, cover and stand, circa 1765, painted with a vine pattern with branches of fruit and insects, stand 9½in. wide. (Christie's) $575

A Worcester teapot and cover, with flower finial, painted in blue with the 'Bird in a Ring' pattern, 13cm. (Phillips) $765

George Owen: a rare Royal Worcester reticulated cup and saucer, the double walled cup with gilt loop handle and supported on three gilt lion paw feet, date code for 1927. (Phillips) $3,060

A fine Worcester basket of circular shape, the interior painted with a large central spray and sprigs on the sides, 19.3cm. (Phillips) $1,836

A Royal Worcester model of George Washington on a dappled charger, modeled by Bernard Winskill, 45cm. high, No. 150 of an edition limited to 750 copies. (Bearne's) $2,142

A Worcester circular basket, the spreading sides pierced with interlaced circles applied with puce and green florettes, 21cm., square mark. (Phillips) $918

Dog Toby, a very rare Royal Worcester extinguisher, the dog wearing an orange Tyrolean hat with a white feather, 7.5cm., probably 1882. (Phillips) $7,038

A Barr, Flight and Barr coffee can and saucer, finely painted with shell panels probably by Samuel Smith. (Phillips) $2,258

A good Worcester King of Prussia jug, of pear shape with a sparrow beak lip, printed in black with a portrait, 1757, 14.75cm. (Phillips) $1,683

WORCESTER

A Worcester blue and white globular teapot and cover painted with prunus issuing from rockwork and with an insect, circa 1754, 12cm. high. (Christie's) $2,496

A pair of Chamberlain's Worcester sauce-tureens and covers, circa 1811, puce printed marks, each with dolphin finial and pierced gallery, 9¹/₈in. high. (Christie's) $3,450

A rare Worcester miniature teapot and cover of globular shape with pointed finial, painted in blue with 'Mansfield' pattern, 8.5cm. (Phillips) $1,451

A mid-18th century Worcester fluted coffee cup, painted in the famille-rose palette with trailing flower sprays, 2¹/₄in. high, circa 1752–55. (Cheffins Grain & Comins) $760

A pair of Royal Worcester vases, oviform with tall slender necks and twin-handled, the handle terminals modeled as swanheads, painted by Sedgley, signed, 14in. high. (Christie's) $3,427

A rare Worcester bell-shaped mug, with ribbed handle, printed on one side in black with the King of Prussia, 14.5cm. (Phillips) $1,484

Flight Barr & Barr Worcester plate, the center painted with a crest and motto, within a floral border in colors, printed and impressed marks, circa 1813/40. (G. A. Key) $231

Very fine pair of Royal Worcester two handled vases, the deep blue grounds decorated in gilt, dated code for 1898, 9in. high, decorator's mark Charlie Deakins. (Ewbank) $4,223

A Worcester blue and white circular pierced basket, circa 1770, blue hatched crescent mark, the interior painted with the 'Pinecone' pattern, 8¹/₂in. diameter. (Christie's) $633

WORCESTER

An extremely rare and early Worcester baluster mug, painted in a pale blue with a Chinese fisherman on the end of a jetty, 9.3cm.
(Phillips) $18,544

A pair of Worcester blanc-de-Chine vases in the form of shells on seaweed supports, 7in. high.
(Anderson & Garland)
                              $367

A very rare Worcester barrel shaped mug, printed in blue with two floral bouquets and smaller sprigs and insects, 14.25cm.
(Phillips) $1,129

Country Girl: a rare Royal Worcester candle extinguisher in Kate Greenaway style, heightened with gilding, 12.5cm., circa 1880.
(Phillips) $1,613

A pair of Worcester (Flight, Barr & Barr) centerpiece bowls, circa 1815, on three fluted tapering legs headed by lion masks, 8½in. high.
(Christie's) $4,025

Royal Worcester peach and ivory ground baluster shaped vase, twin 'seahorse' handles, English, 1889, 13in.
(G. A. Key) $180

Royal Worcester porcelain jardinière by James Hadleigh, reticulated top, circular base with leaf formed and molded feet, 8in. tall.
(G. A. Key) $937

A pair of Worcester (Flight, Barr & Barr) magenta-ground pot-pourri vases, covers and liners, circa 1817, impressed marks, 15½in. high.
(Christie's) $7,475

Royal Worcester porcelain plate, with detail of turkeys to center, 9in., circa 1900.
(G. A. Key) $143

A 16mm. Beaulieu R16 cinematographic camera with film magazine and an Angenieux 12–120mm. f/2.2 lens.
(Christie's) $980

André Debrie, Paris, a 35mm. wood-body hand-cranked Interview cinematographic camera No. 493 with hand-crank, two film magazines.
(Christie's) $1,426

A 16mm. Beaulieu R16 cinematographic camera with an Angenieux Zoom Type 20x12B 12–250mm. f/3.5 lens.
(Christie's) $891

Ernemann-Werke A.G., Dresden, a 35mm. wood-body hand-cranked Aufnahme-Kino model A cinematographic camera no. 1296226 with Carl Zeiss, Jena Tessar f/3.5 5cm. lens no. 509784.
(Christie's) $1,337

Ernemann-Werke A.G., Germany, a 35mm. wood-body hand-cranked Aufn.-Kino Model E cinematographic camera No. 914335 with hand-crank.
(Christie's) $1,693

A 35mm. wood-body hand-cranked cinematographic camera no. 25134 with hand-crank, two film magazines and a Carl Zeiss, Jena Tessar f/3.5 7.5cm. lens no. 453949.
(Christie's) $1,960

Newman-Sinclair Ltd., London, a 35mm. duraluminium-body NS ciné camera No. 742 with a TTH Elc Cooke Speed Panchro 50mm. f/2 lens, in maker's case.
(Christie's) $755

A Lumière Cinématographe camera.
(Christie's) $20,240

Paillard-Bolex, Switzerland, a 16mm. H16 cinematographic camera No. 242488 with a three-lens turret holding a Kern Switar f/1.8 16mm. lens.
(Christie's) $865

BRACKET CLOCKS

English mahogany bracket clock, brass dial with Roman numerals, signed *Matthew King, London.*
(Herholdt Jensen)
$1,628

An impressive ebonized chiming bracket clock, the arched silvered dial with black Roman numerals below a regulating dial, clock 26in. high.
(Spencer's) $3,040

An ebonized and gilt brass mounted basket topped bracket clock, engraved backplate inscribed *Nicholas Massy, London*, 1ft. 2¹/₂in. high.
(Phillips) $3,831

A mahogany bracket clock, John Evans, London, circa 1820, 8in. convex painted dial with Roman numerals, the twin fusée movement striking on a bell, 17¹/₄in.
(Bonhams) $1,170

An attractive 19th century German walnut cuckoo bracket clock, the convex circular white enameled dial with black Roman numerals, 17in. high.
(Spencer's) $1,300

A Regency mahogany bracket clock after a design by Thomas Hope, the dial flanked by canted stiles set with gilt metal sphinx pilasters below anthemion, 52cm. high.
(Spencer's) $2,754

An 18th century fruitwood and gilt brass mounted bracket clock, signed in the arch *Stepn. Rimbault London*, the twin fusée movement with verge escapement and engraved backplate, 42cm. high.
(Phillips) $4,620

A late Victorian oak quarter chiming bracket clock, Parkinson & Frodsham, the five pillar twin chain fusée movement with anchor escapement, oak bracket en suite, 39in. high.
(Christie's) $1,986

George III style japanned bracket clock, early 20th century, retailed by Bigelow Kennard & Co., Boston, parcel-gilt, black and polychrome figural decoration, 15¹/₂in. high with handle.
(Skinner) $747

BRACKET CLOCKS

A mahogany and brass inlaid bracket clock, Stratford, circa 1820, 8in. painted dial with Roman numerals, 19³/₄in.
(Bonhams) **$1,200**

An early ebonized bracket timepiece with alarm, case English circa 1700, movement Continental circa 1700, 14in. high.
(Christie's) **$2,208**

George III mahogany bracket clock, the domed top with brass carrying handle and four finials, by Thomas Harper, London, 21in. high.
(Ewbank) **$10,557**

A late Victorian satinwood bracket timepiece, Jump, 93 Mount St. London, the case with brass ball feet supporting the rectangular break-front plinth, 15¹/₄in. high.
(Christie's) **$3,680**

A George I bracket timepiece in satinwood case, Jno: Wady, London, the case on stepped plinth with fruitwood inlay, pierced wood frets to the sides, the movement circa 1730, 12¹/₂in. high.
(Christie's) **$2,708**

An Italian early 18th century tortoiseshell quarter striking bracket clock, Giovanni Hisla, Napoli, the case on large ormolu mask-and-foliate scroll feet, the caddy-molded top with gallery sound apertures, 26in. high.
(Christie's) **$14,444**

Early 19th century rosewood bracket clock, the stepped top with pineapple finial, painted dial, eight day striking fusée movement by Peterkin, London, 18¹/₂in. high.
(Ewbank) **$1,847**

Dan Quare & Ste Horseman, London, an 18th century ebonized bracket clock, the case with inverted bell top, 46cm. high.
(Phillips) **$7,800**

A George III ebonized striking bracket clock, Robert Best, London, the gilt-brass mounted case with triple-pad to the arched top with handle, 16in. high.
(Christie's) **$8,666**

BRACKET CLOCKS

A George I ebonized striking bracket clock, John Austen Shoreditch, the case with turned handle to inverted bell top, 19in. high.
(Christie's) $3,680

Joseph Knibb, London, a fine Charles II repeating bracket clock, ebonized wood case with gilt-metal carrying handle, 36cm.
(Bearne's) $110,880

A George III brass-mounted mahogany striking bracket clock, Tomlin Royal Exchange, London, 16in. high.
(Christie's) $4,968

A Queen Anne ebonized quarter repeating bracket timepiece, Gabriel Smith, Barthomley, knife-edge verge escapement with later Webster-style backcock, 15¹/₂in. high.
(Christie's) $11,960

A George III ormolu-mounted tortoiseshell and enamel musical bracket clock for the Turkish market, Markwick Markham Perigal, London, the domed top with further flambeau finial and pierced trellis sound frets, 16¹/₂in. high.
(Christie's) $29,791

A Queen Anne ebonized striking bracket clock, Charles Lowndes in Pallmall, the case with foliate-cast basket top with addorsed foliate-tied dolphin handle, 13in. high.
(Christie's) $4,784

A William and Mary kingwood bracket timepiece, Christopher Gould, London, knife-edge verge escapement with Webster-style backcock, pull quarter repeat on two bells, 13¹/₂in. high.
(Christie's) $23,472

A Charles II ebonized striking bracket clock, Joseph Knibb, London, the phase III case with handle and gilt-metal foliate mount to the cushion-molded top, glazed sides, 11³/₄in. high.
(Christie's) $37,916

A fine ebony veneered quarter repeating table clock, Joseph Knibb, circa 1685, the domed top case with gilt mounts and handle, pierced front fret and glazed side panels, 11³/₄in.
(Bonhams) $24,960

BRACKET CLOCKS

A George III mahogany bracket clock, the arched brass dial signed *Wm. Pybus, London*, 1ft. 9in. high.
(Phillips) $3,985

A 19th century mahogany bracket clock, the circular painted dial signed *Jas Henfrey, Leicester*, the twin fusée movement with anchor escapement, 53cm. high.
(Phillips) $2,233

An 18th century walnut bracket clock, dial signed *Thomas Newton, London*, the twin fusée movement with verge escapement, 51cm. high.
(Phillips) $9,961

An early Victorian brass-inlaid mahogany striking bracket clock, Smith, St. Peters, the five pillar twin fusée movement with anchor escapement and strike/trip repeat on bell on plain backplate, 20¹/₂in. high.
(Christie's) $1,083

A mid 18th century walnut and ebonized ormolu-mounted bracket clock, the stepped domed cover surmounted by an allegorical figure, by Pompeo Corsi Rome.
(Finarte) $8,699

A George III mahogany and gilt brass mounted musical bracket clock, the arched engraved silvered dial with subsidiaries for strike/silent and for four tunes signed *Easton, Petworth*, 49cm. high.
(Phillips) $4,928

A George III ebonized bracket clock, dial with date aperture signed on a recessed plaque *Thos Clements London*, with subsidiary strike/silent in the arch, 1ft. 7in. high.
(Phillips) $2,772

A good late Victorian rosewood and satinwood marquetry bracket clock, the breakarch pediment with four gilt metal pineapple finials, 21in. high.
(Cheffins Grain & Comins)
                              $2,280

An 18th century ebonized bracket clock by John Ellicot, London, the five pillared movement with verge escapement and pull quarter repeat on six bells, 42cm. high.
(Phillips) $8,932

BRACKET CLOCKS

A late 17th century walnut bracket clock, the caddy topped case with carrying handle and part glazed side frets on bun feet, 1ft. 2¹/₂in. high.
(Phillips)   **$5,517**

A Gothic Revival oak bracket clock, the lancet-shaped case flanked by cluster columns, the silvered dial inscribed *Webster, Cornhill, London*, 29¹/₂in.
(Hy. Duke & Son)
    $1,001

An 18th century ebonized bracket clock, the arched brass dial with silvered chapter ring signed *Thos Stones, London*, 1ft. 6in. high.
(Phillips)   **$2,222**

An impressive George III mahogany quarter chiming and musical bracket clock, the arched case surmounted by a gilt bronze figure of a lion, dial signed *J. F. Drury, London*, 84cm. high.
(Phillips)   **$8,888**

A 19th century carved wood cuckoo bracket clock, the arched case decorated with squirrels inhabiting oak boughs, 22in. high.
(Phillips)   **$766**

A Regency brass-inlaid mahogany and ebonized striking bracket clock, Trendell, Reading, fishscale sound frets to the sides and handle to top, glazed brass bezel to the cream painted Roman dial, 17¹/₄in. high.
(Christie's)   **$1,173**

A Regency mahogany bracket clock, white enamel dial with Roman numerals with double fusée movement striking on a bell, 16in.
(Hy. Duke & Son)
    $2,160

A George III miniature ebonized bracket timepiece with alarm, the arched silvered dial with concentric alarm set and signed in the arch *Alex R. Hare, London*, 23cm. high.
(Phillips)   **$2,079**

A mahogany chiming bracket clock, Robert Roskell, Liverpool, circa 1830, 8³/₄in. rounded painted dial, the triple fusée movement with an engraved border, 23in.
(Bonhams)   **$1,560**

CARRIAGE CLOCKS

A silver carriage timepiece, English/French, 1904, round enamel dial with Roman numerals, London hallmark for 1904, 2³/₄in.
(Bonhams) $675

An Art Deco gold and enamel miniature tryptich traveling clock, Cartier, No. 9188/183/.10067, European W. & C. Co., 1¹/₂in. high.
(Christie's) $22,080

A gilt-metal miniature oval carriage timepiece, the movement with bimetallic balance to lever platform, plain oval case, 3¹/₄in. high.
(Christie's) $903

A fine large engraved case carriage clock, English, Barwise, London, circa 1840, the five pillar movement double fusée and chain movement with a lever escapement, 9¹/₂in.
(Bonhams) $35,000

A French experimental early grande sonnerie striking chronometer carriage clock, Raingo Frères, Paris, the twin going barrel movement with Earnshaw-type escapement with spring secured at the foot, 6in. high.
(Christie's) $9,930

A silver and enamel minute repeating miniature carriage timepiece, unsigned, the rectangular case covered with yellow guilloché enamel, 3¹/₂in. high.
(Christie's) $4,600

A fine large carriage clock, English, Dent, No. 32571, circa 1898, 3¹/₄in. enamel dial with Roman numerals and fine blued steel fleur-de-lis hands, 10³/₄in.
(Bonhams) $20,100

A gilt-metal striking carriage clock, Henri Jacot, No. 14633, white enamel Roman and Arabic dial with blued moon hands, plain gorge case, 4¹/₂in. high.
(Christie's) $1,806

A French brass and cloisonné enamel grande sonnerie carriage clock, retailed by Friedrich & Winter, strike/repeat/alarm on two gongs, 6¹/₂in. high.
(Christie's) $3,680

CARRIAGE CLOCKS

A French brass carriage clock, the movement with lever platform escapement and push repeat striking on a gong, 18cm. high.
(Phillips) $1,123

A black onyx, gold and coral strut timepiece, Cartier, Nos. 6088/4186, circa 1930, the nickel movement signed *European Watch and Clock Co.*, 3¹/₈in.
(Bonhams) $4,350

A French brass carriage clock, the movement with lever platform escapement and push repeat striking on a gong, 17cm. high.
(Phillips) $905

A 19th century French brass carriage clock, the movement with lever platform escapement and push repeat striking on a gong, with silvered chapter ring signed for *Hamilton & Inches*, 19cm. high.
(Phillips) $893

A 19th century French gilt brass oval carriage clock, the movement with lever platform escapement, the backplate bearing the Drocourt trademark, 19cm. high.
(Phillips) $2,028

A 19th century French giant brass carriage clock, enamel circular dial signed for *Mackay, Cunningham & Co., Edinburgh*, set in a gilt mask within an engraved corniche case, 23cm. high.
(Phillips) $3,696

A 19th century French brass carriage clock, with engraved dial signed for *W. Drummond & Co., Melbourne*, with fruit and foliage decoration, 19.5cm. high.
(Phillips) $1,123

An engraved gilt-brass striking carriage clock, white enamel Roman dial with foliate engraved gilt mask, similarly engraved corniche case, 5in. high.
(Christie's) $1,083

A 19th century French brass petite sonnerie carriage clock, the enamel dial signed *Bourdin Hr du Roi, Rue de la Paix, 24 Paris*, 17cm. high.
(Phillips) $2,496

CARRIAGE CLOCKS

A French gilt brass petite sonnerie carriage clock, the movement signed *Breguet 3593*, in a corniche case, 7in. high. (Phillips) **$1,685**

A 19th century English gilt brass carriage timepiece, signed *James Gowland, London, No. 1108*, the pillared case with engraved top, 6in. high. (Phillips) **$843**

A late 19th century French traveling clock, the brass case with a swing handle above an aneroid barometer, $8^{1}/_{2}$in. high. (Woolley & Wallis) **$680**

A Continental early striking carriage clock, the movement with simple balance to the cylinder platform, strike/repeat/alarm on bell housed in the base, $7^{3}/_{4}$in. high. (Christie's) **$903**

A French gilt brass and enamel combination carriage timepiece and barometer, in a pillared case with T-bar handle and enamel frieze, 6in. high. (Phillips) **$1,349**

A 19th century English nickel chronometer carriage timepiece by F. Dent, the fusée movement with maintaining power, gilt platform, Earnshaw type spring detent escapement, $7^{3}/_{4}$in. high. (Phillips) **$19,923**

A French brass carriage clock, the movement with lever platform escapement with push repeat striking on two gongs, bearing the Jacot trademark, 17cm. high. (Phillips) **$1,109**

A French gilt-brass striking bamboo carriage clock, the movement with bimetallic balance to silvered lever platform, bamboo case of typical form, $6^{3}/_{4}$in. high. (Christie's) **$1,481**

A French gilt brass and enamel paneled carriage clock, the movement with lever platform escapement, push repeat and alarm, 8in. high. (Phillips) **$7,356**

CARRIAGE CLOCKS

A French gilt brass carriage clock, the enamel dial signed for R. Stewart, Glasgow, in a gorge case, 7in. high.
(Phillips) $920

A French gilt brass grande sonnerie carriage clock, the movement signed Breguet No. 1507, in gorge case.
(Phillips) $3,218

A French repeating carriage clock, in a beveled glass and brass case with foliate tied split cylindrical pilasters, 8in. high.
(Spencer's) $765

A 19th century French lacquered brass carriage clock, the movement with lever platform escapement and push repeat striking on a gong, 8in. high.
(Phillips) $1,303

An Edwardian silver and tortoiseshell cased carriage timepiece by William Comyns, the fascia with ribbon tied pendant husk pique decoration, London 1909, 14cm. high.
(Spencer's) $1,364

A French brass grande sonnerie striking carriage clock, the movement with bimetallic balance to gilt lever platform, quarter strike/repeat/alarm on two gongs, 6in. high.
(Christie's) $1,444

A 19th century French brass carriage clock, the movement with lever platform escapement and push repeat striking on a gong, numbered 3560, 17cm. high.
(Phillips) $878

A 19th century French gilt brass carriage clock, with enamel dial signed Charles Frodsham, To the Queen, London, in a numbered corniche case, 16cm. high.
(Phillips) $554

French cast brass and glass cased carriage clock, having front caryatid supports, inscribed Hemry & Co., Paris, mid/late 19th century, 5¹/₂in. high.
(G. A. Key) $585

Aesthetic black marble and cloisonné three-piece clock garniture, late 19th century, with Japanese-style cloisonné bird and floral inserts on turquoise ground, and a pair of covered urns, clock 20¹/₈in. high.
(Skinner) $2,990

19th century French white marble and ormolu mounted clock garniture, the round dial decorated with swags of flowers surmounted by two gilt torches and ribbon tie, the clock 15in. high.
(Ewbank) $1,021

French gilt bronze and champlevé enamel three piece clock garniture, retailed by Tiffany & Co., the dial painted with cherubs and floral swags and surrounded by paste 'jewels', 20¹/₂in. height of clock.
(William Doyle) $6,900

A 19th century French ormolu and patinated bronze garniture, the portico case with stepped top and base with applied foliate decoration, 8¹/₂in. high, together with the matching pair of candlesticks.
(Phillips) $1,042

Louis XVI style ormolu and salmon marble clock garniture, 19th century, enamel dial with zodiac signs, time and strike movement, clock 22⁵/₈in. high.
(Skinner) $6,900

A Second Empire porcelain-mounted ormolu striking clock garniture, unsigned, the foliate-cast case with flanking porcelain columns, 16in. high.
(Christie's) $4,784

A fine French gilt metal clock garniture decorated with Paris porcelain urns, eight-day striking movement by Japy Frères, 27in. high. (Anderson & Garland) **$2,142**

An ormolu and mantel clock garniture, French, circa 1875, 3in. enamel dial with Roman and Arabic numerals, 13³/₄in. (Bonhams) **$1,371**

A late 19th century French gilt metal and enameled garniture de cheminée, the clock with vertical eggshell blue enameled dial, retailer's indistinct name Liverpool, flanked by a pair of two handled pedestal urns, clock 18in. high overall. (Spencer's) **$1,346**

A Sèvres-style composite garniture of two vases and a clock, the clock painted with a central panel of figures in 18th century dress in a rural landscape, maker's mark *MACKAY CUNNINGHAM & CO., EDINBURGH*, 19in. high, 19th century. (Christie's) **$5,412**

A Boulle clock garniture, French, circa 1880, 5¹/₂in., gong striking movement, in a red shell covered waisted case, together with a matching pair of five-light candelabra, 24in. (Bonhams) **$3,900**

A 19th century French ormolu and champlevé enamel clock garniture, in the Oriental taste, the case surmounted by the figure of a stork above a galleried dome, 55cm. high. (Phillips) **$3,696**

A French ormolu garniture, comprising a clock and a pair of candelabra, the clock surmounted by an urn with laurel festoons, the enamel dial inscribed *KREITZ/A ANVERS*, late 19th century, clock 19½in. high. (Christie's) **$5,119**

A large French gilt-bronze and enamel clock garniture, Napoléon III, Paris, circa 1870, in the manner of Barbedienne, the clock with a pierced faceted sphere, 88cm. high. (Sotheby's) **$8,228**

An ormolu and porcelain mounted clock garniture, French, circa 1890, a painted Eastern market scene and mosque beyond, together with a pair of porcelain and ormolu matching urns, 17in. high. (Bonhams) **$1,613**

A French gilt-bronze and onyx garniture, centerpiece and a pair of candelabra, the centerpiece surmounted by a group of Hebe and Jupiter's Eagle, late 19th century, the centerpiece 29¼in. high. (Christie's) **$12,799**

A French gilt-bronze and marble composed clock garniture, Napoléon III, circa 1870, the clock by Barbedienne, finely cast with Mercury's helmet flanked by putti, the clock 40cm. high. (Sotheby's) **$5,303**

A French white marble and gilt-bronze composed clock garniture, Paris, circa 1900, the lyre clock signed *L Leroy & Co, 13 a 15 Palais-Royal*, 56cm. high. (Sotheby's) **$6,583**

LANTERN CLOCKS

A brass lantern clock, English, circa 1870, 6³/₄in. brass chapter ring with engraved Roman numerals and decorated center, 16in.
(Bonhams) $1,209

A brass striking winged lantern clock, the case of typical form with Roman chapter ring signed *Crucefix London*, 13¹/₂in. high.
(Christie's) $2,024

A brass lantern clock, English, 18th/19th century, 6¹/₄in. silvered chapter ring with Roman numerals and foliate engraved center, 15in.
(Bonhams) $720

A brass 30 hour lantern clock, circa 1760, 6¹/₄in. brass Roman numeral chapter ring, signed in the foliage engraved center *Rob' Watts, Stamford*, 13³/₄in.
(Bonhams) $2,258

A mahogany hooded wall alarm timepiece, William Webster, London, circa 1760, the posted weight driven movement with a verge escapement.
(Bonhams) $1,900

A George III brass lantern clock for the Turkish market, the dial signed *Markwich Markham London* on a silvered plaque in the arch, 12in. high.
(Christie's) $1,472

A Charles II gilt-brass striking lantern clock, unsigned, silvered chapter ring with single well sculpted steel hand, 12in. high.
(Christie's) $3,312

A silver plated lantern clock, English/German, circa 1890, signed *Andrew Allan in Grabb St Londini fecit*, standing on ball feet, 15¹/₂in.
(Bonhams) $645

A brass striking lantern clock, *Henry Ireland Londini fecit*, the case of typical form with Roman chapter ring, 16in. high.
(Christie's) $4,416

LONGCASE CLOCKS

A George II walnut quarter chiming longcase clock, Robert Ward, London, 8ft. 6in. high. (Christie's)

$8,280

A mid Georgian mahogany longcase clock, inscribed *Benjamin Barlow, Oldham.* (Locke & England)

$1,683

Late 18th century beech and softwood long case clock, German, 264cm. high. (Kunsthaus am Museum)

$8,162

A mahogany quarter chiming longcase clock, William Jackson, Frodsham, circa 1790, 7ft. 3in. (Bonhams)

$3,850

An 18th century mahogany longcase clock, signed *James Kirkland, Glasgow,* 2.31m. high. (Phillips)

$2,028

A Louis XV ormolu-mounted ebonized pendule regulateur, J. B. Paillard A Paris, 7ft. 3in. high. (Christie's)

$5,888

An oak and mahogany longcase clock, Richardson Waverham, circa 1800, 6ft. 6in. (Bonhams)

$1,300

A George III mahogany longcase clock, signed *J. A. Cawson & Son, Liverpool,* 2.31m. high. (Phillips)

$2,184

LONGCASE CLOCKS

A mahogany longcase regulator, A. L. Howlett, circa 1900, 6ft. 8in. (Bonhams) **$2,750**

A 19th century oak and mahogany longcase clock, signed *Jas Frewin, Hereford*, 7ft. 1in. high. (Phillips) **$1,410**

A mahogany longcase regulator, James Whitelaw, Edinburgh, circa 1800, 6ft. 9in. (Bonhams) **$3,744**

A good 11³/₄-inch symphonion long case clock, German, circa 1910, 78in. high. (Sotheby's) **$14,444**

An ormolu-mounted kingwood and marquetry longcase clock, in the Louis XVI style, 19th century, 94in. high. (Christie's) **$5,851**

A Federal mahogany dwarf tall-case clock, by Reuben Tower, Hingham, Massachusetts, 1816, 50in. high. (Christie's) **$211,500**

A Tempovox grandmother clock radio in simulated figured walnut case of Art Deco design with speaker in trunk, 57in. high, circa 1938. (Christie's) **$389**

A Queen Anne carved cherrywood tall case clock, David Lowrey, Newington, Connecticut, dated *1772*, 7ft. 4¹/₂in. high. (Sotheby's) **$27,600**

LONGCASE CLOCKS

A late George III mahogany longcase clock by M. Bartley, Bristol, 102in. high. (Hy. Duke & Son) **$2,240**

An 18th century oak thirty hour longcase clock, signed *Thos Wood, Tunbridge Wells*, 6ft. 4in. high. (Phillips) **$1,195**

A Louis XV rosewood and ormolu regulator by Balthazar Lieutaud, 205cm. high. (Finarte) **$16,729**

A walnut longcase clock, Thomas Baker, Portsmouth, circa 1740, 7ft. 7in. (Bonhams) **$3,432**

A William IV mahogany and ebony lined longcase clock, the paneled base on a molded plinth, 81in. high. (Christie's) **$2,448**

Figured mahogany Yorkshire longcase clock, with eight day movement and seconds, 95in. high. (Dee, Atkinson & Harrison) **$742**

Pine dwarf clock, Rubin Tower, Kingston, Massachusetts, 1810–30, 48in. high. (Skinner) **$13,800**

A Queen Anne burr walnut longcase clock, the dial now signed *Dan Delander London*, 8ft. 2in. high. (Christie's) **$5,778**

LONGCASE CLOCKS

A mahogany longcase clock, Recorden, London, circa 1790, 7ft. 8in. (Bonhams)
$4,680

A mahogany longcase clock, William Latch, circa 1800, 7ft. 7in. (Bonhams)
$2,096

A good mahogany longcase clock, Grant, Fleet Street, No. 175, circa 1780, 7ft. 2in. (Bonhams)
$8,424

An oak and mahogany longcase clock, W. Toleman, Caernarvon, circa 1780, 7ft. 2in. (Bonhams)
$1,290

A Dutch mahogany and marquetry longcase clock, the dial signed *Phy. Mensenbour Groningen*, circa 1780, 8ft. 4in. high. (Christie's)
$5,778

A Dutch walnut quarter chiming longcase clock, signed *Pieter Swaan, Amsterdam*, 8ft. 4in. high. (Phillips)
$6,743

A Federal mahogany dwarf tall-case clock, Massachusetts, 1790–1810, white circular dial above a blue painted ground with a swagged floral garland, 54¹/₂in. high. (Christie's)
$10,925

A rare carved and ebonized curly maple tall case clock, the dial inscribed *John Foss, Somersworth, New Hampshire*, mid 18th century, 6ft. 9in. high. (Sotheby's)
$13,225

LONGCASE CLOCKS

Grain painted tall case clock, Silas Hoadley, Plymouth, Connecticut, circa 1830, 89in. high. (Skinner)

$3,737

A mahogany longcase clock, Jas and W. Kelley, Glasgow, circa 1830, 13in. round dial, 6ft. 9in. (Bonhams)

$2,184

A walnut Dutch quarter-striking longcase clock, Joan^s Klock, Amsterdam, 18th century, 7ft. 8in. (Bonhams)

$5,304

Victorian inlaid rosewood tall case clock, the silver dial with repoussé floral motifs, 100in. high. (William Doyle)

$17,250

A Federal inlaid mahogany tall-case clock by William Cummens, Massachusetts, circa 1802–1810, 90in. high. (Christie's)

$25,300

A late 17th century walnut and floral marquetry month going longcase clock, signed Daniel Le Count, London, 2.08m. high. (Phillips)

$7,700

A William III seaweed marquetry longcase clock, the 11in. square dial signed John Farewell London, 7ft. 8in. high. (Christie's)

$14,444

A walnut marquetry longcase clock, with pull quarter repeating, signed William Cattel Londini fecit, circa 1685, 6ft. 7in. (Bonhams)

$9,030

LONGCASE CLOCKS

A George III mahogany longcase clock, silvered chapter ring signed *Wm. Hutchings, Cullompton,* 7ft. 4in. high. (Phillips) $1,386

A George II mahogany longcase clock, arched painted dial signed *Jas. Warren, Canterbury,* 6ft. 11½in. high. (Phillips) $4,928

An early 18th century **ebonized** longcase clock, signed *Tho. Tompion London,* 6ft. 10in. high.(Phillips) $29,260

A Regency mahogany longcase clock, the 12in. circular painted dial signed *R. Cole, Ipswich,* 7ft. 4in. high. (Phillips) $2,926

A 19th century mahogany and checker strung longcase clock, signed *Thos. Evans, Bont Uchel,* 7ft. 4in. high. (Phillips) $1,848

Bird's eye maple, tiger maple and maple tall case clock, Silas Hoadley, Plymouth, Connecticut, circa 1825, 85in. high. (Skinner) $2,875

A mahogany and inlaid longcase clock, the 12in. painted arched dial inscribed *Edmonds, Baker Street,* 7ft. 11in. high. (Phillips) $2,772

A walnut veneer longcase clock, circa 1700, 12in. dial with Roman and Arabic numerals, signed *Jamˢ Walker, London,* 7ft. (Bonhams) $4,354

MANTEL CLOCKS

A large Meissen mantel-clock, surmounted by Jupiter seated on clouds, circa 1860, 28in. high. (Christie's) $7,314

An Art Deco nickel-plated timepiece alarm, Cartier 7097, nickel-finished movement jeweled to the third and signed *Lemania Watch Co.*, signed green canvas-covered traveling case, 3½in. high. (Christie's) $1,264

A gilt-bronze mantel clock with figure of George Washington, Du Buc, Paris, circa 1805, 15½in. high. (Christie's) $32,200

A Louis Philippe ormolu-mounted griotte marble urn clock, the revolving enamel circlet rings with individual Roman and Arabic chapters read from the tip of an ormolu arrow, 19¾in. high. (Christie's) $12,639

A Viennese ebonized and parcel-gilt grande sonnerie musical table clock, the break-arch top applied with cast silvered sirens flanking a lunette painted with a landscape and signed *Weillbourg*, 23in. high. (Christie's) $3,430

A Louis XV tortoiseshell boulle month-going bracket timepiece, Julien Le Roy, de la Société des Arts, the case of waisted form with foliate scroll feet, glazed sides, the shoulders applied with foliate eagle mounts, 21in. high. (Christie's) $3,611

A bronze and marked sculptural mantel clock, French, circa 1830, signed *Paris*, set on a shield held by a figure of Minerva, 24in. (Bonhams) $2,258

A neo-Grec ebonized and ormolu-mounted mantel clock, The E. Ingraham & Company, Bristol, Connecticut, circa 1880, 11¾in. high. (Christie's) $368

A Jacob Petit style mantle clock in polychrome enameled porcelain, surmounted by a Turk. (Hôtel de Ventes Horta) $3,579

MANTEL CLOCKS

An ormolu and white marble mantel clock, the enamel dial signed *DURAND A PARIS*, on a canted white marble base and turned feet, 21in. high.
(Christie's) $1,973

A Louis XVI ormolu mantel clock, the glazed circular enameled dial with Roman and Arabic numerals and inscribed *Crosnier/à Paris*, 16¹/₂in. high.
(Christie's) $20,398

An ormolu-mounted black and white marble mantel clock, the glazed circular enameled dial signed *Giraud/A PARIS*, 19th century, 20¹/₂in. high.
(Christie's) $5,382

An important Empire amboyna and ormolu-mounted table orrery clock, Raingo Freres & Leroy et Fils, the Neo-classical case in the form of a Doric rotunda, 26¹/₂in. high.
(Christie's) $149,150

A fine Swiss ormolu grande sonnerie pendule d'officier, Robert & Courvoisier, the case on toupie feet, the sides applied with berried rosettes, circa 1795, 7³/₄in. high.
(Christie's) $11,194

A Louis XVI ormolu mantel clock, the glazed circular enameled Roman and Arabic-chaptered dial signed *In. Fursi/ Le Roux*, the case signed *Osmond*, 20in. high.
(Christie's) $15,762

A Louis Philippe ormolu and bronze striking mantel clock, Bernard Lyon A Paris, the narrow filigree case with D-ended plinth, 16in. high.
(Christie's) $3,430

Liberty & Co., 'Cymric' mantel clock, 1902, in silver with blue-green enameled face with Roman numerals, 19.25cm.
(Sotheby's) $10,433

A gilt metal mantel clock, French, circa 1875, 3¹/₄in., the bell striking movement set into a case surmounted by a Classical lady and putti, 17in.
(Bonhams) $858

MANTEL CLOCKS

A French gilt-metal and Sèvres-style porcelain mounted mantel clock, cast case surmounted by a two-handled urn, 19th century, the clock 14¹/₂in. high.
(Christie's) $452

A 9ct. gold lighter/watch by Dunhill, the plain oval section body with hinged flap containing watch movement, import marked London 1926, 5.5cm. high.
(Cheffins Grain & Comins) $1,900

Empire style patinated bronze mantel clock, 19th century, replaced works, 14in. high.
(Skinner) $431

A mahogany timepiece, W. H. Bailey & Co., circa 1900, 6³/₄in. painted Roman dial, in a tapered case with a glazed door, 18¹/₂in.
(Bonhams) $858

A 19th century satinwood mantel clock, dial signed *Frodsham & Baker, Gracechurch Street, London*, the twin fusée movement with anchor escapement, 15cm. high.
(Phillips) $3,234

A 19th century bronze and gilt brass mantel timepiece, the arched case with carrying handle and bracket feet, signed *Henry Favre, Pall Mall*, 21cm. high.
(Phillips) $3,388

A 19th century French ormolu and rouge marble lyre shaped mantel clock, the two swan side supports surmounted by an anthemion finial, 56cm. high.
(Phillips) $4,138

Louis XVI style gilt and patinated bronze mantel clock, the enamel dial set in a drum shaped case, surmounted by a swag draped urn, 14in. high.
(William Doyle) $2,530

A Louis XVI ormolu musical clock made for the Turkish market, the circular enameled dial with Kufic chapters, lacking musical work, 23¹/₄in. high.
(Christie's) $10,764

MANTEL CLOCKS

A boulle and ormolu mantel clock, French, circa 1880, the bell striking movement (lacking bell) signed *Japy Freres and Hy Marc*, 20½in.
(Bonhams) $1,120

Louis XVI style bronze and painted porcelain mantel clock, late 19th century, the clock face and panels painted with birds and flowers on a white and cobalt ground, gold patinated bronze, 13in. high.
(Skinner) $1,840

Ornate ormolu mantel clock, the finial formed as a winged putto clutching a scroll, by Grotte & Julian of Cannes, 15in. high.
(G. A. Key) $631

A mahogany and gilt grande sonnerie mounted clock, Austrian, Joseph Schwerlin, Wien, circa 1830, the center dial containing two putti at work in Vulcan's workshop, 26in. high.
(Bonhams) $1,935

A 19th century carved wood cuckoo clock, the case of typical chalet form, the twin fusée movement with anchor escapement, 41cm. high.
(Phillips) $708

Large and ornate Victorian American walnut mantel clock, profusely adorned with metal figures of Roman soldiers, striking movement, mid 19th century.
(G. A. Key) $532

A mahogany and ormolu portico timepiece, French, circa 1820, the movement signed *Robert à Paris*, 14in. high.
(Bonhams) $839

A 19th century French bronze and variegated marble mantel clock, the spherical case flanked by seated winged putti, 1ft. 5in. high.
(Phillips) $996

Federal mahogany pillar and scroll clock, E. Terry and Sons, Plymouth, Connecticut, circa 1820, 31in. high.
(Skinner) $4,312

MANTEL CLOCKS

Edwardian mahogany mantel clock having domed hood, decorated with satinwood shells and line inlay, 13in. high.
(G. A. Key) $248

A Continental miniature green onyx and enamelled traveling timepiece, the circular movement with pink guilloche enameled dial, 2½in. high.
(Phillips) $1,042

A late Victorian mantel clock, the case embossed on front with scrollwork, by William Comyns, 1899, 20cm. high.
(Phillips) $1,629

Edwardian mantel clock, mahogany case crossbanded with satinwood and inlaid with marquetry swags, English/French, early part of the 20th century.
(G. A. Key) $456

An Empire ormolu, bronze and marble striking mantel clock, the figures atop a lady seated in a bergère with a dog and cat at her feet whilst winding wool with the help of a young boy, 15½in. high.
(Christie's) $5,417

An early 19th century ormolu traveling clock, the arched case with carrying handle and chased decoration, dial signed *Robert & Courvoisier*, 10in. high.
(Phillips) $1,532

A brass four-glass mantel clock, French, circa 1890, 3½in. enamel dial with Roman numerals, the center containing a Brocourt escapement, in a glazed polished case, 11½in. high.
(Bonhams) $702

A Louis XVI ormolu mantel clock, the glazed circular Roman and Arabic-chaptered enameled dial signed *Frederickduval/a Paris*, 13½in. high.
(Christie's) $12,053

Italian type calendar clock, circa 1864–1903, by Welch, Spring & Co., walnut veneered case with turned columns and brass rims around glass, eight-day time and strike movement, 20in. high.
(Eldred's) $605

MANTEL CLOCKS

French brass four glass mantel clock, late 19th century, with a jeweled bezel, 12in. high.
(Skinner) **$517**

Empire style patinated bronze mantle clock, 19th century, 17½in. high.
(Skinner) **$2,415**

French ormolu-mounted walnut mantel clock, late 19th century, 18in. high.
(Skinner) **$747**

A modern novelty timepiece, in the form of a vintage Rolls Royce car radiator, on a beveled oblong base with enameled Rolls Royce badge, by C. Saunders & F. Shepherd, 1927, 13.5 x 11.5cm.
(Phillips) **$1,912**

A 19th century Continental mahogany and gilt brass calendar mantel clock, the separate gong and strike-calendar movements each mounted in rectangular cases, 12in. high.
(Phillips) **$2,299**

A 19th century Continental organ clock, the thirty hour weight driven movement with wooden plates discharging the weight driven organ movement each hour, with 9in. circular painted dial, 72cm. wide.
(Phillips) **$5,544**

Rare Silas Hoadley mantel clock, in mahogany veneers with painted dial, stenciled pilasters and reverse-painted lower tablet, upside down works and alarm, 26in. high.
(Eldred's) **$2,200**

A French Empire ormolu mantel clock, the case depicting Minerva urging on the horses of Diomedes, signed *Alibert a Paris*, 44cm. high.
(Phillips) **$5,698**

A 19th century French rouge marble, bronze and ormolu mantel clock, the rectangular case decorated with a cockerel and with a figure of a Classical Muse to the side, 69cm.
(Phillips) **$2,156**

MANTEL CLOCKS

A pair of Empire ormolu and bronzed four-light candelabra, each with reeded spreading column on acanthus and stiff-leaf base, 24in. high.
(Christie's) $2,691

A Paris (Nast) ormolu-mounted biscuit clock 'L'amour fait passer le temps', circa 1819, inscribed *Nast*, modeled as Cronus with his arm around the circular face, 16³/₄in. wide.
(Christie's) $5,750

Colonial Revival mahogany inlaid shelf clock, America, late 19th/20th century, with spring driven movements, 16in. high.
(Skinner) $920

A gilt-brass perpetual calendar four-glass table regulator, Brevetté Le Roy & Fils, the massive gorge case with beveled glasses, gilt dial mask finely engraved with scrolling foliage, 7in. high.
(Christie's) $8,666

A French traveling timepiece with R.E.D. escapement, the drum case on toupie feet, the single chain fusée movement with two-plane escapement, 5in. high.
(Christie's) $1,806

A 19th century burr oak mantel chronometer, the rectangular case with molded cornice, beveled glass top and chased gilt carrying handle, 21cm. high.
(Phillips) $5,236

Federal mahogany and mahogany veneer pillar and scroll clock, Seth Thomas, Plymouth, Connecticut, circa 1820, old refinish, 31in. high.
(Skinner) $1,265

Plaue porcelain clock, the drum case striking movement with enameled dial, 12in. high, German, mid to late 19th century.
(G. A. Key) $425

A 19th century German walnut cuckoo clock, with 'tiled' roof, the movement striking the hours on a gong, the cuckoo with bellows operation, 16in. high.
(Spencer's) $1,102

MANTEL CLOCKS

A bell shaped mantel clock, French, circa 1900, 4in. cast dial with enamel reserves, 12in. high.
(Bonhams) **$323**

Black and brown mottled marble mantel clock, inscribed to front *Made In Paris, Wilson and Cander 392 Strand*, English/ French, 20th century.
(G. A. Key) **$214**

A Continental silver traveling timepiece, the arched case with bow handle on bun feet, 4in. high.
(Phillips) **$736**

A 19th century ebonized mantel clock, dial signed *Arnold, 84 Strand, London, No. 736*, and signed on the backplate *Charles Frodsham, 84 Strand, London*, 26cm. high.
(Phillips) **$6,437**

A 19th century Black Forest cuckoo clock, with a cuckoo for the quarters and a trumpeter below for the hours, the three train brass movement stamped *G.H.S.*, 68cm.
(Phillips) **$1,155**

A French gilt metal lyre shaped clock, the drum shaped movement with white enamel dial plate, the case surmounted by eagle masks, no pendulum, 21in. high.
(Spencer's) **$1,148**

A Louis XVI ormolu mantel clock, the circular enamel dial signed *Gudin a Paris*, the signed circular movement with countwheel strike, 30cm. high.
(Phillips) **$4,466**

A mantel clock, the movement with outside countwheel striking on a single bell, inscribed *F. Bohler, Frankfurt, No. 1562*, 16½in. wide.
(Christie's) **$414**

An Empire ormolu pendule d'officier, enamel dial with pierced dial hands and concentric alarm signed *Robert & Courvoisier*, 21cm.
(Phillips) **$6,776**

MANTEL CLOCKS

A Federal inlaid mahogany shelf clock, dial signed by Nathaniel Munroe, Concord, Massachusetts, 1800–1810, 36³/₄in. high.
(Christie's) $36,800

Charles Requier, 15 rue Portefoin 15, Paris, Victorian calendar clock with an aneroid barometer and thermometer, in engraved black marble case, 62cm. wide.
(Bearne's) $857

An unusual chrome timepiece by Jaeger le Coultre, with two colored annular dial on a stepped base, 29cm. high.
(Phillips) $920

An 18ct. gold and enamel miniature traveling clock, signed *Cartier*, case signed *European Clock and Watch Co.*, movement signed *Majestic Watch Co.*, circa 1930, 41mm. high.
(Christie's) $15,500

A mid Victorian ormolu and bronze quarter chiming table clock, Klaftenberger, Regent Street, London, the case emblematic of Learning with flanking female bronze figures, 21³/₄in. high.
(Christie's) $5,520

A palisander and marquetry clock, the sonnerie movement with bronze dial, the base with thermometer and barometer, French, Charles X.
(Galerie Moderne) $1,511

A Federal mahogany giltwood and églomisé banjo clock, Samuel Whiting, Concord, Massachusetts, circa 1815, surmounted by a giltwood acorn finial, 34in. high.
(Sotheby's) $4,025

A black and jasper marble Egyptian Revival clock with bronze mounts, French, circa 1870, 4³/₄in. black chapter ring with stylized Arabic figures, 21in.
(Bonhams) $1,280

A Federal pillar and scroll mahogany shelf clock, by Jeromes & Darrow, Bristol, Connecticut, first quarter 19th century, 29¹/₂in. high.
(Christie's) $1,150

MANTEL CLOCKS

Regency mahogany lyre shaped mantel clock, having circular enamel dial with carved pediment above eight day fusee movement.
(Lawrences) $1,205

A Viennese diamond-set gold and enamel traveling timepiece, unsigned, winding key and brown leather traveling case, 2¹/₂in. high.
(Christie's) $4,784

An ormolu and bronze automaton clock, French, circa 1840, 3¹/₂in. silvered water silk dial with Roman numerals, 21¹/₂in.
(Bonhams) $4,000

A Regency ormolu mantel clock by Robert Philp, surmounted by a square domed roof with pierced chevron gallery and surmounted by an urn, 16in. high.
(Christie's) $12,639

A Reuge electric musical clock, with battery-driven clock movement, in Empire-style brass case with a figure of a musician, 11¹/₂in. wide, modern.
(Christie's) $425

An ormolu and red and green painted marble mantel clock, French, circa 1880, 4¹/₄in. black marked chapter ring with Roman numerals, signed *J. W. Benson, London*, 23¹/₄in.
(Bonhams) $880

A Liberty Tudric pewter clock, designed by Archibald Knox, bowed triangular face with copper dial and blue enamel center, circa 1905, 23cm. high.
(Christie's) $1,817

A Viennese automaton mantel timepiece, unsigned, the arched dial painted with religious scenes, 22¹/₄in. high.
(Christie's) $2,024

A 19th century French patinated bronze and ormolu mantel clock, the case in the form of an urn, 29cm. high.
(Phillips) $1,217

CLOCKS & WATCHES

A Napoleon III year-going great-wheel skeleton timepiece, unsigned, anchor escapement with silk-suspended short pendulum, 17¹/₂in. high. (Christie's) $3,496

A three-train quarter chiming skeleton clock, unsigned, the pierced scrolling brass frame with triple chain fusée movement, 20in. high. (Christie's) $2,392

A 19th century brass skeleton timepiece, the pierced scroll plates with chain fusée and 60 toothed escape wheel with anchor escapement, 39in. high. (Phillips) $847

A skeleton timepiece, circa 1840, 3³/₄in. silvered chapter ring with engraved Roman numerals, the single fusée movement with a lever platform escapement and brass balance wheel, 11in. (Bonhams) $1,872

A Victorian brass skeleton mantel clock, pierced silver lozenge shaped dial, plinth having escutcheon inscribed *F. Thom, Croydon*, 19in. high overall. (Peter Francis) $765

A Victorian striking skeleton clock, the pierced tracery frame with single chain fusée, anchor escapement and passing strike on bell above, 21¹/₄in. high over dome. (Christie's) $1,173

A fine chiming skeleton clock, attributed to Smiths of Clerkenwell, circa 1860, 11in. silvered chapter ring with Roman numeral cartouches surmounted by crosses, 25¹/₂in. (Bonhams) $12,578

A mid Victorian quarter striking skeleton clock, unsigned, the foliate pierced frame with six double-screws pillars and twin chain fusées, 26in. high. (Christie's) $2,944

A very rare and early electric skeleton 'slave' timepiece, Shepherd, circa 1880, 6¹/₂in. silvered chapter ring with Roman numerals, with a mahogany battery box, 14¹/₂in. (Bonhams) $8,708

SKELETON CLOCKS

A 19th century brass skeleton timepiece, the fusée movement with anchor escapement and passing strike, 47cm. high.
(Phillips) $490

Charles MacDowalls, St. John's, Wakefield, a mid-19th century brass skeleton timepiece of simple cut design, 24cm. high.
(Bearne's) $3,696

A brass skeleton timepiece with passing strike, English, 1880, on an oval velvet and rosewood base, 13¼in. high.
(Bonhams) $806

A Victorian striking skeleton clock, Franklin & Co., Manchester, the pierced frame with six double-screwed pillars, twin chain fusées, anchor escapement with steel-suspended pendulum, 18½in. high.
(Christie's) $1,806

A modern reproducion model of Harrison's Timekeeper, Sinclair Harding, Cheltenham, H–020, the seven pillar pierced frame with going barrel and silvered Roman dial with blued moon hands, 18½in. high over glazed case.
(Christie's) $1,986

A Directoire ormolu, white marble and jeweled enamel striking skeleton clock, the enamel by Joseph Coteau, the signature plaque below signed *Laurent à Paris* within a mother-of-pearl border, 17¾in. high.
(Christie's) $64,500

A Victorian skeleton clock, the pierced brass frame with four double-screwed pillars, single chain fusée, anchor escapement, passing strike on bell above, 17¾in. high, over dome.
(Christie's) $812

A Napoleon III great-wheel glass-plate skeleton timepiece of long duration, unsigned, circa 1870, 9¼in. high.
(Christie's) $1,840

A skeleton timepiece with passing strike, circa 1860, 6¼in., the single fusée movement with a half dead beat escapement, 15in.
(Bonhams) $562

WALL CLOCKS

A 19th century giltwood wall timepiece, the case decorated with carved foliate scrolls, signed for *Tree, 121 Gt Dover St, London*, 99cm. high.
(Phillips) $1,195

19th century French clock, mounted on a silvered plaque decorated with flowers, scrolls and foliage, movement by Bion Caburet, Paris, 10in. high.
(Ewbank) $633

A French First Consulate Sedan clock, the movement with a pull repeat ting tang, inscribed *Courvoisier Freres*, 1801–04.
(Woolley & Wallis) $1,582

An early Victorian mother-of-pearl-inlaid ebony and rosewood striking octagonal wall clock, James McCabe, Royal Exchange, London. 2438, the case with rosewood box.
(Christie's) $1,534

A Black Forest walnut quarter chiming wall clock, by Beha, the circular repainted dial inscribed *Morath Bros., Liverpool*, the triple fusée movement with wooden plates striking on two bells, 62cm. high.
(Phillips) $2,926

A George III mahogany wall timepiece, the brass dial signed *Tim Y. Corp London* within the Roman and Arabic chapter ring, 12in. dial diameter.
(Christie's) $2,208

Mahogany cased wall clock, the octagonal surround inlaid with mother of pearl scrolls, by H. Gunton of Norwich, mid 19th century, 19in. high.
(G. A. Key) $418

A late George III mahogany dial clock, convex glazed brass bezel to the convex cream painted wood Roman dial signed *Massey, Strand, London*, pierced blued hands, dial 14in. diameter.
(Christie's) $1,714

A Black Forest trumpeter clock, unsigned, the pierced brass-frame movement with anchor escapement, 17½in. high.
(Christie's) $1,067

228

WALL CLOCKS

Ionic calendar clock, circa 1852–1865, by E. Ingraham Clock Co., walnut veneered case with gold paint around rims, eight-day movement, 30in. high.
(Eldred's) $825

An 18th century circular enameled wall clock, the white enamel face with Roman numerals, 80cm. high.
(Finarte) $10,347

A George II giltwood cartel clock by Thomas Chappell, in a pierced rockwork and flowerhead frame surmounted by a splayed eagle finial, 34 x 24in.
(Christie's) $7,268

A George II black painted pantry alarm wall clock, the 7in. dial signed *John Wood Stroud*, movement with anchor escapement and alarm on bell above, 11³/₄in. high.
(Christie's) $1,563

A Regency mahogany drop-dial striking wall clock, Joel Phillips, London, the cream painted dial with Roman chapters and blued spade hands, 21in. high.
(Christie's) $2,024

A German mahogany wall alarm timepiece with pull quarter repeat, unsigned, the foliate engraved breakarch dial with Roman and Arabic chapter ring, 11¹/₂in. high.
(Christie's) $2,760

Rosewood octagon wall timepiece, Joseph Ives, New York, circa 1830, with thirty day wagon-spring movement, 25¹/₂in. high.
(Skinner) $1,380

A 19th century circular mahogany wall clock, the 14in. circular convex painted dial signed *Whitehurst & Son, Derby*, 41cm. diameter.
(Phillips) $1,309

A 19th century mahogany and cut brass inlaid drop dial wall timepiece, the 12in. repainted dial inscribed *Martin, Baskett & Co., Cheltenham* with later brass bezel, 51cm. diameter.
(Phillips) $462

WALL CLOCKS

A George III ormolu cartel clock by Matthew Boulton, the circular enameled dial with both Roman and Arabic numerals, 8½in. wide. (Christie's)

$30,694

A good Edwardian marquetry rosewood bracket clock with repeat, the arched brass and silvered dial with subsidiary dials, 61cm. and matching bracket. (Bearne's)

$5,049

An oak cased tavern wall timepiece, early 19th century, 30in. painted dial with Roman numerals, signed *Hopkins, Tuxford*, 5ft. 2in. (Bonhams)

$2,419

A Regency mahogany balloon clock, John Johnson, Grays Inn Passage, the waisted brass line-inlaid case with pineapple finial, 28in. high. (Christie's)

$4,784

An attractive late 19th century walnut Vienna regulator wall clock, the circular white enameled chapter ring with black Roman numerals, 43in. high. (Spencer's) $918

A Federal banjo clock, Oliver Gerrish, Portland, Maine, circa 1820, with an eglomisé tablet depicting buildings and a river, 40in. high. (Christie's)

$51,750

A Victorian figured walnut longcase wall clock, the circular cream enameled dial with maker's name *R. Hillaby, Glossop Road, Sheffield*, 62in. high. (Spencer's)

$2,525

An oak gothic wall timepiece, Short & Mason, London, circa 1860, the single fusée movement in a honey oak case, spire pediment, 29¼in. (Bonhams) $774

WALL CLOCKS

A walnut veneered petite sonnerie wall regulator, Austrian, circa 1870, unsigned, the triple-train weight driven movement with a dead-beat escapement, 3ft. 9in. (Bonhams)

$2,419

A black and gold paint Act of Parliament clock, Richd Lord, Farringdon, movement 18th century, case later, 46in. high. (Christie's)

$1,472

A fine Austrian walnut, kingwood, ebonized and parcel-gilt wall regulator, unsigned, circa 1780, 6ft. 7in. high. (Christie's)

$17,152

A 19th century Dutch oak Staartklok, the arched hood above a shaped trunk with glazed pendulum aperture, 97cm. high. (Phillips) $847

A small mahogany weight-driven wall regulator, J. Frodsham, London, circa 1840, 4ft. 7in. (Bonhams)

$3,120

A walnut spring driven wall regulator, Chapman, Oxford, circa 1860, 10in. silvered dial with engraved Arabic numerals, glazed trunk door with Gothic detail, 5ft. 2in. (Bonhams)

$2,258

An Austrian ebonized and parcel-gilt rack clock, the silvered rococo dial with Roman and Arabic chapter ring, circa 1780, 30in. high. (Christie's)

$5,055

A Biedermeier mahogany and boxwood-lined nine-light wall regulator, unsigned, circa 1820, brass trellis-cast bezel to the convex white enamel Roman dial, 38in. high. (Christie's)

$7,360

A Swiss silver keyless double-dialed triple calendar and moonphase world time pocketwatch, unsigned, 56mm. diameter.
(Christie's) $2,944

A Swiss gold hunter cased minute repeating keyless lever watch with perpetual calendar, signed *Henry Capt, Geneve*, 53mm. diameter.
(Phillips) $8,580

A silver pair cased verge alarm watch, the movement signed *Viner Patentee, London, 496*, with enamel dial, 1818, 57mm. diameter.
(Phillips) $1,014

A two color gold keyless openface perpetual calendar dress watch, signed *E. Gubelin, Lucerne*, No. 15420, circa 1930s, 44mm. diameter.
(Christie's) $8,280

A late 17th century quarter repeating verge pocketwatch movement, signed *Decharmes, London*, the gold champlevé dial with Roman numerals, 42mm. diameter.
(Christie's) $1,840

An early 19th century gold and enamel verge pocketwatch, signed *G. Archard & Fils, Geneve*, circa 1810, 48mm. diameter.
(Christie's) $4,416

An 18ct. gold quarter repeating watch, the movement signed *Grimalde & Johnson, London, No. 5619*, the case marked *London, 1811*, 56mm. diameter.
(Phillips) $1,716

A Swiss keyless lever watch of arched design, the bow folding down to provide a stand, 51mm. high.
(Phillips) $296

An unusual 18ct. gold rectangular keyless pocketwatch, unsigned, circa 1930s, the rectangular case with hinged back, 49 x 30mm.
(Christie's) $920

An interesting Adam and Eve automaton and calendar verge pocketwatch, unsigned, the frosted gilt fusée movement with bridgecock, 58mm. diameter.
(Christie's) $2,024

An 18ct. gold half hunter cased keyless lever split second chronograph, signed for *Baume*, the case marked for *London*, *1909*, 52mm. diameter.
(Phillips) $1,716

A fine early 19th century Swiss quarter repeating ruby cylinder in a gold open face case, signed *Vaucher Freres*, circa 1815, 56mm. diameter.
(Pieces of Time) $2,601

An 18th century Swiss verge with calendar in a fine gold and enamel case, signed *Philippe Terrot*, circa 1775, 55mm. diameter.
(Pieces of Time) $5,202

An unusual gold and enamel keyless square dress watch, signed *European Watch and Clock Co. Inc.*, *Cartier* on the dial, 1920s, 40mm. square.
(Christie's) $3,680

A mid 18th century English verge in gilt metal pair cases covered in shagreen, signed *Ben Pullan, Leeds*, circa 1765, 45mm. diameter.
(Pieces of Time) $1,056

A gilt metal pair cased verge stopwatch, the movement with pierced cock signed *Grant, London, No. 2290*, 57mm. diameter.
(Phillips) $1,279

An 18ct. gold and turquoise-set helmet with concealed watch, signed *Tiffany & Co.*, movement signed *Movado*, circa 1960, 43mm. high.
(Christie's) $4,345

A gold skeletonized keyless lever dress watch, signed *Gimeau*, modern, the plain gold case glazed both sides, 15mm. diameter.
(Christie's) $2,944

WATCHES

A silver masonic watch, Solvil Watch Co., circa 1930, triangular mother of pearl dial with masonic symbols, 55mm. (Bonhams) **$1,371**

Swiss, a gold keyless quarter repeating chronograph hunter pocketwatch, unsigned, circa 1900, weep center seconds operated by a button in the band, gold decorative hands, 59mm. diameter. (Christie's) **$1,625**

An open faced gun metal calendar watch, Swiss, circa 1900, enamel dial with Roman numerals, 68mm. (Bonhams) **$564**

A Continental niello and gilt highlighted keyless lever watch, the case depicting a group of card players, and a pair of snooker players, 45mm. diameter. (Phillips) **$262**

An early 18th century silver pair case calendar verge pocketwatch, signed *D. Decharmes, London*, silver champlevé dial with blued steel beetle and poker hands, 55mm. diameter. (Christie's) **$1,625**

A German keyless lever watch, the movement jeweled to the centre and signed *A. Lange & Sohn, Glashutte, Dresden, 30947*, 49mm. diameter. (Phillips) **$1,617**

An 1890s gold openface keyless minute repeating perpetual calendar pocketwatch, signed *Patek Philippe & Co., Geneve*, number 80963, 1890, the plain case with ribbed rim and bezel with cuvette, 54mm. diameter. (Christie's) **$45,138**

A Swiss gold hunter cased minute repeating keyless lever chronograph with calendar, the engine-turned case with stop and repeat buttons in the band, 60mm. diameter. (Phillips) **$3,080**

Swiss, a gold keyless quarter repeating triple calendar and moonphase chronograph hunter pocketwatch, unsigned, circa 1910, repeating the hours and quarters on two gongs, 57mm. diameter. (Christie's) **$3,611**

WATCHES

A late 18th century French gold verge watch, the movement in the form of a twin-handled vase, in a gold case stamped *FLP*, 55mm. diameter.
(Phillips) $3,080

Swiss, an unusual gold crab's-claw duplex and mock-pendulum hunter pocketwatch, unsigned, circa mid-19th century, the white enamel dial painted with the design of a clock, 48mm. diameter.
(Christie's) $1,714

A silver open faced quarter repeating verge erotic watch, French, circa 1820, enamel dial with Roman numerals and concealed through the dial, 54mm.
(Bonhams) $2,258

An 18th century gold pair cased verge watch, the movement with square baluster pillars and pierced bridge cock, signed *Willm Story, London, No. 5180*, 47mm. diameter.
(Phillips) $2,156

A silver pair cased verge watch, Fabian Robins, circa 1700, silver repoussé dial with Roman and Arabic numerals, signed, 55mm.
(Bonhams) $905

A George III gilt metal verge watch and pedometer, the movement with pierced cock signed *Ralph Gout, London 68 'By the Kings letters Patent'*, 54mm. diameter.
(Phillips) $554

A nickel triangular case masonic pocket watch, French/English, mid-19th century, in a case with a red stone set in the pendant, 75 x 85mm.
(Bonhams) $2,741

A fine triple case silver and tortoiseshell verge pocketwatch made for the Turkish market, signed *Isaac Rogers, London*, No. 19135, 1795, 76mm. diameter.
(Christie's) $5,520

A German keyless lever watch, the movement with micrometer regulation, signed *Deutsche Uhren-fabrikation Glashutte 55954*, 49mm. diameter.
(Phillips) $1,232

WATCHES

A late 18th century Swiss verge in a pearl set gold and enamel case, full plate gilt fusée movement, circa 1790, 50mm. diameter.
(Pieces of Time) $5,508

Swiss, an 18ct. gold minute repeating automaton jacquemarts keyless lever hunter-cased watch, circa 1890, 54mm. diameter.
(Christie's) $7,725

A late 19th century Swiss lever in a gold and enamel full hunter case, signed *Gme Hri Guye, Geneve, 8325,* circa 1880, 40mm. diameter.
(Pieces of Time) $2,639

An 18ct. gold half hunter cased keyless lever watch, the movement signed *Dent, London, Patent No. 29085,* the case marked *London, 1878,* 51mm. diameter.
(Phillips) $1,170

An 18ct. gold keyless lever minute repeating, split-seconds chronograph openface watch with perpetual calendar and moonphases, signed *Audemars Piguet,* circa 1979, 50mm. diameter.
(Christie's) $62,000

A gold keyless minute repeating chronograph hunter pocketwatch, signed on the case *Fabrique Germinal, Chaux-de-Fonds,* No. 200575, circa 1890s, 62mm. diameter.
(Christie's) $3,312

A silver gilt and enamel triple time-zone and calendar verge pocketwatch, unsigned, 1800s, the silver gilt case with painted enamel portrait of Napoleon, 64mm. diameter.
(Christie's) $3,680

A Swiss gold hunter cased minute repeating keyless lever chronograph, the cuvette signed *Le Phare, No. 74944,* the case applied with a two-headed Russian eagle, 59mm. diameter.
(Phillips) $3,588

An early silver pair cased verge watch, Peter Perier, London, circa 1680, silver repoussé dial with Roman and Arabic and mock pendulum aperture, 55mm.
(Bonhams) $3,040

WATCHES

An 18th century quarter repeating verge by LeRoy in a gold and enamel consular case, signed, circa 1760, 45mm. diameter.
(Pieces of Time) $5,279

A gold keyless minute repeating chronograph hunter pocketwatch, signed *Le Phare*, white enamel dial with Roman numerals, 59mm. diameter.
(Christie's) $3,680

An early 19th century Swiss quarter repeating automaton verge in a silver open face case, full plate fusée movement, circa 1810, 58mm. diameter.
(Pieces of Time) $4,208

An 18ct. Swiss gold and enamel quarter repeating musical automaton keywound openface watch with erotic scene, unsigned, early 19th century, 58mm. diameter.
(Christie's) $48,300

A late 17th century German silver pair case verge watch, signed *Heinrich Pepfenhauser*, circa 1700, the frosted gilt fusée movement with pierced decorative pillars, 59mm. diameter.
(Christie's) $6,440

An 18ct. gold pair case cylinder pocketwatch, signed *Thos. Mudge London*, No. 553, 1787, the frosted gilt fusée movement with steel cylinder escapement, 52mm. diameter.
(Christie's) $2,299

A 19th century English lever with gold dial in a decorative gold full hunter case, signed *Johnstone, Liverpool, 36824*, hallmarked *London 1865*, 52mm. diameter.
(Pieces of Time) $2,066

An 18ct. gold hunter cased keyless lever chronograph, the movement with visible stopwork signed *T. R. Russell, Liverpool, no. 89844*, marked *London, 1893*, 54mm. diameter.
(Phillips) $1,560

A Swiss quarter repeating cylinder in a gold pearl set case decorated with an enamel miniature, full plate gilt fusée movement, circa 1800, 51mm. diameter.
(Pieces of Time) $5,738

WRIST WATCHES

A gold self winding calendar wristwatch, signed *Piaget*, circa 1970s, the gilt textured dial with date aperture, 33 x 30mm. (Christie's) $2,024

A bi-colour automatic bracelet watch, Rolex Datejust, circa 1980, gilt dial with baton numerals, on a matching Jubilee bracelet, 35mm. (Bonhams) $1,520

Breitling, a stainless steel 'Navitimer' chronograph wristwatch, with milled rotating bezel and snap-on back. (Bearne's) $673

A 1950s pink gold Calatrava wristwatch, signed *Patek Philippe, Geneve*, No. 969056, the signed movement jewled to the center with alloy balance and micrometer regulation, 30mm. diameter. (Christie's) $5,417

An 18ct. gold dodecagonal wristwatch with date, signed *Corum, Admirals Cup*, recent, the matt cream dial with signal flags as the numerals, 34mm. diameter. (Christie's) $2,415

An early gold single button chronograph wristwatch, unsigned, 1930s, the white enamel dial with outer blue, red and green tachymetric scales inscribed *Chronometre 'Le Roy'*, 37mm. diameter. (Christie's) $3,250

An 18ct. gold and diamond set calendar quartz wristwatch, signed *Audemars Piguet*, circa 1980s, with quartz movement, 34mm. diameter. (Christie's) $3,680

An early gold wristwatch, signed *Audemars Piguet, Geneve*, circa 1920s, the nickel finished movement with 19 jewels, 32mm. diameter. (Christie's) $1,840

A white gold wristwatch, signed *Breguet*, No. 2162, recent; the matt silvered dial with Roman numerals, lapis lazuli centerfield, 30mm. square. (Christie's) $6,440

WRIST WATCHES

A gold and diamond set quartz wristwatch, signed *Vacheron & Constantin, Geneve*, circa 1980s, with quartz movement, 30 x 25mm.
(Christie's) $8,832

Patek Philippe, a lady's gold wristwatch, signed, 1970s, the nickel finished movement with 20 jewels.
(Christie's) $2,760

An 18ct. gold and diamond-set self-winding wristwatch, signed *Blancpain*, recent, with nickel finished lever movement, 28mm. diameter.
(Christie's) $8,700

A steel automatic calendar Royal Oak water resistant wristwatch, signed *Audemars Piguet*, No. A930, 1980s, textured gray dial with raised steel baton numerals, 39mm. diameter.
(Christie's) $2,760

A rare gold circular wristwatch with bracelet, signed *Cartier*, model 'Roue Squelette a Heures Points D'or', movement by European Watch and Clock Co. Inc., circa 1950s, 35mm. diameter.
(Christie's) $36,800

An early gold wristwatch, signed *Vacheron Constantin Geneve*, number 386873, circa 1920s, the nickel plated bar movement jeweled to third with bimetallic balance and lever escapement, 30mm. square.
(Christie's) $4,694

A rare steel square chronograph wristwatch, signed *Rolex*, model 3529, 1930s, the nickel plated movement jeweled to the center, 25mm. square.
(Christie's) $10,120

An 18ct. gold self winding moonphase wristwatch with power reserve, signed *Patek Philippe, Geneve*, No. 1959383, recent, 35mm. diameter.
(Christie's) $16,560

A gold self winding calendar wristwatch, signed *Rolex, Oyster Perpetual Datejust*, circa 1950s, with automatic movement, 36mm. diameter.
(Christie's) $6,072

WRIST WATCHES

An early silver wristwatch, signed *Rolex* and *W & D*, 1917, the black enamel dial with Arabic numerals and subsidiary seconds, 32mm. square.
(Christie's) $903

A gold waterproof chronograph wristwatch, signed *Lecoultre Co.*, circa 1950, the nickel-finished lever movement with 17 jewels, 35mm. diameter.
(Christie's) $3,611

Cartier, a gold steel quartz Panthere calendar wristwatch, signed, date aperture at III, secret signature at VII, sweep center seconds, 29mm. square.
(Christie's) $1,806

Swiss, a 9ct. gold masonic wristwatch, unsigned, circa 1940, silvered matt dial with masonic symbols for the numerals, blued steel hands, tonneau shaped case, 30mm. long.
(Christie's) $631

Swiss, an unusual gold wristwatch with enamel dial, unsigned, 1950s, the enamel dial with map of Arabic states at the center, black enamel chapter ring with applied Arabic numerals, 36mm. diameter.
(Christie's) $2,347

A steel limited edition Christobel C automatic astronomical wristwatch, signed *Longines*, No. 5253 0486, snap-on back with enameled insignia and sailing ship motif, 38mm. diameter.
(Christie's) $1,353

Universal, a steel triple calendar and moonphase wristwatch, signed, with mechanical movement, the brushed silvered dial with Arabic numerals, 32mm. diameter.
(Christie's) $1,353

Jaeger-LeCoultre, an unusual gold day/date calendar wristwatch, signed, 1950s, outer date ring with central date hand, aperture below 12 for the day in German, 30mm. diameter.
(Christie's) $867

Rolex, a steel self-winding waterproof bubble back wristwatch, signed *Rolex, Oyster Perpetual*, circa 1940s, with jewled nickel finished lever movement, 32mm. diameter.
(Christie's) $1,806

WRIST WATCHES

A rare special edition Il Destriero Scafusia perpetual calendar, minute repeating, split second chronograph tourbillon wristwatch, signed *International Watch Co.*, 42mm. diameter.
(Christie's) $123,245

A steel chronograph wristwatch, signed *Universal, Geneve, Uni-Compax*, 1940s, circular case with down turned lugs, 35mm. diameter.
(Christie's) $722

A pink gold chronograph wristwatch, signed *Omega Watch Co*, 1950s, the pink gilt movement jeweled to the center with gold alloy balance, 37mm. diameter.
(Christie's) $1,806

Rolex, a 1930s 9ct. gold tonneau wristwatch, signed, 1934, the nickel plated ultra prima precision movement jeweled to the third, with engraved presentation, import mark Glasgow 1934, 29 x 21mm.
(Christie's) $1,083

An 18ct. pink gold automatic calendar water-resistant chronograph wristwatch, signed *Girard-Perregaux, GP4900*, the engine-turned silvered dial with hatched center field and polished Roman chapter ring, 38mm. diameter.
(Christie's) $4,694

A steel self-winding chronograph calendar wristwatch, signed *Breitling, Geneve, model Navitimer Chrono-matic*, the black dial with luminous baton numerals, 48mm. diameter.
(Christie's) $1,083

Swiss, a gold single button chronograph wristwatch, unsigned, circa 1920s, the nickel finished jeweled lever movement with bi-metallic balance, 32mm. diameter.
(Christie's) $1,353

Jaeger-LeCoultre, a gentleman's gold rectangular wristwatch with unusual D-shaped lugs, signed, 1930s, the nickel plated movement jeweled to the third, 28 x 23mm.
(Christie's) $722

Rolex, a steel Oyster Perpetual Explorer chronometer wristwatch, signed, with automatic movement, the black dial with raised luminous baton numerals, 36mm. diameter.
(Christie's) $1,714

WRIST WATCHES

A stainless steel chronograph wristwatch, Jaeger, circa 1940, silvered dial with quarter Roman numerals, 35mm. (Bonhams) **$450**

Rolex, a 9ct. gold Rolex Oyster wristwatch, the cream dial with subsidiary seconds dial and signed *Rolex Oyster Ultra Prima*. (Bearne's) **$2,142**

An 18ct. gold wristwatch, signed *Cartier*, model Vendome, circa 1980, the white dial with Roman numerals, secret signature at VII, 33mm. diameter. (Christie's) **$2,400**

Rolex, a gentleman's gold wristwatch, signed, circa 1945, the circular case with milled bezel and five minute divisions with snap-on back, 35mm. diameter. (Christie's) **$1,986**

A gold and diamond set dresswatch, signed *Corum*, circa 1980s, black dial with diamond set numerals, 40mm. wide. (Christie's) **$4,416**

Patek Philippe, a small 18ct. gold rectangular wristwatch, signed, number 1394678, the nickel plated movement jeweled to the center with 18 jewels, 25 x 22mm. (Christie's) **$2,798**

An 18ct. gold 'Rolls Royce radiator' wristwatch, signed *Corum, Patented*, recent, with jeweled nickel-finished lever movement, 40mm. wide. (Christie's) **$2,898**

A silver and enamel sports watch, Dunhill/Tavannes, circa 1930, in rectangular case decorated in black, blue and green enamel, 45 x 35mm. (Bonhams) **$1,451**

A stainless steel chronograph wristwatch, Longines, circa 1960, the 19-jewel nickel movement in a polished case with stepped lugs, 38mm. (Bonhams) **$830**

WRIST WATCHES

A steel hour angle pilot's watch, signed *Longines*, Lindbergh model, No. 5575308, circa 1930s, the gilt finished movement with 15 jewels, 47mm. diameter.
(Christie's) $6,256

A stainless steel reversible wristwatch with sweep center-seconds, signed *Jaeger Le Coultre*, model Reverso, circa 1945, 33mm. long.
(Christie's) $3,670

An 18ct. gold wristwatch with date and moonphases, signed *Cartier*, model Pasha, recent, with quartz movement, 38mm. diameter.
(Christie's) $8,210

A gold and diamond set ladies wristwatch with bracelet, signed *Piaget*, circa 1980s, mono-metallic balance, gilt textured dial with applied baton numerals, 27mm. diameter.
(Christie's) $4,514

An 18ct. gold and diamond-set 'Mickey Mouse' octagonal wristwatch with bracelet, signed *Gerald Genta, Geneve*, recent, 32mm. diameter.
(Christie's) $9,650

A gold automatic triple calendar and moonphase wristwatch, signed *Gubelin*, 1950s, the square gold case with fluted lugs and domed crystal, 32mm. square.
(Christie's) $7,222

An 18ct. gold 'crash' wristwatch, signed *Cartier*, No. 073/400, circa 1991, with nickel finished lever movement, 17 jewels, 39mm. long.
(Christie's) $13,500

An 18ct. gold rectangular calendar quartz wristwatch, signed *Audemars Piguet*, circa 1970–80s, with quartz movement, 29 x 38mm.
(Christie's) $5,888

A lady's 18ct. gold bracelet watch, Cartier 'Panthère', modern, Swiss made quartz movement, in a polished case, 21mm.
(Bonhams) $5,150

A silver-mounted holly wood salt throne, the mounts cloisonné enameled with scrollwork and flowerheads, St. Petersburg, 1896–1903, 3¹/₂in. (Christie's) $492

An Imperial cloisonné enamel and gilt-bronze vessel and cover modeled as a mythical tiger, the crouching animal with long curling tail, incised Qianlong four-character mark and of the period, 21cm. long. (Christie's) $60,858

A cloisonné enamel and hardwood table screen, of square shape depicting two deer and two cranes in a lakescape, Qianlong/Jiaqing, 47.8cm. high. (Christie's) $3,703

An unusual gilt-metal-mounted cloisonné enamel globular vase, with waisted neck and spreading foot, the shoulders with taotie masks suspending loose rings, Qianlong, 40.5cm. high. (Sotheby's) $20,240

A large cloisonné enamel vase, hu, decorated with birds and bats flying among a fruiting peach tree, citrus and pomegranate, 18th/19th century, 40.5cm. high. (Christie's) $4,629

A cloisonné enamel moonflask, the body with dragons surrounded by continuous lotus meander reserved on a turquoise ground, 17th century, 20.3cm. high. (Christie's) $5,555

A Namikawa oviform cloisonné vase, decorated with various colored enamels and wire with cockerels, chicks and flying sparrows, late 19th century, 17.5cm. high. (Christie's) $22,080

A cloisonné enamel and gilt-bronze incense burner and cover, decorated with a dense archaistic dragon scrollwork design in dark blue on a turquoise ground, Qianlong, 19.5cm. high. (Christie's) $2,222

A cloisonné enamel vase, fang gu, the exterior decorated with archaistic phoenixes and dissolved masks, 17th/early 18th century, 37.5cm. high. (Christie's) $3,703

A silver-gilt beaker, cloisonné enameled with mythical birds within blue and white borders, A. Postnikov, Moscow, late 19th century, 5¾in.
(Christie's) $528

A cloisonné enamel and gilt-bronze flask, loosely modeled after a Han prototype with broad flattened body, garlic neck and phoenix-head handles, 20.7cm. high.
(Sotheby's) $8,830

A Namikawa cloisonné vase, the body separated into panels with the design of butterflies and flowers, signed, late 19th century, 15.5cm. high.
(Christie's) $11,960

A large ormolu-mounted cloisonné enamel alms bowl, decorated around the exterior with cranes, magpies and other birds flying among lotus and other flowers, 19th century, 41cm. high.
(Christie's) $3,703

A massive cloisonné enamel basin, with slightly flaring sides, decorated on the exterior with a herd of deer and a flock of crane in a continuous mountainous riverscape. late 18th century, 64cm. diameter.
(Christie's) $20,367

A large cloisonné enamel vase, hu, decorated with bands of archaistic animal motifs, cicada panels containing masks and formal patterns on a lotus-meander ground, 19th century, 45cm. high.
(Christie's) $5,184

A Meiping shaped cloisonné vase in shaded gray and white with blossom-laden branches of a cherry tree, sealed *Namikawa Sosuke* (1847–1910), 22.8cm. high.
(Christie's) $38,399

A rare large cloisonné enamel and gilt-bronze altar ornament, the lotus flower and pod, top knop raised on a flanged double-baluster stem, Qianlong, 47.8cm. high.
(Sotheby's) $5,900

A cloisonné enamel incense burner and cover, decorated with lotus meander, ruyi bands and lozenges containing wan symbols, Qianlong/Jiaqing, 29.5cm. high.
(Christie's) $2,250

Large ship's wheel, in walnut with brass hub, inscribed *SS Scargo Manor*, 78in. diameter. (Eldred's) $660

A brass hand warmer of spherical form, pierced and engraved with flowerheads and foliage, 19th century, 5in. diameter. (Christie's) $200

Copper jelly mold in the form of a castle. (G. A. Key) $260

Pair of brass candlesticks, 19th century, one push-up missing, 12in. high. (Eldred's) $143

Gustav Stickley hammered copper plaque, No. 344, original bronze patina and decorated with stylized spades on wide rim, impressed mark, 15in. diameter. (Skinner) $10,350

Two brass church candlesticks on tripod base with three ball and claw feet, 59cm. high. (Herholdt Jensen) $332

A chrome and brass coffee machine with porcelain handles by Chardone & Cie, gas powered, 1910–30. (Arnold Frankfurt) $360

A pair of brass Lucas King of the Road No. 621 oil sidelights, each 26cm. high. (Onslow's) $240

Antique cast brass footed candlestick, 9in. high. (Eldred's) $165

Copper and brass kettle, early 20th century, 10in. high. (G. A. Key) $92

A brass Lucifer center acetylene headlight, 27cm. high; together with generator. (Onslow's) $190

Large copper hot water can with swing handle and hinged lid, English, early 20th century. (G. A. Key) $85

A 19th century brass ship's binnacle compass with illumination chamber, stamped *Patt 01151A*, 9¹/₂in. high. (Phillips) $889

A 19th century German brass alms dish with central motif of the Virgin and Child, 40cm. diameter. (Kunsthaus am Museum) $871

A. Reiss brass coffee pot on stand, Austria, orange finial on dome lid and spout, 13in. high. (Skinner) $259

Art Deco brass figural cigarette holder, circa 1935, unsigned, 9³/₄in. high. (Skinner) $173

Pair of oak and brass bound spirit barrels, copper labels inscribed *Gin* and *Rum*, English, 19th century, 12¹/₂in. (G. A. Key) $585

A large oak pitcher, brass-bound, of coopered construction, English, late 19th/ early 20th century, 23in. high. (Christie's) $177

A brass and copper cash register, National Cash Register Co., Dayton, Ohio, late 19th/ early 20th century.
(Christie's) $575

A George III brass bushel grain measure, engraved to one side *Lincolnshire Lindsey, Spilsby, Brackenbury. Clerk. of. ye. Peace 1793*, 25in. diameter.
(Christie's) $4,724

A steel and brass book press, supported by spirally-turned columns on a rectangular base with bracket feet, 9¼in. wide.
(Christie's) $1,560

Two of a set of six Victorian brass altar candlesticks, with dentil-cut drip-pans above cylindrical stems bisected with circular platforms mounted with cabochon paste bosses, 22¾in. high.
(Christie's) $1,700

A pair of brass wall pricket sconces, the scrolling branches on later molded beech brackets, Continental, probably 19th century, 18in. protrudence.
(Christie's) $1,293

A pair of brass floor standing altar candlesticks, the repoussé baluster columns with gadrooned and foliate ornament, Northern European, 19th century, 62½in. high.
(Christie's) $2,957

A brass desk set, English or Continental, 18th century, a circular handle above a brass urn-shaped centerpiece with two urn-shaped candleholders, 7¼in. high.
(Christie's) $4,830

A brass and iron dough-scraper, attributed to Peter Derr, Tulpehocken Township, Berkshire County, Pennsylvania, dated *1847*, 4in. long.
(Sotheby's) $1,495

A copper and brass hot water kettle, signed *E. Miller, Pennsylvania. 1780–1825*, the body with domed lid, 16¼in. long.
(Sotheby's) $920

An early brass tobacco box, English, dated *1716*, of circular form with hinged lid, 3³/₄in. diameter.
(Sotheby's) $11,500

A good set of three William IV brass and copper imperial measures, the largest with loop handle and shield-shaped terminal.
(Bearne's) $672

An Eisenloeffel brass kettle on stand, the tapering cylindrical base with pierced gallery containing spirit burner, 20cm. high.
(Christie's) $460

A rare matching engraved wrought-iron and brass ladle and sieve, probably Pennsylvania, 1750–1800, each with a hook terminal, 15in. and 16³/₈in. long.
(Sotheby's) $575

A pair of covered brass bowls, E. F. Caldwell & Co., Inc., each with circular domed lid centering a grape finial, inscribed *Perrini*, 8¹/₂in. high.
(Christie's) $1,035

A rare brass-inlaid iron, copper and brass spatula, initialed *J.H.*, probably Pennsylvania, dated *1807*, with hooked handle, with date *1807*, 23¹/₄in. long.
(Sotheby's) $1,495

A Regency brass-bound copper oval-bucket of dished oval form, the arched handle above a central armorial plaque, 14¹/₂in. wide.
(Christie's) $1,010

A pair of brass altar candlesticks, with stop-fluted stems, on octagonal gadrooned bases, English or French, 17th century, 18in. high.
(Christie's) $4,965

A fine bright-cut decorated turned cherrywood, brass and wrought-iron clothes iron, American, possibly Pennsylvania, dated *1854*, 5¹/₂in. high. (Sotheby's) $1,265

A dress of saxe blue silk taffeta, trimmed with silk piping and black bobbin lace, with separate peplum, late 1860s. (Christie's) $251

A collared satin cape, printed in pink and blue with flowers, labeled in one tassel *Liberty & Co., London and Paris*. (Christie's) $302

A dress of midnight blue silk taffeta, trimmed with figured silk covered buttons, the skirts trimmed with ruched blue silk piped with satin, mid 1870s. (Christie's) $504

A gentleman's suit of striped cut velvet, comprising coat, the fronts densely embroidered with sprays of spring flowers, probably French, 18th century. (Christie's) $3,000

An unusual sleeved waistcoat, the sleeves and back knitted, the quilted fronts of blue striped satin, Spanish late 18th century. (Christie's) $216

A dress of fine white muslin, the bodice embroidered with whitework flowers, the skirts with climbing fruiting vines, early 19th century. (Christie's) $117

A dress of bottle green wool, printed with red and white striped leaves, with separate cape collar, late 1840s. (Christie's) **$1,082**

A hunt coat of bottle green facecloth and M-notched lapels, trimmed with gilt buttons of Greenock Hunt, first half 19th century. (Christie's) **$800**

A robe of pale gray chiffon, woven with peach and violet leaves and flowers, labeled in shoulder *Becker Fils*, early 1920s. (Christie's) **$755**

An evening gown of ivory silk gauze woven with satin stripes, the puff sleeves, and neck trimmed with pink satin piping, 1820–25. (Christie's) **$1,984**

A young girl's dress of white cotton with wide puff sleeves, trimmed with olive green wool embroidery, circa 1825. (Christie's) **$503**

A dress of white muslin, finely embroidered with silver scrolling leaves, trimmed with rouleaux at the hem, Indian, for a European lady, 1820–1825. (Christie's) **$2,160**

A theater coat of emerald green and black silk crêpe de chine, woven with gilt japonnaiserie chrysanthemums, labeled in sleeve seam *Chanel*, 1927. (Christie's) $9,020

A wedding dress of ivory tulle, embroidered with a border of flowers, the bodice pleated onto a V-shaped waistline, circa 1840. (Christie's) $2,165

A dress of lilac silk gauze, with rouleaux hem, the neck trimmed with twisted mauve and white piping, mid 1820s. (Christie's) $1,714

A hostess evening gown by Givenchy of lilac damask, with boat neck and front opening with four self-covered buttons, circa 1966. (Christie's) $397

A long evening dress by Givenchy of fine cut velvet revealing satin printed with Prussian blue and pale blue flowers, early 1960s. (Christie's) $541

A robe of emerald green velvet, printed in silver and gold, with slit 'mediaeval' sleeves, labeled *Gallenga, Roma, Firenze*, mid 1920s. (Christie's) $6,133

An evening dress by Givenchy of pink satin flocked with Chinoiserie trees in yellow velvet, sleeveless with boat-neck, Automne-Hiver 1967. (Christie's) $722

A jerkin of silver fox, fastening at the neck with white fur ties, labeled *Christian Dior*. (Christie's) $9,775

A long evening sheath dress by Givenchy of blue, mauve and pink vertically striped organza over silk printed with the same design, early 1970s. (Christie's) $325

A long evening dress by Givenchy, the high waisted bodice of crimson velvet with V-neck and bow at waist, the skirt of crimson satin, circa 1964. (Christie's) $433

A sleeveless long evening dress by Givenchy of alternating narrow and wide navy horizontal stripes, over an underdress of jap silk, Printemps-été 1966. (Christie's) $1,353

A 'Delphos' evening dress of pale blue pleated silk, the side seams trimmed with white murano beads, stamped on reverse *Fortuny, Dse*. (Christie's) $5,412

A Chinese bridal robe, of crimson silk satin embroidered with ten dragons among clouds and flowers, over a peony-filled sea-wave border, 19th century. (Christie's) $2,100

An unusual pair of black leather gentleman's shoes, 1720–70, of traditional form with squared toe and brass buckle, 11³/₄in. long. (Sotheby's) $1,380

A Chinese dragon robe, of blue silk worked with couched gilt threads with nine dragons among clouds and emblems, 19th century. (Christie's) $1,144

A baby's bonnet with Hollie Point insertions, worked with urns of flowers, late 18th, early 19th century. (Christie's) $318

A corset of fawn cotton, trimmed with ecru lace threaded with saxe blue ribbon, late 19th century; and a ribbon corset of blue and white bands. (Christie's) $227

A painted composition ceremonial fireman's parade hat, probably Pennsylvania,, mid-19th century, the red painted hat inscribed *Western, 1840*, 8in. high. (Sotheby's) $1,840

A lady's linen waistcoat, finely quilted in pale yellow silk with scrolling flowers, the fronts with twisted linen braid lacing loops, with flaring skirts, early 18th century. (Christie's) $2,435

A lady's corset of ivory sateen, the triangular front panels worked with an embroidered spot motif, 1820–1830. (Christie's) $541

A Chinese ladies' stole, of black silk satin with couched silver and gilt metal threads with dragons over a sea-wave border, last quarter 19th century. (Christie's) $968

A pair of ladies' shoes, of dark blue leather with grosgrain binding, the 1¹/₂in. heel covered with matching blue leather, 1790s.(Christie's) $2,886

A pair of gloves, of light brown leather with long narrow fingers, trimmed with metal lace and spangles, early 17th century. (Christie's) $397

A pair of shoes, of green silk with white brocade with pointed upturned toe, white kid rands, and 2¹/₄in. covered heel, 1730s. (Christie's) $4,329

Carved mallard, *A. Elmer Crowell Maker – East Harwich Mass*, twice marked in rectangle, 13¹/₂in. long.
(Skinner) $1,840

An American widgeon drake, attributed to Tom Wilson, Ipswich, Massachusetts, of sold construction, with glass inset eyes, retains original paint.
(Sotheby's) $1,610

A northern loon, probably Coastal Maine, with inset glass eyes with carved two-piece bill.
(Sotheby's) $10,350

A Canada goose, attributed to Tom Wilson, Ipswich, Massachusetts, of solid construction with inset glass eyes, retains original paint.
(Sotheby's) $8,050

A merganser drake, attributed to Tom Wilson, Ipswich, Massachusetts, of solid construction, with inset glass eyes, retains its original paint.
(Sotheby's) $6,612

A whistling swan, Susquehanna Flats, Maryland, late 19th century, of solid construction with painted eyes, branded *CWJ* on the underside.
(Sotheby's) $6,325

An oversized nail-bill willet, Charles Thomas, Assinippi, Massachusetts, with inset glass eyes and original iron nail bill.
(Sotheby's) $4,887

A swan, possibly by Charles Hart, Gloucester, Massachusetts, of solid three-piece construction with tack eyes and relief carving in the form of a stylized heart on the back.
(Sotheby's) $3,737

A yellowleg, attributed to Tom Wilson, Ipswich, Massachusetts, of solid construction, relief-carved wings and split tail, retains original paint.
(Sotheby's) $1,380

A flying merganser weathervane, A. E. Crowell, East Harwich, Massachusetts, with inset glass eyes and applied carved wings and carved feather tail detail.
(Sotheby's) $17,250

A pair of merganser, George Boyd, Seabrook, New Hampshire, comprising a hen and a drake, each of solid construction with inset glass eyes.
(Sotheby's) $19,550

A swimming black duck, possibly Martha's Vineyard, Massachusetts, retains original lead weight, original paint with scratch feather detail.
(Sotheby's) $3,450

A rare Bähr and Pröschild for Nöckler and Tittel bisque character doll, German, circa 1912, 15in.
(Sotheby's) $3,611

An early Bourgoin C Series Steiner Bébé, with bisque head, lever operated blue yeux fibres, 16in. high.
(Christie's) $3,020

A Jules Steiner pressed bisque doll, French, circa 1892, jointed papier-mâché body with straight wrists, 18$\frac{1}{2}$in.
(Sotheby's) $6,861

A Lehmann waltzing doll, German, early 20th century, with Lehmann mark to shoulder plate, the red-haired celluloid-headed doll in purple and white lace trimmed dress, 9in. high.
(Sotheby's) $1,460

A rare Kämmer and Reinhardt bisque character doll 'Carl', German, circa 1909, impressed *KstarR 107 55*, with closed pouty mouth, dimple in chin, 21in. high.
(Sotheby's) $42,000

A George II wooden doll, English, circa 1880, the painted gesso over wood face with rouged cheeks, pupil-less black enamel eyes, 19$\frac{1}{2}$in., paint rubbed on the nose.
(Sotheby's) $2,700

A Kämmer and Reinhardt bisque character doll 'Gretchen', German, circa 1909, with closed pouty mouth, dimple in chin, painted blue eyes, brown real hair wig, 20in.
(Sotheby's) $4,400

A Kämmer and Reinhardt bisque character 'Marie' doll, German, circa 1909, with closed pouty mouth, painted blue eyes, brown mohair wig, 19$\frac{1}{2}$in. high.
(Sotheby's) $4,750

A Jules Steiner pressed bisque doll, French, circa 1885, with open/closed mouth and dimple in chin, fixed blue glass paperweight eyes, pierced ears, 16$\frac{1}{2}$in. high.
(Sotheby's) $8,775

A rare early standing bisque doll, with molded hat an luster geather, in blue frock, 4¹/₂in. high, 1860s. (Christie's) $622

A large Kammer & Reinhardt 117 character doll, jointed wood and composition body, dressed in blue cotton frock, 28¹/₂in. (Christie's) $8,527

An Emile Jumeau pressed bisque doll, French, circa 1875, with open/closed mouth showing white between lips, 26in. (Sotheby's) $11,194

A Leopold Lambert musical automaton of a flower seller, French, circa 1880, the Jumeau head stamped in red *Deposé TÊTÊ JUMEAU Bte. S.G.D.G. 4*, with closed mouth, 19in., mechanism sluggish. (Sotheby's) $10,600

A rare and fine painted wooden doll, German, circa 1790, the head and torso carved in one piece, painted face with well defined features, 21in., some repainting to head. (Sotheby's) $3,650

A Schmitt et Fils pressed bisque doll, French, circa 1880, with closed mouth showing white between lips, fixed blue glass paperweight eyes, pierced ears, blonde mohair wig, 24in. high. (Sotheby's) $10,600

A Jules Steiner bisque doll, French, circa 1892, with closed mouth and dimple in chin, fixed blue glass paperweight eyes, pierced ears, brown mohair wig, 18¹/₂in. high. (Sotheby's) $7,300

A Gebrüder Heubach bisque character doll, German, circa 1912, impressed *6969 12* with sunburst mark, with pouty mouth, weighted blue glass eyes, 27in. high. (Sotheby's) $5,485

A good Simon and Halbig bisque character doll, German, circa 1920, with open/closed mouth, small weighted blue glass eyes, blonde mohair wig, 19¹/₂in. high. (Sotheby's) $5,485

A Jules Steiner pressed bisque doll, French, circa 1885, papier-mâché body, in blue dress and matching bonnet, 16¹/₂in.
(Sotheby's) $5,055

A Schoenau and Hoffmeister bisque head doll, with blonde mohair wig, sleeping eyes, open mouth with four teeth.
(Woolley & Wallis) $600

Lord Kitchener, a composition-headed doll, stuffed body, dressed in original uniform, 18¹/₂in. high, circa 1915.
(Christie's) $746

A Schoenau and Hoffmeister bisque china head doll, impressed *1909. 3*, having auburn wig, closing brown glass eyes, 52cm.
(Bearne's) $345

Two rare turned and painted wooden dolls, with added arms akimbo, one with wide flat 'straw' hat, 4³/₄in. high, South German, circa 1750.
(Christie's) $497

A Kammer and Reinhardt child doll, with blue lashed sleeping eyes, short blonde wig, jointed body and contemporary embroidered silk frock, 17¹/₄in. high.
(Christie's) $1,410

An early Grodnertal doll, with papier mâché head, high piled elaborate hairstyle, dressed in contemporary cotton print, 12in. high, circa 1830.
(Christie's) $1,155

A bisque headed doll with blue sleeping eyes, smiling mouth, fair hair, stamped *173.3* with jointed limbs, 14in. high.
(Anderson & Garland) $1,938

A Simon & Halbig Kammer & Reinhardt bisque socket head walking girl doll, with long blonde mohair wig, blue glass closing eyes, 15in. high.
(Spencer's) $747

A Käthe Kruse painted cloth doll, German, circa 1928, the head stitched in three sections with painted face, 43cm.
(Sotheby's) $2,347

A bisque china head doll, impressed *K.R.(?) 11*, having blonde wig, closing blue paperweight glass eyes, 58cm.
(Bearne's) $672

A Käthe Kruse cloth doll, German, circa 1930, in white, blue and red printed cotton dress, bonnet and shoes, 38cm.
(Sotheby's) $1,625

A very rare male doll, with bisque head, original khaki officer's uniform from the Boer War, 11in., possibly Simon and Halbig, circa 1900.
(Christie's) $1,066

A pair of Demalcol bisque googly dolls, German, circa 1926, with closed smiling mouths, in traditional Chinese costume, 10in.
(Sotheby's) $1,353

A Martha Chase cloth doll, American, circa 1920, the stockinette head painted with oils, in pink and white striped dress, 40cm.
(Sotheby's) $722

A Käthe Kruse post-war boy doll with painted blue eyes nd brown hair in Tyrolean clothes, 45cm. long.
(Stockholms Auktionsverk) $610

A Swaine & Co. doll, with bisque head, blue lashed sleeping eyes, pierced ears, fair wig and jointed wood and composition body, 26in. high.
(Christie's) $705

A rare bisque character doll of Uncle Sam, attributed to Simon and Halbig, German, circa 1910, well molded face with closed smiling mouth, 13in.
(Sotheby's) $1,806

A Bähr and Pröschild bisque character doll, German, circa 1912, with painted intaglio brown eyes, pouty open/closed mouth, blonde mohair wig, 18in. high.
(Sotheby's) $2,347

A Schmitt et Fils pressed bisque doll, French, circa 1880, with open/closed mouth showing white between lips, fixed blue paperweight eyes, 22in. high.
(Sotheby's) $9,389

A Kämmer and Reinhardt/ Simon and Halbig bisque character doll, German, circa 1911, with closed mouth and dimple in chin, weighted blue glass eyes, 18¹/₂in. high.
(Sotheby's) $3,430

A Kämmer and Reinhardt bisque character doll 'Gretchen', German, circa 1909, with closed pouty mouth and dimple in chin, painted blue eyes, blonde mohair wig 16¹/₂in. high.
(Sotheby's) $5,120

A rare J. D. Kestner bisque character doll with three extra interchangeable character heads, German, circa 1910, 11in.
(Sotheby's) $11,194

A Bébé louvre molded bisque doll and her trunk, French, circa 1880, closed mouth showing space between lips, pierced ears, 15in. high.
(Sotheby's) $1,625

A rare Armand Marseille bisque character doll, German, circa 1910, ball jointed wood and composition body in green floral printed dress, 16in.
(Sotheby's) $2,798

A Käthe Kruse painted cloth doll, German, circa 1928, the head stitched in five sections with finely painted features, 43cm.
(Sotheby's) $2,708

A large Kämmer and Reinhardt/ Simon and Halbig bisque character doll, German, circa 1911, with closed pouty mouth, dimple in chin, 31in. high.
(Sotheby's) $9,140

A Simon and Halbig bisque character doll, German, circa 1920, four ball jointed wood and composition body, 22in.
(Sotheby's) $5,778

A rare Kämmer and Reinhardt bisque character 'Carl' dolls head, German, circa 1919, impressed *KstarR 107 30*, with open/closed pouty mouth, 3¼in. high.
(Sotheby's) $7,300

A good Casimir Bru pressed bisque bébé, French, circa 1875, gusseted kid-leather body with bisque lower arms, 55cm.
(Sotheby's) $16,250

A good boxed Chad Valley pressed felt Snow White and the Seven Dwarfs, English, circa 1938, together with original boxes, each box with 'Chad Valley' label and two dwarves with original tie-on label, Snow White 16in. high.
(Sotheby's) $4,968

A good ventriloquist's dummy with two composition heads, German, circa 1920, the legs able to walk as the shoulders are held, 74cm.
(Sotheby's) $1,625

A Kämmer and Reinhardt/ Simon and Halbig bisque character doll, German, circa 1911, with closed pouty mouth and dimple in chin, 27in. high.
(Sotheby's) $8,775

A Kämmer and Reinhardt bisque character doll, German, circa 1909, with closed pouty mouth, dimple in chin, painted blue eyes, 21in. high.
(Sotheby's) $4,514

An English enamel tape measure of drum shape, inscribed *A Token of Love* in black on a white band, 2cm.
(Phillips)   **$306**

Rare hand-operated tray-type laundry machine, 19th century, 36in. high.
(Eldred's)   **$143**

A Victorian mahogany and brass-mounted mechanical bellows, the ratcheted winding wheel with turned ebonized handle, 20¹/₄in. long.
(Christie's)   **$513**

The Miracle Firemaker, a battery-powered fire bellows by A. Rowley Tool & Eng. Co., Green Lake, Wisconsin, 23cm. high.
(Auction Team Köln)   **$125**

Astron 2000 heater by Albin Sprenger KG, Germany, 1950s, cast aluminium with ivory-gray enamel finish, on chrome stand.
(Bonhams)   **$170**

Pair of gilt metal lady's binoculars, ceramic barrels painted with scenes of courting couples, 'Providence', modeled by Tilden Thurber Limited, 19th century.
(G. A. Key)   **$380**

An Electro-Weld Co. nickel-plated toaster, American, circa 1920.
(Auction Team Köln)   **$288**

Braun, Germany, Multimix Mixer, 1953, burgundy plastic base, blue tinted glass.
(Bonhams)   **$77**

Peter Behrens (attributed), Germany, a chromed metal toaster, for AEG, 1930, hinged sides.
(Bonhams)   **$70**

1930's brassed and bakelite candlestick telephone, 12in. high.
(G. A. Key) $154

American butter churn, 19th century, painted yellow, marked *Davis Swing Churn No. 2., Vermont Farm Machine Co., Bellows Falls, VT*, 40in. high.
(Eldred's) $121

'Radiopur', a chromed metal hairdryer for AEG, 1930s.
(Bonhams) $85

A Schneider Opel Type SO K detector-receiver, desk-form wooden housing, circa 1925.
(Auction Team Köln) $718

Juice-O-Mat, tilt-top juicer by Rival Mfg. Co., Kansas City, Mo, cast aluminium and chrome plate, with an advanced tilt mechanism.
(Bonhams) $201

The Standard Fan, oscillating fan with brass rotor and cage by Robbins & Myers, Springfield, Ohio, 110v.
(Auction Team Köln) $187

Leslie Roberts, UK, table-top or wall mountable fan, silver/green painted aluminium with rubber blades.
(Bonhams) $85

A Marconi Type 23, two-valve receiver with sloping control panel and mahogany case, 1928.
(Christie's) $389

Cape Cod cranberry scoop, 19th century, stamped *F. L. Buckingham, Mfg., Plymouth, MA*, added feet.
(Eldred's) $302

A Viennese giltmetal-mounted enamel dish, of shaped oval outline, the center painted with a scene of girls bathing and resting, late 19th century, 16¹/₂in. wide.
(Christie's) $2,795

Attributed to Koloman Moser, for Georg Anton Scheidt, Vienna, Girl and Mistletoe box, circa 1900, enameled with the head of a young girl with flowing black hair, 7.5 x 5.5cm.
(Sotheby's) $8,197

A gothic style champlevé enamel and ormolu coffer, decorated with polychrome enameled musicians, the corners mounted with semi-precious stones, 12¹/₂in. wide.
(Christie's) $7,475

A French Graeco-Roman style champlevé enamel and ormolu jardinière, late 19th century, enameled throughout in yellow-ground with polychrome swirling foliage, inscribed *F. Barbedienne*, 13in. high.
(Christie's) $4,672

A pair of Viennese silver and enamel 'flower-filled' urns, each on domed foot with maker's mark of Hermann Böhm, late 19th century, 9¹/₄in. high.
(Christie's) $5,216

A Viennese giltmetal-mounted, ebony and enamel casket, the domed lid surmounted by a camel and cherub above a concealed compartment, late 19th century, 10in. wide.
(Christie's) $4,658

A giltmetal-mounted, Viennese enamel and ebonized casket, the domed lid with a concealed compartment above a pair of small doors, late 19th century, 17¹/₂in. wide.
(Christie's) $8,942

Ferdinand von Reznicek, vesta case with secret panel, circa 1911, the lid lifting to release cover on front concealing enameled panel, 5cm. square.
(Sotheby's) $2,049

A Viennese giltmetal-mounted, ebony and ebonized miniature rolltop desk, with a pierced three-quarter gallery, late 19th century, 8¹/₂in. wide.
(Christie's) $7,825

ENAMEL

A miniature ebonized and enamel table casket, Austrian, circa 1880, with numerous panels painted with mythological scenes, 16.5cm. high.
(Sotheby's) $2,025

Attributed to Koloman Moser, for Georg Anton Scheidt, Vienna, triangular box with three girls, circa 1900, the cover with center panel enameled with three young girls, 6.5 x 3.5cm.
(Sotheby's) $2,422

Paul László, cigarette case with woman and plant, circa 1925, the front enameled with the figure of a young woman and a plant, 10 x 7cm.
(Sotheby's) $2,981

A small silver-gilt bowl, the flutes alternating with plique-a-jour enameled panels of scrollwork and sylized foliage, I. Khlebnikov, Moscow 1908–1917, 4¼in.
(Christie's) $1,936

A pair of Viennese silver and enamel 'flower-filled' urn timepieces, with maker's mark of Hermann Böhm, late 19th century, 9¼in. high.
(Christie's) $5,216

A Viennese Renaissance style silver and rock crystal box, 19th century, with engraved panels depicting arabesques within polychrome enameled foliage, 5in. high.
(Christie's) $14,016

A French Graeco-Roman style champlevé enamel and ormolu jardinière, late 19th century, signed F. Barbedienne, 13in. high.
(Christie's) $4,672

An ormolu-mounted enamel rectangular casket, the cover painted with a Watteauesque view of ladies singing and playing the lute, signed L. Cattentz, 12½in. wide.
(Christie's) $2,700

A Viennese silver and enamel timepiece, cast with a winged cherub, the circular dial with an enamel pair of putti above a further smaller panel below, late 19th century, 7½in. high.
(Christie's) $2,236

French Art Deco paper hand fan, designed by Gabriel Ferre for Galeries Lafayette, Paris, circa 1925, lithograph of stylized Oriental woman and foliage, 9¹/₂in. long. (Skinner) **$748**

A fan, the leaf painted with a banquet, the verso with two figures in a landscape, the tortoiseshell sticks carved, pierced and gilt, 10in., circa 1760. (Christie's) **$1,050**

A Canton gilt filigree brisé fan, enameled in blue, green and maroon with sprays of leaves and sprigs of flowers, 7in., circa 1830. (Christie's) **$2,661**

A Canton filigree brisé fan, enameled in blue and green with vignettes with pagodas, 7in., circa 1830. (Christie's) **$1,508**

A fan signed *Lievre*, painted with elegant figures dancing in a park, the mother of pearl sticks carved with four figures with children, 11in., circa 1870. (Christie's) **$670**

Exposition Universelle, Paris 1889, a chromolithographic fan by Barbier, 11 rue Meslay advertising Siraudin, confiseur, depicting a crowded scene outside the Opera, 13in., 1889. (Christie's) **$1,685**

A Grand Tour fan, the chickenskin leaf painted with the Pantheon, Rome, the reserves with brightly colored Etruscan decoration, 10in., circa 1780. (Christie's) **$880**

The Rape of the Sabine Women, a fan, the chickenskin leaf with a pen and ink drawing after Rubens, the ivory sticks carved with chinoiserie figures in gazebos, 11in., circa 1720. (Christie's) **$3,015**

Souvenir du Village Suisse, Exposition de
Geneve 1896, a chomolithographic fan with
wooden sticks, 13in.
(Christie's) $319

Louis Vuitton, a lithographic advertising fan, in
brown published by J. Ganne, overstamped *The
Cunard Steam Ship Company Limited*, 9in., circa
1900.
(Christie's) $302

A fan signed *A. Ledoux*, the silk leaf painted with
gipsy dancers, the verso with a gipsy, the mother
of pearl sticks carved, 11in., circa 1875.
(Christie's) $790

A Canton filigree brisé fan, enameled in blue
and green with the pagoda of Whampoa, 8in.,
circa 1830.
(Christie's) $1,419

A fan signed *A. Lefeve*, painted with a lady
sitting in the clouds amongst blue feathers, the
mother of pearl sticks carved to resemble
feathers, 9in., circa 1890.
(Christie's) $798

Nelson & Victory, a printed fan, the leaf a line
engraving with names and comic choreography
of 18th century fictional country dances, one
guardstick inscribed *E.B. 1799*, 10in., 1798.
(Christie's) $1,330

A fan attached to a pair of opera glasses by
Asprey, the leaf of maroon gauze embroidered
with sequins, the sticks of tortoiseshell, 6in., circa
1900.
(Christie's) $1,064

L'Assemblée de Notables, printed fan, the leaf a
hand-colored etching in brown, and a satirical
verse set to the music of Air de Figaro, with
wooden sticks, with bone filets, 10in., 1787.
(Christie's) $319

A Grand Tour fan, the chickenskin leaf painted with Vesuvius erupting by night, 10in., Italian, 1779.
(Christie's) $1,080

A Canton ivory brise fan, carved and pierced with inscription *Madame F.D.J Card nee Hte Boulanger Souvenir de S.V.C. Canton 1 Janvier 1825*, 7in., 1825.
(Christie's) $2,520

The Coronation of King George II, a printed fan, the leaf a hand-colored etching of the banquet in Westminster Hall with the Champion of England, 11in., 1727.
(Christie's) $2,100

A fine fan of Flemish lace worked with the Arms of the King and Queen of the Belgians, the mother of pearl sticks carved and pierced with trophies of love, 11in., 1853.
(Christie's) $7,200

Queen Isabella of Spain attending a bullfight, a hand-colored lithographic fan, the mother of pearl sticks carved, pierced and gilt, 11in., circa 1860.
(Christie's) $530

Bal de St. Cyr 1906, a lithographic fan celebrating the passing-out bal and commemorating the battle of Austerlitz 1805, indistinctly signed *Louharty, 1906*, 9in., 1906.
(Christie's) $340

A Geslin fan, the leaf of black lace with three black gauze insertions painted with putti, one indistinctly signed *Galichet*, the tortoiseshell sticks carved and pierced with putti, 13in., circa 1885, in satin box.
(Christie's) $704

A silk fan, the leaf painted with an elegant couple with a baby and another lady, the reserves painted with a canary and a finch, roses, carnations, honeysuckle and pansies, 10in., circa 1820.
(Christie's) $1,050

A fan painted with pilgrims, the verso with a viaduct near Compostela, 12in., circa 1750. (Christie's) $5,676

A Japanese ivory brisé fan, lacquered in hiramakie and takamakie with a dragon, 11in., late 19th century. (Christie's) $5,676

A double-side fan signed A. *Lefeve*, painted with three vignettes of young men spying on a proposal scene through net curtains, 8in., circa 1895. (Christie's) $3,548

A ballooning fan, the silk leaf painted with two elegant couples and two further vignettes each of a lady and a gentleman spying a balloon through a telescope, 10in., circa 1175. (Christie's) $3,168

A Royal fan signed *Ussel*, the canepin leaf painted with Spanish dancers with Seville in the distance, inscribed *A.S.A. La Infanta Da Mercedes al ser Reyna de Espana, Ussel '78*, 11in., Spanish, 1878. (Christie's) $11,700

A Chinoiserie fan, the leaf painted with five Chinese figures on a terrace, their faces of ivory, their clothes of mother of pearl, a window of catgut and butterflies applied with feathers, 12in., French, circa 1820. (Christie's) $968

A printed fan, the leaf a hand-colored etching with an allegory of Trade with King George III, the ivory sticks carved and pierced with chinoiserie, painted and gilt, 11in., English, circa 1760. (Christie's) $6,740

A Canton fan with mother of pearl sticks, the leaf painted with three vignettes of figures on terraces against a blue ground, their faces of ivory, their clothes of silk, 10in., circa 1860. (Christie's) $880

Walt Disney (full page), Charles Boyer, Jimmy Durante, Danny Kaye, etc., King Faisal II of Iraq and other Iraqi Royalty, in leather autograph album.
(Neales) $713

An oval black and yellow cast resin badge, 5³/₄in. long, part of a Batman costume used in the 1992 Warner Bros. film Batman Returns.
(Christie's) $354

Abbot and Costello, an album page, signed and dedicated to John in two different blue inks by Bud Abbott and Lou Costello, 10 x 8in.
(Bonhams) $193

A Norfolk shooting jacket of green and fawn tweed, worn by Basil Rathbone in the 1943 Universal film Sherlock Holmes in Washington.
(Christie's) $797

Brigitte Bardot, a full-length dress of printed jersey, worn by Brigitte Bardot in the 1970s with press cutting showing Bardot wearing the dress.
(Christie's) $744

Charlie Chaplin, a bamboo cane, 37in. long, circa 1921; and a pound note, the reverse stamped with Chaplin's facsimile signature.
(Christie's) $3,542

A full head-mask of heavy latex, with elongated pointed bald head, used in the 1994 Paramount film The Coneheads.
(Christie's) $390

Stan Laurel, a black bowler hat signed and inscribed in ink by Stan Laurel on the interior brown leather head band, Thanks Harry.
(Bonhams) $3,220

Charlie Chaplin, a head and shoulders portrait photograph signed and inscribed Yours Faithfully Charlie Chaplin, 1928, 13¹/₂ x 10¹/₂in.
(Christie's) $673

Errol Flynn, an album page, signed and dedicated in blue biro, mounted with a color Picturegoer postcard from Elizabeth and Essex, framed. (Bonhams) $193

Maurice Chevalier, a straw boater, Maurice's trade mark, autographed on inside rim. (Bonhams) $161

Laurel and Hardy, signed dedicated postcard; autograph letter Empire Theatre Nottingham, dated *Dec 30, '53* from Laurel. (Neales) $465

A jumpsuit of gray cotton, worn by Keir Dullea as Bowman in the 1968 MGM film 2001: A Space Odyssey. (Christie's) $3,542

A pair of knee-length tan suede riding boots; and a tan hand-made Damascan camel robe, worn by Peter O'Toole in Lawrence Of Arabia. (Christie's) $6,730

A custom-made folding director's chair with black leather backrest tooled *BARBRA STREISAND*, and a carbon copy of a memo from Dick Rubin to Carl Deere, 1974, regarding the Special Leather Chair. (Christie's) $5,313

Charlie Chaplin, a three-quarter length publicity photograph circa 1920, signed and inscribed by subject *To Wyn From Charlie*, 8³/₄ x 6in. (Christie's) $319

Walt Disney, an album page signed by Walt Disney in blue biro, mounted, framed and glazed, 5³/₄ x 7¹/₈in. (Bonhams) $419

Bela Lugosi, a head and shoulders publicity photograph signed and inscribed *With best wishes Bela Lugosi*, 9¹/₂ x 7¹/₂in. (Christie's) $744

A Star Is Born, 1954, Warner
Bros., U.S. one-sheet, 41 x 27in.
(Christie's) $1,219

Le Sexe Faible, 1933, Nero,
French, 63 x 47in., linen-backed.
(Christie's) $7,504

The Ladykillers, 1955, Ealing,
British one-sheet, 40 x 27in.
(Christie's) $562

Crime School, 1938, Warner
Bros., U.S. one-sheet, 41 x 27in.,
linen-backed.
(Christie's) $5,064

Citizen Kane, 1941, R.K.O., U.S.
one-sheet, 41 x 27in., linen-
backed.
(Christie's) $7,129

Barbarella, 1968, Paramount,
Italian, Style B, 55 x 39in., linen-
backed.
(Christie's) $1,219

Bringing Up Baby/L'Impossible
Monsieur Bébé, 1938, R.K.O.,
French, 65 x 47in., linen-backed.
(Christie's) $15,945

They Died With Their Boots On,
1942, Warner Bros., U.S. one-
sheet, 41 x 27in.
(Christie's) $1,406

High Sierra/La Grande Evasion,
1941, Warner Bros., Belgian,
22 x 14in., linen-backed.
(Christie's) $525

Silly Symphony, 1938, R.K.O./
Disney, French, 63 x 47in.
(Christie's) $6,753

Rocky II, 1979, U.A., U.S. one-
sheet, 41 x 27in., linen-backed.
(Christie's) $450

Lady Sings The Blues, 1972,
Paramount, Italian, 55 x 39in.
(Christie's) $112

The Seven Year Itch, 1955,
T.C.F., British double crown,
30 x 20in., linen-backed.
(Christie's) $1,781

Dr. Jekyll and Mr. Hyde, 1931,
Paramount, Belgian, 33 x 23in.,
linen-backed.
(Christie's) $12,193

On The Waterfront, 1954,
Columbia, U.S. one-sheet,
41 x 27in.
(Christie's) $787

The Man Who Knew Too Much,
1934, British Gaumont, Swedish,
39 x 28in., paper-backed.
(Christie's) $1,876

High Society, 1958, M.G.M.,
U.S. one-sheet, 41 x 27in., linen-
backed.
(Christie's) $1,501

To Have And Have Not/Acque
Del Sud, 1945, Warner Bros.,
Italian, 79 x 55in., linen-backed.
(Christie's) $26,263

L'Inhumaine, 1923, French, 62 x 46in., linen-backed. (Christie's) **$9,380**

Bus Stop, 1956, T.C.F., British quad, 30 x 40in., linen-backed. (Christie's) **$844**

The African Queen, 1957, U.A., U.S. one-sheet, 41 x 27in. (Christie's) **$2,813**

The Story Of Vernon And Irene Castle/La Grande Farandole, 1939, R.K.O., French, 30³/₄ x 46¹/₂in., linen-backed. (Christie's) **$3,563**

Der Goldene Schmetterling/ Papillon D'Or, 1926, Union-Artiste, French, 63 x 94in., linen-backed. (Christie's) **$5,439**

Rose Of Washington Square/Es Mi Hombre, 1939, T.C.F., Spanish one-sheet, 39 x 28in., linen-backed. (Christie's) **$655**

I Met My Love Again/Volvió El Amor, 1938, U.A., Spanish one-sheet, 34¹/₂ x 36³/₄in. (Christie's) **$525**

A Clockwork Orange, 1971, Warner Bros., British quad, 30 x 40in., linen-backed. (Christie's) **$1,312**

Mickey And Minnie Mouse, 1933–34, United Artists, Belgian stock poster, 24 x 33¹/₂in., linen-backed. (Christie's) **$5,253**

Psycho, 1960, Paramount, U.S. one-sheet, 41 x 27in. (Christie's) $1,126

Laughing Gravy, 1931, M.G.M., U.S. title card, 11 x 14in. (Christie's) $2,063

Rebecca, 1940, U.A., U.S. one-sheet, 41 x 27in., linen-backed. (Christie's) $4,877

A Social Celebrity/En Sparv I Tranedans, 1926, Paramount, Swedish, 27¹/₄ x 40in., linen-backed. (Christie's) $5,064

The Rocky Horror Picture Show, 1975, T.C.F., British quad, 26¹/₂ x 36¹/₂in., linen-backed. (Christie's) $1,031

Gone With The Wind/Autant En Emporte Le Vent, circa 1940s, M.G.M., French, 63 x 47in., linen-backed. (Christie's) $6,003

Edouard Bernard, Arlette Montal, lithograph in colors, circa 1914, 119 x 77cm. (Christie's) $319

Singin' In The Rain, 1952, M.G.M., British quad, 30 x 40in., linen-backed. (Christie's) $1,501

Elephant Boy/Sangre Y Marfil, 1937, London Films, Argentinian one-sheet, 42 x 28in. (Christie's) $600

The Thirty-Nine Steps, 1935, Gaumont British, U.S. one-sheet, 41 x 27in., linen-backed. (Christie's) $9,755

Brief Encounter/Breve Incontro, 1945, Eagle Lion, Italian, 55 x 39in., linen-backed. (Christie's) $1,781

It's A Wonderful Life, 1947, Liberty/R.K.O., U.S. one-sheet, 41 x 27in. (Christie's) $5,253

Scott Of The Antarctic, 1949, Eagle Lion, British one-sheet, 40 x 27in., linen-backed. (Christie's) $655

The Third Man, 1949, David O. Selznick/Alexander Korda, U.S. one-sheet, 41 x 27in. (Christie's) $844

Oliver Twist, 1948, J. Arthur Rank, Spanish one-sheet, 39 x 28in., linen-backed. (Christie's) $712

Gilda, 1946, Columbia, Belgian, 22 x 14in., linen-backed, archivally framed. (Christie's) $1,219

Double Indemnity, 1944, Paramount, U.S. one-sheet, 41 x 27in. (Christie's) $2,251

Casablanca, 1943, Warner Bros., Belgium, 22 x 14in., linen-backed. (Christie's) $3,752

Alice's Spooky Adventure, 1924, Walt Disney, U.S. one-sheet, 41 x 27in., linen-backed. (Christie's) $26,263

Sirocco/Siroco, 1951, Columbia, Spanish one-sheet, 39 x 28in., linen-backed. (Christie's) $9,005

The Thief Of Baghdad/Tjuven I Bagdad, 1924, Swedish, 33 x 23in., linen-backed. (Christie's) $1,126

This Gun For Hire, 1942, Paramount, U.S. one-sheet, 41 x 27in., linen-backed. (Christie's) $4,689

City Streets/Les Carrefours De La Ville, 1931, Paramount, French, 63 x 47in., linen-backed. (Christie's) $12,193

The Spy In Black/El Espia Negro, 1938, Alexander Korda, Spanish one-sheet, 39 x 27in. (Christie's) $562

The Lady From Shanghai, 1948, Columbia, U.S. one-sheet, 41 x 27in. (Christie's) $3,002

Shanghai Express, 1932, Paramount, French, $31^{1}/_{2}$ x $23^{1}/_{2}$in. (Christie's) $15,008

The Garden of Allah/El Jardin de Ala, 1936, U.A., Spanish, $39^{1}/_{2}$ x $27^{3}/_{4}$in. (Christie's) $1,594

A gilt-brass-mounted steel fire grate, in George III style, the oval basket with ram's-head masks supporting chains of ribbon-tied laurel, 60cm. high. (Sotheby's) $4,970

Diego Giacometti, one of two fire grates, circa 1955, wrought iron, the supports of each grate modeled as mythical beasts with splayed claw-like feet, 24in. wide. (Sotheby's) (Two) $28,877

A cast-iron and gilt-bronze mounted basket grate, with acanthine scroll handles to the sides, on oval socle and stepped square plinth, 26^{1}/2in. wide. (Christie's) $1,530

A brass and iron fire-grate with bowed slatted front above a pierced anthemion frieze, on ring-turned baluster legs, 19th century, 23^{1}/2in. wide. (Christie's) $460

A Regency 'Gothic' designcast iron fire grate in the manner of A.W.N. Pugin, the basket grate flanked by twin gables with lancet windows, 37in. wide. (Hy. Duke & Son) $4,500

A blackened-iron basket-grate of George III style, the spindle basket surmounted by urn-finials, 19th century, 27in. wide. (Christie's) $1,380

A George III cast iron hob grate, the serpentine railed fire basket flanked by panels decorated with classical figure, 92cm. wide. (Phillips) $560

A cast-iron Egyptian Revival parlour stove, N. Pratt & Company, Albany, New York, circa 1837–1844, 58^{1}/2in. high. (Christie's) $2,300

A polished-steel basket-grate of George III style, the spindle basket with urn-finials, above a pierced shaped frieze, on turned feet, 30in. wide. (Christie's) $5,150

A George III white and Siena marble chimney-piece, the molded inverted breakfront shelf above a dentiled band and Greek-key frieze centered by a floral tabler, overall: 86¹/₄in. wide. (Christie's) $32,499

A George III white and Siena marble chimney-piece, the frieze centered by a rectangular projecting tablet carved in high relief with Hercules and two female attendants, 78in. wide. (Christie's) $11,040

A George III elaborately carved pine chimney-piece, mid-18th century, the breakfront shelf with a molded and dentil-carved edge, above an oak torus reath centered by an eared tablet, 76³/₄in. wide. (Christie's) $16,560

A George III pine and pewter chimney-piece, late 18th century, the rectangular shelf above a patera-enriched frieze with ribbon-tied husk garlands, with a griffin-guarded urn central tablet, 61in. wide. (Christie's) $5,520

A large verde antico and statuary marble chimney-piece, in the George III style, the verde antico frieze centered by a Bacchic tablet and flanked by flowered tablets, 89in. wide. (Christie's) $22,080

A white marble chimney-piece, second half 19th century, the rectangular shelf with a molded edge and rounded corners, above a rectangular frieze, the jambs each carved with foliate motif, 72¹/₂in. wide. (Christie's) $920

A pair of brass andirons, attributed to Daniel King, Philadelphia, 1760–1770, each with spiral flame and diamond finial, 24in. high.
(Christie's) $46,000

A good cast-brass fan fire-guard, late 19th century, the front and back cast with a dancing female figure, 2ft. 6in. high.
(Sotheby's) $2,760

A set of two French steel and brass fire-irons with stand, mid-19th century, the stand 29in. high.
(Christie's) $1,704

A pair of cast brass and enamel andirons, modeled with the Stuart Arms, supported by male and female figures flanking a floral basket, English, second half 19th century, 23¼in. high.
(Christie's) $2,033

A pair of gilt-bronze chenets, in Louis XV manner, each cast with a putto on a leafy scroll base, 33cm. high.
(Sotheby's) $2,392

A set of three George III brass fire-irons, each with ring-turned handle and pointed finial, the poker 29in. long.
(Christie's) $727

A pair of Louis XV style ormolu and patinated bronze chenets, 19th century, each with the figure of Venus and Vulcan respectively, 17in. high.
(Christie's) $6,555

A carved and painted pine and mahogany fire box, Pennsylvania or Virginia, dated 1861, the open square form with turned columnar supports, dated 1861, 7³/₈in. wide.
(Sotheby's) $1,610

A pair of brass andirons, American, 18th century, each section cast in two parts with flame and reeded ball capital above a reeded baluster support, 21¼in. high.
(Christie's) $5,175

A pair of gilt-bronze chenets, in Louis XVI manner, cast with a quiver and swags of roses, 61cm. high.
(Sotheby's) $3,000

A rare painted pine leather and wrought-iron fireplace bellows, probably Mahantongo Valley, Pennsylvania, dated *1847*, 18in. long.
(Sotheby's) $11,500

A pair of Régence ormolu chenets, each surmounted by a seated putto, the putto possibly mid-18th century, 7in. wide.
(Christie's) $4,485

A set of three George IV steel fire irons, the cylindrical shafts with faceted octagonal grips and mushroom finials, early 19th century.
(Christie's) $1,170

A pair of Louis XV style ormolu and patinated bronze chenets, 19th century, after Charles Cressent, each cast as a rampant lion on a scrolling foliate plinth, 23in. high.
(Christie's) $13,800

A brass and wrought-iron fireplace trivet, American, probably Maryland or Virginia, first quarter 19th century, 17½in. long extended.
(Sotheby's) $747

A rare decorated cast-iron fireback, Virginia, circa 1730, of arched oblong form the crest centering a shell flanked by leafage, 30¼in. high.
(Sotheby's) $72,900

A pair of ormolu chenets of a reclining boar and a stag amidst foliage, 17¾in. wide.
(Christie's) $8,073

A Victorian black and gilt-japanned helmet-shaped coal scuttle and shovel, decorated overall with foliage and with adjustable handle.
(Christie's) $920

A Malloch bronze/brass patent casting reel, 4in., in Farlow's black leather case.
(Bonhams) $124

A carved and painted decoy fish, in the form of a pike; together with a similar perch.
(Bonhams) $105

A Walter Stanley prototype reel, for the Allcock Threadline, alloy with brass handle.
(Christie's) $510

A Hardy brass faced 'Perfect' fly reel, 4¼in., with smooth integral alloy foot, strapped rim check, 1896.
(Bonhams) $331

A G. Little all brass plate wind salmon reel, with constant check and horn handle.
(Bonhams) $198

A John Lyden Galway 4in. all brass crank wind trolling winch, with shallow drum, horn handle and constant check.
(Bonhams) $527

Two bream mounted in gilt lined bowfronted case, bears J. E. Miller, Leeds label, 26in. wide.
(Bonhams) $452

An early Scottish trolling winch or pirn, turned and carved hardwood, probably elm, curved iron crank handle, 6¾in. square.
(Christie's) $1,002

W. Blacker: 'The Art of Angling and Complete System of Fly Making and Dying of Colours', 1842.
(Bonhams) $1,815

A Hardy brass 4in. reel, ivory handle, brass strap over rim tension adjuster.
(Christie's) $1,640

A Japanese bamboo and lacquered fishing rod, 14-piece including top holder, silvered end, each section with ebonised reeded bands, 15ft. extended.
(Christie's) $693

A Bowness and Bowness 4in. all brass plate wind reel, with bulbous turned wooden handle.
(Bonhams) $132

A pike, mounted in a setting of reeds and grasses, in a gilt lined bow fronted case, bears J. Cooper & Sons label, 42in. wide.
(Bonhams) $1,403

A 19th century steel adjustable pike gag/scissor; together with a nickel plated spring balance.
(Bonhams) $48

A black japanned fly case containing approximately twenty fully dressed and other salmon patterns.
(Bonhams) $121

An Allcock's Ariel alloy reel, 4in., with smooth brass foot, rim check lever, six spoke drum and tension regulator.
(Bonhams) $429

A Hardy 'Sea Silex' 5in. reel with smooth brass foot, reverse taper handles and horseshoe drum latch.
(Bonhams) $528

A Hardy 'Conquest' centre-pin trotting reel, with ivorine casting brake lever, and two screw drum latch.
(Bonhams) $132

A roach mounted in a setting of reeds and grasses, gilt lined bowfronted case, bears J. E. Miller Leeds label, 18½in. wide.
(Bonhams) $784

An all brass Hardy reel, 2⅝in., plate wind.
(Bonhams) $116

A bream, bears handwritten label *Caught by M. Woodward at Hardley Cross, Norfolk August 28th 1886*, 25½in. wide.
(Bonhams) $422

A brass 1¾in. clamp-foot winch reel, lever handle and a perforated clamp, lacking locking screw.
(Christie's) $273

An Army & Navy angler's knife, with single cutting blade, saw blade, corkscrew, folding scissors and an integral spring balance.
(Bonhams) $362

A G. Little & Co., 2in. brass fly reel, horn handle, engraved address and a smooth brass foot.
(Christie's) $109

An important rare Hardy all brass transitional 'Perfect', with wire cage, dished perforated drum, brass foot with five perforations.
(Bonhams) $1,356

A Hardy 'Silex' No. 2 salmon fly spinning reel, smooth brass foot, pierced drum core, ivorine rim break and dual ivorine handles.
(Bonhams) $196

A Homers 4¹/₂in. mahogany and brass Nottingham Starback reel, with optical check and slater pattern drum latch, and dual white handles.
(Bonhams) $241

A Hardy, the 'Cascapedia', 3³/₄in., multiplying salmon fly reel, size 4/0, ebonite front and back plates, in a Hardy lined canvas bag.
(Christie's) $6,562

A pair of silver presentation plaques, inscribed, *Llandrindod Wells Casting Tournament*, presentation inscriptions to reverse, cased, Birmingham, 1934, 4³/₄in. wide, 15oz.
(Christie's) $292

A Hardy, the 'Perfect', 2¹/₂in., brass-faced wide-drum fly reel, smooth brass foot, brass strap above tension adjuster.
(Christie's) $765

A Hardy all brass 'Perfect' fly reel, 4¹/₂in. diameter, with perforated foot, strap tension screw and ivorine handle, 1896 check.
(Bonhams) $1,320

A rare Hardy 3in. all brass 1896 model 'Perfect' fly reel, with pierced brass foot, strapped rim, check regulator screw, unperforated drum.
(Bonhams) $1,085

An Allcocks Aerial 'Popular' 4in. center pin reel, with brass feet, knarled tension adjustable disc, dual xylonite handles and line guard.
(Bonhams) $136

A gudgeon, in a gilt lined bowfront case, inscribed *Gudgeon 2ozs. 5drms. Caught at 'Ross', by A. Curtis, 11th February 1934*, 13in. wide. (Bonhams) $4,521

A Jones 19th century all brass crank wind reel, 2¹/₂in., with folding handle, locking disc and raised check housing. (Bonhams) $627

Three perch, mounted in a setting of reeds and grasses, gilt lined bowfronted case, 35in. wide. (Bonhams) $1,959

Two pike mounted and inscribed *27lbs. and 19lbs., Caught by E. & A. Price Jnr. at Ross-on-Wye 14th March 1940*, 49³/₄in. wide. (Bonhams) $5,576

A Gregory brass articulated spinning bait, the fin stamped with maker's name, 4in. (Bonhams) $908

Two pike, in a gilt lined bowfronted case, with printed label *Pike taken by A. W. Dane, 5th March 1891, near Crawley Sussex*, 49in. (Bonhams) $3,014

A Hardy all brass 'Perfect' salmon reel, with ivory handle, maker's mark in oval, 4in. diameter. (Bonhams) $1,898

A rare and extensive collection of over three hundred salmon flies, fully-dressed with gut eyes, contained in two oak cases by Farlow & Co. (Bearne's) $6,000

A rare Hardy 'Davy' contracted fly reel, with grooved brass roof, rim check regulator screw, dal ebonite handles and telephone drum latch. (Bonhams) $832

A Spanish 17th century carved, gilded and painted frame, the corners with leaves and berries on plain central plate, raised foliate inner edge, 8³/8 x 6¹/8 x 4¹/4in.
(Christie's) $2,575

A Venetian 16th century carved and gilded cassetta frame, with raised egg-and-dart outer edge, 33 x 24 x 7³/4in.
(Christie's) $25,000

A Louis XV carved and gilded frame, with dentil outer edge and roundel studded rockwork, the flowerhead corners above cartouches in high profile, 14¹/2 x 20¹/2 x 5in.
(Christie's) $22,000

A Spanish early 17th century carved, gilded and painted frame, the central plate with panels of foliage in granito on hatched ground at corners, 37¹/2 x 30 x 7⁷/8in.
(Christie's) $4,600

A French Regency carved and gilded frame, the anthemia corners and centers flanked by interwoven foliage and strapwork on cross-hatched ground, 7¹/2 x 6¹/8 x 4in.
(Christie's) $1,380

A Bolognese 17th century carved and gilded frame, the central torus with imbricated fruit and foliage running from centers to corners, 29³/4 x 23¹/2 x 6¹/2in.
(Christie's) $5,120

An Italian 17th century carved and gilded frame, the central plate with scrolling foliage and berries running to winged cherubs' heads at corners, 6 x 4¹/4 x 2³/4in.
(Christie's) $4,400

An Italian 17th century carved and gilded sansovino frame, the top with a broken pediment, the sides and base with pierced scrolls, 6¹/2 x 5 x 4in.
(Christie's) $2,925

A Venetian 16th century carved, gilded and painted tabernacle frame, the cornice with dentil molding above frieze, 12⁵/8 x 10¹/2 x 4³/4in.
(Christie's) $6,400

An Italian 17th century carved, gilded and painted sansovino frame, the top and sides with polychromed cherubs' heads, 12¹/₂ x 17 x 5in.
(Christie's) $4,600

A Tuscan early 16th century carved, gilded and painted tondo frame, the raised central plate decorated with imbricated oak leaves, diameter 25¹/₂ x 8³/₄in.
(Christie's) $23,750

A Spanish 18th century carved, partly gilded and painted reverse profile frame, with high profile leaves at corners, 13⁵/₈ x 9³/₄ x 3⁷/₈in.
(Christie's) $1,840

A late Louis XIV carved and gilded frame, with raised gadrooned outer edge, the anthemia corners and centers flanked by scrolling foliage and strapwork, 11¹/₂ x 16 x 5¹/₂in.
(Christie's) $7,000

A fine and rare Italian 17th century boldly carved, pierced and gilded frame with pronounced scrolling cornucopean leaves, 28¹/₄ x 21¹/₄ x 15in.
(Bonhams) $10,080

An Italian 17th century carved and gilded frame, the cushion central plate with pierced scrolling foliage running to acanthus leaf corners, 22 x 26⁵/₈ x 4¹/₂in.
(Christie's) $4,022

An Italian giltwood picture frame, circa 1880, with rectangular frame divided by shells and acanthus, 52.5cm. high.
(Sotheby's) $5,668

An Italian 16th century carved, gilded and painted tabernacle frame, with leaf and rosette finials at top and sides, taenia outer edge, 26¹/₂ x 15⁷/₈ x 2⁷/₈in.
(Christie's) $4,410

A Dutch 17th century carved and partly gilded lutma frame, the top with overlapping armor, shields and weaponry in high relief, 25¹/₂ x 20¹/₂ x 5in.
(Christie's) $7,680

BEDS & CRADLES

A classical mahogany sleigh bed, Philadelphia, 1820–1840, the serpentine head and foot board each with scrolling crestrail terminating in swans' heads, 78in. long.
(Christie's) **$4,600**

Painted Windsor cradle, New England, circa 1810, retains old brown paint over blue green, 38in. long.
(Skinner) **$2,300**

George Nakashima walnut slab double bed, New Hope, Pennsylvania, circa 1960, raised on three shaped blade boards, walnut slab footboard, inscribed signature, 82$^{1}/_{8}$in. long.
(Skinner) **$8,050**

An oak tester bedstead, the paneled canopy carved with scrolling stylized foliage and with a lunette-carved cornice, 61$^{1}/_{2}$in. wide, 17th century and later.
(Bearne's) **$5,049**

A 19th century mahogany tester bed with pierced and carved canopy raised on reeded columns decorated with carved acanthus leaves, 4ft. 6in. wide.
(Anderson & Garland) **$2,480**

A tester bed, the front mahogany posts ribbed and carved with leaf petal collars, 4ft. 6in.
(Woolley & Wallis) **$2,763**

Federal birch red stained canopy bed, New England, circa 1815, original finish, 54in. wide.
(Skinner) **$4,025**

One of a pair of fruitwood bedsteads, each with arched paneled headboard and footboard, joined by siderails with shaped spandrels, French, mid 19th century, each 80in. wide.
(Christie's)
(Two) **$1,205**

A Louis XV green-painted lit à baldaquin, with four shaped velvet-covered iron arms supporting a later stepped domed canopy, 75in. long.
(Christie's) **$2,870**

BEDS & CRADLES

An iron camp bedstead, the head and footrails with dolphin head finials, early 19th century, 212cm. long.
(Finarte) $3,311

A Venetian giltwood cradle jardinière, the tapering body carved with stylized foliage and rockwork and decorated with husk-trails, 19th century, 18³/₄in. wide.
(Christie's) $718

A mid 19th century all brass 4ft. 6in. bedstead, having lancet style and circular decoration in the Gothic style.
(Locke & England) $2,325

A Victorian carved walnut high-post bedstead, Southern States, 19th century, with rectangular molded tester above molded tapering posts, 65in. wide.
(Christie's) $3,220

A Gothic Revival carved walnut crib, New York, 1840–1860, the pointed pillar cornerposts joined by slatted sides forming pointed arches, on square legs, 43in. long.
(Christie's) $1,495

A red-painted high-post bedstead, Texas, mid-19th century, the rectangular tester above octagonal tapering headposts, 52¹/₂in. wide.
(Christie's) $3,910

Tall post cherry and maple bed, probably Connecticut, circa 1780, old refinish, 47¹/₂in. wide.
(Skinner) $4,025

Federal eagle-carved mahogany four poster bedstead, attributed to Joseph Barry, Philadelphia, Pennsylvania, circa 1820, on vase-form feet, 63³/₄in. wide.
(Sotheby's) $26,450

A French kingwood-veneered small double bed, Paris, circa 1900, in Louis XV manner, the headboard with a pierced gilt-bronze cresting, 135cm. wide.
(Sotheby's) $5,120

BEDS & CRADLES

One of a pair of Franco-German marquetry beds, circa 1890, possibly by E-J Zwiener, in Louis XV manner, 213cm. wide. (Sotheby's)
(Two) $16,456

A Japanese style bronze-mounted parcel-silvered giltwood bed, late 19th century, with an arched rectangular headboard formed as a pagoda, 61in. wide. (Christie's) $24,294

Pair of beds and bedside tables, from a bedroom suite for the apartment of Dr. Holzl, circa 1904, by Koloman Moser. (Sotheby's) $46,575

A George III satinwood inlaid and decorated tester bed, surmounted by an arched cornice with rounded corners painted on three sides, 210cm. wide. (Phillips) $25,600

A mahogany and brass-mounted bedroom suite, comprising: a double-bed, a pair of bedside cupboards, and an armoire. (Christie's) $6,480

A French red and gray-painted lit à baldequin, 19th century, the domed canopy surmounted by four pineapple finials centred by a domed foliate clasp, 76³/₄in. long. (Christie's) $9,400

Single bed for the country house of the Knip family, circa 1903, by Josef Hoffmann, of ebonized oak, 37³/₈in. wide. (Sotheby's) $5,589

A bleached mahogany tester bed, the front posts probably 18th century and Colonial, the rectangular molded cornice hung with swagged drapes of cream and blue silk, 67in. wide. (Christie's) $12,960

Louis Majorelle, bed, circa 1900, the wooden frame carved with stylized flowerheads, 196cm. long. (Sotheby's) $13,973

BEDS & CRADLES

A Victorian mother-of-pearl inlaid black lacquer papier mâché cast-iron and brass bed, mid 19th century, with a shaped rectangular headboard inlaid, 36³/₄in. wide.
(Christie's) $2,803

A French ormolu-mounted kingwood and tulipwood double bed, late 19th century, the footboard of bombé shape with husk pendants and flanked by Hercules lion's pelt mounts, 82in. wide.
(Christie's) $31,280

An ormolu-mounted mahogany bed of Empire style, each rectangular head and foot with urn-finials and paneled center, late 19th century, 85in. long.
(Christie's) $3,947

A George III mahogany and stained four-poster bed, the waved canopy covered in pale green silk, within a scrolled channeled frame carved with acanthus sprays, the front posts William IV, 75in. wide.
(Christie's) $29,440

A mahogany and gilt-bronze bedroom suite, French, circa 1890, in the Empire style, comprising, a double bed, a wardrobe and washstand.
(Sotheby's) $16,560

A George III style cream, duck-egg blue-painted and parcel-gilt tester bed, with molded canopy with trefoil frieze, on cluster column posts, 71in. wide.
(Christie's) $9,900

An Italian giltwood and green-painted bed, the paneled rectangular headboard with central armorial cartouche, 19th century, 53in. wide.
(Christie's) $6,817

A mahogany four-poster bed of George III style, the molded shaped canopy covered in old gold silk damask, 86in. long.
(Christie's) $12,500

An American late classical mahogany tester bedstead, mid 19th century, by D. Barjon, on columnar feet with casters and shaped rails, 74¹/₄in. wide.
(Christie's) $7,101

BOOKCASES

A Victorian mahogany bookcase with a molded cornice above a pair of glazed paneled doors, 41in. wide.
(Anderson & Garland)
$1,913

A rosewood veneered and ormolu mounted breakfront bookcase, the scagliola top made to resemble lapis lazuli, early 19th century, English, 213cm. wide.
(Finarte) $10,002

A George III mahogany breakfront bookcase crossbanded overall in satinwood, the broken triangular pediment centered by a plinth, 84in. wide.
(Christie's) $17,262

A pine breakfront library bookcase, with a molded cornice, the front with doric capped fluted pilasters and leaf carving, 8ft.
(Woolley & Wallis)
$5,363

Rare and early Gustav Stickley oak two-door bookcase, No. 510, circa 1901, overhanging top above two twelve-pane doors with mitered mullions, 58$^{1}/_{2}$in. wide.
(Skinner) $14,950

A Queen Anne style walnut break-front bookcase with a scrolling pediment decorated with florets and scallop motif, 61$^{1}/_{2}$in. wide.
(Anderson & Garland)
$5,967

A Victorian mahogany bookcase, the molded cornice above a pair of glazed doors and cupboard doors, flanked by pilaster uprights, 50$^{1}/_{2}$in. wide.
(Christie's) $3,188

A mahogany and satin-banded breakfront bookcase, the pedimented cornice above four astragal glazed doors, on bracket feet, 87in. wide.
(Christie's) $2,927

A late George III mahogany bookcase, the upper section with reverse breakfront shallow cornice over a pair of astragal glazed doors, 53in. wide.
(Spencer's) $1,014

BOOKCASES

Federal mahogany veneer glazed desk and bookcase, Massachusetts, 1790–1810, old refinish, 40½in. wide. (Skinner) $4,600

A good 19th century mahogany reverse breakfront library bookcase, with tongue and groove carved stepped cornice, 310cm. wide. (Spencer's) $7,200

A good George III mahogany bookcase, the upper section with dentil carved architectural cornice, 50in. wide. (Spencer's) $8,160

A mahogany bookcase-on-stand, with a pair of astragal glazed doors below enclosing three shelves, above a pair of paneled doors, on bracket feet, 49½in. wide. (Christie's) $3,443

A matched pair of 19th century walnut bookcases, each with an undulating arched paneled back over four graduated rectangular tiers, 30in. wide. (Spencer's) $2,592

A Victorian mahogany cabinet bookcase, with molded pediment, the plain glazed doors enclosing four adjustable shelves, 60in. wide. (Dee, Atkinson & Harrison) $3,060

A large mahogany break-front bookcase with two pairs of full length glazed paneled doors to the center, 104in. wide. (Anderson & Garland) $4,284

A classical carved and figured mahogany bookcase cabinet, probably New York State, circa 1830, the upper section with shaped pediment, 62in. wide. (Sotheby's) $4,025

A breakfront dwarf bookcase, rosewood veneered with brass marquetry inlay and stringing, 6ft. (Woolley & Wallis) $2,031

FURNITURE

A Regency rosewood and brass mounted bookcase, the overhanging molded cornice above a pair of grille doors flanked by turned columns, 110cm. wide.
(Phillips) **$9,517**

A late Regency rosewood chiffonier, with bead mouldings, the shelved superstructure on turned column supports with a mirror back, 44in. wide.
(Christie's) **$5,000**

A George III style inlaid mahogany breakfront bookcase, late 19th century, on square tapering legs with spade feet, 65½in. wide.
(Christie's) **$11,213**

A late Victorian ebony-veneered and ebonized breakfront bookcase, the molded cornice above three glazed panel doors enclosing green-velvet lined shelves, 94in. wide.
(Christie's) **$12,600**

An Edwardian line-inlaid rosewood crossbanded mahogany bookcase, on square section legs, stamped *From S & H Jewells, Furniture Warehouses, Holburn*, 32½in. wide.
(Christie's) **$3,344**

A late Victorian oak library bookcase, by Howard & Son, the upper part with a molded cornice fitted with adjustable shelves and enclosed by roundel-decorated glazed paneled doors, 81in. wide.
(Christie's) **$6,840**

A late George III mahogany and satinwood banded bookcase of bowed breakfront form, the base with a hinged central writing flap above a pair of paneled doors, 128cm. wide.
(Phillips) **$6,140**

An Edwardian, satinwood breakfront secretaire bookcase, inlaid with checker lines, the upper part of stepped outline with a molded cornice, on bracket feet, 76in. wide.
(Christie's) **$27,000**

An Egyptian Revival ormolu-mounted polycgromed ebonized library bookcase, early 20th century, with a rectangular molded cornice carved with Horus, 55in. wide.
(Christie's) **$20,556**

An early 19th century French Provincial oak cabinet, the molded rounded cornice above a pair of glazed doors enclosing two shelves, 53in. wide.
(Christie's) $3,312

A Regency ormolu mounted breakfront dwarf bookcase, the top with paneled platform pediments at each end, the cupboards below with grille doors, 198cm. wide.
(Phillips) $8,443

One of a pair of Franco-Belgian mahogany bibliothèques, circa 1910, the triangular pediment applied with a putto in a heavenly chariot, 4ft. 2in. wide.
(Sotheby's) $4,149

A Dutch oak, parquetry and marquetry bookcase, with gadrooned cornice above a scroll-lined frieze and a pair of arched glazed doors, the base early 17th century and either Zeeland or Antwerp, 56½in. wide.
(Christie's) $7,176

A French ormolu and ebony bibliotheque basse, the rectangular top inlaid with brass lines, above a pair of glazed panel doors, 19th century, 45in. wide.
(Christie's) $3,540

George II parcel-gilt walnut bookcase, the upper case with outset swan's neck pediment and molded leaf-carved edge, raised on hairy-paw feet, 47in. wide.
(Butterfield & Butterfield) $8,625

Gustav Stickley oak bookcase, designed by Harvey Ellis, Model 700, circa 1904, an arched valance below, 4ft. 10in. high.
(Butterfield & Butterfield) $9,775

A 19th century thuyawood breakfront bookcase, the lower section with green marble top, 224cm. wide.
(Finarte) $24,711

A pine cabinet, carved with trailing floral and foliate stems with stiff-leaf and bead decoration, on scroll feet, Normandy, early 19th century, 56½in. wide.
(Christie's) $6,300

A German walnut and oak bureau-cabinet, 18th century, the swan's neck cresting above a pair of paneled doors enclosing two shelves,, 50in. wide.
(Christie's) $2,700

A Chippendale mahogany desk-and-bookcase, Massachusetts, 1760–1780, the upper section with a pair of scalloped paneled doors opening to an interior fitted with shelves, 39³/₄in. wide.
(Christie's) $21,850

A fine mid 18th century mahogany bureau cabinet, with foliate-carved swan-neck pediment, on ogee bracket feet, 50in. wide.
(Bearne's) $4,131

An 18th century Dutch walnut and floral marquetry bureau cabinet, profusely inlaid with urns of summer flowers, birds, flower blooms and angels, 119cm. wide.
(Phillips) $22,400

A George III burr-yew cylinder bureau-bookcase, crossbanded overall in rosewood, the upper section with three-quarter galleried rectangular mahogany top, 36in. wide.
(Christie's) $43,332

A George I walnut bureau cabinet, the featherbanded base with a sloping flap enclosing an interior of pigeonholes and six drawers around a central cabinet, 99cm. wide.
(Phillips) $16,885

A William and Mary walnut bureau bookcase, in three sections, the upper part with a plain molded cornice enclosed by a pair of beveled panel doors, 1m. wide.
(Phillips) $9,600

A mahogany bureau bookcase, the dentil molded broken pediment above a pair of astragal glazed doors and sloping fall, late 18th century, 50in. wide.
(Christie's) $5,000

An 18th century walnut South German bureau cabinet, in four sections, with paper painted linings, banded in purplewood and inlaid with lines, 118cm. wide.
(Phillips) $9,280

FURNITURE

A walnut bureau cabinet, the later molded cornice fitted with a shaped glazed door, on a molded plinth with bracket feet, 26¹/₂in. wide.
(Christie's) $6,620

A George III ivory-inlaid ebony and ebonized bureau-bookcase inlaid overall with foliate marquetry of Indian figures, birds and animals, 41in. wide.
(Christie's) $30,694

A walnut and crossbanded bureau cabinet, the upper part with a broken arched pediment, fitted with shelves and enclosed by a door, on cabriole legs, 18th century, 28in. wide.
(Christie's) $9,900

A mahogany cylinder bureau, George IV, circa 1825, the ebonized molded cornice above a pair of glazed doors, on a bead-molded plinth, 132cm. wide.
(Sotheby's) $23,920

A South German brass-mounted walnut and Karelian-birch bureau-cabinet, crossbanded overall in tulipwood, first half 18th century, 50in. wide.
(Christie's) $43,056

A Dutch satinwood bureau-bookcase, late 18th century, the waved molded cornice centered by an asymmetrical rockwork C-scroll and acanthus cartouche, 57¹/₂in. wide.
(Christie's) $13,540

A north European walnut double-domed bureau-cabinet, the base section with cross and featherbanded fall-front enclosing a close-nailed olive-green velvet writing-surface, 40¹/₂in. wide.
(Christie's) $33,120

A William and Mary walnut and featherbanded double dome bureau bookcase, the upper part with a molded cornice above a pair of arched mirror paneled doors, 100cm. wide.
(Phillips) $22,400

A Dutch ormolu-mounted kingwood and marquetry bombé bureau-cabinet, second half 18th century, inlaid overall with trellis, the superstructure with molded arched cornice, 51in. wide.
(Christie's) $24,375

BUREAU BOOKCASES

A George III oak bureau bookcase, with dentil cornice over pair of solid paneled doors, 3ft. 6in. wide.
(Russell, Baldwin & Bright)
$3,991

William and Mary style oak secretary, 19th century, the cabinet enclosing letter slots, 36³/₄in. wide.
(Skinner)
$1,840

A Louis XVI walnut secrétaire with carved garland motifs and paneled doors.
(Arnold Frankfurt)
$4,813

A fine and attractive tortoiseshell lacquered double domed bureau bookcase in early 18th century style, the upper section with two mirrored panels enclosing a fitted interior, 36in. wide.
(Spencer's)
$3,366

An oak bureau bookcase, the upper section with fitted interior and pair of astragal glazed doors above candlestands, possibly Welsh, late 18th/early 19th century, 46¹/₂in. wide.
(Christie's)
$2,956

A good Victorian mahogany cylinder bureau bookcase, the upper section with stepped molded cornice flanked by fluted curved corbels, 58in. wide.
(Spencer's)
$2,907

A 19th century Continental ebonized mahogany bureau cabinet, shallow cavetto molded cornice over an eight day clock movement, 50in. wide, Italian or German.
(Spencer's)
$3,498

A George I burr walnut bureau cabinet, the upper part with a cavetto molded cornice and a pair of later doors with ogee patterned glazing bars, 106cm. wide.
(Phillips)
$6,908

An Edwardian mahogany and satinwood-banded bureau bookcase, with molded cornice and a pair of geometrically astragal glazed doors, 36in. wide.
(Christie's)
$1,589

BUREAUX

Chippendale mahogany slant lid desk, Newport, Rhode Island, replaced brass, refinished, 40½in. wide.
(Skinner) $2,990

A Georgian oak standing bureau, the interior fittings having two concealed drawers and well, 2ft. 11in.
(Russell, Baldwin & Bright) $1,765

Chippendale maple slant lid desk, probably Massachusetts, circa 1780, 38¾in. wide.
(Skinner) $2,415

Chippendale cherry slant lid desk, Connecticut, circa 1780, refinished replaced brasses, 38in. wide.
(Skinner) $3,737

A Biedermeier mahogany cylinder bureau, with rectangular top, over a central cupboard, 42½in. wide.
(Spencer's) $3,021

Chippendale maple slant-lid desk, Rhode Island, 18th century, original brass, 35½in. wide.
(Skinner) $4,887

An Edwardian line-inlaid mahogany bureau, the sloping fall enclosing a fitted interior above four graduated drawers, 37½in. wide.
(Christie's) $2,066

A Chippendale mahogany slant-front desk, Rhode Island, 1760–1780, the rectangular top above a thumbmolded slant lid, 37½in. wide.
(Christie's) $25,300

A walnut and feather-banded bureau, with two short and two long drawers, on later bun feet, 18th century, 36in. wide.
(Christie's) $2,510

A small French brass tortoiseshell and pewter bureau Mazarin, Paris, circa 1850, in Louis XIV manner, the rectangular top lavishly inlaid, 142cm. wide.
(Sotheby's) $32,913

A French marquetry ladies writing desk, Napoléon III, circa 1860, in Louis XV style, the bombé writing flap with a well and three drawers, 83cm. wide.
(Sotheby's) $7,314

A German ormolu-mounted walnut, amaranth and marquetry bureau, the rounded rectangular top and shaped rectangular fallfront inlaid with floral sprays, 44in. wide.
(Christie's) $25,116

A German ormolu-mounted mahogany and parquetry bureau à cylindre, possibly by Johann Gottlob Fiedler, the rectangular three-quarter galleried top above a solid cylinder, late 18th century, 49in. wide.
(Christie's) $25,116

A Chippendale mahogany reverse-serpentine slant-front desk, North Shore, Massachusetts, 1760–1780, thumbmolded hinged lid opening to a stepped interior, 39⅝in. wide.
(Christie's) $9,200

A brass-bound plum-pudding mahogany and mahogany bureau à cylindre, the superstructure with rectangular gray-veined white marble top, 19th century, 51in. wide.
(Christie's) $7,535

A Portuguese rosewood bureau in the rococo style, the superimposed upper section with a sloping fall enclosing a stepped serpentine interior, top section 19th century, base 18th century, 124cm. wide.
(Phillips) $13,048

A Chippendale mahogany reverse-serpentine slant-front desk, Eastern Massachusetts, 1760–1780, the rectangular hinged lid opening to reveal a fitted interior with central fan-carved drawer, 42¼in. wide.
(Christie's) $10,925

An 18th century South German walnut, olivewood and crossbanded bureau, the serpentine flap enclosing a stepped interior of seven drawers, the bowed front with two long drawers, 79cm. wide.
(Phillips) $4,605

BUREAUX

A George I walnut and burr-walnut bureau, the spreading frieze with two drawers, the sides with lacquered brass carrying-handles, 21³/₄in. wide. (Christie's) $16,250

A chinoiserie decorated lacquered bureau, the turned legs joined by a pierced X-stretcher, Tuscany, 19th century, 122cm. wide. (Finarte) $6,169

Fine antique rosewood lady's writing desk with floral marquetry inlay to the back section, 24in. wide, French, mid 19th century. (G. A. Key) $1,725

A William and Mary desk-on-frame, Massachusetts, circa 1710–1730, in two parts, the upper section opening to a fitted interior, 27¹/₄in. wide. (Christie's) $27,600

A French ormolu-mounted mahogany bureau à cylindre, in the Empire style, the upper part with three drawers, above the hinged front, second half 19th century, 49³/₄in. wide. (Christie's) $6,399

A George I walnut crossbanded and featherbanded bureau, the sloping fall enclosing a central cupboard door flanked by pillared compartments, 94cm. wide. (Phillips) $6,908

A French ormolu-mounted tulipwood and marquetry bureau de dame, of bombé outline, on cabriole legs with foliate-cast sabots, late 19th century, 31in. wide. (Christie's) $7,314

A George II walnut bureau on stand of small size, inlaid with checkered lines and geometric designs, the stand on lapeted turned legs with club feet, 45cm. wide. (Phillips) $2,763

A gilt-metal-mounted, parquetry, kingwood and tulipwood bureau de dame, the fall front with painted portrait medallion, French, late 19th century, 30in. wide. (Christie's) $7,438

BUREAUX

Small Queen Anne style tiger maple desk on frame, 26in. wide. (Skinner)   **$1,495**

A George II mahogany bureau with a fall-flap enclosing a well fitted interior, the exterior with two short and three long drawers, 43³/₄in. wide. (Hy. Duke & Son)

$3,640

Dutch rococo style mahogany and marquetry slant-lid desk, late 19th century, 50in. wide. (Skinner)   **$4,887**

An early 18th century bureau, in Virginian walnut, the fall flap reveals a fitted interior with a well above a girdle molding, 3ft. 2in. (Woolley & Wallis)   **$1,950**

George III mahogany slant-lid desk, third quarter 18th century, 39¹/₂in. wide. (Skinner)   **$2,070**

Louis XV style gilt bronze mounted parquetry bureau en pente, opening to reveal two drawers, above two long drawers and a shelf stretcher, 21in. wide. (William Doyle)   **$1,380**

A George III mahogany bureau, the fall-flap enclosing a fitted interior over four graduated drawers, 39in. wide. (Hy. Duke & Son)

$1,365

A George III mahogany bureau, the fall front above an arrangement of four graduated drawers, 36in. wide. (Hy. Duke & Son)   **$1,468**

A Georgian yellow lacquered bureau ornately decorated in chinoiserie, raised on bracket feet, 33in. wide. (Anderson & Garland)

$918

BUREAUX

A rosewood and foliate-marquetry bureau de dame, the three-quarter brass gallery above a sloping fall enclosing a fitted interior, 29in. wide. (Christie's) $1,332

Louis XVI style gilt bronze mounted mahogany desk, the rectangular top above a tambour slide, raised on tapered square legs, 39in. wide. (William Doyle) $9,775

A feather-banded walnut bureau-on-stand, the sloping fall above a frieze drawer and three short drawers about an arched apron, 28in. wide. (Christie's) $2,204

A mahogany bureau of small size, the sloping fall with inscribed plaque, enclosing a leather-lined fitted interior, parts 18th century, 25in. wide. (Christie's) $1,776

A Biedermeier mahogany cylinder bureau, the slightly raised rectangular top with deep chamfered edge over a cylinder, 123cm. wide. (Spencer's) $3,021

A George III mahogany bureau, the fall front inlaid with oval satinwood stringing, on molded plinth and shaped bracket feet, 37½in. wide. (Hy. Duke & Son) $1,931

A Queen Anne walnut bureau, the herringbone crossbanded fall front above two small drawers, 38in. wide. (Hy. Duke & Son) $5,408

An Edwardian mahogany and satinwood-banded bureau, with three-quarter galleried top, sloping fall enclosing a fitted interior, 30in. wide. (Christie's) $1,412

A George I walnut and boxwood strung miniature bureau, the fall front concealing a fitted interior with a well, 9in. wide. (Cheffins Grain & Comins) $2,736

CABINETS

An English marquetry side cabinet, Victorian, circa 1880, in the manner of Collinson & Lock, 183cm. wide.
(Sotheby's) $11,337

A French mahogany side cabinet, Napoléon III, Paris, circa 1870, attributed to Grohé of Paris, or possibly by Sormani, in Louis XVI manner, 143cm. wide.
(Sotheby's) $10,971

An oak cabinet, designed by Peter Waals, the superstructure with a series of long and short paneled drawers, 1920/25, 106.8cm. wide.
(Christie's) $5,451

A 17th century Indo or Portuguese teak, ebonised and rosewood cabinet on stand, the front with an arrangement of eight drawers inlaid with confronting tigers wearing ducal coronets, 79cm. wide.
(Phillips) $18,420

A French ormolu-mounted walnut, ebony and lacquer meuble-entre-deux, the brocatelle marble top with shaped sides, last quarter 19th century, 49½in. wide.
(Christie's) $2,925

A French pietre dure side cabinet, Napoléon III, Paris, circa 1850, with gilt-bronze egg and dart cresting above alternate sunflowers and acanthus, the whole ebony-veneered, with key, 97cm. wide.
(Sotheby's) $4,206

Oval side cabinet, circa 1925, in the style of Emile-Jacques Ruhlmann, in walnut with silvered wood, half-fluted legs and a bronze lock plate, 65.5cm. wide.
(Sotheby's) $2,236

An Italian ebonised specimen marble and pietra dura inset cabinet on stand, with a molded cornice above a pair of cupboard doors, 19th century, 43in. wide.
(Christie's) $36,570

A Flemish bone-inlaid fruitwood and marquetry cabinet-on-stand, the stand with three drawers and on turned legs, late 17th century, 46in. wide.
(Christie's) $7,176

CABINETS

An English ormolu-mounted walnut side-cabinet, of serpentine outline, centered by a glazed paneled door, second half 19th century, 72½in. wide.
(Christie's) $5,851

A George IV ormolu-mounted Chinese lac burgauté and black and gilt-japanned side cabinet, inlaid overall with mother-of-pearl depicting courtly chinoiserie figures, 90½in. wide.
(Christie's) $15,347

Painted cabinet, circa 1865, in the manner of William Burges, the doors painted with fourteen arched panels of saints, 137.5cm. wide.
(Sotheby's) $3,726

A French ormolu-mounted mahogany and Vernis Martin decorated meuble d'appui, by Mathieu Befort, with a red marble breakfront top and rounded corners, second half 19th century, 41½in. wide.
(Christie's) $5,485

A Regency satinwood cabinet-on-stand, the upper section with rectangular molded cornice above a pair of geometrically-glazed doors with simulated bamboo rounded angles, 33½in. wide.
(Christie's) $7,222

An English ormolu-mounted walnut writing/side cabinet, with a pierced brass gallery above three glazed paneled doors, second half 19th century, 56¾in. wide.
(Christie's) $10,057

A Regency mahogany and ebonized side cabinet, the crossbanded rectangular top above a paneled frieze drawer and a pair of simulated doors, 21¼in. wide.
(Christie's) $4,724

A good English satinwood marquetry side cabinet, London, circa 1900, in George III style, of demi-lune form, 92cm. wide.
(Sotheby's) $10,057

An Italian ebonized wood table cabinet, the carved architectural front inlaid with polychrome marble and hardstones, early 18th century, 78cm. wide.
(Finarte) $11,036

A late Victorian rosewood salon cabinet, the stepped mirrored superstructure with frilled leaf and fret carved swept pediment, 60in. wide.
(Spencer's) $2,080

A South German table cabinet in polished and ebonized palisander, inlaid with ivory, 17th century, 48.5cm. wide.
(Kunsthaus am Museum) $1,368

George III mahogany library cabinet, late 18th century, in two sections, the upper portion with flat molded cornice, 41in. wide.
(William Doyle) $5,175

A late Victorian inlaid walnut sofa cabinet, of bowfronted form, the foliate-carved raised back above three paneled doors flanked by foliate corbels, 59¹/₂in. wide.
(Christie's) $2,657

Edwardian rosewood and marquetry music cabinet, late 19th century, bearing a metal label for *W. J. Mansell cabinet maker upholsterer 266 Fulham Rd. London*, 23in. wide.
(Skinner) $805

A mid 19th century French side cabinet, the sides with serpentine front shelves and gilt bronze mounts to a central mirror door, 4ft. 3in.
(Woolley & Wallis) $4,108

Aesthetic Movement cabinet, 1880s, oak, of asymmetrical construction, the centre with rectangular panel inlaid with bronze and pewter, 79cm. wide.
(Sotheby's) $2,236

An Aesthetic Movement painted, ebonized and mahogany splay-front side cabinet, enclosed by a pair of paneled doors, circa 1880, 60in. wide.
(Neales) $1,040

A Japanese carved and ebonised fruitwood stage cabinet fitted with six open shelves, divided by blue lacquered paneled cupboard doors, 44¹/₂in. wide.
(Christie's) $1,130

CABINETS

A Regency architect's mahogany cabinet, the rectangular hinged and double ratcheted top with a central hinged and ratcheted rectangular panel, 52in. wide. (Spencer's) $13,770

A black lacquered cabinet on stand decorated with chinoiseries, the front shaped as four concave columns, Dutch, 18th century, 120cm. wide. (Finarte) $5,519

Renaissance Revival walnut and marquetry side cabinet, late 19th century, 65in. wide. (Skinner) $1,725

A late Victorian ebonised and amboyna breakfront side cabinet, the paneled door inset with painted ceramic panel flanked by Ionic capital stop-fluted column uprights, 59½in. wide. (Christie's) $2,514

An oak cabinet with a pair of Gothic tracery paneled doors, above a pierced Gothic tracery apron, late 19th/early 20th century, 39in. wide. (Christie's) $1,294

A hardwood side cabinet, with ripple and wave molding, the two doors with raised panels, on bun feet, Portuguese, 19th century, 57½in. wide. (Christie's) $1,682

A mahogany specimen cabinet, the rectangular top above a panel door enclosing thirty-two ivory handled drawers, on plinth base, 17in. wide. (Christie's) $496

A giltmetal mounted, ebonized and brass inlaid scarlet boulle side cabinet of serpentine outline, the central paneled doors flanked by two glazed doors, late 19th century, 83in. wide. (Christie's) $2,582

A burr walnut cabinet on stand, the lower part with four serpentine fronted drawers, on bun feet, Dutch, 19th century. (Kunsthaus am Museum) $4,043

An English walnut small display cabinet, circa 1860, the frieze with a plaque cast in low relief above glazed doors, 93cm. wide. (Sotheby's) $4,526

An American 'Aesthetic Movement' copper-mounted parcel-gilt and lacquered ebonized credenza, circa 1865, by Herter Brothers, 66½in. wide. (Christie's) $14,576

A French painted side cabinet, circa 1890, in Hispano-Moresque style, with a pair of glazed doors flanked by pilasters, 149cm. wide. (Sotheby's) $8,487

Important cabinet with inlaid figures, from a suite of bedroom furniture made for the apartment of Dr. Holzl, circa 1904, by Koloman Moser, 51¼in. wide. (Sotheby's) $537,030

A pair of French marquetry and gilt-bronze encoignures, Paris, circa 1880, in Transitional manner, with a molded veined marble top above a frieze drawer, 80cm. wide. (Sotheby's) $16,974

A Victorian kingwood work cabinet, circa 1860, the hinged quarter-veneered top centered by a porcelain plaque, on cabriole legs and gilt-metal sabots and chûtes, 40cm. wide. (Sotheby's) $2,829

A Napoleon II porcelain and ormolu-mounted tulipwood and mahogany meuble d'appui, third quarter 19th century, with an ormolu-mounted eared rectangular white marble top, 49¾in. wide. (Christie's) $8,409

Cabinet, circa 1904, by Koloman Moser, executed by Caspar Hrazdril, in thuya and lemonwood with brass handles and legs, 39½in. wide. (Sotheby's) $77,274

A mahogany and marquetry bowfront corner cabinet, decorated with foliate scrolls and meandering floral stems, the top with a ribbon-tied roundel, Dutch, late 18th/early 19th century, 36½in. wide. (Christie's) $2,600

CABINETS

A late George III mahogany collector's cabinet, with associated bookcase top, the molded cornice above two glazed panel doors, 33in. wide. (Christie's) **$6,300**

Pair of cabinets, from a bedroom suite for the apartment of Dr. Holzl, circa 1904, by Koloman Moser, with geometric marquetry in exotic woods. (Sotheby's) **$59,454**

A French ormolu-mounted, amaranth and marquetry-inlaid encoignure, with a later white marble top, third quarter 19th century, 30¾in. wide. (Christie's) **$2,795**

A rosewood and brass-inlaid cabinet, the rectangular crossbanded top above a foliate and lion decorated frieze, 56½in. wide. (Christie's) **$2,541**

An English ormolu-mounted marquetry, walnut, thuya wood and coromandel double-doored library folio cabinet, second half 19th century, 48½in. wide. (Christie's) **$7,525**

An English ormolu-mounted, ebonized and pietra dura side cabinet, the paneled door with an oval panel of flowers and fruit within an ormolu ribbon-tied border, second half 19th century, 39in. wide. (Christie's) **$1,677**

A Viennese giltmetal-mounted ebony and enamel display cabinet, of small size, with a three-quarter balustraded gallery above the molded pediment, late 19th century, 17¼in. wide. (Christie's) **$11,550**

A pair of Louis XVI style ormolu-mounted tulipwood and amaranth meubles d'appui, late 19th century, by Paul Sormani, 33in. wide. (Christie's) **$10,278**

A William and Mary black and gilt-japanned double-domed cabinet-on-chest, decorated overall with chinoiserie figures hunting in a watery landscape with island temples and pagodas, 38¾in. wide. (Christie's) **$27,600**

309

CABINETS

A Regency ormolu-mounted and brass-inlaid rosewood side cabinet in the manner of George Bullock, the stepped breakfront portor marble top with pierced anthemion gallery, 72³/₄in. wide.
(Christie's) $21,666

A mid-Victorian walnut dentist's cabinet, with three-quarter pierced gallery above mirrored back, 32in. wide.
(Christie's) $2,869

A 19th century Burmese rosewood serpentine side cabinet, profusely carved and pierced throughout, 71¹/₂in. wide.
(Bearne's) $1,101

A marquetry inlaid walnut demi-lune side cabinet, the top above two frieze drawers between simulated fluted uprights, Dutch, 19th century, 29¹/₂in. wide.
(Christie's) $3,048

One of a pair of Louis XV style Provincial walnut cabinets, 28in. wide.
(Skinner)
          (Two) $3,220

A Regency rosewood parcel-gilt side cabinet, the raised mirror back with carrara marble top on turned supports, 40³/₄in. wide.
(Anderson & Garland)
          $5,202

A Gothic Revival oak cabinet in the manner of A. W. N. Pugin and two matching side sections, with glazed doors and of slightly later date, 54¹/₄in. wide and 28in. wide.
(Bearne's) $6,885

Art Deco sycamore and burr walnut cocktail cabinet, having two shaped doors, flanked by two cupboard doors on 'U' shaped support.
(Lawrences) $2,279

A mahogany side cabinet, applied with gilt-metal mounts, the rectangular top above three frieze drawers, French, late 19th century, 74in. wide.
(Christie's) $1,672

CANTERBURYS

A George IV mahogany rectangular canterbury with four sections and central cut out carrying handle, 18in. wide. (Anderson & Garland) $1,454

A Victorian walnut canterbury with raised pierced back, turned twisted supports, 1ft. 10in. wide. (Russell, Baldwin & Bright) $1,765

Victorian burr walnut veneered music canterbury with fret work sides, turned dividers and corner supports, 21 x 16in., English, circa 1850. (G. A. Key) $654

A Victorian burr and figured walnut canterbury/whatnot of serpentine outline, the top surface with open fret scrollwork cresting, 26in. wide. (Peter Francis) $1,913

A George III satinwood canterbury, the dished open rectangular top with three columnar divisions, above a mahogany-lined frieze drawer and on square tapering legs. (Christie's) $10,970

Victorian mahogany canterbury, the top with pierced scrolled pediment, on two pierced scrolled supports, mid 19th century, 23in. wide. (G. A. Key) $1,186

An early Victorian mahogany canterbury, with four open divisions, on bobbin-turned uprights above a frieze drawer, on ring-turned legs, 20¹/₂in. wide. (Christie's) $1,526

Victorian walnut canterbury of oval form, the base with two scrolled pierced panels and frieze drawer below, circa 1850, 29in. wide. (G. A. Key) $1,771

A George III mahogany canterbury, the open rectangular top with brass angles and three divisions, on square tapering legs, 18in. wide. (Christie's) $4,224

DINING CHAIRS

Walnut carved side chair, Newport, Rhode Island, circa 1750, old refinish, 39in. high. (Skinner) $8,050

Pair of antique American Sheraton fancy chairs, with stenciled decoration, rush seat. (Eldred's) $358

A William IV mahogany hallchair, the scrolling shield-shaped back with castellated top, on turned and reeded legs. (Christie's) $353

One of a pair of giltwood and red painted side chairs, each with arched scrolling toprail, turned splats flanked by spiral uprights with finials, Italian, 19th century. (Christie's) (Two) $293

Two of a set of six Provincial Empire walnut side chairs, early 19th century, each of restrained gondola form, raised on saber legs. (William Doyle) (Six) $2,760

A 1950s Italian side chair, in an elegant organic style, rosewood frame and 'wings' back, upholstered in green and yellow velvet fabric. (Bonhams) $217

One of a set of four ash ladder-back chairs, each with arched splats and turned top-rail surmounted on the uprights, Macclesfield, early 19th century. (Christie's) (Four) $1,108

A pair of Regency mahogany hallchairs, each with reeded top-rail above waisted back and solid seat. (Christie's) $673

One of a set of six early Victorian mahogany dining chairs, each with deep bar toprail above a padded seat on turned faceted tapering legs. (Christie's) (Six) $1,722

DINING CHAIRS

Chippendale walnut carved side chair, Pennsylvania, circa 1780, old refinish, 38in. high.
(Skinner) $4,887

Pair of maple side chairs, New England, circa 1780, old refinish.
(Skinner) $1,610

Mahogany balloon-seat side chair, New England, circa 1750, 40½in. high.
(Skinner) $2,185

One of a matched set of eight elm spindle-back dining chairs, each with eared top-rail and two rows of spindles above a straw seat, North Country, mid 19th century.
(Christie's)
      (Eight) $3,142

Two of a set of eight William IV mahogany dining chairs with curved deep top rails and 'C' scroll crossbars, on turned octagonal tapering legs.
(Phillips)
      (Eight) $3,070

A Queen Anne walnut sidechair, attributed to William Savery, 1721–1728, Philadelphia, the serpentine incised crestrail with shaped ears above a solid vasiform splat, on cabriole legs with pad feet.
(Christie's) $2,990

One of a set of eight beech dining/salon chairs, each with waisted back and scrolled horizontal splat, 19th century.
(Christie's)
      (Eight) $1,894

Two of a set of eight late Victorian oak dining chairs, including two armchairs, each with molded scrolled toprail.
(Christie's)
      (Eight) $2,165

One of a set of seven early Victorian mahogany dining chairs, each with waisted oval back with a coat of arms cresting.
(Christie's)
      (Seven) $1,589

DINING CHAIRS

One of a set of fourteen Dutch mahogany dining-chairs including a pair of open armchairs, on cabriole legs and pad feet, mid-18th century. (Christie's)
(Fourteen) $34,086

A pair of Austrian Biedermeier fruitwood and parcel-gilt side chairs, each with curved tablet toprail, above a pierced lyre-shaped and horizontal back. (Christie's) $5,741

One of a pair of Dutch ivory-inlaid walnut and marquetry side chairs, the foliate waved toprail above a solid vase-shaped splat, 18th/19th century. (Christie's)
(Two) $3,947

One of a pair of Biedermeier burr-elm, ebonized and parcel-gilt side chairs, each with cartouche-shaped back with confronting sphinx toprail, early 19th century. (Christie's)
(Two) $9,867

A pair of Chippendale carved mahogany side chairs, attributed to the Shop of John Goddard, Newport, Rhode Island, 1760–1775. (Christie's) $96,000

One of a set of six George III green-painted and parcel-gilt side chairs in the Gothic style, each with pierced, pointed arched back with a pagoda cresting. (Christie's)
(Six) $13,541

One of a set of six Danish beechwood dining-chairs, each with pierced rectangular back filled with lattice-work, late 18th/early 19th century. (Christie's)
(Six) $6,458

A pair of Chippendale carved walnut sidechairs, New England, 1750–1770, each with serpentine crestrail continuing to molded scrolling ears above a strap work splat, 38in. high. (Christie's) $4,600

One of a set of ten Regency and mahogany simulated-bamboo dining-chairs, each with pierced toprail with three balls above a shaped X-shaped splat. (Christie's)
(Ten) $11,811

DINING CHAIRS

Two of a set of six Regency mahogany dining chairs, including two open armchairs, each with line inlaid bar toprail. (Christie's)

(Six) $3,344

A George II oak chair, the solid vase splat above a needlework drop-in seat. (Christie's) $704

Two of a set of ten Victorian oak dining chairs, including two open armchairs, on ring-turned legs joined by stretchers. (Christie's) (Ten) $1,165

Two of a set of eight mahogany dining chairs, of George III style, including two open armchairs, each wheel-back with central foliate paterae. (Christie's)

(Eight) $4,928

One of a set of six early Victorian rosewood dining chairs, each with scrolling bar top-rail, and foliate horizontal splat. (Christie's)

(Six) $1,972

Two of a set of six Regency dining chairs, including two armchairs, each with a tablet top-rail above paterae-decorated horizontal splat. (Christie's)

(Six) $4,928

Two of a set of ten blue and parcel-gilt decorated dining chairs, including two open armchairs, 19th century. (Christie's)

(Ten) $8,448

One of a set of four early Victorian mahogany dining chairs, each with deep bar top-rail, on reeded tapering legs. (Christie's)

(Four) $1,056

Two of a set of six early Victorian mahogany dining chairs, each with deep undulating bar top-rail. (Christie's)

(Six) $1,972

DINING CHAIRS

One of a set of six mid-Victorian rosewood balloon-back dining chairs, each with molded top-rail and horizontal splat.
(Christie's) (Six) $1,155

Two of a set of four Austro-Hungarian walnut chairs with ox block backs, circa 1825.
(Kunsthaus am Museum)
(Four) $1,749

One of a pair of classical brass inlaid rosewood sidechairs, attributed to William Seavers, Boston, circa 1810, 32¼in. high.
(Christie's)
(Two) $1,265

One of a set of six early Victorian mahogany balloon-back dining chairs, each with foliate horizontal splat, serpentine padded seat, on reeded tapering legs.
(Christie's)
(Six) $1,912

Two of a set of seven Scottish Regency period mahogany dining chairs, the reeded backs with vertical rails and ball decoration.
(Woolley & Wallis)
(Seven) $5,022

One of a set of six mahogany dining chairs, molded overscrolled uprights joined by a turned and fluted top-rail, late 19th century.
(Christie's)
(Six) $1,777

One of a set of six Regency mahogany dining chairs, line inlaid, each with rope-twist and tablet horizontal splats above drop-in seat, on saber legs.
(Christie's)
(Six) $2,334

A pair of Victorian mahogany hall chairs, with shaped and pierced backs on turned legs and thimble feet with hard seats.
(Dee, Atkinson & Harrison)
$216

One of a set of four Regency mahogany dining chairs, including one open armchair, each with bar top-rail and horizontal splat, on ring-turned tapering legs.
(Christie's) (Four) $673

316

Chippendale mahogany carved side chair, 37¹/₂in. high.
(Skinner) $805

Pair of antique American Sheraton fancy chairs, in old yellow paint with stenciled decoration and rush seats.
(Eldred's) $660

Federal mahogany carved side chair, probably New York, circa 1810, old finish, 35in. high.
(Skinner) $862

Frank Lloyd Wright mahogany and upholstered side chair, circa 1955, for Heritage-Henredon Furniture Co., medium finish with brushed green vinyl upholstery, unsigned.
(Skinner) $805

Two of a set of six Regency period mahogany dining chairs, the backs with veneered crests and pierced and reeded horizontal rails.
(Woolley & Wallis)
          (Six) $4,424

A Shaker maple diminutive slat-back chair, early 20th century, with rounded button finials above swelled cylindrical stiles above a trapezoidal cloth-tape woven seat.
(Christie's) $1,610

One of a set of seven late Victorian mahogany dining chairs, each with rounded rectangular back with central reeded splat.
(Christie's)
          (Seven) $2,309

A pair of George III mahogany hall chairs in the manner of Ince and Mayhew, the oval backs inlaid with a panel of satinwood, 19in. wide.
(Hy. Duke & Son)
                          $11,588

One of a set of four late Regency mahogany dining chairs, the paterae-decorated top-rail above scrolling vertical splat, with drop-in seat, and foliate-carved rail.
(Christie's) (Four) $886

EASY CHAIRS

English, eagles head chair, 1880s, oak, the arms with eagle head terminals.
(Sotheby's) $1,677

Marco Zanuso, Italy, Lady armchair for Arflex, 1951, pressed metal frame with rubber webbing.
(Bonhams) $1,160

S.S. Normandy mahogany First Class dining chair, 1934, original woven tapestry upholstery, concave and reeded back with inset panel cushion.
(Skinner) $4,140

Attributed to Charles Rennie Mackintosh, low backed dressing table chair, circa 1905, oak, the low back with vertical slats centered by horizontal elements.
(Sotheby's) $5,589

Early Gustav Stickley oak Morris chair, No. 2341, circa 1901, adjustable back, flat shaped arm over two vertical slats and interior arched corbels.
(Skinner) $2,875

Harden oak slat-sided rocker, Camden, New York, dome tack leather back upholstery and spring cushion seat, Harden paper label.
(Skinner) $805

A Chippendale mahogany wing armchair, New England, circa 1785, the arched crest flanked by ogival wings.
(Sotheby's) $5,462

Art Deco ebonized and upholstered armchair, France, circa 1925, original gold silk upholstery on ebonized wood frame.
(Skinner) $748

A mid-Victorian walnut easy armchair, the upholstered button-back and arms above a serpentine seat.
(Christie's) $1,102

EASY CHAIRS

Victorian mahogany nursing chair, the spoon back crested with floral motif, on short scrolled feet, mid 19th century. (G. A. Key) **$930**

C. Scolari, P. Lomazzi, J. de Pas, D. D'Urbino, Italy, blow chair, for Zanotta, 1967, clear inflatable P.V.C. (Bonhams) **$650**

George II mahogany wing chair, mid 18th century, raised on cabriole legs carved at the knees with acanthus leaves. (William Doyle) **$2,875**

One of a pair of Régence giltwood and gilt-gesso fauteuils à la reine, the arms with ball terminals carved with flowerheads and on scrolled supports. (Christie's) (Two) **$123,034**

Carlo Bugatti pewter and ivory inlaid walnut, copper, ebony parchment and silk corner chair, Italy, circa 1902, shaped continuous arm inlaid with pewter and ivory. (Skinner) **$3,795**

One of a pair of Louis XV giltwood bergères, by Nicolas Quinibert Foliot, each with square padded back, arm-rests, side and squab cushion. (Christie's) (Two) **$112,391**

A George IV mahogany tub-shaped bergère, the outswept arms above padded seat, on ring-turned legs. (Christie's) **$1,286**

Emile-Jacques Ruhlmann, 'Tusks' desk chair, circa 1920, with fluted, curved front legs, upholstered in cream silk. (Sotheby's) **$15,277**

An oak armchair, designed by Alfred Waterhouse for the Council Chamber, Reading Town Hall, on turned legs, 1874. (Christie's) **$726**

EASY CHAIRS

Flemish baroque walnut adjustable armchair, late 17th century, with iron ratchets, upholstered in 17th century tapestry.
(Skinner) $3,738

A pair of beechwood fauteuils, of Louis XV style, each with a cartouche-shaped padded back with outcurved arms, Hungarian.
(Christie's) $2,062

Harden Co. oak arm rocker, Camden, New York, circa 1910, leather upholstered spring cushion, five pierced vertical back slats, four-bowed side slats.
(Skinner) $863

One of a pair of late Victorian mahogany armchairs, each with rounded button back and arms upon ring-turned gallery.
(Christie's)
(Two) $3,198

Charles and Ray Eames Lounge 670 and ottoman, designed 1956, for Herman Miller, Zeeland, Michigan, rosewood veneer on laminated wood shell with original black upholstery, 32¹/₂in. wide.
(Skinner) $1,840

One of a pair of Italian giltwood side chairs, each with cartouche-shaped padded back and drop-in seats.
(Christie's)
(Two) $46,644

A carved oak armchair, attributed to Bembe and Kimmel, New York, circa 1857, the horizontal molded crestrail centering a carved shield above a padded back, on vase shaped lotus carved legs.
(Christie's) $6,325

One of a set of four Regency ebonized and parcel gilt masonic open armchairs, each with paneled curved cresting rail.
(Spencer's)
(Four) $64,000

Important Warren McArthur upholstered aluminium tilting swivel armchair, Rome, New York, circa 1935, original blue leather upholstery on spun aluminium frame with four casters.
(Skinner) $6,325

EASY CHAIRS

One of a pair of grey painted and parcel-gilt fauteuils of Louis XVI style, each frame carved overall with beading and stiff-leaf.
(Christie's)
(Two) $5,023

A pair of walnut open armchairs, of Carolean style, with outswept downscrolled arms, on foliate-carved legs, late 19th century.
(Christie's) $3,168

Large Louis XV style cream painted and parcel-gilt bergère, third quarter 19th century, peach velour upholstery, 45in. high.
(Skinner) $4,312

One of a set of six Louis XV giltwood chaises by Nicolas Quinibert Foliot, each with cartouche-shaped padded back and serpentine squab-cushion covered in pale green suede.
(Christie's)
(Six) $73,369

Rustic carved oak armchair and arm rocker, circa 1907, original medium finish on low-relief carved scenic and oak leaf and limb decoration.
(Skinner) $1,265

One of a pair of Empire mahogany armchairs, 19th century, backs surmounted by triangular section cresting with gilt brass roundel, 27½in. wide.
(Hy. Duke & Son)
(Two) $6,080

One of a pair of Louis XV grained-beech fauteuils à la reine, the channeled frame carved with acanthus and small flowerheads, on cabriole legs headed by a cabochon.
(Christie's)
(Two) $40,796

A pair of green and parcel-gilt decorated fauteuils, each back with needlework medallion depicting 17th century characters.
(Christie's) $1,852

One of a pair of Régence grained fauteuils, each with rectangular shaped back, on cabriole legs headed by flowers and on foliate feet.
(Christie's)
(Two) $117,713

EASY CHAIRS

An ormolu-mounted burr elm
fauteuil, the out-curved arms
mounted with laurel and on
square tapering legs.
(Christie's) $2,691

A pair of Empire white-painted
and parcel-gilt fauteuils, the
stiff-leaf-headed arms
terminating in lioness-masks.
(Christie's) $4,306

A George III mahogany library
open armchair, the downswept
arms carved with stiff-leaf and
flowerheads, on trellis canted
square legs.
(Christie's) $9,930

An Austrian ormolu-mounted
mahogany and figured walnut
bergère, with outscrolled arms
and on a solid X-shaped base,
early 19th century.
(Christie's) $2,153

A pair of 19th century Empire
Revival mahogany and gilt
bronze mounted library
bergères, on square tapering
legs with paw feet.
(Phillips) $9,210

One of a pair of Louis XV white-
painted and parcel-gilt fauteuils,
each with cartouche-shaped
padded back, arm-rests and
serpentine seat.
(Christie's)
(Two) $3,947

One of a pair of Louis XV
giltwood fauteuils, each with
foliate trailed channeled
cartouche-shaped padded back.
(Christie's)
(Two) $19,734

A pair of George III white-
painted and parcel-gilt open
armchairs, each with shield-
shaped channeled back centered
by a fluted scallop-shell.
(Christie's) $11,736

A George III giltwood open
armchair attributed to Thomas
Chippendale, with ribbon-tied
swag cresting and laurel front
seat-rail, on reeded turned
tapering legs.
(Christie's) $10,902

EASY CHAIRS

A Flemish beech wing armchair with slightly arched rectangular padded back, the shaped apron with C-scrolls, early 18th century.
(Christie's) $4,485

A Venetian giltwood open armchair, the shaped seat-rail with central scallop-shell on hipped cabriole legs with pad feet, first half 18th century.
(Christie's) $11,661

A giltwood fauteuil of Régence style, the entrelac carved frame surmounted by a central Apollo mask with acanthus-sprays and espagnolette-masks.
(Christie's) $5,023

One of a pair of George III mahogany library open armchairs, with channeled scrolled arm-supports and bowed channeled apron centered by a cabochon.
(Christie's)
(Two) $36,110

A mahogany library open armchair, the downswept arm-supports carved with flowerhead-filled guilloche, on cabriole legs headed by scallop-shells.
(Christie's) $9,994

One of a pair of George III mahogany library open armchairs, each with slightly arched rectangular padded back, arm-rests and serpentine seat.
(Christie's)
(Two) $123,245

One of a pair of walnut fauteuils, with channeled frame and floral cresting on cabriole legs headed by flowerheads.
(Christie's)
(Two) $4,664

A pair of Louis XV gray-painted and parcel-gilt fauteuils, each with foliate-carved channeled cartouche-shaped padded back, on foliate-carved cabriole legs.
(Christie's) $9,085

One of a pair of Louis XV beech fauteuils, each with cartouche shaped padded back, arm-rests and serpentine seat.
(Christie's)
(Two) $1,794

EASY CHAIRS

A Regency mahogany bergère library chair, with cane paneled curved rectangular back, arms and seat.
(Spencer's) $4,960

A Chippendale mahogany easy chair, Massachusetts, 1750–1780, the canted back with serpentine crest.
(Christie's) $32,200

A Federal mahogany lolling chair, coastal Massachusetts or New Hampshire, circa 1810, the serpentine crest flanked by shaped arms.
(Christie's) $10,925

One of a pair of George II mahogany library open armchairs, each with cartouche-shaped padded back, arm-rests and seat, on cabriole legs headed by elongated foliage.
(Christie's)
(Two) $16,353

IB Kofod-Larsen, Denmark, armchair, for Christensen and Larsen, Copenhagen, circa 1955, teak frame with upholstered seat and back covered in natural fleece fabric.
(Bonhams) $232

A Russian gilt-bronze and lacquer brass-mounted mahogany fauteuil sans accotoirs, the paneled tapering tablet back and squab cushion covered in close-nailed black leather, circa 1800.
(Christie's) $67,548

A pair of French parcel-gilt marquises, Paris, mid 20th century, in Transitional manner, each with an arched flower-carved molded frame, 97cm. wide.
(Sotheby's) $6,034

One of a pair of French giltwood fauteuils, in the Louis XVI style, each with a rectangular padded back, late 19th century.
(Christie's)
(Two) $4,206

One of a pair of beechwood fauteuils, of Régence style, each with an arched padded back carved with foliage and shells.
(Christie's)
(Two) $4,022

ELBOW CHAIRS

A Continental oak open armchair, the shaped foliate-carved toprail centered by a stylized portrait-mask.
(Christie's)   **$188**

A Regency ebonized open armchair, with slightly arched curved cresting rail richly carved.
(Spencer's)   **$1,440**

A 19th century Windsor style rocking chair, with shaped crest rail and bobbin back, with cane seat.
(Dee, Atkinson & Harrison)   **$428**

Alvar Aalto, Finland, cantilevered armchair 406 for Finmar, 1933, laminated wooden frame with cross woven tan leather webbing.
(Bonhams)   **$804**

A carved oak wainscot armchair, Essex County, Massachusetts, circa 1640–1700, the stepped crestrail carved with double arcades, 36¼in. high.
(Christie's)   **$211,500**

One of a pair of George III mahogany open armchairs, each with spindle-turned back, on square section legs joined by stretchers.
(Christie's)
(Two)   **$1,408**

A Shaker rocking armchair, Mt. Lebanon, New York, 19th century, the acorn finials above cylindrical stiles centering a woven back.
(Christie's) ·   **$1,380**

A carved and stained chair, American, 20th century, the rectangular carved and pierced splat of a face with swirling carved hair, 37¼in. high.
(Christie's)   **$345**

A red-painted ladderback rocking armchair, coastal New Hampshire or Southern Maine, 1750–1800, the horizontal slats flanked by cylindrical stiles.
(Christie's)   **$690**

ELBOW CHAIRS

A painted and turned Windsor bow-back armchair, American, circa 1795, on turned legs joined by turned stretchers.
(Sotheby's) $1,495

Two of a set of eight late Victorian mahogany dining chairs of George III style, including two armchairs.
(Christie's)
(Eight) $2,353

Good quality Victorian carved oak armchair, the back with ornate carved top piece, on turned legs, English, circa 1860.
(G. A. Key) $318

Paul McCobb fibreglass armchair, circa 1955, cubist molded orange fibreglass chair with silver finished arched iron legs.
(Skinner) $374

Pair of George III painted beechwood open armchairs, late 18th century, each with a turned crest rail centering a panel ornamented with pinecone finials.
(William Doyle) $9,775

A fine Shaker turned curly maple rocker, New Lebanon Community, New York, first half 19th century, the back comprised of four slats.
(Sotheby's) $6,900

A mahogany open armchair, with arched shell-carved back on eagle head uprights and with central three-pronged splat, late 19th century.
(Christie's) $698

A pair of 'First' chairs by Michel de Lucchi 1983, round painted wooden seats, metal frames, stamped *Memphis Milano Made in Italy*.
(Stockholms Auktionsverk)
                    $607

George Walton, 'Abingdon chair', circa 1895, in oak, with heart shaped tapering back splat, curved arms and rush seat.
(Sotheby's) $1,304

ELBOW CHAIRS

L. & J. G. Stickley oak Morris chair, No. 830, circa 1912, spring cushion seat, 'The Work of...' decal.
(Skinner) $1,265

A pair of Louis XVI white-painted and parcel-gilt fauteuils by Jean-Baptiste-Claude Sené, each with oval guilloche-carved back.
(Christie's) $30,498

Maple and ash turned high chair, Delaware River Valley, late 18th century, 40³/₄in. high.
(Skinner) $920

One of a set of four mahogany open armchairs of George III style, each with pierced cartouche-shaped back, the outscrolled arms with flowerhead terminals.
(Christie's)
(Four) $3,271

A pair of Regency white-painted mahogany bergères attributed to Thomas Chippendale Junior, each with scrolled arched channeled toprail centered by an oval patera.
(Christie's) $16,250

One of a set of eight Italian silvered open armchairs, on cabriole legs headed by scrolls, mid-18th century.
(Christie's)
(Eight) $23,332

An Austrian ormolu-mounted grained fruitwood open armchair, the arched back with pierced flowerhead and entrelac toprail, early 19th century.
(Christie's) $3,229

A pair of yew-wood Grotto armchairs, each with rectangular back and solid splat, flattened arms, slatted seat and knotty uprights, English, 19th century.
(Christie's) $7,392

Norman Cherner laminated and bentwood armchair, circa 1958, for Plycraft, Lawrence, Massachusetts, unsigned.
(Skinner) $575

ELBOW CHAIRS

A George III Provincial mahogany ladder-back armchair, with outcurved arms and drop-in seat, on square legs joined by a stretcher.
(Christie's) $230

An early George III mahogany elbow chair in the Chippendale style, the top rail with acanthus leaf scrolls and pierced vase splat with paterae.
(Phillips) $1,535

A mahogany open armchair, the curved channeled top-rail above an acanthus-carved splat flanked by a pair of downswept arms, early 19th century.
(Christie's) $744

A birchwood and ash rush-seat ladder-back weaver's chair, American, 1800–1820, the back with three slats, the arms and rush-seat below on turned legs joined by stretchers.
(Sotheby's) $1,955

A pair of Regency ebony-inlaid mahogany side chairs, each with deeply-curved arched back inlaid with a central anthemion and laurel spray above a tapering splat.
(Christie's) $16,250

A late Windsor bamboo-turned grain-painted and stenciled child's rocker, American, circa 1820–1829, the crest rail stenciled with flowers and leaves.
(Sotheby's) $1,150

One of a set of four William IV mahogany dining chairs, including an open armchair, each with a boldly-carved tablet top-rail, one with label *Waring & Gillow*.
(Christie's) (Four) $971

A Queen Anne maple corner chair, New England, 1760–1780, the shaped crest above spurred arm rests with rounded handgrips, rush seat with exposed corners, 30in. high.
(Christie's) $863

One of a pair of George III mahogany open armchairs with rectangular spindle backs of slightly differing shape, the padded seats on square chamfered legs.
(Phillips) (Two) $1,075

328

ELBOW CHAIRS

Empire ormolu-mounted mahogany fauteuil de bureau, first quarter 19th century, 32¹/₂in. high. (Skinner) $3,105

Mission oak slat-sided cube chair, 1914, seven vertical back slats, six vertical slats under each arm, inscribed *Made by John Derwallis – 1914.* (Skinner) $575

Bow-back Windsor high chair, New England, circa 1790, original black paint, 33in. high. (Skinner) $19,550

A Chippendale carved walnut armchair, Philadelphia, 1760–1780, the serpentine crestrail centering a foliate and petal carved cartouche above a pierced vase-shaped splat, on cabriole legs with ball-and-claw feet. (Christie's) $20,700

Two of a matching set of five Regency mahogany open armchairs, the curved top rails banded in rosewood above anthemion carved scrolling cross bars. (Phillips) (Five) $4,605

A William and Mary red-painted great chair, Connecticut, 1735–1745, with scrolled and heart-pierced crown crest above four vertical molded banisters over a rushed seat, 46¹/₂in. high. (Christie's) $2,760

A George II walnut and mahogany open armchair, the dished toprail above a solid vase-shaped splat, on cabriole legs headed by acanthus carving. (Christie's) $1,090

William and Mary turned corner chair, New England, early 18th century, original black paint, old leather upholstered seat over original splint seat. (Skinner) $7,475

One of a set of three George III bamboo bergères in the Chinoiserie style, each with canted rectangular back with stepped sides and solid plank seats, on cluster-column legs. (Christie's) (Three) $13,541

CHESTS OF DRAWERS

A Flemish oak chest, the front finely carved with arcaded panels, cast iron fittings, part 16th century.
(Galerie Moderne)
$3,620

Chippendale cherry carved base to chest on chest, probably Colchester, Connecticut, late 18th century, 41in. wide.
(Skinner)
$2,300

An early George III mahogany chest, with two short and five long graduated drawers below, on ogee bracket feet, 112cm. wide.
(Phillips)
$4,605

A fine Federal paint-decorated poplar tall chest of drawers, Schwaben Creek Valley, Pennsylvania, circa 1830, the rectangular top with dentil-carved tympanum, 41in. wide.
(Sotheby's)
$31,050

A carved and painted oak Hadley chest-over-drawers, Hampshire County, Connecticut, 1680–1730, the case with three carved panels, 46in. wide.
(Christie's)
$206,000

A George I walnut and featherbanded batchelor's chest, the hinged top with a quarter veneered and crossbanded interior above two short and three long graduated drawers, 77cm. wide.
(Phillips)
$11,513

A William and Mary maple bun foot chest, Massachusetts, circa 1700–1720, the case fitted with four graduated long drawers, 32³/₄in. wide.
(Christie's)
$40,250

An ebonized and decorated box on stand, the upper section with a sloping fall and fronted with initials I.T within a cartouche, English, the box early 17th century, 29in. wide.
(Christie's)
$1,478

A mahogany chest, of small size, with brushing slide and four graduated drawers, on bracket feet, 18th century, 26¹/₂in. wide.
(Christie's)
$1,408

CHESTS OF DRAWERS

Federal mahogany and mahogany veneer bureau, Massachusetts, circa 1815, 43in. wide.
(Skinner) $690

An oak chest, with four drawers, on bun feet, early 18th century, 36¹/₂in. wide.
(Christie's) $1,614

Antique American blanket chest, in curly maple with lift top, three false drawers over two full-length drawers, bracket base, 37¹/₂in. wide.
(Eldred's) $2,970

A George III mahogany dressing-chest, the rectangular top above a fitted long drawer enclosing a green baize-lined slide, a hinged parcel-gilt mirror with molded frame and lidded compartments and wells, 36in. wide.
(Christie's) $15,347

A George II mahogany bachelor's chest, the hinged rectangular top above two short drawers, one fitted, and two further short and three graduated long drawers, 31in. wide.
(Christie's) $8,125

A Chippendale mahogany reverse serpentine chest-of-drawers, Boston, 1765–1775, with a leather lined writing slide over four graduated long drawers each with cockbeaded surrounds, 41in. wide.
(Christie's) $19,550

A George III cherrywood chest-of-drawers, English, late 18th/ early 19th century, the rectangular molded top over three graduated long drawers, 29¹/₄in. long.
(Christie's) $3,680

A brass-bound mahogany military chest, mid 19th century, the back painted *Leiunt O'Reily R.N. No. 5 Teignmouth, Devon*, 42in. wide.
(Christie's) $3,168

A line-inlaid oyster-veneered chest, the crossbanded top above two short and three long crossbanded drawers, on bun feet, 40¹/₂in. wide.
(Christie's) $1,614

CHESTS OF DRAWERS

A mahogany chest, the
rectangular gray marble top
above three long drawers with
lion mask handles, on lion's paw
feet, French, early 19th century,
51in. wide.
(Christie's) $2,152

Chippendale walnut tall chest of
drawers, Pennsylvania, circa
1780, old refinish, replaced
brasses, 38¹/₂in. wide.
(Skinner) $1,955

A George III oak blanket chest,
the raised back and hinged top
above four dummy and four
true drawers, on ogee bracket
feet, 69in. wide.
(Christie's) $2,514

A Federal cherrywood chest-of-
drawers, New England, 1790–
1810, the case fitted with four
graduated long drawers flanked
by reeded columns continuing to
ring-turned and cylindrical
tapering legs, 44¹/₂in. wide.
(Christie's) $1,610

A late 18th century Dutch chest,
mahogany veneered, the hinged
top with fan inlay and banding,
the apron with brass mounts,
36¹/₂in.
(Woolley & Wallis) $6,320

A Chippendale mahogany chest-
of-drawers, Mid-Atlantic States,
1760–1790, the rectangular top
with line inlaid edge above a
case fitted with four graduated
long drawers, on straight
bracket feet, 37in. wide.
(Christie's) $2,990

A Chippendale maple chest-of-
drawers, Southern Connecticut
or Rhode Island, 1770–1800, the
case with four graduated
thumbmolded drawers, on
shaped bracket feet, 34in. wide.
(Christie's) $2,990

A grain-painted blanket chest,
New England, 1760–1780, on
bracket feet, the drawers sponge
grained and mustard colored,
the case sponge grained and red,
43³/₄in. wide.
(Christie's) $6,900

A William and Mary oyster-
veneered walnut and floral
marquetry chest, two short and
three long graduated drawers,
inlaid with vases issuing foliate
arabesques, 38³/₄in. wide.
(Christie's) $16,353

CHESTS OF DRAWERS

Shaker cherry and tiger maple chest over two drawers, *Built by W. D. Shimnway 1835 when he was 18 years old*, 42in. wide. (Skinner) $1,265

Antique American seven-drawer tall chest in cherry, molded top with dentil molding, molded drawer fronts, 40in. wide. (Eldred's) $1,540

A Federal inlaid walnut child's chest of drawers, Pennsylvania, circa 1820, with four graduated cockbeaded line-inlaid drawers, 18½in. wide. (Sotheby's) $6,325

Continental neo-classical walnut tall chest, possibly South German, early 19th century, the rectangular white veined marble top bordered with a torus molding of green marble, 38in. wide. (William Doyle) $11,500

A 17th century oak straight front chest, the projecting base with two long geometric paneled drawers with grained and stained fascias, two sections, 44in. wide. (Spencer's) $1,280

Federal mahogany and mahogany veneer bow-front bureau, probably Connecticut, circa 1820, with original silver plated pulls, old finish, 41½in. wide. (Skinner) $978

An early George III mahogany chest, the rectangular moulded top above a slide and four graduated long drawers, on shaped bracket feet, 83cm. wide. (Phillips) $2,302

Chippendale maple tall chest of drawers, New England, circa 1780, refinished, brasses appear to be original, 35½in. wide. (Skinner) $4,313

Mahogany Art Nouveau style chest of three long graduated drawers, inlaid with satinwood bands and similarly with Art Nouveau flower decoration, late 19th century, 36in. wide. (G. A. Key) $616

CHESTS OF DRAWERS

Federal mahogany and veneer bureau, New Hampshire, 1815–25, with stringing, beaded and inlaid drawers and escutcheons, saw tooth skirt, 41¹/₂in. wide. (Skinner) **$1,150**

A burr yew-wood chest, crossbanded with two short and three long drawers, on bracket feet, 37¹/₂in. wide. (Christie's) **$2,204**

A George III mahogany serpentine chest of three long drawers and on splayed bracket feet, 43¹/₄in. wide. (Christie's) **$2,544**

An oyster-veneered chest, the crossbanded and geometrically veneered top above two short and three graduated crossbanded long drawers, early 18th century, 38¹/₄in. wide. (Christie's) **$3,099**

An early 19th century Dutch marquetry tallboy, veneered in mahogany, the five inverted graduated drawers inlaid ribbon tied sprays of flowers, 3ft. 5in. wide. (Woolley & Wallis) **$4,536**

A Chippendale walnut chest-of-drawers, labeled Joseph Newlin, Wilmington, Delaware, 1770–1790, the case fitted with two short drawers and three graduated long drawers, on ogee bracket feet, 40in. wide. (Christie's) **$17,250**

Federal mahogany veneer inlaid bow front bureau, Massachusetts or New Hampshire, circa 1800. (Skinner) **$4,312**

A walnut veneered and feather-banded bachelor's chest, with hinged top, side drawer and facing dummy frieze drawer, on bracket feet, 30in. wide. (Christie's) **$2,410**

Walnut sugar chest, Southeastern United States, circa 1820, replaced brasses, 35in. wide. (Skinner) **$1,092**

CHESTS OF DRAWERS

A brass-bound military chest, in two sections with two short and three long drawers, early 19th century, 41½in. wide. (Christie's) $1,201

An Edwardian mahogany chest with mirrored superstructure having a gilt-metal gallery, above brushing slide, 30in. wide. (Christie's) $1,412

An oyster-veneered chest, in olive wood and laburnum, the featherbanded top with central yew-wood lobed panel, 37in. wide. (Christie's) $2,296

A green-painted chest, decorated in the chinoiserie style, three long drawers flanked by paneled ends with molded apron, late 17th/early 18th century, 37in. wide. (Christie's) $1,063

A Federal inlaid mahogany bow-front chest-of-drawers, Newburyport, Massachusetts, 1800–1810, four graduated long drawers each cockbeaded with diamond and bellflower inlaid escutcheons surrounded by stringing, 41⅝in. wide. (Christie's) $9,775

An 18th century chest, veneered in birds eye figured maple, the serpentine edge top with quartering and crossbanded, probably North German, 35½in. (Woolley & Wallis) $3,002

William and Mary oak chest of drawers, late 17th century, 35½in. wide. (Skinner) $2,645

A George II red walnut chest, the rectangular molded top above three graduated long drawers and on shaped bracket feet, 29in. wide. (Christie's) $3,089

Classical mahogany and bird's-eye maple bureau, New England, 1825–30, old refinish, 40½in. wide. (Skinner) $1,840

CHESTS ON CHESTS

A George III elm chest on chest in two stages, the upper part with dentil cornice above a fluted frieze, 44in. wide. (Peter Francis) **$1,836**

A good George III oak chest on chest, the upper section with key pattern carved broken apex pediment centered by a fret carved panel, 46in. wide. (Spencer's) **$5,967**

Carved Chippendale cherry chest on chest, Connecticut, 1760–90, with pin-wheel carved drawer, old replaced brass, 39in. wide. (Skinner) **$12,650**

A mahogany bowfront tallboy, with molded cornice and two short and six long drawers on swept bracket feet, 19th century, 49in. wide. (Christie's) **$2,356**

A George III mahogany chest on chest, the upper section with key pattern carved cavetto molded cornice, raised upon bracket feet, 46½in. wide. (Spencer's) **$3,720**

A George I walnut and burr walnut secrétaire tallboy chest, the upper part with a cavetto cornice above three short and three long cross and featherbanded drawers, 106cm. wide. (Phillips) **$21,490**

A line-inlaid mahogany tallboy, the dentil-molded cornice above two short and three long drawers flanked by fluted angles, 44in. wide. (Christie's) **$1,464**

A fine and rare Queen Anne carved and grain-painted maple chest-on-chest-on-frame, attributed to the Dunlap family, Bedford, New Hampshire, 1777–1792, 36½in. wide. (Sotheby's) **$310,500**

A George III mahogany tallboy with dentil cornice, blind fret-carved frieze and two short and three graduated long drawers, 43¾in. wide. (Bearne's) **$2,268**

CHESTS ON STANDS

William and Mary walnut and walnut veneer and pine tall chest of drawers, New England, 18th century, refinished, 35½in. wide.
(Skinner) **$5,175**

Queen Anne maple bonnet-top high chest of drawers, probably Massachusetts, 1780, old brasses, 38¾in. wide.
(Skinner) **$41,400**

A mahogany chest-on-stand, the cavetto molded cornice above two short and three long drawers, mid 18th century, 40½in. wide.
(Christie's) **$1,599**

An 18th century oak chest on stand, the upper section fitted with two small and three graduated drawers, 3ft. 6in. wide.
(Russell, Baldwin & Bright) **$1,965**

A walnut and feather-banded chest-on-stand, with shaped aprons and cabriole legs with pad feet, early 18th century and later, 108cm. wide.
(Christie's) **$2,572**

A walnut and herringbone crossbanded chest-on-stand, the ogee molded cornice above an ovolo frieze drawer, 18th century and later, 39½in. wide.
(Christie's) **$2,448**

An early Georgian walnut chest-on-stand, the rectangular top with molded cornice above two short and three long drawers, 39¼in. wide.
(Christie's) **$8,722**

A walnut-veneered and floral-marquetry chest-on-stand, burr crossbanded, the top, sides and drawer fronts with panels of foliage and birds, 33½in. wide.
(Christie's) **$2,021**

William and Mary birch and maple high chest of drawers, probably Massachusetts, circa 1730, old refinish, replaced brasses, 36in. wide.
(Skinner) **$5,462**

CHIFFONIERS

A Regency rosewood chiffonier, the gallery back on leaf-carved scroll supports, on platform base, 41in. wide.
(Hy. Duke & Son) $1,313

A Victorian rosewood chiffonier, the raised back fitted an open shelf with turned pilaster supports, fitted one long drawer to the frieze, 46in. wide.
(Anderson & Garland) $1,054

Small mahogany chiffonier, a back single shelf piece with swan supports, having a carved cornice, 3ft. wide, English, circa 1860.
(G. A. Key) $729

A Regency rosewood chiffonier, the tiered superstructure with a quatrefoil pierced gallery above a mirror backed shelf, 92cm. wide.
(Phillips) $4,605

A pair of William IV mahogany dining room chiffoniers, the raised architectural panelled backs each with knulled molded central pilasters, 34in.
(Woolley & Wallis) $6,898

Fine figured mahogany Victorian chiffonier, raised back piece with single shelf, supported by scrolled and pierced designs, 3ft. 6in. wide, English, mid 19th century.
(G. A. Key) $1,246

A rosewood chiffonier, the raised back above two glazed doors hung with green silk flanked by ring-turned uprights, on turned feet, 19th century, 30in. wide.
(Christie's) $2,259

A good early 19th century French mahogany chiffonier, the superstructure with reeded three quarter gallery over two graduated shallow shelves, 56in. wide.
(Spencer's) $954

A Maples Art Nouveau mahogany and marquetry chiffonier, upper section with mirror paneled back, display shelves, and floral marquetry panels, 48in. wide.
(Hy. Duke & Son) $1,236

CHIFFONIERS

A Regency rosewood chiffonier, the raised superstructure above two frieze drawers and two grilled doors, 44in. wide. (Christie's) $4,066

Regency rosewood chiffonier with two paneled doors opening to reveal a shelved interior, 41in. wide, English, circa 1825. (G. A. Key) $794

A walnut buffet, the mirrored back with glazed doors over, stamped *Serrurier à Liège*, 160cm. wide. (Hôtel de Ventes Horta) $2,385

A Renaissance Revival carved oak sideboard, American, 1860–1880, the shaped mirrored back fitted with two shelves supported by scroll-cut brackets, 67in. high. (Christie's) $2,875

A fine Regency rosewood gilt metal mounted chiffonier, the central raised superstructure with pierced gallery and mirrored back, 48in. wide. (Anderson & Garland) $4,900

An oak sideboard, of serpentine outline, the raised mirrored back flanked by a pierced naturalistic fruit-decorated border, mid 19th century, 92in. wide. (Christie's) $1,564

A Regency mahogany chiffonier with a raised panel back fitted open shelf and turned pilasters, 42in. wide. (Anderson & Garland) $1,071

An unusual early 19th century satin birch chiffonier, the superstructure with three quarter gallery over two open shelves, 45in. wide. (Spencer's) $3,672

A William IV chiffonier, rosewood veneered, the raised superstructure with a mirror back, a shelf with pediment and leaf carved front pillars, 3ft. 8in. (Woolley & Wallis) $1,625

CLOTHES PRESSES

A George III mahogany two stage hanging cupboard, the upper part with molded dentil cornice above a pair of crossbanded doors, 48in. wide. (Peter Francis) $1,836

A Dutch ormolu-mounted mahogany clothes-press, the serpentine upper section with scrolled cornice, above a pair of paneled doors, late 18th century, 64in. wide. (Christie's) $10,405

A Regency mahogany clothes-press, the rectangular molded cornice above a pair of paneled doors enclosing three slides, 54in. wide. (Christie's) $3,452

A George III Welsh oak clothes press in two stages, the lower with an arrangement of seven graduated drawers, 54in. wide. (Peter Francis) $2,186

A carved oak and palisander linen press with two paneled doors and on turnip feet, Dutch, circa 1660, 180cm. wide. (Kunsthaus am Museum) $2,623

A George III oak clothes press in two stages, the upper part with inset paneled doors with three dummy drawers beneath, 51in. wide. (Peter Francis) $1,912

A Dutch mahogany clothes-press, the canted rectangular cornice with pierced fretwork gallery above a pair of paneled doors, late 18th/early 19th century, 71in. wide. (Christie's) $5,023

A late Georgian Welsh oak clothes press, the upper part with molded cornice above a pair of paneled doors, 50in. wide. (Peter Francis) $1,255

A decorated press cupboard, with overall graining simulating oak and with striped banding, on bracket feet, English, late 18th/early 19th century, 50in. wide. (Christie's) $2,587

COMMODE CHESTS

A painted black-lacquer commode of Transitional style, decorated with Oriental figures within a floral landscape, 31in. wide.
(Christie's) $1,324

A French breakfront commode, the rouge marble top above two drawers veneered in walnut with ebony line and rosewood banding, 3ft. 1½in. wide.
(Woolley & Wallis) $3,402

An ormolu mounted rose and birchwood commode in Louis XVI style, with rouge marble top above medallion frieze.
(Herholdt Jensen) $1,055

An 18th century Sicilian kingwood and tulipwood banded serpentine commode, the top with quarter veneered and crossbanded rectangles centered with a lozenge, 118cm. tapering to 126cm. wide.
(Phillips) $9,210

A kingwood and floral marquetry bombé petite commode of Louis XV style, the molded serpentine marble top above three long graduated drawers, 29in. wide.
(Christie's) $1,507

A Genoese ormolu-mounted kingwood and tulipwood parquetry commode, the later serpentine-fronted molded mottle pink marble top above three long graduated drawers, mid-18th century, 37in. wide.
(Christie's) $6,817

A late 18th century polychrome commode, the later marbleized rectangular top above two drawers, on square tapering legs, 132cm. wide.
(Finarte) $10,711

A walnut veneered and marquetry inlaid commode, the front centered with a panel of Hercules and the Nemean lion, Lombardy, circa 1800, 121cm. wide.
(Finarte) $34,277

A Dutch mahogany and marquetry commode inlaid overall with swagged urns and ribbon-tied swags of flowers, 19th century, 47½in. wide.
(Christie's) $5,023

COMMODE CHESTS

One of a pair of German ormolu-mounted tulipwood, amaranth and marquetry serpentine commodes, each with breccia marble top with molded edge, third quarter 18th century, 59½in. wide. (Christie's)
(Two) $374,906

Spanish baroque walnut and fruitwood inlaid commode, 18th century, 50½in. wide. (Skinner) $3,450

A Franco-Flemish ebony and marquetry commode inlaid overall with foliage and flowers, the front with three drawers, late 17th/early 18th century, 44in. wide. (Christie's) $19,734

A Swedish ormolu-mounted kingwood and parquetry serpentine bombé commode, the green mottled Swedish marble top above three long drawers inlaid with trellis-work, mid-18th century, 35in. wide. (Christie's) $10,764

A Louis XV ormolu-mounted kingwood and parquetry commode, the molded serpentine-fronted liver marble top above three graduated drawers, 38½in. wide. (Christie's) $11,811

A Transitional ormolu-mounted rosewood, amaranth and green-stained commode, the molded breakfront white speckled gray marble top above two drawers decorated sans traverse, 31in. wide. (Christie's) $11,123

An ormolu-mounted mahogany and parquetry serpentine commode, the brocatelle marble top with molded edge above two drawers inlaid with shaped cartouches, 47½in. wide. (Christie's) $5,023

A walnut and marquetry console cupboard of bombé outline, inlaid overall with hunting scenes, North Italy, mid 18th century. (Kunsthaus am Museum) $6,405

A Swedish ormolu-mounted, tulipwood parquetry bombé commode attributed to Johan Neijber, on splayed feet with pierced foliate mounts, 46¼in. wide. (Christie's) $13,455

A George III mahogany commode with bow front and crossbanded top decorated with inlaid stringing, 22 x 32in. high. (Anderson & Garland) $3,565

A George III mahogany bedside commode, the rectangular top above a hinged front, simulated as four drawers enclosing a ceramic bowl, 25in. wide. (Christie's) $1,063

A George III mahogany bedside commode, the galleried rounded rectangular top with tambour door and a drawer, 20in. wide. (Christie's) $1,635

A mahogany bedside commode, the galleried superstructure with three small drawers raised on concave fronted paneled sides, late 18th/early 19th century, 22in. wide. (Christie's) $2,021

A pair of Georgian mahogany bedside cupboards each with a threequarter gallery over a single paneled door, 40$\frac{1}{2}$in. wide. (Anderson & Garland) $2,295

A George III mahogany bedside commode, the concave-fronted rectangular top with waved gallery above a tambour door and a deep drawer simulated as two drawers, 22$\frac{3}{4}$in. wide. (Christie's) $2,907

A George III mahogany tray top bedside commode with paneled door and pull out drawer below, on molded square tapering legs, 18in. wide. (Anderson & Garland) $949

Hepplewhite tray top commode with open compartment above the commode area, galleried back and sides, 1ft. 10in. wide, English, mid to late 18th century. (G. A. Key) $465

A George III mahogany bedside commode, the galleried rectangular top above a hinged fall-front and pull-out section enclosing a pot, 21$\frac{3}{4}$in. wide. (Christie's) $909

CORNER CUPBOARDS

Antique corner cupboard, circa 1830, in cherry with molded top and foot, paneled doors, 80in. high.
(Eldred's) $1,540

Federal pine glazed corner cupboard, Pennsylvania, circa 1810, 50in. wide.
(Skinner) $2,415

Poplar glazed corner cupboard, probably Pennsylvania, circa 1810, 43in. wide.
(Skinner) $2,645

A George II style green-japanned corner cupboard decorated in shades of gilt and red with Chinese figures and landscapes, 18th century and later, 39½in. wide.
(Hy. Duke & Son) $3,641

A pair of lacquered corner cabinets with marble tops, shaped skirts, on short cabriole legs, signed *L. de Laitre*, Paris 1750.
(Galerie Koller) $40,303

An Edwardian mahogany and satinwood-banded corner display cabinet, decorated overall with scrolling foliage, urns and bellflower swags, 26in. wide.
(Christie's) $3,001

A French Provincial fruitwood vestment armoire with door molded with two panels inlaid with a central sunburst incorporating the letters *IHS*, 18th/19th century, 45¼in. wide.
(Hy. Duke & Son) $910

A Dutch mahogany corner cupboard, with an urn inlaid panelled door below, on square tapering legs, Dutch, 19th century, 32in. wide.
(Christie's) $1,936

An 18th century French oak slightly concave floor standing corner cupboard, with reverse breakfront cavetto molded cornice, 61in. wide.
(Spencer's) $2,340

CORNER CUPBOARDS

A pine corner bookcase of George III style, with open shelves above two paneled cupboard doors, 39in. wide. (Christie's) $1,412

Cherry glazed corner cupboard, Middle Atlantic States, circa 1830, old refinish, replaced brasses, 46½in. wide. (Skinner) $3,450

Mahogany and mahogany veneer inlaid glazed corner cupboard, circa 1800, old finish, 48in. wide. (Skinner) $2,990

American corner cupboard in pine with molded cornice two doors enclosing three shelves, painted blue with yellow interior, New York State, 19th century, 54in. wide. (Eldred's) $1,760

A pair of pine encoignures, painted with vases of flowers and parrots, German, 18th century. (Galerie Moderne) $3,629

A Georgian mahogany hanging corner cupboard, the plain pediment over an acorn and finial frieze, paneled door, 30in. wide. (Dee, Atkinson & Harrison) $618

An oak upright corner cupboard, with molded cornice above a pair of arched twin-fielded paneled doors, English, late 18th century, 42in. wide. (Christie's) $3,141

A kingwood-banded rosewood cupboard, the shaped molded top of serpentine outline with a pair of doors between crossbanded uprights, 33in. wide. (Christie's) $1,355

A paint-decorated poplar corner cupboard, Pennsylvania, circa 1785, the upper section with molded dentil-carved cornice, 46in. wide. (Sotheby's) $6,900

CORNER CUPBOARDS

Cherry corner cupboard, New England, circa 1810, old refinish, 42in. wide. (Skinner) $2,530

A pair of Victorian mahogany, satinwood and marquetry corner cupboards, circa 1860, possibly by Ross, each with a white marble top, 64cm. wide. (Sotheby's) $14,350

An American 'Aesthetic Movement' polychromed ebonized corner cabinet, circa 1865, possibly by Kimbal and Cabus, 39¼in. wide. (Christie's) $16,445

A Venetian green-painted and parcel-gilt corner cupboard, the upper section with a pair of glazed convex-fronted doors with foliate moldings, 19th century, 32¼in. wide. (Christie's) $3,588

A pair of Napoleon III porcelain and ormolu-mounted tulipwood and parquetry encoignures, third quarter 19th century, each with a bowed molded white marble top, 32in. wide. (Christie's) $15,884

An important paint-decorated poplar bonnet-top corner cupboard, Pennsylvania, dated *1817*, the upper section with molded swan's-neck crest, 43in. wide. (Sotheby's) $96,000

A paint-decorated pine corner cupboard, Pennsylvania, first half 19th century, the molded cornice above a hinged glazed door, 44in. wide. (Sotheby's) $2,875

A pair of Empire style gilt-metal mounted mahogany corner cabinets, each with a bowed eared cornice above a conforming case fitted with a glazed mullioned door, 37in. wide. (Christie's) $10,278

Carlo Bugatti, corner cabinet, circa 1900, with mirrored back above single cupboard door, the top with turned rail, 65.5cm. wide. (Sotheby's) $7,079

CREDENZAS

An attractive Victorian walnut credenza, of break serpentine front form, a cupboard enclosed by a paneled door set with an oval ebony fielded panel, 76in. wide.
(Spencer's) $4,590

One of a pair of painted wood credenzas, the front with two paneled doors, Venetian, 17th century, 192cm. wide.
(Finarte)
(Two) $14,536

An attractive Victorian figured and stained walnut credenza, the narrow break 'D' shaped top crssbanded in rosewood and strung with ebony and box, 74in. wide.
(Spencer's) $5,565

A Victorian burr walnut credenza with raised mirror back decorated with fruiting vines, raised on a serpentine-shaped base with bun feet, 60in. wide.
(Anderson & Garland)
$2,754

A Victorian ebonized mahogany credenza, a long drawer to the frieze over a cupboard enclosed by a paneled door, 50in. wide.
(Spencer's) $1,200

An Italian grained pine credenza in the Tuscan style, the rectangular simulated marble top above two drawers and a pair of paneled doors, 102cm. wide.
(Phillips) $1,382

A French ormolu-mounted, kingwood and ebonized meuble d'appui, circa 1850, with a breakfront top above a central drawer with quarter-veneered panels, 188cm. wide.
(Sotheby's) $8,487

Italian Renaissance walnut credenza, 44in. wide.
(Skinner) $3,220

A Victorian burr walnut credenza, with satinwood arabesque inlay, glazed bow front side cupboards on breakfront shaped plinth, 58in. wide.
(Hy. Duke & Son)
$3,840

An 18th century Welsh cwpwrdd tridarn with an open upper section on turned supports, 54³/₄in. wide. (Bearne's) $3,696

A 17th century oak bacon cupboard, with a pair of shaped arched double fielded paneled doors over projecting base, 55in. wide. (Spencer's) $2,306

A late Victorian walnut and burr-walnut cased safe, designed as a Wellington chest, by S. Mordan & Co., London, the outer door with five dummy drawer fronts, 29¹/₂in. wide. (Christie's) $2,833

A red-painted pine cupboard, Texas, mid-19th century, the rectangular projecting cornice above a pair of recessed paneled cupboard doors, 50in. wide. (Christie's) $2,300

A Charles I oak and marquetry inlaid press cupboard, lunette frieze supported upon gadrooned and rusticated 'cup and cover' columns bearing the marriage initials *R.S and E.S*, and the date *1633*, 159cm. wide. (Phillips) $7,675

A 19th century German cupboard, blue painted with polychrome decoration, the central column flanked by two doors, 148cm. wide. (Stockholms Auktionsverk)
                $4,053

A salmon-painted pine cupboard, American, 19th century, the recessed upper section with hinged cupboard doors, 37¹/₄in. wide. (Sotheby's) $4,600

A 17th century oak small press cupboard, raised upon ring turned cylindrical and block supports tied by an undertier, 46¹/₂in. wide. (Spencer's) $1,560

A Chippendale walnut hutch cupboard, Pennsylvania, circa 1790, the molded and dentil-carved cornice above open shelves, 53¹/₂in. wide. (Sotheby's) $3,737

CUPBOARDS

Pine wall cupboard, New England, 18th century, 25in. wide.
(Skinner) $4,025

A 17th century oak food hutch, the rectangular double plank top with molded edge, 59in. wide.
(Spencer's) $4,000

A Gothic Revival oak cupboard, the front with three doors carved with tracery picked out with polychrome and gilt, 59¹/₂in. wide.
(Bearne's) $2,100

An early 18th century walnut cupboard on chest, with a molded cornice and cushion shaped frieze drawer, 44in. wide.
(Anderson & Garland) $4,783

A 17th century oak livery cupboard, the overhanging cornice over a bead and reel carved frieze, on later ball castors, 75in. wide.
(Spencer's) $2,862

A late 17th century South German oak, walnut and fruitwood Schrank, the fielded paneled doors with ripple molded reserves above two short drawers and one long drawer, on turned feet, 155cm. wide.
(Phillips) $4,605

A good Queen Anne paneled walnut Schrank, Pennsylvania, circa 1760, the lower section with two short and three long molded drawers, 5ft. 10in. wide.
(Sotheby's) $17,250

A paint-decorated poplar Schrank, Pennsylvania, dated 1769, in several parts, decorated allover in green, red and orange, 6ft. 6in. wide.
(Sotheby's) $40,250

Burr walnut commode cupboard inlaid with various woods and ivory, the doors with ivory inlay of the virtues Faith and Hope, Brunswick, circa 1720–30, 133cm. wide.
(Lempertz) $24,056

DAVENPORTS

A late Victorian walnut davenport, the shallow ogee molded superstructure with slightly domed hinged cover, 53.5cm. wide.
(Spencer's)   **$1,908**

A Victorian walnut davenport, the cavetto molded superstructure with hinged cover enclosing wells, 21in. wide.
(Spencer's)   **$1,085**

A rosewood and line-inlaid davenport, the sliding top-section with lobed three-quarter gallery and leather-lined slope, on bracket feet, 19in. wide.
(Christie's)   **$1,417**

Fine quality Victorian figured walnut davenport with piano formed front, having a writing slide and fitted interior, 21in. wide, English, early 19th century.
(G. A. Key)   **$4,560**

A mid-Victorian walnut davenport, the line-inlaid superstructure with gilt-metal gallery, with a recess below enclosing a double-hinged compartment flanked by two short drawers, 22in. wide.
(Christie's)   **$1,948**

Late Victorian davenport in walnut and ebonized wood, right hand door with four fitted interior drawers, 1ft. 10in. wide, English, mid to late 19th century.
(G. A. Key)   **$973**

A William IV rosewood davenport, the leather-lined slope enclosing a bird's-eye-maple interior with pigeon holes and drawers, 20in. wide.
(Christie's)   **$1,240**

An early Victorian rosewood davenport, with gilt-metal galleried top, the leather-lined writing slope above a fitted interior, 56cm. wide.
(Christie's)   **$1,056**

A mid-Victorian walnut davenport, the sloping lined fall sliding to reveal an open compartment above a hinged pen drawer, 21in. wide.
(Christie's)   **$1,408**

DAVENPORTS

A Victorian walnut-veneered davenport, with a raised superstructure, on foliate-carved cabriole front supports, 21in. wide.
(Bearne's) $1,606

A mid Victorian burr walnut-veneered davenport, with rising stationery compartment, on a shaped plinth with bun feet, 21³/₄in. wide.
(Bearne's) $1,530

A mid-Victorian walnut davenport, the raised superstructure with three-quarter gallery enclosing a fitted interior, 21¹/₂in. wide.
(Christie's) $1,501

A George IV brass-mounted rosewood davenport, the rectangular three-quarter galleried top above a hinged swivelling leather-lined slope, 14in. wide.
(Christie's) $7,268

A late Victorian rosewood davenport, line-inlaid with three-quarter brass gallery above four short drawers and hinged compartment above leather-lined sloping fall, 22in. wide.
(Christie's) $1,651

A Victorian burr walnut davenport, the forward sliding upper section with slightly sloping hinged and rising top, 23in. wide.
(Spencer's) $1,560

A Victorian figured walnut cylinder davenport/sheet music cabinet, the cylinder inlaid with a foliate medallion in box and amboyna, 59cm. wide.
(Spencer's) $2,544

A good Victorian figured walnut davenport/sheet music cabinet, with sloping hinged and rising top inset with a crimson skiver, 62cm. wide.
(Spencer's) $3,588

An early Victorian mahogany davenport, with balustraded three quarter gallery, sliding back to reveal wells for pens and ink, 62cm. wide.
(Spencer's) $1,113

DISPLAY CABINETS

A French Louis XVI style mahogany pier display étagère, the open mirrored back superstructure with a gilt brass pierced gallery, 22in.
(Woolley & Wallis) $1,027

An English satinwood and painted vitrine cabinet, of serpentine shape, on square-tapering legs, late 19th century, 45in. wide.
(Christie's) $6,583

An Edwardian mahogany display cabinet, with satinwood crossbanding and boxwood and ebony stringing throughout, 39³/₄in. wide.
(Bearne's) $2,984

Viennese glazed cabinet, circa 1905–10, in teak, the lower section with beveled glass doors beneath three cupboard doors, 152cm. wide.
(Sotheby's) $2,981

A French ormolu-mounted kingwood and parquetry vitrine, of breakfront outline, on square-shaped legs with scroll-cast knees, late 19th century, 48¹/₂in. wide.
(Christie's) $5,119

Joseph Maria Olbrich, vitrine, circa 1900, poplar, veneered in burr elm and ebonized gaboon, 102.5cm. wide.
(Sotheby's) $8,384

A good late 19th century mahogany display cabinet in the Chippendale style, the lower panels carved with panels of lyre, ribbon bow and fruiting tendrils, 51in. wide.
(Spencer's) $2,703

A pearwood and fruitwood inlaid vitrine with canted corners, the lower part on bun feet, Bergisch, late 18th century, 140cm. wide.
(Kunsthaus am Museum)
$12,732

One of a pair of satin-veneered and painted display cabinets, each with dentil-molded cornice and a pair of astragal glazed doors, 43in. wide.
(Christie's)
(Two) $5,144

352

DISPLAY CABINETS

A Bugatti display cabinet, large circular mirror with ebonized surround inlaid with pewter, 103cm. wide.
(Christie's) $14,536

An English ormolu-mounted burr walnut, amboyna, calamander, tulipwood and marquetry display cabinet, of serpentine outline, second half 19th century, 79in. wide.
(Christie's) $21,942

A Victorian walnut-veneered marquetry display cabinet, the frieze and uprights inlaid with floral sprays and foliage, 47¹/₂in. wide.
(Bearne's) $2,688

A brass-mounted mahogany vitrine-table, the rectangular glazed top enclosing a well, on square tapering legs, probably French, late 19th century, 17in. wide.
(Christie's) $2,870

A japanned cabinet on stand, the upper section with three glazed doors having polychrome decoration depicting figures, 4ft. 6in. wide.
(Russell, Baldwin & Bright) $1,474

English, Art Nouveau vitrine, circa 1900, in mahogany, inlaid with abalone and fruitwoods in the form of stylized lilies, butterflies and tulips, 136cm. wide.
(Sotheby's) $11,178

A 1930s chinoiserie shagreen and painted hanging vitrine, the elaborate scrolled pediment above asymmetrically glazed doors, 77.5cm. wide.
(Christie's) $7,268

An early 20th century satinwood and marquetry breakfront display cabinet, with kingwood crossbanding and boxwood and ebony stringing, 52in. wide.
(Bearne's) $4,896

A good French kingwood display cabinet, Napoléon III, Paris, circa 1860, of serpentine outline, 116cm. wide.
(Sotheby's) $21,942

DISPLAY CABINETS

George III style mahogany display cabinet, Irving & Cassons, A.H. Davenport Co., early 20th century, 44in. wide. (Skinner) $2,645

Neoclassical style walnut vitrine cabinet, late 19th/20th century, 69in. high. (Skinner) $2,530

An Edwardian mahogany salon cabinet, crossbanded in satinwood and strung with ebony and box, 57in. wide. (Spencer's) $1,908

A Dutch walnut and marquetry display cabinet, the upper glazed section enclosing interior serpentine shaped shelves, 18th century, 56in. wide. (Hy. Duke & Son) $8,034

A pair of Victorian burr walnut display cabinets, the glazed doors enclosing interior silk-lined shelves, 32in. wide. (Hy. Duke & Son) $3,708

A gilt-metal-mounted mahogany vitrine cabinet, of serpentine form, the glazed doors and glazed sides above Vernis Martin painted panels, French, late 19th century, 41in. wide. (Christie's) $2,302

Glazed cabinet, circa 1910, by L. Ernst, the lower section with two doors enclosing shelves, inlaid with geometric motifs, 117cm. wide. (Sotheby's) $2,608

Louis XVI style gilt bronze vitrine, the rectangular marble top with outset center section above a conforming case, 45in. wide. (William Doyle) $5,750

Arts and Crafts oak two-door china cabinet, No. 141, two single pane doors, interior with three adjustable shelves, casters, 36⅝in. wide. (Skinner) $1,610

DISPLAY CABINETS

A late Victorian mahogany salon cabinet, the break bow front center section with rococo scrolling and fret carved diapered cresting, 138cm. wide. (Spencer's) **$592**

An Edwardian mahogany and inlaid display cabinet, with simulated fluted frieze above a central astragal glazed door, 55in. wide. (Christie's) **$3,908**

A Dutch mahogany veneered bombé vitrine in two parts, the lower with two short and three long drawers, on trilobate feet, 173cm. wide. (Finarte) **$10,037**

A Georgian style mahogany display cabinet with a molded cornice above two pairs of glazed paneled doors, 42¹/₂in. wide. (Anderson & Garland) **$1,683**

A pair of Edwardian stained mahogany and gilt-metal-mounted table display cabinets, on short cabriole supports, 13³/₄in. wide. (Christie's) **$1,695**

A late Victorian mahogany cabinet, two short drawers to the frieze with a single paneled door and a pair of glazed paneled doors below, 42in. wide. (Anderson & Garland) **$1,285**

An attractive Edwardian mahogany salon cabinet, the upper section with foliate carved broken arched cresting, 47¹/₂in. wide. (Spencer's) **$1,377**

Fine Edwardian mahogany curio cabinet, late 19th/early 20th century, having twin single door glazed tall cupboards surmounted by pagoda like crests, 6ft. 7¹/₂in. wide. (William Doyle) **$5,462**

A French half vitrine, mahogany veneered, the recessed cornice above a mirror back cabinet with glass shelves, 3ft. 7¹/₂in. wide. (Woolley & Wallis) **$8,216**

DRESSERS

An early 19th century oak dresser, the upper section with a molded cornice and three shelves, 63in. wide. (Bearne's) $5,376

A Victorian pollard oak sideboard in the style of Pugin by Holland and Sons, 63in. wide. (Spencer's) $2,067

A late Georgian Cardiganshire Welsh oak dresser, on baluster turned supports in front united by a potboard, 72in. wide. (Peter Francis) $5,355

A mid 19th century North Pembrokeshire Welsh oak dresser, the superstructure with three shelves, raised on square feet, 68in. wide. (Peter Francis) $2,806

A George III oak dresser, the boarded three-shelf back with flared cornice, circa 1770, 65¹/₂in. wide. (Neales) $4,640

European painted pine cupboard, 19th century, built as one piece with two doors above and two drawers below, with floral and urn decoration, 78in. high. (Eldred's) $2,310

A late Georgian Welsh oak dresser, the superstructure of four shelves, the base having three frieze drawers, 64in. wide. (Peter Francis) $4,437

Antique English two-part pewter dresser, in walnut, with molded cornice above a scrolled frieze, 64in. wide. (Eldred's) $1,430

Pine step-back pewter dresser, New England, late 18th century, old refinish, 46³/₄in. wide. (Skinner) $2,070

356

DRESSERS

George III elmwood Welsh cupboard, late 18th century, 52½in. wide.
(Skinner) $2,990

An oak dresser, the rectangular top above three frieze drawers and ogee shaped aprons, South Wales, early 18th century, 69½in. wide.
(Christie's) $6,283

An oak dresser, the plate rack with molded cornice and three graduated shelves, South Wales, early 18th century, 59in. wide.
(Christie's) $5,544

An oak dresser, the plate rack with molded cornice and shaped frieze above three central shelves, West Midlands, mid 18th century, 79in. wide.
(Christie's) $4,805

Arts & Crafts ebonized oak server inset with Grueby tiles, the server attributed to L. & J.G. Stickley, raised on square posts joined by a platform stretcher, 30¼in. high.
(Butterfield & Butterfield) $1,725

A fine and rare paint decorated pine apothecary chest and cupboard, Massachusetts, 1770–90, the lower section fitted with forty-two small molded drawers, painted allover in blue-green, 41½in. wide.
(Sotheby's) $151,000

A George III oak dresser, with pollard oak panels and columns, the plank back delft rack with two shelves, 65in. wide.
(Hy. Duke & Son) $4,326

An 18th century oak dresser, the later delft rack with shallow stepped molded cornice, 77in. wide.
(Spencer's) $3,021

An early 19th century oak dresser, the upper section with a molded cornice and three shelves, 60½in. wide.
(Bearne's) $4,131

Lady's custom-made kidney-form writing desk, in burled walnut with brass gallery and inset red leather top, 48in. wide. (Eldred's) $3,190

Edwardian mahogany satinwood banded and ebony line inlaid desk with leather inset top with two small drawers, 54in. (Ewbank) $1,760

An English satinwood pedestal desk, Victorian, by Gillow of Lancaster and London, circa 1880, the leather-lined top above three frieze drawers, 130cm. wide. (Sotheby's) $5,120

An early 18th century walnut and featherbanded kneehole desk, the rectangular molded top quarter veneered and crossbanded above a frieze drawer, 76cm. wide. (Phillips) $6,140

A George I walnut kneehole desk, cross and feather-banded overall, central kneehole cupboard with plain interior and with a concealed drawer, 30½in. wide. (Christie's) $13,628

An early 18th century walnut-veneered kneehole desk, six small drawers flanking a recessed cupboard and on bracket feet, 31in. wide. (Bearne's) $4,131

George III mahogany, boxwood urn and swag inlaid kneehole desk, central kneehole drawer and cupboard flanked by six small drawers, circa 1800. (Lawrences) $1,911

A walnut kneehole desk, the superstructure with central shelves and two small drawers, on turned feet, Italian, 53in. wide. (Christie's) $1,470

An Edwardian satinwood kidney shaped kneehole desk, the top inset with gilt tooled brown skiver, within a molded edge, 48in. wide. (Spencer's) $2,184

358

KNEEHOLE DESKS

A late Victorian mahogany kneehole desk with raised gallery back centered by a hinged flap opening to reveal stationery compartments, 54 x 44¹/₂in. high.
(Anderson & Garland)
$2,790

A Victorian carved oak partner's desk with leather lined writing surface above frieze drawers with lions masks, 56¹/₂in. wide.
(Hy. Duke & Son)
$1,545

A Victorian burr-walnut kidney-shaped pedestal desk, the leather-lined top above three frieze drawers and two cupboard doors, 64in. wide.
(Christie's)
$7,920

A Queen Anne japanned kneehole bureau, Boston, 1720–1740, the case fitted with one long drawer over an arched valanced drawer, 34in. wide.
(Christie's)
$96,000

A George III mahogany secrétaire architect's table attributed to Gillows of Lancaster, the molded rectangular green leather-lined double-hinged top above a secrétaire-drawer, 48¹/₂in. wide.
(Christie's)
$5,451

A Chippendale carved mahogany block-and-shell kneehole dressing table, attributed to Edmund Townsend and Daniel Goddard, Newport, Rhode Island, 1768–1779, 35¹/₂in. wide.
(Christie's)
$442,500

A Russian ormolu-mounted Karelian-birch pedestal desk, the frieze with five variously-sized drawers mounted with ferocious birds and palmettes, 49¹/₄in. wide.
(Christie's)
$35,880

A small mid 18th century walnut kneehole desk, the two pillars on a carved apron and short cabriole legs, Venice, 88cm. wide.
(Finarte)
$20,744

A presentation English mahogany cylinder bureau, late Victorian, circa 1897, in the French manner, on circular legs with brass castors, 135cm. wide.
(Sotheby's)
$10,971

LINEN PRESSES

A George III mahogany linen press, the molded cornice above a pair of oval paneled doors with a long drawer below.
(Christie's) **$1,320**

A Georgian style oak linen press, in two sections, the top with rectangular molded overhanging cornice, 39³/₄in. long.
(Christie's) **$552**

A Regency mahogany linen press, the shaped cornice above two line-inlaid paneled doors, 49in. wide.
(Christie's) **$2,572**

A George III mahogany linen press, the molded cornice above a pair of paneled doors enclosing sliding drawers, 62¹/₂in. wide.
(Christie's) **$1,672**

A yellow pine linen press, Texas, mid-19th century, the rectangular molded cornice above a paneled fireze, 60in. wide.
(Christie's) **$2,300**

A George III mahogany linen press, the cavetto molded cornice above a pair of paneled doors, on outswept bracket feet, 51in. wide.
(Christie's) **$3,354**

An early Victorian mahogany linen press, the molded cornice above two paneled doors, two long and two short drawers, 50in. wide.
(Christie's) **$1,294**

A Queen Anne maple linen press, Westchester County, New York, 1750–1785, in two sections, the upper with a molded over-hanging cornice, 42¹/₄in. wide.
(Christie's) **$66,300**

A George III mahogany linen press, later checker-inlaid, the later swan-neck pediment above a molded cornice with paterae-decorated paneled doors.
(Christie's) **$2,833**

LOWBOYS

18th century walnut lowboy, the two part top with herring bone inlay, on plain cabriole legs, 19 x 31in., English, circa 1730. (G. A. Key) $667

Queen Anne cherry base to highboy, Connecticut, circa 1770, old refinish, old brasses, 39in. wide. (Skinner) $1,380

A walnut and mahogany lowboy, two frieze drawers with a wavy apron below flanked by two short drawers, early 18th century, 39in. wide. (Christie's) $825

Antique English Queen Anne style lowboy, with shaped top and three drawers, on cabriole legs and duck feet, 29$\frac{1}{2}$in. wide. (Eldred's) $770

A Queen Anne burl-veneered walnut lowboy, Boston, Massachusetts, 1730–60, the shaped cockbeaded skirt continuing to cabriole legs, width of top 34$\frac{1}{4}$in. (Sotheby's) $9,775

Queen Anne maple base to high chest, Connecticut or Rhode Island, circa 1770, old red stain, original brasses, 37$\frac{1}{2}$in. wide. (Skinner) $2,185

A mahogany lowboy, with crossbanded top above two short and one long drawer, mid 18th century, 30in. wide. (Christie's) $1,837

George II walnut dressing table, 30in. wide. (Skinner) $4,025

A George II mahogany lowboy, the molded rectangular top with re-entrant corners above a frieze drawer, on lappeted turned legs with pad feet, 68cm. wide. (Phillips) $1,995

361

SCREENS

Four panel screen, 1920s, attributed to Emile-Jacques Ruhlmann, painted with a gold abstract design on a mottled black and copper background, each panel 160 x 37.25cm.
(Sotheby's) $6,707

An Empire mahogany fire-screen, the turned toprail above a rectangular banner of foliate needlework, 23in. wide.
(Christie's) $807

A French kingwood three-fold marquetry screen, by Francois Linke of Paris, circa 1900, the central fold with a large gilt-bronze plaque of Diana, largest fold 200cm. high.
(Sotheby's) $67,098

A Chinese five-fold draught screen, the molded arched padouk-wood frame with raised-and-fielded base panels, early 20th century, 69in. high.
(Neales) $2,320

A Louis XV style gilt-bronze fire screen, with scrolling foliate cartouche-shaped frame and conforming feet, $27^{3/4}$in. high.
(Christie's) $681

A giltwood four panel screen painted with chinoiserie scenes and birds in branches, Piedmont, 18th century, each leaf 148 x 62cm.
(Finarte) $3,104

An Aesthetic Movement stained and painted glass screen, the design attributed to J. Moyr Smith, four panels depicting herons, house martins, a kingfisher and other birds, circa 1875/80, 51cm. wide (each panel).
(Christie's) $32,706

A Louis XVI giltwood fire-screen attributed to Jean Jacques Baptiste Tilliard, the arched rising panel covered in yellow silk and in a part-beaded slip, on acanthus-carved scroll feet, $49^{3/4}$in. high.
(Christie's) $22,253

An attractive 19th century leather four leaf draught screen, each vertical rectangular leaf of three panels embossed and painted with stylized shells, approximately 97in. long extended.
(Spencer's) $940

SECRETAIRE BOOKCASES

A Regency rosewood and
mahogany secrétaire-bookcase
inlaid overall with satinwood
and bird's eye maple, 30³/₄in.
wide.
(Christie's) $18,170

A George IV mahogany
secrétaire bookcase, the
triangular pediment with
acroters to the corners, on
reeded bun feet, 46in. wide.
(Bearne's) $2,371

An Empire carved mahogany
secretary bookcase, New York,
1820–1830, the upper section
with a pair of Gothic mullioned
glazed doors, 46¹/₂in. wide.
(Christie's) $6,325

A George III mahogany
secrétaire-bookcase, the pierced
swan's neck cresting above a
pendant frieze and a pair of
geometrically-glazed doors,
43in. wide.
(Christie's) $10,902

A Federal inlaid mahogany
ladies' writing desk and
bookcase, Massachusetts, circa
1805, the lower section with a
baize-lined writing flap above a
case with three cockbeaded long
drawers, on turned tapering
legs, 40in. wide.
(Sotheby's) $5,175

A George III satinwood,
mahogany, parquetry and
painted secrétaire and dressing-
cabinet attributed to George
Simson, crossbanded overall
with tulipwood, 35¹/₂in. wide.
(Christie's) $48,749

A Regency mahogany secrétaire
bookcase, the upper section with
lancet glazed doors surmounted
by domed pediment, 53in. wide.
(Hy. Duke & Son)
$2,472

A fine George III mahogany
secrétaire bookcase, the upper
section with shallow dentil
carved cornice over astragal
glazed doors, 63in. wide.
(Spencer's) $7,038

A late Victorian walnut
secrétaire bookcase, the upper
section with stepped foliate
carved pediment to the molded
cornice, 49in. wide.
(Spencer's) $1,749

A Directoire mahogany secrétaire with a white marble top and three quarter pierced brass gallery, on toupie feet, 94cm. wide.
(Phillips) $3,070

Biedermeier birch and part-ebonized secrétaire, second half 19th century, 43in. wide.
(Skinner) $3,737

A Louis XV lacquered secrétaire, signed *F. Bayer*, Paris, circa 1775–80.
(Galerie Koller)
$59,649

A Federal inlaid mahogany butler's desk and cabinet, New York, circa 1820, the rectangular top above a pull-out writing section, 47in. wide.
(Sotheby's) $2,070

A mahogany secrétaire à abattant, with six graduated drawers flanked by gilt-metal-mounted column uprights, French, second quarter 19th century, 41in. wide.
(Christie's) $1,682

Gustav Stickley oak fall-front desk, No. 729, circa 1912, medium finish, fitted interior in chestnut, Craftsman paper label, 36$\frac{1}{2}$in. wide.
(Skinner) $1,955

An early 19th century Dutch walnut secrétaire à abattant, the polished top surface above a concave frieze with drawer, 38in. wide.
(Peter Francis) $1,772

Federal cherry inlaid sideboard with desk drawer, probably Massachusetts, circa 1810, old refinish, 40$\frac{1}{2}$in. wide.
(Skinner) $2,990

A mahogany secrétaire à abattant, the pedimented cornice with finials and molded frieze drawer above a paneled fall, German, mid 19th century, 42in. wide.
(Christie's) $2,388

A Louis XVI walnut, sycamore and parquetry secrétaire à abattant, the lower section with two doors decorated sans traverse, 31³/₄in. wide.
(Christie's) $9,867

A mahogany secrétaire, in two parts, the rectangular crossbanded and line-inlaid top above a fall front, early 19th century and later, 45in. wide.
(Christie's) $1,501

A late Biedermeier mahogany secrétaire with fruitwood inlay, 101cm. wide.
(Arnold Frankfurt) $2,423

A Transitional kingwood, walnut, marquetry and parquetry secrétaire à abattant, the molded rectangular liver marble top above a frieze drawer with inlaid panel, 30¹/₂in. wide.
(Christie's) $2,153

A George III mahogany secrétaire chest inlaid with boxwood and ebony stringing, on splayed bracket feet joined by a valanced apron, 42¹/₂in. wide.
(Hy. Duke & Son) $1,485

An early George III mahogany secrétaire press cupboard, the upper section with twin figured paneled doors surmounted by dentil carved architectural pediment, 52in. wide.
(Hy. Duke & Son) $3,555

A William III walnut veneered secrétaire cabinet, the pair of rectangular doors with engraved brass hinges and escutcheons, 3ft. 5in.
(Woolley & Wallis) $13,904

A George III mahogany secrétaire, the fall front enclosing a fitted interior above three drawers, on bracket feet, 43in. wide.
(Christie's) $1,063

A walnut-veneered, feather-banded and inlaid secretaire tallboy, with molded cornice above three short and three long drawers, the lower part with fall front, 42in. wide.
(Christie's) $3,443

A Charles X mahogany secrétaire à abattant, with white-marble top and frieze drawer, 43½in. wide. (Christie's) **$2,288**

A Regency crossbanded mahogany secrétaire, the rectangular top above a fall front enclosing a fitted interior, above two paneled doors, 47in. wide. (Christie's) **$2,241**

An attractive 19th century ebonized bonheur du jour in the Louis XVI style, the upper section with serpentine arched top over a cupboard, 30in. wide. (Spencer's) **$729**

A German repoussé giltmetal-mounted mahogany secrétaire à abattant, the stepped rectangular top with central pediment and inset glazed Roman-chaptered clock, early 19th century, 39½in. wide. (Christie's) **$26,910**

An early 19th century mahogany draughtsman's secrétaire table, in the manner of Gillows, with double ratcheted adjustable top with a book ledge, on reeded tapered legs, 1.12m. x 64cm. top. (Phillips) **$8,443**

A William and Mary walnut and featherbanded escritoire, the ogee molded cornice above a convex frieze drawer and quarter veneered fall front, the base with two short and two long drawers, 98cm. wide. (Phillips) **$4,605**

A Queen Anne walnut and burr walnut escritoire, the interior with an arrangement of fourteen various drawers around a central cupboard, on later bracket feet, 108cm. wide. (Phillips) **$8,443**

A mid 19th century mahogany secrétaire campaign chest, with two simulated drawers enclosing a fitted interior, three graduated long drawers below, 40¼in. wide. (Bearne's) **$1,408**

A French marquetry secrétaire à abattant, probably Paris, circa 1880, in Louis XV manner, the brown gray-marble top above a drawer and a fitted secrétaire, 78cm. wide. (Sotheby's) **$8,141**

SECRETAIRES & ESCRITOIRES

Federal mahogany, wavy birch and rosewood inlaid secretary, Massachusetts or New Hampshire, old refinish, brasses appear to be original, 37in. wide. (Skinner) $6,325

An early 18th century walnut cabinet on chest, fitted secrétaire with fall front, two deep drawers under, 43in. wide. (Locke & England) $8,700

Federal mahogany inlaid lady's desk, Massachusetts, circa 1790, original brass pulls, 42in. wide. (Skinner) $4,600

A Queen Anne red and gilt-japanned secrétaire decorated overall with Chinoiserie flowers, foliage and figures, the lower section with three long drawers and on later bracket feet, 41³/₄in. wide. (Christie's) $21,666

A line-inlaid mahogany secrétaire chest, the fall front enclosing a fitted interior of pigeon holes and short drawers, 40in. wide. (Christie's) $1,760

A French ormolu-mounted mahogany petit secrétaire, in the Empire style, with a fossil marble rectangular top above a drawer, second half 19th century, 24¹/₂in. wide. (Christie's) $6,948

A 19th century French mahogany cartonnier inlaid with gilt banding, the marbled topped superstructure with six leather fronted drawers, 153cm. high. (Finarte) $2,759

A Danish mahogany secrétaire à abattant, the eared stepped top above a frieze drawer and a fall-front, mid-19th century, 40¹/₂in. wide. (Christie's) $7,535

A Spanish decorated and parcel-gilt vargueno-on-stand, the front decorated overall with geometric drawers and three doors, late 17th century, 40¹/₂in. wide. (Christie's) $11,123

Classical mahogany carved and veneer sofa, possibly Boston, circa 1825, 84in. wide. (Skinner) **$2,300**

A Chesterfield sofa, upholstered in button-down red-leather, on bun feet, 79in. wide. (Christie's) **$1,496**

A Biedermeier walnut sofa with cornucopia carving on end supports, 192cm. wide. (Arnold Frankfurt) **$2,240**

An aluminium chaise longue, designed by Marcel Breuer, the seat, base and arms constructed from split and bent single strips of aluminium, circa 1935. (Christie's) **$30,889**

An 18th century oak settle, the rectangular back with four angular arched fielded panels, with loose seat squab, one roll-over arm opposing an open arm, 71in. (Spencer's) **$949**

A late Victorian carved giltwood settee of Louis XV style, the molded frame on cabriole supports and scrolled toes headed by flowerheads, 72in. wide. (Christie's) **$1,411**

L. & J. G. Stickley oak couch, No. 291, circa 1910, two-part box cushion, five vertical slats at each end, Handcraft Furniture decal, 72in. long. (Skinner) **$1,265**

Fine quality mahogany three piece bergère suite, the acanthus carved frames of scroll shape with double caned backs and sides. (Lawrences) **$3,800**

SETTEES & COUCHES

A Regency mahogany sofa with stuffover ends covered in striped pink material complete with bolsters, raised on reeded tapering legs and castors, 84in. long.
(Anderson & Garland)   **$1,377**

Richard Rogers, UK, three-seater reversible sofa, for Tecno, circa 1984, tan leather seats and tubular back on black metal frame.
(Bonhams)   **$1,856**

A yellow pine daybed, Texas, mid-19th century, rectangular with outwardly flared ends, on square tapering chamfered legs, 77^{1}/$_{2}$in. long.
(Christie's)   **$518**

Baltic neoclassical fruitwood, gilt-metal mounted and part ebonized settee, second-half 19th century, 71in. wide.
(Skinner)   **$3,450**

A French giltwood canapé, in the Louis XV style, the arched back and serpentine-shaped seat upholstered in a hob-nailed tapestry, the shaped apron pierced with rosettes, late 19th century, 80in. wide.
(Christie's)   **$7,679**

An Austrian walnut sofa, the arm supports in the form of stylized swans, mid 19th century, 183cm. wide.
(Kunsthaus am Museum)   **$2,177**

A classical carved mahogany sofa, possibly Boston, 1815–1830, on stylised foliate carved legs with scrolled returns, 86^{3}/$_{4}$in. long.
(Christie's)   **$2,185**

Harden oak settle, No. 157, Camden, New York, spring cushion seat, twelve back slats, three side slats under each arm, paper label, 79^{3}/$_{4}$in. long.
(Skinner)   **$1,840**

SETTEES & COUCHES

Marcel Breuer, Germany, Isokon long chair, for the Isokon Furniture Company, 1935–36, laminated wood with removable upholstered cushion.
(Bonhams) $8,973

A cherrywood curved center sofa on saber legs, early 19th century, 128cm. long.
(Finarte) $4,828

Chaise-longue, probably early 1970s, a long upholstered form covered in velour orange/brown/cream patterned fabric.
(Bonhams) $278

High-backed settle, New England, 1750–1800, the back with tongue and groove boarding, plank seat, 64¹/₂in. wide.
(Skinner) $1,840

An astronomer's hardwood open armchair, the reclined padded back with revolving headrest, above outswept arms and paneled seat, on square legs with adjustable footrest, Colonial.
(Christie's) $610

Good quality reproduction oak monk's seat, the arm rests encrusted by dentil and rosette and seated lion finials, 36in. wide.
(G. A. Key) $643

An elm high-back settle, with shaped sides and arm rests on turned supports, West Country, early 19th century, 65in. wide.
(Christie's) $2,217

Modern walnut and upholstered lounger, America, black corduroy upholstery on walnut frame, 51¹/₂in. long.
(Skinner) $748

Oak Ecclesiastical style two seater settle with quatrefoil pierced back, trefoil pierced arms, 50in. wide.
(G. A. Key) $400

SETTEES & COUCHES

A Wiliam IV mahogany two-seat settee, the arched padded back in a molded and lotus-carved frame, 45in. wide. (Christie's) $753

One of two oak choir stalls, each with individual seats, flanked by Ionic style columns and carved with figures and animals, French, late 19th century, 129in. wide and 159in. wide. (Christie's) (Two) $4,620

Ron Arad, Israel/UK, Rover 2-seater for One Off Ltd., 1981, a pair of black leather Rover car seats on a chrome-plated steel 'scaffolding' frame. (Bonhams) $1,392

A Flemish oak bench-chest, the straight back carved with arcades and surmounted by angels, part 17th century. (Galerie Moderne) $1,810

A large suede armchair and matching foot stool by Zarach, circa 1969, brown/tan suede covered upholstery, on chromed tubular steel feet. (Bonhams) $557

A late Victorian brass-mounted mahogany hall seat by Urquhart and Adamson, the horizontal pierced baluster back above a molded rectangular seat with circular ends centered by a gadrooned clasp. (Christie's) $6,905

Louis XV style gilt carved wood settee, the back and sides with elaborate pierced foliate and swag decoration, 44in. wide. (William Doyle) $1,840

One of a pair of George III mahogany double-chairback hall benches, each with shaped channeled toprail incorporating two beaded channeled roundels, 54in. wide. (Christie's) (Two) $57,619

A George II mahogany bergère, on cabriole legs headed by scallop-shells and on claw-and-ball feet. (Christie's) $14,444

SETTEES & COUCHES

Painted Windsor bench, signed *J.C. Hubbard Boston, J.M. White Boston*, circa 1840, old red stain with black seat, 95in. wide.
(Skinner) $1,955

A Louis XV giltwood canapé, the channeled molded frame with ribbon-tied flowerspray cresting, 95in. wide.
(Christie's) $8,611

One of a pair of George III giltwood sofas, the arched back carved with laurel and centered by a palmette cresting, with fluted apron, 66in. wide.
(Christie's)   (Two) $19,861

A mid-Victorian walnut sofa, the arched foliate-carved top-rail above button-down padded back and sides, 24in. wide.
(Christie's) $1,722

A Regency mahogany day-bed, the outscrolled padded end with roundel terminals, on reeded saber legs, 71in. wide.
(Christie's) $1,515

A large Italian giltwood settee, mid 19th century, in early 18th century style, the multiple arched back carved with acanthus and an amorial device, 235cm. wide.
(Sotheby's) $6,582

Federal carved mahogany sofa, New York City, circa 1810, with bow knot and sheaves of wheat as well as triglyphs on the crest, reeded arm supports and legs, 78¹/₂in. wide.
(Skinner) $3,450

A George IV mahogany sofa in the Gothic style, the toprail paneled with quatrefoils and rectangles, with pierced arched sides, 82¹/₂in. wide.
(Christie's) $6,178

SETTEES & COUCHES

Federal mahogany inlaid sofa, probably Massachusetts, circa 1815, old refinish, 77½in. wide.
(Skinner) $5,462

A Biedermeier birch sofa, the arms with fluted scroll supports on sabre legs, 19th century, 85½in. wide.
(Christie's) $6,817

An early Victorian rosewood chaise longue, the button-back with foliate arm terminals above a squab cushion, 73in. wide.
(Christie's) $2,472

An attractive Victorian walnut chaise longue, the undulating cresting rail and fluted scroll arm terminals richly pierced and carved.
(Spencer's) $1,539

One of a pair of Empire ormolu-mounted mahogany canapés, the sides with ball-finials and turned supports mounted with lotus-leaves, 59in. wide.
(Christie's)   (Two) $21,528

A white-painted settee, on stop-fluted turned tapering legs headed by flowerheads, on turned feet, possibly English, late 18th century, 76½in. wide.
(Christie's) $5,382

A classical carved mahogany sofa, Boston, 1820–1830, the cylinder crestrail above a quadripartite caned back flanked by caned side with columnar arm supports, 78¾in. wide.
(Christie's) $4,370

A Louis XV serpentine walnut canapé, the back with an undulating top rail carved with shells, on husk carved cabriole legs with scrolled toes, 210cm. long.
(Phillips) $1,458

SETTEES & COUCHES

Carlo Bugatti, bench seat, circa 1900, of rectangular form with vellum covered seat and back panel, 120cm. wide.
(Sotheby's) $4,844

A 19th century cherrywood divan en bateau raised on stylizd legs on a plinth base, 222cm. wide.
(Finarte) $5,019

A mid-Victorian mahogany conversation sofa, of lobed outline, on foliate-capped cabriole legs.
(Christie's) $2,112

A giltwood daybed, the ends carved with an armorial shield and supporters, within a foliate scroll-carved framework, 19th century, 78in. wide.
(Christie's) $3,657

A William and Mary style couch, York, Maine, with adjustable wings, with two upholstered foot stools, 95in. wide.
(Christie's) $3,220

A Louis XVI style giltwood sofa, the oval padded back within a foliate border and raised on leafy supports, $61^1/2$in. wide.
(Christie's) $792

A Lamb of Manchester mahogany corner settle, padded back above sinuous trellis lower frieze, circa 1875.
(Christie's) $1,453

A Regency mahogany hall bench with paneled rectangular top with pierced spirally-fluted arm-rests, possibly Irish, $36^1/2$in. wide.
(Christie's) $13,268

A George III style giltwood two-seated sofa, with padded back flanked by outscrolled arms, on cabriole legs, 48in. wide.
(Christie's) $2,309

SIDEBOARDS

A George III North Country mahogany break front sideboard, a long drawer to the frieze flanked by two deep cellaret drawers, 77in. wide. (Spencer's) **$2,754**

An early Victorian mahogany pedestal sideboard, with paneled ledge back, flanked and surmounted by foliate scrolling decoration, 90½in. wide. (Christie's) **$986**

A Federal inlaid mahogany sideboard, New England, circa 1810, with three frieze drawers above a pair of convex doors, 1.68m. wide. (Sotheby's) **$6,325**

A classical marble-top mahogany pedestal sideboard, branded Wm. Alexander, Pittsburgh, Pennsylvania, circa 1825, on ogee molded plinth and carved paw feet, 1.92m. wide. (Sotheby's) **$9,200**

Lifetime oak mirrored sideboard, circa 1907, hammered copper hardware, arched crest rail over mirror flanked by corbels, Paine Furniture retail tag, 48in. wide. (Skinner) **$575**

A Wylie & Lochhead sideboard, the superstructure with central bow-fronted glazed cabinet flanked on each side by an open shelf recess, 197cm. wide. (Christie's) **$5,451**

A Georgian mahogany pedestal dressing table with seven short drawers, surrounding the kneehole, 45½in. wide. (Anderson & Garland) **$1,408**

An Edwardian mahogany sideboard, the line-inlaid and crossbanded bowfront top above two drawers, flanked by two drawers and a pair of paneled doors, 60in. wide. (Christie's) **$1,345**

A Regency mahogany kneehole-cabinet attributed to Gillows of Lancaster, the eared rectangular top with reeded edge and concave center, 46¼in. wide. (Christie's) **$13,541**

SIDEBOARDS

A late George III mahogany small serpentine front sideboard, the top with narrow walnut crossbanding, 54in. wide. (Spencer's) $2,560

Mission oak sideboard with cutouts, gallery back and sides with vertical slats with spade cutouts, unsigned, 50in. wide. (Skinner) $863

A Federal inlaid mahogany small sideboard, New England, circa 1800, the oblong top with shaped front, 1.8m. wide. (Sotheby's) $9,200

Gustav Stickley oak sideboard, No. 804, circa 1907, designed by Harvey Ellis, original medium finish and hammered iron hardware, red decal, 54¼in. wide. (Skinner) $7,475

A Regency ebonised line-inlaid mahogany serpentine sideboard, the central frieze drawer flanked by two short drawers and a deep cellaret drawer, on ring-turned tapering legs, 48in. wide. (Christie's) $2,238

An Edwardian mahogany sideboard, line-inlaid, the serpentine top above a frieze drawer and apron drawer flanked by a cupboard door and deep drawer, 59½in. wide. (Christie's) $1,651

A mahogany pedestal sideboard, with paneled and shelved ledge back above a central slide drawer and paneled cupboard German, mid 19th century, 75in. wide. (Christie's) $827

L. & J. G. Stickley oak sideboard, No. 734, circa 1912, original medium finish and hammered iron hardware, 48in. wide. (Skinner) $1,610

Hepplewhite revival mahogany sideboard, oval mirrored back with shaped shelf and hatched inlay, 5ft. wide. English, circa 1900. (G. A. Key) $1,421

SIDEBOARDS

Gustav Stickley oak sideboard, No. 814, circa 1910, original medium finish and hammered iron hardware, 66¼in. wide. (Skinner) $3,220

A mahogany sideboard, attributed to Dominique, with a pair of cupboard doors carved with an African scene, 88in. wide. (Christie's) $1,594

A mahogany breakfront sideboard, the bowfront top with three-quarter roundel decorated gallery above three frieze drawers and two paneled cupboard doors, 66½in. wide. (Christie's) $1,738

A 19th century shaped front sideboard, veneered in mahogany with satinwood banding, the edge inlaid stringing, 6ft. 4in. wide. (Woolley & Wallis)
                    $3,240

Federal bird's eye maple and cherry sideboard, Vermont, 1815–25, with old pattern glass pulls, refinished, 42in. wide. (Skinner) $2,645

A line-inlaid mahogany bowfront sideboard, the frieze drawer above a deep arched apron drawer flanked by a deep cellaret drawer and cupboard door, 48in. wide. (Christie's) $1,635

A George III mahogany bowfront sideboard, line-inlaid, with raised back above four drawers and arched apron, 54in. wide. (Christie's) $4,409

A Regency mahogany sideboard, pair of recessed paneled cupboard doors between spiral half columns, on spiral twist legs and tapering feet, 73in. wide. (Christie's) $2,756

A mahogany breakfront sideboard, in Sheraton Revival style, with satinwood banding and stringing, the square tapering legs on socket feet, 5ft. (Woolley & Wallis) $1,593

377

STANDS

A Federal birch stand, New England, 1790–1810, on reeded and ring-turned legs, 15¹/₂in. wide.
(Christie's) $7,475

A Regency rosewood and stained as rosewood folio stand, with two lattice pierced hinged and ratcheted rectangular panels, 29¹/₂in. wide.
(Spencer's) $3,840

A George III mahogany and inlaid plate canterbury, with a pierced carrying handle and pierced spindle galleried divided compartment, on ring turned splayed legs, 63cm. high.
(Phillips) $1,842

An ash pedestal with stepped platform top incorporating a swivel lid and fitted compartments, above four drawers, late 19th century, 20in. wide.
(Christie's) $794

One of a pair of green-painted and parcel-gilt decorated pedestals, each with simulated marble top above a waisted body decorated with flaming torch trophy, 45¹/₂in. high.
(Christie's)
     (Two) $1,232

Gustav Stickley oak slat umbrella stand, No. 100, circa 1907, original medium finish, ten slats riveted to three hammered iron hoops, (missing pan), 24in. high.
(Skinner) $1,265

A mahogany cutlery stand, with open compartment, carrying handle and bowed end, 22in. wide.
(Christie's) $551

Roycroft oak 'Little Journeys' book stand, East Aurora, New York, original medium finish, copper tag, 26¹/₈in. long.
(Skinner) $604

A Chinese red lacquer folding missal stand decorated in gold with a central sunburst halo, 17th/18th century, 32.5cm. high.
(Christie's) $7,314

STANDS

Majolica jardinière stand, the base applied with three seated putti each clutching a grape, 15in. high.
(G. A. Key) $539

A Cotswold School elm bookstand, with bone dot-inlay, the galleried shelf joined by chamfered arched uprights, 19in. wide.
(Christie's) $459

A turned wood yarn winder, New Hampshire, late 18th/early 19th century, the cylindrical winding wheel with four painted cross-members, 42^{1}/$_{4}$in. high.
(Christie's) $2,185

A Regency mahogany folio stand, the adjustable hinged lattice filled flaps on rectangular end supports joined by a ring turned baluster stretcher, 110cm. high.
(Phillips) $5,833

Federal birch and bird's eye maple lightstand, New Hampshire, circa 1825, original finish, 27^{1}/$_{2}$in. high.
(Skinner) $3,220

A Victorian figured-walnut folio-stand, the rounded rectangular four-leaf support with pierced center filled with strapwork, 37^{1}/$_{2}$in. wide.
(Christie's) $7,268

A William and Mary maple candlestand, possibly Dunlap School, Southern New Hampshire, early/mid 18th century, on T-shaped trestle base, 23^{1}/$_{2}$in. high.
(Christie's) $4,025

A painted and decorated hanging shelf, American, early 19th century, the shaped sides joined by two molded shelves, 18^{1}/$_{4}$in. wide.
(Christie's) $805

A Federal painted birchwood tilt-top candlestand, New England, circa 1810, the oval top tilting above a vase-form standard, on downcurving legs, 29^{1}/$_{2}$in. high.
(Sotheby's) $4,025

Gustav Stickley oak foot stool, No. 300, circa 1904, leather upholstery and black-finished dome tacks, through tenon stretchers, unsigned, 20in. long. (Skinner) **$1,380**

Victorian walnut framed large upholstered stool, carved friezes, supported on four cabriole legs, English, mid 19th century. (G. A. Key) **$667**

A George III carved mahogany long stool in the Chippendale style, the rectangular stuffover seat on blind fret chamfered legs, 77 x 42cm. (Phillips) **$2,763**

A classical carved mahogany piano stool, Boston, circa 1830, the circular seat revolving above a conforming molded base, legs with ebonized ball turned capitals and feet, 21½in. high. (Christie's) **$920**

A Spanish walnut stool, and another similar, on pierced scrolled double end-supports with metal stretchers and scroll feet, 16¾in. wide. (Christie's) **$2,332**

A William and Mary turned and black-painted oak joint stool, the rectangular molded top above a plain skirt on ring- and baluster-turned legs, 13½in. wide. (Sotheby's) **$3,335**

A Victorian rosewood X-frame stool, with floral needlework seat, 21in. wide. (Christie's) **$853**

J. M. Young oak and leather upholstered footstool, No. 382, Camden, New York, tacked leather upholstered seat, paper label, 19⅛in. long. (Skinner) **$431**

A Victorian walnut stool, the rectangular padded seat covered in gros point floral needlework on a tan ground, 21in. wide. (Christie's) **$999**

STOOLS

A Charles II beech footstool with a loose cushion cover raised on braganza legs, 18in. wide. (Cheffins Grain & Comins) $1,520

A mid-18th century Welsh oak backstool, the scrolled toprail incorporating a pierced heart. (Cheffins Grain & Comins) $1,034

A Regency simulated rosewood stool, on tapering reeded legs, brass caps and castors, 18in. wide. (Christie's) $817

A classical rosewood piano stool, American, probably New England, circa 1840, the needlework-covered top above a canted seat frame, 19½in. high. (Sotheby's) $402

A pair of white-painted and parcel-gilt stools, on domed patera-headed turned tapering fluted legs. (Christie's) $5,023

A set of Victorian walnut library steps, with two heights of upholstered serpentine treads on shell-carved swept cabriole legs, 20in. wide. (Hy. Duke & Son) $992

A German white-painted and parcel-gilt mahogany stool, on cabriole legs headed by flowerheads and on foliate feet, 17¼in. square. (Christie's) $2,332

An Edwardian mahogany and satinwood piano stool, the padded seat flanked by outcurved sides with padded top-rail. (Christie's) $675

A walnut stool of George II style, the padded drop-in seat above a shaped apron on foliate cabochon headed cabriole legs, late 19th century, 24in. wide. (Christie's) $448

STOOLS

A Franco-Flemish walnut stool, late 19th century, on twist-turned legs and stretchers, 120cm. wide.
(Sotheby's) $5,120

A good Victorian rosewood duet stool, with cavetto molded frieze, raised upon angular scroll end standards.
(Spencer's) $1,377

A William IV white-painted and parcel-gilt stool, the waved apron carved with foliate C-scrolls and acanthus and centered by a foliate cartouche, 52in. wide.
(Christie's) $14,444

A pair of Regency mahogany window stools, each with a curved rectangular top with reeded pole shallow arms.
(Spencer's) $3,021

A rare classical paint-decorated and carved mahogany piano stool, Philadelphia, Pennsylvania, circa 1830, on acanthus-carved legs.
(Sotheby's) $1,380

A pair of Regency giltwood X-frame stools, the turned uprights headed by panther-mask and ring-finials, possibly Continental, 35in. wide.
(Christie's) $11,811

A black-lacquered stool, with overall polychrome and gilt decoration, on scrolling uprights, 18¹/₂in. wide.
(Christie's) $466

One of a pair of Roman simulated-rosewood window seats, the open back with double-arched stretcher centered by a foliate clasp, early 19th century, 40in. wide.
(Christie's)
(Two) $30,498

A George II mahogany stool, on cabriole legs headed by scroll angles and with pad feet, 24in. wide.
(Christie's) $2,362

STOOLS

One of a set of four Swedish Gustaf III white-painted and parcel-gilt tabourets by Johan Lindgren.
(Christie's)
(Four) $14,835

A pair of North European birch stools, with plain frieze and on ring-turned tapering legs, mid-19th century, 50¾in. wide.
(Christie's) $3,050

One of a pair of red-painted and parcel-gilt X-frame stools, with turned arm-rests and paneled supports.
(Christie's)
(Two) $4,664

A carved walnut prie-dieu, the kneeling surface with lid, over molded base, Italian, 16th century, 85cm. wide.
(Kunsthaus am Museum) $1,368

A pair of mid 18th century cherrywood stools with one scrolled arm, on cabriole legs and hoof feet, Venice, 100cm. wide.
(Finarte) $8,030

A North Italian ebony, ebonized and ivory-inlaid fruitwood prie-dieu, inlaid with foliate-arabesques, on a molded spreading base, 19th century, 32¾in. wide.
(Christie's) $3,229

One of a pair of French giltwood stools, by Jansen, in the Louis XVI style, on circular fluted tapering legs, late 19th century, 22½in. square.
(Christie's)
(Two) $8,228

A pair of Italian walnut and parcel-gilt stools, the shaped low scrolled back with rockwork cresting, mid-18th century.
(Christie's) $8,432

An Art Deco ebonized and gilt stool, rectangular padded seat, above four gently swollen fluted legs, 1920/25.
(Christie's) $998

SUITES

An ormolu-mounted walnut salon suite, comprising a sofa, a pair of armchairs, three single chairs and a piano stool, all upholstered in gold silk satin, late 19th century.
(Christie's) $5,485

A Louis XV style giltwood suite, comprising: four open armchairs, each with foliate top-rail, padded arms, serpentine padded seat, on foliate-headed cabriole legs; and a matching canapé, 64in. wide.
(Christie's) $1,975

Gordon Russell, dining room suite, 1925, comprising, extending table, six side chairs, two armchairs and a sideboard, in walnut, the chairs with upholstered drop-in seats, table extending to 273.25cm.
(Sotheby's) $17,140

A suite of Louis XV blue and white-painted seat furniture, comprising a canapé and four fauteuils, the fauteuils en cabriolet each with padded back, arms and seat upholstered in Aubusson tapestry, the canapé 73½in. long.
(Christie's) $26,910

A mid 19th century suite comprising a table, sofa and four chairs in carved and lacquered wood, the table on a simulated tree trunk column and quadruped base.
(Finarte) $25,022

A suite of Russian Karelian-birch seat furniture, comprising a canapé, four small bergères and a pair of larger bergères, each with scrolled arched toprail, first half 19th century, the canapé 56in. wide.
(Christie's) $101,868

SUITES

N. Norman, dining room suite, 1930s, comprising, table, six upholstered side chairs and sideboard, in maple veneer, table 84³/₄in. long.
(Sotheby's) $2,981

An attractive Edwardian rosewood three piece salon suite, with shaped cresting rails and pierced foliate carved splats inlaid with leafy scrolls in ivory and box, comprising a buttoned back two seater settee and a pair of single chairs.
(Spencer's) $1,760

A definitive mid 1970s dining room suite by John Makepeace, comprising: a circular cherrywood table, 5ft. 10in. diameter, together with a set of six chairs.
(Locke & England) $2,900

SUITES

Austrian bentwood five-piece salon suite, designed by Josef Hoffmann, manufactured by Mobile Sighet, circa 1910, comprising a settee and four side chairs.
(Butterfield & Butterfield) $2,875

A maccassar ebony dining suite, attributed to Porteneuve, comprising: extending dining table, ten chairs and a buffet, the rectangular table on four shaped square-section legs, 260cm. wide (the table fully extended).
(Christie's) $8,722

Austrian bentwood four-piece salon suite, designed by Marcel Kammerer, circa 1909, the settee and chairs manufactured by Mundus, the table by Thonet, comprising a settee, two armchairs and a table.
(Butterfield & Butterfield) $5,750

BREAKFAST TABLES

A Regency mahogany breakfast table, of small size, the rounded rectangular tilt-top on four ring-turned uprights, 48in. wide. (Christie's) $1,016

A Regency mahogany breakfast-table, the oval tilt-top above a ring-turned baluster support and on arched square tapering legs, 59³/₄in. wide. (Christie's) $3,089

A Regency mahogany breakfast table, with a reeded edge to the rounded rectangular tip-up top, 48¹/₄in. wide. (Bearne's) $1,725

A George IV mahogany and rosewood breakfast-table, on a concave-sided rectangular foot with inlaid palmettes and scrolling acanthus, extending at two ends, 60in. wide. (Christie's) $29,450

A fine Regency rosewood circular breakfast table, the top decorated with crossbanding inlaid brass honeysuckle motifs, 50in. diameter. (Anderson & Garland) $5,508

An early Victorian mahogany breakfast table, the circular tilt top on lotus lappeted turned column and quadripartite platform with lappeted bun feet, 53¹/₂in. wide. (Christie's) $3,232

A late Regency mahogany breakfast table, on turned and fluted pedestal support and a concave sided tripartite base, 54in. diameter. (Christie's) $3,011

Regency mahogany and ebony strung drop leaf breakfast table, the hinged top with cut corners containing a frieze drawer, on a ring turned quadruple column platform, 90 x 103cm. extended. (Phillips) $2,617

An early Victorian mahogany breakfast table, the circular tilt-top with shaped frieze above faceted bulbous column, 48in. wide. (Christie's) $2,648

An early 19th century Regency pollard oak turnover top swivel action tea table, with ebony stringing, 36in.
(Locke & England)
$1,740

Pair of Regency rosewood and brass inlaid foldover card tables, on square tapering column supports with quadruped platform bases
(Lawrences)
$5,320

A George III mahogany tea-table, the serpentine-fronted beaded rectangular top above a rosette-and-flute channeled lip, 36¼in. wide.
(Christie's)
$5,814

A George I burr-walnut concertina-action card-table, the eared rectangular folding top enclosing a feather-edged green baize-lined playing-surface with circular candle-stands, 36in. wide.
(Christie's)
$64,527

A late Victorian rosewood and marquetry envelope card table, the hinged top inlaid with baskets of fruit and ribbon-tied garlands, above a drawer flanked by corbels, 22in. wide.
(Christie's)
$1,894

A Federal inlaid mahogany demi-lune card table, New York, 1790–1810, the hinged top centering a ring of inlaid bell flowers above a conforming apron, on square tapering bellflower inlaid legs, 36⅛in. wide.
(Christie's)
$5,520

A French boulle card table, Napoléon III, Paris, circa 1855, the hinged multiple serpentine swivelling top on cabriole legs, 92cm. wide.
(Sotheby's)
$6,399

A pair of late Victorian walnut, burr-walnut and inlaid half round card tables, each with foliate edged top and fluted columnar supports, 35½in. wide.
(Christie's)
$5,174

A French ormolu-mounted kingwood and marquetry card table, by Gervais Durand, on cabriole legs headed by foliate-cast clasps, late 19th century, 32½in. wide.
(Christie's)
$5,485

CARD & TEA TABLES

An early Victorian rosewood card table, the rounded rectangular top enclosing a baize lining, 26¹/₂in. wide. (Christie's) $1,244

An early Victorian rosewood card table, the hinged rounded rectangular top enclosing a blue baize lining, 36¹/₂in. wide. (Christie's) $1,942

Classical carved mahogany veneer card table, Boston, circa 1825–35, old refinish, 35¹/₂in. wide. (Skinner) $1,265

A William IV rosewood card table, the rounded rectangular hinged top on turned and gadrooned column and four splayed legs with roundels, 36in. wide. (Christie's) $2,086

A late 18th/early 19th century Dutch mahogany and floral marquetry tea table inlaid with baskets of flowers, birds and butterflies within checker lines, 66cm. wide. (Phillips) $2,916

A late Regency period mahogany card table, with ebony inlay and stringing, the 'D' shape swivel top baize lined, 3ft. (Woolley & Wallis) $2,356

George I mahogany and padouk wood card table, first half 18th century, the rectangular fold over top above a plain frieze, 26¹/₂in. wide. (William Doyle) $6,325

An Edwardian rosewood and inlaid envelope card table, on square tapering legs joined by a concave-sided undertier, 21¹/₂in. wide. (Christie's) $1,421

A George IV mahogany card table, on four fluted square tapering outward splayed supports with turned Regency knees, 36in. wide. (Spencer's) $1,145

Classical mahogany card table, probably Massachusetts, circa 1820, old refinish, 34³/₄in. wide. (Skinner) $1,265

A late Victorian rosewood, bone and boxwood inlaid envelope card table, the rectangular hinged top above a frieze drawer, 22in. wide. (Christie's) $1,695

A mid-Victorian carved rosewood card table, with rounded rectangular top and foliate scroll frieze, 36in. wide. (Christie's) $1,244

A Federal mahogany card table, New York, 1800–1815, the hinged clover-shaped top above a conforming apron, on five reeded cylindrical tapering legs, 36¹/₄in. wide. (Christie's) $2,530

Fine Sheraton Revival rosewood envelope card table of rectangular form, each triangular segment at the top inlaid with bone and marquetry urn of flowers, 22in. square, English, circa 1900. (G. A. Key) $2,064

An 18th century red walnut double folding butterfly top card/tea table, the rectangular top with rounded angles, unfolding to reveal a polished surface, 32in. wide. (Spencer's) $2,907

A German mahogany card-table, the rectangular folding-top enclosing a red baize-lined writing-surface, 19th century, 34¹/₄in. wide. (Christie's) $2,691

A classical mahogany card table, New York, 1815–1825, the rectangular patera veneered top with canted corners above a foliate carved pedestal and quadripartite base, 35³/₄in. wide. (Christie's) $1,840

A George III mahogany card table with concertina action, the hinged baize lined top with a beaded and foliate edge, 91cm. wide. (Phillips) $1,995

CENTER TABLES

An English marquetry center table, possibly by Holland, London, circa 1865, with a triple column support and triple downswept legs, 117cm. diameter.
(Sotheby's) $15,542

An oak draw leaf center table, on elaborately carved mythological grotesque creature supports, joined by arcaded reeded column stretcher, German, 19th century, 113in. fully extended.
(Christie's) $3,703

A 19th century Anglo Indian padouk wood center table, raised upon acanthus sheathed baluster pillar flanked by four undulating scroll angles, 54in. diameter.
(Spencer's) $1,193

A specimen marble topped giltmetal mounted ebonized center table, the rectangular top on paterae headed square section legs, 36in. wide.
(Christie's) $1,291

A classical stenciled mahogany center table, New York, 1810–1820, the circular marble top above a conforming apron with gilt-stenciled edge over a columnar pedestal on a tripartite base, 37½in. diameter.
(Christie's) $4,830

A walnut center table, the shaped rectangular top with cube parquetry inlaid top within a feather-banded border, South German, late 18th/early 19th century, 35in. wide.
(Christie's) $1,505

A walnut center table, the crossbanded serpentine top on foliate-carved frieze and foliate-headed cabriole legs joined by X-shaped stretcher, 50in. wide.
(Christie's) $1,063

An Oriental hardwood center table, the circular top with painted ceramic insert depicting courtly figures in a landscape, late 19th century, 22in. wide.
(Christie's) $883

Heal's, a center table, 1930s, the trestle base with lattice work end panels, in walnut banded with ebonized wood, 137.5cm. wide.
(Sotheby's) $2,608

CENTER TABLES

An Anglo-Indian ebony center table, the rectangular top with inset green marble above a pierced foliate frieze, first half 19th century, 41¼in. wide. (Christie's) $7,268

A good Victorian amboyna and ebony center table, the rounded rectangular top with a central lozenge ebony panel inlaid with delicate foliage in ivory, 48½in. wide. (Spencer's) $2,295

A Spanish walnut center table, on twin pierced end-supports joined by a scrolled stretcher and with metal underframe, late 17th century, 52in. wide. (Christie's) $7,176

An early 19th century Dutch mahogany and marquetry center table, the circular top with cornucopiae, birds and butterflies, on a splayed trefoil pedestal, 1.02m. diameter. (Phillips) $4,605

Mission oak hexagonal top table, circa 1905, brown leather covered top, each leg decorated with incised floral design, unsigned. (Skinner) $863

An Empire rosewood and ebonized center table, ebonized frieze set with classical figures on three turned columns and triform base, 30in. diameter. (Hy. Duke & Son) $10,880

A giltwood center-table, the molded rounded rectangular gray and white marble top above a shaped frieze carved to front and back with a musical trophy, 44½in. wide. (Christie's) $15,787

A mahogany center table, on spiral-turned column and root-carved platform with paw feet, early 19th century, 35½in. wide. (Christie's) $1,194

An Italian oak center table, with foliate scroll frieze with lion masks to the corner angles, 36½in. wide. (Cheffins Grain & Comins) $608

CONSOLE TABLES

Edgar Brandt, console table, circa 1925, marble top supported on two scrolled wrought iron supports with marble bases, 56¹/₈in. wide. (Sotheby's) $4,658

A mahogany console table, the rectangular top on scroll supports, the mirrored back on breakfront plinth base, early 19th century, 69in. wide. (Christie's) $1,688

Console table, 1930s, with single sheet metal scroll support and two stepped thick acid-textured glass shelves, 59¹/₄in. wide. (Sotheby's) $3,353

One of a pair of Continental giltwood console tables, each with later D-shaped occhio marble top with gadrooned edge, early 19th century, 35in. wide. (Christie's)
(Two) $14,352

A pair of South German painted and giltwood console tables, with winged cherub supports, late 17th century, 22¹/₂in. wide. (Hy. Duke & Son) $4,800

A George III pine console table, the white marble top inlaid with geometric Siena marble banding, on reeded turned tapering legs joined by waved flowerhead-carved stretchers, 57in. wide. (Christie's) $6,541

A giltwood console table, the serpentine porta santa marble top above a pierced frieze of rockwork and floral swags, 56¹/₂in. wide. (Christie's) $5,023

A William IV mahogany console table, with ledge back, white-marble top, foliate edge and cushion molded frieze drawer 47¹/₂in. wide. (Christie's) $2,204

A pair of walnut console tables, with ovolo carved frieze on double volute legs joined by stretchers, Lombardy, 17th/18th century, 107cm. wide. (Finarte) $16,452

CONSOLE TABLES

An Italian giltwood console table, the marbled shaped wooden top above a carved frieze on four tapering legs twined with leafy tracery, 18th century, 141cm. wide. (Finarte) $3,011

One of a pair of rosewood console tables, each with simulated marble top, on lion monopodiae, 54in. wide. (Christie's)
(Two) $4,066

A late 18th century lacquered and gilded demi-lune console table, the marble top over a foliate frieze, Naples, 145cm. wide. (Finarte) $14,053

A German bronzed and painted console table, the associated serpentine-fronted gray marble top supported on a splayed eagle resting on a castle, early 18th century, 38¹/₂in. wide. (Christie's) $8,970

A pair of Louis XVI demi-lune giltwood console tables, the white marble tops above a garland hung carved frieze, 72.5cm. wide. (Finarte) $12,045

An Italian giltwood console table, the later portor marble top above a waisted frieze and a free-standing harpie, mid-18th century, 34³/₄in. wide. (Christie's) $4,664

An Irish William IV bronzed console table in the manner of del Vecchio, the rectangular back and white marble top on angled winged lion monopodia and paw feet, 48in. wide. (Christie's) $7,222

A George II pine console table, the later rectangular Siena marble top above a flowerhead-filled trefoil-cornice and supported on two entwined dolphins, 38in. wide. (Christie's) $64,938

A French ormolu-mounted boulle console table, inlaid à conntre partie, by Mignaud, Paris, with a black and yellow marble breakfront top, mid-19th century, 42¹/₂in. wide. (Christie's) $8,228

DINING TABLES

A mid Victorian mahogany extending pedestal dining table, baluster stem and on four foliate-carved splayed legs, 47¹/₂in. diameter.
(Bearne's) $4,200

A twin-pillar mahogany dining table with an additional leaf and two rectangular end sections with rounded corners, 19th century, 77¹/₂in. long.
(Hy. Duke & Son)

$3,186

A late Regency mahogany twin-pedestal dining table, on turned column support with foliate capped hipped downswept legs, with extra leaf, 75in. extended.
(Christie's) $6,732

A small bent and laminated plywood dining table, designed by Marcel Breuer for the Isobar at the Isokon Lawn Road Flats, the top bent to overhang on two sides, circa 1936, 68.5cm. wide.
(Christie's) $6,359

Victorian mahogany circular loo table on tilt mechanism to a cannon column with tricorn base, 3ft. 6in., English, early 19th century.
(G. A. Key) $794

Late Regency mahogany concertina action dining table, the D-shaped foldover molded top on six turned and spiral fluted supports, 80in. fully opened.
(Lawrences) $2,205

Victorian mahogany circular wind-out dining table, supported on four heavy acanthus leaf molded and beaded baluster tapering supports, 52in. diameter.
(G. A. Key) $2,464

Pine and oak table, Pennsylvania, 1760–80, with thumb-molded top and single drawer with old replaced brass, 55¹/₂in. wide.
(Skinner) $2,760

A Regency pollard oak dining table, the base with a triform spreading shaft with anthemion clasps, tripartite platform base, 137cm. diameter.
(Phillips) $15,350

DINING TABLES

A rare English Elizabethan Revival dining table, early Victorian, late 1830s, in well-figured pollard oak, with two leaves, 132cm. wide.
(Sotheby's) $8,228

A Regency mahogany dining table in the manner of Gillows of Lancaster, on turned and reeded legs headed by turned roundels, 98in. extended.
(Hy. Duke & Son) $6,220

L. & J.G. Stickley oak extension dining table, Model 713, 1912–1917, raised on a shaped curved base, with four leaves, 8ft. extended.
(Butterfield & Butterfield) $2,300

Lifetime oak pedestal dining table, No. 9057, circa 1907, round extension top on square pedestal with four radiating legs, three leaves, Paine Furniture retail tag, 48in. diameter.
(Skinner) $1,035

A large early Victorian figured mahogany loo table, the veneered circular tilt top, on turned and petal carved stem, 4ft. 5½in. diameter.
(Woolley & Wallis) $4,375

Painted pine and maple tavern table with drawer, New England, 18th century, top with old varnish and base with old red paint, 37½in. wide.
(Skinner) $2,070

A William IV mahogany extending dining table, the central section with rectangular tilting top on baluster turned column, 92in.
(Hy. Duke & Son) $2,080

An early Victorian mahogany extending dining table, including eight extra leaves of a later date, the lobed top on spiral turned column, 236in. extended.
(Christie's) $14,960

An oak draw-leaf dining table, with a parquetry frieze, above foliate scroll-carved molded apron, English, parts 17th century, 166in. extended.
(Christie's) $12,012

DRESSING TABLES

Classical tiger maple and mahogany veneer dressing table, circa 1825, refinished, 36in. wide.
(Skinner) $1,840

A Charles X elm veneered and ebony banded toilet table, with marble top and raised on lyre front supports, 109cm. wide.
(Finarte) $5,519

An early 19th century mahogany bow-front kneehole dressing table, with an arrangement of five drawers, 39in. wide.
(Bearne's) $1,932

An early 19th century North Italian walnut and marquetry serpentine dressing table, the 'arc-en-arbalette' superstructure with four drawers around a central cupboard, on cabriole legs with pointed pad feet, 118cm. wide.
(Phillips) $3,838

Charles X burl wood dressing table, first half 19th century, the rectangular top lifting to reveal a vanity mirror over a central well and lidded compartments, 21½in. wide.
(William Doyle) $5,462

A Federal paint-decorated pine dressing table, New England, probably Massachusetts or Maine, circa 1825–1828, the shaped splashboard with brass rosette-mounted scrolls above a shelf incorporating two drawers, 33¼in. wide.
(Sotheby's) $11,500

A mahogany and ebony banded dressing table, the mirror flanked by niches with ormolu figures of Cupid, Austria, 19th century, 125cm. wide.
(Finarte) $17,933

A Queen Anne walnut dressing-table, attributed to William Savery, Philadelphia, circa 1770, on cabriole legs with intaglio carved knees, 34½in. wide.
(Christie's) $27,600

A mid 19th century mahogany dressing table with raised beveled toilet mirror on turned supports, 35in. wide.
(Anderson & Garland) $949

DRESSING TABLES

A late George III mahogany and line-inlaid dressing chest, with flame veneered twin flap top, enclosing a fitted interior, 62in. opened.
(Christie's) $1,244

A Robert 'Mouseman' Thompson paneled oak dressing table and stool, central kneehole flanked by three drawers, the sides with adzed paneling, 138cm. wide.
(Christie's) $2,907

A tulipwood poudreuse, the serpentine top with hinged center enclosing a pale blue damask-lined interior and a toilet-mirror, 28¼in. wide.
(Christie's) $9,329

A Queen Anne carved and inlaid walnut dressing table, Portsmouth, New Hampshire, 1735–1760, the concave carved shell and arched and scrolled apron centering two acorn drops, 36in. wide.
(Christie's) $103,700

Classical rosewood veneer cherry and bird's eye maple bureau with dressing glass, Orange, Massachusetts, circa 1835, old refinish, old brass pulls, 41¼in. wide.
(Skinner) $1,955

A Federal bird's-eye maple and mahogany veneered dressing table, New England, circa 1825, the scrolled splashboard with a stepped and conforming bird's-eye maple veneered drawer, 37in. wide.
(Christie's) $3,680

Federal mahogany carved and bird's eye maple veneered inlaid bureau and dressing glass, Boston, circa 1810–20, old brasses, 39in. wide.
(Skinner) $85,000

A late Federal red-painted dressing table, New England, early 19th century, the scalloped splashboard enclosing a rectangular top, 30in. wide.
(Christie's) $1,265

Renaissance Revival walnut and burl walnut drop-well dresser, third quarter 19th century, 50⅛in. wide.
(Skinner) $1,035

DROP LEAF TABLES

Chippendale mahogany drop leaf table, Massachusetts, circa 1780, old finish, 52^{1}/$_{2}$in. long (open).
(Skinner) $690

Classical mahogany drop leaf table with drawer, possibly New York, circa 1815, old refinish, 51^{1}/$_{2}$in. long (open).
(Skinner) $863

Chippendale cherry carved dining table, possibly Rhode Island, circa 1780, old refinish, 52^{1}/$_{2}$in. wide.
(Skinner) $6,900

An early Victorian burr-walnut and simulated walnut Sutherland table, the rounded rectangular twin-flap top inlaid with a geometric quatrefoil border, 41^{1}/$_{2}$in. wide.
(Christie's) $5,088

A George II mahogany drop leaf table, the oval top on shell carved cabriole legs with ball and claw feet, 108 x 136cm.
(Phillips) $2,917

A Federal mahogany breakfast table, New York, 1810–1820, the rectangular top with clover-shaped drop leaves above an apron with a frieze drawer on either side, 40^{1}/$_{4}$in. wide (open).
(Christie's) $5,175

Maple dining table, New England, late 18th century, refinished, 48in. diameter.
(Skinner) $4,312

Directoire walnut dining table, the oblong top with slightly bowed ends banded in brass and crescent form drop leaves, 7ft. 7in. long extended.
(William Doyle) $8,337

Queen Anne walnut dining table, Massachusetts, circa 1760, old finish, 48in. wide.
(Skinner) $11,500

DROP LEAF TABLES

Classical carved mahogany drop leaf table, New England, circa 1825, 50³/₄in. wide (open). (Skinner) $546

A Chippendale carved mahogany dining table, Essex County, Massachusetts, circa 1770, angular cabriole legs on claw-and-ball feet, 47in. wide. (Sotheby's) $5,462

Federal tiger maple drop leaf table, New England, circa 1820, 39in. wide. (Skinner) $2,645

Federal tiger maple drop leaf table with drawer, New England, circa 1820, old finish, 35¹/₂in. wide. (Skinner) $1,092

A Queen Anne figured walnut drop-leaf breakfast table, Boston, Massachusetts, 1740–60, the oblong top with two hinged D-shaped leaves, on cabriole legs ending in pad feet, 27in. long, extended. (Sotheby's) $19,550

William and Mary maple and pine trestle drop leaf table, New England, early 18th century, 38in. wide. (Skinner) $6,325

Federal cherry inlaid drop leaf table, probably Connecticut, circa 1790, refinished, 36in. wide. (Skinner) $2,185

An attractive Victorian walnut Sutherland table, raised upon bobbin turned and tapering outward splayed supports, 43in. long extended. (Spencer's) $905

Chippendale mahogany drop leaf table, Pennsylvania, 18th century, 46¹/₄in. wide. (Skinner) $805

DROP LEAF TABLES

Early 19th century mahogany extending dining table with two drop leaves on reeded turned tapering legs, 55in. long. (Ewbank)　　　　$2,023

A George II mahogany drop-leaf table, the oval twin-flap top above one frieze drawer and on cabriole legs, 62¼in. wide. (Christie's)　　　　$15,347

A Chippendale maple drop leaf table, New England, 1760–1780, the rectangular top above a scalloped apron, 45¾in. wide (open). (Christie's)　　　　$2,760

A William and Mary carved oak drop-leaf table, English, early 18th century, the rectangular hinged top above a baluster turned T-base, 26½in. wide. (Christie's)　　　　$3,680

A diminutive Queen Anne maple drop-leaf table, New England, 1740–1760, on cabriole legs and pad disk feet, 30½in. wide (open). (Christie's)　　　　$74,000

A Federal bird's-eye maple and cherrywood drop-leaf stand, possibly Robert Dunlap (1779–1865), Bedford, New Hampshire, 1820–40, 30¼in. long (open). (Christie's)　　　　$14,950

A Chippendale carved mahogany small drop-leaf table, Massachusetts, 1760–1780, the two drop leaves with cove-molded edges, 35¾in. wide (Christie's)　　　　$51,750

Antique American Sheraton drop-leaf dining table, in cherry with turned legs, top 46 x 18in. with two 20in. leaves. (Eldred's)　　　　$495

A Federal curly maple drop-leaf table, New England, 1790–1810, on square tapering line-inlaid legs, 35½in. wide. (Christie's)　　　　$4,600

A walnut drum table, the circular leather-lined top above four frieze drawers, on reeded column and reeded splayed legs, 56in. wide.
(Christie's) $2,160

A Regency mahogany drum top library table, of small size, on turned column and quadruped legs, 92cm. diameter.
(Phillips) $3,840

A mahogany drum table, Regency, circa 1815, with inset yellow leather top, four real and four dummy drawers, 89cm. diameter.
(Sotheby's) $9,200

A mahogany drum-table, part early 19th century, the circular gilt-tooled green leather-lined top above four paneled frieze drawers and four simulated drawers, 25¹/₂in. diameter.
(Christie's) $6,500

Grosfield octagonal card table and four chairs, original blond finish and blue leather inset top over four drawers, table 36³/₄in. diameter.
(Skinner) $2,013

A William IV rosewood drum top occasional table, the circular top with three drawers divided by dummy drawer fronts, on a polygonal column and trefoil platform, 61cm. diameter.
(Phillips) $1,842

A Regency mahogany drum-table, the green leather-lined top above two slides, with four drawers and four cupboards simulated as drawers, 32in. diameter.
(Christie's) $8,722

A birds-eye maple drum-top library table, inlaid with lines, the top inset with a panel of green tooled leather, on a polygonal tapering column, trefoil platform and gilt paw feet, 48in. diameter.
(Christie's) $8,000

A Regency mahogany drum top library table, inlaid with ebony lines, the top inset with a panel of tooled leather and fitted with four frieze drawers, 48in. diameter.
(Christie's) $5,760

DUMB WAITERS

A Regency mahogany dumb waiter, with reeded edges to the two graduated circular dropleaf tiers, 24¼in. diameter.
(Bearne's) $1,836

A Victorian mahogany extending dumb-waiter, the rectangular top with molded edge extendable to three tiers, the lower two with molded edge, 59¼in. wide.
(Christie's) $11,000

A Regency mahogany two tier dumb waiter, the circular dished shelves on spiral reeded columns, 58cm. diameter.
(Phillips) $798

An early 19th century mahogany metamorphic dumb waiter, the rising mechanism revealing three circular tiers with molded edges, 25½in. diameter.
(Bearne's) $2,524

Edwardian mahogany oval three tier dumb waiter, decorated throughout with line and checkerboard inlay, tray top, 24in. wide.
(G. A. Key) $520

A rare Regency mahogany dumb waiter, the oval mahogany top with a rising center section and milled brass border on a ribbed and ring turned shaft, 79cm. high.
(Phillips) $3,377

A mahogany dumb waiter, George III, circa 1790, the two molded graduated tiers on a ringed tapering column, 110cm. high.
(Sotheby's) $3,680

An early Victorian mahogany dumb waiter with three rounded rectangular adjustable tiers, 41¾in. wide.
(Bearne's) $2,184

An early George III mahogany revolving two tier dumb waiter, on tripod carved cabriole legs with scroll ornament and castors, 61cm. diameter.
(Phillips) $16,000

GATELEG TABLES

A William and Mary maple gate-leg dining table, Massachusetts, 1700–1720, the rectangular top with bowed ends flanked by D-shaped drop leaves, 51in. wide.
(Christie's) $88,300

A large oval oak double-gateleg dining table, in 17th century style, on twelve turned legs with turned stretchers, top 234cm. x 207cm. open.
(Sotheby's) $9,200

A William and Mary maple and birchwood single-drawer gate leg drop-leaf dining table, New England, probably Massachusetts or Rhode Island, 1720–50, 61¼in. wide extended.
(Sotheby's) $79,500

A yew-wood gateleg table, the oval twin-flap above a plain frieze with later drawer, on ring-turned baluster supports with a double gateleg, late 17th/18th century, 45in. wide.
(Christie's) $8,000

A rare William and Mary turned and paint-decorated maple and pine gateleg table, probably Windsor, Connecticut, circa 1760, the rectangular top flanked by D-shaped drop-leaves above a plain skirt, 33½in. wide, extended.
(Sotheby's) $19,550

A J. S. Henry mahogany Pembroke table, designed by George Walton, supported on each side on three slender turned uprights, circa 1900/05, 83cm. diameter.
(Christie's) $1,800

A Georgian oak drop-leaf console table, with demi-lune top lifting to reveal a well above baluster-turned legs, 77.5cm. wide.
(Christie's) $2,990

Antique oval gate-leg table, in pine, bobbin-turned legs, possibly Scandinavian, shows significant restoration, 28in. long.
(Eldred's) $99

Antique English oval gate-leg table, in oak with one drawer, box stretcher, and turned legs, some old repairs, top open, 38 x 43½in.
(Eldred's) $687

LARGE TABLES

A George III mahogany 'D' end dining table in three sections with frieze above chamfered tapering legs.
(Locke & England)   **$2,610**

A mahogany three-pillar dining table, the D-end top crossbanded with satinwood, 118¹/₂in., the bases early 19th century.
(Bearne's)   **$5,712**

Art Deco Biedermeier style tiger maple and ebonized dining table, inverted tripod scroll foliate form pedestals each on stepped elliptical platform base, 75in. long.
(Skinner)   **$5,405**

A Regency mahogany telescopic dining-table, the rounded rectangular reeded D-shaped end-section opening to reveal two further hinged reeded leaves, 87¹/₄in. fully extended.
(Christie's)   **$10,539**

An oak refectory table, the rectangular cleated plank top above arcaded friezes and spiral-twist supports, English, 19th century, 108in. wide.
(Christie's)   **$9,609**

Federal two-part cherry inlaid banquet table, New England, circa 1825, old refinish, 61in. wide.
(Skinner)   **$3,450**

A good early Victorian mahogany serving table, with shallow superstructure, the projecting base with deep molded edge, 229cm. long.
(Spencer's)   **$1,120**

A mahogany triple section dining table, with central drop-leaf section and two D-ends, 109in. extended.
(Christie's)   **$2,656**

LARGE TABLES

Shaker birch and pine trestle foot table, from
Shirley Shaker settlement, 19th century, old
refinish, 102in. wide.
(Skinner) $6,900

Pine and birch harvest table, probably New
England, circa 1830, 81in. long.
(Skinner) $4,945

A George IV mahogany concertina action
extending dining table, on turned ribbed legs
and castors, 203cm. long.
(Phillips) $4,605

French Art Deco black lacquer table, stepped
overhanging extension top on 'U' shaped double
pedestal base, 71in. long.
(Skinner) $978

A Regency mahogany concertina action dining
table, the rounded rectangular reeded top on
spiral turned legs headed by roundels, 185cm.
long.
(Phillips) $4,298

A George III mahogany D-end dining table, with
central dropleaf section and on tapering square
legs, 110in. long.
(Bearne's) $3,825

A George III style mahogany triple pedestal
dining table, with reeded rounded rectangular
top and turned columns with reeded splayed
legs, 132in. extended.
(Christie's) $5,028

A mahogany twin-pedestal dining table,
comprising a pair of drop-leaf tables joined by a
specially shaped extra leaf, on bulbous square
section baluster columns, mid 19th century,
113in. extended.
(Christie's) $2,957

LARGE TABLES

A Regency extending dining table, the rounded rectangular reeded top above a plain molded frieze, on ring turned legs, 256cm. long. (Phillips)   **$9,978**

A George III mahogany serpentine serving table, the frieze inlaid with illusionistic fluting and a central fan on square tapering legs, 182cm. wide. (Phillips)   **$6,447**

George II mahogany D-end dining table on turned legs with one leaf, $46^{1}/_2$ x $62^{1}/_2$in. maximum. (Ewbank)   **$1,200**

An oak dining table, designed by Sir Gordon Russell, rectangular paneled top above octagonal section legs, central chamfered stretcher bifurcating into each leg, 197.5cm. wide. (Christie's)   **$5,087**

An oak refectory table, with one piece rectangular top, on forked end trestle supports, English, the top 17th century, the base 19th century, 113in. wide. (Christie's)   **$12,936**

A Charles X mahogany extending dining-table, the demi-lune drop-ends above a plain frieze and ring-turned baluster legs, with six later leaves, 152in. long. (Christie's)   **$23,322**

An early 19th century extending mahogany dining table, the oval molded top opening with a wind out mechanism to include two extra leaves, 233 x 132 x 77cm. high. (Phillips)   **$6,908**

A large Victorian oak extending dining table with canted corners raised on turned tapering legs and brass castors, 55 x 145 x $28^{1}/_2$in. high, with three leaves. (Anderson & Garland)   **$4,805**

LARGE TABLES

A mahogany extending dining table, comprising two D-ends and three extra leaves, on ring-turned tapering legs, 112in. fully extended. (Christie's) $2,852

E. J. Riley half size oak framed dining snooker table, fitted four leaves, resting on rise and fall patent, slate bed, 83 x 46in. (Peter Wilson) $1,473

A Spanish oak refectory table, on six scrolled legs joined by pierced stretcher with central putto mask flanked by foliate scrolls on scrolled feet, 83³/₄in. wide. (Christie's) $12,558

A Regency mahogany extending dining-table with two extending D-shaped end-sections and six further leaves, on tapering reeded legs, 209³/₄in. long, fully extended. (Christie's) $57,619

A Regency mahogany serving-table, the paneled frieze inlaid with Greek key and with two drawers, on spirally-reeded turned tapering legs, 70in. wide. (Christie's) $16,353

An oak and elm refectory table, the molded rectangular top above a paneled frieze with two simulated drawers, on canted square legs, 19th century reconstruction, 102in. wide. (Christie's) $5,382

A Regency mahogany two-pedestal extending dining-table with two D-shaped end-sections and two extra leaves, each pedestal with ring-turned baluster and downswept legs, 93¹/₄in. long, extended. (Christie's) $10,902

A mahogany three-pedestal dining-table crossbanded overall in kingwood, with two D-shaped end-sections, a central pedestal section and two later leaves, part early 19th century, 138in. long, fully extended. (Christie's) $12,639

LIBRARY TABLES

An English inlaid walnut library or center table, Victorian, circa 1860, on fluted canted carved trestle supports joined by a stretcher, 178cm. wide.
(Sotheby's) $10,971

Limbert oak two-drawer library table, No. 164, circa 1907, original medium finish and copper hardware, branded mark, 48in. wide.
(Skinner) $1,955

An early Victorian mahogany library table, on octagonal gadrooned collared end supports joined by a turned stretcher, 59in. wide.
(Christie's) $1,683

An early Victorian mahogany library table, the rectangular hinged top with gadrooned edge enclosing deep well and plain frieze, 59½in. wide.
(Christie's) $2,510

Limbert oak one-drawer library table, No. 153, Holland, Michigan, circa 1907, shaped top over blind drawer, panel ends with cut outs and medial shelf, 48in. long.
(Skinner) $2,645

A Regency rosewood small library table, raised upon a cannon barrel turned pillar issuing from a concave rectangular platform, 53½in. wide.
(Spencer's) $2,790

Rare Limbert oak six-drawer library table, Grand Rapids, Michigan, circa 1905, panel sides and each end fitted with three graduated drawers, unsigned, 56in. long.
(Skinner) $2,990

Roycroft oak two-drawer library table, No. 75, circa 1906, original medium finish and copper hardware, carved orb mark, 52⅛in. long.
(Skinner) $1,955

A Swedish mahogany writing table, with tambour fronted superstructure to one side, signed *C. D. Fick*, late 18th century, 150cm. wide.
(Stockholms Auktionsverk) $21,532

OCCASIONAL TABLES

A French parquetry tea table, by Linke of Paris, circa 1920, the serpentine top with a crossbanded edge enclosing four hinged sides, 78cm. wide.
(Sotheby's) $4,754

A French occasional table, Paris, 1920, in Empire manner, on turned tapering fluted legs, 79cm. wide.
(Sotheby's) $7,680

A Louis XVI tulipwood and kingwood marquetry poudreuse, the shaped rectangular top in three hinged sections, on square tapering legs, 77cm. wide.
(Phillips) $1,458

An ormolu-mounted Sèvres-style porcelain-mounted guéridon, of oval shape, the upper dish painted with a couple within a pastoral landscape, late 19th century, 24½in. wide.
(Christie's) $3,291

A pair of Regency burr maple occasional or work tables, with rectangular tops each containing a paneled frieze drawer, on ring turned knopped columns, 47cm. wide.
(Phillips) $2,917

A French ormolu-mounted tulipwood, parquetry and marquetry occasional table, in the Louis XV style, 19th century, 26in. wide.
(Christie's) $4,571

A Renaissance Revival rosewood gaming table, American, 1860–1880, the carved apron with single drawer over four tapering cylindrical supports, 26³/₈in. diameter.
(Christie's) $1,495

An Omega Workshops marquetry table, designed by Roger Fry and made by J. Kallenborn and Sons, circa 1913, 75.8cm. wide.
(Christie's) $7,631

A William and Mary painted pine and maple tavern table, New Hampshire, 1740–1770, the oval top above a straight apron on double baluster-turned legs, 31in. long.
(Christie's) $16,100

OCCASIONAL TABLES

Limbert oak occasional table,
No. 146, Holland, Michigan,
circa 1910, original medium-
light finish, branded mark, 45in.
long.
(Skinner) $2,300

Gustav Stickley oak round table,
No. 645, circa 1904, arched
crossed stretchers with dome
finial, red decal, 36in. diameter.
(Skinner) $1,840

Painted tea table, New England,
18th century, old surface with
red paint, 32in. wide.
(Skinner) $9,200

A late Victorian rosewood
occasional table, the
crossbanded kidney-shaped top
with inlaid musical trophy, on
reeded stop-fluted tapering legs
joined by stretchers, 25in. wide.
(Christie's) $1,167

Art Deco maple and veneered
occasional table, America, circa
1930, burr walnut and
fruitwood veneered octagonal
top, five-part pedestal, 28½in.
diameter.
(Skinner) $1,495

A painted and turned maple and
pine oval-top tavern table, New
England, 1730–70, the oval top
above a molded frieze raised
on vase- and reel-turned legs,
23in. wide.
(Sotheby's) $6,900

A mid 19th century walnut
inlaid table, the top inlaid in
fruitwoods with a central panel
of musicians, Sorrento, 60cm.
wide.
(Finarte) $5,353

A Regency pale blue and ivory
painted reading table, raised on
a lyre-shaped base, 29in. wide.
(Anderson & Garland)
                         $3,978

An early Victorian walnut and
specimen marble center table,
the circular top with malachite
center and verde antico border,
37¼in. diameter.
(Christie's) $6,861

OCCASIONAL TABLES

William and Mary walnut tavern table, possibly Boston, early 18th century, 31½in. wide. (Skinner) **$8,050**

An early George III mahogany tilt-top tripod table, the circular top above a bird-cage, on ring-turned column, 34in. wide. (Christie's) **$1,837**

William IV mahogany reading table, second quarter 19th century, 29¼in. wide. (Skinner) **$2,300**

An ebonised and gilt-painted occasional table, the marmo belgio nero top inlaid with pietra dura iceberg roses, above a scrolling frieze, 24½in. diameter. (Christie's) **$1,505**

European Arts and Crafts ebonized and carved table, original ebonized finish with intaglio design highlighted in green, incised *Werderman*, 19¾in. wide. (Skinner) **$316**

A Chippendale walnut tea-table, Pennsylvania, 1770–1790, the circular dished top tilting and revolving above a birdcage support over a ring and bulbous baluster-turned pedestal, 32½in. diameter. (Christie's) **$2,530**

A late George II mahogany occasional or tea table, the circular snap top on a ring and urn turned shaft, 96cm. diameter. (Phillips) **$1,458**

A tulipwood, kingwood and green-stained fruitwood parquetry table en chiffonière, inlaid with cube parquetry, on square tapering legs, 15¾in. wide. (Christie's) **$1,794**

Louis XVI style gilt bronze mounted mahogany bouillotte table, the top with an inset leather panel surrounded by a pierced gallery, 30in. diameter. (William Doyle) **$6,325**

OCCASIONAL TABLES

A Regency ormolu-mounted slate lamp-table, the octagonal engraved slate top with a frieze of classical figures, 18½in. diameter.
(Christie's) $9,994

A mahogany tripod table, the circular tilt-top with pie-crust edge above a fluted columnar stem, 20in. diameter.
(Christie's) $3,089

An Austrian figured-ash tripod table, the octagonal radially-veneered top above two frieze drawers, early 19th century, 24in. diameter.
(Christie's) $3,229

An early 19th century circular table inlaid with palisander and fruitwoods with specimen marble top on addorsed dolphin support and triangular base, Tuscany, 59cm. diameter.
(Finarte) $30,507

A rare imported birchwood tea table mounted with a Rorstrand faience tray, circa 1800, the stand an inlaid-birchwood frame, on shaped legs joined by an X-form stretcher, 30½in. high.
(Sotheby's) $17,250

A Regency kingwood and parcel gilt mounted occasional table with crossbanded mahogany top with a brass edge, on lotus knopped gilt column, 57cm. diameter.
(Phillips) $6,410

A late George II mahogany draughtsman or architect's table, the molded rectangular top with re-entrant corners, adjustable on a ratchet and with a rising book rest, 91cm. wide.
(Phillips) $5,373

A Georgian mahogany tripod table, the circular tilting top with a ribbon and rosette carved rim, the fluted shaft with foliate carved baluster, 75cm. diameter.
(Phillips) $5,833

Egyptian Revival table, circa 1875–80, in ebonized and gilt wood, the columns decorated with palm and lotus leaves, 75.25cm. wide.
(Sotheby's) $7,079

OCCASIONAL TABLES

A parcel-gilt and pale green painted center table, the mottled rouge circular marble top above fluted bulbous column, mid 19th century, 29¹/₂in. wide.
(Christie's) **$1,178**

A Transitional oval gueridon table attributed to C. Topino, Paris, circa 1760.
(Galerie Koller)
$25,023

A Piedmontese circular fruitwood table, with concentric geometric inlay, on baluster column and shaped base, early 19th century, 63cm. diameter.
(Finarte) **$7,198**

A Russian Karelian-birch and parcel-gilt occasional table, the circular top with plain frieze above a turned columnar support, first half 19th century, 21in. diameter.
(Christie's) **$5,382**

Federal carved and figured mahogany drop-leaf library table, attributed to Duncan Phyfe or a contemporary, New York, circa 1815, 46¹/₂in. wide extended.
(Sotheby's) **$9,200**

A Viennese burr-walnut and tulipwood crossbanded occasional table, the circular top inset with a blue ground porcelain roundel, 26¹/₄in. diameter.
(Christie's) **$3,291**

An octagonal walnut table on griffin supports, the specimen marble top with a view of Etna, Sicilian, 19th century, 72cm. wide.
(Finarte) **$27,421**

A George II red walnut tripod table, the dished circular tilt-top on a bird-cage support and ring-turned baluster shaft, 35³/₄in. diameter.
(Christie's) **$22,569**

An Empire ormolu-mounted burr-elm vide-poche, the rectangular top with a laurel leaf band and single mahogany-lined frieze drawer, 19¹/₂in. wide.
(Christie's) **$16,146**

PEMBROKE TABLES

Irish George III mahogany Pembroke table, third quarter 18th century, 30½in. wide. (Skinner) $1,495

A George III mahogany and marquetry Pembroke table, the oval top with a satinwood band inlaid with entwined berried leaves and ribbons, 39in. wide. (Christie's) $16,250

Chippendale mahogany Pembroke table, Rhode Island, 1765–90, with fluted and chamfered legs, 29in. wide. (Skinner) $747

A George III mahogany butterfly top Pembroke table, the serpentine rectangular top inlaid with a band of leafy scrolls in colored woods, 39in. wide extended. (Spencer's) $3,180

An Edwardian painted satinwood Pembroke table, the twin-flap rounded rectangular top decorated with portrait medallions and floral swags, 17in. wide. (Christie's) $1,304

An 18th century laburnum parquetry veneered Pembroke table, inlaid checker stringing and banded in mahogany, pierced 'X' stretchers, 27in. (Woolley & Wallis) $10,432

Chippendale mahogany Pembroke table, New England, late 18th century, old refinish, 37in. wide. (Skinner) $1,265

A George III mahogany and crossbanded Pembroke table inlaid with boxwood lines, on square tapering molded legs with brass caps and castors, 105cm. wide. (Phillips) $3,377

A Federal inlaid mahogany Pembroke table, New York, circa 1810, the rectangular top with hinged lid. (Sotheby's) $1,725

PEMBROKE TABLES

Federal mahogany inlaid Pembroke table with drawer, Middle Atlantic States, circa 1790, old refinish, 40in. wide (open).
(Skinner) $1,610

Federal mahogany inlaid Pembroke table, Massachusetts, circa 1800, (minor restoration), 39in. wide.
(Skinner) $3,450

George III mahogany and inlay Pembroke table, fourth quarter 18th century, 36in. wide (extended).
(Skinner) $1,380

A Federal inlaid mahogany Pembroke table, New York, 1790–1810, the rectangular line inlaid top with two drop leaves and ovolo corners, on square line inlaid legs with cuffs, 37¼in. wide.
(Christie's) $2,760

A George III Pembroke table, veneered in kingwood, the oval drop leaf top crossbanded in ebony with satinwood outer bands, 30in.
(Woolley & Wallis) $4,711

A Chippendale carved mahogany Pembroke table, Portsmouth, New Hampshire, 1760–1780, the serpentine top with two drop leaves above an apron, 33½in. long.
(Christie's) $21,850

A Federal satinwood inlaid mahogany Pembroke table, attributed to William Whitehead, New York, circa 1795, 41in. wide (open).
(Christie's) $85,000

A Federal inlaid mahogany Pembroke table, Mid-Atlantic States, 1790–1810, on square tapering line inlaid legs with cuffs, 39³⁄₈in. wide (open).
(Christie's) $4,025

A George III mahogany and painted Pembroke table, the rounded rectangular twin-flap top with a border of bell-flowers, 37³⁄₄in. wide.
(Christie's) $7,631

SIDE TABLES

A mahogany Empire style ormolu mounted side table with rectangular mottled brown and white marble top, 45¼in. wide. (Anderson & Garland) $1,989

A 19th century Chinese padouk wood altar table, the rectangular paneled top with roll-over ends, 47in. wide. (Spencer's) $2,306

A late 17th century Swiss walnut side table, the cleated rectangular top above a drawer on multi-turned legs joined by flat stretchers, 113cm. wide. (Phillips) $1,535

A Federal paint-decorated pine single-drawer side table, New England, circa 1800, the rectangular top with notched corners above a case fitted with a drawer, on square tapering legs, 28in. high. (Sotheby's) $9,200

One of a pair of giltwood side tables of 17th century style, each with a rectangular inset giallo marble top. (Christie's) (Two) $7,535

A J. & J. Kohn bentwood side table, after a design by Josef Hoffmann, circular top supported on four pairs of legs, circa 1910, 75.2cm. diameter. (Christie's) $1,817

A giltwood serving table, the concave-sided top above paneled friezes with foliate decoration, on angled square tapering legs, with label *Jetley Manufacturer, London*, 55½in. wide. (Christie's) $1,077

One of a pair of George II grey-painted and parcel-gilt side tables, each with an associated rectangular Siena marble top above a foliate cornice and Vitruvian scroll frieze, 62in. wide. (Christie's) (Two) $175,055

One of a matched pair of 18th century cream painted side tables, each with a break front marble top over a plain frieze, 52in. wide. (Spencer's) (Two) $8,262

SIDE TABLES

A white-japanned and parcel-gilt side table, with one side drawer and a scroll-decorated frieze, on cabriole legs, 35in. wide.
(Christie's) $5,023

A 17th century Spanish walnut side table, the rectangular top above a pair of frieze drawers carved with square leaf paterae and centered with brass bosses, 131cm. wide.
(Phillips) $2,917

A late 17th century oak side table, the molded edge top above a drawer, 3ft.
(Woolley & Wallis)
                    $3,169

Lucite and mirrored glass side table, copper mirrored top on clear lucite base, unsigned, 24in. long.
(Skinner) $144

A Swedish Gustaf III ormolu-mounted sycamore, tulipwood, amaranth and marquetry side table by Gustaf Adolph Ditzinger, the rectangular top with white and gray-veined mottled marble top, 34³/₄in. wide.
(Christie's) $357,169

A carved and silvered side table, the rectangular verde antico marble top above profusely foliate-carved frieze, 29in. wide.
(Christie's) $1,219

Sheraton period satinwood, rosewood banded side table, having one long drawer, on ebony lined turned supports.
(Lawrences) $2,720

A diminutive Federal mahogany side table, Salem, Massachusetts, circa 1790, the oval top with inlaid bordered edge, 23¹/₂in. high.
(Christie's) $32,200

A George II red walnut and parcel-gilt side table, on acanthus-carved scrolled cabriole legs and claw feet, 42in. wide.
(Christie's) $11,811

SOFA TABLES

A Regency rosewood and brass inlaid sofa table, the rounded rectangular twin flap top inlaid with brass lines and an ivory leaf border band, 146 x 69cm.
(Phillips) $3,530

A 19th century century Danish maple sofa table, the oblong top with two drop flaps, raised upon plain rectangular end standards, 68$\frac{1}{2}$in. long.
(Spencer's) $1,034

A Regency amboyna-veneered sofa table, with rosewood crossbanding, on hipped splayed feet with anthemion scroll brackets, 59$\frac{1}{4}$in. wide.
(Bearne's) $7,560

A burr-walnut crossbanded rosewood sofa table, the twin-flap rounded rectangular top above two frieze drawers, opposed by two dummy drawers, early 19th century, 59$\frac{3}{4}$in. wide.
(Christie's) $4,304

A rosewood and brass-inlaid sofa table, decorated with lines, flowerheads and foliate scrolls, the rectangular hinged top with two frieze drawers with dummy drawers to the reverse, early 19th century, 60in. wide extended.
(Christie's) $3,600

A Regency brass-mounted rosewood sofa table mounted overall with molded beading, the rounded rectangular twin-flap top above two frieze drawers, 58in. wide.
(Christie's) $21,666

A Regency mahogany and rosewood-banded sofa table, with a rectangular hinged top, fitted with two frieze drawers with dummy drawers to the reverse, 51in. wide extended.
(Christie's) $2,340

An ebonized line-inlaid satinwood sofa table, on lyre supports and splayed legs joined by stretchers, 52in. wide.
(Christie's) $1,766

A Biedermeier mahogany sofa table, on a solid pelta-shaped support and concave-sided canted rectangular platform base, 55$\frac{1}{4}$in. wide, open.
(Christie's) $4,485

SOFA TABLES

A Regency rosewood sofa table, the rounded rectangular twin-flap top and frieze with two drawers, on solid end standards, 60½in. wide.
(Christie's) $6,300

A Regency brown oak small sofa table, the rounded rectangular twin-flap top, above three frieze drawers to each side, 29¼in. wide.
(Christie's) $9,028

A Regency pollard oak and inlaid sofa table, the hinged top crossbanded in purpleheart containing two drawers in the frieze, 1.5m.
(Phillips) $5,200

An Anglo-Indian solid calamander sofa table, the rounded rectangular twin-flap top on single reeded end-supports, early 19th century, 41¾in. wide.
(Christie's) $3,271

A rosewood and mahogany sofa table, George IV, circa 1825, with reeded top and plain frieze with turned and carved pendants, 112cm. wide.
(Sotheby's) $2,390

A Regency brass-inlaid rosewood sofa table, the canted rectangular crossbanded twin-flap top above two frieze drawers, on quadripartite platform, 61in. wide.
(Christie's) $2,992

A George III rosewood and satinwood-banded sofa table, inlaid with lines, on standard and dual splayed end supports terminating in brass caps and castors, 58in. wide extended.
(Christie's) $11,700

A Regency mahogany sofa table, the rounded rectangular twin flap top above two true and two false frieze drawers, on X-shaped end supports, 58in. wide.
(Christie's) $1,738

A Regency rosewood and brass-inlaid sofa table, the top crossbanded in amboyna and with two frieze drawers and opposing dummy drawers, 59in. extended.
(Christie's) $4,320

WORK BOX & GAMES TABLES

A Federal carved mahogany two drawer work table, New York, circa 1815, the oblong top above a two-drawer frieze, 20in. wide. (Sotheby's) **$2,070**

Classical mahogany and mahogany veneer work table, probably Massachusetts, circa 1825, refinished replaced brasses, 18¼in. wide. (Skinner) **$1,840**

An early Victorian mahogany work table, the rectangular twin-flap top above two true and two dummy drawers, 17½in. wide. (Christie's) **$1,194**

A late Federal figured mahogany two-drawer work table, Salem, Massachusetts, circa 1825, on star-punch-decorated reeded tapering legs ending in tapered feet, 22in. wide. (Sotheby's) **$2,070**

A Louis Philippe mahogany work table, the rectangular hinged top enclosing a fitted interior above a frieze drawer and sliding silk upholstered well, 19½in. wide. (Christie's) **$1,345**

A Shaker pine worktable, New York, signed *Anderson*, early 20th century, with detachable long compartmented double shelf above a rectangular top with breadboard ends, 29¾in. wide. (Christie's) **$1,725**

A rosewood work table, the rectangular hinged top enclosing a fitted interior above a crimson floral upholstered sliding well, early 19th century, 21½in. wide. (Christie's) **$2,487**

A Victorian inlaid figured walnut games/work table, the shaped swivelling top opening to reveal a chess board and a backgammon board, 26in. wide. (Peter Francis) **$1,912**

A Federal figured mahogany two-drawer lift-top work table, New York, circa 1815, on circular reeded tapering legs, 20¾in. wide. (Sotheby's) **$2,875**

A late Regency rosewood work table, the rounded rectangular twin-flap top above two frieze drawers with opposing dummy drawers, 27in. extended. (Christie's) $974

A lacquered work table with chinoiserie decoration in red and gold, Dutch, 19th century. (Kunsthaus am Museum) $871

A William IV rosewood work table, the rounded rectangular twin-flap top above a frieze drawer, with pierced end supports, 31½in. extended. (Christie's) $706

A Federal mahogany work table, Newport, Rhode Island, 1790–1810, the case fitted with two cockbeaded drawers flanked by fluted sides, on cylindrical tapering reeded legs, 20⅛in. wide. (Christie's) $1,840

An early Victorian mahogany work table, the serpentine rectangular top with thumb molded edge, with sliding action, 23in. wide. (Spencer's) $1,338

A mid-Victorian black lacquer chinoiserie decorated work box on stand, decorated overall with foliage, on turned column and cabriole legs with paw feet, 15in. wide. (Christie's) $775

Regency burl wood games table, early 19th century, the almost square divided top opening to form a leather backgammon surface, 18in. wide. (William Doyle) $2,587

An early Victorian rosewood work table, the rounded rectangular top over a long frieze drawer with turned knob handles, 22in. wide. (Spencer's) $930

Victorian octagonal work table in burr walnut and ebony, supported on a rosewood swept octagonal column, 16in., English, mid to late 19th century. (G. A. Key) $762

A rosewood games-table, the rectangular sliding chessboard top enclosing a blackgammon well, and with a green silk-lined basket, 27in. wide.
(Christie's) $3,634

A Regency rosewood work table, the rectangular top above a frieze fitted with a single drawer to one side and a false drawer to the other, 20in. wide.
(Christie's) $1,094

An Austrian ash and ebonised work-table, the canted Hungarian ash rectangular top with ebonized edges and enclosing a silk-lined well, 24³/₄in. wide.
(Christie's) $3,588

A fine Federal inlaid mahogany and maple work table, Massachusetts, circa 1800, the square top serpentine on all sides with checkered-inlaid edge, 17¹/₄in. wide.
(Sotheby's) $9,200

An early Victorian mahogany work table, on foliate scroll supports joined by turned stretchers, on scroll feet, 24in. wide.
(Christie's) $1,165

A Federal paint-decorated figured maple and pine work table, decorated by Sarah Eaton-Balch, at Mrs. Rowson's School, Roxbury, Massachusetts, circa 1798–1810, 18¹/₄in. wide.
(Sotheby's) $17,250

Classical mahogany carved and mahogany veneer work table, Massachusetts, circa 1833, 20in. wide.
(Skinner) $1,955

A Federal carved and figured mahogany astragal-end work table, attributed to Duncan Phyfe or a contemporary, New York, circa 1815, 25¹/₂in. wide.
(Sotheby's) $12,650

An early Victorian mahogany drop-leaf work table, on ring-turned tapering supports ending in brass caps and castors, 36in. wide, open.
(Christie's) $819

WORK BOX & GAMES TABLES

A Louis Philippe rosewood work table, the serpentine hinged top above a sliding well, on scroll supports, 19in. wide.
(Christie's) $1,436

A George IV rosewood work-table, the baluster-galleried circular top with removable center enclosing a well, 16in. diameter.
(Christie's) $8,125

A satinwood and mahogany Federal octagonal sewing table, attributed to John and Thomas Seymour, Boston, 1800–1810, 20½in. wide.
(Christie's) $25,300

A George III satinwood and marquetry games-table, the double-hinged rectangular top with two shell ovals and enclosing a green baize-lined playing-surface, 21in. wide.
(Christie's) $11,194

An early Victorian rosewood work table, on reeded column and quadripartite platform with scroll feet, 24in. wide.
(Christie's) $1,653

A Federal carved mahogany work table, attributed to Samuel McIntire, Salem, Massachusetts, 1810–1815, on spiral carved legs, 22in. wide.
(Christie's) $2,990

A Federal inlaid birch and mahogany two-drawer work table, Judkins and Senter, Portsmouth, New Hampshire, 1816, 16⅜in. wide.
(Christie's) $43,700

A French Empire work table, applied throughout with gilt brass edge moldings and mounts, on confronting 'S'-supports, 22in. wide.
(Bearne's) $1,425

Late Georgian mahogany bow fronted sewing table with rising lid, and single fitted drawer beneath, tapering legs, 18in. wide, English, 18th century.
(G. A. Key) $1,350

A German Louis XV bureau plat, ormolu mounted with cabriole legs ending in ormolu sabots, circa 1760.
(Galerie Koller)

$56,425

Ambrose Heal for Heal & Son, a twin pedestal writing desk, 1931, in limed oak, 152cm. wide.
(Sotheby's) $4,099

Edwardian rosewood kidney shaped desk, the drawer fronts inlaid with scrolls, ribbon ties and swags and foliage, 48in. wide.
(Ewbank) $2,200

A Louis XV amaranth and tulipwood parquetry bonheur du jour veneered à quatre faces, on cabriole legs and foliate sabots, 27³/₄in. wide.
(Christie's) $12,199

Ambrose Heal for Heal & Son Ltd., Special Edition writing table and chair, 1931, the limed oak corner writing table with vellum writing surface, limed oak and leather chair.
(Sotheby's) $7,079

A Victorian mother-of-pearl inlaid black and gilt papier mâché writing-table, the rounded top inlaid with a flower-spray flanked by vases of flowers, 35¹/₄in. wide.
(Christie's) $3,634

Attributed to Charles Rennie Mackintosh, desk, circa 1905, oak, of rectangular construction, the top section with four small drawers, 121.75çm. wide.
(Sotheby's) $2,795

A palisander, limewood and marquetry inlaid lady's desk, the lid with mirrored back, inlaid with the arms of Hesse, Darmstadt, circa 1868, 80cm. wide.
(Kunsthaus am Museum)
                    $44,892

An Austrian ebonized Karelian-birch writing-desk, the curved superstructure with ebonized low gallery above four frieze drawers, early 19th century, 47¹/₂in. wide.
(Christie's) $67,548

WRITING TABLES & DESKS

Late Louis XVI bureau plat in the style of René Dubois, Paris, circa 1870.
(Galerie Koller)
$44,334

A Regency mahogany writing-table, the rounded rectangular red leather-lined top with central rising section, on solid paneled end-supports, 58³/₄in. wide.
(Christie's) $6,905

A Regency rosewood library table, the rectangular top with re-entrant corners and banded overall in satinwood, 60in. wide.
(Christie's) $17,152

A Louis XVI giltmetal-mounted tulipwood and marquetry table à écrire in the manner of Charles Topino, the eared rectangular top inlaid with a panel of naif marquetry depicting books, quills and other utensils, 20³/₄in. wide.
(Christie's) $45,425

A Regency brass-inlaid rosewood bonheur du jour, together with an almost identical companion piece, 32³/₄in. wide, possibly by John Maclean.
(Anderson & Garland)
$18,360

A Swedish Adolf Frederick ormolu-mounted mahogany, padouk and lozenge-parquetry writing-table, the crossbanded rounded rectangular top, above a central cedar-lined frieze drawer and a candle-slide to each side, 29¹/₂in. wide.
(Christie's) $9,643

A Russian Karelian-birch and parcel-gilt writing-table, the shaped concave-fronted rectangular stretcher surmounted by a domed plinth and scrolled lyre, early 19th century, 56in. wide.
(Christie's) $32,292

A Transitional ormolu-mounted tulipwood, amaranth, fruitwood and marquetry bonheur du jour, inlaid overall with floral trelliswork, 25in. wide.
(Christie's) $7,535

A Regency rosewood and amboyna writing-table, the rectangular red leather-lined top with oval ends above three frieze drawers, 47in. wide.
(Christie's) $8,722

WRITING TABLES & DESKS

Edwardian satinwood kidney shaped writing table, a curved drawer to the frieze, flanked by four short drawers to the kneehole, 48in. wide.
(Spencer's) $1,628

A Dutch floral marquetry desk, the rectangular top above five drawers to each side with arched apron, on cabriole legs with block feet, 53in. wide.
(Christie's) $3,476

A palisander and marquetry desk, the ends rounded with shelving, with balustrading over, Karlsruhe, circa 1910, 208cm. wide.
(Kunsthaus am Museum)
                              $3,790

An ebonized tortoiseshell and brass-inlaid bonheur du jour, the upper section enclosed by a pair of doors with oval porcelain plaques with two small drawers below, late 19th century, 29¹/₂in. wide.
(Christie's) $2,834

Louis XV style gilt bronze mounted parquetry lady's writing desk, the shaped rectangular top above a frieze set with a single drawer flanked by banks of two drawers, 33in. wide.
(William Doyle) $3,450

An early George III mahogany clerk's desk with later flaps to the side, the slope with a book ledge and shelved open compartment above a drawer, 69cm. wide.
(Phillips) $1,228

An early Victorian mahogany roll-top desk, the front revealing a fitted interior with a pull-out ratcheted leather-lined writing slope, pigeon-holes and drawers, 48¹/₂in. wide.
(Christie's) $2,582

A mahogany folding/travelling writing table, with red-leather fitted interior and inkwell, on X-framed supports joined by a fluted stretcher, 24¹/₂in. wide.
(Christie's) $2,125

An Edwardian mahogany writing desk crossbanded, the mirrored superstructure with two bowed glazed doors and two short drawers above a leather-lined writing surface, 39in. wide.
(Christie's) $2,086

WRITING TABLES & DESKS

An early Victorian oak writing table in the Gothic style, the rectangular leather-lined top above a frieze drawer to each side, 48in. wide. (Christie's) **$1,954**

A walnut and kingwood veneered roll-top desk, of cylindrical form and inlaid with checker lines, and with two drawers to the sides, 46in. wide. (Christie's) **$1,294**

A rosewood writing table of Transitional style, on female mask headed cabriole legs with gilt sabots, 52in. wide. (Christie's) **$2,132**

Roycroft oak writing desk, No. 91, East Aurora, New York, circa 1906, original copper hardware, interior fitted with letter slots and short central drawer, 18³/₄in. wide. (Skinner) **$2,760**

A French bureau plat, veneered in kingwood, brass channeled molding to the edge, cast bronze mounts to the friezes, 3ft. (Woolley & Wallis) **$2,692**

A late Federal carved mahogany butler's desk, New York, 1810–1825, with cockbeaded long drawer over a hinged drawer opening to reveal a fitted interior, 43in. wide. (Christie's) **$4,600**

A satinbirch cylinder desk, the raised superstructure with two glazed doors enclosing two short drawers, on ring-turned tapering legs, 31in. wide. (Christie's) **$3,098**

An early George III mahogany partner's writing table, the molded rectangular leather inset top containing three drawers to either side, 106cm. wide. (Phillips) **$4,605**

A Napoleon III rosewood and line-inlaid bureau, the superstructure with a gilt-metal gallery above two long and three short drawers. (Christie's) **$1,980**

WRITING TABLES & DESKS

A Regency mahogany cylinder writing desk, the tambour slide enclosing a fitted interior with leather-lined ratcheted writing slope above five drawers, 48in. wide.
(Christie's) $2,816

An Italian silvered gesso writing table and armchair, 1920s, the chair with an asymmetric dragon back on shell legs.
(Sotheby's) $4,206

A late George III mahogany line-inlaid writing table, with rectangular leather-lined top above frieze drawer, 24in. wide.
(Christie's) $711

A Louis XV style walnut and gilt-metal-mounted writing desk, the superstructure with a central panel door flanked by three short drawers, mid 19th century, 44in. wide.
(Christie's) $4,526

An Edwardian satinwood roll top lady's desk having shaped broken pediment gallery, the front section decorated with painted designs of garlands, 33in. wide.
(Locke & England) $3,320

A 19th century kingwood bonheur-du-jour in the Louis XV style, raised upon square section cabriole supports, 35½in. wide.
(Spencer's) $2,496

A French ormolu-mounted ebonized and boulle inlaid table à écrire, the frieze inset with two drawers, late 19th century, 42in. wide.
(Christie's) $7,314

A French 'plum pudding' mahogany cylinder desk, circa 1900, in Louis XVI style, the breccia marble top with a three-quarter gallery, 130cm. wide.
(Sotheby's) $5,486

A gilt-metal-mounted and veneered bureau plat, after Riesener, the rectangular leather-lined top crossbanded and with gilt-metal rim, 44in. wide. (Christie's) $1,936

TEAPOYS

Victorian walnut teapoy, late 19th century, with a fitted interior, 29in. high.
(Skinner) $920

An Edwardian satinwood and floral marquetry box-on-stand, with hinged domed lid and frieze drawer, 18in. wide.
(Christie's) $1,059

A George IV rosewood teapoy, the circular top enclosing two caddies, on scroll feet, 20in. wide.
(Christie's) $1,345

A 19th century French kingwood and marquetry teapoy in the Louis XV-style, of serpentine outline and with gilt brass foliate mounts, 20¼in. wide.
(Bearne's) $2,142

A Regency rosewood and specimen wood parquetry teapoy, the hinged rounded rectangular top enclosing a fitted interior with two lidded caddies and openings for two mixing bowls, 15in. wide.
(Christie's) $7,268

A Regency brass-inlaid brown oak and ebonized teapoy, attributed to George Bullock, the hinged rectangular top banded in ivy and enclosing a fitted interior with two red velvet-lined wells, 23in. wide.
(Christie's) $27,400

A mid-Victorian walnut teapoy, the ten-sided hinged top enclosing fitted interior of two glass mixing bowls and two tea caddies, 17in. wide.
(Christie's) $782

Victorian mahogany teapoy, interior of two tea boxes and two mixing bowls, on a fluted column, approximately 18 x 15in., English, circa 1820.
(G. A. Key) $1,292

An Anglo-Indian ivory-inlaid and lacquered brass-mounted rosewood teapot, decorated overall with scrolling foliage, early 19th century, 12¾in. wide.
(Christie's) $4,625

TRUNKS & COFFERS

A brass-bound green-leather coffer, the domed hinged lid above carrying handles to the side, 18th century, 52in. wide. (Christie's) $1,109

South German baroque walnut chest, early 18th century, the oblong domed top ornamented with twin parquetry cartouche panels, 46in. wide. (William Doyle) $5,462

A North Italian walnut and marquetry strongbox with bronze handles, raised on anthropomorphic feet, 16th century, 120cm. wide. (Finarte) $9,812

Antique American lift-top two-drawer blanket chest, in pine with snipe hinges, original brasses, 41in. long. (Eldred's) $715

A Georgian rectangular mahogany brass bound strong box with crossbanded lid, raised on later mahogany stand, 17¼in. wide. (Anderson & Garland) $918

Joined and paneled pine chest with drawer, Hampshire County, Massachusetts, 1710–30, paneled sides, drawer on channel runner, 38in. wide. (Skinner) $5,175

Early Gustav Stickley oak cedar lined chest, circa 1901, original dark finish and black finished iron hardware, unsigned, 40in. long. (Skinner) $7,475

Oak and pine joined chest with drawer, Massachusetts, circa 1650–1700, old finish, 42¾in. wide. (Skinner) $4,600

A late 16th/early 17th century Flemish oak coffer, the later rectangular top above three arched panels carved in high relief with biblical scenes, 88 x 189cm. (Bearne's) $6,750

WARDROBES

A Louis XV style kingwood wardrobe, with beveled glass mirror paneled doors, 48in. wide.
(Hy. Duke & Son) $3,200

A wardrobe, twin paneled doors with elaborate heavy latch device and exposed hinges, above two drawers with 'Celtic' loop handles, circa 1900, 195.2cm. wide.
(Christie's) $5,087

A rare early 19th century Swiss polychrome painted pine marriage armoire, circle of Johannes Bartholomeus Thaler and dated 1829, 138cm. wide.
(Phillips) $24,560

A late Victorian mahogany wardrobe, inlaid marquetry in Sheraton Revival style, pierced fret swan neck pediment, 6ft. 4in.
(Woolley & Wallis) $2,212

A late Victorian walnut wardrobe, of Art Nouveau influence, inlaid with whip-lash foliate marquetry, the central paneled door and open compartment above two drawers, 72in. wide.
(Christie's) $1,240

A Robert 'Mouseman' Thompson paneled oak wardrobe, the doors and sides with adzed paneling, and with wrought iron door furniture, 137cm. wide.
(Christie's) $5,451

Lifetime oak two-door wardrobe, Grand Rapids, Michigan, circa 1910, original medium finish, fitted interior, decal, 38in. wide.
(Skinner) $4,370

A South German kingwood, walnut and marquetry armoire of serpentine shape, with overhanging tapering stepped cornice above a paneled frieze, mid-18th century, 79½in. wide.
(Christie's) $39,468

A late George III gentleman's mahogany wardrobe with molded cornice above a pair of satinwood crossbanded paneled doors, 50in. wide.
(Anderson & Garland) $3,978

WASHSTANDS

Federal mahogany and flame birch veneer basin stand, Boston, circa 1800, old surface. (Skinner) **$3,105**

Antique American dry sink in pine, with two paneled doors and one drawer, 40in. high. (Eldred's) **$825**

A late Victorian mahogany washstand, the foliate-carved superstructure with a streaky yellow marble top surrounding a Royal Doulton basin, 55in. wide. (Christie's) **$1,979**

A mahogany and ebony lined washstand, with eared rectangular white and black veined marble inset top, 19th century, 46in. wide. (Christie's) **$3,500**

A Federal inlaid mahogany and birch veneered washstand, attributed to Langley Boardman, Portsmouth, New Hampshire, 1800–1810, 16½in. wide. (Christie's) **$19,550**

A Regency mahogany washstand, attributed to Gillows of Lancaster, each with waved superstructure with one shelf, the rounded rectangular top above a plain frieze, 41¾in. wide. (Christie's) **$2,575**

A late Federal fancy painted washstand, New England, 1810–1820, with rectangular splashboard above a rectangular top, 27¾in. wide. (Christie's) **$1,265**

A George III mahogany washstand, inlaid overall with boxwood and ebonized lines, the double hinged rectangular top enclosing a fitted interior with white China bowl, 19¾in. wide. (Christie's) **$2,400**

A late Federal fancy-painted washstand, New England, 1820–1830, the rectangular recessed shelf on shaped supports, 20in. wide. (Christie's) **$1,093**

WHATNOTS

Federal mahogany etagère cabinet, New York, circa 1805, refinished, 20in. wide.
(Skinner)   **$5,175**

A George IV mahogany three-tier whatnot, the rectangular platform on S-scroll and ring-turned supports, 24in. wide.
(Christie's)   **$1,800**

19th century walnut and foliage inlaid four tier whatnot on turned supports, 29in.
(Ewbank)   **$852**

Walnut four tier corner whatnot, the top with pierced scrolled gallery back, decorated throughout with baluster finials, 19th century, 52in. high.
(G. A. Key)   **$474**

A Victorian rosewood whatnot, with three rectangular tiers, a drawer to the second, 21in. wide.
(Spencer's)   **$1,872**

19th century mahogany three tier whatnot with one drawer on turned supports and legs with brass terminals and casters, 17in.
(Ewbank)   **$837**

A mid-Victorian burr-walnut four-tier étagère, with line inlay and brass mounts, each bowfronted tier on shaped supports, 24in. wide.
(Christie's)   **$1,756**

A mahogany and amboyna etagère, with three rectangular tiers between turned uprights, the turned tapering legs with brass caps and castors, 19th century, 18½in. wide.
(Christie's)   **$2,520**

19th century rosewood bowfronted four tier corner whatnot, the top tier with fret carved raised back and turned finials, 24in. wide.
(Ewbank)   **$794**

A Regency mahogany cellaret, of sarcophagus form, the hinged top inlaid with a quatrefoil, on lion paw feet, 24in. wide.
(Bearne's) $1,377

A Regency mahogany cellaret, the rectangular hinged top enclosing a fitted lined interior, 18in. wide.
(Christie's) $772

A Regency brass-mounted mahogany sarcophagus cellaret with hinged rectangular top and loop-handle, the front with lion-mask and ring-handle, 22½in. wide.
(Christie's) $3,634

A Regency mahogany brass mounted sarcophagus shaped wine cooler, the front heightened with ivory lines, anthemia motifs and roundels engraved with roses, 77cm. wide.
(Phillips) $2,456

A George III mahogany and brass bound octagonal wine cooler, the molded hinged top enclosing a later zinc liner, the stand on square tapering legs with later castors, 45cm. diameter.
(Phillips) $1,382

A Victorian mahogany sarcophagus cellaret, the canted rectangular hinged top with central panel enclosing a green baize-lined interior, 26in. wide.
(Christie's) $2,544

A George III brass-bound mahogany wine-cooler, the stand with square tapering legs, brass caps and castors, 17³/₄in. wide.
(Christie's) $7,222

An early Victorian oak and brown oak cellaret, the top with stepped center with beaded edge and a ribbon-tied laurel edge, 35in. wide.
(Christie's) $5,814

A George III mahogany and marquetry cellaret, inlaid overall with boxwood lines, on a molded plinth and square tapering legs, North Country, 18in. wide.
(Christie's) $4,361

GARDEN ORNAMENTS

An alabaster sculpture of a bulldog, signed *Y. Otto L,* 23cm. high.
(Hôtel de Ventes Horta)
$785

A pair of plaster busts of Bacchus and Ariadne, probably Italian, late 19th/early 20th century, 28¹/₂in. high.
(Christie's) $2,100

A Victorian brown-glazed stoneware figure of an eagle, with spread wings, on an oval waisted base, 25ln. wide.
(Christie's) $1,794

An Italian white marble and pietra paesina center table, the circular top with a leaf-carved edge, late 19th century, 27¹/₂in. diameter.
(Christie's) $5,119

Pair of cast cement American eagles, 20th century, 29in. high.
(Skinner) $863

A statuary marble figure of the Farnese Hercules, by Pietro Galli, dated *1852*, 32in. high.
(Christie's) $17,600

A sculpted statuary marble bust of Napoleon as Premier Consul, after Canova, with square truncation, inscribed *NAPOLÉON*, Italian, early 19th century, 20in. high.
(Christie's) $4,400

A pair of sculpted serpentine marble models of the dog of Alcibedes, on rectangular plinths, English or Italian, late 19th century, 13¹/₄in. high.
(Christie's) $3,520

A multi-colored marble bust of the Emperor Nero, Italian, 18th century, 15⁷/₈in. high, overall.
(Christie's) $13,200

BASKETS

Monumental Art Glass basket, iridescent green freeblown body with folded rim and applied colorless glass handle, 21½in. high total.
(Skinner) $373

Pair of Victorian satin glass bride's baskets, cased green to white ruffled and crimped bowls with upturned rim, 12in. diameter.
(Skinner) $460

Carder Steuben gold aurene basket, ruffle crimped rim on unribbed version with applied berry prunts on arched handle, 12½in. high.
(Skinner) $1,150

BEAKERS

A Nürnberg amethyst cylindrical beaker engraved in the manner of Paulus Eders with a bird perched on swags of fruit and flowers, late 17th century, 7.5cm. high.
(Christie's) $7,176

A Gallé enameled glass beaker, decorated with gilt rampant lions of Lorraine supporting an armorial shield, circa 1884, 14.5cm. high.
(Christie's) $2,543

An early diamond-engraved beaker with gadrooned lower part, decorated with bust portraits of King William III and Queen Mary within foliate cartouches, circa 1690, 9.5cm. high. (Christie's) $7,176

An Austrian Perlenbecher of Ranftbecher form, the flaring body with a wide band of sprays of red carnations, 10.5cm.
(Phillips) $704

Verlys two women beaker, colorless flared form press molded with woman of the fields obverse, 8¼in. high.
(Skinner) $500

A ruby overlay and sulphide beaker, the small ruby panel with a head of a man in profile flanked by six windows, 13cm.
(Phillips) $774

BOTTLES

A Daum bottle and stopper, cased amethyst glass acid-etched with thistles on scrolling foliage, 7.5cm. high.
(Christie's) $567

'Blue Lagoon', a clear and frosted glass scent bottle and stopper, molded with panels of foliage, 10cm. high.
(Christie's) $2,479

A green glass wine-bottle, circa 1660, found in Stamford, Connecticut, the bulbous body of green tint, 7¹/₂in. high.
(Christie's) $1,150

Daum, Libellules bottle and stopper, circa 1900, in clear glass, overlaid with green and yellow, with two applied dragonflies, cameo mark, 29.5cm.
(Sotheby's) $10,247

René Lalique, pair of bottles and stoppers, 'Douze figurines avec Bouchon figurine', after 1920, in colorless frosted glass molded with dancing couples, 29cm. and 30cm. respectively.
(Sotheby's) $8,570

A large Victorian silver-mounted cologne bottle, cut with stars and with a domed screw cap stamped with arabesques, maker's initials *C.B.*, London 1895, 7in.
(Christie's) $1,136

René Lalique, scent bottle and stopper, 'Rosace figurines', after 1912, molded with a concentric group of female figures and drapery, 11cm.
(Sotheby's) $2,422

A Federal inlaid and veneered mahogany liquor-chest, American, 1790–1810, fitted to hold ten glass bottles and tray, 12¹/₈in. wide.
(Christie's) $12,650

'Nikki', an amethyst tint scent bottle and stopper, made for Orloff, the handles molded in the form of eagles, 11.5cm. high.
(Christie's) $496

BOWLS

An attractive Stevens & Williams Mat-su-Noke and swirl satin bowl in lime green with brown spiral stripes, 20.5cm. diameter.
(Phillips) $581

German 800 Standard silver and cut glass figural centerpiece, B & Z, circa 1895–1915, with diamond and fan cut clear glass oval bowl, 10in. high, 79oz. 10dwt.
(Butterfield & Butterfield)
                            $8,625

'Paradise', an Orrefors engraved glass bowl, designed by Simon Gate in 1919, finely engraved with naked figures in the 'Garden of Paradise', 1928, 29cm. wide.
(Christie's) $817

Two-part cut glass punch bowl on pedestal base, with pinwheel design, 14¹/₂in. high.
(Eldred's) $1,320

Steuben engraved crystal masterwork 'Commerce and Trade' bowl, 1943, George Thompson form with engraving designed by Sidney Waugh, 7¹/₂in. diameter.
(Skinner) $4,888

A lead glass footed bowl, English, circa 1690, with bulbous body and applied gadrooned base, 6¹/₄in. high.
(Christie's) $3,450

A small Décorchement pâte de cristal bowl, clear glass streaked with green and aubergine, circa 1920, 5.7cm. high.
(Christie's) $1,817

René Lalique, coupe, 'Flora-Bella' in original box, after 1930, molded as a large flowerhead with radiating petals, stenciled mark, 39cm. diameter.
(Sotheby's) $2,608

Steuben gold aurene on alabaster bowl, of cream-white crystal lightly overlaid with lustrous gold aurene, acid etched in floral Chinese pattern, 7in. diameter.
(Skinner) $2,415

CANDLESTICKS

A composite-stemmed candlestick, hexagonally molded pedestal section above a triple collar and swelling knop filled with spiral air threads, circa 1750, 19.5cm. high. (Christie's) $2,870

Four Steuben crystal candlesticks, design number 7746, triple ball sticks with central teardrop, 10¹/₂in. high. (Skinner) $1,495

An airtwist candlestick, the cylindrical nozzle with everted rim set on a beaded ball knop, on a domed and terraced foot, circa 1750, 24cm. high. (Christie's) $4,664

Pair of Carder Steuben silverina candlesticks, double layered colorless examples with trapped mica particles, 5in. high. (Skinner) $1,200

Steuben blue aurene on calcite candlesticks, flared mushroom bobeche rim of lustrous blue cased to white, 6¹/₄in. high. (Skinner) $2,070

Pair of Carder Steuben colorless and topaz candleholders, controlled bubble design with applied golden topaz reeding, 5¹/₄in. high. (Skinner) $400

Pair of Steuben olive green candlesticks, variant with deep cupped foot, distinct yellow olive color, 12in. high. (Skinner) $500

Five-piece cut glass console set, centerbowl and four candlesticks, 14in. high. (Skinner) $977

Three matching Steuben pomona green candlesticks, smooth hollow examples, each stamped *Steuben*, 12in. high. (Skinner) $747

DECANTERS

A 'Lynn' carafe, the globular body molded with horizontal ribs and with slender waisted neck, circa 1770, 19cm. high. (Christie's) $1,256

A set of Lobmeyr blown and facet-cut drinking glasses with decanter, designed by Otto Prutscher in circa 1920, 30cm. high (decanter). (Christie's) $2,543

A George III etched glass decanter, Anglo-Irish, 1760–1820, the body centered by an elaborate eagle, 10¹/₈in. high. (Christie's) $5,750

A pair of Dorflinger (Nicholas Lutz) decanters and stoppers of slender baluster form cut with wide flutes, each stopper enclosing a dark-blue double-clematis, circa 1865, 34cm. high. (Christie's) $1,292

Tricorn formed plated decanter stand with cast and gadrooned border, cast paw feet and three cut glass decanters, English, 19th century. (G. A. Key) $245

A pair of late Victorian silver-mounted 'cluck-cluck' clear glass decanters, with stoppers, the mounts pierced and stamped with arabesques, Birmingham 1895, 9³/₄in. (Christie's) $681

A cut ice-decanter and stopper of slender mallet form, the base inset with a slender bulbous pocket for ice, the lower part cut with flutes, early 19th century, 30cm. high. (Christie's) $2,332

Eight brilliant cut glass pieces, decanter with two goblets in Russian cut variation, five fluted champagnes cut in strawberry diamond and fan. (Skinner) $1,840

René Lalique, decanter and stopper, 'Coquilles', after 1920, in clear glass, molded with cockleshell design, engraved mark, 34cm. (Sotheby's) $1,490

DISHES

A French smoked glass dish in the manner of Gallé, trefoil with inverted rim, 24cm. wide.
(Christie's) $739

A Décorchement pâte de cristal vide poche, molded with a mermaid and a crab in brilliant blue, 17.7cm. wide.
(Christie's) $1,998

A small Gallé internally decorated glass coupe, shallow bowl in clear glass with milky pink tint, circa 1902, 12cm. high.
(Christie's) $3,270

A lacy Sandwich glass dish, American, 1840–60, with serrated edge, the sides and center decorated with leafage and tulips, American, 1840–60, 4$^{1}/_{2}$in. diameter.
(Sotheby's) $805

Cut glass centerpiece bowl on silver dolphin supports and trilobate base, German, circa 1820, 14cm. high.
(Kunsthaus am Museum) $342

A J. & L. Lobmeyr engraved circular dish attributed to Franz Ullmann, the center with a scantily draped winged figure of a youth, circa 1885, 23.5cm. diameter.
(Christie's) $12,917

Daum, orchid coupe, circa 1910, clear glass decorated with mottled yellow, orange and aubergine to half height, 20.5cm.
(Sotheby's) $15,735

A rare purple lacy Sandwich glass dish, American, 1840–60, with serrated edge decorated with circles and a central flowerhead, 5$^{1}/_{4}$in. diameter.
(Sotheby's) $805

An 18th century sweetmeat glass, the double ogee bowl with everted rim on a triple-ringed collar, 15cm.
(Phillips) $258

DRINKING GLASSES

Tiffany gold loving cup, three applied handles on vessel with fine iridescence, 6in. high. (Skinner) **$460**

Eleven champagne glasses with engraved festoon ornament, Swedish, circa 1800, 20cm. high. (Stockholms Auktionsverk) **$2,027**

A clear glass tumbler, American, circa 1800, the body with a geometric band centering an inscription *JAB*, 5³/₈in. high. (Christie's) **$115**

A Jacobite firing-glass, the flared bowl engraved with a rose, bud and half-opened bud, the reverse inscribed *Revirescit*, mid-18th century, 9cm. high. (Christie's) **$2,512**

Steuben crystal and silver cocktail set, circa 1950, designed by George Thompson, six teardrop hourglass martini glasses with handled pitcher. (Skinner) **$1,000**

A North Bohemian 'Glasperlen' Ranftbecher decorated in colored glass beads on a band with red flowers and green foliage, circa 1840, 10.3cm. high. (Christie's) **$753**

Carder Steuben verre de soie cordial set, integrated service for six includes stoppered decanter, six glasses and conforming tray, 8¹/₂in. high. (Skinner) **$1,800**

A mammoth engraved rummer, the flared bucket bowl cut with a band of wide facets to the lower part, inscribed *Jem Burn's. Four Pets,/Jack Shepherd. Duchess. Cribb and Ball.*, circa 1840, 25.5cm. high. (Christie's) **$2,870**

Five enamel decorated French glass cordials, three on pedestalled foot, two oval with thistle motif, 3¹/₄in. high. (Skinner) **$230**

FLASKS

Daum cabochon applied cameo glass flacon, flattened oval of colorless glass with interior green webbing, 7¹/₄in. high. (Skinner) $5,000

English cameo glass perfume, brilliant red cased to colorless and overlaid in white, cameo cut overall with spike-leaf foliate elements, 4in. long. (Skinner) $1,035

A soda glass flask, English, circa 1685, the ring-turned lip over a tapering neck above an oval-shaped body, 4⁷/₈in. high. (Christie's) $230

Two Italian hexagonal flasks of straw-tint, decorated in 'cold enamels' with St. Nicholas of Bari, figures, ships and a fountain, 18th century, 30.5cm. and 32cm. high. (Christie's) $1,524

A German dated armorial square flask of greenish/yellow tint and enameled in colors, one side with a coat-of-arms and the date 1664, Saxony or Bohemia, 17cm. high. (Christie's) $5,023

A Central European enameled rectangular spirit-flask with canted edges, decorated with a white bear enriched in black on a green mound below a stylized sun, the flask 14cm. high; and a similar flask, third quarter of the 18th century. (Christie's) $1,435

'Dahlia' No. 616, a frosted glass scent bottle and stopper, of circular shape molded back and front with a flowerhead, stencil-etched R Lalique France, 17.5cm. high. (Christie's) $540

A pair of Gallé scent bottles, decorated in the Persian manner, of stepped bowed rectangular section, sepia tinted glass enameled in colors and gilt, 13.5cm. high. (Christie's) $4,500

Emile Gallé enameled glass flacon, pale blue transparent ribbed body decorated by winged griffin, 6in. high. (Skinner) $2,185

GOBLETS

A lead glass goblet, English, circa 1690, with a flaring lip above a gadrooned body, 6in. high.
(Christie's) $1,150

A rare and fine early 18th century Jacobite goblet and cover with cup-shaped bowl molded with eight engraved panels, 30cm. high overall.
(Phillips) $3,060

A tall German wine goblet with rounded funnel bowl engraved with the coat of arms of England, 22.2cm.
(Phillips) $806

An enameled dated goblet of straw tint, the flared funnel bowl with a standing figure of a man, beside a carpenter's plane, 1674, Bohemia or France, 15cm. high.
(Christie's) $5,741

A plain-stemmed coin-goblet, the hollow knop applied with three raspberry prunts and containing a George III silver three-pence dated *1763*, circa 1765, 19cm. high.
(Christie's) $466

A Dutch-engraved 'Friendship' balustroid goblet, the bell bowl with two figures, one as a warrior with a sword, the other crowned and with a lyre, circa 1740, 19cm. high.
(Christie's) $986

A German engraved goblet, the flared funnel bowl decorated with three flaming urns, circa 1725, Thuringia or Bohemia, 19cm. high.
(Christie's) $1,345

An engraved opaque-twist goblet for 'Perry', the ogee bowl with a fruiting pear-tree growing from a grassy sward, circa 1765, 20cm. high.
(Christie's) $1,041

A finely engraved Bohemian or German clear glass goblet with faceted bucket bowl, engraved in a large panel with the Three Kings, 28.5cm.
(Phillips) $1,097

JUGS

Three-mold green glass pitcher in Sunburst and Waffle pattern, 19th century, 6¹/₂in. high. (Eldred's) $330

Tiffany blue iridescent engraved pitcher, flared tankard of cobalt blue glass with unusual purple luster, 8¹/₂in. high. (Skinner) $3,220

Rare antique pressed glass milk pitcher, in Bellflower pattern with double vine and cut flower, 8¹/₂in. high. (Eldred's) $275

A Stourbridge raisin-ground cameo silver-mounted jug and hinged cover of slender conical form, overlaid in opaque-white, the silver Birmingham, 1886, the glass circa 1886 and perhaps Thomas Webb, 31.5cm. high. (Christie's) $2,691

A rare amber blown three-mold glass pitcher, American, 1830–50, with flared and threaded neck, 6in. high. (Sotheby's) $9,200

A Stourbridge crested ewer of flattened oviform with slender neck, trefoil rim and scroll handle, engraved with two crests, circa 1865, perhaps W.H., B. & J. Richardson, 28.5cm. high. (Christie's) $1,615

Emile Gallé, Magnolias jug, circa 1900, in clear glass overlaid with white, green and pink and carved with magnolias, carved mark *Gallé*, 25.5cm. (Sotheby's) $29,808

Emile Gallé, Algues ewer, circa 1900, in dark green glass and carved with seaweed and shells, carved mark *Gallé*, 20cm. (Sotheby's) $11,178

Large opaque-white and aquamarine free blown glass pitcher, American, probably New Jersey, 1830 –60, with a strap handle, 9in. high. (Sotheby's) $1,265

A Lalique clear glass car mascot modeled as a stylized cockerel's head, catalogued *Tet de Coq*, 18cm. high.
(Bearne's) $413

Emile Gallé, pair of flaçons in original box, 1887 or earlier, one with repoussé flower spray, the other with a dragonfly, 11cm.
(Sotheby's) $10,433

Steuben crystal lion, Lloyd Atkins design, conventionalized reclining animal of solid crystal, original walnut stand and fitted red leather and velvet case, 8¼in. long.
(Skinner) $1,380

Lalique molded and enameled glass ice bucket, Fougères, the slightly tapering cylindrical vessel with flattened rim, 8⁷/₈in. high.
(Butterfield & Butterfield)
                          $1,955

A pair of Victorian silver-mounted glass dressing table jars, the hinged circular cover embossed with a classical scene, 14cm. high, William Comyns, London 1893–4.
(Bearne's) $2,268

A fine German glass tankard, the cylindrical body engraved and inscribed with the portraits of four Saints, 18.5cm. high, 18th century.
(Bearne's) $2,856

Gabriel Argy-Rousseau pâte de verre covered box, blue and amethyst frosted rectangle with feather and swag decoration, conforming stork decorated cover, 5½in. long.
(Skinner) $4,025

Pair of puce glass lusters, scalloped rims, gilt edged, hung with clear glass prismatic drops, 19th century, 10½in. high.
(G. A. Key) $169

Black lacquer liqueur box, 19th century, with brass inlay, removable rosewood interior tray containing four blown glass decanters.
(Eldred's) $605

René Lalique, surtout de table, 'Oiseau de feu', after 1922, in frosted and clear glass, intaglio molded with an exotic firebird, intaglio molded mark, 32cm. (Sotheby's) $16,767

A pâte de verre perfume burner, with stylized decoration in red and brown, on six-footed metal stand, Argy Rousseau, circa 1925, 20cm. high. (Stockholms Auktionsverk) $3,926

Daum applied cameo glass inkstand, cut in fire-polished oak leaves decorated with three foil-backed wheel-carved acorn and insect cabochons, 5in. high. (Skinner) $8,050

A clear glass enamel painted tankard, the pewter lid in the form of a winged helmet, German, late 19th century. (Kunsthaus am Museum) $438

Three 2^1/$_2$ x 2in. erotic lithophanes in maker's box. (Christie's) $913

A sandglass, probably English, 18th century, the case with five columns and two glass bulbs, 19cm. high. (Bonhams) $300

'The Wave', a pâte-sur-pâte plate, painted by Thomas Bott with a loosely-draped female nude issuing from a wave among sea-spray, dated for 1883, 8^1/$_8$in. diameter. (Christie's) $1,172

Large glass ink well, the body molded with wrythen bands, the similar hinged silver lid bearing the London hallmark for 1889. (G. A. Key) $237

Cobalt cut to colorless crystal centerpiece, large heavy walled flared bowl with brilliant blue overlay, 16^1/$_4$in. diameter. (Skinner) $374

A Baccarat dated close millefiori weight, the profusion of colorful canes including the date B 1846, 7.8cm. (Phillips) $3,064

A Clichy swirl weight, the central pastrymold cane in dark red and white enclosing pink and green florets, 6.2cm. (Phillips) $1,613

A Baccarat garlanded buttercup weight with a blue and white flower with yellow center, 7.3cm. (Phillips) $2,258

A St. Louis crown weight with red and green twisted ribbon alternating with entwined latticinio thread, mid-19th century, 7.8cm. diameter. (Christie's) $1,435

A Baccarat blue-ground patterned concentric millefiori weight, the central large green, blue and white cane within a circle of yellow and white star canes, mid-19th century, 6.8cm. diameter. (Christie's) $4,664

A St. Louis large faceted cherry weight, the two bright-red fruit and three green leaves pendant from an ocher stalk, mid-19th century, 9.3cm. diameter. (Christie's) $3,588

A Baccarat dated spaced millefiori weight, including silhouettes of a horse, a stag, an elephant, with the date B 1848, 8cm. (Phillips) $2,096

An attractive Baccarat garlanded primrose weight, the blue and white five-petaled flower with yellow star-dust center, 6.4cm. (Phillips) $3,386

A rare Bacchus concentric weight, the central white flower-like cane encircled by rows of canes within a basket of white staves, 7.8cm. (Phillips) $2,580

PAPER WEIGHTS

A Baccarat butterfly and flower weight, the insect with purple body, turquoise eyes and open wings, 7.6cm.
(Phillips) $5,160

A Baccarat dog rose weight with five pink petals edged in white around a white stardust center, 6.3cm.
(Phillips) $1,290

A rare Clichy garland weight unusually in clear glass set with two interlaced quatrefoils, 7.1cm.
(Phillips) $4,676

A St. Louis jasper-ground yellow dahlia weight, the flower with ten dark-yellow petals striped in black, mid-19th century, 7cm. diameter.
(Christie's) $6,279

A Baccarat faceted flat bouquet weight, the bouquet including a pansy flanked by a dark-red rose, a red bud and a white double clematis, mid-19th century, 9cm. diameter.
(Christie's) $9,329

A Baccarat garlanded butterfly weight, the insect with amethyst body, turquoise eyes and marbled wings, mid-19th century, 7.9cm. diameter.
(Christie's) $2,870

A St. Louis signed and dated mushroom weight, the concentric tuft with four rows of canes, around a central large concentric cane, 1848, 6.8cm.
(Phillips) $3,225

A Baccarat red and white primrose weight, the flower with six large petals striped in white, mid-19th century, 8cm. diameter.
(Christie's) $1,524

A Clichy close concentric millefiori weight, the central moss cane surrounded by six circles of canes, mid-19th century, 6.7cm. diameter.
(Christie's) $3,409

Leaded glass ceiling lamp, composed of predominantly green, red, yellow and amber glass segments arranged as blossoms and leaves in latticework background, stamped *Handel*, 8½in. high. (Skinner) $1,380

Leaded glass and brass ceiling lamp, attributed to Duffner & Kimberly, circular shade with green and amber leaded glass geometric pattern, 20in. diameter. (Skinner) $1,955

A silvered metal and leaded glass hanging shade, designed by Charles Rennie Mackintosh, open cube body with shallow domed overhung top inset with a flat circular disk, circa 1900, 36.3cm. diameter. (Christie's) $8,722

Tiffany favrile glass golden ball shade, cased ambergris to opal and decorated by gold iridescent leaf and vine motif, 12½in. high. (Skinner) $4,140

Gabriel Argy-Rousseau, 'Masques' veilleuse, 1923, the pâte de verre shade divided into six segments with three molded red masks, wrought iron base, 13.75cm. (Sotheby's) $8,384

René Lalique, ceiling light, 'Gaillon', after 1927, in colorless frosted glass, molded with concentric acanthus leaves, wheel cut mark, 45cm. (Sotheby's) $1,677

Four Tiffany gold iridescent shades, ten-rib bell shape, with orange gold iridescent surface, 4¾ to 5in. high. (Skinner) $2,070

Emile Gallé, spherical hanging light, circa 1910, grey glass overlaid with bubble gum pink and fudge brown and etched with ombellifères, 36cm. high, maximum. (Sotheby's) $11,480

Leaded glass ceiling lamp, colorful red, green and purple segments arranged to depict grape cluster and foliate border below, shade 22in. diameter. (Skinner) $690

STAINED GLASS

Scenic leaded glass window, glass segments arranged in the LaFarge layered technique to depict an extensive cliff-side garden scene overlooking Mediterranean-style waterside villa, 39 x 57in.
(Skinner) $5,750

Leaded glass 'Owl' window, with 'jeweled' border and central bead-eyed owl on quarter moon medallion, 46½ x 24in.
(Skinner) $1,265

School of William Morris (British, 1834–1896), 'Design for Stain Glass Window – Two Ships', circa 1910, unsigned, watercolor and graphite on paper, 4 x 4½in., framed.
(Skinner) $115

Leaded glass window, brilliant multicolored and textured glass segments artfully arranged to replicate the 'Vase of Peonies', 57in. high.
(Skinner) $3,737

Intarsia panel 'The Galleon', designed by Frank Brangwyn and executed by A. J. Rowley, England, circa 1923, image 29¼ x 31⅛in.
(Skinner) $978

Leaded glass scenic landscape panel, multicolored and textured segments of glass arranged to depict mountainous landscape, 57in. high.
(Skinner) $1,840

TUMBLERS

A Baccarat molded cylindrical tumbler enameled in colors on gilt foil with a spray of forget-me-not, mid-19th century, 9.5cm. high.
(Christie's) $1,345

A pair of Saxon engraved and facet-cut flared tumblers for the English market, from a set emblematic of the Seasons, of Autumn and Winter, circa 1765, perhaps Glücksberg, 11cm. high. (Christie's) $986

A Charpentier cut cylindrical tumbler with everted rim, the base set with a sulphide portrait of Louis XVIII, circa 1830, 10cm. high.
(Christie's) $1,435

VASES

René Lalique, vase, 'Formose', after 1924, in ruby red glass molded with swimmimg fish, impressed mark, 17cm.
(Sotheby's) $6,334

Argy-Rousseau pâte-de-verre vase, Le Jardin des Hesperides, the ovoid vessel in gray glass splashed with violet, 9¹/₂in. high.
(Butterfield & Butterfield)
                              $24,150

'Les Plumes', a Sabino frosted topaz glass vase, molded in relief with bands of peacock feathers, 19cm. high.
(Christie's) $230

A Eugène Rousseau carved cameo glass vase, rectangular slab body with quatrefoil neck, internally crackled, colored with clear pink and turquoise, circa 1885, 21cm. high.
(Christie's) $7,268

'Oran', a large Lalique opalescent glass vase, in dense milky blue/white glass, molded in high relief with chrysanthemums, circa 1925, 26cm. high.
(Christie's) $11,265

Eugène Rousseau, vase 'Japonais', circa 1880, in clear smoked glass etched and enameled with a Japanese woman under a blossoming prunus tree, 17cm.
(Sotheby's) $3,353

'Médaillons Fleuris', an Argy-Rousseau pâte de verre vase, molded with roundels of stylized flowerheads, circa 1928 26cm. high.
(Christie's) $10,538

Emile Gallé, Chrysanthemum vase, circa 1900, in yellow glass, overlaid with orange and etched with flowering sprays of chrysanthemums, cameo mark *Gallé*, 14.5cm.
(Sotheby's) $1,677

Emile Gallé, Grasshopper solifleur vase, circa 1900, in clear glass overlaid with ruby red with flecks of blue, mustard and green, 15cm.
(Sotheby's) $3,353

VASES

A Schneider cased glass vase, translucent bubbled orange glass internally decorated, 34cm. high.
(Christie's) $3,896

Loetz, dimpled vase with furled neck, circa 1898, in deep red glass washed with peacock blue and gold iridescence, 24cm.
(Sotheby's) $1,081

An Austrian Art Nouveau vase, iridescent pale green glass enameled in colors and gilt with sprays of lilies, 22cm. high.
(Christie's) $443

Emile Gallé, Convolvulus vase, circa 1900, in colorless glass internally decorated with blue, overlaid and etched with convolvulus flowers and foliage, cameo mark *Gallé*, 29cm.
(Sotheby's) $6,707

A Gallé cameo glass 'Polar Bear' vase, aquamarine tinted glass overlaid in cream and etched with a pair of polar bears, circa 1925, 27.7cm. high.
(Christie's) $47,242

Emile Gallé, Fruits of Autumn bottle vase, circa 1900, in blue tinted glass, etched and enameled in shades of green, ochre and sienna with autumnal leaves and berries, etched mark, 14cm.
(Sotheby's) $1,676

A Loetz iridescent glass vase, yellow ground with pink iridescence and blue trailed linear decoration, circa 1900, 16cm. high.
(Christie's) $3,270

A Gallé etched and enameled glass vase, in smoky glass enameled with a spray of delicate blue flowers, circa 1896–99, 28cm. high.
(Christie's) $4,724

A Gallé internally decorated and applied cameo glass vase, in amber glass richly streaked with brilliant blue, circa 1920, 29cm. high.
(Christie's) $36,340

VASES

Emile Gallé, Magnolia vase, circa 1900, in dichroic lime green/amber glass overlaid with red, cameo mark *Gallé*, 43cm. (Sotheby's) **$11,178**

Eduard Prochaska for Loetz, iridescent vase, 1907, in cased iridescent white and green glass, 13.25cm. (Sotheby's) **$3,353**

Loetz, small iridescent vase, circa 1900, in orange glass washed with green/blue iridescence, 10.5cm. (Sotheby's) **$1,396**

Daum, Ombellifères vase, circa 1900, in opalescent glass, etched with cow parsley with carved details against a martelé ground, intaglio mark, 14.5cm. (Sotheby's) **$3,726**

Daum, Hunting Landscape vase, circa 1880, applied with four roundels, each enameled with a lakeside hunting or fishing scene, 15cm. (Sotheby's) **$5,962**

Emile Gallé, Fuchsia 'blow out' vase, circa 1900, molded in high relief with fuchsias falling from the neck, cameo mark *Gallé*, 29.75cm. (Sotheby's) **$7,825**

Emile Gallé, Sycamore vase, circa 1900, in colorless glass overlaid with pink and carved with flowering branches, engraved mark *Gallé*, 13cm. (Sotheby's) **$10,805**

A North Bohemian overlay two-handled oviform vase engraved by Franz Zach, the matt ground overlaid in ruby-red and carved with nude figures and Cupid, signed, circa 1860, 23cm. high. (Christie's) **$3,947**

Loetz, slender waisted vase, circa 1900, in deep red glass, festooned with peacock blue, pale blue and gold iridescence, 13.75cm. (Sotheby's) **$1,490**

VASES

A Gallé multilayer vase with iris decoration, circa 1900, signed, 21cm. high.
(Hôtel de Ventes Horta) $22,334

Emile Gallé, small dragonfly vase, circa 1890, in thick spirally fluted, clear glass internally decorated with purple, 8cm.
(Sotheby's) $12,668

Emile Gallé, Leaves vase, circa 1900, in clear glass, overlaid with red and etched with falling leaves, cameo mark *Gallé*, 30cm.
(Sotheby's) $5,589

Legras, forest landscape vase, circa 1900, in clear glass internally decorated with green, blue and yellow, enameled mark *Legras*, 14.75cm.
(Sotheby's) $1,210

Daum, Autumnal Leaves vase, 1910, in gray glass overlaid with mottled pale yellow and ocher with electric blue at the base, cameo mark, 14cm.
(Sotheby's) $1,528

René Lalique, vase, 'Bacchantes', after 1927, in opalescent glass, molded with a frieze of neoclassical nudes, 24.25cm.
(Sotheby's) $12,296

Emile Gallé, Dragonfly vase, circa 1890, in clear slightly tinted glass enameled in blues, browns and cream, 19.5cm. high.
(Sotheby's) $5,589

Fulvio Bianconi for Venini, handkerchief vase, circa 1955, in incaminciato glass, opaque white glass cased over plum interior, 26cm.
(Sotheby's) $2,795

Emile Gallé, landscape vase, circa 1900, in gray glass, overlaid with purple and etched with a mountain lakeside scene, cameo mark *Gallé*, 19.5cm.
(Sotheby's) $2,608

VASES

René Lalique Nefliers frosted vase, oval bowl form with molded blossoms selectively polished to attract light, 5⁵/₈in. high.
(Skinner) $316

Daum, ribbed vase, 1920s, in pale yellow glass, horizontally ribbed with acid textured ground, etched mark, 20cm.
(Sotheby's) $1,304

Legras enameled scenic vase quatriform bowl of colorless glass with etched surface and enameled polychrome waterfront scene, 5in. long.
(Skinner) $317

Daum 'Summer' enameled cameo glass vase, broad shouldered mottled yellow-green and blue frosted glass body etched and enamel painted in sunny waterfront riverscape, 9⁵/₈in. high.
(Skinner) $7,475

A Webb 'rock crystal' vase engraved by W. Fritsch, the compressed baluster bowl with a parrot perched on a swag of fruit, signed, circa 1900, 19cm. high.
(Christie's) $2,153

Daum and Majorelle blown-out vase, tortoiseshell amber colored glass with silver foil specks by Daum blown into fancy hand wrought iron quatriform framework by Majorelle, 9¼in. high.
(Skinner) $1,035

Emile Gallé cameo glass carved vase, heavy walled ovoid body of champagne color layered in translucent aqua green, 7³/₈in. high.
(Skinner) $4,313

Argy Rousseau pâte de verre vase, sphere of purple, blue and black mottled glass press molded in swirling foliate repeating motif, 5in. high.
(Skinner) $3,105

Emile Gallé carved marquetry Etude vase, onyx-green blossom form vessel with applied petal base, engraved signature, 5¹/₈in. high.
(Skinner) $9,200

Daum, small Winter Landscape vase, circa 1900, in colorless glass internally decorated with yellow, overlaid with orange, **enameled** mark, 7.5cm.
(Sotheby's) $2,236

Pauly & C. Murano motorcycle vase, contemporary Venetian glass bowl-form of pale blue crystal with decoration of six cyclists in simple surrealistic landscape, 5¹/₈in. high.
(Skinner) $863

Gabriel Argy-Rousseau, Anemones vase, 1920, in pâte de verre, molded with a frieze of anemones in deep red with black centres, 8cm.
(Sotheby's) $5,962

Venini Studio glass Pezzato vase, designed by Fulvio Bianconi, freeblown patchwork composition of colorless, turquoise blue, amethyst and topaz-gray squares, 8¹/₄in. high.
(Skinner) $5,462

Frederick Carder Steuben intarsia vase, stemmed bowl-form of colorless crystal internally decorated with true blue repeating leaf and vine design, 6in. high.
(Skinner) $8,625

Rene Lalique amber 'Archers' vase, brilliant amber oval vessel with molded design of nude male archers, impressed molded mark on base, 10⁵/₈in. high.
(Skinner) $3,450

Tiffany favrile glass vase, of baluster form, in gold iridescence with white flowers and green leaves, signed, 12in. high.
(William Doyle) $2,990

Rene Lalique 'Baies' enameled vase/lamp base, oversize spherical vessel decorated with black enameled berries on thorny brambles, 10³/₈in. high.
(Skinner) $1,035

Daum Nancy cameo glass landscape vase, of flattened ovoid form, cut with boats on a river against a red and yellow mottled ground, 12in. high.
(William Doyle) $4,370

WINE GLASSES

A tartan-twist wine-glass, the stem with a laminated corkscrew core edged with translucent red and green threads, circa 1765, 17cm. high. (Christie's) $4,306

The rare Fingask Jacobite wine glass with an enameled portrait of Prince Charles Edward, on an opaque twist stem, 12cm. (Phillips) $16,830

A Jacobite airtwist wine-glass, the funnel bowl with rose, bud and half-opened bud, the reverse with a sun, circa 1750, 17cm. high. (Christie's) $718

A canary-yellow-twist wine-glass with a waisted bucket bowl, the stem with four yellow entwined threads, circa 1765, 15.5cm. high. (Christie's) $12,558

An electioneering diamond-engraved plain-stemmed wine-glass, the funnel bowl inscribed *Our Liberty Preservd* (sic) *by Taylor*, on a plain stem and folded conical foot, 1739–47, 15cm. high. (Christie's) $1,076

A Beilby enameled opaque-twist wine-glass, the ogee bowl decorated with a sportsman shooting duck in flight, circa 1765, 14.5cm. high. (Christie's) $12,199

A Beilby opaque-twist wine-glass, the ogee bowl enameled with a border of fruiting-vine, on a conical foot, circa 1770, 15cm. high. (Christie's) $933

A Beilby enamelled opaque-twist wine-glass, the bell bowl decorated with a pendant branch of fruiting-vine, circa 1765, 17.7cm. high. (Christie's) $2,512

A baluster cylinder-knopped wine-glass, the small straight-sided funnel bowl with a tear to the solid lower part, circa 1715, 13.5cm. high. (Christie's) $4,306

WINE GLASSES

A Jacobite airtwist wine-glass, the bowl engraved with a rose and bud, the reverse with a flowering thistle, circa 1750, 15.5cm. high.
(Christie's) $718

A baluster wine-glass with a bell bowl, supported on an inverted baluster stem, circa 1720, 16cm. high.
(Christie's) $682

An engraved opaque-twist wine-glass, the bell bowl with branches of fruiting-vine, on a conical foot, circa 1765, 17.5cm. high.
(Christie's) $1,041

An electioneering opaque-twist wine-glass, the ogee bowl inscribed *Lowther and Upton/ Huzza*, the stem with a gauze corkscrew core, circa 1761, 15.5cm. high.
(Christie's) $1,165

A color-twist ale-glass, the stem with a pair of entwined gauze spirals enclosed within two cobalt-blue and white ribbed corkscrew ribbons, circa 1765, 18cm. high.
(Christie's) $8,073

A Dutch-engraved balustroid wine-glass, the funnel bowl engraved with a sailing-ship and inscribed in diamond-point above *Salus Patriæ.*, circa 1745, 16cm. high.
(Christie's) $897

An engraved color-twist wine-glass, the funnel bowl with a hatched and dot border, the stem with a brick-red corkscrew core, circa 1765, 15cm. high.
(Christie's) $2,691

A 'Toastmaster's' small baluster wine-glass, the deceptive funnel bowl with slightly everted rim, on a folded conical foot, circa 1715, 11cm. high.
(Christie's) $1,076

An engraved airtwist ale-glass, the slender funnel bowl inscribed *Welcome* on a ribbon cartouche above a punch-bowl, circa 1750, 18cm. high.
(Christie's) $1,220

A plated six-division crossed iron clubs toast rack, 16cm. (Phillips) $162

A large and impressive Heather Club Golf Club Henderson medal, engraved with the winners from 1906 to 1938, with tartan suspension ribbon, cased. (Phillips) $744

Copes cigarette cards, a complete set of Copes Golfers, tab cards, all mint or near mint. (Phillips) $4,044

Peter H. Thomas: Reminiscences of Golf and Golfers (by an old hand), published in Edinburgh by James Thin 1890, 55pp., red cloth. (Phillips) $7,117

A glazed shield-shaped display case, plush lined, containing medals and trophies for the Woodford Golf Club, North London, circa 1899. (Phillips) $647

Murray, Sir Thomas: The Laws and Acts of Parliament made by King James I, II, III, IV and V, 3rd edition, published in Edinburgh by David Lindsay in 1681. (Phillips) $2,264

A brass gutty ball urn and cover, with gutty ball finial, 17cm. (Phillips) $210

Six golf club top spoons, four irons and two woods. (Phillips) $146

A Dunlop mesh dimple pocket watch, winder lacking. (Phillips) $243

A Grimwades 'Sporting Brownies' decorated pedestal bowl, 25cm. diameter.
(Phillips) $971

An edition of the Edinburgh Weekly Journal, October 16th 1816 with notification of a golf meeting at St. Andrews for the Gold Medal.
(Phillips) $582

A four-division crossed clubs and gutty ball plated toast rack.
(Phillips) $291

A Heather Club Golf Club silver medal, presented by Captain Shoolbread, the Handicap Medal, with pierced runic decoration over, with winners from 1906 to 1936.
(Phillips) $728

A 9ct. gold shield-shaped medal for the Newcastle Golf Club, 1922; a gold shield-shaped Inches medal for the Dunbar Castle Golf Club.
(Phillips) $226

A bronzed spelter golfer figurine in plus fours at the end of drive, on circular stone base, 20cm.
(Phillips) $162

A hole-in-one trophy with Spalding mesh dimple ball resting on tripod of three clubs, on ebonized plinth, 14.5cm.
(Phillips) $227

After Zwick: a white metal figurine of golfer in hooped pullover and plus fours, on alabaster oval ashtray base.
(Phillips) $162

A good Britannia metal samovar of pedestal rounded cylindrical form, the cover surmounted by Edwardian golfer at end of drive, 42cm.
(Phillips) $809

A 9ct. gold medal, scroll and shield shape, the circular center engraved a golfer, with crossed clubs and ribbon over, for Thurso Golf Club 1899. (Phillips) **$194**

A Carlton Ware matchpot, the sides decorated golfers, 6.5cm. (Phillips) **$146**

A circular 18ct. gold medal, the Chalmers Cup, of circular form, the center pierced initals H.G.C. and with crossed clubs. (Phillips) **$146**

An impressive Royal Doulton Morrisian Ware flare-mouth vase, decorated 17th-century golfers with Art Nouveau rim and base and gilt edging, 30.5cm. (Phillips) **$2,754**

A pair of saucer dishes, inscribed *Promise little and do much*, each with different decoration, 14cm. diameter. (Phillips) **$226**

A Doulton Lambeth stoneware quart jug, the sides decorated with golfing scenes in white relief, with Art Nouveau floral scrollwork in greens, blues and browns, 24cm. (Phillips) **$728**

A barrel-shaped jug, inscribed *Every dog has its day*, 13cm. (Phillips) **$356**

A square plate with invert corners inscribed *He that always complains is never pitied*, 14.5cm. (Phillips) **$178**

A Burleigh Ware golfing jug, blue glazed and with golfer in plus fours handle, 20cm. (Phillips) **$453**

A 9ct. gold circular medal with scroll loop over, the center depicting golfer and caddy.
(Phillips) $146

A Carlton Ware matchpot, the sides decorated a golfer, 7cm.
(Phillips) $154

A pedestal bowl, inscribed *He hath good judgement* and *Give loser leave to speak*, 21cm. diameter x 10.5cm. tall.
(Phillips) $1,294

A 9ct. gold circular medallion, the reverse with coat of arms inscribed *Presented to the Manchester Golf Club by Alexander Bannerman 1837*, Birmingham 1911.
(Phillips) $582

A pair of Devon brown glazed pottery ovoid jars, slip decorated the 'Scratch Man' and 'One Down', 21cm.
(Phillips) $776

An Austrian Amphora porcelain figurine of goofy caddy in check coat with outsize boots, 34cm.
(Phillips) $1,132

A Doulton Bunnikins jug, decorated golfing rabbits, 13.5cm.
(Phillips) $178

A square base candlestick, inscribed *Promise little and do much*, 17cm.
(Phillips) $243

A Copeland blue pottery baluster vase, the sides decoration royal blue and with white golfers in relief, 12.5cm.
(Phillips) $421

Mitchell: a dark stained beech
play club, with 42in. shaft.
(Phillips) $1,537

A Bussey patent putting cleek.
(Phillips) $162

An unusual hollow iron headed
putter of transitional shape.
(Phillips) $121

A Novakclub adjustable club
with steel shaft.
(Phillips) $113

A Northwood long nosed putter
with green-heart shaft.
(Phillips) $194

A Gibson Princeps 'topspin'
putter with upper flange.
(Phillips) $259

A Rangefinder 'Power 80'
niblick with large head.
(Phillips) $372

A good mid 19th-century rut
iron, with 5in. hosel.
(Phillips) $2,265

A Thornton & Co. 'Mammoth'
niblick.
(Phillips) $776

A Forrester patent topspin wry-
necked putter, the upper portion
of blade curving forward.
(Phillips) $647

A Jack White putter with boat-
shaped duplex head and square
section grip.
(Phillips) $356

Golf Co., St. Andrews: a dark
stained beech putter with
greenheart shaft.
(Phillips) $744

T. Morris: a golden beech late transitional brassie.
(Phillips) $971

A Guss Faulkner outsize Gem putter.
(Phillips) $421

An Auchterlonie brown stained persimmon putter.
(Phillips) $226

A Urquhart adjustable patent iron, the early pattern, no. 1161.
(Phillips) $2,507

A Perwhit convex faced putter with 6½in. hosel.
(Phillips) $307

A Whole-in-One club with steel shaft.
(Phillips) $113

An unusual Ben Sayers Digger niblick, the patent head with reverse tapering blade, steel shafted.
(Phillips) $162

An Auchterlonie Balance putter with persimmon head and brass sole.
(Phillips) $291

A Jean Gassiat persimmon head putter with half brass sole and with patent 'Rib Pad' grip to the top of the dangawood shaft.
(Phillips) $809

A Jackson golden beech headed putter, the sole with extra lead weighting, 36in. hickory shaft.
(Phillips) $4,044

A rolling head putter, after the Payne-Galwey patent, the hosel stamped *Patented July 1907*.
(Phillips) $1,941

T. Morris: a dark stained beech putter, the shaft also dark stained.
(Phillips) $1,294

A G. Forrester dark stained beech putter.
(Phillips) $809

J. Walker: a dark stained beech putter.
(Phillips) $1,051

An Army & Navy beech headed transitional driver.
(Phillips) $971

A. Patrick: a golden beech headed play club, with 42in. shaft.
(Phillips) $3,073

R. White: a lofting iron with 4in. hosel.
(Phillips) $178

J. Anderson: a beech headed mid spoon with leather face insert.
(Phillips) $1,132

A Millar pronounced lump-back mashie with Carruthers hosel.
(Phillips) $113

An unusual Smiths patent deep faced cleek for Forgan with pronounced heel and toe weight, with unusual Fairlie type blade.
(Phillips) $226

J. Gray: a good curved faced lofting iron with 4¹/₂in. hosel.
(Phillips) $1,537

'H. Philp': a golden applewood headed late transitional putter, also stamped *T. Morris*, the shaft stamped *T. Morris, St. Andrews N.B.*
(Phillips) $2,588

A Forgan dark stained beech putter with Prince of Wales feather stamp, and greenheart shaft.
(Phillips) $890

Simpson: a golden persimmon headed bulger driver, the head stamped *Simpson, St. Andrews* in an oval.
(Phillips) $243

J. Morris: a stained beech left handed putter.
(Phillips) $890

T. Morris: a stained persimmon head putter with greenheart shaft, stamped *Tom Morris, St. Andrews*.
(Phillips) $518

T. Morris: a dark stained beech putter.
(Phillips) $971

A Spalding Schenectady putter.
(Phillips) $194

An unusual brass center shafted putter with ring hickory shaft.
(Phillips) $137

A mid 19th-century cleek with 5in. hosel.
(Phillips) $291

A Gibson 'Big Ben' niblick.
(Phillips) $712

A Mills 'B' model driver with a beechwood face insert.
(Phillips) $210

A D. Stephenson long nosed putter with scared joint.
(Phillips) $226

A. Patrick: a dark stained beech play club, the head stamped with owner's initials *W.P.*, the shaft bound.
(Phillips) $1,375

Jackson: a golden thornwood headed short spoon, with leather face insert, the head counterstamped *R. Kirk*, hickory shaft 37in.
(Phillips) $7,764

McEwan: a golden beechwood headed putter, the sole with extra lead weighting, the shaft marked for stymie measure.
(Phillips) $971

A gramophone by the Gramophone and Typewriter Company Ltd., in a paneled oak case of square form, with 7in. turntable.
(Spencer's) $1,836

An EMG gramophone, with four-spring soundbox, spring motor and papier-mâché horn, 29½in. diameter, circa 1935.
(Christie's) $2,833

A Persephone gramophone in a well figured case, with two tone green enameled tin fluted horn.
(Spencer's) $643

A Klingsor gramophone, with Klingsor soundbox and single-spring motor in dark oak Arts and Crafts style case, 41¼in. high.
(Christie's) $1,505

An His Master's Voice Automatic 1 gramophone with 5a (bronzed) and 5b soundboxes, electric motor for turntable and record changing mechanism and walnut case, 42½in. wide.
(Christie's) $3,365

A Klingsor cabinet gramophone, circa 1925, the mahogany case with fall front opening to turntable, 29in. high.
(Sotheby's) $992

A New Style No. 3 gramophone, by The Gramophone & Typewriter Ltd., with beveled 7-inch turntable, Concert soundbox, zinc horn and oak case, 1904.
(Christie's) $1,505

An American Victrola IV oak-cased table gramophone with integral speaker and original pickup, 1915.
(Auction Team Köln) $200

An Edison Bell Electron cabinet gramophone, Model EB248, in black Chinoiserie lacquered cabinet with gilt internal fittings, 28½in. wide, circa 1928.
(Christie's) $1,594

A five-case dark brown lacquer ground inro decorated with a phoenix, signed *Koami saku*, 19th century, 7.7cm. long. (Christie's) $1,280

A four-case guri lacquer inro with sylized scrolling foliage surrounded by key-fret pattern, unsigned, 19th century, 6.2cm. long. (Christie's) $731

A four-case fundame and gold hirame-ground inro depicting a falcon attacking an egret, signed *Shuncho saku* and tsubo seal, 19th century, 8cm. long. (Christie's) $2,194

A four-case gold ground inro decorated in gold hiramakie, takamakie, kirikane and kimpun with a karashishi, signed *Jokasai saku*, 19th century, with a coral ojime, 8.5cm. long. (Christie's) $3,474

A five-case roironuri ground inro, decorated and inlaid in Shibayama style with a behatted Chinese gentleman with two cranes, late 19th century, 8.5cm. long. (Christie's) $2,392

A four-case gold lacquer inro, decorated in gold, silver and iroe hiramakie, takamakie, nashiji and togidashi, with a lacquered netsuke of Hannya, both late 19th century, 10.1cm. long. (Christie's) $12,880

A four-case roironuri ground inro decorated with hydrangeas and a butterfly, signed *Kajikawa*, 19th century, with a carved nut ojime, 8.2cm. long. (Christie's) $1,097

A large five-case roironuri ground inro, decorated with birds and insects around a stone water basin, signed, late 19th century, 14.8cm. long. (Christie's) $7,360

A three-case roironuri ground inro decorated with Seven Sages of Bamboo Grove, signed *Koma Koryu saku*, early 19th century, an agate ojime, 7.4cm. long. (Christie's) $4,023

A lacquered brass barograph with seven tier vacuum in a glazed mahogany case with fitted drawer below, 38cm. wide.
(Phillips) $770

An unusual combination horn handled shooting knife, including knife and saw blades, spike, tweezers, screwdriver, gimlet and scissors.
(Bonhams) $181

A black japanned brass theodolite by Thomas Jones, the sighting telescope with rack and pinion focusing and spirit level, mid-19th century.
(Neales) $930

A mid-18th century mahogany and checkerstrung angle barometer and perpetual regulation of time, by Watkins & Smith, London, the architectural case with triangular pediment, 1.08m. high.
(Phillips) $13,793

A 19th century oxidized brass sextant, the bell frame with seven shades signed *Hezzanith, Patent No. 15917*, in a fitted mahogany box.
(Phillips) $1,001

A 'Sestrel' brass mounted ship's compass by Henry Browne & Son, type 90/315 on square mahogany base, 51in. high.
(Anderson & Garland) $930

Pair of Avery brass pole scales with brass pans and weights, on mahogany base, 21in. high, English, circa 1900.
(G. A. Key) $254

An oak barograph, English, early 20th century, No. 3389, with lacquered brass mechanism, clockwork recording drum and seven aneroid bellows, 36cm. wide.
(Bonhams) $700

A fine early 19th century Cary's celestial table globe, on mahogany tripod base with hoof feet, 50cm. high.
(Bearne's) $3,000

A lacquered brass dial barograph, with ten-tier vacuum and silvered dial signed *Negretti & Zambra*, 42cm. wide. (Phillips) $705

A mahogany cased adding machine by Arth. Burkhardt, Glashütte, circa 1900. (Stockholms Auktionsverk) $1,082

A 19th century brass dipleidoscope by E. J. Dent, London, the adjustable square brass plinth with level and compass, 4in. high. (Phillips) $521

An 18th century mahogany angle barometer and Perpetual Regulation of Time by E. Scarlet, London, the visible angled tube with engraved silvered scale from 28 to 31 inches, 1.02m. high. (Phillips) $36,960

A pair of 12in. library globes by Smith, each set within brass meridians on turned mahogany stands, 2ft. 10in. high. (Phillips) $8,429

An AEG Mignon typewriter with instruction booklet. (Arnold Frankfurt) $205

An early Victorian 12in. diameter Terrestrial Globe, with colored paper gores, inscribed *Kirkwood's New Terrestrial Globe*. (Christie's) $904

A McGregor brass A-frame sextant, Scottish, second half 19th century, signed *D McGregor & C° Glasgow, Greenock & Liverpool*. (Bonhams) $630

A William Bardin 9in. celestial table globe, English, 1785 edition, composed of twelve printed gores, 34cm. high overall. (Bonhams) $830

A Columbia No. 2 typewriter, with upper and lower case on single typewheel, nickeled frame and walnut case. (Christie's) $4,873

An incandescent lamp by Thomas Edison, the blown-glass bulb with platina vice clamps and (detached) horse-shoe carbon filament, on turned wood stand, 7¼in. high, circa 1880. (Christie's) $7,831

A brass helichronometer, by Ross Ltd., with rotating month and hour disks on adjustable stand, 10½in. high. (Christie's) $521

A rare medieval astronomical quadrant (quadrans novus), radius 5¾in., possibly Northern European, 14th century. (Christie's) $22,625

A compound microscope by Giuseppe Campani, with turned ebony body tube in two threaded sections with turned ivory eyepiece cap, bi-convex 13mm. eye-lens, 4⅛in. wide, late 17th century. (Christie's) $31,327

A set of coin scales, by J. P. Aeckersberg, Wichlinghausen, the steel balance with brass pans, with various weights in fitted wood case, dated 1772, 7in. wide. (Christie's) $783

A demonstration electric motor, in lacquered brass and black enamel, the armature with axis driving twin 7¾in. diameter pulley wheel, 14⅛in. wide. (Christie's) $1,740

A universal equinoctial sundial, by G. Adams, London, in lacquered-brass with folding gnomon, silvered hour ring divided VIII–XII–IIII, 4½in. diameter, late 18th century. (Christie's) $1,740

A compendium, by Negretti & Zambra, London, comprising pocket barometer and compass in gilt-metal case, 5in. wide. (Christie's) $693

A rare Hammonia typewriter, with brass 'bread-knife' typeface in sliding carriage and cast-iron base with gilt lettering.
(Christie's) $14,792

A calculator by Seidel & Naumann, with push-button keyboard, thirteen digit capacity and japanned and nickeled case on shaped feet, 21⁷/₈in. wide.
(Christie's) $2,437

A Columbia No. 1 typewriter, with black japanned frame, gilt lining, upper case typewheel (now italic) and varnished pine box.
(Christie's) $6,090

Siemens & Halske, a fine late 19th-century astatic elektro-dynamometer, the vulcanite base with maker's label engraved *SIEMENS & HALSKE BERLIN, No. 29272*, 13³/₄in. high.
(Christie's) $1,392

A Millionär calculator, by Hans W. Egli ... Zürich, No. 4006, in brass and aluminium case with instructions and 1895 patent dates, 21⁵/₈in. wide.
(Christie's) $2,785

A mahogany slide cabinet, with glazed door, carrying-handle and twenty-one drawers containing approximately 160 mostly entomological slides, 10in. wide.
(Christie's) $608

An Apps induction coil, with ivory and ebonite fittings and maker's label *1327, Apps, 433 Strand, London, Patd. 1881–264*, 17in. wide.
(Christie's) $835

A clinometer by Casella, in oxidized-brass, with circular silvered-dial, divided 0°–90° (x 4), clamp and telescope, 3in. wide.
(Christie's) $418

A gilt pocket compass, by Abraham & Co., Glasgow, with white enameled dial, edge-bar needle, clamp and suspension loop, 1³/₄in. diameter.
(Christie's) $487

A Myochin iron model of a shachihoko, finely worked with its fully articulated body, antennae and movable fins, tail and mouth, signed *Munekazu*, late Edo period, 35.5cm. long overall.
(Christie's) $20,873

An iron tripod koro, the body decorated with sparrows among grape vine, late 19th century, 31cm. high.
(Christie's) $10,120

Art Deco wrought-iron console, circa 1930, the bow-fronted rectangular stepped beige marble top trimmed along the front and sides with hammered wrought-iron, 4ft. 9¹/₂in. wide.
(Butterfield & Butterfield)
                               $3,737

The Showman, a metal-body statuette showing a peep box and three figures, 5in. high.
(Christie's) $4,000

A Regency brass-mounted steel sarcophagus coal-shuttle, the domed canted rectangular lid with gadrooned ring-handle and rim enclosing a metal liner, 20³/₄in. wide.
(Christie's) $3,634

A Velocipede Michaux original pedal cycle, with iron-rimmed wooden wheels and bronzed pedals, leather saddle on iron frame spring, 1861.
(Auction Team Köln)
                               $9,324

A pair of moulded and painted cast-iron figural andirons, American, 20th century, cast with the figure of a man, his hands on his knees, 17in. high.
(Sotheby's) $690

A Victorian cast-iron stick stand, modeled as a terrier sitting on its back legs on a socle, the base with removable tray, 24in. high.
(Christie's) $2,388

A pair of cast-iron and molded copper andirons, probably American, late 19th/early 20th century, molded with serpents in relief, 23¹/₂in. high.
(Sotheby's) $2,875

An Indian ivory one piece carving of St. George and The Dragon in European style, with hardwood plinth, 11in. high. (Spencer's) $429

A good late 19th century Japanese carved ivory group of two wrestlers, both wearing grass skirts, 4¹/₄in. high. (Canterbury) $1,185

A carved Japanese one piece ivory group of a dancing bear, on hind legs, holding a large drum, signed, 14cm. high. (Spencer's) $890

A carved ivory figure of Lord Nelson, by John Perron, the Admiral wearing Naval uniform, mid-19th century, 8¹/₄in. high overall. (Christie's) $3,657

A rare large carved whalebone birdcage, New England, mid 19th century, the slightly arched top fitted with a hook, each side fitted with a door, 15in. wide. (Sotheby's) $8,050

An ivory tankard carved with a hunting scene, Germany, 19th century, 23.5cm. high. (Stockholms Auktionsverk) $5,066

An ivory triptych figure of Elizabeth I, her bodice applied with paste jewels, opening to relief depictions of her contemporaries, Dieppe, late 19th century, 7³/₄in. high. (Christie's) $1,430

A pair of ivory vases with wooden stands decorated with inlays of mother-of-pearl, tortoiseshell, ivory, coral and wood, mark *Masamitsu*, late 19th century, 34cm. high. (Christie's) $4,571

A large sectional ivory model of the Shichifukujin in the takarabune, the Seven Gods with their own attributes, 19th century, 46cm. wide overall. (Christie's) $4,023

A German carved ivory lidded tankard, surmounted by a horseman and with three projecting male busts, second half 19th century, 19¼in. high. (Christie's)　$10,971

A Japanese carved ivory 3in. group of two rats and an egg. (Anderson & Garland)　$306

A carved ivory group of Saint Michael slaying the Antichrist, on an octagonal base, Dieppe, 19th century, 9½in. high. (Christie's)　$2,288

A pair of French carved ivory maidens, each nude, one holding a festoon of flowers, the other with her hair falling down her back, late 19th century, the ivory: 8¼in. and 8¾in. high. (Christie's)　$6,948

A carved ivory group depicting Minerva and Fortune, the Goddess of War, gesturing towards the naked Fortune, 19th century, 12½in. high overall. (Christie's)　$7,679

A finely carved gilt-metal lined Austro-Hungarian ivory cup, by P. W. Schutz, carved depicting a military hunting scene, circa 1834, 7in. high. (Christie's)　$14,628

A German silver-mounted carved ivory lidded tankard, surmounted by a figure of Pan seated playing his pipes, second half 19th century, 10in. high. (Christie's)　$3,657

An attractive 19th century green stained and natural ivory chess set of tapering knopped form, 5–10cm., on a stained wood stand. (Bearne's)　$2,520

A 19th century German carved ivory beaker, the interior in gilt metal, the bowl carved with a stag hunting scene in relief, 7in. high. (Spencer's)　$731

A late Chien Lung Dynasty portable black lacquer and Chinoiserie decorated carved wood portable shrine, having elaborate paneled and pierced doors, 19in.
(Locke & England) $496

A roironuri ground gunbai (a military leader's or umpire's fan) decorated in gold, silver and iroe hiramakie, unsigned, 19th century, 54.2cm. long.
(Christie's) $8,228

A fine lacquer zushi-dana, decorated with each tier depicting cranes and minogame among plum blossom, pine and bamboo, late 17th/early 18th century, 71.5cm. high.
(Christie's) $16,560

A roironuri ground suzuribako, decorated with pine, bamboo and plum tree issuing from rockwork, Meiji period (1868–1912), 21 x 19.5cm.
(Christie's) $1,840

A kinji ground lacquer box with tray, decorated with peacocks among rocks and peony, with an inner tray depicting a hawk perched, signed, 19th century, 17 x 13cm.
(Christie's) $7,728

A rare metsubushi or pepper-thrower, the square body decorated with a poem and clouds on a roironuri ground, signed *Sano Tsunetada hatsumei zo kore* (invented and made it), 19th century, 8.5cm.
(Christie's) $5,120

A Shibayama kodansu, the silver ground in relief with cherry blossoms and a stream over hanabishi patterns, late 19th century, 11.5 x 11 x 8.5cm.
(Christie's) $5,520

A small Momoyama chest, inlaid in mother-of-pearl on a roironuri ground, the front with panels of maples and camellia, late 16th century, 22.5cm. wide.
(Christie's) $3,771

A four-case gold lacquer inro, decorated with Itsukushima Shrine in gold hiramakie, hirame and kirikane, 19th century, 8.2cm. long.
(Christie's) $3,312

Handel scenic table lamp, reverse painted dome shade with expansive landscape in earth tone shades, mounted on copper colored metal base, 23in. high. (Skinner) $3,220

A Muller Frères mushroom lamp with lake and alpine decoration, signed, 45cm. high. (Hôtel de Ventes Horta) $6,349

Handel leaded glass lamp, cone shade composed of selected opal and ripple glass arranged as pansy-like blossoms in overall brilliant display, 24in. high. (Skinner) $5,175

Oil lamp, green glass domed shade, earthenware baluster reservoir decorated with ochre and off white floral festoons, possibly Doulton, late 19th century, 27in. high. (G. A. Key) $291

A pair of late Victorian Staffordshire pink luster spirit-jar lamps, each decorated in pink and gilt and with later giltmetal stopper-spout, fitted for electricity, circa 1893, 11¾in. high. (Christie's) $1,454

Tiffany bronze and gold Favrile seven-light lily lamp, raised ribbed base with upright shaft stems supporting ribbed gold iridescent lily blossoms, 25in. high total. (Skinner) $6,900

Handel leaded glass lamp, predominately green, yellow, orange-amber glass segments arranged as bright centered flowers, mounted in bronzed metal, 28in. high. (Skinner) $3,450

Pairpoint miniature puffy boudoir lamp, blown-out rose tree shade with two butterflies above pink and yellow roses, 16in. high total. (Skinner) $3,105

Muller Fres enameled cameo glass lamp, shaped tuck-under glass dome shade of mottled purple shaded to yellow-amber with matching baluster form base, 19½in. total height. (Skinner) $8,625

Daum acid etched Art Deco
lamp, heavy textured colorless
sphere overlaid in emerald
green deeply etched as stylized
blossoms, 28in. total height.
(Skinner) $2,588

Tiffany bronze and Favrile
acorn lamp, bulbous swirl
decorated three-arm bronze
base supporting green leaded
glass shade, 18in. high.
(Skinner) $6,325

Daum, Winter Landscape lamp,
circa 1900, in gray glass
internally decorated with bands
of yellow, orange and pink,
enameled mark, 64cm.
(Sotheby's) $31,671

Bent panel slag glass table lamp,
matching blue slag panels in gilt
metal lighted base and shade
with elaborate repeating urn
and bird scenic framework,
22in. high.
(Skinner) $690

'Fox Women' decorated table
lamp, after 1907 Bertha Lum
color woodcut, hand decorated
porcelain base with repeating
scene of dancing Japanese
women, 22in. high.
(Skinner) $2,070

Pairpoint reverse painted table
lamp, flared dome Copley shade
with green, purple and white
canopy top bordered by
colorful leafy urn and scroll
motif, 22in. high.
(Skinner) $1,610

Unusual slag glass and gilt metal
lamp, shade composed of
reticulated scrollwork frame for
eight green slag panels above
and below eight red rectangular
panels, 28in. high.
(Skinner) $805

Frank Gehry 'Easy Edges'
laminated cardboard table
lamp, circa 1972, stack
laminated shade and base with
plywood capped ends, unsigned,
26½in. high.
(Skinner) $690

Bradley & Hubbard octagonal
slag glass lamp, gilt metal two-
socket base, supporting shade
with eight amber slag glass
panels in floral frame, 22in.
high.
(Skinner) $575

Tiffany Studios Tyler pattern lamp, the domed shaped shade with yellow swirling pattern against a green shaded ground, 27in. high.
(William Doyle) $11,550

Bent panel slag glass table lamp, Pairpoint urn-form pot metal three-socket lamp base mounted with six panel amber slag shade, 25in. high.
(Skinner) $288

Tiffany Studios bronze and favrile glass apple blossom lamp, the shade with pink flowers against a mottled green ground, 22in. overall height.
(William Doyle) $8,625

Handel Treasure Island lamp, textured dome shade reverse painted, depicting tall masted sailing ship at anchor in moonlit lagoon, mounted on metal base, 24½in. high.
(Skinner) $8,050

Onondaga Metal Shops hammered copper and wicker oil lamp, East Syracuse, New York, circa 1904, hammered copper base with original bronze patina, 21in. high.
(Skinner) $2,070

Floral leaded glass table lamp, attributed to Wilkinson Lamp Company, conical shade with amber slag diamond glass segments above wide border of blossoms, 23½in. high.
(Skinner) $1,380

Handel Moserine lamp, moss green cased to opal white tam o'shanter shade, raised on Bradley Hubbard single-socket lamp base, 16¼in. high total.
(Skinner) $1,150

Bronze desk lamp with Daum Art Glass shade, ridged C-shape single-socket base with molded foil decorated frosted glass shade, 13in. high.
(Skinner) $1,265

Tiffany bronze and Favrile glass tulip lamp, dome shade of leaded glass segments arranged as eighteen pink tulip blossoms, 21in. high.
(Skinner) $17,250

Pairpoint square puffy lamp, elaborate four-sided 'Torino' glass shade with blown out pink and red rose blossoms, 20½in. high.
(Skinner) $4,888

Art Deco table lamp, flattened half-oval isinglass shade decorated front and back by red stylized blossoms and leafy Deco devices, 24in. high.
(Skinner) $805

Jefferson reverse painted scenic lamp, angular hexagonal glass shade painted with rolling hillside meadowlands, 25in. high.
(Skinner) $1,093

Jefferson reverse painted scenic lamp, domed glass shade with riverside landscape under yellow and blue sky, mounted on bronzed metal urn-form base, 21in. high.
(Skinner) $978

Carder Steuben yellow Cluthra lamp, gilt metal harp desk lamp with swing-socket fitted with rare Cluthra glass shade of yellow and white mottling, 14in. high total.
(Skinner) $1,725

Handel peacock lamp, by George Palme, domed glass shade decorated with two full length peacocks cameo etched and enamel painted in metallic gold, 24in. high.
(Skinner) $19,550

Handel reverse painted scenic lamp, conical Teroma shade artistically painted with white birches and green tree-filled river scene, 23in. high.
(Skinner) $4,312

Finnish modern brass lamp, severe gilt metal standard lamp base with four-socket wheel supporting original conforming fabric shade, 24¾in. high.
(Skinner) $547

Lily pad leaded glass table lamp, colorful conical shade with drop apron composed of shaded and mottled green and pink glass segments, 21½in. high.
(Skinner) $1,438

French gilt-metal and onyx adjustable candle lamp, winged dragon and double candle sockets, 16⁷/₈in. high. (Skinner) $690

A Gallé cameo glass table lamp, in deep yellow tinted glass, overlaid with rich red/brown, circa 1900, 32.4cm. high. (Christie's) $38,157

Daum, Alliums lamp, circa 1910, in clear glass internally mottled with orange, yellow and aubergine, cameo mark, 35.5cm. (Sotheby's) $15,836

A French gilt-bronze bouillotte lamp, Louis-Philippe, Paris, circa 1845, with four stylized leaf-cast candle-arms above a triform leaf and shell cast socle, with tôle shade, 65cm. high. (Sotheby's) $2,560

A pair of French mounted Chinese cloisonné oil lamps, circa 1880, the mounts possibly by Barbedienne, the light fittings signed *Gagneau*, 56cm. high. (Sotheby's) $5,303

Ettore Sottsass Jr, Austria/Italy, Asteroide Lamp for Poltronova, 1968, arched fluorescent tube covered by pink perspex, on metallic blue painted cast metal base, 74cm. high. (Bonhams) $2,630

A Daum cameo glass table lamp, each piece in mottled brilliant yellow glass shading to blue, overlaid in mottled autumnal red, circa 1900, 47.2cm. high. (Christie's) $64,938

Gustav Stickley oak and hammered copper table lamp, No. 506, circa 1912, amber exterior glass backed with white interior glass, 16¹/₄in. high. (Skinner) $4,600

A Muller Frères table lamp, the silvered metal base supporting domed frosted glass shade in mottled blue and pink 33cm. high. (Christie's) $974

A Tiffany desk lamp, in the 'Grapevine' pattern, on four claw feet, 61cm. high.
(Christie's) $3,188

Franco Albini, Italy, a table lamp for Sirrah, 1969, chrome with white glass shade.
(Bonhams) $201

A 1930s Modernist table lamp, chrome interlocking trumpet-shaped elements raised on similar base, 51cm. high.
(Bonhams) $325

Tiffany Studios woodbine lamp, with leaded shade of predominantly maroon green with pink, blue purple mottled segments arranged as woodbine blossoms, 19in. high.
(Skinner) $11,500

'Papillons', an Argy-Rousseau pâte de verre veilleuse/night light, molded red and amethyst decoration of four butterflies, circa 1924, 11.8cm. high.
(Christie's) $8,721

Gorham Anglo-Japanese mixed-metal oil lamp base, 1881–85, chased copper body with applied silver and brass flowers, fruit, birds and insects, brass burner and copper font, 14in. high.
(Skinner) $3,450

Muller and Chapelle stork lamp, naturalistic bird composed of wrought iron figural cage body with overlapping neck and tail feathers, 15¹/₂in. high.
(Skinner) $7,475

A classical brass two-light argand lamp, by Messenger and Son, English, circa 1830, the urn-shaped font with acanthus finial, 21in. high.
(Christie's) $575

A chromed metal and plexiglass lamp in the Italian style of Stilnovo, this piece believed to be a prototype because of the cost of its production.
(Bonhams) $402

LAMPS

An Argental cameo table lamp, yellow glass overlaid in red, acid-etched and carved with flowers and foliage, 35cm. high. (Christie's) **$4,928**

An Eastern European Chanukkah lamp, the shaped back plate decorated with the Lions of Judah supporting the Tablets of the Law, 10in. (Christie's) **$1,220**

Bradley & Hubbard Art Nouveau table lamp, with patinated floral design and palm leaf imprint, slag glass shade, 21in. diameter. (Eldred's) **$1,870**

Dirk Van Erp warty copper and mica lamp, first quarter 20th century, the conical shade fitted with three mica panels and three riveted battens surmounted by a domical cap, 21^1/$_2$in. high. (Butterfield & Butterfield) **$4,600**

Gallé mold-blown cameo glass rhododendron lamp, early 20th century, overlaid with blue and cut with blossoming rhododendrons and budding leafy stems in low relief, 18^1/$_2$in. high. (Butterfield & Butterfield) **$123,500**

Tiffany favrile glass and patinated bronze clematis lamp, 1899–1928, the conical shade composed of clematis blossoms in streaked and mottled royal blue, 20in. high. (Butterfield & Butterfield) **$29,900**

Austrian patinated bronze and glass table lamp, circa 1910, the waisted green frosted glass domical shade bordered by a pierced bronze band, 23^1/$_4$in. high. (Butterfield & Butterfield) **$2,587**

Tiffany favrile glass and bronze twelve-light lily lamp, 1898–1902, composed of twelve slender cylindrical stems turning outward, 19^1/$_2$in. high. (Butterfield & Butterfield) **$14,950**

French Art Nouveau gilt-bronze, champlevé enamel and alabaster lamp, Louchet Foundry, early 20th century, the waisted ovoid cast with shaped reserves, 12^1/$_2$in. high. (Butterfield & Butterfield) **$805**

Rare Britains Set 171 Greek Infantry Running at
the Trail, with officer.
(Christie's) $355

Rare Britains from Set 94 21st Lancers, steel
helmets, two eared horses, 3rd version, 1919.
(Christie's) $320

Heyde or Heyde like 90mm. Troops: Boer War
Troops and Imperial Yeomanry at the Slope,
circa 1899.
(Christie's) $1,332

Rare Britains Set 1339 Royal Horse Artillery,
with Gun Limber Team (Active Service Order),
at the gallop, 1931.
(Christie's) $888

Rare 60mm. German hollow-cast khaki
infantrymen: ten men Running at the Trail with
officer and bugler, circa 1898.
(Christie's) $231

A rare Britains Set 54 First Lifeguards, Second
Dragoon Guards and Ninth Lancers, fifteen
pieces, in original red box, 1920.
(Christie's) $799

Rare Britains Set 17 Somerset Light Infantry, 1st
version, wasp waisted officer, in original box
with green label, 1894.
(Christie's) $320

Rare Johillco 'Skiing Patrol', types of Finland's
Heroic Ghost Army, in original green box, 1935.
(Christie's) $977

Britains Set 123 Bikanir Camel Corps, 1st
version with wire tails, 1901.
(Christie's) $622

A lifesize white marble group of The Three Graces, after the model by Canova, late 19th century, 68in. high.
(Christie's) $177,285

A Russian ormolu, cut-glass and rhodonite inkstand, the ten-sided inkwell with conforming hinged lid surmounted by a double-headed eagle below a coronet, 19th century, 10½in. wide.
(Christie's) $8,073

A white marble bust of William, 12th Duke of Hamilton and marble pedestal, by Jean-Pierre Dantan, circa 1863, the bust: 22in. high.
(Christie's) $3,657

A pair of 19th century life-size white marble figures of maidens, representing two of the Seasons, 143cm. and 170cm.
(Bearne's) $4,872

White marble vase, decorated with helicoid ribs and a garland suspended from a ram's mask, 72cm. high.
(Finarte) $9,049

A pair of white marble busts after the Antique, one of Diana Chasseureuse, the other of the Apollo Belvedere, second half 19th century, 31¾in. high.
(Christie's) $10,605

White marble sculpture of Ariadne, late 19th century, 18in. high.
(Skinner) $1,093

A French white marble bust of a lady, her hair and dress in the eighteenth century style, second half 19th century, 20in. high.
(Christie's) $1,828

A white marble group of a young naked lady seated on a rock flanked by two swans, 27in. high.
(Hy. Duke & Son) $2,008

Italian white marble bust of a young girl, 20th century, inscribed *Made in Italy* and *Pedrini*, 14¹/₂in. high. (Skinner) $345

An English white marble group, by Richard Garbe, depicting a nude man and woman cradling their infant child, 1913, 37in. wide. (Christie's) $5,119

A white marble bust of Hermes and marble pedestal, after the Antique, second half 19th century, the bust: 21¹/₂in. high. (Christie's) $6,399

A statuary marble figure of Cupid, shown standing, holding a bow to his right (now lacking), a tree trunk to his side, Italian, late 19th century, 30in. high. (Christie's) $704

A pair of Italian white marble sculptures of long-horned bullocks, both lying down, and one with its head mooing, mid-19th century, 30in. wide. (Christie's) $30,498

A French white marble figure entitled 'Fleur d'Hiver', by Louis Ernest Barrias, depicting a young girl wrapped in a shawl, second half 19th century, 31¹/₂in. high. (Christie's) $10,971

A French white marble bust entitled 'Genie de la Danse', by Jean-Baptiste Carpeaux, last quarter 19th century, 26¹/₄in. high. (Christie's) $10,605

White marble sculpture of a mother and child, late 19th century, indistinctly signed, possibly on a later base, 14in. long. (Skinner) $1,035

A French white marble bust of a lady, by Prosper d'Epinay, wearing a cloak and with a flower to her hair, second half 19th century, 29¹/₂in. high. (Christie's) $3,657

A singing bird box, in gilt and enamel case with rustic views in white, blue and gilt surrounds, 4in. wide, mid 20th-century.
(Christie's) $2,479

A tinplate Stollwerk talking machine, with floating reproducer on conical horn, with one 4³/₄-inch wax disk.
(Christie's) $4,958

A musical necéssaire, of carte-de-visite album form with tools, playing Carmen and one other air, 6¹/₄in. wide.
(Christie's) $425

A 9-inch Britannia disk musical box, with twin-comb movement in upright walnut smoker's cabinet, with fifteen disks, 21¹/₂in. high.
(Christie's) $2,125

A Hicks-pattern barrel piano, with twenty-seven note action playing eight airs, in rosewood-veneered case, 38in. high, circa 1830.
(Christie's) $1,328

A B. H. Abrahams 'Britannia' 11³/₄in. disk musical box, Swiss, circa 1900, with single comb movement in a walnut and ebonized case, 64cm. high, and sixteen disks.
(Bonhams) $1,500

The Speaking Picture Book, German, circa 1910, with pull-cords to the side which causes the book to emit the relevant farm sounds, 32cm. long.
(Sotheby's) $1,228

A 'Stella' polyphon patented December 6th 1887, model No. 1510, in 25in. rectangular rosewood case with inlaid panels of flowers.
(Anderson & Garland) $837

A Flight & Robson chamber barrel organ, English, dated 1821, in a mahogany case with painted foliate garlands and checker banded inlay, 70cm. wide.
(Bonhams) $3,650

A table top symphonion, contained in a red stained and parcel gilt walnut case, playing 12in. metal disks, together with a metal disk, 18in. wide. (Spencer's) $1,836

A Columbia Type AT graphophone, No. 267058, in molded oak case with 17-inch red flower horn and table stand. (Christie's) $531

A Tanzbaer accordion, with twenty-eight note trigger-operated action, walnut-veneered case and thirty-two rolls. (Christie's) $1,948

An 11³/₄-inch upright Symphonion, with twin diametric combs and coin mechanism in walnut case, with eight disks, 25¹/₂in. high. (Christie's) $4,605

A 11³/₄-inch Monopol disk musical box, German, circa 1900, the sublime harmonie comb arrangement contained in upright case, with sixteen metal disks, 28in. high. (Sotheby's) $2,167

A 19⁵/₈-inch Polyphon disk musical box, German, circa 1900, the coin operated periphery drive movement, playing on duplex combs, 38in. high. (Sotheby's) $3,250

A small chamber barrel organ, with sixteen-key action playing one rank of wood and one of metal pipes, 29¹/₂in. high, circa 1820. (Christie's) $1,594

A late baroque Toggenburger house organ, signed and dated *1789*, by Joseph Looser. (Galerie Koller) $60,490

A 19⁵/₈-inch Polyphon, with twin comb movement and coin mechanism in typical upright walnut case, 38in. high. (Christie's) $7,438

A physician's instrument wallet, containing various lancets and bistouries by Osborn & Son, Ferguson, Weiss and others, directors and other items. (Christie's) $190

A turned-wood monaural stethoscope, 7in. high. (Christie's) $348

A brass and iron fleam, with trigger and blade-box with floriate engraving, 3³/₄in. wide, 18th century. (Christie's) $557

A surgeon's set, by Evans & Wormull, with metacarpal saw, two Liston knives, trephine, trocar and canulae, 17¹/₂in. wide, dated(?) 1897. (Christie's) $696

Baillière's Popular Atlas, of the Anatomy and Physiology of the Male Human Body, with colored plates and text; and companion volume ... Female Human Body. (Christie's) $104

A comprehensive dental set, by Bucquet, Paris, with fifty-four pluggers, scalers, finger drills, bisturies, lancets and cauterisers, 28¹/₂in. wide. (Christie's) $24,365

A single-claw tooth key, with cranked shaft and smooth ebony handle, 5³/₄in. long. (Christie's) $121

A part-amputation set, by Brown, with metacarpal saw, three Liston knives (one by Arnold & Sons), bone forceps, tourniquet and two tenacula, 16¹/₂in. wide. (Christie's) $557

A tooth chisel, with iron blade, turned stem and ivory handle, 4in. long, 18th century. (Christie's) $418

A metacarpal bow saw, with octagonal wood handle and tension nut, 9¼in. long. (Christie's) $190

A pair of amethyst drug jars, of bulbous form with gilt labels and stoppers, 15in. high. (Christie's) $1,914

A porcelain phrenology seal, the cranium divided in black with the characteristics listed below, with gilt lining on brass seal, 3in. high. (Christie's) $1,392

A homeopathic medicine chest, by Thompson & Capper, Liverpool and Birkenhead, the upper compartment with fifty bottles, in mahogany case, 11in. wide. (Christie's) $956

A cupping set, by Weiss, with lacquered-brass syringe and two cupping glasses with stopcocks, in fitted leather-covered case, 5½in. wide. (Christie's) $418

Queen Victoria's traveling medicine case, the leather-covered case with tooled decoration, with divisions containing fifteen bottles, 10¾in. wide. (Christie's) $8,354

A trepanning set by Erhardt, with steel trepan with mother of pearl infil, trephine, four crowns, Hey-pattern skull saw, etc., 16in. wide. (Christie's) $9,571

A phrenology head by Fowler, with divided cranium, 11½in. high; and a copy of Fowler's New Illustrated Self-Instructor in Phrenology and Physiology. (Christie's) $1,652

A surgeon's set, by J. Millikin, London, with Butcher's-pattern saw with three blades, two Liston-pattern knives, trephine, trocar and cannule, 16½in. wide. (Christie's) $956

A George I style carved giltwood mirror, the surmount with a central cartouche spray flanked by eagle's heads, 27in. wide. (Woolley & Wallis) **$1,134**

A Biedermeier cheval mirror, mahogany veneered, the side supports with chased gilt bronze urn finials. (Woolley & Wallis) **$1,944**

A George III giltwood wall mirror, the vertical rectangular beveled mirror plate within a bead and reel fillet, 52in. high. (Spencer's) **$1,071**

An early George II mirror, veneered in walnut with carved giltwood moldings, a swan neck pediment terminating in florets, 28½in. wide. (Woolley & Wallis) **$3,870**

A dressing mirror, in Stuart style with chinoiserie engraving to the silver cushion frame, 19½ x 23in., probably late 19th century. (Woolley & Wallis) **$3,577**

Federal gilt gesso looking glass, probably Massachusetts, circa 1815, standing figure of America, flanked by eglomisé tablet of urns of flowers, 16in. wide. (Skinner) **$9,775**

Federal gilt gesso looking glass, labeled *E. Lothrop, Boston*, circa 1820, original condition, 14¼in. wide. (Skinner) **$632**

A Queen Anne walnut and featherbanded toilet mirror, with an arched shaped plate tilting between later turned uprights and finials, on bun feet, 93cm. high. (Phillips) **$1,842**

An early 18th century wall mirror, parcel gilt foliate molded fillet and figured walnut fret carved frame, 108cm. high. (Spencer's) **$480**

Walnut looking glass, probably England, 18th century, with beveled two-part glass.
(Skinner) $2,530

Gilt gesso carved girandole looking glass, England or America, early 19th century, 38¹/₂in. high.
(Skinner) $3,450

Walnut looking glass, probably England, 18th century, old refinish, 30in. high.
(Skinner) $1,955

A classical carved gesso and gilt mirror, New England, circa 1815, the cove molded broken cornice hung with gilt spherules, 44in. high.
(Christie's) $1,725

An Italian walnut toilet mirror, the inverted breakfront base with three drawers and central tazza, second quarter 19th century, 27³/₄in. wide.
(Christie's) $2,153

Continental baroque style ebonized and gilt-metal mounted mirror, late 19th century, arched rectangular form, with foliate pierced and pressed gilt-metal borders, 57in. high.
(Skinner) $1,495

Ornate porcelain framed dressing table mirror, encrusted with putti bearing flowers, 13in. high.
(G. A. Key) $229

A Venetian glass octagonal mirror, the frame with angels embellished with carved flowerheads, early 19th century.
(Galerie Moderne) $1,181

Rococo style gilt carved wood mirror, with elaborate pierced foliate and scrolling motif, 34in. wide.
(William Doyle) $2,070

A Regency ebonized and parcel-gilt convex mirror, the cresting surmounted by a splayed eagle flanked by scrolled acanthus trails, 39 x 28¹/₂in.
(Christie's) $4,724

A carved and giltwood framed mirror, decorated with scrolling foliage, 17th century, 36 x 46cm.
(Finarte) $6,905

A Franco-Flemish boulle mirror, circa 1880, the arched cresting surmounted by vases of gilt-bronze flowers, 67cm. wide.
(Sotheby's) $3,840

A massive 19th century Continental porcelain framed mirror with all-over encrustations of flowers, cherubs, birds, etc., 4ft. 6in. x 2ft. 10in. wide.
(Russell, Baldwin & Bright) $5,526

Lebkuecher & Company sterling dressing mirror, circa 1900, retailed by Hodgson, Kennard and Company Inc., engraved floral and scroll design, monogram, 15in. high.
(Skinner) $1,610

A mid 18th century South German polychrome painted and parcel gilt rococo mirror, the pierced asymmetrical rockwork cresting with a basket of flowers with further flowers and pierced apron, 78 x 35cm.
(Phillips) $5,833

A South German repoussé white metal mirror, the waved rectangular plate within a claret silk frame, metalwork 18th century, 70 x 42¹/₂in.
(Christie's) $5,382

An antique Italian wall mirror, the giltwood architectural frame carved equestrian and other figures, 30 x 29in.
(Russell, Baldwin & Bright) $1,151

A William and Mary giltwood and gesso mirror, the divided rectangular plate with shaped arched top and in a molded frame carved on a ribbed ground, 64¹/₂ x 31¹/₂in.
(Christie's) $10,471

A satinwood cheval mirror inlaid overall with ebonized lines, on downswept legs, 29½in. wide.
(Christie's) $16,716

An Italian giltwood overmantel mirror, the later shaped rectangular plate within a mirrored border profusely carved, mid-18th century, 68 x 53½in.
(Christie's) $8,611

An Empire ormolu-mounted mahogany cheval mirror, the rectangular plate in a plain surround mounted with stars, 37¼in. wide.
(Christie's) $4,306

An Empire ebonized, giltwood and eglomisé mirror, American, late 19th century, the steamship 'Citizen' above a rectangular glass plate, 29 x 13½in.
(Christie's) $2,875

A George II giltwood mirror, the later rectangular beveled plate within a gadrooned border, 32¾ x 26½in.
(Christie's) $1,454

Austrian silvered metal figural mirror, Argentor, early 20th century, cast with an Art Nouveau maiden wearing a long flowing dress and sash over each shoulder, 37in. high.
(Butterfield & Butterfield) $2,875

A Continental silver-gilt dressing table mirror, unmarked, circa 1880, on two shell and leaf-capped scroll feet, 25in. high.
(Christie's) $4,773

Fine antique English early Queen Anne dressing mirror, in walnut veneers with five drawers and a small cabinet, 29½in. high.
(Eldred's) $462

A Dresden oval mirror-frame applied with garlands and birds, surmounted by a portrait-medallion of Marie Antoinette, late 19th century, 35¼in. high.
(Christie's) $5,485

A 'Lipsia' steam plant, German, circa 1905, the single cylinder engine with large diameter flywheel, 25.5cm. wide.
(Sotheby's) $1,228

A large hot air engine, German, circa 1900, with vertical engine, 41cm. high.
(Sotheby's) $1,444

A Plank vertical steam plant, German, circa 1920, vertical single cylinder engine with electric generator, 28cm. square.
(Sotheby's) $1,625

A large Doll horizontal stationary steam engine, German, circa 1912, with horizontal boiler, companionways and ladders, 36cm. long.
(Sotheby's) $2,528

A vertical steam engine, German, circa 1905, with single cylinder, lithographed 'wooden' lagging, flywheel and spirit fired vertical boiler, 30.5cm. high.
(Sotheby's) $1,173

A rare J. Schoenner spirit fired traction engine, German, late 19th century, with double burner, flywheel chimney, and whistle, 28cm. long.
(Sotheby's) $2,528

A Bing hot air engine, German, circa 1905, with water reservoir, burner and chimney, 28cm. wide.
(Sotheby's) $1,408

A Bing hot air engine, German, circa 1902, with spirit fired burner, and twin flywheels, 33cm. high.
(Sotheby's) $1,534

A Ernst Plank steam plant, German, circa 1910, with vertical boiler, pressure gauge and safety valve, 41cm. wide.
(Sotheby's) $1,806

MODEL SHIPS

A Bing clockwork 100cm. four-funnel torpedo boat, with original key, circa 1925. (Christie's) $3,375

A Plank steam 39cm. river gunboat, with externally fired boiler and spirit lamp, circa 1905. (Christie's) $1,599

A Bing hand painted tinplate 2nd Series 42cm. four-funnel liner, finished in dark blue, red and ivory, with fore and aft lithographed Italian flags. (Christie's) $1,777

A Bing steam 36.5cm. 3rd Series three funnel ocean liner, finished in red and ivory, with externally fired boiler, circa 1924. (Christie's) $2,132

A painted and lacquered tinplate side-wheel steam gunboat carpet toy, mounted on four revolving spoked wheels, with cannon, probably French, 1880s, 12in. long. (Christie's) $533

A Fleischmann clockwork painted and lithographed tinplate tanker, tabbed construction with details including tank covers, circa 1939. (Christie's) $746

A Bing steam hand painted tinplate four funnel 59cm. torpedo boat, with externally fired boiler. (Christie's) $2,487

A Bing steam tinplate single funnel torpedo boat, with externally fired boiler and spirit lamp, circa 1909. (Christie's) $1,421

A John Harper & Co. Hoop-La Bank, English, circa 1890, the clown with white face, and yellow robes, 22cm. long. (Sotheby's) $4,514

A J. & E. Stevens reclining Chinaman cast iron money bank, American, bearing patent date 1882, 21cm. long. (Sotheby's) $6,139

A J. & E. Stevens Dark Town Battery bank, American, bearing 1875 patent date, the pitcher with articulated arm, 25cm. long. (Sotheby's) $2,076

A Shepard Hardware Co. Punch and Judy mechanical cast iron bank, American, circa 1884, 16cm. long. (Sotheby's) $1,264

A painted cast iron toy bank, American, late 19th/early 20th century, a smiling African-American man, 6$^{1}/_{2}$in. high. (Christie's) $460

A rare 'Four Towers' still bank, probably John Harper, English, 1890s, the iron castle cast with the work *Bank*, 10cm. high. (Sotheby's) $361

A J. & E. Stevens Paddy and the Pig mechanical cast iron money bank, American, circa 1882, 18cm. long. (Sotheby's) $1,083

A rare cast iron pillar box still bank, English, 1880s, the pillar box of traditional form, cast with the initials *VR*, and Royal cipher, 15cm. high. (Sotheby's) $542

A J. & E. Stevens 'World's Fair' cast iron mechanical bank, American, circa 1893, with seated figure of Christopher Columbus, 21cm. long. (Sotheby's) $1,481

A 'Bells in sight' ten-air cylinder musical box, Swiss, 1880's, No. 5183, with 38cm. cylinder, in a burr-walnut case, 65cm. wide.
(Bonhams) $2,500

A silver-gilt 'sur-plateau' snuff box, the movement playing God Save the King, 3¹/₈in. wide, London, 1815.
(Christie's) $7,438

A rare Chancellor's patent enbarmon ikon, Irish or English, circa 1811, in a rosewood and brass inlaid case, 50cm. wide.
(Bonhams) $11,620

A mandarin musical box, accompanied by six saucer-shaped, vertically-mounted bells struck by three seated mandarins with nodding heads, 20³/₄in. wide.
(Christie's) $3,010

An interchangeable cylinder musical box on stand, Swiss, circa 1880, each of the six 28cm. cylinders playing six popular airs, 38in. wide.
(Sotheby's) $10,833

A royal presentation musical box with six-air program, case with brass plaque *Presented by T.R.H.'s The Prince & Princess of Wales … Xmas 1908*, 23in. wide.
(Christie's) $1,417

A twelve-air Harp-Bells zither cylinder musical box, Swiss, circa 1890–1900, No. 53416, with 33cm. cylinder, tune indicator, six saucer shaped bells, 69cm. wide.
(Bonhams) $1,500

A sur-plateau silver snuff box, playing two airs, in reeded silver case with gilt compartment, 3¹/₈in. wide, Birmingham 1815.
(Christie's) $9,740

A sublime harmony musical box, by Junod, with two interchangeable nickel-plate cylinders playing six airs each, zither attachments on each comb, walnut case.
(Christie's) $5,400

A Spanish guitar, by Miguel Simplicio, 1922, the two piece back and ribs of rosewood, l.o.b. 18¹⁵/₁₆in. (Christie's)

$5,144

Dizzy Gillespie, a Martin Committee trumpet, silver plated 4³/₄in. bell set at a forty five degree angle to the body with floral engraving. (Christie's) $63,000

A fine Italian violin, by Giuseppe Ornati, 1920, one-piece back, the l.o.b. 14¹/₁₆in. (Christie's)

$40,250

A cream plastic and brass-lacquered alto saxophone, by Grafton, No. 10169, in the original case. (Christie's)

$1,755

A double action harp, by Sebastian Erard, No. 4842, the reeded column surmounted by caryatids, with an acanthus molded base, 8 pedals. (Christie's)

$1,745

Coleman Hawkins, a Selmer Mark VI tenor saxophone serial No. 126522, gold-plated body and black hardshell case. (Christie's) $19,550

An English serpent (Schlangenrohr), circa 1830, by F. Pretty, the body of hard wood with overpainted light canvas or hide covering, overall length 30in. (Phillips)

$2,496

A fine violoncello, table by Antonio Stradivari, circa 1730, back, ribs and scroll the work of John Lott, the l.o.b. 29¹/₂in. (Christie's)

$464,500

An eight string metal mandolin, by Dobro, No. 6 183 M, the pierced front decorated with stars and moons, l.o.b. 13¹/₈in.
(Christie's) $964

A good Italian violin, Guarneri Model, circa 1760, one-piece back, l.o.b. 13⁷/₈in.
(Christie's)
                    $36,800

A brass bass trumpet, engraved with *GBno.7*, with three rotary valves, diameter of bell 5³/₄in.
(Christie's) $315

A carved ivory treble (alto) recorder, possibly South German, first half 18th century, 19³/₄in. long.
(Christie's)
                        $5,486

A silver soprano saxophone, stamped *V. Kohlert & Sohne/ Graslitz/ Czechoslovakia*, in a case.
(Christie's)
            $455

A decorative four string banjo, by Paramount, labeled *Wm. L. Lange/Art Craft*, the back marquetry inlaid with an urn full of flowers, 11³/₄in. diameter.
(Christie's)
            $2,388

A Boehm system silver-mounted grenadilla flute, by Boehm & Mendler, the sounding length 23¹¹/₁₆in., in a case.
(Christie's)
            $6,981

A good English violoncello, by Thomas Dodd, the two-piece back of medium curl, l.o.b. 29¹/₂in.
(Christie's)
            $26,450

An ivory netsuke of a tiger, his head turned and scratching his jaw with his hind leg, 18th century, 4.2cm. wide. (Christie's) $4,600

A wood netsuke of Okame, clambering on to the top of a huge mushroom, unsigned, early 19th century, 6.3cm. long. (Christie's) $2,277

An ivory netsuke, of a boy supporting the elongated head of Fukurokuju, signed *Masayuki*, 19th century, 4.7cm. wide. (Christie's) $1,288

A wood netsuke of Shoki and oni, Shoki standing holding a scroll in one hand and holding oni by his head, late 18th century, 8.5cm. high. (Christie's) $2,392

A round yamagane netsuke, with stylized aoi (hollyhock) leaves, the himotoshi ringed with the silvered metal, unsigned, 19th century, 4.8cm. diameter. (Christie's) $759

An ivory netsuke, of a half naked woman, a piece of cloth around her shoulder inlaid in aogai, her eyes in horn and the comb in tortoise shell, unsigned, late 18th/early 19th century, 4.8cm. high. (Christie's) $2,371

An ivory netsuke of two musicians, one with a tsutsumi drum, the other holding a fan, signed *Shuraku saku*, late 19th century, 4.5cm. (Christie's) $1,472

A wood netsuke, modeled as two tsuba, one round and and the other square with canted corners, the latter engraved and inlaid with willow branches, an insect cage and a butterfly, unsigned, 19th century, 5.8cm. wide. (Christie's) $949

A wood netsuke of a tiger, seated and his head turned to the left, the claws boldly carved, 19th century, 4cm. high. (Christie's) $1,472

A russet and iron netsuke, with a russet iron wasp perched on a coral branch, 19th century, 5.8cm. wide.
(Christie's) $2,846

An ivory netsuke of mushrooms, signed *Masakzu*, late 18th/early 19th century, 4cm.
(Christie's) $1,097

An ivory netsuke of a grazing horse, standing with its head bowed, 18th century, 5.8cm. high.
(Christie's) $1,463

An ivory netsuke of a tigress by Tomotada, seated licking her raised paw, her cub lies at her feet, signed, late 18th century, 4cm. high.
(Christie's) $14,720

A wood netsuke of Okame, seated with her one knee raised and holding a large wooden pestle, unsigned, 19th century, 3.3cm. high.
(Christie's) $1,139

An ivory netsuke of a man on a large parcel from which tentacles of an octopus are reaching out to him, with signature *Goju-ni sai Mitsuhiro to*, 19th century, 4.5cm. wide.
(Christie's) $3,226

An ivory netsuke of kirin, seated with one foreleg slightly raised and looking up, with signature *Masatomo*, 18th century, 6.3cm. high.
(Christie's) $3,128

An ebony netsuke of a Portuguese, trying to lift a stone, 18th century, 6.5cm. wide.
(Christie's) $2,944

An ivory netsuke of an intoxicated shojo by Yasuyuki, decorated in horn, mother-of-pearl and dyed ivory, signed on a tablet *Yasuyuki*, 20th century, 5.3cm. high.
(Christie's) $2,467

Rudolf Nureyev, a black and white poster of a young Rudolf Nureyev, signed in the top left hand corner in black ballpoint pen, 23¹/₃ x 16¹/₄in.
(Bonhams) $129

Costume for Swan Lake, Act III, Prince Siegfried, 1963 production, tunic of black velvet with epaulettes bound with gold braid, with false shirt.
(Christie's) $29,900

A diamond and gold stick pin, designed as the initial 'R' set with circular-cut diamonds, mounted in gold.
(Christie's) $5,980

Costume for Don Quixote, Act III, Basilio, 1979 production, jacket of yellow wool brocaded in gold lace trimmed with bands of green and gold brocade.
(Christie's) $36,800

Costume for Don Quixote, Act I, Basilio, 1966 production, a bolero of pink ribbed silk trimmed with bands of orange and gold brocade.
(Christie's) $3,220

Costume for The Sleeping Beauty, Act II, Prince Florimond, 1966 production, tunic of pale green silk applied with lace flowers.
(Christie's) $28,750

Daily Mail News Chronicle, London, Saturday June 17, 1961, headline: Nijinsky shouts: I want to be free. SOVIET STAR FLEES.
(Christie's) $863

Costume for Raymonda, Act III, Jean de Brienne, 1972 production, tunic of cloth of gold trimmed with black satin.
(Christie's) $17,250

Richard Avedon, Rudolf Nureyev, gelatin silver print, 1962, signed, dated in ink on reverse, approximately 13¹/₂ x 10¹/₂in.
(Christie's) $4,830

Assorted Nureyev ephemera, including: several personal handwritten letters to Nureyev, a card from Imelda Marcos and an autographed black and white photograph.
(Christie's) $2,300

Headdress for L'Après-Midi d'un Faune, 1979 (?) production, gold and copper wool painted wig with curling horns.
(Christie's) $3,450

A pair of beige ballet slippers, soles stamped with the size 7EEE and inscribed with Nureyev's name.
(Christie's) $6,325

An emerald and gilt-metal neck ornament, designed as a filigree gilt-metal Imperial double-headed eagle set with rectangular-cut emeralds.
(Christie's) $5,175

Costume for Giselle, Act I, Prince Albrecht, 1960 production, tunic of fawn stockinette piped in brown wool with false shirt.
(Christie's) $51,750

Doctorate vestments and Butler University commemorative photo album, worn on the occasion of Nureyev's receiving his Doctorate of Fine Arts in 1988.
(Christie's) $575

Harlequin costume for Petrushka comprising hat, white blouse and orange and yellow breeches.
(Christie's) $2,760

Costume for Les Sylphides, 1932 production, tunic of black velvet with full sleeve shirt and collar of white silk.
(Christie's) $25,300

Richard Avedon, Rudolf Nureyev, gelatin silver print, 1962, approximately $13^1/_2$ x $10^1/_2$in.
(Christie's) $2,070

White Star Line Southampton-Cherbourg-New York, double royal.
(Onslow's) $480

Willem F. Ten Broek, Holland-America Line, 1936, lithograph printed in colors on wove paper, printed by Joh. Enschede en Zonen, Harlem, $23^9/_{16}$ x $36^3/_4$in.
(Butterfield & Butterfield) $862

Odin Rosenvinge, Allan Line To and From Canada, double royal.
(Onslow's) $460

John Gilroy, They Do Look After You On P&O Cruises, double royal.
(Onslow's) $1,520

Brochure, White Star Line The World's Largest and Finest Steamer New Triple Screw SS Olympic, circa 1911.
(Onslow's) $290

Tom Purvis, Canadian Pacific Happy Cruises, 1937, double royal.
(Onslow's) $1,120

Cunard White Star Queen Mary Souvenir Number of the Shipbuilder and Marine Engine Builder, June 1936.
(Onslow's) $100

A Stonier & Co. White Star Line plate, with company burgee, turquoise brown decoration.
(Onslow's) $350

Sandy Hook, Mediterranean Cruises by Messageries Maritimes, on linen, 59 x 39cm.
(Onslow's) $360

Kenneth D. Shoesmith, Canadian Pacific To Canada and USA Great Southern Railways.
(Onslow's) $1,280

A color folding leaflet for the White Star Line Triple Screw RMS Olympic, circa 1920.
(Onslow's) $180

Paul Colin, Cie Gle Transatlantique French Line, on linen, 61 x 40cm.
(Onslow's) $370

White Star Line Mediterranean Service Royal and United States Mail Steamers, double royal, on linen.
(Onslow's) $370

Inman Line Royal and United States Mail Steamers, hanging laminated chromo-lithograph on tin, 69 x 54cm., circa 1890.
(Onslow's) $2,400

Leonard Padden, White Star West Indies Azores and The Spanish Main by Luxury Motor Liner Britannic, double royal.
(Onslow's) $580

CGT Normandie Souvenir Number of the Shipbuilder and Marine Engine Builder, June 1935.
(Onslow's) $240

Odin Rosenvinge, Canada by The Cunard Line, double royal.
(Onslow's) $400

Norman Wilkinson, Blue Star Line De-Luxe Mail Service to South America, double royal.
(Onslow's) $350

Children's toy projector, an Ensign Ltd Mickey Mouse magic lantern and slides, in maker's box.
(Christie's) $142

A metal-body kaleidoscope with turned-wood eyepiece, internally-contained glass specimen rods (lacks stand).
(Christie's) $347

British Mutoscope & Biograph Co. Ltd., London, a wood-body Kinora viewer with hand-crank, metal viewing hood and maker's label.
(Christie's) $980

London Stereoscopic Co., London, a 12-inch diameter Wheel of Life zoetrope with picture disks, instructions for use and List of Designs for the Wheel of Life.
(Christie's) $2,302

A collapsible Kinora viewer with metal body-section, single lens, hand-cranked mechanism, on a wood base with one Kinora reel.
(Christie's) $913

J. Carpentier, Paris, a 35mm. hand-cranked Cinématographe Lumière projection mechanism no. H4225 with hand-crank, on a wood base.
(Christie's) $6,415

Painted metal and brass mounted magic lantern, (electrically fitted).
(G. A. Key) $159

An IMPUU stereo Elmar 5cm. f/3.5 projection lens.
(Christie's) $1,643

Walnut and ebonized and metal 3-D viewer, English, late 19th century.
(G. A. Key) $114

A Kinora Animated viewer, with embossed black metal viewing hood, on a ratcheted oak plinth, together with three picture reels. (Spencer's) **$551**

Topographical panorama, a 4$^{1}/_{4}$-inch wide engraved panorama, backed on linen, in wood holder, mid 19th century. (Christie's) **$708**

A pair of metal-body dissolving lanterns, each with two internal colored filters and a Darlot, Paris lens. (Christie's) **$570**

An early 19th century black enameled tinplate 'Wheel of Life' (Zoetrope), the cylindrical drum sitting in a wrythen fluted cylindrical pillar, 29cm. diameter. (Spencer's) **$398**

E. Reynauld, Paris, a wood-body Le Praxinoscope Théatre with removable screen, a quantity of picture strips and label *The Praxinoscope. New Optical Toy.* (Christie's) **$1,278**

A wood-body Cosmorama-pattern stereoscope with hinged top, rack and pinion focusing lens section and a pair of viewing lenses. (Christie's) **$1,515**

Newton & Co., London, a lacquered-brass patent projecting microscope with rack and pinion focusing. (Christie's) **$475**

An 18th-century lignum vitae scioptic ball, 3$^{1}/_{4}$in. diameter. (Christie's) **$1,370**

A wood-body stereo-graphoscope with internal drawer and a quantity of photographs, in a wood box. (Christie's) **$511**

A Fantascope phenakistiscope, comprising seven 10in. diameter slotted disks, six colored and one monochrome.
(Christie's) **$2,350**

Peep view, a 5-part peep view, mounted in a later display box, 19 x 16 x 28.5cm.
(Christie's) **$540**

A wood-body peep box with single-meniscus viewing lens, colored lithographic sheets depicting trees, animals and railway subjects, mid 19th century.
(Christie's) **$2,125**

A floor-standing wood-body peep box, the front with two 4¹/₂in. viewing lenses, 30in. wide, probably late 18th century.
(Christie's) **$1,170**

A wood-body Kinora viewer with hand-crank, metal viewing hood and seven Kinora reels.
(Christie's) **$1,080**

A wood-body zograscope viewer with decorative cross-banded inlay, 5¹/₂ x 7¹/₂in. mirror and 4in. diameter lens, late 18th century.
(Christie's) **$548**

Smith, Beck & Beck, London, mahogany-body Achromatic Stereoscope no. 1247 with lacquered-brass fittings.
(Christie's) **$720**

Suzuki Optical Co., Tokyo, a metal-body Camera Lite in case with film cassettes, in maker's box.
(Christie's) **$1,450**

A wood-body Graphotrope photograph viewer, the lid with paper label *Manufactured by Wm. Walker & Co., New Haven.*
(Christie's) **$90**

Éclair, Paris, a 16–35 Caméflex Standard cinematographic camera with 35mm. and 16mm. film gates.
(Christie's) $2,000

A 'Kinora' viewer, English, circa 1910, with hand-turned mechanism, black viewing hood and oak frame.
(Bonhams) $500

Houghtons Ltd., London, a Ticka camera, viewfinder, instruction booklets and Ticka film in box, in maker's presentation box.
(Christie's) $744

Jean Schoenner, Germany, a metal-body upright cylinder lantern with chimney, lens, integral spirit burner, and slides.
(Christie's) $540

Georg Carette, Nurnberg, a metal-body cinematographic lantern with hand-crank, chimney, lens, film holder and spirit burner.
(Christie's) $216

A gilt-metal photograph viewing ball, each half with six 1¼in. diameter apertures and one 2¼in. diameter, circa 1870.
(Christie's) $720

A red-painted metal-body Mutoscope viewer No. AB1619 with hand-crank, coin-op mechanism.
(Christie's) $2,600

A wood-body hand-held Claudet-pattern stereoscope with brass-bound dividing viewing lenses and hinged top with foil mirror.
(Christie's) $290

Parker, an experimental metallic oxblood 45, with medium nib, American, circa 1970.
(Bonhams) $86

Parker, a limited edition R.M.S. Queen Elizabeth 75 No. 2022/5000, with box, certificate and 75
leaflet with card covers, American, circa 1974.
(Bonhams) $905

W.V.S. Ltd., a silver filigree overlaid safety pen, with replaced nib, English, 1917.
(Bonhams) $234

Parker, a mother-of-pearl barrel taper cap, with two gold plated bands of flower design and
Parker Fountain Pen No. 2 nib with keyhole vent, Lucky Curve feed, American, circa 1898–1905.
(Bonhams) $1,873

Parker, a 9ct. gold 61 Fine Barley, converter version, with box, English, 1972.
(Bonhams) $374

Parker: a rare yellow metal overlay Jack-Knife safety button filler, engraved with scroll bands,
with a no. 2 nib.
(Christie's) $710

Mont Blanc, a 30 red Masterpiece, with 4810 nib, German, circa 1930.
(Bonhams) $562

Namiki: a Dunhill Namiki Maki-E lacquer lever fill pen, decorated with a wild fowl flying past
reeds, signed in the lacquer, with Dunhill Namiki no. 6 nib.
(Christie's) $3,119

Wahl Eversharp, a burgundy lined Doric lever-filler, with Eversharp nib, American, circa 1932.
(Bonhams) $234

Garrard: a gold slide action pencil, engraved with presentation inscription *From H R H Prince
Alfred to T Michell, August 1862*, in fitted Garrard case.
(Christie's) $1,337

Mont Blanc, a green marble 246, with No. 6 nib, Danish, 1940's.
(Bonhams) $250

Parker, an 18ct. gold 51 pen, ballpoint and clutch pencil trio set, in leather Parker trio box,
English, 1956 and 1959–60.
(Bonhams) $2,340

Parker, a black/pearl Deluxe Duofold Juniorette, with Duofold Deluxe nib, American, circa 1930.
(Bonhams) $187

Waterman: a rare 504 yellow metal 'Repousse' overlay eyedropper, with Waterman no. 4 nib,
stamped *14kt*.
(Christie's) $9,266

Parker, a pearl/green Duofold Junior, with Duofold Deluxe nib, American, circa 1931.
(Bonhams) $140

Mordan, a butter knife pencil, with feather scrolled pistol butt handle, telescopic mechanism
extending the pencil through the handle.
(Bonhams) $452

Parker: a Cordovan brown 51 piston filler with Lustraloy cap, in presentation box.
(Christie's) $160

Namiki: a Maki-E lacquer safety pen, decorated with a Samurai helmet amongst falling leaves,
with Namiki nib.
(Christie's) $2,138

S. Mordan: a gold slide action pen, pencil and paperknife stamped *S. Mordan & Co.*
(Christie's) $285

Mabie Todd, a Swan yellow metal overlay over/under-fed eyedropper, the overlay decorated with
scrolling foliage.
(Christie's) $321

Waterman, a 14S Night and Day filigree, with early threaded turning knob and No. 4 nib, American, French factory overlay circa 1915–20.
(Bonhams) $468

Parker, a silver pearl oversize Vacumatic, with two-color Arrow nib, Canadian, circa 1935.
(Bonhams) $312

Sheaffer, a brown striped Autograph Triumph, with 14ct. clip and band and two-color wrap-around nib, American, circa 1940.
(Bonhams) $133

Mont Blanc, a black 25 Masterpiece, with 4810 nib, German, 1930's.
(Bonhams) $265

Parker, a Mandarin Streamlined Lucky Curve Senior, with Duofold Pen nib, American, circa 1929/30.
(Bonhams) $905

Pullman, a Lapis Pullman automatic pen, with Pullman nib, English, 1930's.
(Bonhams) $1,560

Aiken Lambert, a gold plated eyedropper, with snail design and No. 3 nib, American, circa 1900–10.
(Bonhams) $234

Parker, a green/pearl Duofold Junior pencil, American, circa 1931.
(Bonhams) $94

Salz Brothers, a black eyedropper pen, with high relief pierced rolled gold overlay and No. 4 nib, American, circa 1910.
(Bonhams) $172

Waterman, a silver 402 eyedropper, with early No. 2 nib, English, 1911.
(Bonhams) $312

Dunhill Namiki, a maki-e lacquer Balance, decorated with dragonflies among reeds, No. 3 Dunhill Namiki nib with Alfred Dunhill box, Japanese, Taisho-Showa period, circa 1930. (Bonhams) $1,560

Mont Blanc, a pearl/black Lined III B-EF, with 'b' nib, German, 1930's. (Bonhams) $2,340

Pilot, a maki-e lacquer Balance, decorated with the 'moonscape' design, Red Seal signature, Platinum 3 nib, Japanese, Showa period, 1930's. (Bonhams) $2,964

Mont Blanc, a 25 gray-green Masterpiece, with 4810 nib, Danish, 1940's. (Bonhams) $437

Mabie Todd, a gold plated leverless pen and pencil set, with No. 3 nib and Swan box, English, circa 1935. (Bonhams) $468

Waterman, a 54 Woodgrain, with two bands and No. 4 nib, American/French, circa 1920. (Bonhams) $172

Sheaffer, a gray striped lever-filling Triumph pen and pencil set, with Sheaffer Lifetime two-color nib, American, circa 1942. (Bonhams) $117

Mont Blanc, a red 53 pencil, German, 1920's/30's. (Bonhams) $47

Namiki, a maki-e lacquer pen, decorated with birds in a bush, with Red Seal signature, Namiki 3 nib, Japanese, Taisho-Showa period, late 1920's. (Bonhams) $546

Waterman, an 0552½ L.E.C. 'Pansy Panel', with No. 2 nib and box, American, 1920's. (Bonhams) $406

A pewter pitcher, 19th century, baluster form with scroll handle, 5³/₄in. high. (Christie's) $460

A Kayserzinn pewter tea service, each piece cast in relief with cartouches of stylized foliage, hot water pot 25cm. high. (Christie's) $266

A pewter porringer, Samuel Hamlin, 1746–1801, Providence, Rhode Island, circular with everted brim and curved sides, 5¹/₄in. diameter. (Christie's) $978

A pewter plate, Thomas D. Boardman, 1784–1873, Hartford, Connecticut, circular with single reed brim, 7⁷/₈in. diameter. (Christie's) $920

Pewter square tea caddy, the body decorated in the Art Nouveau manner with stylized flowers etc., 5in. high. (G. A. Key) $291

A pewter basin, Josiah Danforth, 1803–1872, Middletown, Connecticut, 1825–1837, circular with single bead rim, 8in. diameter. (Christie's) $633

A pewter cann, Parks Boyd, 1771/72–1819, Philadelphia, 1795–1819, tapering cylindrical, with a scroll handle, 4¹/₄in. high. (Christie's) $6,670

A pewter inkwell modeled as an owl, with inset glass eyes, Continental, late 19th century, 7¹/₄in. high. (Christie's) $318

A WMF silvered pewter-shaped oval dressing table tray, depicting a young woman with flowing hair, 31.5cm. wide. (Bearne's) $734

A W.M.F. silvered pewter jardinière, the frame and handles pierced and cast in relief with Art Nouveau cartouches of foliage, 30.5cm. long.
(Christie's) $213

A W.M.F. trefoil dish, silvered pewter, the three triangular bowls each cast in low relief with Darmstadt motifs, 27cm. high.
(Christie's) $496

Gerhardi & Cie, tea and coffee service with tray, circa 1900, comprising: teapot, coffee pot, sugar bowl and cover, milk jug and tray, pewter, with repoussé decoration.
(Sotheby's) $1,666

A pewter fluid lamp, William Calder, 1792–1856, Providence, Rhode Island, with double capped wicks above an inverted tapering cylindrical font, 4^1/$_2$in. high.
(Christie's) $437

Continental pewter plate, 18th century, engraved decoration depicting a feast, 13in. diameter.
(Skinner) $1,035

A pewter chalice, Timothy Brigden, 1774–1819, Albany, New York, with tapering cylindrical cup over a baluster stem, Laughlin touch 519, 8^7/$_8$in. high.
(Christie's) $4,600

W.M.F., wine jug, No. 138D, circa 1900, Britannia metal with antique silver finish, the body decorated with low relief flowers and leaves, mark for 1880–1925 manufacture, 39cm.
(Sotheby's) $3,310

A pewter teapot, George Richardson, 1782–1848, Boston, pear shaped with hinged domed lid, and scroll handle, 8in. high.
(Christie's) $1,035

A James I pewter lidded flagon, the hinged bun cover with a turned finial, the cylindrical body on a skirt foot, 13in. high.
(Woolley & Wallis)
                             $4,199

Duplex disk phonograph, Duplex Phonograph Co., Chicago, Illinois, with quarter-applied colonettes, turntable and two cast-metal and brass horns. (Butterfield & Butterfield) $2,070

An Edison red Gem phonograph, Model D, No. 319799D, with Combination gearing, K reproducer and two-piece maroon Fireside horn with part crane. (Christie's) $1,328

An Edison Standard Phonograph, in an oak case, numbered S58081, with aluminium turned horn and approximately twenty four cylinders. (Spencer's) $413

An Edison Phonograph, the small brass horn set with an oval black enameled plaque *Made by Powell & Hammer Ltd Birmingham*, 13in. wide. (Spencer's) $520

Ferry lamp phonograph, Burns Pollack Electrical Manufacturing Co., Indiana Harbor, Indiana, circa 1915, the turntable contained in an octagonal fabric-covered tasseled bowl. (Butterfield & Butterfield) $3,737

An Edison Opera phonograph, Model A, No. 2851, with mahogany Music Master horn, in mahogany case with oxidized handles. (Christie's) $6,198

Edison concert phonograph, Thomas A. Edison, Orange, New Jersey, circa 1899, together with one cylinder. (Butterfield & Butterfield) $3,162

An Edison Standard Phonograph, with flared octagonal black tinplate horn with gilt lines, together with fifty three records. (Spencer's) $612

An Edison fireside phonograph model A, American, circa 1909, No. 115709 with No. 10 Cygnet horn and approximately one hundred cylinders. (Bonhams) $1,360

Decorative portrait of a girl, gelatin silver print, 7½ x 5½in., mounted on card, decorative gilt frame.
(Christie's) $250

William Henry Fox Talbot, The Woodcutters, circa 1841–1843, calotype, 5⅞ x 8⅛in., mounted on card with ink wash border.
(Christie's) $5,589

William Henry Fox Talbot (1800–77), Leaf study, circa 1839, photogenic drawing negative, possibly salt-fixed, 7³/₁₆ x 4⅜in., mounted on card, inscribed in ink on mount.
(Christie's) $32,453

Herb Ritts, Djimon (three-quarter nude), Hollywood, 1989, platinum print, image size 22¼ x 19in.
(Christie's) $1,583

Frederick Henry Evans (1853–1943), Aubrey Beardsley, 1894, two portraits comprising a platinum print, 5⅜ x 3⅞in. and a photogravure, 4⅞ x 3¾in.
(Christie's) $20,493

Norman Parkinson, Imperial Airways Flying Boat, 1939, printed later, gelatin-silver print, 40 x 30cm., signed in pencil.
(Bonhams) $630

Japanese, Portrait of a Japanese man, seated holding an umbrella, circa 1860s, ambrotype, 3¼ x 2½in., in original balsa-wood case.
(Christie's) $1,582

William Henry Fox Talbot, Lace, 1845 or earlier, photogenic drawing negative, 6⅞ x 8¾in., mounted on card.
(Christie's) $10,247

Francis Frith & Co., English life, 1880's–1910, one hundred and thirty-four prints, mostly 15 x 20cm., includes villages, towns and cities.
(Bonhams) $600

Herbert List, Ritti, Nordsee (North Sea), Germany, 1933 printed 1988, gelatin silver print, image size 11⅛ x 9¼in., photographer's monogram blindstamp in margin.
(Christie's) $838

John Benton-Harris, 'Be kind to your husband day', May 1977, printed later, gelatin silver print, 12½ x 8¼in., signed, dated and inscribed in pencil on verso.
(Christie's) $763

John K. Hillers, 'Moki hairdresser', circa 1880, albumen print, 9 x 7¼in., signed and titled in the negative, mounted on gray card with decorative border.
(Christie's) $2,100

American, Portrait of a Chinese boy, seated holding a fan and scroll, late 1860s–early 1870s, sixth-plate tintype, in modern custom-made balsa-wood case.
(Christie's) $1,024

Frank Meadow Sutcliffe, 'In Puris Naturabilis'; The Storm family of Robin Hood's Bay, late 19th century, printed early 1900s, two warm-toned matt gelatin silver prints, 9¾ x 11¼in. and 9 x 11¼in.
(Christie's) $1,304

British, John T. Campbell, Feb. 1858, half-plate ambrotype, mounted as oval, gilt-metal surround, inscribed in pencil on verso.
(Christie's) $241

André Kertész (1894–1985), Circus Budapest, 1920, printed later, gelatin silver print, 9¾ x 7¾in., dated and inscribed *Kertész* in pencil.
(Christie's) $1,396

Alvin Langdon Coburn (1882–1966), St. Paul's Cathedral from Ludgate Circus, 1905, large-format photogravure, 15⅛ x 11¼in., matted, framed.
(Christie's) $5,962

?Stratford, Young Cantonese girl in American dress, 1850s–60s, sixth-plate ambrotype, lightly hand-tinted, oval gilt-metal mount.
(Christie's) $837

Anonymous, possibly Baron Von Stillfried, Semi-nude Japanese lady, late 1870s or 1880s, albumen print, 9 x 7¹/₄in., lightly hand-tinted, mounted on paper, matted.
(Christie's)   **$558**

Eve Arnold (b. 1913), 'Studying lines, Marilyn Monroe on location in Nevada for the Misfits, 1960', printed later, gelatin silver print, 15¹/₂ x 10¹/₄in.
(Christie's)   **$1,396**

Man Ray, Cecil Beaton, F. S. Lincoln and others, Portraits of Helena Rubinstein, early 1900s–circa 1940s, thirty-eight gelatin silver prints, sizes approx. 14 x 11in. to 7¹/₂ x 4¹/₄in.
(Christie's)   **$2,049**

Margaret Bourke-White (1904–1971), 'Plow Blades, Oliver Chilled Plow Company', 1930, warm-toned matt gelatin silver print, 13¹/₈ x 9¹/₄in.
(Christie's)   **$35,397**

Margaret Bourke-White, U.S.S. Akron, World's Largest Airship, 1931, warm-toned gelatin silver print on matt textured paper, 17¹/₄ x 23in., signed in ink on recto.
(Christie's)   **$3,353**

Richard Avedon, 'Jeanette-Chanel, 1958', gelatin silver print, 12³/₄ x 10¹/₂in., flush-mounted on card, signed and dated *Avedon 59*.
(Christie's)   **$2,236**

Lai Chong (Shanghai), General Ko-Lin, Sept. 1853, daguerreotype, 2¹/₂ x 1³/₄in., the robes and accessories hand-tinted, gilt card mount.
(Christie's)   **$10,246**

William Wegman (b. 1935), 'Address Stand, '89', unique polaroid polacolor II print, image size 26 x 21in., signed, titled and dated.
(Christie's)   **$4,844**

Brassaï (1899–1984), 'Couple fâché! (Quarrel), 1932', printed later, gelatin silver print, 10⁷/₈ x 8³/₈in., signed, titled, dated, and annotated.
(Christie's)   **$1,583**

Herb Ritts (b. 1952), 'Fred with Tires, Hollywood', from Bodyshop series, 1984, toned gelatin silver print, image size 22¹/₂ x 18¹/₄in.
(Christie's) $2,673

Lewis Carroll, 'Alexandra Rhoda ('Xie') Kitchin', 18 May 1874, albumen print, 4¹/₈ x 5⁷/₈in., sitter's family tree in pencil on verso.
(Christie's) $3,054

Two gentlemen in military uniforms embracing, 1850s, quarter-plate daguerreotype, in ebonized wood and plaster frame, French.
(Christie's) $955

Brassaï [Gyula Halász] (1899–1984), 'Jeune couple habillé d'un seul complet au bal du Magic-City', circa 1931, gelatin silver print, 11⁵/₈ x 8⁷/₈in., signed in pencil.
(Christie's) $3,436

Death portrait of a gentleman, 1850s, sixth-plate daguerreotype, gilt mount, in folding morocco case, American.
(Christie's) $611

Dennis Stock, Audrey Hepburn on 'Sabrina Affair' set, 1953 printed 1994, gelatin silver print, image size 13¹/₄ x 9in., signed and inscribed in pencil *Audrey Hepburn. Sabrina. 1953* on verso.
(Christie's) $1,336

Lewis Carroll [Charles Lutwidge Dodgson] (1832–98), Xie Kitchin in white hat and coat, circa 1873, albumen print, 5⁵/₈ x 4in.
(Christie's) $2,100

Female nude reclining on a settee, 1850s, sixth-plate daguerreotype, in folding morocco case with original red silk lining, French.
(Christie's) $4,199

Angus McBean (1904–90), Flora Robson, London, 1938, gelatin silver print, 14³/₄ x 11¹/₂in., mounted on card, signed in pencil on mount.
(Christie's) $955

Peter Henry Emerson (1856–1936), 'Setting up the bow-net', 1886, platinum print, 10³/₈ x 8⁵/₈in., mounted on card, matted. (Christie's) $1,336

E. J. C. Puyo, Sacred Song, late 1890s, albumen print, 6⁵/₈ x 8⁷/₈in., mounted on gray card, matted. (Christie's) $1,145

Rudolph Koppitz (1884–1936), Study of movement, 1933, photogravure, 9³/₈ x 6³/₄in., signed on recto, mounted on card. (Christie's) $2,291

Portrait of a student holding a sextant, circa 1850s, sixth-plate daguerreotype, lightly hand-tinted, cartouche-shaped gilt mount, in folding case, American. (Christie's) $858

John Deakin (1912–1972), portrait of John Minton, circa 1952, gelatin silver print, 14¹/₂ x 11³/₄in., mounted on card, matted; with *The Independent Magazine*, 11 May 1991 where this portrait was used as front cover illustration. (Christie's) $3,245

Irving Penn (b. 1917), Alfred Hitchcock, New York, May 23, 1947 printed 1948, gelatin silver contact print, 9⁵/₈ x 7³/₈in., signed, titled, dated, and numbered *21*. (Christie's) $3,627

Bill Brandt, Bais des Anges, France, 1959, printed mid 1970s, gelatin silver print, 13 x 11¹/₂in., mounted on card, signed in ink on verso. (Christie's) $3,436

Auguste Belloc (d. circa 1867), female nude sitting on a bed, 1850s–60s, salt print and albumen print, 8¹/₄ x 6¹/₄in. and 8 x 6¹/₈in. (Christie's) $3,245

Jacques-Henri Lartigue, Zissou in rubber ring, circa 1910, printed later, gelatin silver print, 11³/₄ x 9³/₈in., signed on recto, matted. (Christie's) $1,718

Art Deco ivory lacquer baby grand piano, America, circa 1937, made by Joseph Adnet, Gaveau, Paris, 52in. long.
(Skinner) $2,990

M. H. Baillie-Scott for John Broadwood & Sons, 'Manxman' piano, circa 1900, the back panel inset with enameled floral motifs, 135cm. wide.
(Sotheby's) $12,110

A Bluthner boudoir grand piano, No. 68195, the rosewood case on tapering turned and fluted legs.
(Bearne's) $2,268

A baby grand piano by J. & J. Hopkinson, London, No. 80012, the rosewood-veneered case on fluted and acanthus-carved tapering square legs, 5ft. 2in.
(Bearne's) $1,101

A mahogany upright piano, the front with relief decor of a sunrise, marked D. Hansson, Lund, 158cm. wide.
(Stockholms Auktionsverk) $2,027

A painted and giltwood clavichord decorated with polychrome floral swags, the interior with an allegory of Music, 18th century, 200cm. long.
(Finarte) $16,452

A Bluthner boudoir grand piano, No. 83556, the ebonized case on tapering square legs, 5ft. 8in.
(Bearne's) $1,848

An Art Nouveau mahogany upright piano by C. Bechstein of Berlin, the iron frame overstrung with rail blind fret fascia backed by gold cloth.
(Spencer's) $1,148

An English cased Steinway boudoir grand piano, circa 1911, the walnut case inlaid with eclectic 17th century style foliage, 150cm. wide.
(Sotheby's) $38,399

Noah Seaman (fl. 1724–1741), King George II, facing right in red coat, enamel, gilt-metal frame, oval, 1⁷/₈in. high. (Christie's) $2,668

Christian Friedrich Zincke (1683/4–1767), a lady, in white dress with white underslip, enamel, oval, 2³/₈in. high. (Christie's) $3,380

Henry Edridge (1769–1821), a gentleman, facing right in moss-colored coat and cream waistcoat, oval, 2¹/₈in. high. (Christie's) $1,245

Philip Jean (1755–1802), a gentleman, in blue coat with gold buttons, frilled white cravat, gold frame with blue glass borders, oval, 1³/₄in. high. (Christie's) $2,846

English School, circa 1655 after Samuel Cooper (1609–1672), Oliver Cromwell, facing right in armor, lawn collar, oval, 1⁵/₈in. high. (Christie's) $6,405

Richard Cosway, R.A. (1742–1821), a child, facing right in white shirt with frilled collar, signed and dated 1789, oval, 2⁵/₈in. high. (Christie's) $7,472

English School, 19th century, a lady in period dress, in giltmetal mount, on ivory, oval, 15cm. high. (Finarte) $1,172

English School, circa 1800, an eye with a blue iris, gilt-metal frame mounted as a stick pin, oval, ⁷/₈in. high. (Christie's) $1,156

John Smart (1742–1811), a gentleman, in blue-lined red coat, signed with initials and dated 1774, oval, 1¹/₂in. high. (Christie's) $16,011

Abraham Daniel (died 1806), a lady, in white dress with frilled neckline, gold frame, oval, 2³/₄in. high.
(Christie's) $978

George Engleheart (1750–1829), a gentleman, in blue coat, white waistcoat and cravat, signed, oval, 3¹/₂in. high.
(Christie's) $3,380

Nathaniel Plimer (1757–1822), a lady, in brown dress with fichu, signed with initials and dated *1786*, oval, 2in. high.
(Christie's) $1,957

Henry Bone, R.A. (1755–1834), after John Smart (1742–1811), John Clements, in blue coat, enamel, signed and dated *January 1818*, oval, 3in. high.
(Christie's) $3,024

Richard Crosse (1742–1810), a gentleman, in scarlet coat and cream waistcoat, gold frame with split-pearl border, oval, 1³/₈in. high.
(Christie's) $2,313

Peter Paillou (died after 1820), a gentleman, in blue coat, white waistcoat and frilled cravat, signed and dated *1804*, oval, 2³/₄in. high.
(Christie's) $1,334

Christian Friedrich Zincke (1683/4–1767), a gentleman, facing right in gray coat, white cravat, enamel, gilt-metal mount, oval, 1³/₄in. high.
(Christie's) $1,689

Christian Friedrich Zincke (1683/4–1767), a lady, facing right in lace-bordered white dress, enamel, gold frame, oval, 1³/₄in. high.
(Christie's) $1,779

Jean Roughet, a nobleman, facing right in silver-embroidered scarlet coat and cream waistcoat, enamel, fitted fishskin case, oval, 1³/₄in. high.
(Christie's) $15,656

John Smart (1742–1821), a lady, in frilled white dress and yellow surcoat, signed with initials and dated *1785*, oval, 1⁷/₈in. high. (Christie's) $12,453

Sir William Charles Ross (1794–1860), a lady, in black dress, her fair hair dressed in ringlets, oval, 3³/₄in. high. (Christie's) $1,511

George Chinnery (1774–1852), Sir John Hadley D'Oyly, in gray coat, silver-gilt frame, oval, 3⁷/₈in. high. (Christie's) $6,049

J. Heughan (fl. circa 1800), a gentleman, in blue coat with black collar, signed, located York and dated (180)6, oval, 2¹/₂in. high. (Christie's) $1,423

Nicholas Hilliard (1547–1619), George Clifford, 3rd Earl of Cumberland, facing left in cut white doublet, on vellum backed with playing card, oval, 1³/₄in. high. (Christie's) $16,011

Edward Lobo Moira (1817–1887), Marie Evelyn Moreton, later Viscountess Byng of Vimy full face in white dress, oval, 4in. high. (Christie's) $11,564

English School, circa 1768, a gentleman, facing right, full bottomed powdered wig, signed with initials *J.S.* and dated *1768*, oval, 1¹/₂in. high. (Christie's) $463

Horace Hone (1754–1825), Mrs Maquay, in white dress with frilled collar and blue bodice, signed with initials and dated *1792*, oval, 2¹/₂in. high. (Christie's) $4,625

Samuel Cotes (1734–1818), a lady, facing right in décolleté pink dress, signed with initials and dated *1780*, oval, 3⁵/₈in. high. (Christie's) $1,957

English School, circa 1770, a lady, facing right in lace-bordered pink dress, gold frame, oval, 1¼in. high.
(Christie's) $1,689

John Smart (1742–1811), a young boy, full face in blue coat, signed with initials and dated 1777, oval, 1½in. high.
(Christie's) $3,202

Andrew Plimer (1763–1837), a lady, in white dress, white bandeau tied under her chin, oval, 2⅞in. high.
(Christie's) $3,024

Patrick McMoreland (1741–1809), a gentleman, facing right in brown coat and waistcoat, signed with initials, oval, 1½in. high.
(Christie's) $747

Samuel Shelley (1750–1808), two brothers, in red and blue coats respectively, holding their young sister in white dress, 3½in. diameter.
(Christie's) $1,067

School of Christian Friedrich Zincke (1683/4–1767), a lady, facing left in white dress with blue stole, enamel, gilt-metal mount, oval, 1⅝in. high.
(Christie's) $1,511

Henry Kirchoffer (circa 1781–1860), a gentleman, in black coat and frilled cravat, the reverse with initials GEEH, oval, 3⅛in. high.
(Christie's) $1,689

Henry Spicer (1743–1804), a gentleman, facing right in blue coat and waistcoat, enamel, gold frame with split-pearl border, oval, 1½in. high.
(Christie's) $1,511

Mrs Barou (fl. 1797–1801), Mr Campbell, facing right in black coat and white waistcoat, signed on the reverse, gold frame, oval, 3in. high.
(Christie's) $4,448

English School, circa 1720,
Prince James Francis Stuart, in
gilt-studded armor, oil on
copper, oval, 3¹/₈in. high.
(Christie's) $1,601

Reginald Easton (1807–1893),
Miss Jacqueline Isabel Loraine
as a child, holding a posy of
primroses, oval, 3¹/₂in. high.
(Christie's) $1,601

George Patten (1801–1865), a
gentleman, in blue coat with
black collar, gold frame, oval,
2¹/₂in. high.
(Christie's) $978

Horace Hone (1754–1825),
George Maquay, in blue coat,
white waistcoat and frilled
cravat, signed with initials and
dated 1785, oval, 2¹/₄in. high.
(Christie's) $1,957

John Wright (died 1820), Lady
Charlotte Jane Dundas, facing
left in brown dress, signed and
dated 1803, 5in. diameter.
(Christie's) $1,601

Irish School, circa 1790, a
gentleman, in black coat and
waistcoat, white cravat, the
reverse with gold initials JOC,
oval, 3in. high.
(Christie's) $1,032

Jean Roughet (1701–1758), a
noblewoman, facing left in blue
dress with white underslip,
enamel, gold frame, oval, 2³/₄in.
high.
(Christie's) $3,202

Rupert Barber (fl. 1736–1772), a
gentleman, facing left in gold-
bordered blue coat, enamel, gilt-
metal mount, oval, 1⁷/₈in. high.
(Christie's) $978

Henry Burch (born 1760), a
young girl, in white dress with
yellow sash, the reverse with
gold initials AC, hair border,
oval, 2¹/₂in. high.
(Christie's) $1,334

John James Audubon (After), American
Woodcock, hand colored etching, engraving
and aquatint, by R. Havell, 1835, plate 374 x
519mm.
(Sotheby's) $4,887

Currier and Ives (Publishers), 'Wooding Up' on
the Mississippi, hand colored lithograph, with
touches of gum arabic, 1863, image 454 x
703mm.
(Sotheby's) $9,200

N. Currier (Publisher), American Winter Sports.
Trout Fishing 'On Chateaugay Lake', hand
colored lithograph, with touches of gum, arabic,
1856, after the painting by Arthur F. Tait, image
453 x 652mm.
(Sotheby's) $5,750

Currier and Ives (Publishers), Winter Morning,
hand colored lithograph, 1861, F.F. Palmer
del., image 287 x 388mm.
(Sotheby's) $1,495

Currier and Ives (Publishers), American Express
Train, hand colored lithograph, with touches of
gum arabic, a fresh impression, 1864, 451 x
705mm.
(Sotheby's) $12,650

John James Audubon (After), Great Northern
Diver or Loon, hand colored engraving, etching
and aquatint, by R. Havell, 1836, sheet 668 x
1003mm.
(Sotheby's) $18,400

John James Audubon (After), White Heron, hand colored engraving, etching and aquatint, 1837, by R. Havell, sheet 637 x 962mm. (Sotheby's) **$14,950**

John James Audubon (After), Roseate Spoonbill, hand colored engraving, etching and aquatint, 1836, by R. Havell, sheet 650 x 965mm. (Sotheby's) **$26,450**

John James Audubon (After), Buffel-headed Duck, hand colored etching, engraving and aquatint, by R. Havell, 1836, plate 374 x 520mm. (Sotheby's) **$13,800**

John James Audubon (After), Canada Lynx, hand colored lithograph, by J.T. Bowen, Philadelphia, 1843, sheet 534 x 673mm. (Sotheby's) **$3,737**

Currier and Ives (Publishers), The Life of a Fireman. The Metropolitan System, hand colored lithograph, with touches of gum arabic 1866, after John Cameron, image 437 x 671mm. (Sotheby's) **$2,587**

N. Currier (Publisher), High Pressure Steamboat Mayflower, First Class Packet between St. Louis and New Orleans on the Mississippi River, hand colored lithograph, 1855, image 414 x 712mm. (Sotheby's) **$2,530**

'Leda and the Swan' by Louis Icart, etching and drypoint, framed and glazed, circa 1934, 52 x 79cm. plate size.
(Christie's) $6,359

Currier and Ives, Publishers, Life of a Hunter. 'A tight fix.', after A. F. Tait, lithograph with hand-coloring and touches of gum arabic, 1861 on wove paper, 18³/₄ x 27in.
(Christie's) $34,500

Louis Icart, Melody Hour (H. C. & I. 437), 1934, etching and aquatint printed in colors with touches of hand-coloring on wove paper, signed in pencil, with the artist's blindstamp, 18⁷/₈ x 23⁵/₈in.
(Butterfield & Butterfield) $4,312

Louis Icart, Perfect Harmony (H. C. & I. 417), 1932, drypoint and aquatint printed in colors with touches of hand-coloring on wove paper, signed in pencil, with the artist's blindstamp, 13⁵/₁₆ x 17¹/₄in.
(Butterfield & Butterfield) $4,025

Currier and Ives, Publishers, The 'Lightning Express' Trains. 'Leaving the Junction.', by F. F. Palmer, lithograph in colors with hand-coloring and touches of gum arabic, 1863, on wove paper, 17¹/₂ x 27³/₄in.
(Christie's) $9,775

Currier and Ives, Publishers (active 1857–1907), Across the Continent. 'Westward the Course of Empire Takes Its Way.', after F. F. Palmer, by J. M. Ives, lithograph with hand-coloring, framed, 17³/₄ x 27¹/₄in.
(Christie's) $20,700

A fine pieced and appliqued Baltimore album quilt, dated *March 4, 1841*, 96 x 97in. (Sotheby's) $5,462

Applique quilt, America, 19th century, rose wreath worked in red and green heightened with parallel line quilting, 88 x 84in. $1,035

An appliqued and stuffed cotton quilted coverlet, by Diana Morse, Tyrone, New York, circa 1861, the inscription *Presentated to M.P. Morse.* 74 x 28in. (Christie's) $7,475

A pieced and appliqued cotton quilted coverlet, Baltimore, dated *1848*, the central square with spreadwing bird grasping the inscribed banner in its beak, 108in. (Christie's) $59,700

A pieced and appliqued coverlet, American, 19th century, worked twenty blocks of Log Cabin variation pattern, in variously colored fabrics, 75¼ x 60¾in. (Christie's) $483

A pieced and appliqued cotton quilted coverlet, Ohio, circa 1880, worked in sixteen blocks of red, blue, yellow and checkered cotton 64 x 79in. (Christie's) $437

Pieced Star quilt, America, late 19th century,
77 x 65in.
(Skinner) $431

A 'Meadow Lily' quilt, of cream cotton with olive
green flower stems and Turkey red flowers and
large diamond border, 79 x 98in., late 19th
century. (Christie's) $805

A pieced cotton coverlet, Philadelphia area,
dated *1844*, worked in 85 offset chintz squares
each centering a six-pointed chintz star with
printed pictorial interior each with inscribed or
printed name, 113¹/₂ x 118in.
(Christie's) $4,600

An Amish pieced and quilted cotton coverlet,
Indiana, dated 1931, worked in plain and satin
woven cottons centering a multi-colored
Lonestar, 84in. square.
(Christie's) $1,380

Red and blue jacquard coverlet, 19th century,
with Boston town border, 83 x 88in.
(Skinner) $805

Applique autograph quilt, America, dated
January 10, 1893, 84 x 100in.
(Skinner) $2,875

A pieced, appliqued and trapunto cotton
Baltimore album quilt, circa 1850, worked with
the figure of an American eagle, flag and shield
at center, approximately 80 x 80in.
(Sotheby's) $11,500

An Amish pieced and quilted cotton coverlet,
Indiana or Ohio, circa 1910, worked in twenty
blocks of Basket pattern in purple and black
plain and satin woven cottons, 81 x 70in.
(Christie's) $1,495

A pieced and appliqued cotton quilted coverlet,
inscribed *Baltimore*, and dated *1845*, comprised
of thirty-six variously appliqued squares of
green, red, yellow, and blue cotton printed
calicoes, 90³/4 x 102¹/2in.
(Christie's) $2,300

Pieced geometric quilt, America, early 20th
century, worked in vivid orange and brown
cotton patches, 79 x 84in.
(Skinner) $690

Applique quilt, 19th century, Wreaths of Lilies,
91 x 77in.
(Skinner) $690

Applique quilt, mid 19th century, Rose of
Sharon pattern, 95 x 96in.
(Skinner) $920

Fada 'Bullet' Catalin table radio, model 1000, circa 1946, cabinet green with yellow marbling, 6in. high.
(Skinner) $1,093

Marco Zanuso, Richard Sapper, Italy, Algoll 11, portable black and white television for Brionvega, 1964, black ABS housing with smoked acrylic front.
(Bonhams) $217

A Marconiphone Model 709 television, No. 1925, with 9-inch screen and radio in walnut-veneered cabinet, 39$^{1}/_2$in. high.
(Christie's) $1,417

Westinghouse 'Little Jewel/ Refrigerator' portable plastic radio, Sunbury, Pennsylvania, circa 1946, green plastic cabinet, two knobs and swing handle, 9in. high.
(Skinner) $259

Sparton 'Bluebird' table radio, Jackson, Michigan, circa 1936, designed by Walter Dorwin Teague, for the Spark-Withington Co., blue lettered yellow marb, bakelite dial face, 14$^{1}/_2$in. diameter.
(Skinner) $1,725

A transparent plastic Bubble television by Zarach, UK, circa 1970, Sony color television elements housed in and visible through a brown tinted plexiglass sphere, 68.5cm. high.
(Bonhams) $1,702

A Philips Model 6–20–A super inductance dual circuit straight receiver with typical Philips two-button control, with Philips bakelite loudspeaker, circa 1932.
(Auction Team Köln) $315

A Bush type 22 television, English, 1940's, in mahogany bakelite case with 11in. screen, 44cm. high.
(Bonhams) $380

A Seibt VE 301 GW bakelite all-mains receiver, complete with Membra aerial switch/circuit breaker, circa 1935.
(Auction Team Köln) $294

N. Cramer Roberts, Dungeness by The Romney Hythe & Dymchurch Railway, double royal.
(Onslow's) $500

Frank Newbould, The Electrical Plant of the LNER Automatically Coals The Flying Scotsman in Six Minutes, LNER, quad royal, on linen.
(Onslow's) $830

B. Grey, Connemara The Old Bog Road, pub by Great Southern Railways, double royal.
(Onslow's) $380

N. Cramer Roberts, Greatstone by The Romney Hythe & Dymchurch Railway, double royal.
(Onslow's) $470

Gregory Brown, Conducted Rambles All The Year Round, pub by Southern Railway, double royal, 1937.
(Onslow's) $300

V. L. Danvers, The High Street Guildford, London Underground, double royal, 1922.
(Onslow's) $240

Walter Till, Killarney Heavens Reflex, pub by Great Southern Railways, double royal.
(Onslow's) $410

Frank H. Mason, Clacton On Sea, LNER, quad royal, on board.
(Onslow's) $480

C. Norwich, Canadian National Railways A Great Railway In A Great Land, double crown.
(Onslow's) $260

Beatles, the program and press pack synopsis for the world premier of 'Help', London Pavilion 29th July 1965.
(Bonhams) $816

Beatles, 'Help' L.P., signed in three different inks on the back cover.
(Bonhams) $980

A black and white photograph of Jim Morrison, mounted with paper, signed in black ink *Jim Morrison*, 15$^{1}/_{2}$ x 11$^{1}/_{2}$in.
(Christie's) $805

A Yellow Submarine production celluloid of John Lennon, framed and glazed.
(Bonhams) $408

A pair of Dolce & Gabbana shoes worn by Madonna, of purple platform style with pink, purple and white rhinestones.
(Christie's) $5,750

An 11 x 14in. color calendar page showing Michael Jackson, signed boldly across the image.
(Bonhams) $131

Beatles, a Capitol Records R.I.A.A. gold 45 disk presented to Capitol Records for selling over one million copies of the pop single 'I Feel Fine'.
(Bonhams) $1,224

A collection of backstage passes, photographs, tickets and memorabilia from Bruce Springsteen's 1980/1981 World Tour, 21$^{3}/_{4}$ x 21$^{1}/_{2}$in., framed.
(Christie's) $978

A presentation 'gold' disk, Blood, Sweat and Tears, R.I.A.A. certified, white mat format, *Presented to Fred Lipsius*, 19$^{1}/_{2}$ x 15$^{1}/_{2}$in., framed.
(Christie's) $633

An old matted style R.I.A.A. gold award for the Apple L.P. 'Rubber Soul' presented to the Beatles.
(Bonhams) $1,388

Elvis/T.V. Guide presents, the 45 that the Elvis Presley Record Price Guide rates as 'The Most Valuable Record in the World'.
(Bonhams) $1,796

David Bowie, a presentation 'gold' disk, The Rise and Fall of Ziggy Stardust and the Spiders from Mars, R.I.A.A. certified.
(Christie's) $920

A copy of the 'Moody Blue' L.P. signed *My Best Wishes, Elvis Presley.*
(Bonhams) $327

A green American army style jacket, owned and worn on stage by Jimi Hendrix.
(Bonhams) $3,592

Beatles, 'From Then To You', Beatles Fan Club L.P. 1970, LYN 2/53.
(Bonhams) $310

A color advertisement from Billboard, featuring Eurythmics – They've got the Golden Touch; signed *Annie Lennox*, 19 x 15^{1}/$_2$in.
(Christie's) $230

Beatles, a page from Freddy Frinton's autograph book (the drunk comedian) with all four Beatle signatures in blue biro pen.
(Bonhams) $1,061

A black and white photograph of Jimi Hendrix performing, signed in silver felt pen *Leonard J. Eisenberg Carousel, MA. August 26, 1968.*
(Christie's) $403

Jimi Hendrix, a stage shirt, circa late 1960s, with signed letters of authenticity.
(Christie's) $2,300

An early press book for The Doors, featuring color photographs of the band, poetry and drawings; together with a piece of original Jefferson Airplane stationery for Spencer · Dryden.
(Christie's) $552

Bob Dylan 1960's 'Blowing in the Mind' poster in red, black and gold.
(Bonhams) $375

Michael Jackson, signed color 8 x 10in., three quarter length standing.
(Vennett-Smith) $205

A green fringed cowboy jacket owned and worn by Jimi Hendrix on stage.
(Bonhams) $6,857

Jimi Hendrix, signed 3 x 4in. newspaper photo, half length holding guitar.
(Vennett-Smith) $394

A signed postcard collection in Bad Nauheim Germany 12 Oct. 1959, mounted with a brass plaque and color print of the young Elvis.
(Bonhams) $490

A pair of Dolce & Gabbana platform shoes; with a 1993 black and white photograph of Madonna wearing the shoes; inscribed and signed, 10 x 8in.
(Christie's) $3,450

A portrait painting of the Rolling Stones by Ronnie Wood, inscribed *To Suné, Happy Christmas 1988, Ronnie Wood*, signed and glazed.
(Bonhams) $653

Fats Domino, self portrait cartoon drawn in ink by Fats Domino.
(Bonhams) $424

Sid Vicious, a note pad page in Sid's hand, titled 'What makes Nancy so great'.
(Bonhams) $1,061

Beatles and Frank Ifield, L.P. Vee-Jay VJLP 1085.
(Bonhams) $196

The Beatles, a black and white band photograph, signed in black felt pen *Paul McCartney*, *George Harrison* and *Ringo*, 7 x 5in.
(Christie's) $1,495

Elton John, a pair of black patent leather lace-up platform shoes, trimmed in silver, with black and white striped laces.
(Bonhams) $571

Frankie Lymon, a color theatre poster from The London Palladium, circa 1950s, announcing the first London visit of 'America's Sensational Young Stars', 29½ x 19¾in.
(Christie's) $690

A heart-shaped satin cushion, fringed with embroidered message 'Our hearts are 1' and Elton John's name.
(Bonhams) $49

A REMO Weather King drumskin, signed in black felt pen *Larry – Thanks for your help! Luv Phil Collins 88*.
(Christie's) $978

Rolling Stones, a green velvet jacket made by Granny Takes a Trip, owned and worn by Keith Richards.
(Bonhams) $4,245

A 1953 Humes High School, Memphis, Tennesse school yearbook, features graduate Presley, Elvis Aron, who inscribes and signs *Best Wishes to a swell athlete, Elvis.*
(Christie's) $4,025

Elton John, a pair of brown leather open backed platform shoes.
(Bonhams) $147

Beatles, a Beatles rug with all of the Fab Four printed in the weave, 3 x 2ft.
(Bonhams) $359

Beatles, a good set of signatures on the back of one of the vendor's own Lloyds Bank checks collected in 1965.
(Bonhams) $1,959

Elton John, a telephone in the shape of a grand piano, the numbered keys playing notes.
(Bonhams) $245

A black t-shirt worn by Eric Clapton; inscribed and signed in silver felt pen across the front.
(Christie's) $1,380

Madonna, a two piece stage outfit from the 1993 'Girlie Show' World Tour.
(Christie's) $8,625

John Lennon's American Express bill, annotated by John Lennon *Who screwed up John.*
(Bonhams) $1,306

Jimi Hendrix, hand drawn sketches and doodles mounted on A4 yellow notepaper with *You Can't Tell Me That,* written in pen at the top of the sketch.
(Bonhams) $1,306

The Beatles, an original color album slick, Apple/Electrola, Let It Be, 17 x 17in., framed.
(Christie's) $138

Delaney and Bonnie, Apple, acetate for the Delaney and Bonnie L.P. on the Apple Custom label.
(Bonhams) $359

An unpublished lyric by John Lennon 'When a Girl Begins to be a Problem'.
(Bonhams) $12,081

Beatles, a square faced 'Apple' watch on a black suede strap, issued only to members of Apple staff.
(Bonhams) $686

The Apple dartboard given to Elton by the Beatles and used at his Windsor home.
(Bonhams) $947

An autograph book containing the signatures of all four Beatles on one page with other signatures of sixties pop stars throughout.
(Bonhams) $1,633

Rolling Stones, a postcard autographed in blue biro by all five Stones, circa 1964.
(Bonhams) $424

Beatles, copy of 'Sergeant Pepper's Lonely Hearts Club Band', signed in blue biro across each image.
(Bonhams) $1,877

A black and gold satin stage bustier worn by Madonna during The Blonde Ambition Tour.
(Christie's) $4,025

Woodstock, 1969, the original sign from the Woodstock Exit on the New York State Thruway, 4 x 8ft.
(Christie's) $7,475

A black and white photograph of Elvis Presley, mounted with a piece of paper, signed in black ink *Elvis Presley*, 16¼ x 11in.
(Christie's) $748

A color photograph of Sam Cooke mounted with a 'gold' disk of You Send Me, signed *Lots Of Luck Sam Cooke*.
(Christie's) $575

Paul McCartney, a black and white 10 x 8in. print, signed in blue pen with an earlier print.
(Bonhams) $261

A color advertisement sheet for Bob Marley & The Wailers Rastaman Vibration, inscribed and signed, 22^1/$_2$ x 29^1/$_2$in., framed.
(Christie's) $1,840

The Grateful Dead, a 'Dead in Vermont' t-shirt; inscriptions and signatures across the front.
(Christie's) $575

A black and white photograph of Jim Morrison, mounted with a Willie Mitchell LIVE advertisement, signed, 14^1/$_4$ x 19^1/$_4$in.
(Christie's) $575

A color photograph of Fleetwood Mac, inscribed and signed by Mick Fleetwood, Stevie Nicks, Christine McVie and Lindsey Buckingham, 13^1/$_2$ x 10^1/$_2$in.
(Christie's) $518

A color photograph of Eric Clapton performing, signed in black felt pen *Eric Clapton*; together with a REMO Weather King drumskin, inscribed and signed.
(Christie's) $978

A guitar strap used by Jimi Hendrix, circa late 1960s, with letter of authenticity from Experience bass player Noel Redding and two color photographs.
(Christie's) $11,500

A handwritten and drawn 'announcement' by John Lennon, originally taped to a hallway wall on the 17th floor of the Queen Liz Hotel in Montreal, Canada, 24^3/$_4$ x 30in.
(Christie's) $18,400

Elton John, a pair of blue leather side-zip knee-length boots, on silver leather platform.
(Bonhams) $522

The Rolling Stones, an early black and white publicity card; inscribed and signed *Keith Richards, To Linda – Brian Jones, Bill Wyman, Mick Jagger,* and *Charlie Watts,* 4^1/$_4$ x 5^1/$_2$in.
(Christie's) $1,150

Paul McCartney, a black and white 8 x 10in. signed print matted with the 'Friends of The Earth World Tour 1990 L.P. Flyer'.
(Bonhams) $751

A black fedora, the underside of the brim inscribed and signed in silver felt pen *Love Michael Jackson*, accompanied by signed color photograph.
(Christie's) $748

Elvis, an extremely rare 10in. acetate on the associated label of the Hill and Range song 'Where Could I Go To But The Lord', mounted with photograph of the young Elvis.
(Bonhams) $1,306

The cover of Madonna's 1992 calendar, signed in black felt tip pen, mounted and framed, 16 x 19in.
(Bonhams) $457

Duane Allman, a circa late 1960s custom designed black and brown leather guitar strap, engraved on the interior *Dwane* (sic) *with everlasting love Dixie*, 44in. in length.
(Christie's) $3,220

The Rolling Stones, an early color photograph of the band mounted with a yellow piece of paper; inscribed and signed, 16 x 12in.
(Christie's) $805

A color photograph of Cream signed in blue felt pen *Eric Clapton, Ginger Baker* and *Jack Bruce*, 10½ x 13½in.
(Christie's) $575

A black satin stage brassiere, worn by Madonna during The Blonde Ambition Tour; with color photograph, 9½ x 11¾in.
(Christie's) $1,150

A Rawlings official American League baseball, signed in blue felt pen on the 'sweet spot' *Eric Clapton E.C. 94.*
(Christie's) $690

Red suedette and silver stage suit worn by Gary Glitter on the Red Hot Reputation tour and a letter of authenticity.
(Bonhams) $653

Beatles, a female record stamper made of plate metal with the Beatles signatures scratched on both sides.
(Bonhams) $1,633

A color advertisement from Billboard, featuring Queen – The Works, signed by Freddie Mercury, 19$^{1}/_{2}$ x 15$^{1}/_{2}$in., framed.
(Christie's) $633

Freddie Mercury tribute poster promoting the concert for Aids Awareness at Wembley Stadium, signed by the band members of Queen.
(Bonhams) $424

Jimi Hendrix/Wobern Festival 1968, a set of four black and white 8 x 10in. limited edition prints, mounted and glazed, 30 x 36in.
(Bonhams) $261

A Beatles Book, Issue No. 12 July 1964, featuring John Lennon on the cover, inscribed and signed *Love John Lennon 79*, 8$^{1}/_{4}$ x 6in.
(Christie's) $1,035

A black leather pouch with leather drawstring, used by Cher to hold coins/keys, 13$^{1}/_{2}$ x 10$^{1}/_{2}$in., framed.
(Christie's) $518

The jacket from the album Walls and Bridges; signed *Love John Lennon* with a doodle in the image of two faces, 12 x 12in.
(Christie's) $1,495

John Lennon's 1968 signed tax form 1968–69 with a receipt from the Inland Revenue and a letter from Bryce Hammer.
(Bonhams) $1,306

A color photograph of Mick Jagger, signed *Mick Rock 9/79*; and a color photograph of Joan Jett, signed *Mick Rock 8/82*. (Christie's) $437

The Beach Boys, a black REMO Weather King drumskin, gold felt pen inscriptions and signatures. (Christie's) $863

A 1968 concert poster for Jimi Hendrix's appearance at City Park Stadium in New Orleans, LA, 22 x 13^{3}/4in. (Christie's) $575

Janis Joplin, an original 1968 performance contract for Big Brother & The Holding Co. to appear at the Electric Factory in Philadelphia. (Christie's) $805

An uncut sheet of the proposed 1978 Elvis Presley Tour Book, unpublished due to the singer's death in August 1977, 57^{1}/4 x 41^{1}/2in., framed. (Christie's) $460

The 'Elvis in Person' program for the Las Vegas Hilton concert, signed on the front cover *To Pat from Elvis Presley*. (Bonhams) $555

A black and white photograph of Buddy Holly, mounted with a yellow piece of paper, signed in black felt pen, 15^{1}/2 x 10^{1}/2in. (Christie's) $748

Elvis Presley, a wide ranging collection of L.P's, boxed sets, E.P's, 45's, books, magazines, newsletters and posters. (Bonhams) $1,224

A 'grapefruit' t-shirt worn by John Lennon, mounted with a color photograph of John Lennon, 35^{3}/4 x 24in. (Christie's) $575

An antique Daghestan prayer rug, north East Caucasus, the ivory mihrab with characteristic leaf latticework containing stylized shrubs, 1.45m. x 1.12m. (Phillips) $1,228

Yomud Ensi, West Turkestan, early 20th century, staggered bracketed diamonds in blue, red and brown on the quartered rust field, 6ft. 2in. x 4ft. 9in. (Skinner) $977

Shirvan rug, East Caucasus, late 19th century, rectangular grid of branching plants in midnight blue, red and gold, ivory meander border, 5ft. x 3ft. 8in. (Skinner) $1,495

Yomud Ensi, West Turkestan, last quarter 19th century, diagonal rows of midnight blue, red, and blue-green plant motifs on the quartered aubergine field, 5ft. x 4ft. 2in. (Skinner) $2,070

Qashqai kelim, Southwest Persia, early 20th century, vertical stripes in midnight and royal blue, red, gold, ivory, brown, and blue-green, 7ft. 4in. x 5ft. (Skinner) $1,035

Hamadan rug, Northwest Persia, early 20th century, staggered rows of delicate blue, gold, and ivory floral groups on the terracotta red field, 4ft. x 3ft. 4in. (Skinner) $863

Shirvan rug, East Caucasus, late 19th century, hexagonal lattice with flowering plants in red, rose, sky blue, and gold on the rust field, 3ft. 2in. x 2ft. 5in. (Skinner) $518

Anatolian Prayer kelim, last quarter 19th century, red shaped mihrab on the light aubergine-blue-green field, 4ft. 7in. x 3ft. 6in. (Skinner) $460

Baluch rug, Northeast Persia, last quarter 19th century, serrated diamond lattice with large flowering plants on the camel field, 4ft. 8in. x 3ft. 5in. (Skinner) $2,760

An antique Daghestan rug, North East Caucasus, the ivory field with a characteristic stylized latticework with stylized shrubs, 1.97m. x 1.24m. (Phillips) $1,151

Senneh mat, Northwest Persia, early 20th century, small boteh and vines in red and orange on the midnight blue field, 3ft. x 2ft. 2in. (Skinner) $374

A fine Isfahan rug, Central Persia, the rose field decorated with flowerheads and vines around an indigo, rose and ivory floral medallion, 2.08m. x 1.49m. (Phillips) $2,303

Kazak rug, Southwest Caucasus, last quarter 19th century, concentric gabled square medallions and small geometric motifs, sky blue 'arrowhead' border, 5ft. x 3ft. 10in. (Skinner) $1,610

Afshar rug, South Persia, last quarter 19th century, red and sky blue serrated octagonal medallion and matching spandrels on the midnight blue field, 6ft. 5in. x 4ft. 8in. (Skinner) $1,265

Kuba rug, Northeast Persia, last quarter 19th century, two radiating medallions and small geometric motifs on the midnight blue field, 5ft. 4in. x 4ft. 2in. (Skinner) $4,600

Southwest Persian kelim, late 19th/early 20th century, overall zig-zag design in navy blue, red, gold, and abrashed blue-green, 4ft. x 2ft. 9in. (Skinner) $863

Bidjar mat, Northwest Persia, early 20th century, circular sprays of blossoms on the red field, midnight blue floral meander border, 2ft. 5in. x 2ft. (Skinner) $1,495

Sarouk rug, West Persia, late 19th century, midnight and sky blue circular medallion and blossoming vines on the very pale tan field, 6ft. 7in. x 4ft. 2in. (Skinner) $1,610

RUGS

Sewan Kazak rug, Southwest
Caucasus, late 19th century,
8ft. x 5ft. 6in.
(Skinner) $8,050

A wool and cotton hooked rug,
American, early 20th century,
with brown and black ground
centering two white cats facing
each other, 31¼ x 53½in.
(Christie's) $1,955

Kazak rug, Southwest Caucasus,
last quarter 19th century,
6ft. 6in. x 5ft. 10in.
(Skinner) $5,750

Karabagh rug, South Caucasus,
late 19th century, two
medallions inset with
'cloudbands' in midnight blue,
red, gold and ivory on the red-
brown field, 7ft. 9in. x 4ft. 3in.
(Skinner) $575

A Bidjar Wagireh, Persian
Kurdistan, comprising part
decoration in herati pattern,
ivory border with meandering
vine and a wide ivory palmette
end skirt, 2m. x 1.42m.
(Phillips) $998

An antique Kazak rug, the
brick-red field with four sea-
green and indigo gabled
medallions, each containing
small brick-red panel, 7ft. 6in. x
5ft. 3in.
(Christie's) $1,672

A fine Shirvan rug, the shaded
indigo field with stylized animal
figures, small serrated panels,
large jewelry motifs and
hooked bars, 6ft. x 4ft. 1in.
(Christie's) $1,167

An antique Kazak Karatchopf
rug, the brick-red field with
variously colored panels
containing hooked motifs and
hooked lozenges, 7ft. x 5ft. 9in.
(Christie's) $792

Roger Fry for the Omega
Workshop, rug, 1914, worked in
wool with an abstract pattern on
a chocolate ground, 189 x
240cm.
(Sotheby's) $5,030

552

Mudjar prayer rug, Central Anatolia, third quarter 19th century, 7ft. x 5ft. 2in. (Skinner) $5,750

Tekke Torba, West Turkestan, last quarter 19th century, six navy blue, apricot, and ivory chuval guls on the rust field, 3ft. 10in. x 1ft. 5in. (Skinner) $1,380

Kansu rug, Northwest China, 20th century, 8ft. x 5ft. 5in. (Skinner) $4,025

A fine Qum Garden carpet, the field with overall square floral lattice of light blue, ivory, brick-red, indigo and yellow-beige panels containing flowering vines, 11ft. 7in. x 7ft. 11in. (Christie's) $1,975

A fine Kazak rug, the field with column of large charcoal-black and rust lozenges containing similar concentric camel, blue and sea-green motifs flanked by angular floral sprays, 5ft. 1in. x 3ft. 11in. (Christie's) $1,077

Aubusson rug, France, mid 19th century, large scalloped ivory medallion in dark rose, violet, olive, light green and brown on the aubergine field, 8ft. 10in. x 7ft. 4in. (Skinner) $8,625

Navajo rug in Chief's Blanket design with red, black and white colors, circa 1920, 5ft. 8in. x 6ft. 7in. (Eldred's) $1,650

A Khoum floral silk rug with central medallion, the white ground decorated with arabesques and flowerheads, 156 x 110cm. (Galerie Moderne) $960

A Sennah Kurd rug, step sided indigo field with triple pole center medallion in pale blue and brick, 4ft. 10in. x 3ft. 6in. (Woolley & Wallis) $745

Northwest Persian fragment, 18th century, (pieced together, backed with fabric), 8ft. 2in. x 5ft. 4in.
(Skinner) $5,750

Shirvan rug, East Caucasus, dated *1913*, Perepedil design in sky blue, light green, gold, ivory, and blue green on the abrashed dark red field, 6ft. x 4ft. 3in.
(Skinner) $2,875

Sarouk rug, West Persia, late 19th century, large midnight blue diamond medallion, on the ivory field, 5ft. 4in. x 3ft. 7in.
(Skinner) $1,495

A fine Tabriz carpet, the shaded raspberry-red field with meandering vines connecting various multicolored palmettes, flowerheads, serrated leaves and cloud bands, 10ft. 3in. x 8ft. 7in.
(Christie's) $654

A Shaker wool ravel-knit shirred rug, American, late 19th early 20th century, the rectangular form worked in conforming graduated borders of blue, taupe, red, gray, mint green, burgundy and black wool threads, 27 x 43in.
(Christie's) $748

A fine and unusual antique Heriz rug, North West Persia, piled in silk and cotton on a silk foundation, indigo field with Persian garden design of flowering trees and shrubs, 1.84m. x 1.31m.
(Phillips) $5,373

Anatolian kelim, last quarter 19th century, concentric radiating diamond medallion on the red field, ivory palmette and vine meander border, 5ft. 2in. x 4ft.
(Skinner) $748

An antique Heriz carpet, North West Persia, the terracotta field with stylized vines around a large pendant medallion in indigo, ivory, pale yellow and pale blue, 4.24m. x 3m.
(Phillips) $3,070

Bakshaish rug, Northwest Persia, late 19th century, three midnight blue and ivory stepped diamond medallions on the terracotta red field, 5ft. 10in. x 4ft. 6in.
(Skinner) $1,725

Bessarabian kelim, last quarter 19th century, rectangular grid of summer blossoms on the black field, 8ft. x 7ft. 4in.
(Skinner) $6,325

Verner Panton, Denmark/ Switzerland, Pebbles, a woollen rug, for Art Line by AGE Axminster, 1960s, 198 x 138cm.
(Bonhams) $1,238

Afshar saddle cover, South Persia, late 19th century, empty midnight blue field, narrow gold floral border, 3ft. 3in. x 3ft.
(Skinner) $1,840

Hereke silk prayer rug, West Anatolia, contemporary, vases of flowers and a hanging lamp in dark red, rose, sky blue, deep gold, green and blue-green on the ivory field, 4ft. 10in. x 3ft. 3in.
(Skinner) $4,025

A Tabriz carpet, the ivory field with overall design of scrolling vines connecting bold multicolored serrated palmettes, leaves and flowerheads, 12ft. 10in. x 9ft. 6in.
(Christie's) $620

Gendje rug, South Central Caucasus, last quarter 19th century, diagonal stripes with small hooked square in midnight and navy blue, red, tan-gold, and blue-green, 5ft. 4in. x 3ft. 2in.
(Skinner) $1,150

Central Anatolian village prayer rug, 18th century, two columns and small floral motifs in sky blue, gold, aubergine, and blue-green on the red field, 5ft. 2in. x 3ft. 7in.
(Skinner) $2,645

A European (probably Spanish) piled needlework rug, 18th century, the soft powder-blue field with an all over design of stylized tulips framed by a border, 2.25m. x 1.73m.
(Phillips) $2,149

Daghestan rug, Northeast Caucasus, third quarter 19th century, hexagonal lattice with cruciform geometric motifs in red, royal blue, and blue-green on the gold field, 7ft. x 4ft. 10in.
(Skinner) $1,840

18th century silk sampler decorated with birds, flowers, figures and animals, dated *1785*, 12¹/₂ x 13in.
(Ewbank)   **$1,020**

Needlework sampler, wrought by *Margaret Rimmington 1842*, 16¹/₂ x 12¹/₂in., framed.
(Skinner)   **$1,150**

A George III sampler worked in fine needlework on a colored ground, by Betty Bridger aged 11 years 1772, 12 x 9¹/₂in.
(Hy. Duke & Son)   **$759**

Needlework sampler, *Rosamond Lamb her sampler in the year of our Lord 1799*, polychrome silk threads on linen ground, 15 x 12³/₄in., framed.
(Skinner)   **$1,035**

Needlework sampler, Pennsylvania, *Ann Mayron aged 13 Edmond Iley School 1827*, 16 x 16in., framed.
(Skinner)   **$1,092**

A needlework sampler, signed *Ellen Farrar*, probably Pennsylvania, circa 1840, worked in a variety of wool threads on a linen ground, 17 x 17¹/₄in.
(Sotheby's)   **$1,725**

Needlework family register, probably Massachusetts, records births and death dates of the Isaac Fish family, 1782–1824, 15¹/₄ x 15³/₄in.
(Skinner)   **$690**

A sampler by Rachel Hook, 1853, worked in colored silks with a verse 'Give first to God...', and alphabets and floral motifs, 12 x 11¹/₂in.
(Christie's)   **$1,510**

'A Map of England and Wales' by Philippa Jane Wilcock, 1836, the oval map sampler worked in black and brown silks, 20 x 22¹/₂in.
(Christie's)   **$1,510**

Needlework sampler, *Julia O'Brien Washington City, June the 4th 1812*, polychrome silk threads on a green linen ground, 18 x 18¹/₂in., framed.
(Skinner) $34,500

A sampler by Rachel Hook, 1805, worked in colored silks and gilt metal threads, with a verse 'Next unto God...', 11¹/₂ x 14¹/₂in., framed and glazed.
(Christie's) $2,852

An early Victorian sampler, by Hannah Arnott dated *1823*, flowers, birds, sailing ships, dogs, 20¹/₂ x 20in.
(Dee, Atkinson & Harrison) $541

A silk-on-linen needlework sampler, Roxana M'Gee, Franklin, Tennessee, August 1839, worked in cream, light and dark green, yellow, black, brown and red silk threads in a variety of stitches, 16¹/₄ x 16¹/₄in.
(Christie's) $2,070

A George II sampler worked in fine colored thread on a linen ground, with The Lord's Prayer by Elizabeth Ginger aged 10, 1735, 13 x 12in.
(Hy. Duke & Son) $1,820

A silk-on-linen needlework sampler, Lydia Swain, Nantucket, Massachusetts, dated *1803*, comprised of three cursive and plain alphabetical registers above the cross-stitched verse flanked by butterflies, 13¹/₂ x 12in.
(Christie's) $6,900

A sampler by Elizabeth Goodman, 1796, finely worked in brightly colored silks with a verse 'On Mortality', 13¹/₂ x 16in.
(Christie's) $923

A sampler by Mary Payne, 1846, worked in shades of green, cream and brown silks, the upper band with Adam and Eve flanked by a verse, 15¹/₂ x 12¹/₂in. (Christie's) $705

A sampler by Margaret Moffitt, Gateshead, 1819, worked in colored silks with a short verse about spot motifs including Adam and Eve, 13 x 19¹/₂in.
(Christie's) $923

Raymond Household-Type American transverse shuttle machine with gold foliate decoration, circa 1880. (Auction Team Köln)
$272

An American F & L treadle machine with unusual head, instruction booklet and wooden cover, circa 1880. (Auction Team Köln)
$323

English sewing machine by Jones, with gilt decoration to the cast iron frame, circa 1890. (Auction Team Köln)
$160

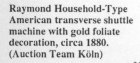

An Original Brunonia oscillating shuttle sewing machine, with shuttle, by Bremer & Brückman, Braunschweig, 1895. (Auction Team Köln)
$272

A Legat-System Avriel French oscillating shuttle machine on cast iron plinth, with unusual pumping mechanism, circa 1875. (Auction Team Köln)
$1,435

A Little Europa sewing machine, by Smith & Starley, Patentees, Coventry, with shuttle, enclosed gear drive to upper and lower shafts, 13in. wide. (Christie's)
$3,915

A Taylor's twisted loop, chainstitch sewing machine No. 1854, with belt drive, faded gilt and 1875 patent date, 8¹/₂in. wide. (Christie's)
$1,131

Sewing machine on cast iron frame by Clemens Müller, Dresden, complete with shuttle, circa 1882. (Auction Team Köln)
$160

A lockstitch sewing machine, of Wanzer pattern, with slender-spoked handwheel, vine-leaf transfer on stitch-plate, patent date July 27 1867. (Christie's)
$243

A scrimshawed oval lidded box, American, 19th century, the oval hinged and bezeled lid opening to a conforming interior, 4¹/₈in. wide.
(Christie's) $2,760

A whalebone and mother-of-pearl jagging wheel, American, 1850–1870, in seagull head-shaped mount with mother-of-pearl eyes, 8¹/₂in. long.
(Christie's) $1,725

A scrimshawed whalebone and baleen box, American, 19th century, the circular baleen lid engraved with a fully rigged ship, 5³/₄in. diameter.
(Christie's) $1,150

Scrimshawed whale's tooth, probably late 19th century, depicting scenes of American Eagle and shield, stars and foliage, unusual elephant and man with palm trees motif, 5¹/₄in. high.
(Butterfield & Butterfield)
                                 $605

A painted and scrimshawed pair of sperm whale teeth, probably American, mid-19th century, on shaped wood base, 7⁵/₈in. high.
(Sotheby's) $11,500

A whalebone hourglass, American, 19th century, the central hollow joined double-bellied glass flanked by four ring and baluster-turned columns, 6³/₄in. high.
(Christie's) $1,610

Unusual Australian whale's tooth scrimshaw inscribed *This tooth was taken from a monstrous whale struck by the ship 'John' of London, Australia, July 1821*, 8in.
(Ewbank) $1,760

A scrimshawed whalebone box, American, 19th century, the circular lid with pinprick decoration in the form of two interlocking hearts, 4in. diameter.
(Christie's) $1,610

A whalebone bird cage, America, circa 1870, of individual cylindrical and bent whalebone spokes, with domed top and straight sides, 29in. high.
(Christie's) $13,800

Miss Jane Read (1773–1857), a naval officer, profile to right, on glass, black papier-mâché frame, oval, 3³/₈in. high.
(Christie's) $640

American School, 19th century, a hollow-cut silhouette bust portrait of a young girl, in a sunburst églomisé frame, 4¹/₂ x 3¹/₈in.
(Sotheby's) $460

A hollow-cut silhouette portrait of Robert Wright, 1830, in a stone carved frame, 4¹/₂ x 3in.
(Sotheby's) $805

Jacob Spornberg (1768–died after 1840), a gentleman, profile to left, on glass, signed and dated *Bath 1792*, oval, 3¹/₂in. high.
(Christie's) $1,334

John Miers (1758–1821), Mr Knapp and Miss Harriet Knapp, in profiles; in frilled cravat, wearing falling veil headgear, respectively, oval, 3¹/₂in. high.
(Christie's) $3,380

John Miers (1758–1821) and John Field (1772–1848), Thomas Bridge, profile to left in coat, bronzed, on plaster, oval, 3¹/₂in. high.
(Christie's) $640

Arthur Lea (1768–1828), a naval officer, in naval uniform, on glass, plaster background, oval, 3¹/₄in. high.
(Christie's) $1,779

Mrs Jane Read (1773–1857), General Charles Dixon, seated in a chair before a curtain, on glass backed with wax, 3¹/₈in. high.
(Christie's) $3,024

Arthur Lea (1768–1828), a lady, profile to right, on glass, plaster background, verre églomisé border, oval, 3³/₄in. high.
(Christie's) $640

Mrs Jane Read (1773–1857),
Louisa Dixon, in lace-bordered
dress, wearing necklace, on
glass, backed with wax, 3¹/₈in.
high.
(Christie's)   **$3,914**

American School, 19th century,
a hollow-cut silhouette of a boy
in a top hat, cut paper mounted
over black, oval: 3¹/₂ x 3in.
(Sotheby's)   **$575**

American School, 19th century,
a hollow-cut silhouette of
Captain Jesse Collins, North
Truro, Massachusetts, with
églomisé panel, 4³/₄ x 3³/₈in.
(Sotheby's)   **$690**

Mrs Isabella Beetham (1752–
1825), Miss Baxland, profile to
right in dress with frilled collar,
on glass, plaster backing, oval,
2¹/₂in. high.
(Christie's)   **$3,202**

A pair of silhouette portrait
miniatures, American, circa
1820, comprising two profile
silhouettes each a young woman,
impressed *WKING*, 3¹/₄in. long,
each.
(Christie's)   **$345**

Everett Howard (1787–1820), a
young boy with tousled hair and
frilled white stock: a hollow-cut
silhouette portrait, cut-paper
mounted over black fabric, oval:
3³/₄ x 3in.
(Sotheby's)   **$1,955**

William Wellings (fl. circa 1778–
1796), Mr J. M. Days, profile to
left, holding a cane and hat,
landscape background, dated
7 July 1788, 10in. high.
(Christie's)   **$5,692**

J. Thomason of Dublin (fl. 1786–
1800), a gentleman, profile to
left, on plaster, hammered brass
frame, oval, 3¹/₂in. high.
(Christie's)   **$1,245**

Jacob Spornberg (1768–died
after 1840), a lady of the Anstey
family, in plumed hat, signed
and dated *Bath 1793*, oval, 3¹/₄in.
high.
(Christie's)   **$2,313**

BASKETS

A fine early Victorian silver-gilt fruit basket, Barnard Bros., London, 1847, with reeded simulated basketwork, 11½in. diameter, approximate weight 39½oz.
(Bonhams) $5,760

Pair of sterling silver fenestrated baskets, by Gorham, 10in. long, 25.2 troy oz.
(Eldred's) $880

Victorian silver cake basket, having cast scrolled and foliate edge, pierced and embossed center, Sheffield 1852 by Henry Wilkinson and Co., 10½in. diameter, 22oz.
(G. A. Key) $775

A fine George II Irish bread basket, applied scroll border interspersed with Bacchus and Ceres masks, Dublin 1743, maker Robert Calderwood, 15¾in. long, approximate weight 80oz.
(Bonhams) $96,000

An Edward VII swing-handled vase-shaped sugar basket, the undulating rim and spreading pedestal base, 18.5cm. high overall, Birmingham 1905, 220gms.
(Bearne's) $403

A fine early George III 15½in. shaped oval cake basket with gadroon and shell cast rim, London mark 1770, maker William Penstone, 45oz.
(Anderson & Garland) $5,967

A George III swing-handle bread basket, William Plummer, London, 1786, pierced with an inner border of vertical slats and scrollwork patera, 14½in. long, approximate weight 27oz.
(Bonhams) $2,400

A silver cake basket, Van Voorhis & Schanck, New York, 1791–1793, flaring octagonal, on an oval foot pierced with pales, 13½in. long, 34oz.
(Christie's) $85,000

A swing-handled oval basket, sides pierced with slats, the edge with scrolls, rosettes and laurel leaves, by The Goldsmiths & Silversmiths Company Ltd., 1913, 37.5cm. long, 37.25oz.
(Phillips) $1,373

BASKETS

A George IV cake basket probably by Richard Gregory & Co., Sheffield 1826, raised on a cast floral foot ring with four shell feet, 29cm. diameter, 31.5oz.
(Cheffins Grain & Comins)
$1,262

A George III simulated wickerwork basket of circular form, London 1760, maker's mark of John Parker I and Edward Wakelin, 11¹/₂in. diameter, approximate weight 29oz.
(Bonhams)
$2,560

An early Victorian cake basket by Henry Wilkinson & Co. Ltd., Sheffield 1846, engraved in the center of he bowl with two crests, 25.5cm. diameter, 17.25oz.
(Cheffins Grain & Comins)
$562

A Victorian swing-handled shaped oval pedestal sugar basket with thread edging and bright-cut decoration, J. E. Bingham, Walker and Hall, Sheffield 1890, 298gms.
(Bearne's)
$773

An early 19th century Russian oval swing-handled basket, the sides pierced with honeycomb decoration, assay master Alexander Yashinov, St. Petersburg, circa 1820, 30.2cm. long, 33.25oz.
(Phillips)
$1,373

Attractive large Victorian sugar basket with finely pierced sides, beaded rims, beaded swing handle, London 1846 by Charles T. Fox and George Fox, 3¹/₂in. high.
(G. A. Key)
$517

A George III swing-handled shaped oval cake basket, the sides pierced with fretwork and embossed with beaded 'swags', by William Plummer, 1765, 35cm. long, 37.5oz.
(Phillips)
$4,156

Fine George III silver sugar basket, boat shaped to an oval foot, reeded swing handle, London 1783 probably by Burrage Davenport.
(G. A. Key)
$666

A George III oval swing-handled cake basket, center engraved with the armorials of Congreve of Staffordshire, by Burrage Davenport, 1780, 35.9cm. long, 30oz.
(Phillips)
$5,819

BEAKERS

A Charles II beaker, of flaring circular form, on a skirted foot and engraved with strapwork and scrolling foliage, London 1683, 3¹/₂in.
(Christie's) $3,001

A late 17th century German parcel-gilt covered beaker, on three fruit ball feet, by Matthäus Schmidt, Augsburg, circa 1685, 15.5cm. high, 8oz.
(Phillips) $3,276

A Danish 17th century beaker, engraved with initials and a date 1654, Hans Clausen, Aalborg, second half 17th century, 5¹/₄in., 8oz.
(Christie's) $662

A late 17th century German parcel-gilt covered beaker, sides embossed with profile busts of King Henry II, Emperor Constantine II, and Sultan Mohammed II, probably East German/Silesian, circa 1695, 12.5cm. high, 6.5oz.
(Phillips) $1,247

A pair of Victorian gilt-lined beakers, chased with roundels and cartouches on a matted ground, Robert Hennell, London 1845, 5³/₄in., 16.5oz.
(Christie's) $1,328

A Commonwealth beaker of tapering shape with flared lip, on molded foot, engraved with a band of strapwork, maker's mark DG with an anchor between, London, 1665, 9.9cm. high, 4.25oz.
(Phillips) $4,212

A French 18th century beaker, the upper part of the body engraved with a frieze of strapwork, flowers, foliage and trelliswork, maker's initials J.F.R., Paris 1788, 2³/₄in.
(Christie's) $662

A German parcel-gilt beaker, the tapering circular body chased with architectural vignettes divided by bow-tied fruit and foliage, Nuremburg circa 1680, 2¹/₂in.
(Christie's) $907

A 19th century Russian silver-gilt and niello beaker, decorated with an extensive architectural scene, maker's mark G. Sch. (Cyrillics), Moscow, 1834, 7.1cm. high, 3.75oz.
(Phillips) $593

BOWLS

A late Victorian fruit bowl, the sides with floral and foliate-stamped panels incorporating vacant rococo C-scroll cartouches, Roberts & Belk, Sheffield 1897, 6³/₄in., 11.75oz.
(Christie's) $398

A large Charles II bowl, by Jacob Bodendick, London, 1680, circular and on spreading domed foot chased with a band of acanthus foliage, 19¹/₂in. wide, 169oz.
(Christie's) $38,942

A German parcel-gilt brandy bowl, the center chased in relief with a bowl decorated with a swag, maker's initials *H.B.* conjoined, Augsburg, circa 1680, 5¹/₄in.
(Christie's) $2,093

An Edwardian Scottish pedestal fruit bowl, of molded circular form, the bowl and the foot each decorated with piercing, Hamilton & Inches, Edinburgh 1910, 8¹/₄in., 13.5oz.
(Christie's) $398

A pair of late Victorian rose bowls, chased with female masks surrounded by flowers and foliage and with vacant cartouches, Wakeley & Wheeler, London 1894, 7¹/₂in., 53oz.
(Christie's) $2,171

An Edwardian pedestal fruit bowl, on a rising circular foot pierced with shells, foliage and trelliswork, Jackson & Fullerton, London 1905, 11in., 21oz.
(Christie's) $869

Two Edwardian rose bowls, of tapering circular form, each decorated with arabesques, Sheffield 1904 and Birmingham 1906, 8¹/₄in. and 7¹/₄in., 27.75oz.
(Christie's) $1,086

A Victorian Monteith rose bowl, applied stylized shell and C-scroll rim, one side with oval cartouche with presentation inscription, Gibson & Langman, London 1891, 10¹/₄in., 38oz.
(Christie's) $1,832

A spot-hammered rose bowl, of tapering molded circular form, with two applied lion's mask and ring-drop handles, London 1918, 7³/₄in., 23.25oz.
(Christie's) $470

BOWLS

Fine Art Nouveau two handled silver pedestal fruit bowl on a circular foot, London 1903 by the Goldsmiths and the Silversmiths Co., 22¹/₂oz.
(G. A. Key) $492

Quezal gold iridescent punchbowl, eighteen-rib bowl with attached matching stand, 13in. diameter.
(Skinner) $805

Silver pedestal fruit bowl with pierced trellis top, cast laurel handles, plain circular foot, Chester 1913, 17¹/₂oz.
(G. A. Key) $325

A Victorian circular two-handled punch bowl in Monteith style, 32cm. diameter, Robert Garrard, London 1881, 66oz.
(Bearne's) $3,360

An early 19th century Portuguese covered sugar bowl, of tapering bellied oblong form on ball and claw feet, by José Joaquim Antunes Ribeiro, Lisbon, circa 1830, 18cm. high, 23.5oz.
(Phillips) $599

An Edwardian silver rose bowl, one cartouche engraved with *The John Birkerdyke Challenge Cup*, the other engraved with *The British Sea Anglers Society*, London 1901, 8¹/₄in. diameter, approximate weight 21oz.
(Bonhams) $422

Art Nouveau silver rose bowl, circular shaped with embossed stylized floral decoration, 8in. diameter, London 1910, 19oz.
(G. A. Key) $520

An Edward VII two-handled circular vase-shaped sugar bowl, 14.2cm. high, Nathan & Hayes, Chester 1906, 291gms, with a blue glass liner.
(Bearne's) $437

A Georg Jensen silver bowl, supported on stylized branches, raised circular foot, London 1937, 16.5cm. high, 575 grams.
(Christie's) $1,998

BOWLS

A Queen Anne covered sugar bowl, of fluted hemispherical form chased with acanthus leaves around the rim, by Philip Brush, 1707, 11.9cm. diameter, 8oz.
(Phillips) $1,496

A Continental silver two-handled brandy bowl, unmarked, 19th century, the bracket handles cast and chased with cherubim and scrolls, 7¼in. wide, 10oz.
(Christie's) $400

Tiffany sterling round fruit bowl, 1907–38, applied scroll border, scroll feet, 9½in. diameter, approximately 29 troy oz.
(Skinner) $1,955

Important Georg Jensen sterling silver bowl, no. 445, Denmark, circa 1930, hammered bowl with flaring rim, impressed marks, approximately 18 troy oz. 6⅞in. high.
(Skinner) $1,495

A decorative pair of William IV bowls, with pleated sides, twin foliate handles and circular pedestal bases, by Charles Fox, 1833, 17cm. diameter, 29oz.
(Phillips) $1,995

John P. Kohler repoussé sterling bowl, circa 1910, shaped reserve engraved *M.L.J. Oct. 29, 1915*, 6¼in. diameter, 12 troy oz.
(Skinner) $460

A large Chinese punch bowl, inscribed *Royal Bombay Yacht Club 1901 Challenge Cup 'Sapphire' E. S. Luard*, circa 1900, 37.5cm. diameter.
(Phillips) $5,460

Reed & Barton sterling bowl, Francis I pattern, monogram, 11½in. diameter, approximately 21 troy oz.
(Skinner) $402

A late Victorian Monteith bowl, Robert Garrard, London, 1888, part fluted and applied with cast ribbon tied husk swags, 10¾in. high, approximate weight 126oz.
(Bonhams) $10,400

SILVER

A 19th century Viennese sugar box, gilt lined, with maker's mark *AH*, 11cm. high, 310gr. (Arnold Frankfurt) $485

A good late 17th century spice box, the cover raised in centre and engraved with a dove amidst foliage, circa 1695, 4.7cm. long. (Phillips) $1,529

An 18th century Dutch biscuit box of rectangular shape with bead borders, by Jacobus L. Van Velthoven, Utrecht, 1787, 14.8cm. long, 17.25oz. (Phillips) $1,950

Cardeilhac, circular box and cover, circa 1925, silver-colored metal, the cover with a large flat knop in green hardstone, 14cm. diameter. (Sotheby's) $5,589

Continental 13 Standard silver soap box, 18th century, engraved with armorials and initials, 4¼in. high, 9oz. 12dwt. (Butterfield & Butterfield) $1,840

A Victorian sugar box of semi fluted ovoid form, the hinged semi fluted domed cover with melon fluted finial, London 1888, 265gr. (Spencer's) $398

An Edwardian bright-cut biscuit box, of oval form, the integral tray on pad feet and with a molded rim, William Hutton & Sons Ltd., Sheffield 1902, 7in., 23oz. (Christie's) $807

Jean E. Puiforcat, box and cover, circa 1925, the cover decorated with a frieze of cornelians, maker's mark, 14.25cm. (Sotheby's) $4,099

A George II oval tobacco box, the lid inset with an agate panel, the base with mirrored initials *MH*, probably Robert Cooke, London 1739. (Woolley & Wallis) $7,680

CADDY SPOONS

A Victorian leaf caddy spoon with bifurcated openwork vine handle, by George Unite, Birmingham, 1855.
(Phillips) $283

A George III caddy spoon with rounded tapering handle stamped with bead borders, by Samuel Wintle, circa 1790.
(Phillips) $233

A George III primula leaf caddy spoon, the matted bowl stamped with veins, by Matthew Linwood, Birmingham, 1808.
(Phillips) $366

A Victorian caddy spoon, the thistle or bell shaped bowl embossed with fruiting vines and parcel-gilt, Birmingham, 1852.
(Phillips) $216

An early Victorian caddy spoon, the flower shaped bowl stamped with decoration simulating filigree, by Taylor & Perry, Birmingham, 1837.
(Phillips) $366

An attractive George III fiddle pattern caddy spoon, the scallop shaped bowl engraved with a songbird, by Thomas Freeth, 1818.
(Phillips) $366

A William IV hour glass pattern caddy spoon, the fluted stamped-out bowl with a large scallop shell in center, by Taylor & Perry, Birmingham, 1836.
(Phillips) $183

A George III caddy spoon with wide scalloped bowl and tapering handle, by Wardell & Kempson, Birmingham, 1818.
(Phillips) $183

A Victorian buttercup caddy spoon, with stamped parcel-gilt bowl and leafy stalk handle, by Hilliard & Thomason, Birmingham, 1852.
(Phillips) $432

CANDELABRA

Sheffield plate pair of large four-light candelabra with a pair of finials, Matthew Boulton & Co., Sheffield, circa 1810, 26in. high.
(Butterfield & Butterfield)
$4,312

A Victorian trailing vine six-light candelabrum, on a trefoil base with scrolling foliate feet, 29¼in.
(Christie's)
$3,312

Sheffield plate pair of three-light candelabra, the arms with mark of Matthew Boulton & Co., Sheffield, circa 1800, 19½in. high.
(Butterfield & Butterfield)
$1,150

A pair of late Victorian four-light candelabra, the domed circular bases resting on a pierced apron of foliate scrolls and anthemion feet, by the Goldsmiths & Silversmiths Co. Ltd., 1900, 50cm. high, 189oz.
(Phillips)
$7,648

German 800 Standard silver menorah, late 19th/early 20th century, and a matching servant lamp, 12¼in. high, 25oz. 10dwt.
(Butterfield & Butterfield)
$805

A decorative pair of late Victorian parcel-gilt five-light candelabra, the column modeled as a standing child, supporting scroll branches, by Elkington & Co., 1888, 26½in. high.
(Bonhams)
$5,600

Danish sterling pair of two-light candelabra, Georg Jensen, Copenhagen, Denmark, post 1945, numbered 324, 75oz. 18dwt.
(Butterfield & Butterfield)
$11,500

A five-light candelabrum, with a baluster stem, scrolling branches, waisted sockets and plain circular drip pans, Henry Eyre Ltd., Sheffield 1936, 20in.
(Christie's)
$2,964

A pair of George III silver two-light candelabra, by John Schofield, London, 1795, on spreading circular base and with plain tapering cylindrical stem, 17in. high, 93oz.
(Christie's)
$13,908

CANDLESTICKS

A **pair** of cast candlesticks, in the 17th century taste, each on a part-fluted shaped square base, Sheffield, 6¼in., 29oz.
(Christie's) $628

James Gould, a George II taperstick, the faceted knopped stem with a paneled shoulder and spool holder, 4¼in., London 1747, 3.75oz.
(Woolley & Wallis) $1,312

A pair of Old Sheffield plate candlesticks, on rising square bases stamped with satyr's masks and trailing vines, 12¼in.
(Christie's) $618

A pair of George II cast candlesticks, each on a shell-decorated rising shaped square base and with a knopped stem, William Cafe, London 1754, 9in., 38.25oz.
(Christie's) $2,895

A pair of candlesticks, on rising shaped square bases, the bases, shoulders and nozzles die-stamped with flowers and foliage, Viners, Sheffield 1928, 6in.
(Christie's) $717

A pair of Victorian candlesticks, in the mid 18th century taste, each on a shell-decorated rising shaped square base, Henry Wilkinson & Co., Sheffield 1845, 9¼in.
(Christie's) $869

Isaac Liger, a pair of William III cast candlesticks, the holders of slight campana form, 6in. high, London 1693, 24oz.
(Woolley & Wallis)
                            $15,200

A pair of Edwardian dwarf candlesticks, on reeded and fluted rising shaped oblong bases, Martin Hall & Co., Sheffield 1903, 9.5cm.
(Christie's) $507

A pair of Swedish silver candlesticks, by Olof Yttraeus, Uppsala, 1784, spirally fluted and on circular domed base, 9⅛in. high, 32oz.
(Christie's) $11,497

CANDLESTICKS

Two of four George III cast candlesticks, on stepped square bases with gadroon borders and knops, by William Cafe, 1766, 26cm. high, 83oz.
(Phillips) $7,800

A George I cast taperstick with hexagonal sconce, baluster stem and spreading base, 11.5cm. high, Richard Bayley, London 1722, 100gms.
(Bearne's) $918

Pair of candlesticks on rectangular scalloped bases, domed foot and tapering ovoid baluster columns, hallmarked for London 1936, 11¹/₂in.
(G. A. Key) $352

A pair of George III table candlesticks, monogrammed below a crown on the bases, 24.7cm. high, Thomas James & Nathaniel Creswick, Sheffield 1819, weighted.
(Bearne's) $1,848

A pair of late Victorian candlesticks, on gadrooned stepped square bases, with fluted tapering columns, Gibson & Langman, Sheffield 1896, 5¹/₂in.
(Christie's) $850

A pair of Swedish silver candlesticks by Jonas Thomasson Ronander, Stockholm, 1757, each on shaped-circular base and with baluster stem, 9¹/₄in. high, 27oz.
(Christie's) $33,379

A pair of plated on copper candlesticks in the neo-classic style, flared cylindrical stems with urn shaped knops, loaded, 30cm. high.
(Spencer's) $279

A pair of Victorian Corinthian column dressing table candlesticks, the square bases with acanthus edging, 17.5cm. high, Martin Hall & Co., London 1891, loaded.
(Bearne's) $907

A pair of George II cast rococo candlesticks, with swirling baluster columns and domed bases, 30cm. high, by Lawrence Johnson, 1752, 66.5oz.
(Phillips) $6,983

CARD CASES

An early Victorian silver castle top calling card case, pierced, chased and repoussé with a view of Warwick castle, Birmingham 1838, by Nathaniel Mills.
(Spencer's) $955

A Victorian card case, cover decorated in high relief with the Burns Monument and Brig o'Doon, by Nathaniel Mills, Birmingham, 1849.
(Phillips) $1,279

An Edwardian silver calling card case, chased and repoussé with a view inscribed *Nile (Philae)*, Birmingham 1905, makers mark *R.P.*
(Spencer's) $462

A late Victorian silver calling card case, with bright cut engraved decoration of convolvulus, roses, and scrolling foliage, London 1876, by Sampson Mordan & Co.
(Spencer's) $400

A Victorian 'castle-top' card case, chased in relief with a cathedral on cover, probably Lichfield Cathedral, by Yapp & Woodward, Birmingham, circa 1850.
(Phillips) $2,340

A mid Victorian silver castle top calling card case, chased and repoussé with a view of Osborne House, Isle of Wight, Birmingham 1860, by Frederick Marson.
(Spencer's) $924

An early Victorian silver calling card case, pierced, chased and repoussé with fruiting vine, and flowers, Birmingham 1837, by Nathaniel Mills.
(Spencer's) $554

A mid Victorian silver castle top calling card case, chased and repoussé with a view of York Minster, Birmingham 1853, by Hilliard & Thomason.
(Spencer's) $893

An Edwardian silver calling card case, chased and repoussé with fighting lions opposing a cartouche, Birmingham 1904, by Chrisford & Norris.
(Spencer's) $431

CASTERS

Unusual caster of ovoid form, on three animal feet, pierced lid with turned finial, Birmingham 1908.
(G. A. Key) $122

A set of three George II silver casters, by Pezé Pilleau, London, 1732, of plain octagonal vase form and on spreading foot, 7³/₄in. and 6¹/₄in. high, 28oz.
(Christie's) $5,563

Large caster, the wrythen body supported on trumpet base, hallmarked for Birmingham 1910.
(G. A. Key) $107

A pair of George II casters, of vase shape, each on a rising circular foot and with a baluster finial, maker's mark indistinct, London 1735, 5in.
(Christie's) $1,095

A set of three important Queen Anne silver-gilt casters, unmarked, circa 1705, attributed to Philip Rollos, vase-shaped and on spreading circular base, 10¹/₄in. and 8in. high, 56oz.
(Christie's) $224,138

A George II and a George III caster, of inverted pear shape and with a baluster finial, London 1758, 4³/₄in., the latter with a vase-shaped finial, London 1790, 5in.
(Christie's) $618

Fine Omar Ramsden and Alwyn Carr silver caster, lighthouse shaped with wide circular foot, inscribed to base, 5in. tall, London 1911, 6oz.
(G. A. Key) $926

A pair of George II casters, of plain vase shape, each on a rising circular foot, Samuel Wood, London 1743 and 1744, 4³/₄in.
(Christie's) $1,148

A sugar caster, chased with fluting, flowers and foliage and with vacant C-scroll cartouches, Goldsmiths & Silversmiths Co. Limited, London 1919, 7³/₄in., 8oz.
(Christie's) $390

An American silver centerpiece, Bailey, Banks & Biddle, Philadelphia, circa 1890, of rectangular form, embossed with rococo ornament, 111oz., 18¼in. long.
(Sotheby's) $6,325

Sterling chased centerpiece with plated pierced cover, Gorham Mfg. Co., Providence, Rhode Island, 1919, 8in. high, 45oz. 12dwt.
(Butterfield & Butterfield)
                              $1,610

An American silver large circular centerpiece, Redlich, New York, circa 1900, the domed sides embossed and applied as a rose trellis, 98oz., 19½in. diameter.
(Sotheby's) $4,600

A good centerpiece épergne, with central vase flanked by three smaller vases and two sweet dishes, by Walker & Hall, Sheffield, 1910, 40.3cm. high, 74.25oz.
(Phillips) $4,655

J. E. Caldwell sterling centerpiece and tray, late 19th and early 20th century, reticulated rims and base, monogrammed, tray 13½in. diameter, approximately 74 troy oz. weighable silver.
(Skinner) $2,070

A Victorian three-light candelabrum centerpiece épergne, on fluted circular base, the vine tendril stem applied with a cherub, 22in. high.
(Christie's) $2,260

Fine early 19th century silver plated table centerpiece, rising to a central boss emitting four branches with large center trumpet, 14in. high.
(G. A. Key) $746

Sterling basket form centerpiece with plated liner and wire frog fittings, Shreve & Co., San Francisco, California, circa 1909–22, 10in. high, 45oz.
(Butterfield & Butterfield)
                              $2,587

A Victorian table center piece, one side chased with a vignette of a racing scene with two jockeys up, Messrs. Barnard, London 1845, 22¾in., 152.25oz.
(Christie's) $7,844

CHAMBERSTICKS

A French 19th century chamber candlestick, with an 18th century style rococo stylized shell and scrolling foliate handle, 6½in. overall. (Christie's) $436

A rare pair of American silver candlesticks, Obadiah Rich, Boston, circa 1830, each scalloped circular, with lobed and molded rim, 2⅝in. high. 6oz.
(Christie's) $11,500

George II silver chamberstick, with bobeche, hallmarks for London, 1730, marks of James Goulet, 9.4 troy oz.
(Eldred's) $990

A pair of George II chambersticks, molded borders, spool shaped capitals, raised on three ball feet, circa 1750, by Richard Calderwood, approximate weight 16oz.
(Bonhams) $3,520

A pair of George III chamber candlesticks, rising scroll handle with beaded shaped thumb piece, probably Daniel Smith & Robert Sharp, London 1784, 6½in. overall, 19.75oz.
(Christie's) $2,800

A good pair of George IV chamber candlesticks by Matthew Boulton, each with gadroon and shell cast border, Birmingham 1823, 680gr. approximately.
(Spencer's) $1,837

A William IV circular chamber candlestick with knopped stem, 11.2cm. diameter, John Wrangham & William Moulson, London 1834, 254gms.
(Bearne's) $605

A pair of George III chamber candlesticks, of gadrooned circular form, each with a rising handle with foliate thumb piece, probably Edmund Vincent, London 1766, 14.75oz. gross.
(Christie's) $2,268

Early George III silver chamber candlestick of plain circular form with reeded edges, plus matching snuffer, London 1772, 7oz.
(G. A. Key) $357

SILVER

F. Zwickl, blue Daimler racing car cigarette case, 1931, silver-colored metal, enameled panel, 8.25 x 11.5cm. · (Sotheby's) $3,353

A Continental silver colored metal cigar case, embossed and chased to one side with a fallen angel, 4^1/$_2$ x 3^1/$_2$in., approx. 7oz. (Neales) $672

After Franz von Stuck, 'The See-Saw' cigarette case, 1901, enameled with two women with drapes on an improvised see-saw, 7 x 8.5cm. (Sotheby's) $2,422

After Alphonse Mucha for Louis Kuppenheim, Girl Smoking cigarette box, 1900, the hinged cover enameled with a draped female nude with a lighted cigarette, 8.5 x 5.25cm. (Sotheby's) $3,167

Georg Anton Scheidt, Vienna, box with cabochon, circa 1900, the hinged lid with organic, whiplash design incorporating a green hardstone cabochon, 9cm. square. (Sotheby's) $1,267

Russian 84 Standard cigarette case, G. Samomin, Moscow, circa 1908–17, with a cast oval relief plaque of a group of young girls' faces, 4^1/$_2$in. long. (Butterfield & Butterfield) $517

F. Lodholz, Bi-plane cigarette case, circa 1920, enamel panel with plane above clouds, 8.75 x 8cm. (Sotheby's) $1,490

An Austro-Hungarian white-metal cigarette case, circa 1910, the hinged cover enameled, depicting a young man and woman in evening dress, embracing, 3^1/$_2$in. high. (Bonhams) $1,120

An electroplated cigarette box, of rounded rectangular form, the lid with engraved initials R.N. by R. & D. Ltd., 1^1/$_2$ x 6^1/$_2$in. (Christie's) $3,680

CIGARETTE CASES

A late Victorian cigarette case, the cover enameled with a blonde girl dressed in a pink tutu siting upon a white horse, Birmingham, 1896.
(Phillips) $749

Ferdinand von Reznicek, Lovers, cigarette case, circa 1890, enameled with a pair of lovers flirting in the boudoir, 9 x 7.5cm.
(Sotheby's) $2,422

A Japanese silver cigarette case decorated in relief, the details heightened with coloured metals, Meiji, 10cm.
(Bearne's) $688

A green guilloche enamel lady's cigarette case, maker's mark of Fabergé, workmaster August Hollming, 1896–1908, silver mounts, 5 x 8.2cm.
(Bonhams) $1,920

Franz von Bayros, cigarette case with woman and white peacock, circa 1900, silver-colored metal, enameled in soft shades of cream and sepia, 8cm. square.
(Sotheby's) $2,422

Russian gentleman's 84 Standard silver souvenir cigarette case, P.J.S., circa 1896–1907, 4in. long.
(Butterfield & Butterfield)
                         $1,610

A late 19th century electroplated cigarette case, in polychrome enamel with the portrait of a terrier, marked *Alpacca*, 7.5 x 8.5cm.
(Phillips) $599

Russian cloisonné enamel gilt 84 Standard silver cigarette case, maker's initials *PR*, Moscow, 1887, 3³/₄in. long.
(Butterfield & Butterfield)
                         $920

An American white-metal cigarette case, circa 1900, the hinged cover enameled with the bust portrait of a semi-nude blonde young woman.
(Bonhams) $1,760

CLARET JUGS

A Victorian mounted cut-glass claret jug, with a pierced girdle of trailing scrollwork, by Charles Edwards, 1888, 33cm. high.
(Phillips) $3,990

A late Victorian silver-mounted clear glass claret jug, with cut tapering oval body with star-cut base, William Comyns, London 1899, 12in.
(Christie's) $1,255

A clear glass claret jug, of barrel shape, cut with vertical staves and applied with hoops with bosses, 9³/₄in.
(Christie's) $390

A Victorian silver-mounted clear glass claret jug, of oval bellied form, on a star-cut base and with a beaded mount, W. & G. Sissons, Sheffield 1879, 9¹/₂in. high.
(Christie's) $1,794

A Victorian presentation baluster claret jug, richly chased with scrolling foliage, dated *1860* by J. & W. Marshall, Edinburgh, 1859, 10in. high, 32oz.
(Christie's) $1,168

An Edward VII silver-mounted cut-glass claret jug, the cylindrical cut-glass body with bulbous base, 27.5cm. high, Charles Boyton and Sons, London 1907.
(Bearne's) $1,008

German 800 Standard silver and cut glass claret jug, circa 1900, finished in alternating vertical panels of plain polished and diamond cut, 11in. high.
(Butterfield & Butterfield) $1,955

A late Victorian silver-mounted cut glass claret jug, the neck mount die-stamped with rococo scrolling foliage and C-scrolls, W. & G. Sissons, Sheffield 1901, 9³/₄in.
(Christie's) $995

A mid-Victorian claret jug by Elkington & Co. 1869, the mount and spout chased with Bacchanalian figures and vines, 27cm. high.
(Cheffins Grain & Comins) $547

COASTERS

A pair of George III decanter stands, with pierced fret sides and silver covered mahogany bases, probably by William Parker, London 1791/93.
(Woolley & Wallis) $1,280

George III silver and wood set of four wine coasters, Solomon Hougham, London, 1800, 5in. diameter.
(Butterfield & Butterfield) $4,600

A pair of George III wine coasters, the sides pierced with geometric designs and engraved with crests, Edward Aldridge, London 1766, 4³/4in.
(Christie's) $1,324

Russian silver teacup holder, possibly Frolov Sergei Alexevich, St. Petersburg, circa 1900, engraved floral design, 4¹/2in. high, approx. 4 troy oz.
(Skinner) $115

A set of six George III silver wine coasters, London, 1798, maker's mark indistinct but probably that of Samuel Godbehere and Edward Wigan, 4¹/2in. diameter.
(Christie's) $9,163

An Art Nouveau two-handled syphon stand, pierced with broad frieze of stylized scrolling foliage, Goldsmiths & Silversmiths Co. Limited, London 1904, 7in.
(Christie's) $567

A pair of George IV Scottish decanter stands, serpentine edge pierced fret sides, engraved paterae, crested with motto, maker J. McKay, Edinburgh 1823.
(Woolley & Wallis) $1,306

A pair of George III wirework wine coasters, of circular form, each applied with two oval cartouches, William Vincent, London 1889, 4³/4in.
(Christie's) $1,810

A pair of George III wine coasters, of circular form, the turned wood bases with unmarked vacant circular bosses, maker's marks indistinct, Sheffield 1775, 5¹/2in.
(Christie's) $1,374

COFFEE POTS

A three piece sterling coffee service, stamped *Wiwen Nilsson*, Lund 1956–7, of octagonal form with C-handles, 26cm. height of pot.
(Stockholms Auktionsverk)
$11,652

A German style coffee pot, with a rising curved spout with lion's head terminal, 8¼in.
(Christie's) $732

Pair of George II style large silver coffee pots of circular baluster form with leaf capped spouts, Birmingham 1970, 64oz. all in.
(G. A. Key) $1,292

A George II coffee pot of baluster circular form with fluted acanthus decorated swanneck spout, 25cm. high, Robert and Albin Cox, London 1759, 727gms.
(Bearne's) $2,142

A pair of café au lait pots, each of plain tapering cylindrical form and on a flaring foot, D. & J. Wellby, London 1934, height of coffee pot 7¾in., 32.25oz. gross.
(Christie's) $840

George III silver coffee pot, Sutton & Bult, London, 1782, with domed lid, 12½in. high, gross weight 27oz. 16dwt.
(Butterfield & Butterfield) $2,300

Austrian silver matching coffee pot and ewer, circa 1872, maker VDC, ovoid baluster form, carved ivory handles and finial on post, applied crest on side, 9⅝in. high, approximately 36 troy oz.
(Skinner) $805

A George III silver coffee jug, stand and lamp, by Paul Storr, London, 1808, the vase-shaped jug applied with a band of anthemion ornament, 11¾in. high, 55oz. gross.
(Christie's) $13,908

A pair of early 18th century café au lait pots, of molded oval form, each applied with cut card stylized soliage, S. Garrard, London 1913, height of coffee pot 8½in.
(Christie's) $1,412

581

COFFEE POTS

A George III coffee pot of tapering cylindrical form with paneled straight spout, 25.5cm. high, Thomas Farren, London 1725, 782gms.
(Bearne's) $4,590

A George III coffee pot of plain tapering form, with bell-shaped finial, by Aymé Videau, 1750, 20.5cm. high, 21oz.
(Phillips) $3,276

A Victorian coffee pot, of baluster form, Robert Hennell, London 1855, 9¼in., on a similar fluted and molded circular warming stand, 35oz.
(Christie's) $1,569

A George III coffee pot, the domed hinged cover having artichoke finial, engraved with a coat-of-arms, London 1764, maker Ebenezer Coker, 10¾in. high, approximate weight 28oz.
(Bonhams) $3,840

A George III 11in. plain baluster coffee pot, the spout with acanthus leaf mount, wood scroll handle on stem foot, London mark 1776, maker John Kentenber, 29oz. 10dwt.
(Anderson & Garland)
                              $2,015

An 18th century Channel Islands coffee pot of tapering shape, with leaf-capped scalloped spout, by Jean Gavey, Jersey, circa 1740, 25cm. high, 34oz.
(Phillips) $10,920

A George III coffee pot, James Young, 1769, baluster form, scroll mounted spout, domed hinged cover, 11⅝in. high, approximate weight 30oz.
(Bonhams) $4,160

A George III silver coffee pot, Paul Storr, London, 1817, the vase-shaped body with mask and acanthus foliage spout, 10¾in. high, 38oz. gross.
(Christie's) $9,607

An 18th century style coffee pot, polished wood scroll handle and domed hinged cover with baluster finial, London 1934, 9in., 27.75oz. gross.
(Christie's) $847

COFFEE POTS

A Sheffield Plate vase-shaped coffee pot, crested, with bead edging and scrolling acanthus spout, 30.5cm. high.
(Bearne's) $597

A George II ovoid coffee pot with thread edging, 26.5cm. high, Peter, Anne and William Bateman, London 1800, 726gms.
(Bearne's) $1,454

A George II coffee pot, one side chased with a vignette of two figures, the other side engraved with a crest, Isaac Cookson, Newcastle 1758, 8^{1}/$_{2}$in., 20.75oz.
(Christie's) $974

A fine silver coffee pot, Myer Myers, New York, circa 1750, engraved on side with script initials *PCW*, 11in. high, 34oz. 10dwt. gross.
(Christie's) $77,300

A silver and mixed-metal coffee pot, Gorham Mfg. Co., Providence, 1881, the sides applied with a copper tree branch, a lizard, three birds and a butterfly, 7^{1}/$_{8}$in. high, 16oz. gross.
(Christie's) $6,325

A George III baluster coffee pot, having a cast leaf spray decorated swan neck spout, maker John King, London 1771, 26oz. all in.
(Woolley & Wallis)
                              $2,644

Regency silver coffee pot, Robertson & Walton, Newcastle, 1818, with shell thumbpiece, 10^{5}/$_{8}$in. high, 30oz. 2dwt.
(Butterfield & Butterfield)
                              $920

An 18th century German coffee pot, Johann Pepfsenhauser, Augsburg, 1737, domed hinged cover with faceted finial, 5^{1}/$_{4}$in. high, approximate weight 8oz.
(Bonhams) $2,720

Queen Anne style silver coffee pot of plain tapering cylindrical design with domed lid, composition handle, London 1964, 24oz.
(G. A. Key) $403

CREAM JUGS

A George II cast cream jug of auricular or mollusc form, with eagle head handle, unmarked, circa 1735, 10.2cm. high, 2.5oz. (Phillips) $1,061

William IV silver cream jug, melon shaped with heavy reeded rim, leaf capped scrolled handle, Birmingham probably 1831, 9^{1}/$_{2}$oz. (G. A. Key) $258

Attractive George II silver cream jug, the body chased and embossed with flowers, leaves, vacant cartouche, London 1759. (G. A. Key) $385

A George III pedestal cream jug, of vase shape, on a reeded rising square base and with a reeded rim and spout and fluted scroll handle, Henry Chawner, London 1792, 5in. high. (Christie's) $454

A Continental late 19th century cow cream jug, the hinged cover applied with a stylized bee and chased with flowers and foliage, bearing import marks for London 1895, 8.75oz. (Christie's) $1,416

A silver cream jug, attributed to Thomas Sparrow, Philadelphia or Annapolis, circa 1765, pyriform, on three ball-and-claw feet, 4^{1}/$_{4}$in. high, 4oz. (Christie's) $6,325

An American silver creamer, William Ball, Philadelphia, circa 1760, of pear form with waved rim, 2oz. 10dwt., 4^{1}/$_{8}$in. high. (Sotheby's) $3,565

A George III gilt-lined cream jug, of helmet form, on a beaded and engraved rising square base, Peter & Ann Bateman, London 1791, 7in., 5.5oz. (Christie's) $924

A silver cream-jug, Benjamin Burt, Boston, 1765, pyriform, on three scroll legs with trifid feet, 3^{5}/$_{8}$in. high, 3oz. (Christie's) $3,220

CRUETS

A George III eight-bottle cruet, of oval form, on curved feet and with a central tapering stem, probably George Brasier, London 1789, 10¹/₂in. overall. (Christie's) $1,306

Sheffield silver plated caster set, Colonial Revival style, cut glass bottles, 10¹/₄in. high. (Skinner) $489

A George III oval cruet with eight mounted glass bottles, the stand with reeded rim, by Hester Bateman, 1790, 19.6cm. long. (Phillips) $2,028

A George IV oil and vinegar frame, with a leaf-capped scroll handle, scroll pierced sides and four cast feet, by Charles Fox, 1826, 20cm. high, 14cm. wide, 13oz. weighable. (Phillips) $2,078

A George III four-bottle cruet frame, the wirework frame having a central foliate scroll handle decorated with a mask, London 1817, by William Burwash, 6³/₄in. high, approximate weight 16oz. (Bonhams) $768

A George II Warwick cruet, with three casters and two mounted glass bottles, the handle engraved with the crest of Congreve, by George Greenhill Jones, 1738, 52oz. (Phillips) $4,988

An early Victorian 8-bottle cruet frame by the Barnards, 1850, of oval shape with pierced compressed gallery, 26cm. high, crested. (Cheffins Grain & Comins) $1,216

Victorian trefoil silver cruet stand with beaded edges, twist and bead handle and containing three faceted glass bottles with silver mounts, London 1875. (G. A. Key) $170

George III oval silver cruet frame with reeded gallery supported on four oval stays, inset mahogany base, London 1803 by Alice and George Burrows. (G. A. Key) $1,034

A large caudle cup, Gerrit Onckelbag, New York, circa 1700, the sides applied with two cast caryatid scroll handles, 6½in. high, 27oz. 10dwt. (Christie's) $23,000

An early 18th century Norwegian parcel-gilt tumbler cup, engraved with script initials *FHS:MMD*, by Niels Andersen Wibe, Larvik, circa 1730, 7.7cm. diameter, 2.25oz. (Phillips) $1,530

German silver-handled kiddush cup, with repoussé decoration and inscription, 3in. high. (Skinner) $863

A Charles I communion cup, maker's mark *I•M* above a bear, London, 1637, raised on a trumpet foot terminating in a domed circular base, 4⅝in. high, approximate weight 8oz. (Bonhams) $2,480

An American silver-gilt three-handled cup, Tiffany & Co., New York, circa 1890, embossed and chased with a continuous circle of dancing maenads, 43oz., 9in. high. (Sotheby's) $3,450

A fine George III regimental presentation cup and cover, by Paul Storr, of campana form, the pedestal foot decorated with a border of laurel leaves, 1809, 40cm. high, 140oz. (Phillips) $14,131

A George II Irish two-handled cup and cover of inverted bell form, engraved with the coat-of-arms of Sir Richard Meade, Dublin 1728, 11in. high, approximate weight 48oz. (Bonhams) $4,480

A Victorian stirrup cup, finely modeled as a fox's head, also engraved with a presentation inscription, 1864, by George Fox, approximate weight 7oz. (Bonhams) $4,000

The Hawkstone Cup, a William IV silver-gilt horse racing trophy cup and cover, the cover with cast finial of a mare and foal, by William Bateman, 1834, 46.5cm. high, 120.5oz. (Phillips) $8,313

CUPS

Goodnow & Jenks sterling loving cup, retailed by Bigelow, Kennard & Co., monogram, 8in. high, approximately 34 troy oz. (Skinner) $402

A silver handled cup, John Coney, Boston, circa 1690, the scroll handle with beaded rattail, 2¹/₈in. high, 1oz. 10dwt. (Christie's) $4,830

A George I cup and cover, of inverted bell shape, on a spreading foot, Samuel Lea, London 1719, 12³/₄in., 79oz. (Christie's) $2,930

A late 17th century ox-eye or college cup of baluster form with 'ox-eye' side handles, front engraved with the armorials of a lady, circa 1685, 13cm. high, 18oz. (Phillips) $14,040

An American silver large three-handled cup, Tiffany & Co., New York, 1902–7, partly chased with scrolling foliage, 178oz., 14⁵/₈in. high. (Sotheby's) $6,325

Sterling floral chased three handled cup, circa 1900, with chased blossom and leaf bands, 6in. high, 20oz. 4dwt. (Butterfield & Butterfield) $1,150

A Commonwealth gilt-lined wine cup, tapering circular bowl, pricked with initials and a date 1666 above a punch-beaded frieze, maker's mark indistinct, London 1654, 6.25cm. (Christie's) $1,395

An American Indian style silver, copper and horn-mounted cup, Tiffany & Co., New York, 1905, the neck inlaid with Navajo-inspired zig-zag designs, 12⁷/₈in. high. (Sotheby's) $48,875

Montefiore Anglo-Palestinian silver kiddush cup, circa 1867, with three applied Montefiori crests, 8in. high. (Skinner) $6,900

DISHES

A George III swing-handled bob-bon dish, the lower part of the body decorated with beading and fluting, Arthur Annesley, London 1762, 6¹/₂in., 6oz. (Christie's) $879

A German silver-gilt dish, maker Johann Martin Satzger, Augsburg, circa 1765, of shaped oval form, chased with floral scrollwork and birds. (Bonhams) $3,520

A late William IV butter dish, cover and liner, the frosted glass bowl cut to simulate staved wood, London 1836, by the Barnards, 355gr., 7in. diameter. (Spencer's) $796

A pair of Victorian sweet dishes, the bases with laurel leaf and ribbon borders, on ball and claw feet, by Robert Harper, 1881, 17.4cm. long, 18.75oz. (Phillips) $1,120

German reticulated silver compote, late 19th century, the oval bowl decorated with scrolls, flowers, putti and eagles' head handles, on a pedestal base, 12in. high, approximately 24 troy oz. (Skinner) $690

A good pair of Victorian butter shells, on mollusc feet, the handles with shell and scroll borders, by Messrs. Barnard, 1843, 14.2cm. wide, 11.25oz. (Phillips) $1,413

A two-handled dish, Paris, circa 1910, signed *Boucheron, Paris*, the lug handles, each set with rose quartz. (Bonhams) $2,400

A pair of Victorian oval breakfast dishes, with double crests to the revolving covers, bead edges, detachable liners, 14in. (Woolley & Wallis) $933

One of a pair of boat-shaped dishes, with floral-embellished scroll handles, by Mappin & Webb, 1916, 27cm. long, 42.5oz. (Phillips) $1,716

EPERGNES

A post Regency Sheffield plated épergne, applied with broad borders of acanthus and shells, circa 1830, 14in. high overall.
(Neales) $1,200

An American silver eight-branch épergne, Gorham Mfg. Co., Providence, RI, circa 1889, of circular form, the domed centre pierced and cast, 232oz., 31.8cm. high.
(Sotheby's) $8,625

Sheffield plate four-arm épergne frame with associated later glass fittings, circa 1820, 13¹/₂in. high.
(Butterfield & Butterfield) $2,587

An Edwardian table centerpiece, with a fluted central vase and three openwork scrolling branches, each fitted with a conforming smaller vase, maker's intials H.M., Chester 1906, 14in.
(Christie's) $814

An early Victorian candelabrum/épergne, with three cast Classical female figures, one representing Justice, by John Edward Terrey, 1837, 71cm. high, 325oz.
(Phillips) $21,613

A George V table épergne, the central trumpet shaped vase with pierced border, supporting two circular sweetmeat dishes and two tapering smaller vases, Chester 1912, 910gr. approximately.
(Spencer's) $836

A George V épergne, the scrolled mounts supporting four trumpet shaped vases with frill lips, Sheffield 1910, loaded, 38cm. high.
(Spencer's) $616

An American silver épergne, Gorham Mfg. Co., Providence, RI, 1901, on shaped square base, partially chased with flowers, 170oz. 10dwt., 50.2cm. high.
(Sotheby's) $6,325

An Edwardian table centerpiece, fitted with four detachable tulip-shaped vases with molded waved rims, maker's initials J.G., Birmingham 1908, 15¹/₄in.
(Christie's) $543

FLATWARE

A Charles I Provincial Apostle spoon of good gauge, the gilt cast figure probably representing St. Matthew, possibly Aberystwyth, 7¹/₂in. long. (Hy. Duke & Son) **$1,840**

Interesting Charles II silver tablespoon, trefid and rattail pattern, York 1679 maker Thomas Mangy.
(G. A. Key) **$813**

An American silver soup ladle, Joseph Lownes, Philadelphia, circa 1790, with rounded end, bright-cut and engraved, 6oz., 13¹/₄in. long. (Sotheby's) **$862**

A Victorian silver sifting spoon, Francis Higgins, London, 1847, the shaped oval bowl pierced with scrolls, 6³/₄in. long, 3oz.
(Christie's) **$272**

A Victorian fish slice and fork, the ivory handles carved with stylized dolphins amidst bullrushes, Hilliard & Thomason, Birmingham 1857. (Christie's) **$797**

A mid-17th century Provincial apostle spoon with gilt terminal figure, maker's mark *E.A.*, Exeter, circa 1650.
(Bearne's) **$1,932**

Fine Victorian silver soup ladle, double struck King's pattern, London 1874 by G. Angell, 10oz. (G. A. Key) **$456**

A Victorian fish slice and fork, the ivory handles carved with entwined dolphins and other fish.
(Christie's) **$850**

Three American 'Japanese style' silver servers, Gorham Mfg. Co., Providence, RI, 1892 and circa 1890, with bamboo-form handles, 11oz. (Sotheby's) **$4,887**

An American silver flatware set, Tiffany & Co., New York, circa 1885, Lap Over Edge Etched pattern, 133 pieces.
(Sotheby's) **$20,700**

A William and Mary silver basting spoon, maker's mark of Benjamin Bathurst, London, 1692, deep oval bow and tapering octagonal handle, 18in. long, 9oz. (Christie's) **$7,472**

A William and Mary silver-gilt trefid spoon of good gauge, the unusual cleft terminal having vacant cartouches, in a shagreen case, London 1689, by Thomas Issod, 6³/₈in. long.
(Bonhams) **$2,240**

FLATWARE

A late George III Old English pattern punch ladle, with shell bowl, possibly by Simon Harris, London 1814, 142gr.
(Spencer's) $199

A Charles II dog nose (wavy end) rat tail pattern spoon by John Sutton, London possibly 1696, 50gr., 18.8cm. long.
(Spencer's) $199

An early/mid-17th century Provincial Buddah knop spoon, the terminal figure with traces of gilding, 18.3cm. long, circa 1630, 48gms.
(Bearne's) $4,452

A rare silver spoon, Jeremiah Dummer, Boston, 1680–1710, the wavy-end handle engraved on reverse *Mary Webster*, 7¼in. long, 1oz. 8dwt.
(Christie's) $4,370

A pair of Danish fish slices, realistically cast and chased as flat fish, maker's mark *M. Aase*.
(Christie's) $620

A rare Chinese silver marrow scoop cum sucket fork, Old English reeded pattern, stamped once with maker's mark *KHC* (Khecheong), circa 1850, 12in. long.
(Bonhams) $512

A George III Irish soup ladle, with scalloped bowl, bright-engraved with star decoration, by John Sheils, Dublin, 1791, 5oz.
(Phillips) $437

A Portuguese 19th century fish slice, with octagonal handle and pierced blade engraved with a fish, Lisbon.
(Christie's) $230

An attractive pair of late Victorian fish servers, with acanthus leaf and anthemion pierced blade and tine, Sheffield 1892.
(Spencer's) $217

Fine example of an early George III scroll and shell backed silver tablespoon, London 1762.
(G. A. Key) $137

A pair of Victorian fish servers, the blade pierced and engraved with foliate enclosing a roundel, Sheffield 1855, by Martin Hall and Co., cased.
(Spencer's) $543

A good early 18th century Channel Islands basting spoon of French fiddle pattern, engraved with baroque armorial above initials, by Jean Gavey, Jersey, circa 1735, 35cm. long, 7.5oz.
(Phillips) $2,340

GOBLETS

A George III silver-gilt goblet, decorated in relief with stiff leafage, by Peter Podio, 1793, 18.1cm. high, 13.5oz.
(Phillips) $2,660

George III silver assembled pair of similar goblets, London, Hester Bateman, 1787; and Robert Hennell, 1783, 13oz. 6dwt.
(Butterfield & Butterfield)
                                $1,380

German hevra kadishah silver and silver-gilt memorial goblet, Berlin, circa 1833, 10³/₄in. high.
(Skinner) $2,645

A pair of Regency goblets, the part-fluted inverted bell-shaped bowls each engraved: *Gage D'amour Conjugal*, probably William Elliot, London 1818, 5¹/₄in., 12.25oz.
(Christie's) $799

A mid 18th century Irish silver mounted coconut goblet, mark of Michael Cormick & Charles Townsend only, Dublin, circa 1770, crested, 6in. high.
(Bonhams) $1,040

A pair of Continental marriage goblets, the paneled etched bowls on cast figure stems of a lady and gentleman in period costume, 7in., London import mark 1895, 9oz.
(Woolley & Wallis) $480

A small and attractive goblet, the trumpet foot chased and set all around with cabochon set chrysoprase, by Ramsden & Carr, 1917, 9.5cm. high, 2.5oz. gross weight.
(Phillips) $1,496

Two Victorian goblets and an Edwardian example, each decorated with flowers and foliage, London 1863 and 1873 and Birmingham 1902, 8³/₄in. and smaller, 27.75oz.
(Christie's) $543

A Regency gilt-lined goblet, the part-fluted campana-shaped bowl decorated with a frieze of trailing vines, Emes & Barnard, London 1812, 6in., 10.25oz.
(Christie's) $724

INKSTANDS

An Art Nouveau inkstand, on a shaped oak base, molded with stylized shells and with a pen rest and inkwell, Birmingham 1909, 21cm.
(Christie's) $532

A Victorian inkstand on scroll feet, with a central circular box and a taperstick cover, by John S. Hunt, 1863, 27cm. long, 28oz. weighable.
(Phillips) $1,829

A Victorian scallop-shaped inkwell, engraved with panels of anthemion, by Brook & Son, Edinburgh 1865, 9½in. wide, 10oz.
(Christie's) $791

A George III inkstand, the central box having a later chamberstick, flanked by two silver mounted and glass ink bottles, Birmingham 1821, by Matthew Boulton.
(Bonhams) $1,920

A late Victorian two-bottle inkstand, the square cut glass inkwells with shaped square hinged covers engraved with crests, Thomas Bradbury, London 1901, 11¾in., 21.25oz. free.
(Christie's) $784

A George III navette-shaped inkstand with reeded rim, on fluted bracket feet, complete with three mounted diamond-cut glass bottles, by John Emes, 1806, 19oz.
(Phillips) $1,560

An Edwardian inkstand, of shaped oblong form, on pierced rococo shell feet, James Dixon & Son, Sheffield 1902, 7in., 8oz. free.
(Christie's) $850

A George IV partner's inkstand, with foliage borders, 11½in., makers Samuel Roberts and George Cadman & Co., Sheffield 1822, 30oz.
(Woolley & Wallis) $1,711

An Edwardian novelty inkstand modeled as a sofa, the two shield-shaped 'chair backs' centered by a watch holder, Sheffield 1908, 7¼in., with a white metal watch.
(Christie's) $976

A late Victorian two-bottle inkstand, with everted pierced gallery, by J. & W. Deakin, Sheffield 1898, 10in. wide, 22oz.
(Christie's) $1,281

A Victorian naturalistic inkstand, modeled with rocks and foliage and applied with a recumbent stag, John S. Hunt, London 1852, 10½in.
(Christie's) $1,484

A silver gilt octagonal inkwell, modeled as the Old Cowdray Fountain, by C. & R. Comyns, 1920, 8in. wide, 58oz.
(Christie's) $1,318

JUGS

An Edwardian hot water jug, with a molded body band, and gadrooned domed hinged hinged cover, London 1907, 8³/₄in., 17oz. gross.
(Christie's) $407

A George III hot water jug, gadrooned domed hinged cover decorated with spiral fluting, Parker & Wakelin, London 1771, 9³/₄in., 18.5oz. gross.
(Christie's) $3,011

A George II silver beer jug, Richard Bayley, London, 1740, of plain baluster form and on spreading circular foot, 6³/₄in. high, 24oz.
(Christie's) $7,472

An Edwardian hot water jug, on a gadroon and scroll-stamped rising square base, Goldsmiths & Silversmiths Co. Limited, London 1904, 9in., 18.25oz. gross.
(Christie's) $620

Austrian silver-gilt kohanims laver, Vienna, early 19th century, three-handled, marked *Schill*, bearing a dedicatory text inscribed to the Horowitz family, 8¹/₂in. high.
(Skinner) $6,095

A Scottish Victorian wine jug, virtually the entire surface with neo-Gothic or Tudor style chasing, Edinburgh 1866, 10¹/₄in. high, 29oz.
(Dee, Atkinson & Harrison) $2,781

A George III Irish hot water jug, of baluster form, the front with a rococo C and S-scroll cartouche, Dublin 1805, 7¹/₂in., 19oz. gross.
(Christie's) $633

An early 19th century Italian water jug, Carto Balbino, Turin, 1792–1824, of squat baluster form, with a heavy gadroon border, 7¹/₂in. high, approximate weight 34oz.
(Bonhams) $7,680

Diamond patterned cutglass beer jug, the hinged cover with pierced thumb piece, stamped *A. Bruce, Manchester*, 10¹/₂in. high.
(Ewbank) $141

MISCELLANEOUS SILVER

A late George III pap boat, with slightly raised rim, London 1816, maker's mark rubbed, 50gr., 5in. wide.
(Spencer's) $334

A 19th century novelty container, possibly a table snuff mull, modeled as a ram's head with curling horns, 7³/₄in.
(Christie's) $784

A silver table bell, maker's mark probably that of Job Hall, London, 1915, modeled as a pig, 6¹/₄in. long.
(Christie's) $3,818

A William III style toilet mirror, walnut with applied silver, the cushion rectangular swing frame with chased corner mounts, 17¹/₂in., Lionel Alfred Crichton, London 1933.
(Woolley & Wallis) $4,320

A Victorian parcel-gilt four-piece christening set, the mug Frederic Elkington, London 1887, the knife, fork and spoon Francis Higgins, London 1874/88.
(Bearne's) $538

A Victorian silver-gilt, gilt-metal and cut-glass traveling dressing table service, by William Thomas Wright and Frederick Davies, London, 1875, the medicine spoon with maker's mark of George Adams, London, 1874, weight of covers 10oz.
(Christie's) $7,047

A Victorian hunting horn shape scent phial and vinaigrette, the sky blue glass body decorated with swallows in flight, by S. Mordan, London 1871.
(Woolley & Wallis) $768

A William IV gothic toast rack, with six double arched divisions and a central oval shape ring handle, maker Henry Wilkinson, Sheffield 1834, 10oz.
(Woolley & Wallis) $512

A silver presentation flask, Gorham Mfg. Co., Providence, 1888, applied with cactus issuing from shrubbery, 7¹/₂in. high, 19oz. gross.
(Christie's) $7,475

MISCELLANEOUS SILVER

Rebecca Emes and Edward Barnard, a George IV brandy saucepan, with a detachable lid and finial, a hinged cover to the spout, London 1822, 12oz.
(Woolley & Wallis) $1,024

A pair of Continental model pheasants, with realistically-chased plumage, import marks, 7¹/₂in., 9.25oz.
(Christie's) $971

German repoussé silver charity container, 19th century, Nuremburg, inscribed *Charity Shall Avert Death*, 7¹/₄in. high.
(Skinner) $3,450

A set of twelve American silver dinner plates, Howard & Co., New York, 1886, with scalloped shell and foliate scroll rims, the borders chased with flowers, 254oz., 10³/₈in. diameter.
(Sotheby's) $5,175

A pair of large Victorian silver pilgrim bottles, maker's mark of George Fox, London, 1870, each on spreading fluted foot and applied with a broad band of lobes and strapwork, 21in. high, 234oz.
(Christie's) $36,271

A George III swing-handled sugar basin, of tapering boat shape and on a conforming rising beaded foot, Henry Chawner, London 1787, 6¹/₄in. overall, 5.25oz. free.
(Christie's) $688

Louis Kuppenhaim, Cat vanity case, 1920s, cast front and back with stylized cat, ruby red gem set eyes and collar, 8 x 4.5cm.
(Sotheby's) $1,490

Fine George V silver backed dressing table set, the backs inlaid with silver and mother of pearl decoration, in Adam style, Birmingham 1912.
(G. A. Key) $462

A Russian 19th century swing-handled ice pail, with molded body bands and with a broad frieze of engraved foliage and strapwork, Moscow 1876, 7³/₄in. overall, 16oz.
(Christie's) $847

MISCELLANEOUS SILVER

A good Edwardian novelty stationery box modeled as a stylized replica of the Oken chest in St. Mary's Church, Warwick, by James Dixon & Sons, Sheffield, 1906, 30.5cm. long.
(Phillips) $2,411

A late Victorian silver-gilt three-piece christening set with matching Edwardian mug, the former of King's shape with stamped rococo decoration, Hunt & Roskell Ltd., the set London 1897, the mug London 1905.
(Christie's) $918

A decorative Edwardian jewel casket, modeled as a side table with a single serpentine drawer and four foliate cabriole supports, by William Comyns, 1901, 28.5 x 21cm.
(Phillips) $1,363

Belgian 835 Standard silver cocktail shaker, Wolffert, of canopic form with rope borders, 9in. high, 22oz. 14dwt.
(Butterfield & Butterfield) $747

A set of twenty dessert plates, by Sebastian Garrard, London, 1928, circular form, ropework border, crested, 9in. diameter, approximate weight 306oz.
(Bonhams) $4,640

A George II chocolate pot of baluster circular form, the spout cast with stylized acanthus, London 1759, 28cm. high overall, 729gms.
(Bearne's) $1,912

An Edwardian silver-gilt pomander, domed hinged cover with stylized artichoke finial, Nathan & Hayes, Chester 1908, 3½in., 6.25oz.
(Christie's) $448

A 19th century six-division toast rack, of shaped oblong form, on dolphin feet and with applied rococo shell and scrolling foliate decoration, 7¾in., 18.25oz.
(Christie's) $628

A pierced dish ring, in the Irish 18th century taste, of waisted form and decorated with laurel swags and foliage, 8in., 13oz.
(Christie's) $932

MISCELLANEOUS SILVER

Edwardian circular silver covered sugar basin, the base and top profusely fluted, standing on a circular foot, Chester 1908.
(G. A. Key)   **$175**

A George III wax jack, on a dished reeded circular base engraved with a crest, Henry Green, London 1792, 6in.
(Christie's)   **$1,948**

An Edwardian novelty table lighter modeled as a carriage, with vesta compartment in front and scroll-edged bar at back, 1907, 13.7cm. long, gross weight 8oz.
(Phillips)   **$562**

An Art Deco cocktail shaker, in the form of a zeppelin, the electroplate body fitted with four spoons and beakers, 31cm. high.
(Christie's)   **$1,240**

A pair of Victorian silver-gilt scent bottles and stands of baluster shape, in the Oriental taste, by George Fox, 1871, 12.3cm. high.
(Phillips)   **$1,123**

An unusual Victorian novelty double spirit flask, of heart shape, chased with rocaille borders, C.H. Cheshire, Birmingham 1888, 5$\frac{1}{2}$in., 8.25oz.
(Christie's)   **$1,594**

A Victorian novelty scent atomiser, realistically modeled as a watering can, by Thomas Johnson, 1882, 16.5cm. high, gross weight 30oz.
(Phillips)   **$1,794**

Mid 19th century silver encased folding traveling corkscrew with engine turned decoration and foliate engraving, Londn 1856 maker T J.
(G. A. Key)   **$627**

A George III cream pail, engraved with crest and having a chainwork swing handle, by Walter Brind, 1770, 10.5cm. high, 3oz.
(Phillips)   **$1,014**

MISCELLANEOUS SILVER

A Victorian novelty elephant's head table bell, with upcurving trunk, the bell activated by depressing the ivory tusks, 6in. (Christie's) $673

A Victorian masonic jewel, formed as a cornucopia of fruit, by William Platt, 1864, also an earlier parcel-gilt masonic jewel. (Phillips) $499

A German or Austrian model of a fox, realistically chased with hair, 13in. (Christie's) $673

An American silver flask, Meriden Britannia Company for International Silver Company, circa 1900, with engine-turned pales on one side, 6⅝in. long, 7oz. 10dwt. (Christie's) $368

An imposing pair of Victorian boat-shaped jardinières, each end terminating in scrolling foliage, the sides with oval cartouches, by Gibson & Langman, 1891, 37cm. high, 137.75oz. (Phillips) $7,488

Fine George III silver two part wine funnel with gadrooned edge, marked for London 1812 by Rebecca Emes and Edward Barnard. (G. A. Key) $540

An Edward VII bottle-shaped wine decanter, chased all over with flowers and scrolling foliage, 23cm. height of decanter, T. W. Dobson, London 1904, 22oz. (Bearne's) $873

A silver ice bucket and tongs, designed by Professor Gerald Benney, with small flat flange handles, rosewood cover, London 1972, the tongs 1971, 16.5cm. high, 835 grams. gross. (Christie's) $4,724

A Victorian novelty scent bottle, the hinged cover concealing an interior glass stopper, Birmingham, 1884, 6.5cm. long. (Phillips) $1,092

MUGS & CANNS

A George II mug, later-chased with rococo flowers, foliage, C-scrolls and scale-work, W. Shaw & W. Priest, London 1753, 5in., 11.75oz.
(Christie's) $799

A George II mug, maker's mark rubbed 1750, of plain baluster shape, 12.25cm., 12.25oz.
(Cheffins Grain & Comins) $608

A George I Provincial mug of tapering shape with skirted foot and narrow applied girdle, by John Elston, Exeter, probably 1720, 11cm. high, 9oz.
(Phillips) $749

An early 18th century Provincial mug, probably West Country, engraved on front with a Baroque armorial for Hough, and later Latin presentation inscription, Penzance, circa 1720, 10.6cm. high, 12.5oz.
(Phillips) $1,912

A George III mug, leaf-capped double scroll handle later scratch-engraved with initials and a date *1800*, Hester Bateman, London 1790, 5¼in., 11.75oz.
(Christie's) $958

A Victorian gilt-lined christening mug, the body engine-turned and bright-cut with strapwork, flowers and foliage, Thomas Smiley, London 1870, 3¼in.
(Christie's) $496

A George III mug, with a molded rim and scroll handle scratch-engraved with initials, John Langlands, Newcastle 1774, 3¾in., 5.75oz.
(Christie's) $711

A Regency gilt-lined christening mug, of baluster form, on a rising circular foot, George Knight, London 1820, 3¾in.
(Christie's) $638

A George IV silver-gilt mug, by Benjamin Smith, London, 1827, formed as a thistle and on spreading circular foot, 5⅓in. high, 24oz.
(Christie's) $12,053

MUSTARDS

A George III silver mustard pot by Thomas Hyde, London, 1792, plain octagonal and with hinged cover, 4in. long overall, 5oz. (Christie's) **$545**

An early George III drum mustard pot, with pierced quatrefoil decoration and small shell thumbpiece, 1766, 5in. diameter; and a mustard ladle. (Christie's) **$2,760**

A large and unusual George III mustard pot, of good gauge, by Richard Cooke, London 1811, 4½in. long, 7oz. (Tennants) **$581**

A George III drum mustard pot, pierced shell thumbpiece, and bright engraved mustard spoon, the mustard pot by Jabez Daniell & James Mince, 1770, 5oz. (Phillips) **$698**

A pair of George IV mustard pots with later spoons, gilt-lined and of cauldron form, Waterhouse, Hodson & Co., Sheffield 1826, 3¼in., the two Victorian spoons Queen's pattern, London 1890, 23.5oz. (Christie's) **$2,381**

Large 18th century oval silver mustard with liner, Adam style chased decoration, maker's mark for Stephen Adams, circa 1780. (G. A. Key) **$200**

A George III silver mustard pot, London, 1813, tapering cylindrical and with bracket handle, 2¾in. high, 3oz. (Christie's) **$654**

A Victorian novelty three-piece condiment set, Charles Thomas Fox and George Fox, London, 1859, modeled as owls, height of large owl 3¾in., approximate weight 10oz. (Bonhams) **$2,880**

An American silver and other metals 'Japanese style' mustard pot, Tiffany, New York, circa 1885, 3oz. 10dwt., 3¼in. high. (Sotheby's) **$10,350**

Continental silver pitcher of cylindrical section, the sides with lozenges set with flowers, the lid set with a cupid, 13¹/₂in. high, 60oz. approximately. (William Doyle) $632

A Gorham Martelé sterling silver ewer, of undulating form, worked in relief with scrolling foliage and flowers, 10in. high, 28oz. (William Doyle) $4,887

George III hot water pitcher, William Holmes, London, 1769, with wrapped scroll handle, 11¹/₂in. high, 23oz. 14dwt. (Butterfield & Butterfield) $3,450

Sterling hand wrought water pitcher, Allan Adler, Los Angeles, California, with C-scroll strap handle, 8¹/₂in. high, 30oz. 8dwt. (Butterfield & Butterfield) $977

Sterling floral chased water pitcher, Dominick & Haff, New York, New York, 1886, retailed by Bailey, Banks & Biddle Company, Philadelphia, Pennsylvania, 8⁵/₈in. high, 34oz. 2dwt. (Butterfield & Butterfield) $2,070

An American silver and mixed metals pitcher, Gorham Mfg. Co., Providence, RI, 1880, of baluster form with spot-hammered surface, 21oz., 6³/₄in. high. (Sotheby's) $5,462

Sterling water pitcher in the Japanese taste, Gorham Mfg. Co., Providence, Rhode Island, 1883, 7¹/₂in. high, 18oz. (Butterfield & Butterfield) $1,725

A late Victorian ewer, signed *Gilbert Marks 1900*, the lower body chased with flower motifs, 14¹/₂in. high, approximate weight 53oz. (Bonhams) $8,320

Whiting sterling water pitcher, raised and chased design, acid etched inscription *Larchmont Special Regatta, For Forty Footers, Sept. 28th 1889*, 9³/₄in. high, approximately 31 troy oz. (Skinner) $2,760

SILVER

Archibald Knox for Liberty & Co., 'Cymric' pitcher, 1903, silver with two cabochons of orange and amber stones, 16cm.
(Sotheby's) $10,060

An American silver water pitcher, Tiffany & Co., New York, circa 1880, embossed and chased all over with water lilies, 31oz., 7³/₄in. high.
(Sotheby's) $7,475

A late 19th century American ewer, Tiffany & Co., circa 1880, elaborately chased with various flowers and acanthus leaves, 17¹/₄in. high, approximate weight 50oz.
(Bonhams) $4,800

A Georg Jensen silver pitcher, designed by Jorgen Jensen, fluted ebony handle with a leaf and berry cluster below the rim, London 1970, 17.5cm. high, 650 grams. gross.
(Christie's) $2,362

An ewer and basin in the 17th century Portuguese manner, the ewer embossed with two friezes of scrolling flowers and terminating in a bird's head spout, probably Goanese, early 19th century, ewer 31cm. high, 123.5oz.
(Phillips) $8,645

Sterling floral chased water pitcher, Whiting Mfg. Co., Providence, Rhode Island, late 19th century, 7³/₄in. high, 16oz. 18dwt.
(Butterfield & Butterfield) $1,495

An American silver covered pitcher, Ebenezer Moulton, Boston or Newburyport, circa 1820, the scroll handle with heart-shaped terminal, 10in. high, 34oz.
(Christie's) $8,625

Sterling silver water pitcher, American, circa 1920, by Baltimore Silversmiths, engraved decoration, 8in high, 28 troy oz.
(Eldred's) $440

A mid-Victorian wine ewer of vase form, the domed hinged cover having a finial formed as a vine tendril, London 1867, by Henry Wilkinson, 13¹/₄in. high, approximate weight 24oz.
(Bonhams) $2,400

A Queen Anne two-handled circular porringer, crested, initialed and dated below a beaded band, 7.5cm. high, John Elston, Exeter 1708, 92gms. (Bearne's) **$1,346**

Paul Revere II, Boston 1782, an important and documented porringer of plain circular form, the pierced keyhole handle engraved, length to handle 8¼in., approximate weight 9oz. (Bonhams) **$16,000**

Irish George III silver porringer, John Laughlin, Jr., Dublin, 1795, engraved with period armorial, 7oz. 12dwt. (Butterfield & Butterfield) **$1,495**

A Charles II silver porringer, maker's mark WG, trefoil below, London, 1673, with cast beaded and leaf-capped scroll handles, 3³/₄in. high, 7oz. (Christie's) **$3,627**

An American silver porringer, Samuel Minott, Boston, circa 1780, keyhole handle engraved with contemporary initials IP to LC, 7oz. 10dwt., 5in. diameter. (Sotheby's) **$1,840**

A William III silver porringer and cover, maker's mark of Joseph Ward, London, 1698, Britannia Standard, on fluted spreading foot, 8in. high, 28oz. (Christie's) **$7,254**

An American silver large porringer, Paul Revere Jr., Boston, circa 1760, the keyhole handle engraved with contemporary initials E S, 8oz. 10dwt., 5⁷/₈in. diameter. (Sotheby's) **$13,800**

A Charles II silver-gilt porringer and cover, London, 1671, maker's mark IH or TH in monogram, 5¼in. high, 16oz. (Christie's) **$17,180**

A late 17th/early 18th century Provincial porringer or bleeding bowl, the circular body with pierced handle, probably West Country, circa 1700, 12cm. diameter, 5.5oz. (Phillips) **$964**

SALTS & PEPPERS

A set of four silver salt cellars, James Howell, Philadelphia, circa 1810, shaped oval, on bat's-wing supports, 3⁷/₈in. long, 11oz. 10dwt.
(Christie's) $5,060

A pair of Victorian novelty pepperettes, modeled as a seated pug dog and a seated cat, dated 1879 to 1882, E. H. Stockwell, London 1877, 2¹/₂in. high, 6oz.
(Christie's) $2,456

A set of four silver salt cellars, Tiffany & Co., New York, circa 1870, circular, on three paw supports headed by rams' heads, diameter of bowl 2³/₄in., 9oz.
(Christie's) $2,300

A pair of Victorian silver salt cellars, maker's mark of John S. Hunt, London, 1856, each formed as a standing figure in 18th century costume, 6³/₄in. high, 27oz.
(Christie's) $17,563

A set of four George IV silver salt cellars, by Paul Storr, London, 1824, on three lion's mask and paw feet and with fluted everted rim, 3¹/₄in. diameter, 21oz.
(Christie's) $5,749

A pair of Austro-Hungarian 19th century salt cellars, each on a conforming rising foot and with a floral and foliate-chased border, 3¹/₄in.
(Christie's) $226

A set of four William salt cellars, the tapering gadrooned circular bowls cast with rising stiff foliage, bases engraved: *Arthur's Club*, probably William Bateman, London 1835, 3¹/₄in., 40oz.
(Christie's) $2,171

A silver pepper box, Elias Pelletreau, Southampton, New York, circa 1770, the pierced cover with molded bands and baluster finial, 3³/₈in. high, 3oz.
(Christie's) $8,625

A set of six George III 3¹/₂in. half-fluted oval boat shaped pedestal salts with straight gadroon borders, two London mark 1803, four London mark 1807, maker A.K., 16oz.
(Anderson & Garland) $775

SAUCE BOATS

A George II sauceboat, with wavy rim on shell and hoof feet, with leaf-capped scroll handle, by Thomas Collier, 1756, 11oz. (Phillips) **$865**

A George II Scottish sauceboat, on paw feet, leaf-capped scroll handle, by William Aytoun, Edinburgh, 1746, 19.6cm. long, 8oz. (Phillips) **$2,652**

Good quality Georgian silver sauce boat with card cut rim, leaf capped flying scrolled handle, circa 1753. (G. A. Key) **$429**

A pair of George III sauceboats, the feet and scroll handles decorated with overlapping scale decoration, by William Robertson, 1765, 29.5oz. (Phillips) **$5,320**

A pair of George II oval sauceboats, with scroll-edged shaped rims and leaf-capped scroll handles, by George Methuen, 1746, 15.5cm. high, 35oz. (Phillips) **$5,616**

Fine quality pair of hallmarked silver double lipped sauce boats with side handles, shaped reeded rims, oval feet, London 1937, 8oz. (G. A. Key) **$554**

A pair of early George III 6½in. plain gravy boats with gadroon borders, on shell cast scroll legs, London marks 1761, maker William Sampel, 26oz. (Anderson & Garland) **$1,913**

An early 19th century Dutch oval sauceboat and stand, the body half fluted, with loop handle and bead borders, circa 1825, 23cm. high, 27oz. (Phillips) **$1,081**

A pair of fine silver sauceboats, John Coburn, Boston, circa 1750, oval, on three scroll legs and fluted shell-form feet, 8½in. long, 29oz. (Christie's) **$32,200**

SNUFF BOXES

An early Victorian table snuff box of rectangular form with raised border, the cover inscribed, by Edward Edwards, 1838, 10cm. long.
(Phillips) $1,404

A French 18th century snuff box, the hinged cover with a vignette of three bucolic figures, Antoine Daroux, Paris circa 1780, 2½in.
(Christie's) $907

A good 19th century Chinese Export snuff box of rectangular shape with foliate chased sides, maker's mark *IW*, probably for Ing Wo, Hong Kong, circa 1845, 7cm. long, 2oz.
(Phillips) $499

A good George IV 'Pedlar' snuff box, the rectangular box with reeded borders, plain base and gilt interior, by John Linnit, 1824, 9.9cm. long, 6.5oz.
(Phillips) $6,318

A silver snuff-box, Zachariah Brigden, Boston, 1760–1780, the lifting cover engraved with foliate scrolls terminating in a bird's head, 2¼in. long, 1oz.
(Christie's) $14,950

A George III Irish Provincial mounted cowrie shell snuff box, the cover bright engraved with a script monogram, by Carden Terry & Jane Williams, Cork, circa 1810, 6.4cm. long.
(Phillips) $936

A good William IV rectangular snuff box, the cover engraved with a rampant gryphon within a shield, inscribed inside, by Joseph Willmore, Birmingham, 1833, 3.5oz.
(Phillips) $1,092

A George IV silver-gilt snuff box, maker's mark Charles Rawlings, London, 1824, marked on base and cover, 3¼in. wide, 5oz.
(Christie's) $3,436

A George III silver-gilt snuff box, a cast plaque on the cover, depicting a classical battle scene, by John Linnit & William Atkinson, 1812, 8cm. wide, 5.5oz.
(Phillips) $665

TANKARDS

Silver tankard, Freeman Woods, New York, New York, circa 1791–94, of tapered cylindrical form, 7¹/₂in. high, 39oz. 4dwt. (Butterfield & Butterfield)
$21,850

Attractive Victorian silver christening tankard of inverted bell form to a circular foot, London 1852 by E. & J. Barnard. (G. A. Key)
$245

A George I tapering cylindrical tankard with reeded girdle, domed hinged cover, dated 1769, 19cm. high, Thomas Coffin, Exeter 1724, 790gms. (Bearne's)
$3,978

A William & Mary lidded tankard, of plain tapering circular form, on a skirted foot and with a molded rim and scroll handle, London 1692, 6¹/₂in., 22oz. (Christie's)
$5,297

A George III tankard of baluster cylindrical form, 19.5cm. high, Richard Bentley, London 1749, converted for use as a jug, with hallmarks for Robert Hennell, London 1866, 858gms. (Bearne's)
$1,148

Victorian silver christening tankard, engraved with scrolls and featuring a monogram, Birmingham 1869 by G. Unite, 5¹/₂oz. (G. A. Key)
$186

A George II lidded tankard, the front engraved with an armorial within a floral and foliate cartouche, a crest above, possibly Thomas Whipham, London 1755, 7in., 23.75oz. (Christie's)
$2,198

A George II Provincial tankard, John Langlands I, Newcastle, 1757, tapering circular form, central girdle, 7³/₄in. high, approximate weight 24oz. (Bonhams)
$2,080

A silver large tankard, Simeon Soumaine, New York, circa 1730, on a molded circular base with an applied band of leaf-stamped cut-card decoration, 8in. high, 48oz. (Christie's)
$195,000

TANKARDS

A Norwegian silver peg tankard, maker's mark HM only, circa 1860, cylindrical and on three pomegranate feet, 6³/₄in. high, 28oz.
(Christie's) $23,180

George III silver tankard, London, 1770–71, maker J.S. engraved cartouche, 7³/₄in. high, approximately 25 troy oz.
(Skinner) $1,495

A mid-19th century American silver tankard of tapering cylindrical form, 19cm. high, Bailey and Kitchen, Philadelphia, circa 1840, 30.5oz.
(Bearne's) $1,377

A George III lidded tankard, of tapering circular form and on a flaring foot, later-chased with rococo flowers, James Mince, London 1795, 7¹/₄in. high, 26.75oz.
(Christie's) $1,416

A George III baluster tankard, the body and domed hinged cover subsequently chased, with later added spout, 21cm. high, the base and hinged cover Samuel Godbeher and Edward Wigan, London 1787, 850gms.
(Bearne's) $1,224

Sterling tankard, Gorham Mfg. Co., Providence, Rhode Island, 1885, of plain cylindrical form excepting acid etched alligator at the base behind the handle, 8in. high, 27oz. 14 ł vt.
(Butterfield & Butterfield) $3,000

Victorian silver baluster formed pint tankard, leaf capped scrolled handle, domed foot, London 1900, stamped to base *Wilson and Gill, London.*
(G. A. Key) $135

A late 17th century Kinsale tankard, stamped for William and/or Joseph Wall, circa 1690, plain tapering cylindrical body, 6¹/₂in. high, approx. weight 23oz.
(Bonhams) $13,600

Queen Anne silver tankard of tapering cylindrical design, reeded base and handle, later embossed, probably London 1705.
(G. A. Key) $240

TEA & COFFEE SETS

An Art Deco four-piece tea service, the teapot and hot water jug with composition angular handles, Elkington & Co., Birmingham, height of hot water jug 7in., 49.25oz. gross.
(Christie's) $1,080

Sterling four piece tea and coffee set, Moore for Tiffany & Co., New York, New York, circa 1870, the surfaces engraved with panels of ivy leaf sprays, 104oz. 2dwt.
(Butterfield & Butterfield) $3,450

A George V four piece tea service, of canted slightly tapering rectangular form, slightly everted rim, Sheffield 1931, maker's mark *C.B.* and *S.*, 1813gr. total gross.
(Spencer's) $1,002

A George IV three-piece tea set, the teapot with rising curved spout, and domed hinged cover, Joseph Angell, London 1820 and 1821, height of teapot 5³/₄in., 34oz.
(Christie's) $1,275

A three-piece tea service, of compressed molded circular form, each on a rising circular foot and with an applied stylized shell, C-scroll and foliate everted rim, 6¹/₄in., 38oz. gross.
(Christie's) $717

A French three-piece tea service, of molded circular form and on scrolling foliate feet, each decorated with tied foliate branches, height of teapot 6³/₄in.
(Christie's) $807

A George IV three-piece teaset, the teapot with a chased rising curved spout, the gilt-lined milk jug and sugar basin with foliate and flute-decorated scroll handles, Hyam Hyams, London 1823, height of teapot 6¹/₄in., 47.25oz.
(Christie's) $1,682

A Victorian three-piece tea service, engraved with foliage and strapwork and with conforming cartouches, each engraved with a monogram, Charles Hawksworth & John Eyre, London 1866 and 1868, height of teapot 6¹/₂in., 40.25oz.
(Christie's) $1,324

TEA & COFFEE SETS

A George VI tea service in Victorian style, comprising: teapot of compressed globular form, with flower knop, ivory insulators and scrolling feet, Sheffield 1946, 2240gr. approximately. (Spencer's) **$1,520**

German 800 Standard silver four piece tea and coffee set with matching tray in the 18th century taste, 20th century, 113oz. 16dwt. (Butterfield & Butterfield) **$2,070**

An attractive George V tea service in William IV style, comprising teapot and cover of compressed globular form, Sheffield 1932 and 1933, makers Walker & Hall, 2700gr. gross approximately. (Spencer's) **$2,128**

Sterling five piece tea and coffee set with matching tray, after Georg Jensen's Blossom pattern, probably Japanese manufacture, gross weight 241oz. 10dwt. (Butterfield & Butterfield) **$5,175**

A George V tea service and tray, the lightly hammered ground decorated with stylized strapwork in relief, London 1930 and 1934, 3900gr. approximately gross, makers Goldsmiths & Silversmiths Company. (Spencer's) **$2,128**

An Art Deco style five-piece tea service, comprising: a tapering shaped oblong hot water jug, teapot, milk jug and sugar basin on pad feet and with engraved decoration, 21in., Viners, Sheffield various dates, 131.75oz. gross. (Christie's) **$3,376**

A late Victorian composite three-piece teaset, of rounded molded oblong form and on bun feet, Samuel Watton Smith & Co., the teapot London 1899, the milk jug and sugar basin Birmingham 1900, 39oz. gross. (Christie's) **$944**

A Victorian four-piece tea and coffee service, of tapering molded circular form, each on a rising circular foot and chased with rococo flowers, shells, foliage and trellis work, John S. Hunt, London 1860, height of coffee pot 9in., 66.75oz. (Christie's) **$2,913**

TEA CADDIES

A late Victorian tea caddy, on bun feet and with a shaped rim, maker's initials *H.F.*, Sheffield 1889, 3½in., 7.75oz. gross. (Christie's) $301

A cased pair of George II tea caddies, with bombé shaped bodies and vertically reeded corners, by Thomas Heming, 1752, 12.5cm. high, 14.5oz. (Phillips) $3,990

A late Victorian tea caddy, of bombé-shaped oblong form, on scrolling foliate feet, Chester 1895, 5½in., 7oz. (Christie's) $390

A Dutch early 19th century tea caddy and cover, with a reeded body band and rim and dished hinged cover with pineapple finial, Theodore Gerard Bentvelt, Amsterdam 1807, 6in., 11.75oz. (Christie's) $1,412

A pair of George II caddies, the rectangular bodies and hinged stepped covers chased with rococo scrollwork, by Thomas Heming, 1747, 15cm. high, 43oz. (Phillips) $718

A German gilt-lined tea canister, with a flattened screw cap with swing scroll handle, Augsburg, 6in. overall, 11.25oz. (Christie's) $5,509

An Edward VII tea caddy, of bombé rectangular form, with hinged slightly domed cover, London 1904, by Thomas Bradbury, 256gr. (Spencer's) $413

A pair of Victorian tea caddies, engraved with Chinese characters, vignettes and monograms within oblong cartouches, Daniel & Charles Houle, London 1868, 5in., 27oz. (Christie's) $3,021

A Victorian tea caddy and cover, on openwork scrolling foliate feet and with a flower finial, Samuel Watton Smith, London 1895, 5½in. wide. (Christie's) $532

TEA KETTLES

A George III silver tea kettle, stand and lamp, maker's mark of John Edwards, London, 1810, 15³⁄₄in. high, 80oz. gross. (Christie's) **$2,864**

A Victorian Irish tea kettle, of compressed pear shape, chased and embossed with rococo flowers, foliage and strapwork, maker's initials *J.S.*, Dublin 1874, 18in. overall, 71.5oz. (Christie's) **$3,024**

A silver hot water kettle, stand and lamp, Gerardus Boyce, New York, circa 1840, bulbous fluted urn form, with fluted spout, 14in. high, 64oz. gross. (Christie's) **$1,725**

An early 18th century style tea kettle, stand and burner, domed detachable cover with turned wood finial, Crichton Brothers, London 1911, Britannia Standard, 12¹⁄₄in. overall, 54oz. gross. (Christie's) **$1,395**

Victorian silver kettle on lampstand, Benjamin Smith, London, 1838, the pot engraved with full armorial in a side panel reserve, 15¹⁄₂in. high, 114oz. 8dwt. (Butterfield & Butterfield) **$2,300**

An 18th century style tea kettle, stand and burner, the stand on rococo scroll and pad supports, the kettle and stand Goldsmiths & Silversmiths Co. Limited, London 1928, 12¹⁄₂in. overall, 48.25oz. gross. (Christie's) **$1,680**

A Victorian 7in. oval tapered and half-fluted tea kettle, domed fluted cover with ivory urn shaped finial and handle, London mark 1889, maker Messrs. Barnard. (Anderson & Garland) **$1,054**

George V Britannia standard silver kettle on lampstand in the Queen Anne taste, F. Higgins & Son Ltd., London, 1910, 16¹⁄₄in. high, gross weight 89oz. 2dwt. (Butterfield & Butterfield) **$2,500**

A Continental tapering circular tea kettle, stand and lamp richly chased and embossed with flowerheads and matted foliage, possibly Austro-Hungarian, mid-19th century, 14in. high, 54oz. (Christie's) **$1,281**

T. and J. Settle, a George IV teapot, the circular compressed body chased with repoussé flowers to a matt ground, Sheffield 1821, 29oz. all in. (Woolley & Wallis) $746

A Victorian compressed circular teapot, engraved with panels of fruit and flowers, fruit finial and strawberry thumbpiece, by Stephen Smith, 1870, 22.5oz. (Phillips) $686

Christopher Dresser for James Dixon & Sons, electroplated teapot, 1879, shallow drum-shaped body with hinged lid and angular ebonized handle, 12cm. (Sotheby's) $105,786

A William IV teapot, of melon-fluted compressed pear shape, on berried foliate feet, Richard Atkins & William Somersall, London 1835, 7¹/₄in., 24.25oz. (Christie's) $986

A late Victorian teapot, decorated with beading, flowers and foliage and with a rising curved spout, Charles Stuart Harris, London 1898, 5¹/₄in., 17.5oz. gross. (Christie's) $283

A George IV partly-fluted squat circular teapot, on foliage and paw feet, the finial formed as a seated Chinaman, by Samuel Dutton, 1824, 26oz. (Christie's) $791

A George III oval teapot with vacant wreath cartouches and amoeba-like decoration, by Alice & George Burrows, 1803, 13.25oz. (Phillips) $686

A George IV silver teapot of paneled pear shape, with leaf capped spout, London 1822, 25oz. 10dwt. gross, 8in. high. (Locke & England) $480

A Victorian teapot, of fluted elongated spherical form and on a rising shaped circular foot, Joseph & George Angell, London 1847, 7¹/₂in., 25.75oz. (Christie's) $1,050

E. and J. Barnard, a Victorian bachelor teapot, the paneled ogee body with crested cartouches and engraved foliage, London 1851, 12oz. all in. (Woolley & Wallis) $653

A Victorian teapot, of melon-fluted compressed shaped circular form, on scrolling foliate feet joined by openwork C-scroll aprons, W. W. Harrison & Co., Sheffield 1869, 6in., 22.75oz. (Christie's) $789

Important Gorham coin silver teapot, by Jabez Gorham, founder of the Gorham Silver Co., for his second wife, Lydia, dated 1857, 21 troy oz. approx. (Eldred's) $825

TEAPOTS

A George III teapot, of shaped oval form, with tapering angular spout, John Langlands, Newcastle 1796, 6in.
(Christie's) $1,209

A George IV circular teapot, the everted rim with rose and shell edging, London 1825, 774gms.
(Bearne's) $571

A George IV teapot, of inverted pear shape, on a circular foot, Charles Fox, London 1824, 7in., 29oz.
(Christie's) $974

A George III teapot, of plain oval form, with beaded border mounts, Daniel Smith & Robert Sharp, London 1788, 5¹/₂in., 16.25oz. gross.
(Christie's) $1,243

English silver teapot with gadroon body and ball feet, hallmarks for London, 1812, maker's mark untraced, 6in. high, 22 troy oz.
(Eldred's) $357

An American silver teapot, Paul Revere Jr., Boston, circa 1798, of straight-sided oval form, deeply fluted and engraved, 22oz. 10dwt. gross, 6in. high.
(Sotheby's) $34,500

A silver teapot, John Brevoort, New York, circa 1740, compressed pear form, on molded circular foot and with molded midband, 7¹/₂in. high, gross weight 22oz.
(Christie's) $145,500

A Victorian teapot, of globular form, engraved in the Aesthetic style with birds, butterfly and prunus, Frederick Elkington, London 1878, 7¹/₄in., 19.5oz.
(Christie's) $620

A George I silver teapot, maker's mark of William Fawdery, London, 1717, with curved octagonal spout terminating in stylized bird's head, 6in. high, 13oz. gross.
(Christie's) $16,227

A Victorian melon pattern teapot, the bulbous body with fluted spout and scroll handle, 14.5cm. high, John Tapley, London 1851, 23.6oz.
(Bearne's) $605

A Liberty's teapot designed by Archibald Knox, of flattened globular form, with conical spout, domed lift-off cover and wicker covered handle, Birmingham 1900, 465gr. gross.
(Spencer's) $1,463

A George III oblong teapot with reeded and bright-cut bands of acanthus, 17cm. high, Alice and George Burrows, London 1811, 545gms.
(Bearne's) $605

TRAYS & SALVERS

A Victorian two-handled tea tray, applied and chased with a bead and scrolling foliate border, Charles Boyton, London 1895, 27³/₄in. overall, 93.5oz. (Christie's) $2,834

A George IV rectangular Sheffield Plate tray, in the style of Robert Gainsford, the raised molded border with leafy scrolls and two handles, 28in. (Woolley & Wallis) $768

George III silver two handled oval tray, William Bennett, London, 1800, 21¹/₂in. long, 63oz. 18dwt. (Butterfield & Butterfield) $2,185

A George III salver, later-chased with a broad frieze of arabesques and also later-gilt, Thomas Hannam & John Crouch, London 1806, 9³/₄in., 21oz. (Christie's) $688

A large, early Victorian presentation salver, the center flat-chased with stylized honeysuckle foliage centred by engraved armorials of G. E. Russell, and inscription, by James Charles Edington, 1837, 59cm. diameter, 150oz. (Phillips) $3,990

An early Victorian 12in. circular salver, engraved foliated scrolls, flowers and crest, London mark 1842, maker William K. Reid, 30oz. (Anderson & Garland) $667

A Regency salver, of shaped circular form, on scrolling foliate feet and with a floral and foliate rim, S. C. Younge & Co., Sheffield 1817, 10¹/₄in., 18.75oz. (Christie's) $660

George IV silver platter, Philip Rundell, London, 1823, of oval form with shell and gadroon border, 23in, long, 100oz. 16dwt. (Butterfield & Butterfield) $2,300

A George II waiter, of shaped circular form, on hoof feet and with a molded rim, Robert Abercromby, London 1735, 6in., 6oz. (Christie's) $724

A George IV two-handled rounded rectangular tea tray, engraved at the center with armorials, 75.5cm. over handles, John Edward Terry, London 1828, 4411gms.
(Bearne's) $7,728

A late Victorian two-handled shaped oval tray, with scroll and floral border, center engraved with armorial, by Langley Archer West, 1896, 77cm. long, 167.75oz.
(Phillips) $3,900

A 19½in. plain rectangular tray engraved monogram with gadroon and shell border, Edinburgh mark 1910, maker Hamilton & Inches, 89oz.
(Anderson & Garland)
                              $1,426

A Victorian salver, Robert Garrard, London, engraved with a coat of arms and crest, on four asymmetrical bracket feet, 17¾in. diameter, approximate weight 74oz.
(Bonhams) $2,560

A George III silver salver, by James Sutton and James Bult, London, 1782, engraved with a coat-of-arms within a foliate scroll cartouche, 18in. diameter, 78oz.
(Christie's) $5,563

English silver salver, 20th century, Cheltenham and Co. Ltd., round form with a shaped molded rim, on four scroll feet, 16⅛in. diameter, approximately 50 troy oz.
(Skinner) $805

A silver salver, John Coburn, Boston, circa 1760, on three cabriole legs with pad feet, the rim of applied scrolls, 13in. diameter, 29oz. 10dwt.
(Christie's) $145,500

An American silver, gold and copper 'Japanese style' circular waiter, Tiffany & Co., New York, circa 1880, inlaid with gold swallows, 19oz., 9⅛in. diameter.
(Sotheby's) $12,650

A George III salver, Ebenezer Coker, London, 1772, crested, with a gadroon border, on three feet, 12¼in. diameter, approximate weight 28oz.
(Bonhams) $960

TUREENS

An American silver two-handled covered vegetable tureen, Tiffany & Co., New York, 1902–7, Chrysanthemum pattern, 57oz., 11½in. long over handles. (Sotheby's) $6,325

A George III Irish soup tureen of plain oblong form, with gadroon border, drop ring side handles, by Robert Breading, Dublin, 1808, 28cm. long, 83.5oz. (Phillips) $4,056

A George III silver soup tureen and cover, by Paul Storr, London, 1803, the bracket handles with lion's mask terminals, 12½in. high, 113oz. (Christie's) $25,961

A Regency soup tureen and cover, the part-fluted domed cover with detachable floral, foliate and C-scroll handle, London 1811, 15¼in. overall, 92.75oz. gross. (Christie's) $5,313

A George IV silver soup tureen, cover, liner and ladle, by Joseph Craddock and William K. Reid, London, 1816, the liner by William Eaton, London, 1824, 17in. long, 136oz. (Christie's) $6,676

A late 19th century American soup tureen and cover, P. L. Krider, Philadelphia, circa 1880, chased with flowers and acanthus leaves, 12¼in. high, approximate weight 76oz. (Bonhams) $4,480

A Victorian electroplated novelty soup tureen and cover, of compressed circular shape with stag head handles, raised on four stag hoof feet, circa 1875, 26cm. high. (Phillips) $865

Christopher Dresser for Hukin & Heath, tureen with associated cover, designed 28th July 1880, the electroplated metal cauldron shaped body with ebony handles, 23.5cm. diameter. (Sotheby's) $2,049

A George III silver soup tureen and cover, by Andrew Fogelberg, London, 1776, chased and applied with a band of waterleaves and anthemion ornament, 15¼in. wide, 92oz. (Christie's) $20,398

URNS

Antique Sheffield silver plated hot water urn, in bulbous form with paw feet, handle missing, 16in. high.
(Eldred's) $242

Copper samovar, globular form on square base with ball feet, ring handle, with tap, English, early 19th century.
(G. A. Key) $293

A Regency Sheffield Plate samovar, of ogee form with leaf embossed borders and handles, 17in.
(Woolley & Wallis) $608

A George III tea urn of hemispherical shape, by Paul Storr, the front engraved with the armorials of Sir William Congreve, the cover domed and fluted, 1805, 40cm. high, 174.5oz.
(Phillips) $22,444

A large Old Sheffield Plate tea urn of compressed circular shape below a foliate gadrooned edge, 43cm. high.
(Cheffins Grain & Comins) $380

A silver coffee urn, stand and lamp, Gorham Mfg. Co., Providence, 1886, baluster on four plain bracket supports with stiff leaf decoration and plain circular lamp, 13in. high, 72oz. gross.
(Christie's) $1,495

An American silver hot water urn, Tiffany, New York, circa 1875, of two-handled vase form, lightly flat-chased, 90oz., 18¾in. high.
(Sotheby's) $5,462

Sheffield plated coffee urn, circa 1840, in ovoid form with fluted lid, pedestal foot with four supports, 15in. high.
(Eldred's) $660

An electroplated two-handled vase-shaped tea urn, with beaded edging, on spreading circular base, 55cm. high.
(Bearne's) $672

VASES

Spahr silver overlaid ceramic vase, stylized decoration in light blue and pink outlined in silver overlay against black enamel ground, 12¹/₈in. high. (Skinner) $978

An Edwardian silver-gilt 'Warwick' vase, Goldsmiths & Silversmiths Co., London, 1910, with a beaded and ovolo border, entwined vine handles, 10³/₄in. high. (Bonhams) $6,400

A Eugène Feuillatre silver vase, front stamped in relief with a cartouche of an Art Nouveau maiden, 11cm. high. (Christie's) $673

Athenic sterling vase, Gorham Mfg. Co., Providence, Rhode Island, on a skirt base with wave edge finished with molded rim, 11⁷/₈in. high, 15oz. 18dwt. (Butterfield & Butterfield) $2,070

A pair of Italian silver 5in. two handled campana shaped vases, part fluted and embossed with acanthus leaves, 19th century. (Anderson & Garland) $209

Cut glass brilliant butterfly vase, bulbed goblet-form with cut and engraved design including butterflies, daisy blossoms and herringbone stepped stem, 14¹/₂in. high. (Skinner) $690

An American Art Nouveau vase, of baluster form, stamped, chased and embossed with flowers and foliage, 14¹/₄in., 32.25oz. (Christie's) $1,112

Gorham sterling and mixed metal footed vase, 1381, copper birds and branches on hammered silver ground, approximately 10 troy oz. (Skinner) $1,380

A Continental vase, in the form of a rising fish with open mouth on an oval foot, Bernhard Muller, import marks, Chester 1900, 10³/₄in., 20oz. (Christie's) $1,594

VESTA CASES

Fabiano Tango, enameled vesta case, 1920s, the cover enameled with a couple dancing the tango, 7.5 x 5cm.
(Sotheby's) $1,341

A vesta case enameled in front with the medal ribbon of the British War Medal 1914/20, by A. & J. Zimmerman Ltd., Birmingham, 1919, 5.4 x 4.4cm.
(Phillips) $359

A late Victorian novelty vesta case, possibly Henry Jackson, Birmingham, 1888, the hinged lid set with a plaque depicting Punch and his dog.
(Bonhams) $480

VINAIGRETTES

An early Victorian 'castle top' vinaigrette, cover chased in low relief with a view of Abbotsford, by Nathaniel Mills, Birmingham, 1837, 3.7cm. long.
(Phillips) $599

A Victorian shaped oval vinaigrette with rounded ends, engraved with the Scott Memorial, by Frederick Marson, Birmingham, 1856, 5.4cm. long.
(Phillips) $432

A large Victorian shaped rectangular vinaigrette, engraved with an unidentified scene on rayed background, by Nathaniel Mills, Birmingham, 1850, 5.3cm. long.
(Phillips) $1,131

An early Victorian silver-gilt 'castle top' vinaigrette, the cover depicting a view of the Royal Exchange building, by Taylor & Perry, Birmingham, 1839, 4.75 x 3cm., 1oz.
(Phillips) $1,297

Fine pendant vinaigrette in the form of a strawberry, Birmingham 1888, maker's marks E.S.B.
(G. A. Key) $435

A George III oblong gaming scorer vinaigrette, the cover set with a gold arrow pointer on revolving rayed disk, probably by John Carey, 1802, 3.5cm. long.
(Phillips) $1,123

WINE COOLERS

Sheffield plate wine cooler, circa 1810, of campana form and plain design, 9³/₄in. high. (Butterfield & Butterfield) $460

A pair of Warwick Vase wine coolers, on rising square bases, each with entwined foliate and flute-decorated handles, 15³/₄in. overall, with foliate-decorated square plinths. (Christie's) $7,531

A William IV campana-shaped wine cooler, profusely chased in relief with fruiting vines, by Robert Garrard, 1831, 26cm. high, 127.75oz. (Phillips) $14,963

Pair of William IV silver plated wine coolers, second quarter 19th century, each of cylindrical form, surmounted by a gadrooned disk above the bellied base, 10in. high. (William Doyle) $2,070

An Old Sheffield plate wine cooler, of campana shape, on a part spiral-fluted rising circular base, 10¹/₄in. (Christie's) $861

A pair of George III silver wine coolers, collars and liners, by William Pitts and Joseph Preedy, London, 1793, the cylindrical body cast and chased with a band of laurel leaves, 7⁷/₈in. high, 82oz. (Christie's) $37,088

A rare silver wine cooler, Jones, Ball & Poor, Boston, 1847–1851, the base engraved *James Lawrence from his Mother 1851*, 38oz. 7dwt., 8in. high, 37oz. 10dwt. (Christie's) $8,050

A pair of Old Sheffield plate wine coolers, modeled as tapering circular two-handled pails, with simulated reeded hoops, probably circa 1805, 8in. overall. (Christie's) $2,472

A Continental silver wine cooler, the sides worked in repoussé with bacchanalian scenes, ram's head handles, 9in. high, approximately 69oz. (William Doyle) $2,760

An Aubusson tapestry depicting Moses at the Well, the borders later, late 17th century, 109 x 192in.
(Christie's) **$21,528**

A Brussels tapestry, woven in wools and silks, depicting the Story of Roxanne Before Alexander, mid-17th century, 136 x 208in.
(Christie's) **$18,837**

A late 17th century Flemish verdure tapestry, depicting a woodland scene with a moorhen and crane to the foreground, with a small hamlet in the background, 2.45m. x 3.35m.
(Phillips) **$10,745**

A Brussels tapestry, woven in wools and silks, depicting an episode from the Flight of Darius, the wide border with central landscape cartouche, early 17th century, 134 x 157^1/$_2$in.
(Christie's) **$25,116**

A Felletin verdure tapestry fragment, woven in wools, of two geese in a wooded landscape, within a floral and foliate border, late 17th century, 67^1/$_2$ x 82^1/$_2$in.
(Christie's) **$5,741**

A Brussels Biblical tapestry, depicting the Passover and the death of the firstborn, woven in wools, silks and metal-threads, mid-16th century, 136 x 178^1/$_2$in.
(Christie's) **$91,572**

A Farnell teddy bear, with golden curly mohair, large painted glass eyes with black button pupils, 15in. tall, 1930s.
(Christie's) $617

A white Steiff center seam teddy bear, with large black boot button eyes, cone shape nose, 23in. tall, circa 1908.
(Christie's) $705

A Steiff teddy bear, with pale golden curly mohair, brown and black glass eyes, 19in. tall, 1950s.
(Christie's) $564

'Pery', a Steevans teddy bear, with pale golden mohair, 9½in. tall, circa 1918, wearing a collection of Henley Regatta badges and medals.
(Christie's) $2,820

A white Steiff teddy bear, with black boot button eyes, pronounced clipped snout, hump, growler and button in ear, 13in. tall, circa 1910.
(Christie's) $3,878

A beige plush covered teddy bear, with amber and black glass eyes, small swivel head with cut muzzle, 16in. tall, unmarked.
(Woolley & Wallis) $387

A Steiff cinnamon teddy bear, elongated jointed shaped limbs, large shaped paws and feet and hump, 20in. tall, circa 1910.
(Christie's) $4,231

A Steiff cream plush teddy bear, German, circa 1908, with brown stitched snout, black shoe button eyes, 41cm.
(Sotheby's) $2,528

A Steiff teddy bear, with golden mohair, deep brown and black glass eyes, pronounced snout, 20in. tall, circa 1920.
(Christie's) $2,115

A Steiff teddy bear, with honey golden mohair, felt pads, hump and button in ear, 13in. tall, circa 1906.
(Christie's) $2,468

An Ideal teddy bear, with golden mohair, wide-apart ears, black boot button eyes, 15in. tall, circa 1905.
(Christie's) $1,322

A large Steiff teddy bear, with pale golden curly mohair, large brown and black glass eyes, 30in. tall, 1950s.
(Christie's) $2,115

A Steiff center seam teddy bear, with golden curly mohair, elongated jointed shaped limbs, large shaped paws and feet, 19in. tall, circa 1907.
(Christie's) $2,468

A Steiff center seam teddy bear, with golden mohair, large black boot button eyes, pronounced clipped snout, 22in. tall, circa 1910.
(Christie's) $3,173

A Hermann teddy bear, with pale golden mohair, deep amber and black glass eyes, jointed limbs, gray felt pads and growler, 17in. tall, 1950s.
(Christie's) $353

A good Steiff dual plush 'Petsy' teddy bear, German, circa 1928, brown-tipped silver plush, red stitched snout, 30cm.
(Sotheby's) $7,222

A Steiff teddy bear, with rich golden brown mohair, cream felt pads, hump and button in ear, 15in. tall, circa 1908.
(Christie's) $3,173

A Steiff teddy bear, with honey golden mohair, cream felt pads, hump and button in ear, 11in. tall, circa 1910.
(Christie's) $2,115

A white Steiff teddy bear, with black boot button eyes, pronounced clipped snout, brown horizontally stitched nose, 12in. tall, circa 1910. (Christie's) $1,062

A white Steiff teddy bear, with beige horizontally stitched nose, beige stitched mouth and claws, hump and blank button in ear, 12in. tall, circa 1905. (Christie's) $1,682

A rare black Steiff teddy bear, with rich black curly mohair, large black boot button eyes, pronounced clipped snout, and hump, 20in. tall, circa 1912. (Christie's) $35,420

A rare blue Schuco 'Yes/No' teddy bear, with bright blue and pale blue tipped mohair, growler and tail operating teddy's 'Yes/No' head movement, 20in. tall, 1930s. (Christie's) $9,740

A teddy bear purse, with honey golden mohair, purse opening to back of teddy lined with rexine, 6$\frac{1}{2}$in. seated, circa 1918, accompanied by a photograph of the bear in his youth being held by his original owner. (Christie's) $5,667

'Sir Randolf', Canterbury Bears, Limited Edition 1 of 1, with gray mohair, large amber and black glass eyes, pronounced clipped snout, black stitched nose, 34in. tall. (Christie's) $319

'Teddy Girl', a Steiff cinnamon center seam teddy bear, with thick curly mohair, black boot button eyes, pronounced clipped snout, large 'spoon' shaped feet and hump, 18in. tall, circa 1904. (Christie's) $177,100

A Merrythought 'Punkinhead', with brown mohair, golden mohair chest and inner ears, Mohican-style scalp lock of long white mohair, 16in. tall, circa 1950. (Christie's) $1,594

An early Steiff teddy bear, with rich golden mohair, 'cone' shaped face, large 'spoon' shaped feet, felt pads, hump and black button in ear, 28in. tall, circa 1905. (Christie's) $6,730

A Farnell teddy bear, with long white curly mohair, clear and black glass eyes, cream felt pads and label stitched to left foot pad, 13in. tall, 1930s.
(Christie's) **$1,771**

A rare Steiff black teddy bear, German, circa 1912, with blonde stitched square snout, and cream felt pads.
(Sotheby's) **$6,861**

A rare black Steiff teddy bear, with large black boot button eyes backed with red felt, cream felt pads and hump, 15in. tall, circa 1912.
(Christie's) **$6,199**

'Rupert', a Steiff teddy bear, with golden mohair, black boot button eyes, pronounced clipped snout, felt pads, hump and button in ear, 19in. tall, circa 1910.
(Christie's) **$3,188**

'Gilbert', a rare Steiff 'Bär Dolly' teddy bear, with red mohair covered body and limbs, white mohair covered face, white wool neck ruff, slight hump and button in ear, 12in. tall, circa 1913.
(Christie's) **$16,825**

A Steiff 'Dual' mohair teddy bear, with dark brown tipped cream mohair, large brown and black glass eyes, pronounced snout, hump and button in ear, 17in. tall, circa 1926.
(Christie's) **$10,626**

An American teddy bear, with short golden mohair, pinched ears, small black shoe button eyes, pronounced snout, swivel head, jointed limbs and hump, 24in. tall, 1920s.
(Christie's) **$336**

A Steiff cinnamon teddy bear, with rich cinnamon mohair, black boot button eyes, pronounced clipped snout, felt pads, hump and button in ear, 13in. tall, circa 1910.
(Christie's) **$3,188**

An early metal-rod jointed Steiff teddy bear, with golden mohair, ears sewn across facial seams, thin pronounced snout, hump and elephant button in ear, 20in. tall, circa 1904.
(Christie's) **$4,428**

An early American 'Stick' teddy bear with honey golden mohair, black boot button eyes, and jointed limbs, 10in. tall, circa 1910.
(Christie's) $230

'Edwin', a Chiltern teddy bear, with golden curly mohair, pronounced clipped snout, black stitched nose, 28in. tall, 1930s.
(Christie's) $1,151

An early German teddy bear, with golden mohair, black boot button eyes, cardboard reinforced feet and slight hump, 22in. tall.
(Christie's) $1,063

'Auction Bear' Bond B, light brown filled with English oak shavings, amber glass eyes, large black wool nose, signed by John and Maude Blackburn, 24in. tall.
(Christie's) $98

A Peacock & Co. Ltd. teddy bear, with golden mohair, large cupped ears, large deep amber and black glass eyes, felt pads and embroidered label stitched to left foot pad, 27in. tall, 1930s.
(Christie's) $974

A Gebrüder Bing clockwork teddy bear, with pale golden mohair, slight hump and key-hole to right side of body, 12in. tall, circa 1910, clockwork head movement inoperative.
(Christie's) $1,682

Kathleen Wallace, 'Samuel', with cream and brown tipped mohair, large black glass eyes, and growler, wearing hand knitted jumper, 23in. tall.
(Christie's) $460

An English teddy bear, with pale golden mohair, clear and black glass eyes, pronounced clipped snout, 23in. tall, 1920s, wearing a blue and white sailor's suit.
(Christie's) $460

'Peter', a Steiff teddy bear, with beige mohair, brown and black glass eyes, cream felt pads and button in ear with yellow label, 11in. tall, circa 1948.
(Christie's) $673

An early teddy bear, with golden mohair, black boot button eyes, swivel head, elongated jointed limbs, and growler, 18in. tall, circa 1910, possibly American. (Christie's) $354

An early German teddy bear, with golden mohair, wide apart eyes, black boot button eyes, elongated jointed limbs and hump, 21in. tall, circa 1910. (Christie's) $566

A German teddy bear, with pale golden short clipped mohair, amber painted and black glass eyes, brown stitched nose, 22in. tall, 1920s. (Christie's) $319

A Farnell teddy bear, with golden mohair, pronounced clipped snout, linen pads, webbed paw claws, cardboard reinforced feet and hump, 20in. tall, 1920s. (Christie's) $1,063

'George', an English teddy bear, with golden curly mohair, dark brown, black and white 'peoples' eyes, large round tummy, brown felt pads, 20in. tall, 1930s. (Christie's) $496

A Merrythought panda, Registered Design No. 821561, with black and white mohair, black cloth pads and label stitched to left foot pad, 13in. tall, circa 1931. (Christie's) $319

A Steiff center seam teddy bear, with golden mohair, pronounced clipped snout, elongated jointed shaped limbs, large shaped paws and hump, 25in. tall, circa 1910. (Christie's) $4,250

A teddy bear purse, with short golden mohair, black shoe button eyes, felt pads and purse opening to back of teddy lined with rexine, 9¹/₂in. tall, 1920s. (Christie's) $1,063

An American teddy bear, with golden mohair, wide apart ears, jointed shaped limbs, felt pads and slight hump, 16in. tall, circa 1912. (Christie's) $708

Terracotta bust of a lady, on stepped circular marble base, 80cm. high.
(Finarte) $2,035

A pair of polychrome terracotta female busts personifying France and Spain respectively, French, late 19th century, 18in. high.
(Christie's) $742

A polychrome terracotta pug, with inset glass eyes, Austrian, late 19th century, 9¹/₄in. high; and a miniature beechwood Windsor armchair.
(Christie's) $1,374

Monumental glazed terracotta bust, designed by Haig Patigian, from the Atlantic Richfield Building, Los Angeles, circa 1930, the muscular winged male depicted looking downward, 24in. high.
(Butterfield & Butterfield) $3,737

A pair of terracotta figures of winged sphinx, with painted finish, one French, 19th century, the other of a later date, 30in. high.
(Christie's) $3,170

A plaster terracotta-look sculpture of a young girl's smiling face with grapes, signed *Géo Verbanck*, and dated *1921*, 33cm. high.
(Hôtel de Ventes Horta) $537

Arthur Craco, Symbolist sculpture, circa 1898, terracotta, modeled as the draped head and shoulders of a young woman with long hair, 35.75cm. high.
(Sotheby's) $1,118

Two painted terracotta figures, one of a fisher-girl, the other of a lady with a basket of flowers, late 19th century, 61in. and 60in. high.
(Christie's) $9,508

A terracotta bust of Sir Joseph Edgar Boehm, the reverse inscribed *J. Edgar Boehm Bart, R.A., Died Dec. 1890.,* ... *Glassby, Sc. 1891,* 23¹/₂in. high.
(Christie's) $401

A novelty purse or scent sachet, in the form of a bunch of grapes attached to a vine leaf behind, 4 x 3¹/₂in., English, mid 17th century.
(Christie's) $2,706

A needlework picture in colored silks and metal threads depicting scenes from the life of a Biblical figure, 17³/₄ x 11¹/₂in., English, 17th century.
(Christie's) $2,165

An embroidered bedhead elaborately scalloped, 64 x 49in., and a pair of matching pilasters with similar embroidery, middle European, 1730s.
(Christie's) $2,165

A crewelwork hanging, the exotic leafy trees filled with various flowers and birds, the hillocky ground with leaping stags, 82 x 80in., English, 19th century.
(Christie's) $3,443

A mummy face mask composed of multi-colored beads, with stylized beard, Ptolemaic after 300 B.C., 6¹/₈in. high.
(Bonhams) $598

A fine needlework picture, worked in tent and cross stitch in colored silks and wools depicting Elijah ascending in a chariot of fire, 18 x 24in., early 18th century.
(Christie's) $1,342

A beadwork picture, depicting a basilisk flanked by the initials M B, within a field of flowers and insects, 9¹/₂ x 7in., English, 17th century.
(Christie's) $1,263

Tent-stitch pocketbook, wrought by Deborah Rogers 1769, worked with vivid polychrome wool yarns on linen ground, 10³/₄ x 8¹/₂in., unfinished.
(Skinner) $805

A needlework portrait of Charles II within a wreath of oak leaves, worked in petit point, inscribed, 37 x 34cm.
(Bearne's) $428

THIMBLES

A silver thimble, the sides with two oval cartouches, one with study of Charles II, the other with the Boscobel Oak, English, 1665, 2.4cm. (Christie's) $3,205

A Chelsea thimble painted with an exotic bird on a branch beneath the inscription *FIDELLE EN AMITIE* in iron-red, circa 1760, 1.9cm. high. (Christie's) $8,950

A Meissen thimble painted in Schwarzlot on a pale-green ground with a shepherd and two shepherdesses with their flock, circa 1745, 2cm. high. (Christie's) $4,845

A Worcester thimble, circa 1890, painted with a bird with a yellow breast and red head perched on a blossoming branch of pink and lilac flowers. (Christie's) $330

A French (hard paste) yellow-ground thimble painted with iron-red scrolling foliage, with inscription *A TOUTES HEURES BONHEUR*, 19th century, 2.3cm. (Christie's) $315

An ivory combination thimble and needle case, the top unscrewing to reveal an ivory thimble with plain border, French, early 19th century. (Christie's) $590

A silver thimble, the oval cartouches depicting Charles II and Queen Katherine of Braganza, English, early 1660's, 2.3cm. (Christie's) $2,530

A Meissen chinoiserie thimble painted in the manner of J. G. Höroldt with a band of chinoiserie figures, circa 1735, 2.3cm. (Christie's) $7,825

A French brown-ground thimble painted with sprigs of flowers within heart and diamond-shaped gilt line panels, early 19th century, 2.1cm. (Christie's) $600

A Meissen thimble painted with bouquets of fruit, and with scattered fungi and cherries below a gilt line, circa 1750, 2.3cm. (Christie's) $4,470

A gold thimble, of domed design, the border applied with a twisted wire-work design, Turkish, possibly 16th century. (Christie's) $6,750

A Continental green-ground thimble painted with a pink rose within an oval puce line panel, circa 1800, perhaps Naples, 1.9cm. high. (Christie's) $1,300

A tortoiseshell and pinchback Piercy's Patent thimble, with tortoiseshell liner, English, circa 1825, 2.8cm. (Christie's) $5,905

An ivory thimble, the border carved with flowerheads studded with cut steel, French, early 19th century, 2.6cm. (Christie's) $1,012

A silver thimble, made to commemorate Queen Victoria's Diamond Jubilee, Birmingham, date letter indistinct Deakin and Francis, 2.3cm. (Christie's) $607

A silver thimble, the sides engraved with strapwork over waffle-type indentations, English, maker's mark *IC* conjoined, early 17th century, 2.7cm. (Christie's) $1,518

A child's steel-topped gold thimble, the sides engraved with four cartouches, English, late 18th century, 1.2cm. (Christie's)
$1,855

A Tunbridgeware thimble, decorated with mosaic work, the top with concentric carved circles, English, circa 1820, 2.5cm. (Christie's)
$3,712

A silver thimble, decorated overall with punched indentations, English provincial, maker's mark a quatrefoil, probably 17th century, 1.2cm. (Christie's)
$370

A tortoiseshell thimble, the sides plain, the wide border carved with a geometric design, English, late 18th century, 2.2cm. (Christie's)
$1608

An iron thimble, cast overall with floral scrollwork and with a reeded rim, Italian, probably mid to late 18th century, 2.4cm. (Christie's)
$1,324

A silver thimble, the sides part decorated with nielloed scrollwork and bright-cut engraving, Russian, probably Moscow circa 1910, 2.1cm. (Christie's)
$287

A Sèvres thimble painted with two puce bands, the upper one entwined with blue cornflowers, circa 1772, 1.9cm. high. (Christie's)
$4,475

A silver thimble, the border engraved with the legend, *Be Not Idell*, English, probably early 17th century, 2.4cm. (Christie's)
$1,265

A Meissen thimble painted with two panels with gallants and companions in landscapes, circa 1745, 2cm. high. (Christie's)
$5,960

A Derby thimble painted with a band of garden flowers within gilt line borders (gilding rubbed), Robt. Bloor & Co., circa 1830, 2.6cm. high. (Christie's)
$688

A bronze thimble, of bulbous form, the border marked with facets within reeding, Turkish, circa 15th century, 3.7cm. (Christie's)
$1,855

A Meissen thimble minutely painted in the manner of B. G. Häuer with a continuous harbor scene, circa 1735, 2.2cm. high. (Christie's)
$8,385

A silver thimble, the sides nielloed with checkerboard design strapwork, English, early 17th century, 3cm. (Christie's)
$3,712

A cast bronze thimble, Hispano-Moresque, circa 12th century, inscribed in Arabic script, *The maker Mohamed* at top, 5cm. (Christie's)
$2,868

A silver thimble, the border engraved with the legend, *Be Trw In Love As Tvrtvl Dove*, English, early 17th century, 2.9cm. (Christie's)
$4,725

A coral thimble, the border carved in relief with scrollwork and foliage, French, early to mid 19th century, 2.5cm. (Christie's)
$4,387

THIMBLES

A gold thimble, the border applied with deep red guilloche enameling, possibly French, early 19th century, 2.3cm. (Christie's) $438

A wooden child's thimble and case, each turned with concentric rings, English, mid-19th century, height of case 2.2cm. (Christie's) $270

An enamel thimble, with applied brass top and rim, English, South Staffordshire, circa 1760, 1.9cm. (Christie's) $1,350

A gold thimble, the border applied with a yellow gold frieze over an engraved bark effect, French, late 18th century, 2.4cm. (Christie's) $843

A silver thimble, the border applied with a shaped oval cartouche and two flowers, English, mid 19th century, 2.4cm. (Christie's) $303

A silver filigrée thimble, decorated with heavy scrollwork panels enclosing lighter filigree work, English, circa 1760, 2.4cm. (Christie's) $473

A silver thimble, made to commemorate the birth and christening of Edward Prince of Wales, English, circa 1842, 2.3cm. (Christie's) $759

A silver thimble, heavily chased overall with flowers and scrolled foliage, Indian (Kutch region), late 19th century, 2.1cm. (Christie's) $252

A brass thimble, the top engraved with a stylized flowerhead, English, early 17th century, 3cm. (Christie's) $1,265

A French (hard paste) thimble painted in the Sèvres style with bouquets of pink roses, circa 1800, 2.2cm. high. (Christie's) $930

A Copenhagen thimble painted with three flower-sprays above a gilt line, circa 1780, 2cm. high. (Christie's) $1,025

A silver thimble, made to commemorate the marriage of Queen Victoria to Prince Albert, English, circa 1840, 2.4cm. (Christie's) $810

A 15ct. gold thimble, the border applied with a ring of set turquoises, with a matching finger guard, English, Charles May, London 1867, thimble 2.2cm. (Christie's) $1,518

A Meissen chinoiserie thimble painted in the manner of J. G. Höroldt with a continuous band of Orientals at various pursuits, circa 1735, 1.7cm. high. (Christie's) $15,800

A gold thimble, with a complementary six-sided velvet lined tortoiseshell and bone thimble case retailed by Lund, 57 Cornhill E.C., English, circa 1880, 2.3cm. (Christie's) $1,096

A silver thimble, in the form of a thistle, stamped with a Registration number 222445, English, maker's mark indistinct, Birmingham 1893, 2.5cm. (Christie's) $1,855

THIMBLES

A gold thimble, the sides engraved with a crest and coronet supported by foliage, English, late 18th century, 2.4cm. (Christie's) $675

A mother-of-pearl thimble, applied oval shield enameled with a pansy and foliage, French, circa 1820, 2.1cm. (Christie's) $590

A Derby blue-ground thimble gilt with foliate swags on a Smith's blue ground, circa 1785, 2cm. high. (Christie's) $1,490

A coquilla thimble, carved from the nut, the border applied with two gilt rings, French, early 19th century, 2.4cm. (Christie's) $270

A silver thimble, the circular indentations extending to a plain border, English, maker's mark *N*., mid 18th century, 1.9cm. (Christie's) $270

A Worcester thimble, circa 1890, painted with a spray of apple-blossom and with a bird in flight, 7/8in. high. (Christie's) $460

A Mennecy small thimble painted with a band of pink roses and green foliage, circa 1760, 1.6cm. high. (Christie's) $1,110

A French (hard paste) thimble painted with a bird perched on a leafy branch, circa 1780, 2.1cm. high. (Christie's) $1,025

A silver thimble, the border engraved with the legend, *I Live In Hope*, English, early 17th century, 2.9cm. (Christie's) $4,050

A silver thimble, the border engraved with the legend, *Soe Not Sleping*, English, early 17th century, 2.8cm. (Christie's) $3,712

A Meissen thimble inscribed in black *Kleines Andenken* between gilt lines, circa 1800, 2.3cm. high. (Christie's) $1,490

A Meissen thimble painted with harbor scenes with merchants on quaysides, circa 1745, 2cm. high. (Christie's) $5,600

A gold and tortoiseshell Piercy's Patent thimble, the tortoiseshell body applied with a gold tip, rim and the Royal Coat of Arms, English, circa 1825, 2.7cm. (Christie's) $2,362

A silver combination thimble and seal, the thimble unscrewing from its seal base to reveal a clear cut-glass scent bottle and stopper, probably Thomas Bartleet, early 19th century, 2.9cm. (Christie's) $878

A gold thimble, the border applied with alternate flowerheads and garnet settings, French, maker's mark for Michel Veyder, early 19th century, 2.3cm. (Christie's) $1,012

A silver-gilt thimble, the sides cloisonné enameled with strapwork, flowers, foliage and spot-work, maker Ovchinnikov, Russian, circa 1910, 2.3cm. (Christie's) $6,750

635

TIN

Nirona tinplate toy gramophone by Nier & Elmer, Beierfeld i.S., with typical bell shaped horn, spring-driven, German, circa 1915.
(Auction Team Köln)
$430

A wrigglework tinware coffee pot, serpents maker's mark, probably Pennsylvania, early 19th century, the conical form with hinged lid, 11in. high.
(Sotheby's)
$8,050

Paint decorated tin pig trade sign, 19th century, 16 x 35in.
(Skinner)
$3,105

Paint decorated tin coffee pot, Pennsylvania, early 19th century, polychrome decoration on asphaltum ground, 10in. high.
(Skinner)
$1,495

A pair of gilt-japanned red and gilt-japanned tôle jardinières, each with cylindrical body with satyr-mask handles and brass interior bucket, 19th century, 9¹/₂in. diameter.
(Christie's)
$9,867

A painted tin 'Tin Man' carnival figure, Asbury Park, New Jersey, circa 1920, his mouth opened to receive a ball, 80¹/₂in. high.
(Sotheby's)
$6,325

Smoke decorated tin house bank, America, 19th century, 7¹/₂in. high.
(Skinner)
$431

Pair of tin chamber sticks, designed by Christopher Dresser, for Perry Son and Co., England, circa 1883, inverted sphere with ceramic bobeche, 5¹³/₁₆in. high.
(Skinner)
$460

A Regency green and gilt-japanned coal-scuttle decorated overall with chinoiserie birds in a landscape, on paw feet, 21¹/₂in. wide.
(Christie's)
$4,724

Postcard, RMS Titanic woven silk by T. Stevens, embossed mount, pre sinking.
(Onslow's) $530

RMS Titanic, a color art postcard, from Fred to Miss Ida Wright, Great Billing, Northampton, dated *Wed Southampton*.
(Onslow's) $510

White Star Line RMS Titanic receipt *Received from the Purser the sum of £ rebate for taking meals in the Restaurant.*
(Onslow's) $350

On Board RMS Titanic, an autograph letter on three sides of embossed official writing paper with company burgee in red, signed *Fred*, Thursday 11th [April] 1912.
(Onslow's) $2,240

A souvenir printed paper napkin *In Memory of the Captain Crew and Passengers Who Lost Their Lives By the Wreck of the Titanic*, 38cm. square.
(Onslow's) $140

On Board RMS Titanic, an autograph letter on three sides on embossed note paper with company burgee in red, signed *Uncle Harry* [Chief Officer Harry Wilde].
(Onslow's) $4,560

White Star Line Olympic and Titanic, a sheet of company notepaper, pencil note addressed to Mr Brown Sailors Home.
(Onslow's) $340

Titanic, Captain Edward Smith, drowned on the Titanic, signed document, one page, 1st March 1895, being a certificate of Discharge from the Britannic.
(Vennett-Smith) $853

SS Titanic Southampton Dock April 6th 1912, contemporary bromide photographic on card mount, 21 x 15cm.
(Onslow's) $320

A good Bing limousine, German, 1920s, inserted chauffeur in gray uniform, orange painted wheels, 32cm. long.
(Sotheby's) $1,806

A vintage boxed game, 'The Game of the Goose'.
(Dee, Atkinson & Harrison) $92

A Gunthermann clockwork Napier Campbell Bluebird III tinplate landspeed record car, German, circa 1930, lithographed with American and British flags, 51cm. long.
(Sotheby's) $1,895

A Märklin miniature pram, in painted tinplate with gilded decoration and spoked wheels, 9in. long; and a bisque-headed doll.
(Christie's) $1,763

A rare Britains Set No. 1413 police car with two officers, in original box 1936–41.
(Christie's) $338

A Carette limousine, German, circa 1910, with clockwork mechanism, brake and reverse levers, 32cm. long.
(Sotheby's) $3,430

A Tippco clockwork lithographed tinplate German Army motor ambulance, with opening rear doors and composition driver.
(Christie's) $462

A Spot-On 'A' presentation set, with five vehicle picture cards and Fleet Owners' Club leaflet, in original box.
(Christie's) $391

A Tipp & Co. Royal Mail van, German, circa 1930, lithographed in mainly scarlet and yellow with driver, 24cm. long.
(Sotheby's) $1,264

A rare Dinky US export-issue 581 'Express Horse Van Hire Service' horsebox, with special US market transfers.
(Christie's) $622

A pre-war Dinky 1st Type 28f 'Palethorpes' delivery van, cast lead with blue wheels, circa 1934.
(Christie's) $529

A Schuco green painted tinplate and plastic 5700 Synchromatic Packard Convertible, with battery operated remote control.
(Christie's) $675

A Märklin model gunboat painted red and white, circa 1900, 88cm. long.
(Stockholms Auktionsverk)
$6,486

A 1950s Maserati pedal car.
(Arnold Frankfurt) $602

A cycling Jeu de Course, probably Gunthermann for the French market, circa 1905.
(Sotheby's) $5,417

Four Chad Valley dwarfs, Doc, Grumpy, Happy and Dopey, with pressed and painted cloth faces and stuffed bodies, 6in. high.
(Christie's) $317

A fine Märklin gauge 1 onion dome central station, German, circa 1900, telegraph office and waiting room to each side, 43cm. long.
(Sotheby's) $2,347

A Steiff pullalong toy, with Puck figure sitting in cart pulled by two ducks and two pigeons, 1920s, 51cm. long.
(Stockholms Auktionsverk)
$2,480

A DRGM tinplate limousine, German, inserted lithographed chauffeur, clockwork mechanism activating rear axle, 13in. long.
(Neales) $356

A Märklin gauge 1 tinplate station, German, circa 1904, with stamped stonework and bricks, 34cm. long.
(Sotheby's) $506

A Carette Limousine, handpainted green roof, with functioning back doors and handbrake, circa 1911.
(Stockholms Auktionsverk)
$2,417

A Carette clockwork lithographed tinplate four-light limousine, finished in ivory lined out, circa 1912.
(Christie's) $1,688

A Linemar friction-powered lithographed tinplate 'Mickey Mouse Mouseketeers Moving Van', in original box.
(Christie's) $391

A grey and green Bing clockwork lithographed tinplate open tourer, with driver dressed in tan colored suit, circa 1914, 10in. long.
(Christie's) $533

An early Steiff monkey, with cinnamon mohair, black boot button eyes, felt face with center seam, 13in. tall, circa 1905. (Christie's) $705

A Lehmann Mandarin tinplate novelty toy, German, circa 1910, the oriental bearers in blue and white lithographed robes, 18cm. long. (Sotheby's) $631

A painted and decorated rocking horse, American, 19th century, with leather saddle and bridle mounted on a green-painted rocker, 21in. high. (Christie's) $1,610

A blue, pale blue and yellow Nomura battery operated Batman, with walking movement, illuminating face and fabric cape, 11½in. high. (Christie's) $1,599

A rare Spot-On No. 0 presentation set, with four vehicle picture cards, Fleet Owners' and Magazine Club leaflets, in original box. (Christie's) $568

A Schuco 'Yes/No' monkey, with brown tipped white mohair, tail operating monkey's 'Yes/No' head movement, 9in. tall, 1920s. (Christie's) $423

Corgi diecast gift set No. 38 (Monte Carlo Rally) 1965, boxed. (Neales) $480

A Roullet et Decamps clockwork automaton of an Egyptian character, French, circa 1910, 31½in. high. (Sotheby's) $758

A Lehmann zig-zag vehicle, the driving wheels supporting gondola containing two figures, circa 1910, 5in. diameter. (Spencer's) $795

A German clockwork lithographed tinplate ice cream vendor, the boy pushing a two-wheeled cart, circa 1912, 7¹/₂in. long.
(Christie's) $622

A Dinky 919 Guy 'Golden Shred' van, in original box.
(Christie's) $622

A rare Arnold clockwork lithographed tinplate German army motorcycle, with rider and rear passenger soldiers dressed in Wehrmacht uniforms, late 1930s, 7¹/₂in.
(Christie's) $391

A Corgi 266 'Chitty Chitty Bang Bang', with inner card and plastic clouds, in original box.
(Christie's) $300

Lehmann, Alabama Coon Jigger, a rhythmically walking Negro, spring wound mechanism, 1920–30s, 25cm. high.
(Stockholms Auktionsverk) $636

Mickey Mouse Theatre, characters include Donald, Minnie, Goofy, Mickey, Pluto and Chip n' Dale.
(Christie's) $249

A carved and painted wooden Ayres of London rocking horse, with original tack, saddle, mane and tail, 34in. high.
(Christie's) $640

An early Steiff dog on wheels, with pale golden mohair, standing on four-spoked metal wheels, 11in. tall, circa 1910.
(Christie's) $388

A Distler free-wheeling lithographed tinplate elephant and howdah novelty toy, on four 'Dunlop Cord' wheels, 11in. long.
(Christie's) $675

Large wood gliding rocking horse, glass eyes, 49in. high. (Skinner) $1,092

A Nomura 'Robbie' mechanized robot, Japanese, 1960s, with clear plastic visor, 34cm. high. (Sotheby's) $1,264

A Günthermann clockwork lithographed and painted tinplate Vis à Vis motor car, finished in blue, circa 1898. (Christie's) $4,264

A Gottschalk dolls' house, German, early 20th century, the façade with central arch flanked by dormer windows, red painted roof and two chimneys, 39in. wide. (Sotheby's) $1,840

A rare Dinky US-export issue Set No. 6 Commercial Vehicles, in original checkered-blue box, circa 1946–1948. (Christie's) $4,619

A painted and carved dolls' house named 'Ivy Cottage', English, 20th century, the façade painted to resemble brick, the gray painted slate roof with two chimneys and central gable, 36in. wide. (Sotheby's) $3,310

A Marx Merrymakers mouse band, English, 1930s, with pianist, violinist, percussion and tap dancer, 16cm. wide. (Sotheby's) $1,444

A scarce Shirley Temple paper doll cut-out book, American, circa 1930's, The Saalfield Publishing Company, Authorized Edition No. 1765, the cut-out doll 34in. high. (Sotheby's) $736

A miniature mahogany half-tester bed, late 19th century, the tester and end with carved finials and pilasters, complete with later mattress and hangings, 20in. high. (Sotheby's) $552

A steamer trunk, vertical opening, circa 1925. (Auction Team Köln) $129

A Louis Vuitton trunk, the hinged top enclosing a plain mustard canvas interior with nailed fruitwood bands, one handle lacking, 56½in. wide. (Christie's) $2,576

A Kelly handbag of dark brown leather with padlock and keys, Hermès Paris, 12½in. base. (Christie's) $1,161

A vanity case of black crocodile leather, with fall front to reveal pocket and jewel drawer below, with key, Lederer de Paris, 11 x 8 x 8½in. (Christie's) $537

A Napoleon III ormolu-mounted ebonized Palais-Royal necessaire de voyage by Boudet, the hinged lid with central emblem of two crossed Ps centered by a flaming torch shaped as a J, 19¼in. wide. (Christie's) $3,975

A Kelly handbag, of burgundy colored leather with gilt metal fastenings, Hermès Paris, 11¼in. base. (Christie's) $705

An early Victorian mahogany and brass-bound campaign box, with recessed handles to the sides and vacant brass cartouche to the cover, 15¼in. wide. (Christie's) $1,009

A Louis Vuitton cabin trunk, covered in LV fabric and bound in black painted steel and wooden banding, 43½ x 22½ x 22½in. (Christie's) $1,174

A dressing case, of brown crocodile leather with foul weather cover, stamped *Asprey, London*, with key, 17½ x 13½ x 7in. (Christie's) $1,080

A. R. Thomson, Fighting Fit In The Factory, double crown. (Onslow's) $210

Beware of the Butterfly Bomb Don't Touch It, double crown. (Onslow's) $150

Britain Is Pledged to Smash Japan, double crown. (Onslow's) $290

'Let Us Go Forward Together', (Churchill) photomontage, double crown. (Onslow's) $340

H. M. Bateman, Coughs and Sneezes Spread Diseases, double crown. (Onslow's) $500

Charles Wood, The Life-Line is Firm Thanks to the Merchant Navy, double royal. (Onslow's) $260

Zec, Women Of Britain Come Into The Factories, double crown. (Onslow's) $1,340

Beat Firebomb Fritz Britain Shall Not Burn; and Fall In The Firebomb Fighters, both double crown. (Onslow's) $220

Tom Curr, The Finest Job In The World Join The Army, circa 1925, double crown. (Onslow's) $340

An 18th century forged iron weathervane as the wind god, 70cm. high.
(Arnold Frankfurt) $480

Copper horse and rider weathervane, America, late 19th century, painted yellow, 31in. long.
(Skinner) $1,495

A gilt-painted running horse weathervane, American, 19th century, mounted on an iron rod with directionals, 38in. wide.
(Christie's) $2,530

An unusual gilded copper cock weathervane, probably Massachusetts, circa 1850, the swell-bodied figure with molded wings, 30½in. high.
(Sotheby's) $1,725

Copper rooster weather vane, America, 19th century, 19½in. high.
(Skinner) $862

Large sheet metal Gabriel weather vane, America, early 20th century, with vestiges of paint, 48in. high.
(Skinner) $3,335

American eagle weathervane, 19th century, full-bodied eagle mounted over an arrow, 26in. high.
(Eldred's) $935

Gilt copper running horse weather vane, America, 19th century, bole and verdigris surface, 29in. long.
(Skinner) $747

A molded copper Hamburg rooster weathervane, Harris & Co., Boston, Massachusetts, circa 1880, 31in. high.
(Sotheby's) $7,475

A carved and painted wood weathervane, Tom Swan, Pennsylvania, circa 1889, white painted and shaped in the form of a swan, with hole eyes, open beak and articulated four-finger tail, 70in. long.
(Christie's)   **$8,280**

Copper black hawk horse weather vane, America, 19th century, verdigris surface, (bullet hole), 26in. long.
(Skinner)   **$2,185**

A molded and gilded copper peacock weathervane, attributed to A. L. Jewell and Company, Waltham, Massachusetts, 1852–1867, the shaped body with applied legs resting on a spherule, 21in. high.
(Christie's)   **$9,775**

A rare painted copper steer weathervane, Cushing & Co., Waltham, Massachusetts, third quarter 19th century, swell-bodied figure with applied ears and horn, 30in. long.
(Sotheby's)   **$8,625**

A molded copper running horse weathervane stamped *A. J. Harris and Co.*, 19th century, the fully extended horse with articulated mane and tail, 31½in. long.
(Christie's)   **$2,875**

A molded copper horse and sulky weathervane, American, 19th century, the full bodied figure of a jockey seated in a buggy, 33¾in. wide.
(Christie's)   **$1,495**

A carved, painted and gilded pine cod fish weathervane, American, third quarter 19th century, the fish carved in the round with stylized scales, 29¹/₂in. long. (Sotheby's) $6,900

A molded cast zinc quill pen weathervane, possibly J. Howard & Co., Bridgewater, Massachusetts, third quarter 19th century, the silhouette of a quill pen with molded zinc point, 50in. long. (Sotheby's) $1,725

A molded and gilded copper horse and rider weathervane, American, 19th century, depicting a seated man above a trotting horse, 26in. high. (Christie's) $6,325

A fine molded and gilded copper leaping stag weathervane, attributed to L. W. Cushing & Sons, Waltham, Massachusetts, third quarter 19th century, 38in. long. (Sotheby's) $8,050

An unusual painted sheet iron pig weathervane, probably Pennsylvania, circa 1880, the silhouetted figure painted white with brown spots, 34¹/₂in. long. (Sotheby's) $7,475

A molded and gilded copper bull weathervane, attributed to J. Howard & Co., Bridgewater, Massachusetts, circa 1875, the full bodied bull depicted standing in profile, 24in. wide. (Christie's) $3,450

Rare cabinet photo of Judge Roy Bean and his Rail Road Store, circa 1895, exterior view, subject shown standing in front of store with group, 5 x 8in. (Butterfield & Butterfield) $4,125

Autographed letter from Frank James to his wife Annie, July 23, 1883, from prison and details his daily routine. (Butterfield & Butterfield) $5,500

Cabinet photo of Pat Garrett and posse holding Billy the Kid after his arrest at Stinking Springs, New Mexico, circa 1880. (Butterfield & Butterfield) $19,800

One pair of shotgun style chaps by L. D. Stone of San Francisco, California, circa 1900, of cowhide construction with straight apron belt,, reinforced gusset and fringed welt. (Butterfield & Butterfield) $605

Autographed target playing card and business card of John Wesley Hardin, circa 1895, shot through during a shooting exhibition sponsored by Hardin and his partner Mike Collins at the grand opening of the Wigwam saloon in El Paso on July 4th, 1895. (Butterfield & Butterfield) $5,225

Rare letter from Jesse James' widow, circa 1882, with letterhead reading *Jesse James Lecturing Company*, explaining that she has embarked on a lecture tour in order to support her children. (Butterfield & Butterfield) $6,050

Black silver mounted parade saddle by Visalia Stock Saddle Co., circa 1930, mounted with German silver ornaments engraved with Western motifs. (Butterfield & Butterfield) $3,300

Rare Buffalo Bill Wild West Show poster 'A Close Call' by A. Hoen & Co., Baltimore, Maryland, circa 1894, depicting Colonel Cody in the center of the action, firing from his fallen horse, 41 x 28in. (Butterfield & Butterfield) $7,150

Letter by Buffalo Bill, Feb. 26th 1901, one page written entirely in his own hand on *Buffalo Bill's/Wild West* embossed letter head. (Butterfield & Butterfield) $1,430

William F. Cody's Fraternal hat, circa 1905, Knights of Templar hat made by the M. C. Lilley Co. (Butterfield & Butterfield) $4,400

Colt single action army revolver with antique Western holster and gun belt, circa 1876, serial No. 23026, .45 caliber, 5¹/₄in. barrel, single line barrel address. (Butterfield & Butterfield) $1,210

Wells Fargo strongbox, circa 1875, of wood and metal construction, size: 20 x 12 x 10in. (Butterfield & Butterfield) $9,250

Rare Wells Fargo & Company Express mug book, circa 1890, a folio of sixty pages filled with photographs of wanted or known criminals. (Butterfield & Butterfield) $33,000

Historic pair of frontier revolvers once owned by Jesse James, comprised of U.S. Colt single action army revolver, cavalry model, Merwin Hulbert & Co. single action army model revolver, serial No. 5704. (Butterfield & Butterfield) $71,500

Buffalo Bill Wild West Show poster 'Perils of the Cowboy' by Courier Lithographic Company of Buffalo, New York, circa 1902, depicting cowboys and cattle herd fleeing from a prairie fire. (Butterfield & Butterfield) $6,600

Rare American walnut Wells Fargo desk, circa 1860–1880, the rectangular top above central letter slots above two small drawers with scalloped shelf below, 4ft. 6in. wide. (Butterfield & Butterfield) $3,025

Original pin and autographed membership card in the Fraternal Order of Eagles belonging to Virgil W. Earp, circa 1905, bronze FOE membership pin with screwback clasp attached to a frayed yellow pillow. (Butterfield & Butterfield) $6,600

Western saddle by G. Thissel, Cottonwood, California, with wide swells, saddle constructed of russet leather, hand tooled in floral pattern. (Butterfield & Butterfield) $715

GENERAL CUSTER

Captain Thomas Ward Custer's cased Galand & Sommerville revolver, circa 1870, serial No. 572, .44 Webley caliber, 5in. octagonal barrel marked on top flat *J.D. Dougall London & Glasgow*.
(Butterfield & Butterfield)
$77,000

Important pipe tomahawk belong to Chief Black Kettle, circa 1868, central portion inscribed, *Pipe Axe Taken From The Lodge of Black Kettle by Pvt. Frederick Klink, Co. E. 7th U.S. Cavalry. Battle of the Washita Nov. 27, 1868*.
(Butterfield & Butterfield)
$38,500

General George A. Custer's 3rd Division, Cavalry Corps designating flag, circa 1864, hand sewn of composite construction.
(Butterfield & Butterfield)
$38,500

Letter from General Custer to his mother, circa 1872, four handwritten pages written from Elizabethtown, Kentucky sometime between March 1871 and January 1872.
(Butterfield & Butterfield)
$7,700

General George A. Custer's pocket Bible, circa 1859, thought to be a gift from his mother, it was stored with other personal items in the rear supply train during Custer's final campaign.
(Butterfield & Butterfield)
$46,750

Mounted photo of Major General George A. Custer, his brother Thomas W. Custer and wife Elizabeth B. Custer, circa 1865, size: 5 x 7in.
(Butterfield & Butterfield)
$1,320

Autographed Custer CDV photo, circa 1865, photographic vignette of steel plate engraving, by Brady, size: 2½ x 4¼in.
(Butterfield & Butterfield)
$7,150

Historic Arapaho war shield used at the Battle of Washita, circa 1868, the buffalo hide war shield with painted totemic image of buffalo on a red field.
(Butterfield & Butterfield)
$66,000

Cabinet photo of Lieutenant Colonel George A. Custer by William R. Howell, circa 1876, bust view, 4 x 6in.
(Butterfield & Butterfield)
$1,540

GENERAL CUSTER

Custer CDV photo, circa 1865, classic seated view by Brady, size: 2³/₈ x 3⁷/₈in. (Butterfield & Butterfield)

$1,320

General George A. Custer's personal map case, circa 1876, Elizabeth Custer commented "General Nelson Miles obtained this from the Indians and gave it to me on the fifth anniversary of the battle." (Butterfield & Butterfield)

$13,200

Lieutenant Colonel George A. Custer's U.S. 7th Cavalry Model 1872 shoulder knot, intact, circa 1876. (Butterfield & Butterfield)

$66,000

Tintype photo of Custer scout Lonesome Charley Reynolds, circa 1875, pictured with Chief Charlie Hogg, Hogg's Indian wife and child, size: 2³/₈ x 3¹/₄in. (Butterfield & Butterfield)

$2,750

The Custer portrait vases, circa 1865, of baluster form with bouquets of pink roses tied with blue ribbons, 11in. high, the vases were commissioned by General Custer while on vacation with his wife in New Orleans. (Butterfield & Butterfield)

$46,750

Original tintype photo portrait of Elizabeth B. Custer, circa 1865, bust view, possibly an unpublished image, size: 2 x 2¹/₂in. (Butterfield & Butterfield)

$2,475

Custer cabinet photo, circa 1876, rare three-quarter bust portrait of Custer wearing 1872 dress uniform. (Butterfield & Butterfield)

$2,750

Rare early autographed letter signed by Lieutenant George A. Custer, dated: *Camp Clind's Mills/Aug. 15. 1861.* (Butterfield & Butterfield)

$7,150

Letter by George A. Custer to Tom Custer with tintype photo, April 28, 1867, a plea for information on the whereabouts of his wayward wife Elizabeth. (Butterfield & Butterfield)

$20,900

GENERAL CUSTER

General George A. Custer's military footlocker, circa 1876, of wood construction stenciled on front *G. A. Custer* with later addition *Monroe Mich.*
(Butterfield & Butterfield)
$30,250

Rare 1872 pattern wool campaign hat, circa 1876, of black wool composition with eye hooks for support of brim, typical of those worn by soldiers of the 7th Cavalry.
(Butterfield & Butterfield)
$7,700

Rare mounted albumen photo of General and Mrs. Custer in their Home at Ft. Abraham Lincoln by Orlander Scott Goff, circa 1873, size: 8 x 10in.
(Butterfield & Butterfield)
$6,600

General George A. Custer's campaign shirt made by Elizabeth Custer, circa 1873, navy wool bib front shirt with white trim and pearl buttons, and worn by General Custer on the Black Hills expedition of 1874.
(Butterfield & Butterfield)
$46,750

General George A Custer's Civil War era dress epaulettes, circa 1862, numeral 5 signifying the U.S. 5th Cavalry, to which Custer was assigned before receiving command of the Michigan Volunteer regiments in the Civil War.
(Butterfield & Butterfield)
$12,100

Unique original tintype photo portrait of Major General George A. Custer, taken July, 1865 while Custer was in New Orleans, Louisiana by photographer R. T. Lux, $3^{1}/_{4}$ x $4^{1}/_{4}$in.
(Butterfield & Butterfield)
$17,600

CDV photo of Brigadier General George A. Custer by Matthew Brady, circa 1864, signature reads: *Gen. Custer* and is possibly in Custer's own hand.
(Butterfield & Butterfield)
$1,430

Lot of personal items belonging to George A. Custer, circa 1876, comprising of red cravat, lock of Custer's hair, clipped signature and cabinet photo of Custer, authenticating letters.
(Butterfield & Butterfield)
$35,750

Custer CDV photo, circa 1876, rare three-quarter bust view of Custer in civilian dress, marked: *Howell-867 & 869 B'way* on front, $2^{3}/_{8}$ x 4in.
(Butterfield & Butterfield)
$1,100

GENERAL CUSTER

General George A. Custer's personal Civil War cavalry guidon, circa 1863, 6th Michigan Cavalry swallowtail guidon, handmade by Elizabeth B. Custer, size: 32 x 67in.
(Butterfield & Butterfield)
$165,000

Sharps four barrel derringer, circa 1861, .22 caliber, 2¹/₂in. barrels, Model 1A, inscribed on backstrap *Friends of the Academy/to Lt. G.A. Custer 1861*.
(Butterfield & Butterfield)
$16,500

Custer's dog calling horn, circa 1865, polished steer horn with turned mouthpiece, braided leather thong attached, size: 3¹/₂ x 13¹/₂in.
(Butterfield & Butterfield)
$8,250

First edition book, Life on the Plains by George A. Custer, circa 1874, My Life on the Plains: or Personal Experiences with Indians by Gen. George A. Custer, U.S., single volume, 256 pages, illustrated.
(Butterfield & Butterfield)
$660

Rare and unique framed presentation American flag autographed by General George A. Custer and other noted individuals while with President Johnson's railroad election tour, circa 1866.
(Butterfield & Butterfield)
$22,000

Albumen print of Major General George A. Custer, circa 1885, 12 x 9in. print, studio view, subject is seated, taken January 4, 1865.
(Butterfield & Butterfield)
$2,475

General George A. Custer's autographed Bible, circa 1874, embossed leather cover, inside flyleaf inscribed: *G.A. Custer U.S. Army Fort Abraham Lincoln Dacota Oct. 1, 1874.*
(Butterfield & Butterfield)
$30,250

Pair of hide gauntlets belonging to General George A. Custer, circa 1869, Indian War era lambskin gauntlets decorated in ornate green, purple and white stitching.
(Butterfield & Butterfield)
$24,750

Autographed letter signed by General George A. Custer, circa 1874, from Headquarters, Fort Abraham Lincoln, December 12, 1874, to 1st Lieutenant William Winer Cook.
(Butterfield & Butterfield)
$10,450

John Begg Gold Cap, circa 1940, John Begg Ltd., Glasgow and London *By Appointment to the Late King George V.*
(Christie's) $243

Talisker, 1887, Selected and bottled for Peter Thomson, Perth, single malt, about 20° under proof.
(Christie's) $4,701

The Dew of Ben Varen, early 20th century, *By Appointment to The King and The Prince of Wales*, Collier & Co., Plymouth.
(Christie's) $680

The Macallan-Glenlivet, 189–, Selected by Proprietors R. Kemp, Macallan-Glenlivet and Talisker Distilleries Ltd.
(Christie's) $6,111

Wright & Greig, early 20th century, cut glass decanter and stopper accompanied by two thistle-shaped drinking glasses.
(Christie's) $235

Glen Grant, 1892, bottled 1904, by John Bisset & Co. Ltd., 10 Links Place, Leith , Edinburgh.
(Christie's) $4,701

Isle of Skye Liqueur Scotch Whisky, *From the lone sheiling and the misty island*, blended and bottled by Ian MacLeod & Co. Ltd., Isle of Skye.
(Christie's) $405

Glenlivet, Guaranteed 25-year-old, early 20th century, Distilled, Bonded and Bottled By Proprietors George & J. G. Smith's, single malt, 80°.
(Christie's) $2,194

Dewar's White Label, 8-year-old, 1939, *By Appointment to The Late King George V 50 Gold and prize medals*, John Dewar & Sons Ltd., Perth.
(Christie's) $2,106

Rosebank, 1923, bottled by Matthew Gloag & Son Ltd., Perth.
(Christie's) $891

B.O.S. Blended Old Scotch Whisky, T. Pease, Son & Co., Whisky Blenders, Darlington, Leith and London.
(Christie's) $211

Talisker, distilled by Dailuaine-Talisker Distilleries Ltd., Isle of Skye.
(Christie's) $680

Macallan-Glenlivet, 15-year-old, early 20th century, Liqueur Scotch Whisky, bottled in Inverness for J. Leslie, Wine Merchant, Fort Augustus, single malt, 75°.
(Christie's) $2,507

The Macallan, 50-year-old, distilled 1928, bottled 1983, bottled number 184 of 500, in wooden presentation case, single malt, 38.6% vol.
(Christie's) $4,231

Macallan-Glenlivet, 15-year-old, early 20th century, Liqueur Scotch Whisky, bottled in Inverness for J. Leslie, Wine Merchant, Fort Augustus, single malt, 75°.
(Christie's) $1,724

Meg Dods' Blend, *When the cork's drawn; The bottle maun be drunk oot; And what for no,* **A. Bennett, Traquair Arms, Innerleithen.**
(Christie's) $211

Glen Grant-Glenlivet, 1889, Glen Grant Distillery Ltd., Rothes, Morayshire, three piece molded glass bottle, driven cork, foil capsule.
(Christie's) $2,977

19th century Kentucky Bourbon, Belmont Straight Bourbon Whiskey, 18 Summers Old, distilled 1899, bottled 1917, 1 gallon jar.
(Christie's) $972

Maden's Special Scotch Whisky, Maden & Co., Wine and Spirit Merchants, Wigan. (Christie's) $292

Drambuie, circa 1940, *A Link With The '45'*, shoulder, neck and main labels. (Christie's) $518

N.E.D., bottled by Urquhart & Fraser, Seagate, Montrose, Scotland. (Christie's) $178

Gilbey's Spey Royal, 10-year-old, circa 1930, bottled and guaranteed by W. & A. Gilbey *By Appointment to His Majesty King George V Government tax 8/5¹/₂ on this bottle.* (Christie's) $308

Believed Glenfarclas, circa 1910, glass embossed *'Imperial Half Gallon' The XL Patent, D. Rylands, Barnsley*, green glass vessel, glass stopper, 1 imperial half gallon. (Christie's) $502

Black & White, circa 1910, *As selected for The House of Commons*, James Buchanan & Co. Ltd., Glasgow and London, Glentauchers-Glenlivet Distillery, Mulben, Speyside. (Christie's) $486

K.O.S.B., 25-year-old, pre 1930, *King's Own Special Blend*, J. J. Blanche & Co., Distillers, Glasgow and London. (Christie's) $680

White Heather De Luxe, circa 1930, square-shaped bottle, distilled and bottled by White Heather Distillers Ltd. (Christie's) $162

Bagots Liqueur Irish Whisky, Guaranteed 15-year-old, early 20th century, Bagots, Hutton and Kinahan Ltd., Dublin. (Christie's) $518

Very Old Specially Selected, 12-year-old, George Morton Ltd., Distillers, Dundee.
(Christie's) $616

McKay's Glenlee Very Old Scotch Whisky, John McKay, Burnbank.
(Christie's) $324

Glen Garroch Liqueur Scotch Whisky, early 20th century, T. B. Hooper & Co. Ltd.
(Christie's) $518

The Macallan-Glenlivet, 28-year-old, bottled by Row & Company (Distillers) Ltd., Glasgow, imported by British American Importation Co. Ltd., Los Angeles.
(Christie's) $1,458

Huntly Blend Fine Old Scotch Whisky, 1896, wire mesh covered bottle, lead capsule embossed *Huntly Old Scotch Whisky* on top, 1 half bottle.
(Christie's) $616

The Macallan-Glenlivet, 30-year-old, bottled by Row & Company (Distillers) Ltd., Glasgow, imported by British American Importation Co. Ltd., Los Angeles.
(Christie's) $1,377

Clynelish, 14-year-old, bottled by Royal Marine Hotel, Brora, Scotland, not less than 92° proof.
(Christie's) $308

House of MacDonald, 26-year-old, 1933, *Kept in wood over 26 years, From the private stock of Henry Clayton Esq.*
(Christie's) $680

Fine Old Glenstrath Liqueur Scotch Whisky, Proprietors: Wallace, Robertson & Co., Edinburgh.
(Christie's) $292

A carved handle burl bowl, American, 18th century, with hand holds on either side, 18³/₄ x 17in. (Sotheby's) $2,300

One of a pair of Regency carved giltwood wall brackets, the bowed friezes mounted with spheres. (Anderson & Garland) (Two) $2,295

A funerary figure of a horse's head with traces of red and white, Han-Wei dynasties. (Stockholms Auktionsverk) $506

A painted wood canteen, American, possibly 18th century, the circular form blue painted with large central white star surrounded by a rosette border on one side, 6¹/₂in. diameter. (Christie's) $1,265

A pair of Victorian treen pounce pots, with ring-turned stems, incised to the underside with the Royal cypher *VR* with crown above, 3¹/₂in. high. (Christie's) $443

A rare small-size carved and painted pine ship's figurehead, New England, circa 1840, finely carved bust portrait of a dark-haired lady wearing a blue-green dress, 16in. high. (Sotheby's) $19,550

A carved oak relief figure of the Virgin, shown standing, robed and crowned within an arched niche, Northern European, 17th/18th century, 30¹/₂ x 16³/₄in. (Christie's) $1,570

A Louis XVI carved and stained-wood relief of a basket of flowers, the tapering trellis-pattern body issuing pomegranates, and other foliage, 16in. high. (Christie's) $2,691

A carved pine parrot in a wrought-iron cage, probably Southern, circa 1880, with eyes fashioned from abalone. (Sotheby's) $1,495

Painted and carved wood whirligig figure of a sailor boy, early 20th century, 12¹/₂in. high. (Eldred's) $715

A carved and painted pine and gesso elephant trade sign: Ellie, carved in the round and painted on both sides, 28¹/₂in. high overall. (Sotheby's) $20,700

A carved and painted pine show figure, attributed to Samuel Robb, New York, third quarter 19th century, 25¹/₂in. high. (Sotheby's) $12,650

A Norwegian birch peg tankard, the hinged cover carved with bird alighted on a shrub, scrolling foliage surround, 7in. circa 1700. (Woolley & Wallis) $29,444

A pair of pine and parcel-gilt urn-stands, each with circular tray-top with gadrooned edge and plain frieze centered by foliate masks, 19th century, 15in. diameter. (Christie's) $2,726

A North Italian triptych portable altar, the frame of Alacertosina decoration centered by bone reliefs of the Virgin and Child flanked by a bishop and a monk, basically 15th century, 13in. high. (Hy. Duke & Son) $4,248

A pine tobacconist's figure of Sir Walter Raleigh, shown wearing a cape, his right hand raised to his chest, English, late 18th/early 19th century, 53in. high. (Christie's) $4,435

A carved and stained-wood relief in the manner of Grinling Gibbons, with a spindle-galleried rope-twist basket, supported by twin seraphim, 19th century, 17in. high. (Christie's) $2,512

A lignum vitae wassail bowl, with banded ornament, on a stepped spreading foot, English, mid 18th century, 8¹/₄in. diameter. (Christie's) $2,956

A burlwood bowl, American, 19th century, circular form with rounded sides, 15in. diameter. (Christie's) $1,955

A carved walnut bellows, attributed to Samuel McIntire, Salem, Massachusetts, circa 1800, 20in. long. (Christie's) $23,000

A carved and painted eagle, attributed to John Bellamy, Portsmouth, New Hampshire and Kittery Point, Maine, mid/late 19th century, depicting a spreadwing eagle, 25in. long. (Christie's) $20,700

A carved and painted figure of Uncle Sam, American, 19th century, holding a thirteen-star American flag in his right hand, 20¼in. high. (Christie's) $4,600

A pair of giltwood wall brackets, the D-shaped plateaux with fluted supports, 7⅞in. high. (Christie's) $528

A polychrome carved wood figure of King David, shown standing, robed and crowned, his right hand raised to his breast, South German, 17th century, 44¼in. high. (Christie's) $2,494

A brass and mahogany gameboard, the rectangular base with oval end, with a brass rim, 23¾ x 16¼in. (Christie's) $81

A carved and painted wood box, New England, 1800–1820, circular, the cover carved with the seal of the United States, 10½in. diameter. (Christie's) $11,500

A polychrome carved tobacconist's figure, of a native of Guinea, his right arm articulated and part lacking, English, late 17th/early 18th century, 21¼in. high. (Christie's) $2,217

A bamboo cage, Chinese, late 19th century.
(Hôtel de Ventes Horta)
$695

A red and black-painted gameboard, American, 19th century, with chess/checkerboard flanked by molded reserves for games pieces, 19 x 29in.
(Christie's) $633

One of a pair of cream painted door surrounds, late 19th century, 103³/₄in. high, 55¹/₂in. wide.
(Skinner)
(Two) $4,887

A carved and painted eagle, American, 19th century, the gray-painted full bodied form with open beak, outstretched neck, spread wings and articulated feathers perched on a red-painted sphere, 38in. high.
(Christie's) $6,325

Continental, Art Nouveau Symbolist fireplace, circa 1900, sculpted wood with spiral side supports and centered by a female head in a cloud of stylized hair, 139.5cm. wide.
(Sotheby's) $31,671

A carved and painted equestrian portrait of George Washington, American, 19th century, depicting George Washington on his charger Jack, 26¹/₄in. high.
(Christie's) $4,600

A pine door, Newbury, Massachusetts, 17th century, the rectangular door with arched fielded panels, 68 x 33in.
(Christie's) $3,450

A mid-18th century giltwood wall bracket with satyr masks and flower head supports to the pierced diaper back, 14³/₄in. high.
(Bearne's) $1,764

A carved and painted counter top cigar store Indian, American, late 19th century, depicting a full-bodied carved figure wearing a ceremonial headdress, 27¹/₂in. high.
(Christie's) $4,370

An Austrian carved boxwood casket, the oval top carved with game birds within a naturalistic setting, 19th century, 19in. wide. (Christie's) $603

Hand carved wooden bust of William Shakespeare, 19th century, 17½in. high. (Eldred's) $1,375

A carved and painted wood model of a salmon, mounted on a rectangular backboard inscribed *P. D. MALLOCH (?). PERTH*, the fish 41¾in. long. (Christie's) $1,151

A carved bear hall stand, the growling bear holding a tree with cub on top, with drip-pan below, 71in. high. (Christie's) $1,722

A Federal cherrywood and curly maple miniature one-drawer side table, New England, circa 1825, on ring-and-spirally-turned legs, 10¼in. wide. (Sotheby's) $575

Alabaster on wood private altar, Mecheln 1605–10, 39.2cm. high. (Lempertz) $13,990

A carved and painted architectural figure, American, 19th century, carved in the round as a woman with her arms outstretched, 36in. high. (Christie's) $12,650

A carved and painted figural group, American, 20th century, depicting a man and woman locked in a kiss, 26in. high. (Christie's) $1,380

A painted papier-mâché wig stand, probably French, late 19th century, in the form of a bust of an elegantly dressed gentleman wearing white tie, 17½in. high. (Sotheby's) $3,105

INDEX